To Monica, with love.
Without you there would be nothing.

# PREFACE

"I'll bet you're scared to walk home alone now, aren't ya?" Jimmy mocked Rex, his friend.

Rex didn't reply. His head was down, and he walked beside Jimmy with his shoulders hunched over to ward off the cold and the mist. Gray clouds hung overhead so close they were suffocating.

"I can't believe your dad doesn't just pick ya up in his squad car. He could do that, couldn't he?" Jimmy asked.

Rex lifted his head. "Sure he could, ya moron. He's Sheriff of Salem Township," Rex exclaimed. "He can do whatever he wants."

Rex shoved Jimmy toward his school bus.

"Watch it, pal, or I'll have ta beat on ya again."

"Oh, I'm so scared. You're epileptic, ya know it?" Rex laughed.

"Hey, can ya show me some a those wrestling moves Migisi used the other night?"

"Oh, I dunno, you're kinda spastic—you know—dis ... discabobyoulated, Sara says."

"What's discabobyoulated?" Jimmy wanted to know.

"You're a spaz." He shoved Jimmy again as they approached Bus 33.

"You don't even know what discabobyoulated means, do ya?"

Rex didn't reply and his head went down again.

"Hey! I still think your bow and arrow are way out. Who cares if Mrs. Tharp didn't like 'um?" Jimmy tugged the tip of the wooden hunting bow Rex was carrying in his left hand.

"Aw, I just think Mrs. Tharp is prejudiced of me being half Indian," Rex commented, but he raised his head.

"Hey, I think that's far out that you're part Indian," Jimmy said. "It kinda shows that you're—ah—you're unique, ya know."

Rex smiled and gave Jimmy another shove.

"So will ya show me those wrestling moves again?" Jimmy persisted.

"Yeah, sure." Rex laughed.

The buses started their engines.

"You're gonna miss your bus and I gotta get going before Sara shows up and I have to walk home with her," Rex said.

"Yeah, see ya tomorrow, but ya should wait for Sara to walk home with ya like your Officer Madison said, or you could be the next one to disappear from Napier Road."

Rex turned back toward Jimmy with his lip curled in a snarl, his black eyes squinted, and his brow knitted together.

"Deputy Madison wasn't joking about the weirdos out there that grab kids and kill'um—kill'um dead," Jimmy continued.

Rex calmed his face and shrugged his shoulders.

"You saw the film this afternoon, same as me. You saw that molested girl floating down the stream. That was gross," Jimmy exclaimed in a sudden adult seriousness.

"I'm no sissy." Rex waved him off. "Besides, I've got these." He held up his bow and arrow in a show of defiance. "See ya tomorrow, ya wet-head."

Rex turned his back and ran before Jimmy could say more.

"Here I go—

"Playin' star again—

"There I go—

"Turn the page..." Rex softly sang his rendition of a Bob Seger tune that was breaking the charts of his favorite radio station, WRIF, the RIFF, Detroit's home of rock'n roll, YEAH BABY!

"That's what I'll do!" Rex puffed to the icy wind. "If any stranger tries to pick me up, I'll call the RIFF and sic Dick the Bruiser on'um. YEAH BABY!

"I doubt Dick the Bruiser makes house calls, but then no stranger's gonna try and pick me up." Rex made his decision and trucked on down Gibbon Street toward his home. He'd forgotten about Napier Road for now.

"Here I go—

"Playin' star again—

"There I go—

"Turn the page..." Rex sang for no one to hear while he walked along with the hope his mental jukebox would keep his imagination from reviewing the film Deputy Madison had shown during his last period of school. Deputy Madison had made his presentation and showed a film to the students and faculty of Salem Middle School about why children should not talk to strangers when they were alone. Rex thought Deputy Madison's presentation came a little late—at least for the two kids from school that were believed to be dead.

"It's kinda like closing the barn door after the ponies escaped." Rex puffed in the freezing air. That was one of Migisi's sayings. Rex felt a warm comfort when he thought about Migisi. Migisi was Rex's live-in grandfather who was a Native American of the Chippewa-Ojibwa Tribe. Migisi was a scholar of Chippewa-Ojibwa history and lore. He also knew neat wrestling moves he claimed were part of any young Chippewa's arsenal of self-defense. Rex's fear returned when he thought about what Migisi's reaction would be when he showed up at home without Sara doggin' his heels. Rex was supposed to walk home from school with his older sister, Sara. Rex knew Migisi would never say a word to discipline Rex or Sara, but Rex hated the disappointment that would show in Migisi's elderly black eyes when Rex broke the rules.

"Here I go—

"Playin' star again—

"There I go—

"Turn the page." Rex slowed his pace for a moment to untie the loose knot that kept his black hair in a ponytail that could flop down between his broad shoulder blades once it was clean and combed. He figured the least his black mane could do was hang over his ears to keep them warm. Rex whipped his head back and forth to disperse his tangled mop. This made him dizzy and he took a few wobbly steps to maintain his balance. He steadied his stance as he came to the crossroads of Gibbon Street and Napier Road. He gazed downhill with keen eyes along Napier Road and hesitated as his stomach did a curious tumble, and he found his mouth was dry. Rex beheld the dark dense foliage of oak, maple, and pine trees that loomed over Napier Road to form a subterranean-like entrance through which he must pass. Above this gloomy route home, Rex espied a red-hawk circling in search of a mouse or a rabbit hidden among the decaying muck below. The hawk was circling beneath the steel-wool clouds as the blusterous dripping mid-afternoon threatened winter. Rex saw the depressing truth of late November in southeastern Michigan before him—all the summer's life with its sea of emerald, jade, and olive had turned a milky coffee dullness of death, rot, and decomposition. The forest floor was a matted disarray of dead branches and soggy compost that was covered with splotches of snow and ice which wouldn't liquefy until the rebirth came in the spring.

The branches on the trees were naked and sagging, and Rex was thankful to trod Napier Road during the day when there remained splashes of the sun's illumination to steer his path. Rex also spied the figurines of his schoolmates pacing home along Napier Road in clusters of two or three like Deputy Madison had advised them during his presentation.

A flurry of sleet replaced the ignorable mist as Rex peered down his trail to be. He lowered his head to protect his squinting eyes from the blast which threw its icy needles into his lofty rosy cheekbones, his pointed nose, and slender lips. The weather seemed to lay emphasis on how his day had gone so far. Rex turned up the collar of his denim jacket in hopes of keeping the cold's fingers from gripping his large boned body.

Rex turned right off the wet pavement of Gibbon Street and jumped onto the slushy gravel mud of Napier Road. He wore his green rubber boots over his Keds that laced up his calves with real leather strings, and he normally enjoyed stomping through the chocolate milk-filled potholes in the packed earth of Napier Road since he knew his feet wouldn't get wet.

"Out past the cornfields where the woods got heavy—

"Out in the back seat of my '60 Chevy ..." Rex continued his Seger renditions—his traveling tunes—but he was unable to find happiness in puddle jumping this day.

"I was a little too tall—

"Could've used a few pounds ..."

To allay his disturbed thoughts Rex imagined a summer-like day where he was flying down Napier Road on his butt-kicking bike. In his mind he could see himself on his rough and tough dark blue speedster with its knobby tires, slightly rusted chrome fenders, its silver metallic banana seat, and its four foot sissy bar. If he had his bike right now he would be cruising home while popping wheelies, jumping mud puddles, and skidding burn marks without noticing the dullness of his surroundings. But Rex didn't have his bike, and he couldn't peddle out of his depressing mood.

Sheriff Bana had stored away Rex's bike when the problem on Napier Road had raised its murderous head. It was a problem so horrid in its nature it caused a grieving expression on Sheriff Bana's face that Rex hadn't seen since his mother died. Even Migisi had grown tense when asked about this problem and he said little except that children should heed Sheriff Bana's warning.

"Don't walk home alone! Beware of strangers!" Migisi told Rex. Then he had shuddered and gone tightlipped.

Sheriff Bana declared it would be safer for Rex to walk to and from school with Sara, who was sixteen, three years older than Rex. Rex enjoyed Sara's company, but she wasn't a puddle jumper, nor would she ride her bike to school. Rex had to hoof it if he wanted to get to school and back home again with Sara. "Hoof it" was a phrase Migisi used which Rex was keen on and used whenever he could figure out a way to use it.

Today something had happened in class that made Rex more upset than the problem on Napier Road. Today his teacher, Mrs. Tharp, made Rex so mad that he broke the rules and didn't wait for Sara to meet him in front of Salem Middle School so they could walk home together.

Rex reminded himself Sara was often late linking with him for their journey home. Sara was in high school and Rex didn't mind waiting for Sara in front of the middle school while she was "shooting the breeze" (another of Migisi's sayings) with her friends. Rex knew everyone liked Sara as much as he did, and he knew she often got to yakitty yak with some of her scary looking girlfriends after school. But today Rex had been so frustrated and confused—no, he was down right mad—by Mrs. Tharp's actions that he didn't feel like waiting in the cold mist for Sara's glowing enthusiasm to join him and warm his afternoon. Instead, he thought he'd take the opportunity to puddle jump and sulk by his lonesome. He didn't know what he wanted to prove by this act of defiance, but just as he thought it was every kid's right to puddle jump, he thought it was every kid's right to stomp off and sulk by his lonesome.

As Thanksgiving Day had approached, Mrs. Tharp had offered Rex's class a chance to earn extra credit in social studies. The students were to draw, paint, or create something from the Thanksgiving Banquet where the Pilgrims and Native Americans had celebrated life together. Rex didn't need the extra points, but he found the task exciting to his creative mind. It would give him a project to work on, and it would be a way he could show off his Chippewa heritage of which he was so proud.

Rex's mother, Namid, had been a full-blooded Chippewa, and during Namid's sickness, Migisi, her father, came to live with the Banas to help bare the burden of Namid's long illness. Migisi had stayed on with the Banas after Namid's death; and although Migisi could not replace the hole left in the lives of the Banas by Namid's passing, he grew to be a warm and much appreciated addition in their hearts and home. Migisi had the heart of a youngster and was just as active.

Rex told Migisi about his idea for the social studies project, and together they made a youth size version of a Chippewa bow and arrow. It was Rex's first usable bow and he was proud to stand in front of his class to show them the things Migisi taught him about the bow's making and usage. It never entered Rex's mind the bow and arrow might be considered a "weapon," or something inappropriate to have in a seventh grade classroom.

Rex's friends were awed by the bow and arrow just as he figured. And just as Rex planned, the girls turned squeamish when he described how the arrow could crack a rabbit's back, or be shot through the animal leaving a nasty hole with blood and guts spilled all over the place. But Rex had not planned on Mrs. Tharp's reaction. Mrs. Tharp found Rex's presentation "a little too authentic."

"Take it back home. I'm sure your grandfather could use it," Mrs. Tharp had said as she looked down at Rex with what he felt was a sarcastic smile and it was in front of the whole class. Rex thought he heard a few snickers from his classmates as he returned to his desk with his project. He felt they were laughing at his darker skin and his lengthy black hair. Rex thought the funny part about the bow and arrow was that they could be seen as authentic Native American tools. Migisi was a member of the Chippewa-Ojibwa Tribe, thus according to Rex's logic, the tools Migisi made were real Native American products.

*Geez*, Rex thought. *How authentic could one get for Thanksgiving?*

"Show it to your father. He'll understand," Mrs. Tharp said to Rex after class. Rex kept his mouth shut, but Sheriff Bana knew about the bow and arrow all along and had proclaimed them, "Neat-o."

How'd Mrs. Tharp think Rex could have gotten a bow and arrow out of the house if big daddy-o hadn't given his a-okay to the project?

"You're as cold as ice. You're willing to sacrifice our love …"

As Rex continued down Napier Road, he switched his mental jukebox to the song, "Cold as Ice," sung by a new group calling themselves, "Foreigner." Foreigner's album had been released last summer, and it was still getting a lot of playing time on the RIFF—WRIF—Detroit's home of rock'n roll. YEAH, BABY!

Rex was still saving his allowance to buy that record.

Rex figured Mrs. Tharp should know Sheriff Bana was not a dummy, especially when it came to allowing his children to handle weapons.

Jimminy Christmas! Every Sunday after church, Rex would race upstairs, leap into Migisi's bed, and they'd wrestle for who was cleaning the breakfast dishes. After the dishes and other shenanigans (as Walter would call them) the sheriff, Migisi, and Rex would head down to the Salem Township Sheriff's Office, open the weapons safe, and they would clean the weapons. Walter or Migisi would show Rex the finer points to gun safety and a gun's proper usage during these times. Sheriff Bana would occasionally take them over to the HUNT & GRUNT CLUB, where they would practice shooting at the gun range.

Sheriff Bana gave Rex a .22-caliber Winchester Model 70 Featherweight rifle on his eleventh birthday. Rex went "spastic," as Sara would say. He spent hours getting the feel of the rifle as he cleaned and oiled it, then he'd clean and oil it again. At the shooting range, Migisi declared Rex had the sharpest eye he'd ever seen. Rex even beat Sheriff Bana in accumulative accuracy with a target rifle.

Rex maintained his Winchester in such fine condition, and he showed such responsibility handling firearms, Walter allowed his son to work and clean his service revolvers. Sheriff Bana also taught Rex and Sara how to use a hand gun in self defense. Sheriff Bana was a big supporter of Michigan gun control and education, especially when it came to having teenagers and guns in the same household.

But there was this murderous problem along Napier Road that had everyone worried and scared. For Rex, fear of this problem was becoming mind consuming at times. At other times the problem hovered in the back of his conscious like a monster lurking beneath his bed ready to grab his ankles if Rex dropped his feet to the floor.

Rex had just been getting over his embarrassment in front of the class when Mrs. Tharp announced they would be spending their final forty-five minute period of the day in the gym to hear a "special announcement." Rex had raised his head again with excitement upon hearing this since doing anything outside his stuffy classroom meant a change. He had hopped to the front of the line and dared to face Mrs. Tharp's big and smelly bottom as he followed her with the rest of the class to the gym.

Then Rex had seen the hall to the gym was crammed with kids from other classes, and he had known it was going to be another one of those general announcements for everyone in the middle school to hear. Rex's excitement had dwindled since he knew this meant forty-five minutes of sitting on the hard wooden floor wondering if the bones in his butt were going to cut through his skin as he sat and listened to a lecture from an adult telling him what he should or should not do. With his emotional bubble popped, Rex had followed Mrs. Tharp's big bottom into the gym. He found a spot on the dusty parquet floor and held another spot free until his buddy Jimmy could join him.

Much to Rex's delight, Jimmy Swanson had sat beside him to pester and poke him. Rex recalled that most of the kids sat cross-legged on the gym floor with big eyes as they listened to Deputy Madison from Salem Township's Sheriff's Office make his presentation.

Deputy Madison had walked back and forth beneath the basketball net and given them a warning to avoid strangers that approached them when they were alone. He stated they should NEVER—Never get into the car of a grown-up they didn't know, unless it was a police car and there was a policeman dressed like him driving the car.

It was scary stuff when a deputy came to their school to tell everyone to BEWARE! Rex had seen Deputy Madison wore a shiny black utility belt that creaked when he moved about. Deputy Madison had carried a gun holster which held a real gun strapped onto his creaking belt. Not that Rex had been afraid of the gun; he'd known about guns.

The special announcement had turned out to be a tummy-tumbler. Rex had been shocked when Deputy Madison barked out a statement concerning the two children from Salem Middle School which had disappeared over the last six-weeks. These were kids from Rex's own school. Deputy Madison had confirmed two children, each walking home by themselves along Napier Road, had never made it to the warm safety of their households. The whereabouts of each child was unknown, but Deputy Madison had claimed they were believed to have been kidnapped and were now dead.

It had not been until then, when Deputy Madison had stalked back and forth before the entire middle school that Rex realized what happened to those children. Everyone had known kids were disappearing. It was still at the top of everyone's neat-things-to-know list.

Rex hadn't known either of the missing children personally, and he didn't want to think about where they had gone. Most of all, he'd tried not to think about the queer adult who was grabbing kids walking home on Napier Road, molesting them, and then killing them—killing them dead.

"Molesting" was another word Rex knew from asking Sara to define after one of Sheriff Bana's lectures on this same subject. Sara explained about molestation with a serious expression on her face, and by the time she finished Rex understood why.

Sheriff Bana had been warning Rex and Sara against accepting rides or taking things from strangers for as long as Rex could remember. Rex always treated the warnings as if the problem was one of those things that would never happen to him. It was a warning that went in one of his ears and out the other. Rex had never associated the disappearance of the two children from his school with his father's words of caution. Yet after the gym lights were dimmed, and Deputy Madison had shown his short film, Rex had found the meaning behind his father's words. He understood why his father tried to drill these warnings into his noggin.

The film had shown a naked child's body, from a distance, as it floated down a stream surrounded by trees. The film had been in black and white and it was splotchy as if it was homemade. The sense that the film appeared homemade made it more realistic to Rex and drove home what Deputy Madison said about molesters. Deputy Madison had told them the floating body was what happened to children that accepted rides from strangers. Rex had seen the kid in the movie was dead, really dead. It had been the first time he'd seen a body that wasn't an actor pretending to be dead. This made the special announcement a lifetime experience for Rex.

During the film, Rex had not liked to see the child's body floating down the stream, so he poked back at Jimmy Swanson and examined the wooded area in the film instead. Rex saw the stream and the woods in the movie produced a scene he could easily find in rural Salem Township. He had even been able to imagine the scene coming from somewhere on the Bana's wooded fifty acres. He couldn't shake the feeling he might have been the kid in the film, and this idea had both scared Rex and set the reality in his mind. Rex recalled that death was real as he had been reminded of the pain he still felt from losing his mother.

These thoughts led Rex to imagine what it must be like for the families of these dead or missing children. What hit Rex the hardest was he knew the murdered kids would not be going home. For the first time since his mother died, Rex had that terrible feeling in his stomach which felt as if molten lead was burning out his innards. He knew what it was like being a close family member of someone who'd died.

Deputy Madison had emphasized this point by shouting that any of the children in the gym could be the next kid floating down that stream if they didn't heed his warning. He said one of them might be the child that doesn't return home after school to be with their families.

Rex had stopped pestering Jimmy and listened to Deputy Madison as he gave his presentation in a dramatic fashion that was obviously meant to scare the children. After the film, Rex had noted the deputy's face was hot and sweaty. Rex had gotten the feeling the deputy enjoyed scaring the bajeebees out of the kids with his loud scary tone. When Deputy Madison glared down at his audience some the girls had cowered away from his gaze—some of the younger children had cried.

Jimmy had pestered Rex all the way back to class saying: "Did ya see that kid floating in the stream? Nobody could hold their breath that long. That couldn't be an actor. No way, José. I tried it once. That had to be a real—dead person—dead kid. Did ya see how that kid's butt floated? Did ya see how white that kid was?"

"Of course I saw," Rex had replied as he elbowed Jimmy's skinny ribs in an attempt to get him off his back. "But the movie was in black and white so anything dead would have looked white, ya moron."

Jimmy said he wasn't a moron, but he wouldn't let up either. "Oh, that was so gross. That kid was really dead. Did ya see?"

Rex had seen, but he remained silent.

Rex knew about death.

Rex stopped singing as he got about halfway home going down Napier Road. His head was down as the gusts of wind picked up icy raindrops and drove them into his body, face, and eyes. As the ice pelted off Rex's jacket, he huddled his shoulders together in an attempt to keep warm. His exposed left hand, which carried his possessions, was numbing in the chill of the wind. His other hand was in his pocket, bunching his jacket close to his body. As his boots crunched through a shallow mud puddle of ice, Rex felt a shadow cross his path and he looked up.

Two figures hopped out from behind an oak tree with a stumble and a push. It took Rex a moment to identify them, and to his dismay, he recognized Kevin Greer and Bobby Higgenson, two of his classmates. Rex would have laughed at the duet's comic bound onto the road, but he sensed trouble if only from their reputations.

Rex didn't care for either Kevin or Higgy, and as far as he knew, neither did anyone else. Rex thought it odd to see Kevin and Higgy together since he was under the impression they hated each other's guts just like everyone else did. The alliance of these two outside a structured environment could only lead to disaster. Rex felt his muscles stiffen with tension at the thought of trouble. It occurred to him, that if there was trouble, he could outrun these two without much effort.

But then, why should he?

It had been a poor day at school, and Rex was in the mood to vent some frustrations. If these two clowns were going to start something, he'd be happy to give them all they wanted.

Rex knew kids disliked Kevin Greer because he was a mischievous troublemaker with never a kind thing to say, but Rex avoided Kevin because Kevin didn't bathe or scrub his teeth. Kevin's presence took all the freshness from the air. Yet as far as being an opponent in a fight, Rex thought Kevin appeared scrawny and was no match for his size and strength. Kevin was nothing to fear.

Bobby Higgenson was a troubled story for Rex. He knew Higgy was the only child of an alcoholic and abusive father—getting the goods on other kids in town was one of the perks of being the sheriff's son—and Rex knew Bobby was frequently absent from the classroom. Even when Bobby came to school he was a bully and spent much of his time in the principal's office. Rex also knew this was Bobby's second attempt to pass the seventh grade due to his absence from school. Higgy was a big dummy at times, but Rex had wondered if Higgy wasn't stupid, he just didn't want to be in class and he didn't apply himself.

When Bobby was in class, Rex noticed his face usually carried the same slack expression. Normally, there was no facial tone in Bobby's face, and his pale freckled skin hung beneath his carrot top. His eyelids would fall to half mast and his yellow brown eyes would remain dull in appearance. But the reason Rex always felt Bobby's expression was so creepy was because it seemed as if Bobby had no emotions, and this was a theory he was about to test.

Right now Rex could see Bobby's eyes bulge as if it was Monday morning and he was gazing at a sixth grader with a week's worth of milk money. Rex also noted Bobby's grin was wide, exposing his beaver-like teeth. Rex smirked at this thought and it brought a smile to his face.

Rex came to a halt as he observed the devilish intensity of Bobby's eyes.

Rex realized he was still smiling and his slowness might be seen as a sign of fear. Then Rex's pride turned his grin into pressed lips of determination and got him moving again. Rex glared defiantly at Kevin and Bobby as he restarted his advance, daring them to stall his path. Rex caught sight of Greer's grimy grin as he neared the unlikely duo. Kevin must have noticed Rex's look of repulsion since he stopped smiling and got down to business.

"Hey, Tonto. Ya wanna play Cowboys and Injuns with me and Higgy?"

Again Rex slowed to a halt, now just a few feet from these highway hoodlums.

"No thanks—it's too wet and cold," Rex responded before lowering his head and continuing his march. Rex walked between the roadblock, knocking Kevin out of way and bouncing off Bobby's belly.

As Rex pushed Kevin aside he could smell the boy's stench, and he heard Higgy "Oooaff" through his beaver teeth as Rex elbowed a clearing. Rex knew he was picking a fight with this bold move, and his heart pounded with anticipation of what was going to happen next. While continuing his determined pace down Napier Road, Rex expected to be jumped from behind at any second. Rex didn't believe he could get away with just blowing through Kevin and Higgy. He decided they hadn't expected him to pass right through them without an ounce of fear or respect. Rex figured they were too dumb to have decided what to do if he failed to be petrified by their unexpected appearance.

Rex didn't get too far down through the slush and mud before Kevin recovered his wits and chased after him. Kevin caught up with Rex and grabbed the end of his bow. As Kevin pulled the bow out of Rex's hand, he spilled Rex's books and the arrow onto the muddy sludge of the road. Rex whipped around to recover his bow, but Bobby had snuck up behind him and shoved Rex in the back. Bobby's shove caught Rex off balance and sent him slip-sliding into the icy muck. Rex came down hard on his books and the arrow. The shaft of the arrow snapped in two.

"That does it," Rex growled, rising from the ice puddle which had soaked the side of his jacket and jeans. He turned and planted his feet shoulder width apart the way Migisi had taught him. Migisi, a master of Indian wrestling, taught Rex one of the keys to winning a fight was remaining calm and not wasting energy. Rex calmed himself through deep breaths, and he took the time to tie his pony tail in a knot. Rex glared into Bobby's eyes.

Kevin danced in small circles off to Rex's right with Rex's bow held high in one hand while he popped his revolting mouth with his other palm and yelled, "… Aw wah wah wah—Aw wah …" in his imitation of a cinematic Native

American. Rex ignored the idiot and concentrated on his main target, big Bobby.

"What's ya gonna do now, Bana baby?" Bobby crumpled his face in his best cry baby act. Bobby never finished his act as Rex ran two-steps forward and kicked Bobby in the crotch as if he was trying to punt a football out of the stadium. One of the things Migisi taught Rex was there were no rules in a street fight.

Rex thanked his lucky stars that he was wearing his boots to support his ankle and foot which went numb after his stellar kick. He'd kicked Bobby so hard he was afraid he'd broken his ankle.

It was then Rex noted Bobby was capable of real facial expressions of emotion and pain. He decided Bobby just needed the proper incentive.

Bobby's first expression was one of surprise as his eyes popped open wide and his mouth formed a big O of intestinal suffering.

"Owww—that musta hurt." Rex grimaced as he watched Bobby's face take on new expressions reflecting his internal pain. Rex could not enjoy Bobby's mimics as Bobby clawed at his crotch with both hands and doubled over as if he was a bobbing for apples. Rex walked around in an effort to regain feeling in his lower extremity. He worked his foot and ankle which seemed to do the trick as he shook off the numbness.

During Rex and Bobby's brief entanglement, Kevin had continued his sleet dance. He was oblivious to Bobby's demise. Rex figured Kevin depended on big Bobby's bulliness to straighten things out if something went wrong with their scheme—if they ever had a scheme.

Later, Rex figured Kevin and Bobby had been waiting on some smaller targets to be walking home from school, but in the foggy sleet they'd been surprised to come across Rex alone with his bow and arrow. Still, Kevin must have expected Bobby to take on Rex without a hitch since Kevin's expression was one of comical surprise when he saw Rex charging toward him to retrieve his bow and deliver some punishment in compensation for his wet delay.

After stalking down Kevin, Rex grabbed back his bow and glared down at the cowering beagle-faced kid with a look of gleeful anticipation. Having learned and practiced many wresting moves from Migisi, Rex rarely had a chance to practice on anyone other than Migisi or Jimmy Swanson. So it was with a manner of glee that Rex took out his day's frustrations on Kevin Greer.

Laying his bow next to his soggy math book and broken arrow, Rex rose again to look down at Kevin. To his disappointment, Kevin had used Rex's moment of distraction to turn and run.

Kevin only ran a few steps before Rex leaped forward and grabbed him from behind. Kevin squealed like the dirty pig he was as Rex wrapped his right arm under Kevin's armpit and around his bony chest. Then Rex threw his butt into Kevin's rear while bending over at the same time to lay Kevin across his back. Rex flipped Kevin over his back before he body slammed him onto the icy mud of the road. To Rex, Kevin felt as light as a feather as he whipped him over and threw him face first into the cold sludge of the dirt road.

"YEAH!" Rex yelled in a shout of triumphant celebration. If Kevin made any sound, Rex didn't notice.

Rex kneeled on Kevin's back and heard an "Oaffff" escape from the boy's thin chest. Rex grabbed Kevin's greasy hair and lowered his mouth next to Kevin's left ear. He got a whiff of Kevin's filth even through his own excitement before saying, "Okay, white boy! Let's see how you like the feel of some darker skin."

Rex slammed Kevin's face into a muddy puddle. With his free hand, Rex scooped sludge from the road and smeared it over Kevin's face, neck, and down his shirt. Rex felt his hand enter Kevin's mouth with a handful of gravel and mud, but he kept Kevin's head out of the puddle since embarrassment was his goal—not drowning.

Rex sat on Kevin and slapped mud on Kevin's head when Bobby came back, grabbed the collar of Rex's jacket with both hands, and hauled him off Kevin's struggling body.

"Ya shouldn' of done that, Bana," Bobby growled as he wrenched Rex off Kevin's back. Rex whipped his right arm out of his jacket, and then threw his fist, arm, and shoulder between Bobby's legs. Rex used the same move he'd practiced on Kevin. He flowed with the momentum of his throw and lifted Bobby across his back while wrapping his left arm and shoulder beneath Bobby's left armpit. As the momentum of Rex's move lifted the startled Higgy off the ground, Rex pushed up hard with his right foot and dropped to his left knee. Using their combined weight allowed Rex to flip Bobby over his body and slam him on Napier Road stretched out on his back. Bobby landed with a muddy splat, but Rex was unable to untangle himself and crashed butt first onto Bobby's belly facing Bobby's feet. Rex didn't see Bobby's open mouth expression of terror as Bobby flew through the air, but Rex got the full effect of Bobby's flagellation when he landed on Bobby's belly and squished his intestines.

With his emotions running full tilt, Rex laughed at Bobby's gaseous release, but he maintained his weight on Bobby while he twisted around and placed his knees on Bobby's armpits. Then Rex sat upon Bobby's chest and leered down at him. Now Rex was able to see an expression he'd never experienced on Bobby's face—he saw fear.

Rex had been upset enough to mess up Bobby the way he was sure Bobby would have done to him if their places were reversed, but after seeing the fear in Bobby's eyes like a frightened child, and having heard the flapping cheeks of Bobby's defeat, Rex settled for the humiliation of his wet and mud-covered opponent.

Rex satisfied himself with playing "Chinese torture." He rapped the knuckle of his index finger hard on Bobby's breastbone while he maintained his weight on Bobby's stomach so Bobby couldn't catch his breath.

Rex had been in Bobby's position before, and he knew this torture to be more frightening and humiliating than a couple knocks on the side of his head. Rex had just sat down for a good session of humiliation when he saw Kevin Greer take off running down Napier Road. Rex considered giving Bobby a break so he could chase after Kevin when the blurp of a police siren behind Rex surprised him. Rex leaped off Bobby and spun around only to be blinded by a searchlight pointed into his face.

Rex put the back of his hand across his brow to block the brightness of the spotlight, and he saw a police cruiser had snuck to within ten-feet without being noticed. Rex recognized the car as one of Salem Township's cruisers. He knew he would be recognized and made no attempt to run away.

Rex hoped to keep his trouble to a minimum when he grabbed Bobby by the hand and hauled him out of the muddy goo as only a gentleman would do. If there was trouble, he wanted to make sure Bobby got his share of it as well. Now the two of them stood there in the same taut position and faced the police cruiser. They had their hands over their brows in an effort to see what was going on without being blinded by the spotlight.

"Aw shit," Bobby grumbled. The seriousness of Bobby's tone cracked a smile on Rex's face. He hadn't expected to hear the "S" word come so easily from Bobby's mouth.

"Nice one, Higgy. I'm sure talking like that will get us out of trouble," Rex said openly.

"Ya gotta save me, Bana. If my dad finds out I've been messing around after school again he'll whip me bad," Bobby whined out of the side of his mouth.

Rex figured Bobby should have thought of that before he pushed and shoved Rex about, but just then the cruiser's door opened and Deputy Madison climbed out.

Rex knew he'd been recognized when Deputy Madison shut off the cruiser's light show. The sight of Deputy Madison didn't lessen Rex's anxiousness. He felt a queer chill at the sight of Deputy Madison that he couldn't identify, and his stomach continued its tummy-tumbling of the molten lead.

"You boys getting into trouble?" Deputy Madison asked.

Rex had dropped his hand and now looked down at his possessions scattered about the road. Deputy Madison was determined to have their attention, and he marched toward them through the sleet in the parade uniform that he'd been wearing at school. Rex looked up at the officer's steps in time to see a powerful gust of wind rip the hair off the top of Madison's head. Rex would not have believed his eyes if Deputy Madison hadn't slapped the top of his bald head while making such an openmouthed expression of horror.

Rex had never seen a toupee up close and personal like this, and having seen it fly off Deputy Madison's head at such a moment seemed the funniest thing in the world. Rex exploded with roaring gales of laughter as Madison shuffled and kicked after his hairpiece.

Bobby wasn't a fool. Rex saw Bobby must have thought the dancing toupee was a sign from heaven the way he turned and raced toward the nearest trees. For some reason the vision of Bobby high kneeing it across the road made Rex laugh even harder. But Rex's laughter came to an abrupt halt.

Rex watched as Deputy Madison caught the mucky sounds of Bobby's running footsteps. Deputy Madison whipped around, and glared at Bobby's running figure with a look of hatred Rex could imagine on a devil. Madison's lips were pulled back in a snarl, and his exposed forehead was pushed down, making his eyes inhuman slits of loathing. Rex thought he could even see Madison's nostrils flaring.

"HALT!" Deputy Madison yelled with the authority an officer might yell at an armed felon before shooting to kill. It was certainly not a shout to use on an escaping seventh grader. To Rex's amazement, Deputy Madison snapped open his holster and pulled out his gun.

Deputy Madison's intentions became obvious and Rex yelled, "Hey! You can't shoot Bobby!"

Madison ignored Rex and continued to draw his revolver from his holster with the practiced efficiency of an officer tracking a deadly criminal. As

Deputy Madison brought up his gun, he assumed a shooter's stance to target Bobby's fleeing backside.

"What are you doing?" Sara shouted from behind the police cruiser.

The affects of Sara's voice were instantaneous. It spelled relief for Rex, but he saw it affected Deputy Madison as if Sara had plunged a knife into his back. Madison shot out his arms and threw back his head as if he was in terrible pain. Madison's act was so quick Rex wasn't sure that he saw it before Madison had lowered his arms and spun his revolver back into his holster. The whole motion happened so fast that Rex couldn't believe Deputy Madison as he did an about face to greet Sara with a smile on his face as if she had just accepted his invitation to a dance.

"Sara, I'm so glad I caught up with you." Deputy Madison gleamed. Rex knew Madison must have just passed Sara on Napier Road and obviously had not stopped to greet her then.

Sara walked around the police car towards Rex without saying a word, but Rex saw the scolding look she gave Deputy Madison, and he knew she was thinking, "What a creep!" Rex watched Madison's lizard eyes fall toward Sara's breasts through her half buttoned jacket.

Sara gave Deputy Madison a wide berth as she walked over to Rex with her back to Madison. Rex envied Sara's tallness, like her father, yet she carried the beauty of her Native American mother even in the foul weather. Sara looked at Rex with concern in her black-brown eyes that were so similar to his. Her thick black hair was matted over her head and shoulders like a mantle. She wore a denim jacket similar to Rex's except hers was made for girls, and Rex thought she looked ten times better than he did in his. Her smooth coffee-colored complexion, high cheekbones, and forehead were held aloof by a cream colored turtleneck sweater. The sweater appeared so soft and cozy to Rex he wanted to bury his face in her chest. He wanted to hug her tight so he could feel her warmth and the safety of her strong heartbeat. Sara raised her hand, with her straight thick fingers and long sharp nails, and she cupped the side of Rex's face as she looked down on him.

"Are you all right?" she asked and pulled some hair away from his face.

"Yeah—sure," Rex replied before turning his face away. He didn't need to be mothered in public.

"Are you sure? I'm sorry I'm late," she said with a smile and showed a set of teeth which brightened the day for Rex.

"Yeah, no problem," Rex said and smiled despite himself. It had only taken the warm touch of Sara's hand to make him forget the troubles over which he'd been sulking.

"Hey, kids?" Deputy Madison hollered from behind Sara's back.

*Oh yeah*, Rex thought, *forgot all about him*. Sara made a reverse pivot to stand at Rex's side so they both faced the bald and wet Deputy Madison. "That's a new look for you, isn't it, Deputy Madison?" Sara said with a sarcastic grin.

"Ah, I hope you won't mention this minor incident to your father." Madison grinned, avoiding Sara's gaze and comment. Fog blossomed from his mouth from his short and hot breaths. Rex knew he'd be telling his father every detail of Deputy Madison's behavior the moment he met up with big daddy-o. Rex didn't like Deputy Madison at all—especially after the way Madison gazed at Sara with hungry eyes that disgusted Rex.

Apparently Madison wasn't happy with Sara's lack of response, and he took an aggressive step closer to Rex and Sara.

Sara wrapped her arm around Rex's shoulder and drew him back from Deputy Madison's advance. Rex sensed Sara's fear, and it confused him. As they retreated, Madison bounded forward to close his position on them. Rex looked into Deputy Madison's eyes and was shocked to see Madison's expression had reverted to that loathing snarl.

"Nooooo—ha!" Sara exclaimed as she squeezed Rex tighter and pulled him back in retreat. Rex saw his chance to retrieve his books, bow, and broken arrow and ripped away from Sara to retrieve his ruined belongings. As he bent Deputy Madison seized his chance and grabbed Rex by the arm in a manner that was not polite or friendly.

Rex heard Sara gasp with surprise as Madison gripped his arm and twisted it behind his back. Rex was now facing Sara and his arm was being pushed up his back enough to be painful and add a shocked expression to his face.

Rex could see the surprised look on Sara's face. He noted she still had her books in one hand while she glared back at Madison with her other hand covering her open mouth.

Rex was so shocked by Deputy Madison's actions he didn't struggle since he knew he had to be polite and obey the deputy. Rex figured he was in enough trouble as it was. Yet, he started to get scared when Deputy Madison reached into his utility belt and pulled out a set of handcuffs. In one fluid motion Madison threw a handcuff around Rex's wrist and locked it.

"Give me your wrist, Sara. Come on, play along. You won't get into any trouble," Deputy Madison said as he held out his palm to Sara while maintaining a pinching grasp on Rex's arm.

This was all wrong, thought Rex, very wrong. A picture of the child's body floating down the stream and the anxious feeling that the child might have been him returned to Rex's mind. He thought of the two children who disappeared while walking home from school on Napier Road. Deputy Madison had said the children were dead, but how would he know the children were dead if their bodies had not been found?

*Hold-on! This isn't right!*

Now Rex could see Sara giving in to Deputy Madison—moving toward him. *No Way José!*

Rex jerked on Deputy Madison's arm and yelled, "Run Sara! Run!"

Deputy Madison jumped at the fierceness of Rex's warning and his light body frame was pulled forward by the vigor in Rex's yank. As Deputy Madison regained his balance, he threw a bony fist into the side of Rex's head and growled, "That'll be enough outta you, boy."

Rex saw the punch come, and he had time to avoid it. Yet he was so surprised an officer of the law would swing at him, he stood there and got clobbered. For a second, Rex was paralyzed. Everything went white. He couldn't see, hear, or move. There was a feel as if hot water ran down the side of his head from his temple to his jaw line. Rex had the impression this feel of hot water was blood, and he felt his knees weaken. He momentarily fell into Deputy Madison … he leaned his back into Madison's chest.

Rex blinked a few times, and his vision returned to normal in time to see Sara's face take on an expression of loathing not too different from Madison's a moment ago. Her eyes lit up with the fury of a mother seeing her child slapped by a monster. A snarl took form on her lips. Sara dropped her books and leapt toward Madison and Rex with her hands stretched out as if they were an eagle's talons and she bored down to rip out Madison's neck.

Rex watched the fury of Sara as his mind tried to correlate information from his bruised senses. Rex watched Sara, and he saw every detail of her assault, from the wrath in her eyes, to the spit that escaped her exposed teeth. This was a side of Sara that Rex had never imagined. Rex felt Deputy Madison wrap his arm around his chest and draw him closer into his body at the same time.

Rex was back to his alert self when he felt Madison jam his gun barrel against his head. Rex watched Sara skid to a halt as she saw the threat that Madison would shoot Rex. Rex looked up at Sara to know what to do, but she had become a quivering statue of rage. Her dark eyes cooled to black coals as she squinted with frustrated anger. She pressed her lips together so hard her mouth disappeared, and she dropped her hands to her sides where they clenched and unclenched.

"What are you doing?" Sara pleaded. Deputy Madison adjusted his hold as Rex came alive and started to struggle.

"Come on, into the car," Deputy Madison commanded.

"And if we don't?" Sara retorted.

Deputy Madison didn't answer vocally, but Rex heard the trigger of his gun click into firing position. Madison punched the barrel of his revolver into Rex's head to emphasize his point.

Sara looked into Rex's eyes. Rex could never be sure what she saw there. Sara's eyes were defiant, but Rex winced as the gun was poked harder against his head. When Rex opened his eyes, he could see Sara maintained her defiance, but she had started to move toward the cruiser. Rex wondered if this was her plan to run away.

Rex was disciplined by Migisi's first rule of fighting and that was to remain calm. Rex remained calm which allowed him to think. Rex thought about the outcome of them getting into that cruiser if Deputy Madison was the killer of children along Napier Road. Rex knew they were dead if they got into that cruiser. Rex figured he and Sara had to make their fight now while they were on the open road and there remained some freedom of action.

If anything, Rex figured Sara should run for help while he kept Madison busy since he was entangled with the officer. Rex knew there were other kids walking home along Napier Road that would hear Sara's cries for help. Rex had passed a neighborhood not too far back. Someone there could call for big Sheriff Bana.

Knowing he must have patience, Rex waited for his opportunity to arise. Deputy Madison had to shuffle both Rex and himself to open the passenger door of the cruiser if he wanted to get Sara and Rex into the backseat. Rex knew Sara would not open the car door herself. She'd stall getting into the car as if her life depended on it.

Rex played along, waiting for their positions to be right. He needed Deputy Madison's attention to be off for a second while the Deputy's weight was above him. Rex figured that moment would come when Deputy Madison had to use one of his hands to open the backdoor.

Sara moved slowly toward the cruiser as if she was thinking about what to do just as Rex hoped she would. Sara neared the front passenger door, with Rex and Deputy Madison shuffling close behind, and then she came to an abrupt halt and started to whirl around.

This was Rex's chance. He couldn't believe Sara was trying some stunt on her own, but he wasn't about to let an opportunity pass.

Madison was momentarily occupied with what Sara was doing. Rex felt the pressure of the arm around his chest loosen, and the gun was pulled away from his head. Rex latched onto Madison's arm and threw his weight back into Madison's knees while he ducked forward.

Madison was caught off guard, and he threw his revolver hand toward the sky in an attempt to maintain his balance. Madison fired his pistol by accident while he tried to regain his balance.

"Run, Sara, run!" Rex shouted as the gunshot deafened his ears.

Deputy Madison quickly recovered and he pulled Rex tight to his body again. Rex turned his head to see if Sara would get away but there was a sharp pain behind his right ear and he was blinded by whiteness before everything became black and he knew no more.

---

Rex awoke abruptly to consciousness as he gagged and coughed for breath. His eyes popped wide, yet he sensed pain as if his arms and legs were torn from his body as they were each pulled in a different direction at once. The pain was so bad, and the gagging feeling was so urgent, that Rex didn't notice Deputy Madison's face so close to his own. Rex felt Madison's hot wet breath spew across his facial skin before Madison laughed and pulled away from him.

Suddenly it all came back to Rex ... the fight with Higgy ... Deputy Madison grabbing him away from Sara ... did Sara escape? He knew he was hit by something hard in the back of the head. Ow—how his head hurt behind his ear.

Rex realized he was being held in a standing position upon the wooden supports of a wall. His arms were stretched in their respective directions by something wrapped around each wrist. His feet were being pulled so far apart Rex felt he was doing splits like he'd seen Sara do in cheerleading practice. Rex discovered there was a rope tied around his neck which choked him whenever he tried to relax the stretch of his arms or legs. He found he could only loosen the rope around his neck and catch his breath while contracting his chest and groin muscles and trying to bring his arms and legs together. Yet it took a tremendous amount of strength to contract either his legs or his arms. He understood it wasn't going to be long before his muscles failed and he hung himself.

Rex twisted his elbows outward to put some of the strain on his wrists while he bent his knees inward. When he did this, he discovered an awkward holding position which was endurable and allowed him to breathe. It was a painful position, and Rex was frightfully aware he could not maintain it all day, but at least now he could think and figure out what was going on around him while he determined a method of escape from this bind.

Given a moment to concentrate on something other than himself, Rex's ears perked and his eyes focused to discover a violent struggle that was taking place only feet away.

"Sara?" he croaked, but he was unable to make himself heard due to the dryness in his throat and the noise of the fight. A bare light bulb was swinging within an inch of his head. Rex was blinded by the light's glare as it swooped back and forth. The bulb's heat and glare were terribly frightening in unison with the noises of the struggle. Rex figured Sara had been tied and gagged since she didn't give him a direct response.

Rex could hear Sara's muffled screams between his own strangled breaths as they echoed off the close walls of their closed confinement. The sounds of Sara's struggles awoke the rage in Rex. He fought with all his might against his restraints, but he only managed to choke himself with the rope around his neck.

Rex searched desperately for a way to see Sara, and he became aware of cruel instruments of destruction hanging on the wall to his left. Rex found he could almost grasp one of the homemade knives, cleavers, and hooks of medieval torture when he thrashed about. And his heart soared with hope when he spied the modern day tool of their salvation hanging from a hook next to the other tools of death. Madison had hung his gun belt and his revolver in its holster with the rest of his deadly devices.

Rex heard Madison's grunts and groans amid Sara's muffled pleas and knew Madison was a monster beyond his wildest dreams, beyond anything he'd seen in a horror film, or read about in a comic book. Madison was a monster of reality. Rex understood that if he and Sara were going to survive that he'd have to renew his efforts to release himself.

Rex bowed and bucked his body as much as his neck would endure. At the same time his eyes searched for a mode of escape—a door from this confined room. He heard Sara's cries as well as Madison's bestial grunts and groans as they reached a fevered pace.

Just when Rex thought his muscles were going to give out the light either flickered or he had started to faint. Rex first assumed he was on the verge of passing out and he moved to his holding position so his muscles could rest.

Rex was able to think after a moment of rest. He realized he'd caught a brief glimpse of the prone figure of Deputy Madison on top of Sara on the floor not ten feet in front of him. This fact told Rex that it was the light bulb that must have gone off for a second before coming on again and blinding him.

Rex renewed his efforts to escape his restraints as the need to defend Sara exploded through his youthful muscles. As he viciously assaulted his restraints, and endured the pain around his neck, Rex discovered that he could loosen the hold around his right wrist. When he relaxed and stretched the muscles across his left shoulder and back he could straighten his right arm beyond a point his restrain was pulling on his wrist. But as Rex attempted to repeat this move, Madison broke into the glare of the light bulb and scared him back to hanging himself.

Initially, Rex thought Madison was some horror film monster, something from a nightmare, and he struggled and gagged to breathe. Then Rex recognized Madison's evil grin and was surprised by his face and uneven teeth which were smeared with the bright red of blood and bubbly drool. Fortunately, Rex's mind was in no position to determine what the gruel dripping off Madison's chin and chest might mean in terms of his or Sara's life. Madison kneeled in front of Rex and pulled upward on a large rusty ring attached to a trapdoor in the floor that Rex had not noticed before.

Rex felt relief from the cold draft of air which blew through the trapdoor. This relief was short lived as Madison slipped down the hole in the floor before reaching back up and quietly returning the door into place.

After Madison closed the trapdoor, Rex realized something was different. Something just happened which his muddled mind couldn't grasp. The room had fallen silent. Rex's rage exploded—he could no longer hear Sara's cries or movements.

"Sara?" Rex tried but discovered he was not capable of more than a whisper, and even his attempt to speak burned this throat. Again, the strength to survive combined with his love for Sara flowed through his muscles and he tried his relax/stretch technique to lift his wrist out of its restraints. These efforts made the rope around his neck burn into his flesh more and more, yet he hardly noticed his pain and gagging as he felt his wrist moving toward freedom. Rex's arms and legs burned beyond their ability to function before Rex slumped into his holding position. The rope around his neck had tightened further, causing him to wheeze for breath and the blood in his temples to pound.

Rex felt his head about to explode, yet the pain in his joints slipped away and his hearing dulled to deafness. A euphoria began to build through his body and the bright light before his eyes darkened. Rex welcomed this darkness and ease of his suffering. Rex felt he could just go to sleep now and forget all his troubles.

Slowly, the darkness lightened but Rex wasn't sure whether his eyes were even open or if he was dreaming. He decided he was dreaming as the light grew brighter and he found himself seated in the aisle seat of a movie theatre.

Rex bounced up and down on the cold vinyl seat just to ensure he was really there. He discovered that he seemed to be floating up and down as he tried out the seat, and he felt very happy and content with himself.

Rex looked up to see what movie was playing. Rex loved movies, and he hoped they were playing something he wanted to see. Rex was astonished to see the movie appeared to be scenes of his life. Rex watched these times in his life and felt the joy of living them again. He watched himself opening presents during his birthdays and Christmas in front of family and friends. He watched himself scoring touchdowns in flag footballs games, and running the 100-yard dash to take first-place. Rex saw moments of total happiness, peace, and security while cuddling in his mother's arms—moments of playing catch with big Sheriff Bana and he heard the easy laugh of his father when he told some silly story—moments of wild laughter as Migisi tickled him and the joy of pillow fighting and wrestling in bed on Sunday mornings—moments of amusement and goofiness with Jimmy Swanson and his other friends. And there seemed to be an infinite number of scenes of the times Rex had spent with Sara whether he was laughing or crying. Rex felt his heart swell at moments of basking in the radiance of Sara's warm personality and beauty. Rex realized Sara was far more than a sister to him, more than a mother. Sara was a counselor, a protector, and a close friend.

Rex took his eyes off the big screen and saw there were others in the movie audience around him. Rex moved his head slowly with the expectation that the rope around his neck would tighten further. To his surprise the euphoria that was passing through his mind and body continued.

Rex was shocked to see the two children who had disappeared from his school sitting a few rows in front of him. Rex recognized them as they turned their heads and stared back at him with expressions of accusation as if he'd done something wrong. Rex tried to return their stare since he didn't understand why he was guilty of something, but he was unable to make out the details of their faces, as if his memory of them was vague and he couldn't recall what they looked like in life. He shuddered to think the two were dead and he wondered what right they had to be here where they destroyed his peaceful reverence. Rex decided he must look away from the two corpses to regain his serenity. He felt a presence at his side, and he looked to his left and saw Sara. No, it wasn't Sara; it was his mother, Namid. Rex was jolted as he saw how much Sara had grown to appear like his mother. Namid was there in all her beauty that Rex recalled before cancer had sucked away the life in her body. Rex took in every feature of his mother's face, as he wanted to remember it forever. He took in the black velvet sheen of her long hair, her brown-black eyes so much like his own, the milky coffee color of her complexion, and her straight full nose which fit in beautiful proportion with her round cheekbones and razor sharp jaw line.

Many questions rushed into Rex's thoughts with this image of Namid whom he saw in his most cherished dreams. Yet Rex's voice continued to elude him and he felt pain in his throat. Namid hushed his questions by turning, looking down into his eyes, and placing the tips of her fingers on his lips then resting her hand on his own. For a time Rex felt as if he was in Heaven. His mother's hand rested on his own with only the armrest between them.

Suddenly, something shook the whole theatre. Rex felt he had to turn away from the comfort of his mother toward the source of this danger. Rex was amazed to see a huge white-tailed buck, with a magnificent rack, as it walked/ pounded down the theatre aisle and snorted an icy bloom that frosted Rex's skin. As Rex marveled at the marble sculpture of the deer's shoulder and neck muscles, and the power of its huge body, the deer paused and slowly turned its head to gaze upon him. Rex was captured by the brown-black beauty in the buck's eyes, and he saw there was a deep sadness in those eyes.

Rex saw life from the angle of the buck. He saw how the buck fought for life from day to day, sometimes from minute to minute. From this angle Rex felt stripped from the comforts of his life as a child and was thrown into the coldness and realness of life's struggle against death. Even as Rex struggled to break from the buck's gaze and return to the warm comforts of his mother's hand he felt Namid's touch turn cold as the frozen soil of a Michigan winter and her hand pin his hand to the armrest like a spike of ice driven through the back of his wrist. Rex felt the agony of the icy spikes driven through his other wrist and his ankles. He felt the agony of his arms and legs back in their stretched positions. Straining painfully, Rex felt his sense of serenity drain and his mind was dragged further into the depths of the buck's gaze as if he was hypnotized. The deeper Rex was lost into the pool of the deer's brown black orbs, the more he felt the pounding strength of the great beast's heart and its will to live. He felt his heart pitter-patter in comparison with the buck's mighty throb. Rex felt his desire to live grow, swell in his body to match the mammoth size and strength of the beast. Feeling immensely powerful, Rex became aware of Sara's desperate pleas ringing in his ears. Rex's serenity and comfort disappeared as the huge bull's desire to live filled his own heart and joined his desire to save Sara's life. Rex contracted the muscles in his chest, arms, and legs with such force that he broke the icy bonds of death's embrace. Suddenly Rex was released from the buck's gaze and felt himself falling from a tremendous height into bright light.

"Oaffff!" Rex heard himself exclaim through his dry painful throat. The sharp hurt of his strains acted as smelling salts to clear his mind, and Rex was alert when he opened his eyes. He found his right hand was free of its restraints and now his body was bent to the left as if he was doing toe touches to his left foot while only using his left arm. Rex's legs remained in a split position and he was suspended a few feet above the wooden floor. He had no idea how he had managed to break his restraints, but the power of the buck's desire to live still pounded in his heart and he wasn't going to sit around all mystified while Sara was hurt and Madison was loose. Now he had a free hand to loosen the rest of the straps that had him doing a gymnast's stretch.

Rex undid the restraint about his left wrist, and for a moment, Rex felt like a genie floating in the air while doing the splits. He quickly used both hands to loosen the rope around his neck and pull it over his head. But Rex gave up on the notion he could magically release himself and he stretched his torso to his left ankle. As much as he struggled and stretched to reach it, he couldn't grasp the strap to manipulate it out of the buckle.

Rex didn't get frustrated. Migisi had taught him that he must relax in a crisis so his mind could act clearly, and his body could react accordingly. Rex knew that allowing his emotions to run amok would only tighten his muscles and make it harder to stretch out to release that strap. Rex took a few deep breaths and concentrated on having calm emotions and relaxing his muscles. After a few moments, he was able to stretch out and release the strap around his left ankle. But this proved a life threatening move since as soon as the weight was released from his left ankle, all the weight strapped around his right ankle yanked him skidding over to a hole in the wall. Rex was slammed painfully into the wall and the restraint around his ankle wrenched hard enough to nearly break a bone. Rex cried out in pain, yet it only came out in a rush of air.

Rex bent down and released the strap, and he was free of all restraints. Rex felt the urgency to escape before Deputy Madison returned was increasing, or he feared there would be no escape at all. The fact that Sara remained so still and wouldn't answer him had Rex's heart busting.

Rex jumped to his feet, felt unsteady, and threw out his hand for balance. Rex found his hand resting on Madison's gun holster almost as if he'd planned it that way, and he was lost in thoughts of how to use the gun when he felt a sizzling pain burning his skull. Sweeping his hand over his head, Rex hit the light bulb which had rested on top of his head.

"Oh yeah! The light bulb—why'd Madison leave after the light flickered?" Rex whispered to himself. He knew this question was important somehow.

The boards beneath Rex's feet abruptly rocked and he was almost thrown off the trapdoor. Rex realized Madison had returned before he could free Sara. He ripped Madison's gun out of its holster as the trapdoor was slowly lifted again. Rex knew he wouldn't be able to hold the door closed and he wasn't sure he wanted to. Stepping off the door meant letting in Madison, but now Rex felt he was on better terms to deal with the insane prick. "Prick" was a word Sara occasionally used and Rex was delighted to find his own use for it.

Rex quickly examined the gun. It was a Smith and Wesson like his father's service revolver. It was loaded. The safety was on. It felt heavy and the weight of what he might do with this weapon slowed Rex's actions and thoughts. The bucking trapdoor got his attention in a hurry. Rex turned to look at Sara and saw she lay naked on her side curled up like a baby trying to hide. This pitiful picture sealed Rex's determination. He jumped from the trapdoor and bounded over to kneel to Sara's side, fully aware Madison would be coming right behind him.

Rex was unable to learn Sara's condition before the trapdoor slapped open, and Madison's bald and grotesque head emerged from the dark cavity. Madison stopped there, and his wedge-shaped head swivelled on his scrawny neck as his dark beady eyes blinked to adjust to the light. Madison searched the room until he saw the black hole of his own gun barrel pointed at his head, and then his eyes moved up to meet Rex's black stare.

Madison put on the wide smile Rex saw him wear for Sara on Napier Road, only this time Rex caught the red tint of blood, Sara's blood, on his crooked teeth.

Madison jumped through the door with his steely eyes trained on the gun barrel. He backed off and held up his hands giving Rex a chance to study his meager appearance. Rex took in the rumpled and stained police shirt with its badges of authority Madison had so thoroughly abused, yet Rex felt no fear. Rex felt urgency for Sara, but he had never been afraid of this monster.

Madison bent and closed the trapdoor, nearly causing Rex to pull the trigger.

With the door closed, Madison stood again and raised his hands, knocking the light bulb. The hatred expression appeared on Madison's face as his hand sizzled from the heat of the light bulb. Abruptly, the snarl on Madison's face returned to his insincere grin.

Madison whispered, "Come-on Rex—the game's over and you caught me. Now gimme the gun and we'll call it quits. The fun's over and we should all go home now." Madison continued to flap his lips but Rex could see him inch closer with each word.

Rex was kneeling in front of Sara with both his hands firmly holding the grip of Madison's gun and his index finger curled around the revolver's trigger. Rex knew he wasn't in a perfect shooter's stance, but his kneel provided him with a stable platform to maintain his grip on the weapon when he pulled the trigger. If for some reason Rex missed Madison with his shot, he wanted to be able to squeeze off another shot before Madison was on top of him. Rex had never shot a person, and had thought he never would, but with each passing word Deputy Madison was making himself the prime candidate to be Rex's first victim. As Madison jabbered, Rex was watching the man's eyes and body movements the way he might hunt an animal in the forest. Rex hoped Madison would not notice the safety of his gun was still in place.

Rex was startled when Sheriff Bana bellowed his name from somewhere beneath him. Rex didn't know where he was being confined, but now he understood why the flickering light had caused Madison to leave their confinement. The light was a warning, a silent doorbell that told Madison there was someone outside. Rex knew he was unable to answer his father's call vocally due to his throat, but he felt no compulsion to try any other method of communication. As Madison continued to move closer, Rex remained silent and kneeling at Sara's side. His urgency increased not from Madison, but from Sara's silence

"See, I just called your daddy and he's here to get ya. I'm sure he wouldn't approve of you handling such a dangerous weapon and pointing it at a person," Madison stated in hushed tones while he continued to inch closer.

"At least you have the safety on." Madison was so close; Rex could see the sweat beads breaking out on his face. Rex felt frigid.

Sheriff Bana hollered for Sara from so close Rex thought his father might be directly beneath him. Still, Rex coldly studied Madison as if he was a young scientist examining an especially large experimental rat that disgusted him.

Rex inched his thumb up to push off the gun's safety. Madison jumped at this signal and gave Rex his perfect shot.

Rex was already pulling the trigger as Deputy Madison lunged at him with his savage snarl and outstretched claws. There was an explosive flash from Rex's hands before a black hole punctuated Madison's wrinkled brow. Madison continued to fly toward Rex as the bullet jerked his head back and his skull, flesh, mangy hair, and brain matter were splattered about the wall and light. The concussion and results of Rex's shot blew away the light bulb and pitched the torture chamber into darkness. Rex tried to duck beneath the onslaught of Madison's airborne body, but Madison hit him head first with the force of a cannon ball and the feel of a bucket of hot stewed tomatoes. Madison's momentum plowed Rex against the wall.

Madison's gory and defecating body pinned Rex beneath its dead compost in the darkness. Rex tried to scream as Madison's hands spastically grabbed and clawed him, but his cries came out no louder than Madison's whispers had been earlier. Rex thought he would scream forever, until he heard the slap of the trapdoor being thrown back and he saw a smoky pillar of light stab through the horror of his darkness. Rex heard his dad call his name as it thundered off the close walls. Sheriff Bana squished into the darkness to find his son and daughter.

Walter quickly threw Madison's remains aside and lifted Rex into an embrace so tight Rex nearly despaired. His body was covered with the hot soup of blood, urine, and shit from Deputy Madison's corpse, but his father ignored the stench.

"Are ya hurt!?" Sheriff Bana asked with urgency. "Did he do anything to you?"

Sheriff Bana looked long into Rex's face as if searching for some lie, but all Rex could do was open his mouth, point his index finger at his tonsils, and then run his finger across his throat to show that he couldn't talk. Old Daddy-o picked up on this right away.

"You're hoarse. Ya can't talk. But you're okay?" asked the sheriff, and Rex nodded to the latter with a worried glance at Sara's prone figure.

Sheriff Bana whispered words of love and thanked his lucky stars before concerning himself more about his son's condition. Although Rex whispered to his father that he would live, he was more concerned about Sara. Her silent stillness through the end of this ordeal continued to terrify him.

Sheriff Bana helped Rex out the trapdoor and down a ladder. At the bottom of the shaky ladder, Sheriff Bana had to leave Rex to return up the ladder after Sara. Rex was left alone briefly in the night's frigid cold without his shirt. He found himself standing on top of a creaky barn loft. Rex looked upon an eerie scene of the ancient barn below that was lit by a multitude of whirling red, white, and blue lights from police cruisers and an ambulance which had just arrived. Now Rex understood how Sheriff Bana had called his name from directly beneath him when he was holding the gun on Deputy Madison.

Rex stood there shaking in the cold with his arms wrapped around himself, but even in the frigid darkness, Rex could smell the remains of Office Madison oozing off his body in a death stench.

Rex figured someone must have tipped his father about him and Sara being grabbed by Deputy Madison. Sheriff Bana had called in an army to find his children. Rex figured that someone that tipped Sheriff Bana had to be Bobby Higgenson unless someone else had been watching from the woods when Madison had grabbed them. Otherwise, Bobby was the only one of the bunch to make it home from school reasonably untouched. Recalling his bout with Bobby, Rex felt he got in good use of Migisi's wrestling techniques. *Migisi would have been proud*, he thought, *but not of this stench.*

Rex peered over the side of the loft and out the open doors of the barn. It seemed to him that an army of men with flash lights, police badges, and guns poured from their vehicles in a carnival atmosphere. The emotional tension in the air felt electrifying.

A tower of State Trooper in blue uniform approached Rex and surrounded him with his arms and body to protect him and keep him warm. Rex never said a word, but he kept thinking the trooper had to be sorry for sharing his body warmth with a dirty kid that smelled like shit.

The trooper carefully ushered Rex across the loft. The boards beneath their feet creaked in protest, making Rex wonder if they might not fall through. They came to a squared hole in the loft that at first appeared to fall into more darkness. Then, another trooper showed up at the bottom of a wide but rickety wooden ladder. He had a flashlight that he flashed into Rex's face. Rex was left seeing spots when the trooper behind him gently nudged him toward the ladder.

"Think you can manage the ladder okay?" the trooper asked in a voice which surprised Rex with its youthful strength.

Rex looked up at the trooper's face and decided he'd make it down one way or another. The trooper's face looked creepy in the light that was shining from the hole and under the trooper's chin, making him look as if he had deep holes for eyes and the cheekbones of a cadaver. Rex had seen enough scary stuff for one night.

Cold or not, Rex slid down the ladder with surprising ease while the trooper thundered down after him. They had come to the dirt floor of the old barn that was full of shadows formed by headlights of the cars. Rex had little time to look around as the trooper who had appeared at the ladder bottom with the flashlight seemed to have come better prepared than the trooper that had escorted him down the stairs.

This guy was as tall as the original trooper, but he looked much bigger in his blue arctic coat with a hood trimmed in fur. Probably fake fur, Rex figured.

This new trooper didn't smile any more than his current trooper had. Their faces were grim, and Rex saw they still had morning stubble on their faces. By their expressions Rex almost felt as if he was in trouble. He knew enough to keep quiet and do as he was told even if he could talk.

Rex was thankful of this new trooper as he wrapped Rex's shaking body in a wool blanket. In fact, the trooper wrapped Rex so tightly he felt as if he was a caterpillar spun in the silk of its cocoon. His personal stench, combined with the smell of the blanket that he figured was last used on a horse, brought Rex back to reality. His thoughts were scrambled when a big hand dug through his horse blanket to grab his arm and shove a burning cup of hot chocolate into his frozen fingers. Rex had no chance to whisper thank you as he felt someone gently push him toward the barn doors.

Outside the barn, the night appeared as crazy as a circus crowd on a mid-summer Saturday night. The trooper guided Rex through a zigzag maze of police vehicles and running men while Rex passed the foam cup of scalding coco back and forth between his burning fingers and managed to keep most of the chocolate lava in its cup.

Rex was escorted to the side of a van-like ambulance before he was brought to a halt. The blanket was folded away from his face, and the trooper did an about face to rush back to his duty. Before Rex stood Migisi wearing a concerned expression, but then his face burst into a wide smile as he spied Rex beneath his wrappings. Rex was never so happy to see a set of stained false teeth, and he would have jumped in Migisi's arms if not for the hot chocolate held before him, beneath his wrappings.

Rex wasn't too surprised to see Bobby Higgenson bouncing from one foot to the other in a borrowed arctic coat while puffing white clouds into the night from his beaver mouth. Before Rex could ask if Bobby was the one that tipped off Sheriff Bana, Higgy leaped forward to squish Rex in a bear hug not unlike the crusher Sheriff Bana had given him only moments before.

"Thanks for saving my life, Bana," Bobby puffed out from inside a ring of fur. "Where's Sara?"

In response, Rex could only emit a hiss. Hot chocolate bathed his bare chest from the crumpled cup in his now fisted hand. When Bobby released him, Rex disappeared into his wraps to use a portion of the horse blanket to sop up the scolding milk on his torso before it seeped lower and made him look as if he'd wet his pants. Briefly, Rex had a mental image of himself stretched across Deputy Madison's wall as he caught a whiff of Madison's stench that also covered his torso. His two watchers turned away as if they felt Rex was releasing the emotions of his escape and he was embarrassed to show them in public.

Presently, Rex popped out of his warm hideaway with only his face showing. Neither Bobby nor Migisi seemed to know what to say, so Rex rubbed his throat and croaked, "How did you two get here?"

Migisi nodded with a smile as if to admit Rex was okay, but Bobby was full of the excitement of having survived a life threatening situation. Bobby gave out a wild and frightening yarn of how he hid behind a tree after he heard Rex and Sara challenge Deputy Madison and stop Madison from shooting him in the back. Bobby said he saw Madison club Rex and Sara before throwing them into his car and driving off. He was afraid about how to respond since no one would believe him. He had always had trouble with the law. How was he going to go to the law for help?

Bobby said he was scared, so he went home. It wasn't until Sheriff Bana showed up at his house to check on Bobby, and tell him his father was down at the county clink, that Bobby had asked how Rex and Sara were doing. Surprised at Bobby's concern, Sheriff Bana questioned the boy, so Bobby recanted what he'd seen happen on Napier Road.

Taking Bobby with him, Sheriff Bana returned home, making a skidding halt in his wildly lit police cruiser that Bobby described as, "... really neat. When I get old enough, I wanna be able to drive around like that."

Sheriff Bana rushed into his house to see if Sara and Rex had returned from school. Bobby followed and was asked to tell what he'd seen a second time. This time Migisi was present, and Bobby said he was scared he'd done something wrong the way Sheriff Bana looked down upon him, but Migisi interrupted Bobby's story to say Sheriff Bana was only concerned about the situation and was very happy Bobby had told them what he'd seen. Rex wondered why Bobby took everything as if he was going to get in trouble.

Bobby said after he'd told Sheriff Bana his story again, and the sheriff seemed both scared and worried as he thought of what to make of these facts. "I can't believe your grandfather and the sheriff trusted me right off," Bobby exclaimed.

Bobby claimed even he could have figured out that the first place to look for Sara and Rex was at Madison's farm. It was right on Napier Road and not far from the place where Madison had picked up Rex and Sara. So that was how they had found Rex and Sara.

"Thanks, Bobby," hissed Rex in a tone he knew couldn't convey his entire sincerity and thankfulness. It was the only thing Rex could think to say, but Rex thought Bobby's acceptance and trust from Sheriff Bana was enough of a thanks to Bobby.

Rex peered up from his vantage point into the expression on Migisi's face. Abruptly, a dense snow began to fall with large flakes. Migisi appeared not to have heard Bobby's monologue, but was concentrating on what was occurring behind Rex—in the barn.

Rex felt his own concern for what was happening with Sara, and he shuffled about to see Sheriff Bana directing two medics with a gurney through the barn doors before he turned and headed towards them. Sheriff Bana marched with a slow gait and with his head down in such a way it appeared the sheriff was being pulled to the gallows for his own execution. The snow became so thick it became hard for Rex to see his father, but Rex could read his posture as the sheriff slowly came through the muck and falling snow.

Rex erupted from his cocoon and ran towards his father. He didn't want to believe what his mind had been telling him since he had kneeled at Sara's side and confronted Madison. Rex hit big Sheriff Bana's body while still running full tilt, and he nearly knocked over the mountain as he questioned, "Sara? Where's Sara?"

Sheriff Bana hugged Rex tightly, but he did not answer his boy's question. He said, "Ya know you did a very courageous and brave thing back there. I couldn't be more proud that you're my son."

Then, the sheriff pulled Rex to his side and continued the march toward Migisi and Bobby. When they reached the end of their march, Sheriff Bana turned Rex to face him; there were tears in his eyes, and he held tight to Rex's shoulders. His father looked into Rex's eyes before he spoke. "Sara is dead."

# Chapter One

"Happy Birthday to me. Come-on, Cappy, sing along. Happy Birthday to me. Happy Birthday dear Reeexxxx. Happy Birthday to me! All right, everybody!"

Rex took a swig of his frosty Stroh's long-neck and looked over the hood of his mud-splattered Hummer to gaze at the "everybody" he was talking about. He tipped his beer at his deaf and dumb companion.

"Here's to my thirty-third birthday, and the only pal present to help me celebrate."

Rex took a long swig of the Strohs, smacked his lips, and then belched.

"Pardon me," he grumbled and leaned back against the warm hood of his truck. The Hummer's 5.7 liter diesel was still tinking as it cooled.

After peeking up at the frigid sky, Rex sighed, blowing a plume of white smoke when he said, "What a life, Captain. What a life."

Not expecting or getting a response from Captain Thrifty, Rex took another swig of his beer.

"Boy, that sure hit the spot after hauling your heavy ass out here to the middle of nowhere." Rex drew another sigh, formed another misty cloud and contemplated his surroundings.

He'd driven into the backwoods of the Bana fifty acres to look for the fence damage done by poachers and trespassers that knocked down the fence during the deer season. Lord help the person caught poaching on the Bana acres while Walter Bana continued as Sheriff of Salem Township.

"Do you realize, Captain, it's possible that parts of these woods have never been explored by any white men except big Walt?" Rex asked before taking another long swig of his beer and blowing out with contentment.

"Now these woods, these fifty acres, are all mine, boy." Rex raised himself to his full six foot four height, and then he raised his muscular arms with a huge yawn as he did a slow turn around. He gazed upon the naked maple, oak, and elm trees that stood about him. He was standing in a clearing near his fence line. The ground surrounding him was the muddy compost of a northern fall. The whole scene signaled death and decay of another approaching Michigan winter.

"I think I'll leave you here as a warning to any white men that trespass here while hunting deer on my property." Rex laughed at the thought and sipped on his beer.

"What's that, Cappy?" Rex tilted his head and cupped his ear for a moment.

"Sorry, Captain. I refuse to waste any of this fine Detroit brew by sharing it with you." Rex grinned as he eyed his bleeding companion.

"Now that I've got you wired up tight to that fence beam, I do believe it's time to party!" Rex started to rally as he opened the driver's door to his truck, reached in, fiddled with some audio buttons, pushed a CD into the player, and cranked up the volume.

Stepping back a moment, Rex listened as the southern rock band, MOLLY HATCHET, blasted out of 400-watt JBL audio speakers loud enough to cover the sound of a twenty-one gun salute. The racket didn't disturb a soul. Rex figured there wasn't anyone except him and the "Captain" for miles around. This is precisely the way Rex intended it to be.

"My horse is kicking dust up off the trail..." Rex began singing along with the tune entitled "Bounty Hunter" as he started digging through his arsenal of weapons in the Hummer's cargo area.

Pulling the cover off his modified Remington 870P Police shotgun with its six shot shell carrier, Rex broke open his battered ammunition box and loaded the gun with 12-gauge shotgun shells.

"Blue steel flashing, hot lead flying..." Rex sang and danced out one legged from behind his Hummer. Rex used the Remington as if it was an air guitar. "I wonder what they feel like when they're dying..." Rex howled.

If his Native American ancestors were watching they might have thought their tall descendent was imitating a rain dance as he hopped and twirled around strumming his shotgun while yelping like an injured dog.

Hop skipping to the music, Rex danced and yelled his way to a position ten feet from where a bleeding "Captain Thrifty" was barbed wired to a fence beam. Abruptly, Rex's motions became purposeful and as fluid as a snake about to strike—all in perfect sync with the thundering music as it hit the lead break.

Rex swung around as his hands turned the Remington from an imaginary guitar into a deadly weapon. Rex followed in tune with the musical beat as he leveled his weapon to shoot Captain Thrifty in the "chest" with lethal accuracy. Captain Thrifty took the blast with a jolt but remained at his post duly wired.

Rex dove to the hard wet ground and rolled with the thrill of the hunt boiling in his blood. He quick pumped the shotgun, and unloaded a second shot into the Captain's "belly" while still pulling the trigger in sync to the drumbeat. Again, the Captain jumped at the impact but appeared no worse for the wear.

Rex quickly rolled back and hopped to a squatting position before he pumped the Remington and it exploded a third time. Rex's aim was a shade off and the shotgun pellets struck the Captain in the right shoulder, ripping away the Captain's empty shirt sleeve.

"Shit!" Rex growled, seeing that his aim was off.

Rex twirled around and sprinted away as if Captain Thrifty had the capacity to chase him. Rex continued to holler in sync with the thundering music. "Did you know five hundred dollars will get your head blown off?"

Rex gained five yards, skidded to a halted, turned, and then belly flopped to the earth. "It will—ha, ha, ha." Rex shot, and then grinned as Captain Thrifty's head exploded into a hundred plastic pieces.

"Yeah!" Rex hollered.

"Now that was a nifty shot, Rex old buddy."

Rex was content for the moment as he slowly got to his feet, wiped away the mud and compost from his hands and arms, and went back to the Hummer where he turned down the music.

"I'm a bounty hunter, gonna hunt you down..." he sang along to the end of the song.

Rex put on the safety, and then he unloaded the Remington. Satisfied with his shotgun accuracy, Rex wiped down the shotgun with an oily cloth before re-casing it. Rex packed the Remington back into the truck.

"Poor Captain Thrifty, you are no more." Rex sighed as he reached into his travel cooler for another Strohs long-neck. "... but it ain't nothing to me..." Rex vocalized in tune with the next song on his Molly Hatchet CD called "Gator Country." After twisting off the beer cap and taking a long swig, Rex retrieved his empty shell casings.

"Now, Captain Thrifty, lets see how that body armor you're wearing protected the full side of beef I strapped onto your bones." Rex took his Strohs and approached his target—Captain Thrifty.

"… I'm going back to the Gator Country where the wine and the women are free …"

"Hmm …" Rex mused as he pulled back the bloody shirt Captain Thrifty wore in between the Special Ops Armored Vest Rex was testing, and the side of beef Rex had wired to a life-size plastic skeleton the mail order catalog prenamed as "Mr. Thrifty."

"… There's a gator in the bushes …" Rex murmured.

"Oh, shit," Rex exclaimed when he saw the jagged edge of white cow bone sticking out of Captain Thrifty's chest. Rex could see that the armored vest protected Captain Thrifty from the shotgun pellets entering into the side of beef, but the force of the shots had broken some bones.

"But I guess that makes sense. Hopefully my live muscle will absorb a shotgun blast better than a half frozen side of beef wired to a beam of wood. But then, I guess you wouldn't know since I went and blew your head clear off—ha, ha, ha."

Rex let go of the bloody shirt and examined the other impact areas on the body armor. He grunted and nodded his head as if he was accessing the damage as acceptable.

"But, I ain't done yet." Rex grinned and strode away from Captain Thrifty and he finished his icy long-neck. "There's many roads I've traveled but they all kinda look the same."

Rex spun quick as a flash as he threw a five point metal star that sawed off the remainder of Captain Thrifty's plastic neck and sank deep into the wood of the fence post.

"Bingo!" Rex hollered while Captain Thrifty remained speechless.

Putting his empty beer bottle back in the Hummer, Rex wiped his hands together before he strolled back out in front of the remains of Captain Thrifty.

Rex squared himself and said, "Hey, Captain. Check out this Robert DeNiro imitation." Rex figured everyone had to do their mutilating imitation of Robert DeNiro sometime in their life. Rex did his.

He threw back his shoulders and tried to act tough looking. "You talkin' ta me. I say—are you talkin' ta me? Cause if ya are …" In a swift movement there was a handgun in Rex's right hand that seemed to be blasting fire and lead before it was out of his holster. Twelve paces away the fencepost holding the headless Captain Thrifty snapped and did a jig as the slugs smashed into the body armor throwing the Captain back five yards. In less than two seconds it was over. Captain Thrifty lay on the frosty ground with smoke and steam rising from the slugs lodged in its chest.

"Wooo-weee!" Rex hollered as he clicked the safety on his Glock 20, spun it once and jammed it neatly into its well oiled holster. "Now that was fine shooting, even if my acting does suck the big whazoo." Rex laughed as he approached the downed Captain.

"Oh, Gator Country, a little bit of that chomp chomp."

"Damn, Captain, you done falled down." Rex laughed after examining the bullet holes in the armored vest.

"Shit, boy, now I see why you lost your footing." Rex stuck his finger through a ragged puncture in Captain Thrifty's chest. He counted four such holes. This told Rex this body armor might hold off a shotgun blast, but it'd never stand up to something like his Glock 20 which was rated the most powerful handgun in the world when loaded with MageSafe 10 loads.

"Well, Rex old buddy, if you see someone pointing a Glock 20 at ya, you better run like hell and hope they can't shoot worth a shit."

Rex grunted with effort as he heaved his armored side of beef back to its feet, fence post and all.

"Well, Cappy—let's—ah—stand ya—over here!" Rex maneuvered the three hundred pounds of headless beef and accessories next to a huge oak tree. Rex had chosen the weight of the beef to match his own weight when he was wearing all his equipment and he was on the hunt for a serial killer—his chosen profession.

Pulling out some heavy gauge wire cutters from his duty belt, Rex wired the Captain up to the tree. "There ya go, Captain. Old Mr. Oak is your new dance partner. Don't you go getting fresh with him 'cause I got a few more tests I'd like to complete. In the meantime, I's feeling another beer coming on."

Rex stepped back up to the Hummer and picked up on the next song on the Molly Hatchet CD, "The Creeper."

"Life is getting stranger, baby..." Rex reached back into that icy cooler and tapped off another Strohs long-neck while contemplating how to handle these next tests.

After rummaging through a second deployment bag, Rex pulled out a .22 caliber target rifle, a .32 midnight special, and a .357 Magnum. He carefully loaded each weapon with three loads and holstered the two revolvers on his body. Rex finished his beer, and then he cranked up the CD player to thundering levels again as he prepared for a grand finale.

"Well, I been stepped on, baby..." Rex sang as he jogged a good twenty paces away from Captain Thrifty. "By people I thought were my friends..."

Rex turned and squatted into a shooting stance as he raised and aimed the .22 target rifle, took a deep breath, and relaxed. Then in quick succession, he squeezed the trigger, pulled back the bolt, shoved it back in place and fired again. Rex repeated this action one more time. He dropped the rifle and made a controlled run at Captain Thrifty, never getting out of his firing position. Rex planted hard on his right foot, and then dodged left and rolled once on the ground. He came to a shooter's squat again, and he had the .32 caliber revolver in his left hand to shoot at Captain Thrifty as soon as his firing platform was stable. Captain Thrifty convulsed three times as all the shots were on target.

Rex didn't see the last shot hit as he had already dropped the .32 and was sprinting and somersaulting forward. As Rex came to his feet in a shooter's squat six feet in front of Captain Thrifty, the .357 Magnum was in his right hand and blazing with three quick shots. All three slugs hit Captain Thrifty dead center.

Rex took a few deep breaths to catch his wind and relaxed as the gun smoke cleared. He returned to the Hummer, and punched the off button to the CD player. The woods went silent with a sudden heaviness.

Rex picked up his weapons and cleaned up his cartridges. He wiped down his weapons with an oil cloth and restored them in the back of the truck. Silently, he chugged another beer and took a few deep breaths of contentment.

He still had to check the results of these last weapon tests on the body armor, but overall he was satisfied with his shooting effort's accuracy and speed. Rex felt confident he could physically outmaneuver, out draw, and out shoot any serial killer he approached. Now he just had to make sure he had enough protection if he was shot at—which was the case more often than not. Rex knew statistically that serial killers did not use guns to kill, but he also knew that when he cornered a killer, the killer came up with all sorts of weapons to defend himself.

After approaching his target for the day, Rex examined the impact points of the shots on the Special Ops Vest. He knew the .22 caliber target rifle was a joke, but since a serial killer had shot at him with one a few years back, he'd tried it on this new armor just to be sure.

"Ya can never do enough tests on defensive equipment when it's your life on the line," Rex told Captain Thrifty. Rex had trouble even finding the impact points from the .22 caliber, although he knew all his shots were on target.

Rex found that the .32 caliber and the .357 Magnum had both left lasting impressions on Captain Thrifty and the armor. One of the .357 slugs almost penetrated through to the bloody side of beef. "But almost doesn't cut it in this league," Rex mused.

Slapping Captain Thrifty on the "shoulder," Rex said, "Thanks, compadre, you've done your job in a stand up manner. I feel much safer knowing what this armor can handle, and more importantly, what it can't handle. Let's just hope this next serial killer isn't a militant freak like me and owns a Glock 20."

Rex realized he was standing there jawing at no one in the middle of nowhere. "Looks like it's time to head on in."

Rex turned slowly and reviewed the area which he'd been using. Then he finished his beer before starting up the Hummer.

"Now I gotta get home and pack," Rex said to no one. "I do believe it's time to visit old Bobby-o and make a trip to Kalamazoo."

# CHAPTER TWO

"Detective Higgenson, please," Rex asked on his cellular phone. The breath from his question formed a cloud of fog below his face.

"Michigan State Police, Detective Higgenson. How may I help you?"

"It's Rex."

"That you, Rex? Ya sound kinda squirrelly."

"Yeah, it's me, Bobby. Your suspect, Norman Lipshitz, he just left for work. Do you have a search warrant for this property?"

"All I have to do is stop down at the courthouse to get it. Ya really think Norman is the killer, huh?"

"He's hiding something in this house, Higgy. All his lower windows are boarded up. It even looks like a murder scene. Have you been out here yet?"

"Naw, the locals brought him in to ask a few questions, but he didn't give' um anything to use, and they don't have any direct evidence."

"He's your man, and if I've ever seen a place to live in isolation, this is it. The man lives in an old farmhouse that sits on a dirt road. The house is surrounded by farmland and forests. The nearest neighbor is about ten miles away, and there's a rickety barn out back that's leaning and about to fall over. You talk about isolated. If it wasn't for Lipshitz and the mailman, I haven't seen another human being while watching this place. To add to that, I'm freezing my ass off in this tree, and we're not any closer to finding the killer."

"You're still up in that tree, huh?" Higgy asked with a laugh.

"Damn right, and if my butt wasn't numb with frostbite, I know it'd be sore."

"You asked for the job, so don't start bitching ..."

"I know, and I appreciate the work and all the tips you give me, Bobby. I'll appreciate the two hundred and fifty thousand dollar reward even more if I catch the right suspect. But I think it's time to shut this one down. Norman Lipshitz has something to hide and we need to get into his house to find out what it is."

"Well this must be your lucky day," said Bobby on a high note. "We had a friend of the last victim come in last night to make a statement. We showed him some of those pictures of Lipshitz and he claims he saw Lipshitz in the same bar as Lewis Spence on Saturday night. That's the last time anyone saw Spence."

"Hot diggity dog!" Rex exclaimed with so much excitement he nearly lost his balance and fell out of the tree.

"I guess that gives me a good enough reason to drive out there and search the place," Higgenson remarked.

"You bet your buns it does. Now I can finally get outta this freakin tree."

"Don't go busting into anything till I get there. I'll grab a few troopers for back-up, so it'll be about thirty minutes or so. You can reach me on the cell phone or on the police ban in the mean time. You haven't seen Lipshitz take anyone into his house?" Higgenson asked. Rex thought he sounded worried.

"Nope, and that's the stumper. I figure Norman does his killing somewhere else and just brings home trophies. I've seen Norman carrying a lot of those plastic grocery bags into the house, but I can't tell what he's got in 'um. For all I know Norman could just be grocery shopping. He's certainly fat enough to be an eater."

Higgy laughed. "I'll be there in a bit. And remember; don't go breaking into the house unless it's an emergency."

"If something comes up, I'll be sure to call. Besides, you know me better than that." Rex laughed.

"Yeah, right."

"Use your siren," Rex added, but the detective had rung-off.

"Well ... I'm sure as hell not going to sit in this tree for another thirty minutes. I know Lipshitz is the killer, so let's start acting as if he is. All this sitting around baloney is why I quit the Troops in the first place," Rex grumbled as he shook his head and stowed his three sets of binoculars. "Three days in a tree and I'm talking to myself."

Rex put his binoculars in his basket and lowered the basket down to the ground using a thin nylon rope. Once on the ground, Rex tilted the basket and dropped out the binoculars. Bringing the basket back up, he packed his thermos and lunch box and repeated the same routine that he'd done with the binoculars. Rex took a peek about the confines of his deer blind to insure that nothing had been left behind other than his rifle.

"It appears I won't be using this just yet," he mumbled as he safetied and cased his rifle.

With a grunt, Rex rose to his full height and rolled his shoulders to work out the stiffness in his neck. Peering out upon the frosty landscape with his black eyes, Rex wondered how his ancestors survived this desolation.

"They were idiots ... should've gone south for the winter. It's too damn cold around here." Having said his peace to any kindred spirits which might be in the vicinity, Rex straightened his ponytail with a yank and grabbed his rifle case.

Rex gathered his possessions once he was down the ladder, and he began the mile jog to the dirt road where his Hummer was hidden beneath a huge camouflage tarp. He figured he had just enough time to pack away his scouting stuff, load up his body armor, arms, and munitions, and drive closer to the scene when Higgenson would arrive with the search warrant and backup.

As Rex jogged along, he reviewed the slayings in his mind. The authorities speculated, and Rex agreed, that Norman Lipshitz murdered his parents six months ago by disguising a fatal auto accident. Now Rex was hunting Norman in the developing cases of four missing young men from the gay community in the Kalamazoo, Calhoun County area. All four men had been students or teaching assistants at Western Michigan University—a close-knit group.

Rex could have picked up the basic information about the cases by being attentive to the news, but he had a wealth of connections in the State, County, and Kalamazoo Police Departments that sought him out for his expertise in this unique and highly publicized mode of crime.

Rex mentally reviewed his sheet on Lipshitz. It read: Norman was a beer guzzling Caucasian twenty-three-year old. He was fat and balding, out of physical condition. Norman had no relatives or close friends. He lived alone, without pets, on the farm he'd inherited from his dead/murdered parents. Yet it was well known that good old "Stormin' Norman" had a passionate desire for young men.

Rex got to the Hummer and quickly packed it up. After packing, he dug through the arsenal in the back of the Hummer to get his duty belt that held his night-vision goggles and his holster containing his Glock 20. He also insured he had two extra mags of nineteen rounds. Finally, Rex put on his body armor which consisted of a Kevlar helmet, a new Special Ops vest, and a pair of black baseball shin guards.

Hoping to get into action, Rex jumped into the driver's seat and drove past Norman's house before pulling into the woods a couple hundred yards down the road. Rex never parked the Hummer where a killer might see it, or worse, shoot at it. But Rex knew from experience, most serial killers weren't into the heavy artillery. They preferred to do their killing up close and personal with knives, clubs, drills ...

Checking the time, Rex saw it had been about thirty minutes since he'd last talked to Detective Higgenson. As Rex jogged back to the Lipshitz farmhouse, he thought it funny how small the world was, and how long it had been since he and Higgy encountered Deputy Madison, their first serial killer.

"Shit," Rex cursed as he caught his breath. He arrived at the farmhouse but there was no Detective Higgy.

Slowly, with the caution of a dog sniffing for landmines, Rex crossed the frosty grass of Lipshitz's front lawn. He approached and stepped onto the front porch. The porch boards bowed beneath Rex's weight as he planted his assault boots shoulder width apart. He gazed upon the fossilized door in front of him with its chiseled crystal doorknob.

"Geez ... you'd think Moses brought this door off the mountain," cracked Rex with a puff. To his left was the boarded up parlor window. Rex noticed Norman didn't waste any time or money on porch furniture or even the frontal appearance of the house. What paint that remained on the gray wooden siding was flaking or peeling off.

Rex decided he was stalling, so he pounded on the door to see if someone was home that he'd missed in the last three days. He had not sat in the tree the entire three days, and it was entirely possible someone else had entered the house. Rex did a slow about face when he heard someone cry out from behind and above him.

Rex backed off the porch and looked up to the second level of the house. He yelled, "Hello ... Is anyone in there!"

Again, what sounded like a human voice responded, but it was so weak Rex wasn't sure if he was hearing things or if it was just the wind. He had no idea what the voice might be saying.

"Hello!" Rex bellowed as loud as he could.

This time there was no answer at all.

Rex was getting frustrated now, so he walked around to the right side of the house. This side looked as dilapidated as the rest of the house with its peeling white paint and warped wooden siding. Yet there were two upper story windows that weren't boarded up, and since they were on the downwind side of the house, Rex thought he might be able to hear better from here.

No sooner had he thought of this when he could have sworn he heard a faint scream coming from inside the house.

"That does it," grumbled Rex. He plugged his miniature microphone headset into the battery powered cellular phone in his duty belt. After putting the phone on speaker and punching the speed-dial for Detective Higgenson, Rex gazed at the dark upper windows of the house wishing he could see inside.

"Detective Higgenson."

"Higgy. There's someone in Lipshitz's house screaming for help," Rex blurted out while he danced from one foot to the other, both to ward off the cold, and to work off some of the nervous energy building in his stomach.

"Rex? Is that you? I've got a problem," Higgenson rushed.

"You and me both." Rex waited for a response, but he didn't get any, so he asked, "What's your problem?"

"I'm stuck monitoring a traffic accident that happened right in front of me. I'm going to have to wait here for the Sheriff's Department or the Kalamazoo Police to arrive to handle this mess ..."

Rex listened while keeping his eye on those windows as if someone was going to abruptly appear and glare down at him, or maybe leap through a window to their death.

" ... Some jackass in a beat-up Buick ran the red-light at the intersection of M-59 and Old US-23 ..."

An alarm went off in Rex's head. "Did you say a beat-up Buick?" he asked.

"Yeah. It was a late-seventies model, brown or rust colored ..." Higgenson laughed at his own joke. "The guy tore through here like a bat-outta-hell and didn't even stop when a milk tanker and a pig trailer collided when they swerved to miss him. Man, you've never seen a bigger mess than this red sea of milk."

"Was it a two-door, or four-door?" Rex wanted to know.

"What?"

"The beat-up Buick."

"It was a two-door, but what's the big deal? Oh damn, now we've got pigs running around on the highway."

"That was Norman Lipshitz!" yelled Rex.

"Norman Lipshitz is a pig?"

"No ... in the Buick!"

"Oh, you mean the car that caused this accident?"

"Yeah. The car is heading in my direction, isn't it?"

"Yup. He zipped right passed me to run the light. Damn, Bana, one a those big sows is chasing a fat lady on high heels past my car." Detective Higgenson sounded as if he was fading away—lost in thought.

"Why is Norman Lipshitz rushing home?" Rex asked although he thought he knew the answer.

"Oh shit, Bana." Higgenson came back right away this time and Rex thought he heard a whine in Higgy's voice. "It's probably my fault. The judge ordered that Lipshitz be notified of the search warrant before we used it, and I ..." Higgy trailed off.

"You called him at work, didn't ya?"

"Well, I thought Lipshitz would come home so we could make an arrest if we found any evidence. Now I'm stuck in this traffic mess, and I can't leave the scene of an accident ..." Higgy trailed off again, so Rex knew there was more bad news coming. He stopped his dancing. It sounded as if he should be conserving energy to fight off the upcoming storm.

"What other surprises do you have for me?" Rex growled.

"Well, figure it out yourself, partner. The backup team that was going to sweep Lipshitz's house is busy chasing pigs right now and getting statements."

"From the pigs?"

"No! From the accident victims."

"So, no Higgy ... no backup team." Now it was Rex's turn to whine.

"It gets worse."

"How's that? We're not about to have an earthquake or some other catastrophe, are we?"

"Nope. It's just that the Kalamazoo Police Department can't spare any men to check out your situation because they have to clean up this mess first."

"In other words, there's a maniac driving home with death on his mind and I'm the only one at his house?"

"You're always free to run away now, and as the one in authority in this case, I'd suggest that route."

"We've been down that road many times, Detective Higgenson, and it's a no go."

"Then I suggest you go to the assistance of whomever is screaming in that house."

"Oh, so you did hear me earlier. Does this qualify as an emergency?"

"As long as you'll take the witness stand and state under oath that you heard screaming ... hell yeah ... that qualifies as an emergency."

"Kick-ass! I've been itching to get into this house for three days. Tell ya what. I have you on speaker phone so we can talk all the way through this mess."

"If that really was Lipshitz, I'd at least like to hear what's going on."

"Okay, partner, here we go."

Rex returned to the rickety porch and front door since nothing appeared to be happening in the second floor windows. After squaring himself with the door, Rex reared back and kicked it with a "Yahhhhh," right next to the door knob. The kick jarred Rex's bones and ran like a tuning-fork up his leg to give his testes a little jiggle.

"Shit ..." Rex hissed through clenched teeth.

The door stood solid as it had for a hundred years. The only satisfaction Rex received was watching the doorknob tilt, and then fall off onto the porch with a clang.

"Did ya get the door down?" Higgy asked with what Rex thought was a laugh.

"No ..." Rex hissed. "Dag-gummit, this isn't supposed to happen to the good guys. It's supposed to splinter into toothpicks like in the movies."

"Sorry, Charlie," Higgenson said snidely. Rex began to wonder if this speaker phone stuff was such a good idea.

Pride got the better of Rex as he squared up to the old door a second time. He reared up with his left foot when suddenly the boards beneath him gave way and he plummeted two feet to the ground.

"Shit!" Rex yelled into his microphone.

"Ouch ... What happened?"

All Detective Higgenson got in response were some rude grunts as Rex kicked his way out of Lipshitz's rotting front porch.

"Good thing I'm wearing baseball shin guards and steel-toed assault boots," Rex came back.

"Still being dressed by Darth Vader and Batman, aren't you?"

"Hardy har har. You're a regular comedian today, Detective Higgenson," Rex growled as he made his way along the right side of the house. "Looks like I'll have to try the rear door. It's the only door I've seen Lipshitz use. I guess I should have thought of this in the first place."

Rex could feel Norman storming home to protect what he would consider his property and treasures. Rex was aware serial killers kept trophies of their kills after they'd disposed of their victim's remains. If Norman was a killer, and he kept trophies, then he would horde these prizes with all the tenacity and viciousness of a spoiled child. Certainly, Norman would not want his possessions to be touched and soiled by a stranger.

Rex rounded the corner of the house with a sharp eye on the leaning barn. There was just something about that barn Rex didn't feel right about and he prayed he wouldn't have to find out what it was. He also kept a keen ear listening for more cries for help, or something that would tell him he didn't imagine that scream. It seemed he heard talking, but it could just be his imagination and the wind blowing through his helmet. Rex couldn't identify or single out a voice or decipher anything that was said.

Reaching the back door, Rex thought it looked as fallible as the front door had appeared, but was probably just as indestructible. Rex yelled, "Hello!"

Immediately his own ears were rung by Higgenson yelling back, "Damn-it, Rex! Quit yelling into your microphone!"

"Oops, sorry." But he didn't hear any other response from inside the house.

Rex marched up the two crumpling and lichen-covered cement steps and banged on the back door with his fist. To Rex, the door felt as if it was made of solid wood and there were no windows, so it was impossible to see into the house from his vantage point. Rex was surprised the way the door shook in its frame when he pounded. To him, this meant the entryway was not bolted with a deadbolt.

Rex figured he could out muscle this door. He backed down the steps. He sucked in his stomach and took a deep breath. Then he charged up those steps with his head and shoulder down and————*WHAM!*

"Look, Bullwinkle, I'm flying through the stars," Rex babbled as he spun off the step and did a belly-flop onto the frosted lawn. The door remained untouched.

"Bullwinkle? Rex, are you okay?" Higgy squawked.

"Bullwinkle?" Rex repeated. He lifted himself from the lawn and realigned his helmet and shoulder armor.

"What are you jabbering about?" Rex asked after taking a few wobbly steps. "Boy, this door is something else." Rex tried to clear his head, but knew better than to shake it and make his head ache more than it already did. He rolled his neck and was satisfied with a snap, crackle, and pop.

"You said something about Bullwinkle."

"Are you watching cartoons on your police monitor again, Detective Higgenson?"

"No, you started this."

The sense of danger approaching and the need to assist who was inside gripped Rex with the desire to get going, but he also remembered Lipshitz was driving home like the mad-hatter, and it might be his own life on the line if he continued. Sweeping his hand across his utility belt Rex knew it was time to get serious.

"Higgenson, I'm going to quit playing around here and force my way into this house," Rex said in a manner that pointed out he was taking charge here and things were going to be done his way.

"Okay ... It's all yours," Detective Higgenson responded a bit too quickly for Rex's liking. "I'll be away from the phone for a few minutes until I can get things straight here. Ten-four, big buddy, and drive safely," Higgenson cracked an old joke from their patrolling days. Rex knew it was Bobby's way of saying, "Be careful and take care of yourself."

"See ya!" Rex clicked off his phone and unplugged his headset. He unbuckled his helmet and removed it. Setting the helmet on the crunchy grass, Rex donned his night vision goggles, then returned the helmet to his head and buckled it down tight. He knew he appeared as if he was a two-legged crab like an alien in a black shell and with prolonged eyeballs.

It took a moment for Rex to adjust to the vision of the night goggles. Now he saw everything in green and magnified 3X. Rex stepped back to give the door plenty of room. Things would be farther away than they appeared.

Rex unsnapped his holster, and set his feet apart to make a solid stance. In one swift motion Rex squatted while his hand was pulling out the Glock from his holster. He straightened his arm as he squeezed the trigger.

The blast from the gun temporarily blinded him as he forgot he was wearing the goggles and he was supposed to close his eyes when he shot. The curse he yelled from his mistake was louder than the gunshot.

Ripping goggles down to his neck, Rex had to wait a moment and look at the door from a side glance to examine his accuracy. He grinned to see a hole the size of an orange where the door knob had been. Then he realized the door remained in place and his grin disappeared.

"Oh that really rips my shorts."

Shifting position, Rex raised his arm and shot the door three more times along the places he figured the hinges would be. Rex was gratified by the wood's splintering destruction from his shots, but he became a little peeved to see the door remained solid in its frame.

"Oh, horse-hockey." Rex huffed a cloud as he jammed his Glock back into his duty belt. For a moment he thought of jogging down to the Hummer for his fireman's ax, but then he decided he wouldn't give the door that much credit.

With a huff and a puff, Rex charged the door a second time. He put his head and shoulder down and flew up the stairs as if he was rushing for the goal line defended by a row of concrete giants. He bashed down the door but it carried him belly first across the kitchen floor surfing in a sea of old linoleum.

*Twang ...* **THUNCK!**

Even as Rex hit the floor he heard the singing of a bowstring and the thuncking of an arrow sticking into something solid.

Rex burst up drawing his revolver as he stood. He settled into a squatting position and cautiously looked about. His gun arm led the way of his sight, and Rex saw the bolt of a crossbow still quivering in the wood of the kitchen cabinets. Rex realized that if he'd walked through that entryway, an arrow would have been shot through his side and skewered him like Norman's next treasure.

"Booby traps," Rex grumbled. He thought one might admire the ingenuity behind them, but one couldn't admire the contraptions if he was caught in the trap. Rex let out a sigh of relief over this one and thanked his lucky stars. Someone up there must be looking out for him, and he knew it wouldn't be the last time he would need their help. He made himself a mental note to test his Special Ops Vest against a bolt shot from a crossbow when he got home. "Might as well try a bow and arrow as well," he said to the kitchen. "Migisi will get a kick out of that."

# CHAPTER THREE

"What's that smell? EEE-Gad. Ack ... something smells like shit ... worse than shit ... Ewe-wee! Retreat! Retreat!"

He jumped back to the entryway and stuck his helmeted noggin back into the crisp, clear, and partially clean air blowing outside. He gulped the fresh air as if he was a drowning person. Rex had forgotten what a house could smell like when all the windows were closed and it was never aired out. The smell of human occupation, waste, and possibly the decomposition of flesh was a brutal force to contend with in this house. It was a physical power that could knock one off their feet.

Judging the time it would take Norman to drive his beat-to-shit Buick from the M-59 intersection, where he'd caused the accident, Rex gave him another eight to ten minutes to reach home at his bat-out-of-hell pace. Rex decided it was to hell with Pepé le Pew, it was time to get through.

Rex pulled his head back in and pulled up his night vision goggles. He was thankful everything turned greenish from his perspective while he wore the goggles. The goggles also had an infrared ability which allowed him to see heated areas in red.

"Hello!" Rex called out.

Waiting a moment for a response but not getting any, Rex gave the kitchen a good look-see. He had to wonder what he'd been hearing since the house was as silent as the inside of a tomb at midnight. His sense of urgency pressured him, but he felt the house was empty of anything living. Rex decided the screams he'd heard were probably wind noises. One starts to hear a lot of strange things after sitting in a tree for three days.

Rex was glad the goggles eliminated the color details of this world. While looking through the goggles everything appeared in flat green without depth perception. This meant it didn't affect the mind or the stomach with the same impact as a true view in living color and depth. But the goggles didn't protect his nose. Rex pulled his travel tub of medicinal vapor rub out of his duty belt, and smeared some of the goo under each nostril. His sense of smell would be eliminated for the next few days, but anything was better then smelling the decay and decomposition of Norman's nauseous kitchen.

Stepping around the ruins of the back door, Rex thought of what a pigsty Norman wallowed about in. The kitchen cabinets were cluttered with dirty dishes, pots, and pans. Rex kicked aside a couple black Hefty barrel bags with his assault boots.

Rex was here to gather evidence. Was it possible that the evidence he sought was the trash?

Naw, Norman wasn't one to throw anything good away. This trash-filled kitchen was evidence of that.

Rex looked to his right at the gas stove and the General Electric refrigerator-freezer. Rex gazed at the GE fridge. For some reason the refrigerator looked familiar to him even though it appeared to have predated the invention of the appliance. It occurred to him the refrigerator appeared to be an appliance stolen from Fred Flintstone's kitchen, and Rex decided he'd been watching too many cartoons lately—time to get a real life.

Rex wasn't finished with the fridge yet. He wanted to examine what was in that freezer. It wouldn't be the first time a serial killer kept parts of his victims in the freezer. The killer would like to pull out the frozen limbs, heads, organs, and so forth to play with them at his own leisure. Rex figured he might hit the jackpot just by taking a look-see into the Lipshitz deepfreeze.

Rex made for the GE, but to get there he had to go through an obstacle course of trash. Flies buzzed about a sink filled with a swampy soup of dirty dishes and lumps of spoiled food. It appeared as if it was something the authorities might tape off as toxic waste.

As Rex passed the sink's pool he swore he saw something dive beneath the surface, like a startled frog leaping for the safety of the depths of its pond. He noticed a ripple on the surface of the semi liquid pool in the sink.

"Hard telling what sort of monstrosity's living in there," Rex muttered to the silence of the dark kitchen. He consoled himself that the thing in the sink was only a gas bubble rising from below.

Making as wide an arc around the sink as possible, Rex bumped into the stove and disturbed a leaning tower of dirty pots. He whipped around and caught the tower before it crashed, but he maintained his distance from the sink since he had no desire to get close enough to prove his bubble theory.

Rex imagined an evil organism with a nasty octopus tentacle living in the bottom of the sink bowl. He knew it would be dark green and slimy with suction cups that had fanged mouths. Rex imaged this grotesque tentacle as it rippled silently out of the sink, miraculously expanding to monster proportions before tapping him on the shoulder from behind. Rex saw himself turning in surprise just before the savage worm wrapped its bulging muscle around his neck, and then it would yank him struggling into the swampy waters and squeeze him down through the sink's drain.

Rex huffed in disgust at his imagination, and he decided he'd have to cut the cable service when he got home. Suddenly, another bubble burped in the sludge of the sink. Rex yelped and jumped sideways, drawing his Glock in self defense. He came to a bone jarring halt when he bumped into the kitchen wall in front of the refrigerator—his eyes never left the sink.

The murk settled again, so Rex holstered his gun and returned his attention to the top door above the refrigerator. Rex figured this was the freezer section. Taking a deep breath to relax, Rex decided he was overreacting about the thing in the sink. He decided he was stalling when he knew there was a killer due to arrive at any minute.

Not knowing what he expected to find, but still feeling spooked after the potential sink incident, Rex retrieved the Glock and pointed it at the freezer door. Slowly, Rex watched his left hand creep up and grasp the freezer handle. He wasn't sure what he expected to find. Worst would be something like a sawed off human leg, or a cut off arm with a claw-like hand. *Probably nothing but frozen vegetables in there*, Rex told himself while managing a fake smile of confidence.

In his mind's eye, Rex could see a hairy arm clawing through the frost and trying to escape the frigid freezer. Rex could almost hear it knocking on the inside of the door to be let out.

"Let me out ... pleasssse!" cried the frozen arm in Rex's imagination.

"Oh, quit being such a sissy," Rex muttered to himself.

He yanked open the door.

"AHHHHaaaaa ..." Rex screamed as something lunged at him from the depths of the freezer.

Rex pulled the trigger of the Glock. The blast in closed quarters was painful, blinding, and deafening.

The kitchen filled with gun smoke, and Rex felt ice slivers splatter the unprotected parts of his face. He had been jumping back in retreat even as he fired the Glock, but he didn't know what had leaped out at him before he shot it. Seeing he wasn't in immediate danger, Rex took a second to collect his wits and figure out what had happened. His heart was doing a jig in his chest, and only years of experience kept his hands from shaking. Rex holstered the Glock before he blew off his foot.

Rex tried to look into the open freezer, but his goggles were dripping from what he'd shot. Wiping clean the goggles with his gloved hand, Rex could tell whatever he'd shot, it was sticky to the touch and pulpy. Rex couldn't make out the color of the substance, yet one fact stood out. Norman was going to need a new freezer. After Rex managed to get his goggles cleaned, he could see there was a gaping hole in the back of the freezer unit that allowed one to look directly into the backyard.

"Wow," Rex said. He was always amazed by the amount of destructive power packed into the Glock using MagSafe loads. In this case, the blast had provided so much punch Rex couldn't find anything else in the freezer. Whatever had been in there had been blown into the next dimension.

Stepping in something sticky, Rex pointed his goggles downward. On the floor, Rex discovered what had attacked him.

It wasn't a creeping hand seizing its chance for freedom. It wasn't a sawed off leg either. On the floor were the remains of the cardboard wrapper that had once held frozen orange juice concentrate. Rex concluded his yanking open of the freezer door caused a container of frozen orange juice to roll out of the freezer towards him. Rex had blasted Norman's breakfast drink to kingdom-come.

"Oops," was the only thing Rex could think of saying.

*Hey, the thing was just in the wrong place at the wrong time, accidents happen*, Rex parlayed with himself. Norman could sue Rex for destruction of personal property, but Rex still had him for that episode where he'd fallen through Norman's front porch.

Rex slapped the freezer door shut in disgust. Hell, the kitchen was such a mess he figured it'd be a week before Norman noticed he had a new rear door to his freezer unit. It wasn't like there was anything in there to spoil. On the other hand, Rex hadn't found the quick evidence he'd sought. This meant a continued search through the house and time was running out.

Satisfied with his destruction in the kitchen area and lacking any evidence that might connect Norman Lipshitz to any murders, Rex turned toward the hallway that was directly across the ruined backdoor.

The hallway led toward the front of the house. Rex's night vision goggles proved indispensable at this point. The entire house was as dark as a bear's cavern. The only light in the kitchen came from the door Rex had broken down. He could always turn on some lights, but that would be too easy.

Kicking rubbish out of his path, Rex made his way down the hallway. To his left was a half size door with a deadbolt used to close it.

Looking up the hallway, Rex could see nothing unusual, but he moved cautiously, always wary of booby traps. Rex knew Norman wouldn't set traps around the avenues he normally tramped about the house, but there was always the trap in the most obvious of places that one would stumble over and get caught.

Rex knew there was no way to prepare for these house traps, as they were as original and deadly as the mind of their maker. Yet, the fact that Norman had set a trap at the back door was encouraging to Rex. It told Rex there was something in this house Norman was serious about keeping hidden or protected. A normal person doesn't set-up a crossbow to pin an intruder to the door like a bug for examination. Norman was a killer, of that Rex was sure. He just had to find the proof.

Rex moved down the hallway. The walls were covered with peeling wallpaper, and the pattern was so faded that Rex couldn't make it out. The paper certainly wasn't something that Norman had put up or even tried to repair.

On his left, beyond the cellar door, were two wooden steps that led to the landing of a staircase.

Time was ticking away.

The staircase ran along the sidewall of the house and went up to the second level. Beyond the staircase, along the left wall, was a door which Rex figured to be the front closet since it was right next to the front door and there wasn't room for anything else to be there. Directly in front of Rex was the front door that had done such a marvelous job of turning back his attempts of entering the house in a more standard fashion.

Gazing at the front door, Rex chuckled. There was no doubt in his mind why he was unable to kick down this old wooden door with a single kick. The door was braced with 2x6 inch planks that were nailed into the structure of the house itself. The planks had been placed horizontally across three quarters of the door making it impenetrable. Again it occurred to Rex that Norman must really be trying to hide something in here.

"Norman … Norman … Aw shit!"

Norman was only about five minutes away and Rex still hadn't found anything. It was time to move. Along the right wall of the hallway there were two parlor doors that were so finely carved they were beautiful even in the green of Rex's night vision. Maybe this was what Norman was trying to hide from everyone, Rex wondered—antique doors that would cost a fortune if bought today. Naw, they were a fluke … dinosaurs hidden in this ancient house. Norman didn't care about them any more than he cared about the rest of the house.

Running his hands over their delicate craftsmanship, Rex found the French door handles were locked. No way was he going to waste time trying to pound through these suckers given the fortitude Norman had embraced upon the other doorways.

With so many other places still to investigate, Rex turned his back on the parlor doors to study the staircase landing. He decided to try the upstairs first. Something told him he was making a mistake the moment he turned his back on the parlor doors, but Rex felt the rest of the house beckoning to him. "Come on, Rex, we're waiting—Come on, Rex, let's play—Oh, Rex, baby …" the house cooed in soft undertones in the back of his mind.

He thought about peeking into the front closet, but the thought of a booby trap was enough to talk Rex out of his curiosity. He figured no one kept their bodies in the front closet anyway. He returned his attention to the staircase, ever thoughtful of time passing—tickity—tickity—tock …

Rex's experience had taught him staircases were the perfect location in a house for booby traps since he was confined by the walls of the staircase. This was where he was most exposed, and probably in his most vulnerable position as he climbed the stairs. Not only did he have to move cautiously up the stairs, but he was also exposed from above if someone was waiting to attack.

Although Rex was aware of the passing time more than ever, he crept up the first two stairs at a snail's pace and stopped on the landing. Now he was able to see into the hallway of the second level.

"Hello!" Rex's voice echoed off the close walls hurting his ears.

In response, Rex heard something behind one of the doors upstairs—a dialogue he was sure, but in a normal tone. He didn't hear screams for help. Rex couldn't understand what was being said or even the sex of the speaker, but someone was yakitty yaking. Why didn't they respond to his calling out?

It occurred to Rex that he was hearing a TV or radio making all the noise.

He saw there was nobody there waiting to bash his noggin, but that was about it. Rex counted nine stairs leading to the second level. Rex knew he would have to examine each and every step for a trap. He wasn't too worried about Norman getting home now. Rex knew he could handle Norman by one method or another. It was the hiding, and possibly fatal, booby trap that Rex couldn't afford to be careless in handling. He couldn't afford to give in to the voices upstairs that might be a TV—voices that seemed to urge him on.

Getting down on all fours, Rex examined every wooden fiber of the first step from the landing. Nothing. Okay—He examined the second step as if he had a mother-in-law coming to check on his dust. There wasn't anything that appeared like it would trigger a trap, but his mother-in-law wouldn't be impressed since the steps had plenty of dust.

Slowly, Rex turtled up the rest of the steps doing the same close examination. He was beginning to think that he'd given Norman too much credit until he came to the seventh and eighth steps.

Running across each of these steps was a clear fishing line which ran into holes in the walls. Norman was smart enough to put these triggering devices in midair, and on two consecutive steps to catch someone that might go up or down the steps two at a time.

Pretty tricky. Rex gave Norman credit. That was another thing Rex had learned about serial killers. Typically, they had above average intelligence, and were so paranoid they were difficult to fool or approach.

Since the ninth and final step appeared okay from a short distance, Rex figured they were okay to use. Otherwise, he didn't think Norman would be able to use the stairs at all. One would have to be an athlete to jump all three stairs to make it to the second floor, and from what Rex had seen of Norman Lipshitz, he was no athlete. He must use the upstairs if there was a TV left on. Yup, those stairs were okay, Rex figured, the TV's the clincher.

Time was passing—tickity—tickity—tock ...

Standing up again with caution, Rex was able to take in the second level hallway to insure that there were no traps evident once he gained the hallway itself.

The hallway was as narrow as the downstairs hallway, and it had a hardwood floor as well. Rex could see there was a doorway directly in front of him, and there were two more doors on the wall to his left. To the right side of the stairs and hallway was a solid wall that made up the side of the house. There was one of the windows Rex had been staring at earlier on the right wall. He'd been right. There was nothing to see in or from the windows anyway.

Rex assumed there was a fourth door at his end of the hall to his left that he couldn't see at the moment. This doorway would lead to the third bedroom that was over the parlor at the front of the house.

Rex was assuming this was a three bedroom house and the two doorways on the wall to his left were bedrooms. The door at the end of the hallway was probably the bathroom. That way the toilet and bath plumbing would go straight down and meet with the kitchen sink plumbing below it.

Rex saw nothing unusual about the hardwood floor. Except maybe the crack that ran the length of the hallway on his right, in between the wall and the floor, where there should have been wooden molding. Rex couldn't tell if it was missing the molding between the floor and the wall, or if the floor was settling away from the wall. Considering the condition of the rest of the house, Rex thought the crack looked natural and harmless enough. His main concern was getting to that ninth step without tripping either of the wires going across steps seven and eight.

Time was passing—tickity—tickity—tock ...

Standing on his left foot, Rex stretched and gently placed his right foot on the ninth step. As Rex started to put his weight on his right foot, the step sank and he heard a snapping noise as if a pencil had been broken in two. Rex looked down to see what he'd stepped on while he could hear something—or someone—running.

Rex's stomach sank and his testicles curled up inside him. He realized the sound was coming from beneath the stairs. Suddenly, the door in front of him burst open and a man with a pitchfork under each arm charged at him. Rex heard someone scream.

Rex leaped to the ninth step, drawing his gun in mid-leap. Fire exploded from the gun as it spit its destruction before the rampaging pitchforks could skewer him like meat on a shiskabob. As Rex fired a second shot, he realized he wasn't shooting a real person, and the Glock would not stop the approaching Grim Reaper less than five feet away.

Rex's first shot hit a mannequin on wheels in its molded chest and blew right through it as if it was paper—the dummy kept charging without a hitch. Rex watched with increasing terror as his second shot blew the mannequin's head into splinters. Still, the pitchforks rolled toward him with remarkable speed.

Rex realized he was the one screaming while the mannequin continued its charge drawn by a steel cable that ran through the crack in the floor. Terror stalled his movement.

Rex wasn't about to run away from a dummy, pitchforks or no pitchforks. He hopped onto the second level in time to dodge left of the charging mannequin. His dodge was only a partial success as Rex was pronged by the dummy's right pitchfork and thrown against the closed door behind him. Rex hit the door with enough force to take his breath away and seat him hard on the floor. The mannequin swerved sideways after pronging Rex. It reached the ninth step only to break apart and tumble down the stairs pitchforks and all.

For a moment, Rex sat against the door trying to catch his breath as he checked his chest for holes. He was sure he'd find blood pumping out of his chest from jagged wounds after being stuck by that pitchfork. To his relief, Rex found that his Kevlar vest no worse for the wear.

"Son-of-a-bitch packed a wallop," Rex cussed when he managed to get up off the floor and catch his wind. "Nifty freakin' trap, Lipshitz, I'll give ya that much."

Rex holstered the Glock, and then straightened his helmet and goggles. Next, Rex thanked his lucky stars for Kevlar body armor and the twenty-eight piles of it that were tightly strapped into his Special Ops Vest. The vest covered Rex from his neck to his crotch, both front and back, and it had just saved his life—although, not for the last time.

Rex was also thankful that he'd spent the time to test this vest beforehand. Those tests had given him the confidence in the armor's protective ability, and allowed him to make that dodge while knowing he was still going to get pronged by a pitchfork no matter what he did. Looking down the stairs, Rex realized if he had stayed on the staircase and tried to duck under the pitchforks, he would have still gotten tangled up with the dummy and broken a few bones, if not his neck, as they both fell down the staircase.

As Rex peeped down the hallway again his ears picked up a distant bangitty-clank of a miss-firing car engine.

"Hot-damn, how time flies when you're having fun," Rex hollered before turning and kicking in the bedroom door that he'd been thrown into by the motoring mannequin. Rex had heard the sounds of talking like a TV when he'd been leaning against the door.

Rex knew he'd have to hurry now as the sound of Lipshitz's Buick came thundering down the dirt road, alerting the entire countryside. Norman had arrived sooner than expected, and before Rex had found his evidence. At this point, Rex had no legal reason to be in the house since there didn't appear to be anyone screaming, nor was he ready for Norman.

As the door splintered off its frame and flew into the room, Rex stood back and wasn't surprised when a spring loaded two by four came whooshing down from the ceiling into the center of the doorway about chest high and with deadly force. The two by four slammed into the top of the doorframe and wall, coming to a halt with a loud bang. Rex saw that the board had rusty nails sticking out to quill anyone that entered the room not expecting a trap.

"Oh, that's rookie material, Lipshitz, rookie material, tsk, tsk," Rex grumbled and shook his head. After the stairway booby trap, Rex thought Norman would have come up with something more original for the rest of the upstairs. Still, he remained cautious.

Having learned from the last booby trap, Rex didn't enter this front room fearing that this first trap was a decoy. Norman hadn't boarded up the windows on the second level, and there was enough light coming through the dirty window curtains even without his goggles for him to see that this room wasn't used.

Six months of dust covered the ancient bedroom furniture. Rex figured this was Lipshitz's parents' room before their fatal auto accident. From other serial killer's psychological profiles, Rex knew that sometimes serial killers lived at home with one or both of their parents. While living at home, the serial killer often hated and worshiped the parents at the same time. Rex figured that Norman hated and feared his parents enough to never be able to enter their bedroom or touch their earthly possessions. Rex figured Norman feared his parents enough to not be able to come in and turn off their four foot high Philco radio in a walnut cabinet which sat just inside the doorway of the master bedroom. The old radio was still broadcasting on some AM station. Rex shook his head, thinking that radio had been on for six months or whenever Norman's parents had last turned it on.

Rex stood looking through this doorway, lost in his own thoughts, as the sound of Lipshitz's Buick reached a thundering crescendo outside the house. It sounded to Rex like the engine had been driven to Hell and back, and it was on its last breath.

Rex looked out the front window in time to catch Lipshitz's beat-up Buick trailing a cloud of black smoke as it came rampaging off the dirt road like a comet. Norman's car turned onto the front lawn, swerving and tearing up frosty grass and dirt, before straightening out, and heading for the house. The engine shot off an acceleration of explosions and black fumes. Norman must have put the pedal to the metal, kicking the Buick through its last gasps. Rex watched this flaming metal monster until it disappeared beneath the roof of the front porch and out of his view. Strangely, he couldn't see Lipshitz in the car since the inner cabin was filled with churning black smoke, and Norman was driving with all the windows rolled up. The car never slowed down as it rammed onto the front porch and through the front door, rocking the house. Rex was thrown off his feet as Lipshitz drove his burning car into the front hall and parlor, directly beneath where Rex was standing.

"Wow, what an entrance," Rex managed to exclaim before sucking in a lungful of oily smoke and starting to cough with intensity. With watering eyes, Rex looked up in time to see the bedroom floor collapse onto the smoking car beneath it with a scream of tearing wood that sounded human, and with an ending crash that sounded explosive.

Rex watched as the bedroom furniture slid across the slanting hardwood floor, broke through the wall beneath the window, and sail out onto the front lawn.

"Kick-ass! Home demolition derby time!" Rex coughed in excitement.

Rex couldn't appreciate Norman's attempt to redecorate since the dark smoke thickened and drove him back down the hallway. As Rex backpedaled in a crab-position and tried to get a glimpse at the condition of the staircase, he heard an inhuman screech of rage from Lipshitz on the first floor.

Rex looked down the staircase and saw there was no exit that way. He saw flames lapping around the front quarter panel and hood of Lipshitz's now really beat-to-shit Buick. The car had rammed all the way through to the staircase landing and set fire to the house along the way.

Rex shouted, "Oh SHIT!"

This scenario was not in his game plan. The gas tank in that burning hunk of junk could explode at any time. An explosive Buick would kill both of them. Unfortunately, Rex had shouted loud enough to draw Lipshitz's attention and now Stormin' Norman as alert to Rex's presence.

Lipshitz slid across the hood of his car on his back, screaming with madness. His head popped out between the car's left front quarter panel and the stairway wall so he could leer up at Rex. Rex stared back down for a moment at Lipshitz—Lipshitz's face appeared green and magnified 3X. Rex screamed at the ugly sight just on general principals. Lipshitz screamed right back at Rex.

Rex imagined how he must appear to Lipshitz with all his equipment on, and he figured Lipshitz had reason to holler. Still, Rex knew Norman was as crazy as a loon even if he had never murdered anyone. Rex had peered into Norman's eyes and he saw the raging torment of Hell.

Norman's eyes changed from those of a lunatic to those of someone surprised by a sudden pain. Rex saw why. The long and greasy hair on the back of Norman's balding head was on fire. Rex sat in fascination as he watched Norman's head burn and blacken like the head of a match. Norman continued to scream the whole time. Abruptly, Norman withdrew his blackened head into the hallway.

Rex realized that could be him burning down there, and he scrambled for an alternate escape from the second level. The smoke was growing so thick that he had to stay on all fours and crawl. Rex headed to the first bedroom thinking to escape the same way the furniture had gone through the wall, but then he saw he was too late since the slanting floor of the bedroom was engulfed in flames. Rex couldn't trust the floor to hold his weight even though his clothing was fire resistant and he didn't fear getting burnt.

Rex knew he was in trouble, and he started to feel terror building inside him. The smoke was so heavy each breath was coming as a cough, and his eyes burned as if his eyelids were on fire.

Rex turned about and crawled toward the second doorway. He came to a halt when the floorboard between his hands exploded. A bullet passed through the floor directly in front of his face. Rex cried out both in surprise of being shot at and because wood splinters peppered his nose, cheeks, and ricocheted off his night vision goggles.

Rex thanked his lucky stars for his goggles. If he hadn't been wearing them he was sure he would have been blinded by splinters. Still, he remembered to turn them off in case he was blinded by the brightening environment of the flames filling the house. He sat back on his haunches briefly and coughed while gently patting his chin and nose to check for facial disfigurement. Rex decided Norman's shot had caused more fear than damage since his gloves came away from his face clean of blood.

Lipshitz must have heard Rex's cry of pain above the roar of the flames because Rex heard a savage cry from below that sounded more triumphant than Norman's previous squeals of rage. Lipshitz fired five more shots through the floor in direct line to the first, but moving in an opposite direction of Rex's reclined position.

Rex thought about his profile on Lipshitz to remember what kind of weapons Norman had registered with the State of Michigan. Lipshitz had legally registered only one weapon. It was a Rossi Model 851 revolver that he'd bought a few months ago, around the same time as the first victim disappeared.

Rex knew the Rossi was a .38 Special 6-shooter his armored vest and helmet could handle, but Rex wasn't in the mood for further testing. Even if the Kevlar held the slug, the blast force would be similar to being kicked by a mule. Rex knew the feel of that kind of blast and didn't care to experience it ever again.

Rex concluded Lipshitz was firing the Rossi six shot and was now reloading. The stinging in his lower face seemed inconsequential, the black smoke was thickening, and his rump was warming up from the flames in the first bedroom—it was time to boogie.

Rex saw no other options and he crawled to the first of the two doors on the left wall. He grasped the doorknob, and it felt cool through his gloved hand. At least this suggested there wasn't a fire in this room. Rex hadn't forgotten the booby traps either. He tested the knob, but he couldn't open the door. Rex concluded it was locked with a deadbolt.

"Shit." Rex coughed, not daring further speech. He held his breath and stood up in the thick smoke. He kicked the door. The door bowed but didn't break, and Rex was forced to the floor again. Rex landed, and there was an explosion as a bullet smashed through the floorboards right where he had been standing. If Rex had enough wind, and he had kicked the door a second time, he would now be sporting a .38 caliber enema.

"Well, two can play this game." Rex coughed. He drew his Glock, and fired two rounds blindly through the floor. Rex was deafened by the blasts in closed quarters, so he heard no response from his shots. He turned his gun toward the door he'd just kicked, and he shot off the door handle. The door swung open as if to invite him in. Below, Rex heard Lipshitz continuing to howl like the lunatic he was, but at least he wasn't shooting anymore.

Rex couldn't tell if it was pain or rage that kept Lipshitz hollering, but he no longer cared. His eyes burned from the smoke, and he was forced to remove his helmet and night vision goggles. He shoved his night vision goggles back into his duty belt.

Rex returned his helmet to his noggin, and buckled down his chin strap. He closed his fire-resistant balaclava as close around his face as possible, sat up in a frog's position, and then dove through the dark hole of the opened doorway.

Rex landed on his hands first, but they slipped and slid on the floor. Rex realized the floor had been greased or oiled down even as his knees hit. His momentum carried him toward whatever doom awaited him in the darkness.

Rex's hands slid out from beneath him, and he belly-flopped into the dark room with the flames following his entrance. The fire ate up the greased surface, but Rex was sliding faster than the flames could ignite around him.

Abruptly, the floor beneath Rex opened and he fell into empty space with a surprised, "Yaaaoooo!"

His yell died when he landed on his hands upon a huge couch with trampolining springs. Bouncing, Rex turned his body in mid-air so he came down on his butt and in a seated position. He made a smaller bounce before settling down with an, "Oaff," and he saw that he had his own personal seat in Hell.

Rex briefly lost interest in Norman as he felt the intense heat of the burning room around him; and he saw everything was roaring, spitting, and popping with dancing flames. He felt every pore in his body erupt with sweat to protect his body from the heat.

In front, and to his left, Rex saw Norman's Buick. The front of the house that had collapsed was being consumed in a huge bonfire before him. Rex thought it was a shame the beautiful parlor doors had been ruined by Lipshitz's entrance, as they now burned like any other piece of wood.

Something slimy smacked against the side of his face. Feeling repulsion of a cold and clammy thing like a raw oyster, Rex batted it away before looking to see what he was pushing. When Rex turned to glance at what had slimed him he looked into the decomposing eyes of a dead man. Rex tried to draw a breath, but couldn't. He went ballistic trying to shoot himself out of the couch cushions which were clutching him closely. In his flailing about, the corpse plopped over into his lap, and Rex thought he'd start screaming like Stormin' Norman.

Rex was grunting and groaning and tangled in his one-sided wrestling match, when he felt something plop with a burning ooze onto his right shoulder. He twisted about and threw off the head of a second cadaver which was in flames. The second body appeared as an angel from Hell. Rex could see this cadaver was more decomposed than his current wrestling partner, but its entire torso was dripping in flames as decaying skin and clothing melted off the skeletal features. Rex watched, struck still in horror, while the fat on the corpse's facial features sizzled and popped. Briefly the cadaver appeared as a blinded king as its hair rose in a fiery crown. The burning skull stared back at Rex with molten orbs and a jawbone ajar in a silent scream.

Rex had found his evidence, or the evidence had found him, and in his horror he decided that Lipshitz had been more productive than the authorities believed or were telling the public at large. Now that Rex had found the evidence he'd risked his neck to obtain, he decided he didn't care about Lipshitz at the moment. He would give anything to get off this couch of repugnance.

Rex fought to get away from his companions as a new chorus of screaming erupted. This new round of bellowing seemed to be coming from behind him. Lipshitz had renewed his screeching solo and Rex regained his concern for the lunatic's whereabouts.

The flaming cadaver's head exploded like a rotten melon and the rest of the body was thrown clear of Rex before he recognized the boom that caused the ringing in his ears was the sound of a gunshot. A second boom came simultaneously with an explosion of goose feathers which erupted from the huge hole in the back of the couch to the right of Rex.

Rex discovered getting out of the couch was easier than he thought as he bounded out and upward. He realized this move could prove fatal since the fire silhouetted his figure to Lipshitz who was behind him with a loaded gun. As Rex turned his flying body while reaching for his gun in hopes of spotting Lipshitz, that mule kicked him in the back. Rex didn't hear the gunshot as the force of the bullet added to his forward motion and sent him headfirst through the flames at the front of the house. Rex's flight came to a landing as he swan dived onto the dead grass of Norman's front lawn and slid to a painful halt clear of the fire.

After Rex landed in a crumpled heap, he was barely conscious, and he couldn't breathe. Rex heard the welcome sound of sirens coming to the rescue. The world was blackening in and out around him, and he thought at least Higgy was about to arrive to save the day.

Rex regained consciousness after an unknown amount of time. He coughed and it immediately reminded him where he was and that he was still in danger. Rex willed himself to his hands and knees like a sick dog. During this time he continued to hack and wheeze from the smoke he'd inhaled.

Every hack or wheeze was a nightmare of stabbing pain in his back muscles and ribs. It wasn't the smoke inhalation that was so painful as much as the bullet in the back that was making breathing an undesirable necessity.

When Rex regained consciousness again it was accompanied by a string of hacking coughs and pain in his back, chest, and shoulder. Rex found himself on his back with a hand trying to hold him down. He felt the roaring heat of a huge fire, and his thoughts returned to where he was and what had happened.

Rex tried to get up, as he thought it was Lipshitz that was holding him down, but his eyes focused and his ears cleared so Rex could understand the man wearing a fire helmet was trying to tell him to relax and stay still. Rex looked into the scared eyes of the young man and saw an unwrinkled face that could have passed for a boy's. What was this boy doing so close to an armed animal, Rex wondered?

Coughing, Rex asked, "Where's Lipshitz?"

"Who?" the boy fireman asked. Then Rex was aware of more shots being fired from behind him.

"Him ... you idiot!" Rex yelled as he ignored his pain and swung his body around to leg whip the fireman down to the ground. "Now stay on the ground before you get your ass killed." Rex grunted with labored breath.

The boy saw his danger and stammered, "I ... I ... think I'll do just that!"

Rex fought his pain and got on all fours in a squatting position. He recalled the pain he'd felt after a 280-pound defensive lineman had speared him in his back with his helmet during the Michigan State Vs Purdue football game eleven years ago. It hurt like hell to inhale, and every time Rex coughed it was as if someone was stabbing him in the back with a knife. Rex had gotten up and played the rest of the game eleven years ago and he knew he'd have to get up now. Rex knew his life, and now the lives of others, were in danger. This had not been the game plan. Innocent people were not supposed to get involved. It was time to suck it up and get back into action.

"I'm gettin' too old for this shit." Rex wheezed, and then he coughed as if he was a lifetime smoker.

Looking around from his squatting position, Rex saw a lone fire truck with three other firemen standing at its side. Higgy had not arrived. The firemen had stunned and scared expressions on their faces as they tried to comprehend what was occurring. It was obvious to Rex a neighbor saw the smoke and called the local volunteer fire force. This fire equipment and personnel were what was left after the accident Lipshitz caused earlier. These were farm boys with no law-enforcement training, much less experience in dealing with a raving lunatic like Lipshitz.

"Get down!" Rex tried to shout, but his voice sounded weak in comparison to the noise of the fire, and the pain in his back exploded, making him wince. Trying to wave his arms, Rex discovered he could barely raise his right arm. Still, Rex managed to get the three firemen's attention by waving his left arm.

Five more shots exploded from the house in rapid succession. Rex had been looking at one of the firemen as he took a slug in the shoulder area that threw the boy against the fire truck. Two more slugs hit the truck around the fireman. A fourth bullet exploded the tire on the fire truck's front passenger side. The fifth bullet missed altogether. The firemen got the message in a hurry and dove to the ground. The two uninjured firemen scrambled to aid their fallen comrade, and Rex understood it was still him against Lipshitz—only now Rex had more responsibilities and Lipshitz had more targets.

Getting down next to the fireman on the ground, Rex told him, "The police are on their way."

The boy just returned Rex's gaze. Rex could see he was terrified as his body shook and the huge helmet rattled on his head.

"Yeah ... Yes ... All alarms are automatically called into the police station," the scared boy said in a mechanical voice as if he was giving his memorized speech to the second graders when they visited the fire station.

Rolling off his right arm, Rex reached down and pulled out his Glock. His right arm was becoming stiff and useless. He popped out the gun's magazine, and then pulled out a spare clip from his duty belt. Slamming in a full magazine, Rex was sure he had nineteen loads to shoot. Then he returned the partially used clip to his mag holder and said to the boy firefighter, "I want you to crawl on your belly back behind the truck and watch carefully to see if that maniac tries to make a run for it. If he does, take cover and stay away from him cause he'll kill you if he gets the chance."

"What ... What ... are you gonna do?" the boy asked, looking so scared Rex felt sorry for the young man.

Catching the boy's eye, Rex said, "I think it's time to even the score." He felt the fire of the hunt begin to pump through his veins and the pain from his injuries fade. He wheeled around and up into a squatting position. Rex was about to make a charge on the house when muscle spasms in his back halted the advance and left him squatting and in danger.

Rex took a few deep breaths to stretch his back while relaxing in a kneeling position to control the pain. He peered into the burning inferno and tried to decide where Lipshitz was and how best to approach him.

Rex switched the Glock to his left hand. His right arm was feeling so weak Rex knew he couldn't count on it. Since even squatting was agony at the moment, Rex could not provide a stable firing platform to shoot back. His pain was becoming crippling, and Rex knew that would never do.

Rex knew pain was a mind game at times. Sometimes it led to healing and health. This was a time when it wasn't helping the situation. Concentrating on turning his pain into a controlled anger, Rex thought about how Lipshitz had gotten the best of him and what he could do to settle the score. It didn't take long for Rex's emotional rage to override any pain he was feeling.

Having made his decision, Rex got up from his squatting position and began shuffling to his right like a crab. Before Rex had taken two shuffles, he heard the fireman hiss, "Fry his ass," and Rex cracked a smile. The kid had some spunk.

A shot exploded from the right side of the house and Rex felt the heat of the bullet pass by the left side of his head even as he heard the slug hitting the fire truck behind him. The shot was enough to scare Rex into sprinting head down toward the gunfire. He knew his helmet and vest were able to withstand a bullet from Lipshitz's gun, but he had no idea how his baseball shin guards would fare.

More explosions rang out, but Rex didn't know where they hit. Diving and rolling, Rex reached the burning corner at the right side of the house. His back exploded with pain during the roll, and Rex felt something pop in his right shoulder as well. He momentarily felt that queasiness again but he knew it would settle.

Rex felt relief from the stabbing pain along his right shoulder and arm. He realized his shoulder must have been dislocated and the hard roll on the ground had thrown it back into its socket.

"Good deal." Rex grinned, now shrugging his shoulder with soreness rather than the stabbing pain he was feeling before. "I always enjoyed using both hands to beat my meat." Rex grinned.

The heat close to the house was staggering, but Rex had to rest for a moment. Gunshots rang out and Rex turned to see the ground exploding in front of the fireman he had left behind. The idiot had gotten up and was high-knee sprinting for the protection of the fire truck.

Rex figured the boy had not liked his advice on crawling. It was just as well. The boy turned out to be a world class sprinter when someone was shooting at him. He rounded the bend behind the fire truck untouched. Rex was happy to see that the other firemen had pulled their fallen comrade beneath the truck to the other side as well.

While feeling the heat of the fire on his face, Rex looked back into the flames and realized he'd made a big mistake. The flicks of fire were now dancing around the rear of the Norman's car and its gas tank. The wreck was ten feet from his position.

Rex got up and sprinted alongside the right side of the house toward the rickety barn. From the barn he might have some cover to fight Lipshitz. Rex figured Lipshitz must be in the kitchen area at the rear of the house because the flames had engulfed the entire front half. As Rex ran, he saw the shutters of the side kitchen window explode outward. Glass and splintered wood blasted out onto the lawn and Lipshitz's black head popped out to gaze about with his kooky eyes. This was quickly followed by a gun poking out of the broken window and it was pointed directly at Rex. Rex took another dive to the ground and rolled even as three more shots exploded from the gun.

Rex began to wonder how much ammunition this asshole had as he hopped up into a shooter's squat and returned fire with the Glock still in his left hand. His shots were fired with the same accuracy as when he'd practiced against Captain Thrifty a few days before.

Rex's heart soared as he made these shots. He was back into the heat of the battle and defending himself instead of being laid out or running away. His four shots were right on target as the window frame exploded into a cloud of splintering wood and broken glass.

Rex heard a scream of pain come from the kitchen area, and the arm with the gun disappeared from the window. Rex smiled with the satisfaction of knowing he was using a handgun that could blow right through the side of a house to find its target.

Feeling he had a moment of safety, Rex turned and ran across the backyard. Since the barn doors were closed, Rex knew he'd have to ram through the rotting wood rather than expose himself as he tried to open the damn things. Putting his head and left shoulder down, Rex knew he'd have to try his charging-the-goal-line technique again as he dove into the lower part of the left door.

Rex hit the door at full speed and he was seeing his lucky stars before he realized he'd landed with only half his body through the door. He tried to raise his head and discovered this was a big mistake. Around him the barn pitched and dropped as if he was lying on a ship deck in troubled waters. Closing his eyes again, Rex could only lay his head in the hay-covered muck until the world stopped moving beneath him. Having his bell rung was another familiar feeling from his football days, so the feeling wasn't new or scary to him. He knew it would fade to a dull headache in a moment.

A voice in the back of his mind reminded him that his rear was still exposed outside the door. The explosion of a gunshot, and a bullet blasting through the rotted wood just over Rex's fanny, told Rex just how exposed his butt was hanging out the barn door. Lipshitz must have recovered enough to take another shot at him. Rex yelped as if someone had just branded his behind with a burning iron, and he squirmed the rest of the way through the door.

After taking a moment, Rex got to his knees and opened his eyes. Slowly the world came into focus as it was no longer spinning. Trying to rid himself of the rest of the cobwebs clouding his mind, Rex made another mistake by shaking his head. His thick neck cramped while his brain felt as if it was bouncing about the walls of his skull. At least the pain seemed to clear his senses, and he was able to get to his feet.

Looking about, Rex saw that he was in front of a window that looked toward the rear of the house. The window was so dirty he couldn't make out any distinct shapes through the clouded glass. Still, Rex didn't want to expose himself to gun fire from the house so he stepped back to the protection of a barn beam.

Rex gazed about the floor to find something to break the window, but Lipshitz beat him to the punch by shooting the window out. Rex threw himself against the thick wood of the barn frame before peeking around the corner to admire his view of the burning house through the broken window.

While in relative safety for the moment, Rex figured he was going to have to use his right arm to shoot through the window frame if he wanted to keep this barn beam in between himself and Lipshitz.

"I ought to just let the fucker burn his way to Hell. Surely he's earned the invitation," Rex said to no one. He watched the fire grow to consume most of the house. It was then that Rex remembered the different entryways along that first level hallway inside the house. The cellar entryway beneath the staircase stood out in his mind in particular.

Rex recalled that the cellar door had been off to the left of the kitchen entryway—not more than a couple of steps from the window through which Lipshitz had been shooting.

It occurred to Rex that if Lipshitz had an ounce of sense remaining, he'd go down into his cellar to find something to hide beneath while the rest of the house burned down. Lipshitz would probably never survive the heat, but who knew what a madman could do. For all Rex knew, Lipshitz might have a well designed hiding place in the cellar with this type of situation in mind. Lipshitz had proved to be an intelligent killer so far—one that was paranoid and thought in advance.

It also occurred to Rex that if Lipshitz found a hiding place, the police wouldn't realize that Lipshitz wasn't among the charred remains they would find after this inferno turned everything to ashes. The police might find one of the unknown cadavers Rex wrestled with in the parlor and they might assume the cadaver was Lipshitz.

Rex stood hypnotized by the fire as the flames engulfed the entire house, and he knew Lipshitz was either dead or had escaped to the cellar. There was no longer anywhere for Lipshitz to hide on the first level and the second level was history.

"Shit!" Rex hissed.

He stepped out from behind the barn support as he thought of his alternatives. Rex didn't care about losing the reward money; he could drop his weapons right now and live in style off his investments. Yet he did care about not being able to extract his pound of flesh from an animal that'd shot him in the back and killed so many innocent people. There was no way Rex was going to allow Lipshitz to just walk away from this. As he looked at the blazing woodpile again, Rex spied the storm doors at the rear of the house. These would lead to the cellar. Bingo!

"Yes ... Yes, those will do nicely ..." Rex said as the grin resurfaced on his face..

Heedless of possible gunfire, Rex strode out of the leaning barn, across the backyard, toward the intense heat of the burning house. The pain in his back was all but forgotten as he concentrated on Lipshitz's escape possibilities. He stopped momentarily as more of the house collapsed into the fire. Rex lowered his head; sparks and small pieces of burning wood rained off his helmet and armored shoulders. The clouds of smoking ash blocked out the sunlight as the whole scene took on the cataclysmic appearance of a small volcanic eruption.

Rex heard the sound as more sirens approached from a distance. He hoped big Bobby was behind the wheel of one of those approaching vehicles.

Hopping back into action, Rex made for the slanting storm doors at the rear of the house. Fortune would have it that the wind was blowing against his back, thus blowing the flames and a good deal of the heat away from him.

Arriving at the storm doors, Rex had his gun out and shot off the lock and chain that kept the doors secured. Rex was glad his right arm had regained the strength to handle the Glock 20. He had an itching feeling that this case was far from closed.

He threw aside the broken chains, and pulled open one of the storm doors. Rex was thrown back as smoke came billowing out this new exit. Rex stepped forward again and took a glimpse of what it might be like to descend a stairway into Hell. The cellar was a roaring inferno of fire. The wind was sucked down the opening from the cellar doors and fueled the flames from below. Rex stepped up to the cellar staircase, but he was thrown back again as the first level floor buckled and crashed into the cellar below.

The heat was so intense that Rex felt his body sweating and continuing to sop his undergarments. Rex waved his hands to dismiss the whole mess. He wasn't suicidal enough to go down there after Lipshitz even if he could manage it.

Rex stood back and sighed as he watched the fire consume every inch of the house. He turned away and headed toward the barn, but he hadn't gotten more than a few paces before he was hurled to the ground by a gigantic hand of heat as Lipshitz's Buick blew up and the explosion threw burning debris in every direction.

Rex was on all fours and crawling towards the barn as fast as he could as burning pieces of the house rained all about him. Although better judgment would have told him to stay away from the leaning disaster, the barn was the only cover Rex could find.

A shattered toilet crashed into the ground just in front of Rex, and he was forced to dive over the hot porcelain into a somersault that racked his painful back. Right away Rex was up and scrambling through the barn door where he threw himself face down onto the cool and smelly dirt floor.

Remaining stretched out on the barn floor for a few moments, Rex caught his breath. Then he sat up to look around the barn and muttered, "I gotta get into better shape if I'm gonna be doing all this running around shit. What happened to the days when they seemed to stand there and let you catch'um or shoot'um?" He shook his head and reminisced.

Slowly getting to his feet, Rex peeked out the barn window again. The entire house was a shambles—one big burning pit. Rex saw that the police had arrived and were just getting out of their cars. An ambulance had also arrived. Two of the firemen, including the one that had tried to help Rex, were pulling a fire hose and carefully making their way towards the barn while giving the burning pit a wide berth.

Blowing out a deep breath, Rex leaned up against the barn support thinking maybe this was another job done.

# CHAPTER FOUR

Rex turned back into the barn. He wasn't satisfied—not by a long shot. He leaned his aching back against the barn support that he'd been using as cover earlier. The relief of leaning against the beam was heaven on his bruised back muscles, so he closed his eyes and held up the barn while he thought.

Rex knew no one could survive that fire. Lipshitz must have surrendered to his wounds, the heat of the fire, his own madness, and was dead. That is, unless there was another exit, stated a voice in Rex's mind. Oh come on, Rex, he told himself. He'd seen all the doors and windows—the guy was dead, toast even. A charcoal biscuit would be a better description.

Still, something was missing. Who were the cadavers Rex had wrestled with on the couch? When had they died? Where had they died, and how did they get to be sitting in Norman's parlor? The how and the why they died didn't seem important to Rex at this moment. There was something going on here Rex had never experienced and he couldn't imagine what it was. Drawing a heavy sigh, Rex opened his eyes when he heard the creaking of a hinge followed by the sound of running footsteps approaching him.

Lipshitz charged Rex with a pitchfork cradled under his arm.

Rex lifted his Glock out of his holster and fired before Lipshitz drove the pitchfork through his exposed neck.

Rex's shot hit the pitchfork with such force it was blown out from under Lipshitz's arm and up into the air. A prong from the pitchfork tweaked the tip of Rex's nose on its way up. Lipshitz's momentum carried him directly into Rex, and for a nasty moment, Rex was staring eyeball to eyeball with the crazy bastard.

Rex was at a loss. His right hand, and his gun, was pinned between this maniac's beer belly and himself. The gun was pointing upward so Rex didn't dare pull the trigger in fear of blowing off his own head. Rex looked into the eyes of Norman. He breathed in the air Norman had exhaled. Rex saw the hate, the anger, and the repulsion that Lipshitz saw while looking back at him. In that puffy, black, and blister-covered face, Rex saw a need to kill—both the killer's desire to kill him, and the raging desire it invoked in Rex to blow this shithead to kingdom come.

Not allowing this animal to make the first move, Rex swiftly brought up his knee into Lipshitz's groin. Rex barely felt a thing since it was his baseball shin guard that pummeled Norman's balls. The bad-boy's look of anger and hate quickly changed to one of shock and pain. Lipshitz's grimace turned into surprised anguish as he hopped away from Rex and before he bent double with his hands going to his groin. Rex noted Lipshitz's left arm and hand were functional despite the gory shoulder wound.

Lipshitz staggered back two paces. Rex reholstered his gun as he decided to finish this job by hand. Rex squared up to Lipshitz and threw a right cross which hit the killer's face square between the jawbone and the ear.

Rex intended his punch to be a knock-out blow, but it came at only half strength as his back muscles were simply too bruised to put the power into the punch. Still, the blow had its effects as Lipshitz was rocked and fell to his knees.

"Ouch!" Rex groaned as he rolled his right shoulder around and prepared to give Lipshitz a good left upper-cut to finish the job.

Rex was waiting for Lipshitz to stand up, when a hand grabbed onto his left arm from behind. Rex whipped around, pulling out his gun in one fluid motion. Fortunately, Rex looked before he shot or the kid fireman would have a new breathing hole in the middle of his forehead.

"Whoa ... Whoa ..." the fireman jumped back with his hands up.

Rex holstered his weapon. He was aware the police were finally arriving on the scene and he didn't want to draw on one of them in this tense situation. Rex's experience with jumpy policemen had been that they shot before they identified a target. This was especially true when it was known that gunshots had been fired.

"Sorry," Rex said. "I get a little cranky when I haven't had my lunch."

The kid laughed and came forward again. His smile dropped dead when he spotted Lipshitz, who was still kneeling and holding his crotch with both hands.

"Is that the fucker who was shooting at us ... that shot Jerry?" asked the kid.

"One and the same," said Rex looking down at the pitiful sight of Lipshitz clawing his balls. Just seeing him made Rex's testes ache as he thought of the intestinal pain Lipshitz must be feeling. It was a low blow, Rex knew, but he'd take them any way he could get them.

"That's the asshole that killed Jerry?" shouted a new voice Rex didn't recognize. But Rex knew madness quivering on murder when he heard it. Suddenly, a yellow blur whipped past him as a fireman threw his body on Lipshitz in a tornado of kicks and punches.

Rex made a move to stop the onslaught. Once again, a hand fell on his arm, and Rex turned to look into the teary eyes of the boy fireman. "Don't stop him, mister." Rex looked long into the sad blue-eyes of this country boy, not understanding what was going on.

The boy looked straight back at Rex. Slowly a tear ran down the boy's dirty face that was shadowed beneath the boy's huge fire helmet. He muttered with quivering lips, "Jerry was his brother, and a close friend of mine."

Rex heard these words, and took in their meaning. He bent over with his hands on his knees and blew out a breath as if he'd been punched in the stomach.

"Dear God," Rex whispered as a sadness struck him deep in his belly reminiscent of the times he remembered learning Sara was dead. With his head hung low, Rex stood straight and began his march out of the barn, sickened by another pointless death and the sorrow it caused.

As Rex passed the boy fireman, he heard him answer, "I don't believe God had anything to do with this."

Rex stopped for a moment as he listened to the punching and kicking going on behind him and he figured the boy might be right.

Rex attempted to exit the barn when two uniformed policemen whisked passed him and descended upon the fighting pair. Rex watched as the three men pinned Lipshitz and seemed to have him under control. Something in Rex's stomach turned while looking at the scene, so he did an about-face and left the barn.

After taking off his helmet and balaclava, Rex stepped away from the crowd that appeared out of nowhere. He turned and squatted on the grass where he could still see the barn door and the continuing festivities. Running his gloved hand through his sweat soaked hair, Rex knew he wasn't leaving until he saw a handcuffed Norman Lipshitz put into an ambulance with a police escort. He sat there taking slow deep breaths to ease away the pain in his back.

While Rex waited, it occurred to him Lipshitz had a tunnel from the house to the barn. Norman could have still gotten away had he not had such a lust for murder that he charged Rex with a pitchfork.

Rex didn't find the idea of this old farmhouse having an underground escape route such a farfetched idea. He recalled the hype during the 1950's and early 60's about nuclear war with the USSR, and the scramble to build personal bomb shelters that had occurred. It annoyed him that he hadn't thought of an escape tunnel from the start when he'd noticed Norman hadn't taken anyone inside the house and he'd found the two bodies on the couch. He had to be looking for those kinds of things when hunting a serial killer. No, that wasn't what annoyed him. Rex decided what really crunched his nuts was that he underestimated Normal Lipshitz, and it nearly cost him his life.

While Rex contemplated the complications of escape tunnels, a voice behind him hollered, "Rex Bana, did you cause all this mess?"

Rex didn't waste the energy or desire to feel the pain of turning about with his response. He remained kneeling as he watched the barn door with an eagle's eye, and said, "Ya know, Higgenson ... one of these days I'm going to kill your fat ass."

As Rex finished, a shadow joined his on the frosty lawn to form a stretched out shadow of a blimp man with wide hips and multiple appendages beneath the waist.

"I'm sorry to hear that, Bana."

Rex heard the tired weariness in that voice, but he still couldn't stop himself. He whirled up to face Bobby Higgenson with a look of determined destruction, and yelled, "You set me up, man!"

Bobby didn't flinch, fade, or fiddle. His yellowish eyes blazed as they glared down into Rex's burning red face, and said, "You got ... Oh shit." Higgy's eyes had flicked over Rex's head, and he must have seen something more interesting than Rex, because he pushed Rex aside in his haste to head for the barn.

"That's it, just push the peons aside once ..." Rex trailed off as he noticed the commotion at the barn which caused him to pull out his gun no matter how many police were around.

Rex watched Higgy trotting toward the two policemen that were coming from the barn with Lipshitz held-up between them. Rex thought the entire scene looked WRONG, WRONG, WRONG. Rex's feelings that the fun wasn't over deepened when he saw the lawmen hadn't handcuffed Lipshitz's hands behind his back.

One of the officers had hand-cuffed his wrist to Dipshitz's right wrist while his other hand was under Norman's right armpit supporting Norman as they shuffled toward the road and Rex. Rex saw that Lipshitz's left arm was free. This was not standard procedure for handling a murderer and all-out wild man.

Rex saw the officers thought Norman's left arm was harmless due to the bullet wound. "Well, at least there's some payback for shooting me in the back, ya ass-wipe," Rex mumbled. Rex was proud to have dealt this wound, but he knew it didn't incapacitate Norman's left arm.

While watching Lipshitz's eyes, Rex could see the officer on Lipshitz's left side dig through his first-aid kit in his duty belt to pull out a wad of white sterile cloth. Rex thought the officer planned to bandage Lipshitz's shoulder. Rex saw Lipshitz's shoulder was bleeding profusely after his fight with the firemen. In the lower part of Rex's vision, he saw Bobby shrug his shoulders as if he was satisfied with the situation. Bobby did an about-face and came walking back towards Rex.

Rex was not satisfied.

That was when the shit hit the fan and spread it about for everyone to experience. Rex caught sudden movement by Lipshitz and was sprinting toward Bobby with his gun out since Bobby had his back turned to Lipshitz and was in Rex's direct line of fire.

Rex had been keeping a sharp eye on Lipshitz's facial expressions ever since the police officers had been dragging him from the shadows of the barn. Rex could see the madness hadn't left those charred, now beaten, features. There was a wildness that remained unchecked in Lipshitz's expression ... like he knew something everyone else didn't know and he couldn't wait until it exploded. Rex looked into Norman's eyes, and he followed their gaze. Rex knew more people were going to die.

Rex was helpless to do anything but watch tragedy unfold as he dashed to save Bobby. Stretching his legs in bounding leaps, Rex looked past Bobby to see the officer on Lipshitz's left try to compress the shoulder wound and stop the bleeding. Lipshitz had spotted the officer's unsnapped holster, and Rex had seen Norman's eyes light up as if he was a kid at Christmas time as he eyeballed an accessible weapon.

The officer tried to compress Lipshitz's wound, but Lipshitz screamed and stepped back while pushing the handcuffed officer into his partner. The two policemen collided in a tangled bash one might see in a comedy act. Rex watched Lipshitz's left arm regain its usefulness as the policemen appeared to be doing a waltz. Norman was shooting the officer's revolver even before he yanked it from the holster. The shot blew a notable hole in the officer's right foot and sent him to the ground in howling agony. Now Lipshitz had a loaded revolver in his free hand, and he was looking around with crazed glee as he decided who to shoot at next.

It never occurred to Rex to yell for Bobby to get down as he rushed forward. Rex had his gun out and he was tackling Bobby while Lipshitz's first shot punctuated the patrolman's foot. In relative time this gave Lipshitz ample opportunity to shoot his next victim. Fortunately, the officer handcuffed to Lipshitz's right arm was off-balance and in front of Lipshitz as he was pushed toward his partner. Being handcuffed to this officer forced Lipshitz's body into a twirling action even as Lipshitz's wild eyes zeroed in to catch the fire in Rex's glare. Lipshitz did a neat pirouette and spun his head, ignoring the other policemen while trying to maintain his scowl on Rex.

Rex struggled to bring up his right arm to shoot Lipshitz, who was close enough to spit on, but Bobby was delaying Rex's shot by grabbing Rex's arm in an effort to raise himself and draw his service revolver from his belt holster.

For a moment the hunter and the hunted stared at each other.

They both knew what they wanted to do—kill.

The killers each drew their weapons towards the other. One did so with practiced speed and experience; one did so with TV-watching experience. One was as calm as a long practiced killer; one was as wild as a lunatic. They were both killers.

Lipshitz shot first. Rex fired as Bobby pulled him down. Rex's tousled hair was yanked and his head was pulled back in a whiplash motion before he fell to the ground. Rex never lost eye contact with the crazed orbs of Norman Lipshitz. Rex had a perfect view. He watched as Norman's right eyeball darkened into a neat hole, and the back of Norman's head exploded like a huge zit being popped under pressure.

The firefighters behind Lipshitz were awarded their piece of meat from Stormin' Norman. It was their good fortune they were wearing their yellow slickers and fire helmets which could be easily cleaned of sticky debris. Norman Lipshitz was dead, but his body continued its pirouette and fell upon the two officers who were lying on the ground beneath him.

Norman's dead right hand, which continued to clutch the stolen revolver, was buried between the pile of the two officers on the ground with Norman's corpse on top. Norman's dead hand continued to carry out its final order and shot the gun in what Rex would have called a "spastic" fashion. Norman's corpse continued to shoot itself in the belly five more times, and it would have continued to kill itself for another few moments but the gun ran out of ammunition.

For a few seconds Rex was dazed as time and reality raced back to normal in his mind and he consciously recognized what had happened—that he'd escaped Death's cold grasp yet again. He squeezed his eyes shut for a moment and an involuntary shiver shook his entire body as if he'd just been plunged naked into the Arctic Ocean.

Regaining control of himself, Rex stood up and was bewildered when he heard laughter erupt from behind him. He wondered what kind of fool would be laughing in this kind of situation. Rex turned to see Bobby Higgenson on the ground yucking it up with gales of laughter while pointing at Rex's head. Now Rex recognized the fool.

"Your ... ha ... head's ... ha ... smoking ... Tanto ..." Bobby rolled about.

Rex's senses recovered enough to the point he felt a tingling sensation running down the middle of his scalp. Rex recalled the feeling of having his hair and head being yanked back as he fired his gun. He raised his hand to feel his head, and his gloved fingers touched a strip where the Grim Reaper's sickle had grazed his head, removing his hair and scalp.

Rex blurted, "Holy shit, Tonto been scalped."

Bobby went silent for a breath, and then he exploded with a renewed exhalation that sounded like laughter. Rex started laughing himself after a moment of pondering why he should be laughing. It occurred to him that he had plenty to celebrate and laugh about. He was alive.

Rex's laughter was the best healer for a body and mind, and he thought he could use a heavy dose of this kind of medicine. Rex knew this release of emotional tension was more involved than this episode with Lipshitz. It'd been a while since his emotions had been allowed to run so freely.

Between teary eyes, Rex watched the police, firemen, and medics give them a wide berth as they moved about their duties. Eventually, Bobby and Rex came together physically to sit back to back on the front lawn laughing, crying, and hooting out emotions until they were emotionally and physically drained.

During one of their moments of reasonable sanity, Bobby asked a medic to fix the damn Indian's head and give Rex some painkillers for his multiple bruises. Rex was thankful to Bobby for many things besides his continued caring and consideration, plus he managed free medical attention and medication while a nervous medic stitched his scalp closed.

Their emotional escape leveled off to sanity as the medic tied strands of Rex's hair together to add strength to the stitching job. Finally, the medic added white medicated powder to Rex's scalp to give him a punk-rocker appearance, or at least of a man with serious dandruff. When Bobby saw Rex's new do there was another bout of laughter followed by poor jokes.

Finally, the ordeal was over. Rex felt wasted, tired, and abused. So much so, Rex refused Bobby's invitation to follow him home to see the wife and his kids. The moments of life Rex shared with Bobby were over and best left locked away and not reviewed or remembered with others. When the moments of remembrance and review did come, and Rex was sure they would, he preferred to do it alone as he always had. Rex told Bobby he'd give him a call.

Bobby made attempts to thank Rex for covering his life, but Rex reminded Bobby that if he hadn't been yanking on Rex's arm as Lipshitz took his shot, Rex's head might have been a quarter of an inch higher and it wouldn't have just been his hair the bullet parted. Plus, Rex reminded Bobby of times he'd done the same for Rex and how they agreed long ago it was all in the line of duty. Rex gave Bobby a bear hug, a slap on the back, and said goodbye while promising to call him soon. They both knew they'd run into each other before that call was made. The line of killers never ended.

# CHAPTER FIVE

After collecting his gear and counseling the grieving young firemen, Rex gave the smoldering pit from Hell a final look over. Rex pondered how messy this episode had gotten, and how near to Death he'd come. Becoming hypnotized by the remaining flames of the house, Rex thought of how he could have done better closing this case down in a way that was less life threatening and costly.

Most of all, Rex knew that he'd just taken another human life and another innocent human life had been taken. The taking of human life was a practice that hit Rex hard even though he realized this was a case of necessity and there would have been more people killed if not for his actions. Once started, serial killers didn't stop killing and go away. After a long hour in his hotel's hot Jacuzzi, Rex felt relaxed enough to go out for a cold Strohs and a fine steak dinner at a local grill.

That night Rex slept like a baby. The horrors of the day were filed away somewhere in his mind as they had been for the last twenty-five years. Rex was able to accept the horrors of mankind in a way that allowed him to continue, and there was always the burning vengeance in his heart for the innocent victims, for Sara. He'd learned to put off his thoughts of evil and evil doing or not exist at all.

This was a solitary, lonely world for a man to live. Rex was maturing and he wasn't ignorant of the desires of his manhood. He watched families around him always, conscious of the life he was missing. Rex longed to toss a football to his growing son, and go to bed at night wrapped in the arms of the woman he loved.

A few years back these feelings of loneliness were meager scratches in his raw desire to continue the hunt, in his desire to avenge the innocent. Yet, every day the feelings of solitude and the desire for a family seemed to be gaining strength until Rex was aware that at some point he'd have to make a decision of what his existence was all about.

Was he no more than a killer of killers?

Was he no better than the men he killed?

Could he be a creator of life as well?

Could he assist in the creation of healthy souls to replace the sick tormentors he destroyed?

The following day, Rex squared away the Norman Lipshitz case with the Kalamazoo and State police, and loaded the Hummer before heading home. He was not a content man. He was not a satisfied man, but he was a richer man. Rex was a man who'd finished one of life's many projects. This chapter of his life was complete and he was looking forward to seeing what the next few pages entailed.

So it was with a smile on his face when Rex got home and received his phone messages from his answering service. Knowing there was a five hour time difference between Maui and Michigan, Rex waited until almost midnight to return the call to his oldest and dearest friend, Joseph Tweedy.

During a two hour phone conversation, Deputy Sheriff Joe Tweedy and Rex caught up on old times. Joe had been a Collegiate All american Wrestler and was Rex's roommate while Rex played football during their four and a half years at Michigan State University. After college, Joe had returned to his home on Maui to join the Maui County Sheriff's Department. Rex had remained in Michigan to join the Michigan State Troopers. They'd kept in contact ever since. Rex tried to visit Joe at least once a year, and he loved the island of Maui. They had often discussed different cases and used each other on how to solve a case. Joe released his current nightmare on Rex, his old buddy.

During their phone conversation Joe faxed Rex some preliminary file material regarding a case which was proving hellish for himself, but not the rest of the Maui County Sheriff's Department. This case wasn't even supposed to be a case according to Maui County's newly elected Sheriff—a man whom Joe considered less than a burro's bottom. Joe was always the polite one.

The phone conversation ended with Joe's pleas for some hands on assistance from an expert in catching serial killers. Rex assured Joe he never had to plea for anything from him; whatever Joe wanted, Rex would be there. Joe was the only family Rex could relate with anymore. Hunting serial killers was a solitary occupation and Rex had never stopped to form friendships. Migisi was over eighty years old and less conscious of the world around him every day. Sheriff Bana wouldn't retire from law enforcement, but he didn't approve of Rex's vigilante and profit making approach to crime solving. Rex assured Joe he'd be on a plane sometime the next day. It was already past 2 a.m. in Michigan.

Rex needed at least one day to get his gear together and have it shipped two-day delivery to Maui. Some of the things Rex felt were indispensable to solving a case couldn't be carried aboard a passenger plane. Besides, he had way too much equipment to carry on a commercial airplane by himself.

Hanging up the phone, Rex knew this was a time he was happy for the freedom his solitary lifestyle provided. If he'd been responsible for a wife and family like Bobby, Rex would never be able to pick up and leave as he was doing now. Another reason his spirits had risen was it appeared he'd get the vacation he'd been planning for months—a trip to Maui, an island of paradise.

# CHAPTER SIX

"Sara?" Rex murmured, gazing down in disbelief at the beautiful girl seated in the window seat of the airplane. Rex was standing in the aisle securing his carry-on in the overhead compartment when he noticed his seat partner for the short flight from Honolulu to Maui's Kahului airport on Hawaiian Air. The young woman had flowing black hair and brown-black eyes that were so similar to Rex's as she looked up at his questioning face.

"Qué?" she asked in a frightened tone like she'd been caught doing something wrong. Rex shook his head as he knew this couldn't be his dead sister Sara and he realized he was scaring this girl.

"Would you like a pillow?" Rex asked, trying to shift the attention away from his strange query. He forced a smile on his face while trying to not show his teeth. He raised his eyebrows and lowered his arms and head since all these gestures would be seen as non-aggressive and submissive. Otherwise, Rex knew his size, Native American features, and long black hair would appear intimidating in these confined quarters.

"No, gracias." The girl shook her head. She dismissed Rex and returned to looking out the window as if she was looking for someone to board the plane and haul her off again.

Searching in his carry-on, Rex grabbed a well used deck of playing cards and shut the overhead compartment. A three hundred pound Polynesian grandmother was bumping Rex with her straw bag of groceries to get him out of the aisle. Mentally, Rex giggled to himself as he pictured this huge woman trying to squeeze herself into the space-saving economy seats of the airplane.

The thought of her trying to wrap a seatbelt over her Budda-belly almost sent Rex into physical laughter that would have been embarrassing since it would have been obvious Rex was laughing at the woman.

Having had his fun, Rex contained himself. He swung his large frame into his seat and cleared the aisle for the backup of sweating passengers. Rex knew the flight was going to be loaded when he checked in. There wasn't a first-class or even a seat assignment on these short flights so he had to duke it out in the economy section. No biggy, Rex figured. It was only a forty minute flight. Besides, this had allowed Rex to encounter this pretty Latin girl who was the spitting image of his dead sister Sara.

Rex knew that thinking of Sara wasn't healthy for him, but shit happens sometimes that can't be avoided. It had taken Rex years to get over the trauma of his sister's horrible death and Deputy Madison's hideaway. Rex had discovered in many ways he wasn't over Sara yet. There would have been no way his ever watchful eyes could have missed this Sara lookalike.

He often caught fleeting glimpses of Sara out of the corner of his eye in grocery stores or while walking the open street. Rex had long since given up on chasing these passing spirits, and figured it was Sara's way of reminding him that she was still there watching over his hazardous lifestyle.

Given the reason that Rex was flying to Maui, he didn't feel this direct encounter with a Sara lookalike was coincidental. Fate had placed Rex next to a young girl that was his sister's double from twenty-five years past for reasons yet unclear to him. Rex felt his destiny was going to be intertwined with the frightened girl seated next to him, since it was obvious this girl wasn't a spirit, but a warm-blooded body. Although he did not dabble in New Age hocus-pocus, neither was he so blind to not see some significance in this meeting at such a time. Rex was happy to follow along, knowing something was going to happen, and he would be wary with an open mind to the possibilities. If someone upstairs was trying to tell Rex something, he was all ears.

Rex tried to settle into his seat, but his long legs were crammed into the seat in front of him. The three hundred pound grandmother sighed into the seats directly behind him. Rex knew this island hop was going to be a noteworthy ride as Grandma started to slam her hammer-fist into the back of his seat to make sure it was up as far as it would go and she had all the room possible. The seat provided Rex with little protection and he swore as he felt every one of Grandma's knuckles punching into his spine. It had only been three days since Rex had last looked death in the eyes in the face of Norman Lipshitz, and Rex was still sore from the bullet Norman had shot into his armor plated back.

"Thanks for the massage, Granny," Rex said to no one in particular.

"Qué?" asked the Latin girl, turning toward Rex.

"Nada ..." Rex mumbled in time to see the Latin girl's seat taking a similar beating as his had gotten.

"Hey ... Watch it back there," the Latin girl turned around and yelled while giving Granny a nasty look. As she turned back around, her eyes met with Rex's, then quickly returned to looking out the window. Rex thought of how beautiful those eyes appeared, even if they looked troubled. Rex knew he must know more about this young lady and why she was here. He was eager to fall into whatever traps awaited him. The whole situation felt as if it were supposed to happen.

Rex studied his seat companion in more of a professional manner while pretending to gaze out the window. He went about analyzing what kind of a person he was seeing and what her circumstances might be. Rex had years of experience hunting and studying people and their actions.

In addition, he had been educated by the FBI while he was a Michigan State Trooper. This experience and training had shown Rex how to form a "profile" on a subject based on his physical observations and the facts Rex knew about that subject. This profile could be used to categorize a person with other known profiles to make assumptions regarding the person being studied based on the characteristics of the known profiles. It was not a perfect system, but it was a start and a method of gathering information when no other method was obvious.

Rex guessed the Latin girl's age to be between fifteen and twenty years old. He briefly wondered if she was old enough to be traveling alone, or if she had needed written consent from a parent or guardian.

She wore blue jeans that were too tight and faded through use. They didn't have a store-bought look. Her short sleeve shirt had frayed elastic around the arms and the waist. Rex could tell the shirt had seen years of wear by the thinness of the material. It was probably a hand-me-down like her jeans, he figured. Leaning forward with a fake cough, Rex caught a glance at the girl's feet. She was wearing plastic sandals that were worn away on the sides. Her bare feet seemed to be the girl's main mode of transportation. Rex saw that her feet were calloused and her toes were a dirty brown with broken and cracked nails.

Finally, Rex examined the girl's hands. Rex had always been a "hand" person, and believed that while a person's eyes might betray their emotions, a person's hands told of their experience in life. This girl's hands were meaty with thick, bare fingers, suggesting hands of a manual labor person. Her nails were short, yet clean. She wore no jewelry, and in her nervousness, the girl's right hand was pinching at the calluses on the palm of her left hand.

Rex smiled, as this was a nervous habit he had himself. An avid weightlifter, Rex's hands were callused from his tight grip on the weight bars. Rex caught himself mimicking the girl's callus picking and he wondered what he had to be nervous about.

Putting his nervousness down to the anxiety of plane travel, Rex was sure that the calluses on the girl's hands were from long hours of manual labor, not from lifting weights for pleasure. The cleanliness and thick tough appearance of the skin on her hands suggested they spent a long time in either dish water or a bucket scrubbing floors ... probably both. Rex had no doubt that she had callused knees from the amount of time she spent scrubbing floors by hand.

Then Rex noticed an interesting thing about the young lady. There was a deep bruise on the girl's right arm that was barely covered by her short shirt sleeve. A frown set into Rex's face at the sight of this bruise. In his line of business, Rex understood what that bruise meant on a girl of her apparently poor social status. This led Rex to examine the girl's hands and bare arms more closely. As he suspected, the girl's brown skin was scarred and scratched. The knuckles Rex could see were scarred and there were scabby nicks that remained along the back of her right hand.

As the plane took off, Rex sat back to form his profile of this beautiful, yet haunted, seat partner.

By the time they were at 30,000 feet, Rex had a good make-up on his seat companion. He first thought she was a Mexican/American from the eastside of Los Angeles based on her language, brown skin and facial features. Rex figured she came from a poor background based on her general appearance, and this was only the second time she'd been on an airplane. Her first plane trip was the flight from Los Angeles to Honolulu that she'd made sometime this morning.

Rex knew this inexperience with plane travel might explain the girl's nervous appearance, but he didn't think it accounted for the terrified look she had given him initially. This girl had a tough personality that didn't scare easily. Rex knew this from the way she'd told off the grandmother behind them. Yet it was obvious to Rex that she was scrappy and a fighter from all the marks on her hands and arms. It also appeared that she'd recently lost a fight based on the bruise on her arm. Given the girl's toughness, Rex figured this fight was against a larger opponent or one that held authority over her.

The girl's clothes were probably hand-me-downs or clothes that she'd worn for some time. To Rex this would confirm the young lady came from a poor background. Being Mexican/American, Rex knew the girl was probably a staunch Catholic that came from a large family. Obviously this wasn't a set rule, only a generalization from which to start. Rex couldn't tell about the length of her pants since she was seated, but he had seen that the hems were frayed and came well above her ankle, and they were shorter than the current style.

The girl's beautiful long hair was clean, yet the cut was uneven and held back by a cheap elastic band instead of a pretty bow or ribbon that one might expect a girl to wear if she was traveling to meet relatives and make a special impression. Although the girl's hair and overall hygiene told Rex she had pride in herself, it suggested she didn't have the money for store-bought haircuts. Rex decided her mother or a sister did the girl's hair.

Rex smelled cheap soap and no deodorant when he sniffed the air. Yet this was a difficult call in the confined space of the aircraft combined with his stench after a day of long flights. Plus there was still the aura of the vapor rub he'd applied under his nostrils in Lipshitz's kitchen.

The girl's wiry arms and her thin body told Rex she'd known hunger, and often went without meals. Rex reminded himself to watch her eat if they served any complimentary food on this short flight. This would show her degree of hunger and her table manners. Coming from a poor background, she would probably hoard her food and show few manners while eating. Yet Rex also knew with girls her age it was hard to tell if their thinness was due to dieting or starvation. Based on the girl's clothes, Rex had to assume the girl didn't eat because there was no food to be eaten.

Rex considered the girl's mannerisms as the next part of his mental checklist. He noticed the way the girl clung to her large cloth handbag like it contained all her possessions. He thought that, typically, one would stash a bag this size under the seat. This girl maintained a white-knuckle grip on the bag's handles. Rex considered the facts he'd seen, and decided the bag probably did hold everything the girl owned.

His second observation was that the girl looked terrified and looked out the window as if someone was following her; almost like she had done something wrong and she was worried someone would catch her and take her home. This brought Rex to the conclusion the girl was running away from home, and he figured she was running away for a good reason. She was beaten by her parents. She might be sexually abused, but Rex doubted it. He knew sexual abuse is nearly impossible to see from a brief glance at a person, so Rex was up in the air on that one.

Rex concluded this girl was running away from a poor Hispanic family in east LA, since they had come from LA and he knew eastside held the highest population of Hispanics. Rex figured the prideful father might beat his family, but he didn't think the father would sexually abuse his own children. The large family would suggest the father could get plenty of sexual satisfaction from his wife, but then one never knows these days.

Somehow this girl had gotten enough money to escape her home and buy a plane ticket to Maui. Rex figured the girl saw Maui as an island paradise as it was shown in the glossy pages of fashion magazines she might have discovered in the stacks of the high school library where Rex figured she escaped to eat her frugal lunch. Rex thought she probably saw Maui as an escape from the terror of her home, and somewhere she could start her own life anew.

Rex had no doubt that she was beaten at home by one or two alcoholic parents. This would account for the bruise on her arm and the terror she showed when Rex was stowing his carry-on. She probably had a brief glimpse of her father standing over her about to beat her. This made Rex glad he'd quickly lowered his arms and assumed a submissive pose when first speaking with the girl—besides the fact that his armpits probably stunk after a long day of flying.

To test his personal stench, Rex covertly lifted his right arm and sniffed his armpit. As his luck would have it, he raised his eyes in time to look directly into those of the lady across the aisle. Rex put down his arm and raised his face with a sheepish grin, but the lady looked away with a huff of disgust.

Rex stuck his foot further into the dumper by whispering to the lady, "I couldn't remember whether I used my deodorant this morning." The lady chuckled and returned to her magazine.

Sighing, and thinking it had been a long day since leaving Detroit Metro, Rex was relieved to see the beverage cart making its clumsy way down the aisle. He thought a nice refreshing Strohs would go a long way toward putting him in a comfort zone, so Rex lowered his tray and waited.

As soon as Rex lowered his tray, his seat companion followed suit. Yet, as the cart got within earshot and the stewardess announced the prices of the beverages, the girl pushed her tray back into place with an oath.

Rex saw his introduction.

When the stewardess asked Rex what he wanted, he asked for two Strohs, but he wasn't surprised to have to settle for another brand. Along with his beers, the stewardess gave Rex a wink and a handful of beer nut bags. Rex did a double take on the wink, but the stewardess had turned her head.

Rex imagined what it would be like making out with a stewardess in an airplane's restroom during flight, but he pooh-poohed the idea since the flight was too short to make the workout worthwhile. With his large frame, Rex found it hard to use the facilities for their intended purposes, let alone cramming a second body in there to do aerobics.

Seeing his seat companion eye his tray, Rex turned and asked if she would mind sharing with him. Rex was delighted as a beautiful smile lit up the girl's face as she accepted and pulled down her tray.

"My name's Rex Bana," he said, passing her a beer and most of the beer nuts. Rex thought he heard a hissing noise being expelled from the Granny behind him when he said his name, but he couldn't tell whether she had something against him personally or she'd merely passed gas.

"Ester Gomez," said the girl, sticking her hand out for Rex to shake.

"Pleased to meet ya." Rex shook the offered hand and was not surprised by its thickness and strength. This confirmed his thoughts this girl was no stranger to long hours of manual labor. Rex figured the manual labor might explain how Ester obtained the money to purchase a ticket to Maui.

Ester proved she was no stranger to beer. Grabbing her beer with confidence, she thumped the top of the can and popped it open with a minimum of foam. Bringing the beverage to her mouth, Ester opened her throat and downed half the can. So much for table manners, thought Rex. She drank that beer like a woman discovering a water hole after a long haul across the desert.

While Rex sipped his beer, Ester inhaled two packs of beer nuts and washed them down with the rest of her beer. Rex snickered after Ester heaved up a healthy belch.

"Disculpa mí," Ester whispered with her laugh.

Rex burped, and said, "No pardons necessary."

They laughed together.

*This is good*, thought Rex. *Ester is relaxing and she seems to have a sense of humor.*

He went for broke.

"How did the barber win the race?" Rex asked.

"Como?" Ester looked confused.

"It's a riddle. How did the barber win the race?"

Ester giggled. It was delightful music to Rex's ears.

"I have no idea." She laughed.

"He took a short cut. Yuck, yuck, yuck." Rex laughed and Ester laughed in earnest with him. This was a first. Normally, Rex got odd stares after trying to lighten the atmosphere with a child's riddle. Letting the good feeling hang in the air, Rex quit while he was ahead.

As the beverage cart returned, Rex grabbed Ester's beer can so it didn't appear Rex was contributing to the delinquency of minors. Then, Rex asked for two more beers. The stewardess gave Rex more than a wink this time, as it didn't take a Sherlock Holmes to figure Rex wasn't going to drink four beers during this short flight. It became obvious Rex was sharing his appetizer with the young señorita. Giving Rex his change, without beer nuts, Rex thought the stewardess stuck up her nose as she continued down the aisle.

Ester accepted the second beer and gave Rex another lovely smile with her thanks. She finished the beer and the rest of her nuts with the relish of her first beer. Rex had trouble keeping up with the girl's drinking, which in itself was surprising, so he gave up.

Rex cleaned up his tray and pulled out the playing cards.

"Care for a game of cards?"

"I'm sorry, señor. I don't know any card games."

"Not even Go Fish?" Rex laughed.

"Sí ... Everyone knows Go Fish." Ester joined in his laughter.

Rex shuffled the cards, trying to remember how to play Go Fish. He knew the basics, but he couldn't recall how many cards to deal each hand. Figuring Ester had no clue either, Rex dealt two seven-card hands—his lucky number. Rex was feeling lucky today. Either that or he was feeling tipsy from the beer.

Ester had taken off her seatbelt, thrown off her flip-flops, and turned to face Rex. Good, this was the way Rex wanted her—up close and personal. This way, he could get her to open up and talk to him. An idea had surfaced in his head and the cards were the perfect diversion. They allowed an avenue of communication to begin.

After Ester had matched up the cards in her hand, she asked Rex if he had any kings. Rex had two. Ester was delighted. Rex asked for jacks, but Ester told him to Go Fish, and he began to pick up cards.

As the game progressed in Ester's favor, Rex asked, "So what're ya going to do on Maui?"

He laughed and looked at his cards, not wanting to appear as if he was prying. If Ester was a runaway, Rex knew she'd be suspicious of anyone digging into her personal life.

For a brief moment, Rex felt a snag in the happy connection he had developed with Ester. Her smile disappeared. She looked frightened again. Ester shrugged in response, and asked if he had any eights.

"Go fish." Rex laughed in attempt to smooth over his intrusion of her private life.

"I'm going to Maui to work a job. I'm not going to get much fun in the sun," he said.

Ester jumped at the chance to talk about something besides her. "What kind of work do you do, Señor Bana? Oh ... do you have any sevens?"

"Go fish." Rex laughed again at Ester's dismay. "Please, call me, Rex. Do you have any fours?" Rex was delighted to get some cards out of Ester for a change. "Oh ... You could say I work for myself. I track down bad people."

Lowering her hand and gazing at Rex with renewed interest, Ester asked, "You mean you're a policeman?"

Surprised by the girl's perceptive insight, Rex looked long into Ester's eyes, and saw an intelligent mind behind that pretty face. Ester returned her look towards her cards.

They were interrupted by the Captain's announcement that they were passing over the island of Molokai, and that the island of Lanai was just off to their right. They were starting their descent to Kahului International Airport on Maui.

Rex had so much to communicate to this girl and so little time to do it. He noticed that Ester hadn't turned away to ogle out the window the way the other passengers were doing. Her attention was on him. With the droning airplane engines masking any commotion around them, Rex felt they had their own private universe. The closeness of the seating and the high seats didn't hurt either.

Lowering his own hand, Rex said, "Well ... Ya might call me a bounty hunter. I'm a person who hunts criminals for the reward money. I don't hunt down criminals who've run out on their bondsman. I hunt a much different type of animal. I hunt serial murderers."

There, he'd spit it out.

It was Rex's experience that when he told people what he did for a living, they either moved on their way, or they were intensely curious. Ester proved to be the curious type.

With a naiveté that was scary to Rex, Ester bought his story without question. Rex was glad that she did, given his time limitation.

"You mean like the killers I hear about in LA, where they stalk innocent women when they're alone?" Ester faked a shiver, or maybe it wasn't faking.

"Something like that. So you're from LA, huh?"

"Si." Ester looked down at her lap. Rex knew he didn't have time to play games if his plan was going to work, so he went for it all.

"You're running away from abusive parents, aren't you?"

Ester's face shot up and she glared at Rex as if he'd accused her of a horrid crime. She went from appearing relaxed, to appearing tense, as if she was a trapped animal.

"It's okay. I'm not going to turn you in or anything." Rex held up his palm and laughed. "It's just that in my line of work, I meet people such as yourself all the time. Unfortunately, I also find them after they've been abused or murdered."

Rex could see what he was saying was doing little to ease Ester. She curled up into a fetal position with her arms around her knees. The plane was descending rapidly now. Rex was having to pop his ears. If there was a serial killer on Maui, Rex knew he had little time to try and save this girl from what might be a terrible death.

"Ester, listen to me for a moment," Rex whispered as he leaned toward Ester. She refused to meet his eyes again. Rex knew he was losing their bond. "I lost someone very close to me to a serial murderer. She was so dear to me that I'd give my life to have her back. But that's not possible, so now I hunt people like the animal who took her away.

"I'm going to Maui to help a close friend catch one of these murderers." Ester looked up at Rex now. "Yes, my friend believes there's a serial killer loose on Maui." Some of this was starting to sink into Ester's intelligent mind. Rex could see her thinking. He hoped she realized the place where she was running to wasn't the safe haven she'd talked herself into believing. They had monsters on Maui too.

After a pause, Rex continued. "You see, these murderers thrive on people who have no safe haven, the homeless, and the runaways. Runaways are easy pickings for them. And if I can figure out that you're a runaway, so can a killer. Serial killers are usually very intelligent." Ester's face took on the look of someone being hunted. Rex knew he had her.

"So what's a girl like me to do?" asked Ester on the brink of tears.

"Oh, now... The world is not as horrible as you think, there are good guys out there as well. People like my friend, Deputy Sheriff Joseph Tweedy, who's picking me up at the airport."

Rex paused when the Granny behind them punched his chair.

"You don't have anywhere to go once this plane lands, do you?"

"No …" A single tear ran down Ester's face.

"Well then, you're in for a big surprise," said Rex in a bright tone intended to dispel her fears. "A few years back, me, my friend Joe, and his brother, Moe …" this made Ester laugh, "… and some other people, set up a shelter on Maui for runaways and abused children just like you. It's called 'Sara's Garden.'"

"Named after the close one you lost. After the dead one you mistook me for when you first boarded the plane. She was your sister," stated Ester.

These weren't questions. The intelligent look Ester gave Rex rocked him in his seat.

"Touché," said Rex with a grin after a moment. "Well, I guess I deserved that for scaring you. But I wanted you to see the necessity of having safe shelter until you've established yourself and made friends who can accompany you around the island. It's safer to travel in groups or with someone else."

"I know how to defend myself," Ester said with pride and a stiff upper lip. *Yeah,* thought Rex, *it's that's the kind of pride that can get girls raped and murdered.*

"Well, let me tell you about Sara's Garden anyway, and then you decide if you want to go there."

Ester nodded her head.

"It's a lovely old church from Maui's whaling days just outside of Lahaina. It's run by nuns and there's a big stone wall that surrounds it. It's about the safest place on the island.

"They have twenty beds in ten separate rooms, three bathrooms, a common room, a kitchen and lots of other things. The medical examiner of Maui County has volunteered to be on call 24-hours a day for emergencies. Sometimes they get women and children that are pretty beat-up and abused, so they need medical attention.

"Everything is free, and you can stay there as long as you like. They even have a job placement counselor for those that are old enough to work and looking to go out on their own. That would be the perfect place for you to start if you're looking for a job."

At this Ester nodded her head and her face brightened. Rex smiled since he'd guessed she wasn't afraid of manual labor.

"They only ask that you abstain from abusing drugs and alcohol while you're there, and that someday, when you've made it on your own, that you return some of the love and caring that you received at the Garden."

Rex had finished his speech.

Ester had returned to looking down at her hands. Rex reached out and gently took Ester's hands into his own. She didn't resist him, but she still would not look into his eyes.

"Ester ... I would feel so relieved if you would come with me and stop at Sara's Garden before you go anywhere else. Just have a look around ... meet the nice people. They're there to help those that haven't gotten a fair shot at life's goodness. If nothing else, this will give you a ride into Lahaina in the safety of a police car."

After a pause, Rex said softly, "I'm not sure I could live to see Sara killed a second time. Please come." With that Rex removed his hands, but Ester quickly grabbed them back and held them tightly in her own.

A warm tear fell onto his hand. "I will come. Do you have any sixes?"

"Go fish."

# CHAPTER SEVEN

The plane landed at Kahului Airport. Rex climbed out of his seat and felt a wave of weariness from the intense plane ride following such a long day.

He returned his playing cards to the pocket of his carry-on and retrieved the bag from the overhead compartment. While blocking the three hundred pound grandmother with her grocery bag, Rex allowed Ester into the aisle before him. Ester only carried her "bolsa," as she called it.

Peeking out a window, Rex saw their plane had parked on the airport tarmac, not up to one of the terminals that led inside the airport itself. Rex was happy to not have to fight the crowds inside the terminal. Having already shipped everything he needed for this trip, Rex didn't have any baggage to recover. Even if his shipment was lost, Rex had enough in his carry-on to make it through a day or two. His clothes might begin to stink after a while, but he'd survive.

The downside of the plane not parking at a terminal was that the passengers had to debark from a mobile staircase onto the tarmac. Rex had always hated these staircases because the steps were steep and small for his big feet. Rex thought mobile staircases were accidents waiting to happen. He envisioned himself tripping on the top step and bouncing down the stairs starting a domino effect of tumbling passengers. He could see the baggage flying and hear the screams as passengers tumbled down the stairs. They'd all end up on the tarmac in a tangled heap of limbs and luggage.

What really terrified Rex was the thought that this three hundred pound grandmother was right behind him. Rex envisioned Big Momma catching her foot on the top step and steamrolling down the staircase wiping out everyone before her. He figured they'd have to use a bucket and a squeegee to clean up that mess.

Rex pushed Ester down the aisle a little faster.

"Qué? Why so pushy?" Ester turned to ask.

Rex bent down and whispered, "Look what's behind me."

Ester craned her neck to gawk behind Rex for a moment.

"So ... It's the fat mamasita ... so what?"

Rex pushed faster and said goodbye to the stewardess before answering.

When they were out in the open, and at the top of the staircase, Rex said, "Now imagine your mamasita tripping on this first step. Would you like to be in front of her when that happens?"

Ester was no dummy. She started pushing the old man in front of her. A Japanese man a few steps ahead of them pulled out his video-camera to make sure he had a complete cinematic version of his vacation on Maui. Rex turned around to see Granny ooze out the airplane door and make for the first step.

With no hesitation, the three hundred pound Polynesian and her bag of groceries came moving on down the line. Given her girth and multiple chins, Rex didn't think she could look down far enough to know where she was going. She let gravity do its thing.

Turning back to see how the line was progressing, Rex saw he was the one holding up the works. The line was slowly moving, but he could step near the tarmac without worrying about old Fatty.

Rex zipped on down the steps, happy to be moving about. To his amazement, Granny zipped right on down the stairs as well. Rex tried to do some mass velocity calculations to determine the impact intensity of being rammed by this three hundred pound whale, but then gave up, figuring he'd have to be Albert Einstein to make all the necessary calculations before being flattened.

Rex figured Granny had to use the facilities in a big way since she was willing to risk life or limb to get there. Rex didn't even want to think about this woman using the facilities. But then he figured that's why they made the handicapped stalls so big.

To his ultimate horror, Granny came right down the stairs as if she was on a mission from a Polynesian god. Once she got her momentum going she couldn't stop, and she pushed Rex hard enough to make him lose his balance going down the last five steps.

Shooting out his arms to maintain his balance, Rex's left fist whooshed over the top of Ester's head. Shooting out in the opposite direction, Rex's right hand sank into something soft and squishy.

Initially Rex was confused about the signals his right hand was sending to his brain. As Rex turned, he was horrified to find that his right palm was resting on the boob of the three hundred pound grandmother behind him.

"Ugh," was the only thing that came out of his mouth in this highly embarrassing situation.

Retracting his hand as if he'd been touching fire, Rex made to apologize. Before he even got his mouth open Granny hauled back and clubbed him with a right hook to the chops.

For a moment, Rex listened to the bells ringing in his ears and counted the little birdies flying around his whirling noggin. Now Rex knew he'd felt all Granny's knuckles. Later Rex would wonder if she'd been holding a roll of quarters in that fist as well. If Ester hadn't been there to catch Rex, his image of tumbling down the staircase might have come true.

After a shake of the head, Rex got the planet to stop whirling around, and he managed to shoo away most of the birds. He was left with an aching pain set into his jaw.

Ester kept Rex steady as they finished the last five steps, but she wasn't strong enough to hold up his two hundred and twenty pounds. Once on the tarmac, Rex had to stop for a moment to shake out the cobwebs. He hadn't had his bell rung like this since college football. It was worse than ramming the Lipshitz barn doors and that was only three going on four days ago. His head began to ache again.

Ester pulled the leaning Rex out of the line once they'd reached the tarmac. Rex shut his eyes for a moment in the hope his lucky stars would be gone when he opened them. He'd dropped his carry-on at his feet, and was holding on to Ester's shoulder as if he was a blind man.

Apparently, Granny wasn't finished. She ambled past Ester and Rex, and stiff armed him for an extra measure.

Ester lit out in pursuit of Granny, but Rex grabbed her around the waist after a couple steps. Rex felt bad enough he'd copped a feel off a grandmother's breast, he didn't need to add to the delinquency of a possible minor by siccing her on the old lady.

"Take it easy, Ester. She didn't hurt me, see?" Rex smiled and did a little ballerina dance step that belied his feelings. He had to stop after one twirl since his head started to spin again and there were still a couple birds fluttering around his watchtower.

"Come on, ya look like such a goof." Ester was laughing again. That was all Rex had wanted. Still, Rex was touched by Ester's instinctive urge to protect him. He knew that somehow, in just the last half hour, he had gained a friend for life. Now, it would be his responsibility to protect her life—if he could.

Rex discovered that Ester didn't have any luggage either, so they were able to skip the baggage claim crowd. It was with sadness Rex made this discovery. It proved to him how desperate Ester's escape must have been. She had fled with the clothes on her back, and they were well-worn clothes that needed to be replaced if she was to interview for a job.

Stopping outside the airport, Rex approached another subject which had bothered him. "Ester, I hate to put a strain on our relationship already, but I have to ask a personal question."

Ester looked into his eyes. This was the sign Rex was looking for. He knew she wouldn't lie. "Since I don't want to be arrested for kidnapping and hauling a minor out of state, how old are you?"

Ester laughed. "Silly Rex, don't you think I would have thought of that before making off on my own?"

Ester dug into her bolsa and came out with a worn wallet. Flipping through the pictures, which Rex tried to see, Ester fished out a California driver's license. Showing this to Rex, he saw she was eighteen years old ... older than Rex had guessed. He also noted a large wad of money inside her wallet. That showed she wasn't desperate. Smart girl, he thought, but they'd have to find a better place for her to put her money.

"Good," Rex smiled. "You're not a minor. That'll solve a lot of problems. Now you're truly a woman on your own."

"I hope I'm not completely alone ..."

"No ... you'll never be completely alone."

Rex put his arm around Ester and gave her a brief hug. Ester surprised Rex by wrapping her arms around him and squeezing him back. *Lord, I think I'm falling in love*, thought Rex.

"Come on." Rex started to lead Ester toward the street. "We've got to find my friend, Detective Tweedy."

"What a goofy name," laughed Ester.

"It goes with a goofy guy," admitted Rex.

"Does he look like a tweedy bird?"

"I'll let you decide. There he is."

"REX BABY!" boomed a huge Hawaiian.

"Dios mio," Ester whispered as the six foot six inch, three hundred and fifty pound Polynesian in a loud Hawaiian shirt, complete with leis of Hawaiian flowers, came bulldozing at them like a charging rhinoceros.

"JOE BABY!" Rex bellowed with equal enthusiasm.

Ester watched in awe as the clash of the titans smashed together a few feet in front of her. Joe, a mountain of beef standing on telephone pole legs and with tree trunks arms, hugged Rex in a crushing wrestler hold. Joe lifted Rex clear off his feet as if he were a child.

Putting Rex back on the ground, Joe's expression turned serious while he gazed into Rex's eyes as if seeing something that troubled him. Then the shadow on Joe's face passed, and he burst into a wide smile that brightened the day. "Ah, Rex my friend," he said. "I have missed you."

"And I you." Rex laughed.

After looking Rex over again, Joe's eyes fell on Ester. Ester returned the curious look, and she watched Joe's expression change from one of astonishment to one of curiosity.

Seeing his friend's curious look, Rex said, "So you noticed it too."

Stepping around Rex and approaching Ester, Joe asked, "Sara?"

"No, mi nombre es Ester ... my name is Ester Gomez," she said with pride.

Stepping to Joe's side, Rex explained, "Ester was my joyful seat companion on the flight from Honolulu. I made the same mistake as you. For a moment there I was twelve years old again."

"Now I understand the look of sadness I saw in your face when we met."

"Ester is searching for a new beginning on this island of yours. I told her about Sara's Garden and she'd like to take a look at it."

"Great!" Joe's smiled returned. "But don't you think you should introduce us first?"

"Oh, I'm sorry." Rex acted embarrassed. "Ester Gomez, this is my longtime friend, Joseph Tweedy. Joe, this is my new friend Ester Gomez."

"Aloha, Ester." Joe beamed. Then he took off the lei from around his neck. "Welcome to Maui, Ester. My home is your home. May the sun warm your soul and the sand rest your feet." With that, Joe placed the beautiful lei over Ester's neck and bent over and lightly kissed each of Ester's cheeks.

Ester looked down at the flowers and touched their delicate pedals. With her head down, she said something that neither of them could catch. Rex saw more tears fall from Ester's face, and he prayed they were tears of happiness.

"You just made up that pretty speech," Rex punched Joe in the arm. Joe shrugged, but he said nothing.

"JOSEPH TWEEDY!" a voice thundered behind them that made all three of them jump. Rex turned to see the Granny from Hell, his continuing nightmare, standing there with her grocery bag and a scolding look on her face.

"Oh no," Rex muttered.

Ester hissed.

"MOM!" Joe bellowed, knocking Rex out of the way to get to his ... mother?

"Mom?" Rex asked while shaking his head in disbelief.

"Su madre?" Ester covered her giggle with her hand.

Joe reverently approached the equally huge woman. Though he towered over his mother, Rex could see a physical resemblance. Rex thought of their confrontation on the airplane stairs, and he was deeply embarrassed. Rex had punched his friend's mother right in the boob. That was sacrilege—an impious act against the brotherhood of friendship—and Rex felt like scum. He should chop off the hand which had committed the offense. Hopefully, Joe's mother would have the good grace to not mention the incident.

"That's Rex Bana?" Joe's mother bellowed as Joe put a lei over her head in welcome. She didn't even wait for the traditional "Aloha" ... she looked straight at Rex. Rex felt like a worm.

"Yeah ..." Joe acknowledged with confusion. "Mom?"

"Come here, Rex Bana." It was an order, not an invitation.

Rex's steps came slowly and kept his head down. Mom Tweedy set down her bag of groceries. This signaled trouble to Rex and he prepared for the worst. His muscles knotted, and his face was as red as Rudolph's nose. Rex prepared to die.

When Rex was before the three hundred pound woman, she said, "Look at me in the eye, boy." Rex felt his head snap up by its own volition, and he found himself staring into two chocolate brown eyes almost identical to Joe's and that made him hungry rather than scared.

"Rex Bana! You and your family cared for my son while he was in college?" Rex was so surprised by the question all he could do was nod.

"You are the one that taught my son the ways of the World?" To this, Rex had no answer, so he stood there looking down at Granny. Rex felt as if he was a five-year-old in front of the principle after hitting the teacher in the fanny with a spit-wad.

"Bend down, please ..." Rex bent toward Granny with a stiff jerky motion.

He was waiting for her to pull out a knife and slit his throat. Rex had faced mass-murderers with more eagerness than he was feeling at the moment. "… Closer, please …"

Rex bent closer.

Granny wrapped her tree trunk arms around Rex's neck and dragged his face next to hers. "Thank you, Rex Bana, he came back a better man," Granny whispered into his ear before planting a wet and sloppy granny kiss on his cheek.

Taking all this in, Ester made a face as if she was about to say "yuck" but then thought better of it.

While Rex remained stunned in his bent position, Granny took off the lei Joe had given her and placed it around his neck. "Aloha. Welcome, Rex Bana, our home is your home. May the sun warm your soul and the sand rest your feet." Then she smiled, and Rex saw where Joe got his warm and beautiful smile.

"Thank you very much. I'm honored," Rex mumbled in relief.

"Oh … and since you already fondled my breast, you can call me Lilly," Granny slipped in loud enough for all to hear.

"WHAT?!" Joe exploded. "…fondled … your brea …" Joe couldn't bring himself to finish the sentence, much less say the "boob" word.

"Oh, pipe down, son … no one's molested me." Lilly waved off Joe's charge. "It was an accident, and if it wasn't, Rex has paid the price for his touch."

"Have I ever," said Rex, rubbing his jaw.

Lilly hadn't finished. "I heard every word you said on the plane, and you did a nice thing there." Joe looked confused.

Lilly turned to Ester for the first time, and said, "Ester, I think you'll find Sara's Garden the most perfect place in the world. It's so peaceful there I could stay forever." Then she winked at Rex.

"Ah … Ummmm … Isn't 'forever' kind of long, Mom? You're not really going to stay forever, are ya?" Joe whined.

"Just long enough to see how you and Moe are making out. I haven't bought a return ticket yet. Now I see that I have work to do. We have to put some meat on this girl." Lilly pointed at Ester and picked up her grocery bag. Joe took the bag from his mother while she came over to Ester and put her arm around the girl. "You're safe woman now. Just let these big men worry about the bad guys. I think you'll be very happy here."

"I already am," smiled Ester, looking at Rex.

# CHAPTER EIGHT

Rex settled into his second floor room at Tweedy Manor, his name for the estate owned and run by Joe and Moe Tweedy, and then he met with Ester and Joe back downstairs. Rex figured the Tweedy house was the perfect place for his retirement, if he lived that long. For the moment, he simply enjoyed being in such a comforting home with its relaxing atmosphere.

The house sat on a five acre plot on the northwestern side of the Puu Kukui volcano, which is dormant. The plot began where the volcano met the Pacific Ocean making a beautiful beach, and it went up the side of the volcano.

It had been decided that Ester would stay with the Tweedys for the weekend. It was late afternoon on a Saturday, and there wasn't anyone at Sara's Garden on Sunday to take care of Ester's induction. This was Lilly's idea, and Rex figured Lilly loved the prospect of showing the girl around her kitchen. She had raised two boys whose only interest had been eating. While Lilly made a late lunch, the county gossip continued in the living room over Strohs and sodas.

"Rex, you're gonna love this new coroner," said Joe.

"What happened to Meat?" asked Rex, while sipping on the beer he'd waited the entire day to savor.

"Meat?" asked Ester. "You have a medical examiner named Meat?"

Rex nodded with a grin, but Joe huffed.

"His given name is James Cook ... as in the first white man to discover these islands," put-in Joe. "He was an abandoned baby found in the leper colony over on Molokai. The missionaries who raised him determined he was born on the anniversary of the English Captain James Cook coming to the islands, so they named him after the explorer. But he's not a leper," Joe was quick to add.

Rex watched Ester as she had the classic reaction to the mention of a leper colony. Her face puckered, and she shivered. Rex had the same reaction every time he met Meat, although there was no physical reason for Rex to react that way.

"So why do you call him Meat?" asked Ester, looking reluctant to continue this conversation.

"I don't call him Meat," answered Joe. "Rex calls him Meat."

Rex told Ester, "I thought it only fitting, him being a county coroner and all. And wait till you meet the guy." Rex grinned and drank some beer before continuing. "He's huge. He's a bodybuilder, which in itself is ironic to me. A man who examines decomposing meat for a living, builds his own meat for a hobby?"

Rex saw that Ester was sucking in her cheeks and trying to ignore his commentary, but he continued to enlighten her for her own good since she might meet the man if she went to Sara's Garden.

"After I saw pictures of the slashed messes he'd made of some autopsies I got the idea of calling him Meat." That was enough for Ester. She turned her back on Rex and started to walk away.

"Rex, you really shouldn't antagonize Dr. Cook." Joe followed after Sara. "The Doctor does provide free medical attention for those living at Sara's Garden."

"I know. It's just that he gives me the willies." Rex shivered for no reason. There was just something unclean, unhealthy, whenever Rex thought of the medical examiner. Maybe it was just his occupation that disturbed Rex—playing with dead bodies. Ester did an about-face and started back, almost running into Joe.

"Well, Meat ..." Joe caught himself, "... Dr. Cook is moving off to do some charity work, or something, so now Maui County has a brand spanking new medical examiner fresh out of residency from the University of Hawaii." Joe said all this with his chest puffed out and his nose in the air as if he'd sired, raised, and educated this new doctor all by his lonesome. Rex figured this doctor had to be a hot tamale for Joe to be all struty about him.

"Is this new guy gonna continue helping out at Sara's Garden?" Rex asked.

"I have no idea what the new doctor's personal life will entail," Joe stated, still acting snobbish.

"A lot of dead bodies, I'd wager," Rex mumbled. Ester caught this remark and started to giggle.

Joe just shook his head and said, "Well, you're going to meet the good doctor at five o'clock."

"Does this good doctor have a name?" Rex queried.

"Certainly. It's Doctor J. Achew."

"Gesundheit."

"God Bless you," Ester put in.

"No, no, no. That's the doctor's name."

"What is?"

"Achew."

"Gesundheit."

"God Bless you."

"Would you two stop it!"

"Gee. I's just being polite."

"Me too."

"Maybe you should see the new doctor for that nasty cold you're getting," said Rex as he went over to feel Joe's forehead. Joe pushed him off. "That's the second time today a Tweedy has stiff armed me," Rex complained. "I'm beginning to feel as if I'm not wanted."

"Well, I suggest you take the hint and go shower. You've got half an hour before the new medical examiner arrives, so you might want to be presentable." Rex thought Joe would make a good mother.

"Why should I get all dolled up for someone that plays with dead people?" Rex asked.

"There are a number of reasons, and they'll come to you while you shower. But the best reason is the doctor is a she. Her name is Dr. Jessica Achew and she's almost as good looking as Ester." Joe winked at Ester.

Rex perked up. Ester gave Rex a long glance.

"Come on to the kitchen, Ester. Mom will have some lunch ready by now."

"Aren't I invited?" Rex asked. His stomach even grumbled.

"Not the way you smell, little brother," answered Ester, returning his grin from earlier as she followed Joe out of the room.

Rex went upstairs again with a whirl of thoughts running through his mind. First and foremost, he decided to watch his words around Ester. She certainly knew how to pay him back for his poor attempts at humor by referring to him as her "little brother."

Rex thought about Sara's Garden as he showered and made himself presentable. Joe was right, he thought. There were multiple reasons for him to want to make a good impression on the new coroner/medical examiner.

The first reason was Sara's Garden needed a licensed physician to be on call if they wanted continued support from the county and state governments for Sara's Garden. Rex knew the support Sara's Garden received from the Benedictine Sisters and St. Anthony's Church in Lahaina alone was not enough to keep the facility running. Joe and Rex couldn't spend all their resources to maintain the place, so the government support was vital for Sara's Garden to function as it should.

Rex also wanted to make a good impression on the new medical examiner because she was the one who noticed the alarming number of deaths by drowning in Maui County over the last year. This was the reason Rex had come to Maui—to assist a friend in solving a case that supposedly wasn't recognized by the Maui County Sheriff's Department.

# CHAPTER NINE

As Rex entered the Tweedy's foyer after his shower, he picked up a husky woman's voice he hadn't heard before, and it occurred to him Dr. Achew had arrived early.

Rex followed the voice with interest and entered the living room to find Ester and Joe standing next to a tall woman dressed in a billowed black wind suit and white cross trainers. Rex came to an abrupt halt and he felt like his heart had skipped a beat as he gazed at this new woman that was about to enter his life. Immediately his mind went about profiling Dr. Jessica Achew.

Rex saw the doctor was a tall Caucasian woman with a deep tan from spending a lot of time outdoors and in the Hawaiian sun. She had thick brown hair that was swept behind her head. Rex concluded that Dr. Achew had driven to this appointment in a convertible or in a vehicle with all the windows rolled down. This would explain how her hair appeared such a windblown mess. Unfortunately, Rex could only see Dr. Achew's profile and not her eyes. Rex guessed that she was the athletic type since she appeared muscular and thin beneath the expensive wind suit she was wearing. But he reminded himself that wind suits could distort a person's figure. Rex noticed her cross trainers were Adidas with their trademark of three stripes down the side of the shoe. Adidas were comfortable and expensive shoes for someone serious about their footwear.

"Rex, buddy," Joe hollered. "Why don't you close your mouth and come meet the doctor."

Rex felt he'd been standing there for an hour staring. He glanced at Ester and caught an angry glare from her. He avoided Ester's jealous look and glanced back at Dr. Achew to find her green eyes piercing his with what he felt was warmth and interest.

Dr. Achew came forward to meet Rex with the kind of athletic stride Rex associated with a person of high self-confidence. Rex thought, *Here is a person that knows what she wants and gets it in a hurry.* Rex thought her squared-off features, sharp nose, and edged chin were attractive and went well with her windswept hair. Dr. Achew broke into a dazzling smile of straight white teeth that contrasted her deeply tanned features as she confronted Rex with her right hand extended. Rex noticed she wore no jewelry on either hand, which suggested she wasn't married.

"Mr. Bana, I've heard so much about you. I'm Jessica Achew, but my friends call me Jesse."

"Gesundheit," Rex blubbered. He shook Jesse's firm hand but he dropped it quickly with embarrassment. He hadn't meant to say that, it just came out.

"REX!" Joe looked aghast.

Ester giggled.

"Pardon me?" asked Dr. Achew. She squinched up her face and appeared puzzled to Rex.

"Please, call me, Rex," he managed. But that was all he managed. The room fell silent with an uncomfortable air as everyone glanced about but didn't know what to say next. Rex felt shy and out of character.

Jesse broke the ice, but her voice boomed like a gunshot after the silence. "You're much taller than you appear in your magazine pictures."

Rex smiled and nodded at this. "You're not just making fun of my pigtails are you?" Rex laughed and pointed at the three short pigtails where the medic had sewed his scalp back together. The pigtails were sticking up on the top of his head like a miniature Mohawk. Rex felt awkward meeting a beautiful lady with his goofy do.

"Oh God no," Jesse exclaimed and looked horrified as if she'd spoiled the whole party. But she did appear to be peeking at Rex's head while trying not to notice. This did diddly squat for Rex's confidence or his thought of winning Jesse over quickly.

"I've been meaning to ask you about those, Rex," Joe put in. "Are you sporting a new hairstyle, or is this some Indian thing?" Joe asked with a laugh to show he was teasing.

"Naw," Rex said as his face darkened. "It's the way the tribal doctors in

Michigan stitch up head wounds. They haven't introduced the use of surgical thread, and I know they didn't use Novocain." Rex laughed a bit too loud, trying to blow this thing away, but Jesse stayed serious on him.

"Actually," Jesse said, "I had my scalp sewn up like that when I was a kid after I banged my head on the end of a table." She patted her head. "But I don't suppose you banged your head on the corner of a table."

"Ah, no," Rex tried to pat his head like Jesse, but as soon as he touched those crop ups they stung him and made him wince.

"Still hurts, huh?" Jesse asked squinching up her face and hissing as if it had hurt her. Later, Rex decided Jesse didn't work on live patients because she made too many faces.

"Yeah, I'll put some cream on it before I go to bed and I'll be fine."

"Oh, men," Ester exclaimed and everyone laughed.

"But I'm sure you didn't come here to talk about my head," Rex said, trying to change the subject away from him.

"I read that your mother was a Chippewa Indian and your father was, or is, a sheriff," Jesse smiled. Rex was impressed that Jesse had done some nosing into his background.

"Yeah, family reunions have always been a riot." Rex laughed. "Still, I was closest to my grandfather on my mother's side, Migisi, as I was growing up. My mother died before I really knew her, and my father was more involved with his work." Rex felt he was in the spotlight and uncharacteristically began to babble.

"Migisi has taught me a great deal about the ways of the Chippewa—their philosophy of living. Much of this applies to life today." Rex nodded and tried to shut up. He wasn't accustomed to saying so much about himself to another person and it made him uncomfortable.

"I understand you're also active in our local charities. You and Joe helped found Sara's Garden, a safe house for abused women and children. Yet you live in Michigan."

"Oh, I spend some time in Maui as well, but like I said, I'm still very close to Migisi although he's older than the Great Lakes. I feel responsible for him in the nursing home even though my father is still there and takes care of him since I'm away from home a great deal."

No one said anything, so Rex let his mouth run on. "My father deeded over our fifty acre farm to me long ago. I think he was hoping I'd get married and settle down. He doesn't approve of my method of living. So at the moment, I feel sort of obligated to stay in Michigan. Besides, it's where I lived all my life, the work's plentiful, and while some might not agree, I think Michigan has some of the most beautiful places in the world."

Rex managed to shut his mouth. He rubbed his nose. He looked down at the ceramic tiled floor, stuffed his hands in the back pockets of his blue jeans, and kicked an imaginary can across the floor as he thought of something new to say. "Ah, Sara's Garden is one of the things I hope we can talk about since I understand you're Maui County's new Medical Examiner."

"Congratulations, by the way," Rex said as his raised his head and smiled. His eyes were caught in Jesse's as he continued, "We need a physician to be on call to keep our state funding for Sara's Garden."

Joe interrupted. "Well, I'm sure you two will get plenty of chances to talk since you'll be teamed together, if Rex decides to take this case, that is."

"Well, I didn't travel halfway across the world to tell you I have no interest in your circumstances."

"No ..." put in Ester, "... you flew across the country to be my escort and to protect me."

Laughing, Rex nodded again and said, "That's right."

"Ester is a new arrival on the island," Joe said to Jesse. "She has expressed an interest in checking out Sara's Garden." After a short pause Joe continued, "Ester, I'm going to ask you to help my mother prepare dinner while we show Rex the case files we've gathered."

Ester pouted at this. Rex felt sorry for leaving her out, but if the files contained gory details it was best that she not be around. Rex put his arm around Ester and led her off toward the kitchen with a promise that he'd tell her what he could when they were done.

"I don't want you having nightmares over things you don't need to see, my little chickadee," Rex told Ester on the way to the kitchen.

"Well, you just make sure it's your little chickadee that you come back to, not the mother hen with the head cold," giggled Ester. Before Rex could ponder a proper response to this new advance, Ester reached up and pecked him on the cheek, then she ran off to the kitchen.

*Oh shit*, thought Rex. *What have I started now?*

Returning to the living room a bit flustered, Rex was again taken by the beauty of Jesse's physical presence. Rex couldn't foresee any problems in being teamed up with her. She appeared outgoing and eager to work to get the job done. Joe motioned them over to the "game room," as Joe liked to call it.

Following Jesse, Rex could see that Joe had used their mahogany pool table to spread out the case files of the victims. It was apparent to Rex that Joe and

Jesse were about to make their case that a serial killer was loose on Maui—their sales pitch that there was work available to Rex should he be so inclined.

Rex cut them off at the knees. "I hate to spoil any presentation you might be about to make, but I'd prefer to look at the files alone before talking to anyone."

Jesse raised her eyebrows and puffed out her cheeks. Joe smiled since he and Rex did their Criminology degrees together at Michigan State University and Joe was familiar with Rex's work methods. Joe also knew this was one of the reasons Rex left the Michigan State Troopers—Rex was a solitary hunter.

After a glance at the other two, Rex continued. "It's critical if I'm going to form an unbiased opinion of your situation before you say anything." Rex stated this in a stern manner while looking back and forth at his partners. "One person's wrong perception of the facts could taint the perceptions of the other people working the case.

"A wrong perception could have us hunting in the wrong direction. This would waste valuable time, resources, and possibly cost lives. Furthermore, a new perception of the facts, that's not tainted by other theories, might reveal a key element you may have missed—something that solves this case."

Joe brought Rex another Strohs, and then he took Jesse under one arm and headed back to the living room to go over the latest county gossip. Rex thought Joe would have been a good bartender or a barber.

Two frosty Strohs later, Rex called Joe and Jessie back into the game room. Joe and Jesse appeared as expectant as children waiting to open their birthday presents as they circled the pool table. Rex understood this was a big case for his friend, and certainly for the new medical examiner, so he tried to keep them as involved as possible in his thought processes and how he arrived at his conclusions.

Rex did this not only so they understood his method of thinking, but so they could poke holes in his theories as well. This would allow Rex to see different angles on the case he might have missed, or didn't have the experience to see, since he obviously didn't have Jesse's pathology experience, or Joe's experience of the demography of the area. Rex knew every case was a learning experience, particularly one that appeared to have so many victims.

"Okay," Rex started. "Based solely on the forensic and post-autopsy reports, I've eliminated four of your files as properly closed cases." Rex burped. "Excuse me. Obviously you have some drowned victims in here that are really accidental."

"Four? Were there really that many?" Jesse seemed surprised. "Well, I guess I just pulled all the drown victim files in the last year whether they were suspicious or not. We thought there might be something we were missing in all the files."

Rex sifted through the files. "You did right, but I think these are similar cases of neglect, old age infirmity, and sickness. The other reason I took these files out is because they all have verified witnesses to the victim's deaths. There isn't anything hidden in these files. Maui County did their usual superb job of covering all the bases and closed the cases properly." Rex looked up at Joe who smiled in appreciation.

"Maui County did such a fine job on those files it's readily apparent these other files don't fit into the same categories.

"Just looking briefly at these files one can tell they're incomplete—that all the bases haven't been covered. There's reason to question all these cases." Rex sighed and took a long drag on his beer before continuing. Joe and Jesse remained expectant and silent.

"I think I have fourteen files here that should never have been closed." Rex frowned at Joe.

Joe shrugged his huge shoulders. Finally he spoke. "That's why we called in a freelance consultant like you. Jesse and I are old friends from back when she was an intern. She brought me those files since she noticed their oddity when she took over the job and was learning the ropes you might say.

"I agreed with her, but my boss, the sheriff, has the policy we should let a sleeping dog lie. Why create more work for an already overworked staff of detectives?

"You know how small the detective staff is here in Maui County, Rex. When Jesse and I presented our case to the sheriff, who is just as new to his job as Jesse is to hers, he basically threw us out of the office," Joe said with a firm nod from Jesse.

This didn't surprise Rex.

"So what's the next step you'd take?" Jesse asked. Now that Rex felt more confident to meet her eyes, he was struck by the piercing dark green sparkle in them. They were a color he'd never seen before, and he was momentarily lost in their beauty. They stood there looking into each other's eyes for a moment before Rex continued.

"Ah ... Oh, I know what I was going to do." Rex grabbed all the rejected files and set them on the other side of the pool table—out of the way.

"Anyone for a beer?" Joe asked. Rex gave him a glance that said, "Need you ask?"

"Jesse?"

"Need you ask?" she said making Rex grin.

"Geez, what a bunch of lushes." Joe laughed.

"Jesse, could you help me put the rest of these files in chronological order—according to suspected date of occurrence?" Rex asked.

"I'd be more than happy to help. It'll give me a chance to do something right for a change."

"Hey, as far as I can see you've not only done the right thing here, but you've gone above and beyond the call of duty." Rex smiled as he looked through a file.

"What do you mean?"

"I don't see Meat standing here, sticking his professional nose out to cry 'foul'. You were the one that picked up on this oddity and have stuck it out so far. Most people would have blown this off from the beginning, or not even cared.

"They blew *you* off, and yet you continued beyond what was called for to find an answer."

Jesse was snickering and not listening to Rex's attempt to praise her.

"Meat. You mean Dr. Cook?" Jesse laughed.

It was a long hearty laugh Rex was glad to have started.

"Meat ... Oh, I love it. And it fits him so perfectly."

Unconsciously, Jesse put her warm hand on the back of his. She didn't notice the touch, but Rex noticed it and felt as if he was a kid again going out on his first date.

"What's with her?" Joe asked returning with the beers.

"Meat!" Jesse answered while she continued to giggle.

"Oh," Joe snickered. "Yeah, the name does kind of fit the man, doesn't it?"

Stopping for a moment in the comfortable silence, Rex drank his beer and thought that ... *Yeah; we might be able to form a crime team here. This might even be fun.* But there was still the question in his mind if these two would stick it out.

"Okay ... while we're figuring out the chronological order here, I need to ask you two some questions," Rex said seriously.

"Uh oh. This sounds serious." Jesse grinned. "I have to warn you, I don't do anything serious on the first date."

"In your dreams, Achew." Rex laughed and Jesse punched him in the arm. *Yeah ... this might work.*

"Okay, this is serious." Rex sobered. "Assuming we're looking for a killer or killers, how far are you two willing to go? I need honest answers here."

Rex knew Joe was an officer of the law and used to putting his life on the line if necessary. Jesse was not. Both Joe and Rex looked at Jesse for an answer.

Noticing she was in the spotlight, Jesse began. "Yeah well, I guess I'm the rookie here. You two have known each other for ages."

Joe interrupted with a laugh. "Hey, I don't think anyone will ever know Rex." Rex shot him a cockeyed glance, then rolled his eyes back to Jesse—a more pleasurable sight.

"But I think ..." Jesse continued, "... that I'm committed to whatever it takes to catch this killer. I mean, have either of you thought of the economic ramifications to the State of Hawaii if the media gets hype of this, and announces a killer has run amok on Maui for the last year totally unnoticed?

"Hawaii's economy is in its sixth year of decline. Unemployment is skyrocketing, and the state can't afford a bad rap about some killer on the loose. The tourists would scatter like wildfire and no one would come back. This is especially true since some of the victims were mainlanders and could be considered tourists."

"That may be a reason the sheriff doesn't want us opening a can of worms here," Joe put-in. "It doesn't take tourists much to decide they'd like to take their vacation somewhere more hospitable. Tourism accounts for at least twenty-five percent of the state's economy. Without it, we could all be looking for new jobs."

"This is my point," Rex stated. "Before we begin, are you two sure you're committed to digging up something that's already closed? Something that might cost you, and a lot of other people, their jobs, or worse?"

"I guess I hadn't thought of it in quite those terms, but it doesn't change my resolve," Jesse said with grim determination.

"Joe?" Rex looked over at his friend knowing his answer. Joe would never have called Rex if he wasn't ready to go all out.

"Come-on, Rex. Need you ask? Hell, yes. Charge! Damn the torpedoes and full speed ahead!" Joe rallied. Rex thought he might have to start monitoring Joe's beer consumption. He was getting too enthusiastic.

"My motives for being here are largely personal," Rex stated. "I made an oath to myself to do my part in eliminating the senseless slaughter of innocent people by serial killers on the day I was unable to save my sister, Sara." Rex kept his head low and spoke in a soft voice as he thought of Sara with reverence.

Raising his head, Rex continued. "To make my living, I collect rewards and donations for the capture or killing of serial murderers. I've already made enough money to last me a few lifetimes, so I don't need this case. I'm taking on this job for personal reasons. I came at the request from a special friend in need, and I'm neither looking for nor do I want a reward." Rex looked up at Joe to be sure this was understood. Joe nodded with a faint smile as if he understood.

"I'm glad you two are sincerely interested in seeing this case through, because I think there's a sophisticated killer or killers loose on Maui, and since the Sheriff's Office is not involved, I think you're gonna need all the help you can get."

"You mean I did right?" Jesse jumped up and down and clapped her hands as if she was a cheerleader.

Rex had to snicker at Jesse's exuberance. "As far as I can tell, you've done superbly," he told her.

Jesse continued to bounce before she surprised the shit out of Rex by giving him a crushing hug. Rex felt this tight embrace for the rest of the night, plus his back popped to give the hug bonus points.

Once the emotion had settled a bit, Rex got back to the brass-tax—the concept of a killer being loose on Maui.

"First off; do either of you have experience in serial killer cases?" Rex asked. Both Jesse and Joe shook their heads. "Okay. We need to define what a serial killer is. How are you classifying someone as a serial killer?"

"I thought it was a murderer who'd killed more than three victims," Jesse stated.

"That's a very good start," Rex indicated. "Joe?"

"What she said," Joe shrugged.

"Okay. Since I received most of my technical training regarding serial killers from the FBI, let's use their basic definition." Rex looked at the other two for their agreement before going on. "The experts define a serial killer as: Any murderer who randomly slays more than one victim with a break of time, a 'cooling off' period, in between the time he murders. Usually, it takes three murders for him to be classified as a serial killer, and the emotional 'cooling-off' period can be hours, days, weeks, or even years."

"Okay, that conforms to our profile so far. Each of these victims died with at least three weeks to a month apart from the next victim," stated Joe.

"I assume you called the killer 'he' for a reason," Jesse stated.

"Yup. Basically, there are very few female serial killers. To date, under the FBI's classifications, almost all multi-murderers that are called serial killers have been men. Let me explain why.

"This trend may be shifting, but for this case I'm assuming the killer's a man. Especially since all these victims are female except one, I believe."

"Are you saying a woman couldn't be a serial killer?" asked Jesse.

"Not at all. It's just that the methods of a serial killer don't usually match those of female multi-murderers. The Modus Operandi, the MO, the ways women kill, are completely different than a serial killer's."

Rex settled in to make his practiced speech.

"A serial killer, whether organized—he plans his murder and who the victim will be—or not organized—he slashes out at a random moment against any victim that fits his criteria—will always degrade his victims, violate them in unspeakable ways, and use the victim as his tool to release his hostility—to gain his satisfaction. The victims, and the actions of the murder in themselves, are the goals of a serial killer. The serial killer enjoys doing it, and if not stopped, will continue to murder ..."

"Almost like a drug addict needing a fix?" Jesse interjected.

"That's not exactly correct. A serial killer doesn't have physical withdrawal symptoms if he doesn't kill again as a drug addict might have if he didn't get his next fix. Yet a serial killer might be driven like an addict for his next murder; he feels he needs to do it.

"And all this is done in a close up and personal manner, using knives, hand tools, sticks, whatever is available to torture and control his victim. A serial killer gets off on these close confrontations where he can torture his victim, where he can watch their fear, feel their life and his domination over that life."

As Rex said these things, he could see Jesse was taking it all to heart. Her beautiful facial expressions snarled and squinched as she was apparently picturing a serial killer's torture. This surprised Rex since he figured a pathologist would know the effect of different weapons used on the human body, but he didn't slow down any as he gave her the woman's side of the story. She'd asked for it, he figured.

"On the other hand, a woman multi-killer tends to do all her killing at once, to a close relative or associate, while using weapons with minimal personal interaction, like poisoning.

"Women murder to achieve a separate goal other than the murder itself. She murders to get an inheritance, or to get rid of her screaming brats so she can have her freedom. Women murderers are after something they will gain as a result of the murders, while the serial killer will slay a victim to satisfy a psychological need that provides personal satisfaction. Serial murders are almost always sexual in nature.

"Still, this isn't to say that a woman killer couldn't take on the characteristics of a serial killer. There have been cases where women systematically kill men over a period of time. Again, this is usually sexual in nature, and the percentage of women serial killers is so low it's negligible."

"So ..." Joe asked, "... by classifying a killer we're trying to determine the MO, and then use the previous killer's MOs to figure out what our killer will do next?"

"Exactly." Rex smiled and mentally thanked Joe for adding in. Rex noticed that Jesse was nodding her head in agreement to show she understood.

"You see, the FBI has done extensive research into the characteristics of serial killers. They've gone into the jails and interviewed these murderers. They've gotten to know what makes them tick, one could say. They've tried to understand why the men kill so they can establish the patterns and lifestyles of serial killers.

"If we can categorize these murders as the work of a serial killer, then we can use the FBI's data and reasoning to construct a physical description of our serial killer and where he might strike next."

"Oh really?" Jesse asked.

"Sure, just as your forensic evidence can give you a profile of the killer; like whether the murderer was left handed or right handed, weak or strong, male or female, etc; serial killers generally are of a particular breed and can be profiled. This will be vital for directing our manpower and resources in the right direction toward finding our suspect. It narrows down the criminal population considerably."

Rex stopped to take a sip of his beer and wet his whistle before continuing. "According to the FBI's historical data about eighty-five percent of serial killers are Caucasian males between the ages of thirteen and thirty-eight. Although, as it was proven by the highly publicized Atlanta child murders in 1981, about fifteen percent of the serial killers are black males."

Rex stopped a moment to let this sink in to his listeners, and to sip his Strohs. He wasn't accustomed to making long-winded presentations, but he felt Joe and Jesse should see where he was coming from since they were the ones that brought him here.

"Another characteristic of these killers is that they kill within their own race. Whites tend to kill whites, and blacks kill blacks. But again, this is not a solid rule either.

"Jeffrey Dahmer killed seventeen men. He was a white male, soft spoken, even meek. Yet most of his victims were young black males that he picked up in gay bars."

"Yeah, Dahmer was a case I studied in school," said Jesse as she hid her face behind her hands. Peeking out from behind her fingers, she added, "I had nightmares for weeks after learning about the things he did. Stuff like drilling holes through a live victim's skull and injecting muriatric acid into their brain to see if he could turn the victim into a zombie." Jesse dropped her hands away from her face.

"And the whole reason he wanted a zombie was to have unlimited sex without the wine and dine charade."

"Yup," said Rex as he recalled the famous case. "Dahmer is a classic one to study. As a child he enjoyed killing and dissecting the neighborhood strays, even road kills. By the time he was eighteen he moved up to human beings. He picked up a male hitchhiker, took him home for sex, bludgeoned him to death, dismembered the body, and buried the parts in the woods."

Rex stopped when Jesse shut her eyes and shook her head. *This woman is going to have to develop some callousness if she's going to continue to be a medical examiner*, Rex thought. But he recalled his first years hunting serial killers, and the fact that he was still squeamish around cadavers.

"Sorry, I tend to be a little callous and verbal since I have a keen interest in these kind of murders. I've studied all the data I can get, and sometimes I forget people aren't aware of this situation.

"I read one book that claimed, statistically, that at any given time there are between fifty to three hundred and fifty serial killers on the loose in the United States—although Hawaii is one of the safest states, I'm sure."

"You're kidding!" exclaimed Jesse. "Well, of course you're not kidding, but that's amazing."

"Isn't it? See, that's one of the biggest problems about tackling this issue. People are not aware of what the world is really like. They don't believe the statistics. Most people in America say, 'That can't happen to me.' They go through their life on a daily basis simply reacting to what occurs to them, and no one takes responsibility for their own actions or reactions. But now I'm getting off track."

There was a pause as Rex inhaled, exhaled and sucked down more beer. Geez, just this woman's physical presence was getting him all hot and bothered as if he was a teenager with something to prove. Calm down, boy, Rex told himself.

"One point I skimmed over is that a serial killer will have a history of being a troublemaker. Serial killers aren't made overnight. Normal twenty-five-year old men don't wake up in the morning and say they're going to start to rape, strangle, and mutilate women.

"These are men who've assaulted and raped. They have similar problems building up to their first murders. Many of them started out torturing animals, or molesting other children."

"Do serial killers come from abused childhoods?" asked Jesse.

"That's a good question." Rex smiled and was glad to see the medical examiner had thought of the root of these problems.

"No. The trend leans toward troubled childhoods, and certainly the defense attorneys would like to create the picture of a tortured man who didn't know what he was doing, but that's not always the situation.

"I remember reading a case where the killer grew up in the back seat of his father's car while his father beat and raped prostitutes in the front seat.

"The kid grows up with no mother or normal interaction with females. He goes through puberty, and what is he supposed to think of women?"

Jesse and Joe both nodded. They'd both seen of cases of abuse and neglect that lead to disaster in the future.

"On the other hand, there are many cases where there's no evidence of abusive parents. The killer grows up in what can be called a typical environment.

"But even in these cases, there's evidence the child is not normal. He's the bully on the block, the neighbors find their pets missing, and there's always evidence of past wrong doing."

"How about another beer, guys?" Joe asked.

"Yeah, I could use an intermission. It's been a long day," Rex said, blowing out his cheeks.

"That's right, you flew all the way from Detroit this morning," Jesse said. "I guess I was getting all caught up in this."

"Dinner should be about ready anyway." Joe smiled.

"Joe, you haven't changed one bit. Always thinking with your stomach," Rex noted.

"I'm a growing boy. I need to keep up my strength if we're going on a manhunt."

"Isn't Moe coming home tonight?" Rex asked.

"Yeah, I think that's what's holding up dinner."

"Well if you gentlemen will excuse me, this fine Detroit brew we've been inhaling has presented some problems which need relief," Jesse said as she made her way for the bathroom.

"Hey … I like this woman," Rex laughed. "Anyone who likes Strohs can come to my house anytime."

"As long as they bring the beer, right?" Jesse asked.

"You betcha." Rex grinned.

After Jesse shut the bathroom door and was out of ear shot, Rex asked, "Hey. Is Moe still working for the FBI?"

Joe's head popped up and he looked around to make sure no one was listening.

"Yeah, but how did you know?" Joe whispered. "No one knows about that."

"Oh, keep your pants on." Rex laughed. "No one's gonna learn it from me. Besides, I didn't know for sure until just now."

"Oops." Joe slapped his hand over his mouth in a fashion so comical it made Rex laugh again.

"I ran into Moe some years ago at FBI headquarters in Quantico while I was doing some training at their facilities. We got together that night at one of those sports bars where he said the food would be delicious—and he was right, the food was great.

"We threw down some beers, and Moe eventually opened up to me about what he was doing at Quantico.

"I asked him if he was working for the FBI since I had no idea he was even into police work, and he said, 'Yeah. I get a paycheck from here …' but he described his living as running a dive shop in Lahaina. After that he went tight lipped about anything else he was doing."

"Yeah, Moe told me about meeting you. He said he was glad you work for the good guys, cause he never wanted to face you on the other side of a fight." This made Rex laugh. "I think Moe's work is more dangerous than what he lets on—you know Moe."

"No, not really. I know what you told me about him in college, years ago, and what I learned through our brief interaction. The only reason I bring him up at all is because I'm surprised you didn't get him involved with this."

"Oh, I've told him about it, and he agreed something is going on." Joe stopped to lick his lips. His eyes flickered back and forth. "But he's not in a position to break his cover, and I'm not even supposed to be working on this case. This case doesn't exist for the Maui County Sheriff's Department, and the sheriff would cut off my right testicle if he thought I was wasting county dollars to build a case. That's why I'm taking my vacation now."

"You hurt my feelings, Joe. I came so we could vacation together and catch up on old times," Rex stated in a joking manner.

"We are, but it's a different sort of vacation." Joe looked around again. He was so jittery Rex had to look around just to see if anyone was listening. There wasn't.

Jesse returned and Rex remembered Joe had never gotten their beers. Now Joe headed off for the refrigerator.

"What were you two talking about?" Jesse asked. "Joe's sweating."

"About you, of course." Rex laughed to show he was joking.

"No, I'm serious. Did I miss something important?"

"Nope. We were just gossiping about Moe, and where little brother was tonight. I thought maybe he had a lady friend and something serious was going on. You know, as in wedding bells." Rex was impressed with the smoothness of his lie. Then he decided he didn't like lying to Jesse. He tried to change the subject.

"So tell me about yourself. Here I've done all the talking, and I don't know a thing about you," Rex pried.

Jesse smiled, and for a change she blushed under his scrutiny. "Well," Jesse said just as the phone rang on the table next to her. She picked it up.

"Tweedy residence," Jesse answered as Joe returned to get the phone. "It's me, Jesse." She turned to look at Joe. "Sure, just a second," Jesse handed the phone to Joe. "It's Moe."

"Hey, brother ..."

Rex watched Joe's face start to crease and his brows begin to furrow.

"Yeah ... go on ... and they didn't find anything else ..."

Joe's features began to gravitate together towards his nose.

"Sure, I'd love too, but I'm supposed to be on vacation. I can't just pop into a crime scene and demand to know what's going on ..." Joe was shaking his head.

"Yeah, all right. Ya know Mom's here, and she's been holding dinner ... nope, no way pal, you tell her ... hold on a second." Joe huffed before turning tail and taking the cellular phone into the kitchen.

Joe disappeared around the corner. Jesse made a similar worried face and asked, "I wonder what that was all about?"

Rex made no response, but he thought he could make an educated guess.

"When was the last victim?" Rex asked.

"I'm not sure exactly." Jesse sighed. "It's all been such a hurried mess since we decided to call you." Jesse went through the files. "Ah ... it looks like ... ah, let's see ... I'd have to say it's been three weeks, a little longer. But that doesn't sound right. It seems like there was one more recent."

"I'd say we've got another murder victim on our hands, and our evening's going to be spent viewing a body," Rex said with a frown since he disliked the idea of disappointing Lilly after all the trouble she went through to make a special dinner.

"How do you figure that?"

"You saw how distressed Joe got, and you heard him talking about going down to a crime scene. Moe would have called only if it was an emergency that was related to Joe in some way. Otherwise he'd be home to eat Lilly's delicious dinner.

"Besides, the murderer is due for another victim." Rex smiled at Jesse as if this was obvious. Jesse pouted with her face down to say nothing was obvious.

"Did you notice after we put the murder files in chronological order that, at first, the killings occurred with wide periods of time passing before the next one?"

Jesse made no indication to answer, so Rex went on.

"It appears that about eighteen months ago the killer was testing the waters to see if it was safe?" Jesse smiled grimly at his analogy.

"But recently the murders are occurring at a more fevered pace. It's as if the killer has perfected his methods and doesn't believe he'll be caught." Rex took a drink of beer and studied Jesse who appeared to be studying him.

Rex continued. "And yet, there's another unusual characteristic about this case that bothers me. It's uncharacteristic for a serial murderer to not want notoriety for their actions—to not desire the media's theories about who's killing people. This one has been very quiet and concealed. Still, I'll betcha there's another drown victim out there tonight."

"I heard that," said Joe as he returned. "You're right. That was Moe calling to say that they found another body."

"Oh no," sighed Jesse looking defeated. Rex had an urge to give her a gentle hug and pat on the back, but he held off.

"What happened? Do you know?" Rex asked.

"Moe's still down at his shop. Ya know how his dive shop sits kitty corner to the Lahaina pier?" Jesse and Rex nodded. "Well, Moe was in the shop when an ambulance pulled up to the pier a minute ago and a Coast Guard boat off loaded a body bag. Moe saw the ambulance and turned on his police scanner to find out what happened. The ambulance was responding to a ten thirty-two, possible one eighty-seven."

"Drowning, possible murder," Rex said, not surprised.

"Hey, you're still up on your codes." Joe nodded.

"That also means they're taking the body down to the morgue." Jesse sighed again.

"Do you have to go?" Joe asked.

"No, I've got a resident working nights right now." Jesse turned to Rex.

"Ya wanna head on down to the pier?" Joe asked.

"You think there'll still be anyone there by the time we get there?" Rex asked.

"Rex, this is Maui. Remember, around here, everything happens less often and at a slower pace."

"Even if no one's there, we can go down to the morgue and you can get a firsthand look at the body instead of these pictures in file folders," Jesse suggested.

"Gee ... that'll make my day," Rex said jokingly. "You pathologists are all the same. Always trying to share the fruits of your labor, aren't you?"

"You're not squeamish, are you?" Jesse laughed.

"No. I've seen my share of death," Rex said in sudden seriousness. "I've never turned my back on it."

Joe interrupted. "Come on; let's break the news to Lilly and Ester. I know they're not gonna be happy about everyone missing dinner."

They arrived at the Lahaina pier in Joe's sedan twenty minutes later. Rex saw that the ambulance was still there parked at the gate of the pier, but its lights were off. He also noted two Maui County Sheriff's cruisers and two deputies moseying around and talking to the ambulance personnel. Rex couldn't see anything that looked like a body. Rex was surprised there wasn't a news crew hovering about the pier taking pictures and asking questions. Then it occurred to him that this was Maui where everything happened slower, and it wasn't like everyone wanted the news live and up to the minute.

"Jesse, you're the only one that has a right to be poking around down here without causing suspicion," Joe said as they got out of the car and started walking toward the pier.

"Gotcha," Jesse said and hurried off. Then she stopped and turned around. "Is there anything you want me to ask?"

Rex approached Jesse, and said, "Yeah. Find out the circumstances of the discovery."

Jesse gave Rex the okay sign and looked at Joe. Joe just shrugged and said, "Yeah. What he said." Rex thought, *Good Lord, she looks nice even in the darkness of a moonless night.*

Rex watched Jesse approach the deputies who seemed to know her, and then he and Joe took a seat on the crumbling remains of a corral wall that had been part of a fort years ago.

"She seems like a good egg," Rex said after a while.

"Huh? Oh, Jesse?" Joe seemed lost in thought. "Yeah, she's young, but I think she can handle it."

"Hell of a way to break in a rookie."

"Yup."

Rex saw the ambulance depart before Jesse reached the deputies.

"HANDS IN THE AIR MOTHER-FUCKER!" someone shouted out of the darkness behind them.

Rex jumped and nearly shit his pants.

"Hey, Moe," Joe said calmly while watching Jesse with the two officers.

"Shitttt," Joe's double swore as he stepped out of the shadows. "Brother, doesn't anything get you riled?" Moe asked. There was a smile on Moe's face. Rex thought it was one of the better features of the Tweedy brothers. If there wasn't a smile on their lips, it wasn't too far away.

"Only when you do something stupid," Joe answered, still chewing his fingernails and watching the scene. There wasn't a smile on his lips at the moment.

"Rex Bana! How do?" asked Moe.

"Moe, good to see ya. But I do believe I'll have to check my skivvies after that one," Rex said with laughter.

"Ah, you mainlanders always were too hyper. Didn't scare Joe in the least," Moe pointed out.

"That's cause I saw ya coming," Joe said in an even tone. "If I hadn't, I would have jumped just as far as Rex, but when I came down I wouldn't be laughing the way Rex is. I'd be beating your ass."

"In your dreams, sugar-bear," Moe sneered. Joe was over the wall and chasing Moe quick as lightning. Rex figured a half a ton of prime Hawaiian beef thundered by him, and he didn't want any part of it. He knew brothers had their own way of sorting things out—even when they were "adults," and big ones at that.

Rex heard a skirmish take place in the shadows where he couldn't see what was happening, but it wasn't long before he heard, "UNCLE ... UNCLE ..."

Moments later, Joe reappeared looking as thoughtful as before, but Rex thought he caught the memory of a grin on Joe's lips. Moe wasn't too far behind. But Rex thought Moe's legs had either grown or his shorts were riding high around his waist. Since Moe was clawing at his crack, Rex assumed Moe's legs remained the same length and it was his shorts that were lifted towards his armpits.

"So how's things back in Michigan?" Moe asked in a strangled voice.

"I'm doing fine. And I'm glad to see you whole and happy," Rex said and laughed at Moe's efforts to dig his underwear out of his heinie.

"I'm whole maybe, but I'm not too happy," Moe grunted. His smile was gone as his face seemed lost in concentration.

"What's her name this week?" Rex asked.

"Oh, Rex," Moe faked deep insult. "You've been talking to my brother too much."

Rex thought of how much Moe and Joe looked alike. Rex saw how much their bodies appeared as if they were twins, but Moe's face was wider, he had a flatter nose, and thicker lips. Rex noted that Moe had a small and shiny scar on the curve of his right jaw line that was shaped like a *C*. He didn't see any distinguishing marks on the smooth skin of Joe's face. Rex knew Joe's eyes were chocolate brown, and it appeared that Moe's eyes were black, which matched their hair color. They wore the same haircut that was parted in the middle and covered their ears.

Rex noticed how intently Joe remained vigilant on the pier area. "What's up, Joe?"

"I was thinking about what you said regarding us having a sophisticated killer..."

"Oh, so you think there's a killer?" interrupted Moe.

"Yeah, there's someone, or ones, that are responsible for some of these deaths. There's no doubt about it. And not only do I believe it, but I'd say Joe and Jesse's speech to the sheriff about there being a murderer that drowns his victims has been heard by other people in the department."

"Why do you say that?" asked Joe.

"Wasn't this called in as a drowning, possible murder?" Rex asked.

"That's what I heard over the scanner," Moe responded. He drew closer to Rex as if he didn't want to miss anything. Rex figured his low deep voice was easily carried off by the Pacific breeze.

"Those deputies came here with the preconceived notion this was a possible murder." Rex paused to let them think about this for a second. When no one interrupted, Rex continued. "When was the last time there was that kind of thinking on Maui? I mean, that a drowning might be a murder?"

Joe shook his head. "Never. Murder's not a vacationing sport, Rex, and the Polynesian culture is too easy going to be thinking that way."

Joe stopped for a moment considering where Rex was going with this. This was good. Rex wanted Joe to think, rather than become dependant on him like a partner. Joe might spot something Rex had missed.

"You said this killer was a sophisticated murderer," continued Joe.

"Don't hang me on one word," said Rex, "but I'd say we're looking for a killer or killers that are mature, have done extensive planning about their murder, and may have even practiced this killing to get it down to their satisfaction.

"These murderers are definitely of the organized sort. One doesn't go out, grab someone, and then take that person out to sea to drown.

"Planning had to go into the murder, making the whole affair premeditated. This might seem a minor point, but I don't think it is."

Rex felt claustrophobic as the Tweedy brothers had closed in on him during his lengthy monologue. He spoke in a loud tone to back them off when he continued, "As you both know, for someone to sit down and plan a murder, and plan to get away with it, they have to be intelligent, and have a sense of what's going on around them in the world." Rex took a deep breath when the Tweedys retreated.

He exhaled, making his next statement loud and carrying. "The murderer is not a raving lunatic." The Tweedys stayed back, allowing Rex to talk in a normal tone. "Serial killers are intelligent, mentally, and morally unbalanced human beings with no concern of right or wrong."

Joe leaned in Rex's direction, and said, "It occurred to me when we got down here …" Joe looked around again, "… that if the killer is covering his murder by making it appear the victim has drowned, then he probably takes the victim out in a boat and does the killing out in the sea."

"Yeah, that makes sense." Rex nodded. He was glad to see that Joe was following his own thinking.

"Well, if the murderer takes the victim out in a boat, then they'd have to leave from Lahaina pier. There's no other harbor on the northwestern side of Maui where we're finding all these victims," Joe deduced.

"In other words, you think one of those boats out there is where these murders are taking place." Rex pointed at the enclosed marina in front of them where some fifty vessels, from luxury yachts to dive boats, were tied up.

"Or at least starting out on one of those boats. Yes," Joe acknowledged.

Rex knew this could be a weak link in their killer's plan. They had narrowed down one of the places the killer had to travel with his victim if he was going to get them very far out to sea.

"Damn fine observation, brother." Moe gave his brother a thumbs-up. "But what if the murderer pushes them off from shore somewhere?"

"That wouldn't work. The bodies would wash up on the beach in no time. In all these cases, the bodies have been found pretty far offshore and in the Lahaina area," pointed out Rex.

The threesome momentarily went silent to gaze out upon the marina, and to ogle at Jesse.

"Hey, Moe. Do you still have that apartment above your shop?" Rex asked. Moe gave Rex a wary look.

"Yeah," Moe said slowly. Rex was grinning because he knew what Moe was using the apartment for.

"Don't have any girls stashed up there right now?" Rex asked, just joking.

Moe did his innocent, hurt look, before stating, "Come on Rex, I'd never have a woman up to that dingy place."

"Aw, cut the crap," Joe said. "What'd you have in mind, Rex?"

"Nothing really, it's just that from Moe's apartment I would be able to see which boats come in and out of Lahaina harbor during the night, wouldn't I?"

"Sure, that's how I happened to see this episode before I called you tonight," Moe stated. "I've got a bird's eye view of the whole marina from up there."

"What? Are you thinking of making a stakeout in my apartment?"

"It's a possibility," Rex said. "If Joe's right about the killer using a boat, and I think he is, and the only boats on this side of the island are parked right here, then it's conceivable we can watch the killer take his next victim onto one of those boats. Of course that means we have to wait till the killer strikes again." Rex knew this was a long shot and meant another death, which was something none of them wanted to see happen. Still, Joe jumped on the idea.

"And we may have a good idea what the killer looks like already, and what kind of victim he's stalking," Joe put in.

"Lighten up, Joe. I hadn't finished telling you everything when we got called out here," Rex exclaimed.

"What do ya mean?"

"Well, based on the forensic evidence I've seen so far, and the circumstances of the victims, I'd say you don't have a serial killer on the loose on Maui." Rex cringed even as he said this since it might seem contrary to what he'd been telling Joe. He wanted to keep an open mind until he knew more.

"WHAT?" Joe blew up on Rex.

"Settle down, Joe. Let's wait to see what our dear doctor finds out first. She appears to be coming back," Rex said, seeing Jesse had left the deputies and was walking around the pier for a moment.

"Now you've got me confused," Joe huffed.

"Didn't take much," Moe commented while taking a step in retreat in preparation for flight.

"Well, I don't want to limit our options before all the facts are in and we've had a chance to sort through what we know versus the histories we've studied so far."

In an attempt to gain some additional information that might fit a theory brewing in his mind, Rex asked Moe, "You still working that case we talked about in Virginia, Moe?"

Moe did a 360° turn to see if anyone was within hearing distance. Rex had checked before he said anything, so he knew no one could hear them but Joe.

"Ah ... yeah," Moe said slowly.

"Any progress?"

"Certainly," Moe said quietly.

Rex saw Moe's smile had disappeared and he'd gone tightlipped.

"Not going to elaborate, huh?"

"Let's just say things are reaching a boiling point. Something's gonna happen soon."

"Got all your bases covered?"

"Damn ... I hope so."

Rex thought he saw sweat building up on Moe's brow.

"What you're working on wouldn't have anything to do with this string of murders over the eighteen months or so, would it? Something that's picking up its pace recently?"

"Gee, I hadn't even thought of that." Moe whispered.

"The time table sort of fits. The little operation that you're investigating started about the same time these murders started in earnest."

"Damn, Bana, how is it you spend five minutes on this island and come up with theories I haven't figured out in over a year?" Moe whined.

"I guess it just takes an outsider's view sometimes."

"Howdy, Moe," Jesse said upon her return.

"Well if it isn't Maui's beautiful medical examiner. How do, Doc?"

"Just fine, Moe. Are you having a problem with your shorts there?"

"Aw, Joe thought he'd show off what an adult he is by giving me a wedgee."

"I see," said Jesse. Rex saw that Jesse laughed and seemed amused over this problem.

"Well?" Rex asked impatiently.

"Well, according to Deputy Frommer and Dell, someone spotted a body floating outside the harbor and the Coast Guard was called in to fish it out.

"All the two deputies knew was that it was the body of a Caucasian male wearing some scuba gear. His name was Burt Rogers, and he had an Indiana driver's license. There was still a wallet in the guy's swim shorts pocket. The deputies said it was apparent Rogers had drowned and no one saw it or has reported Rogers missing."

"Then why the code 187, I wonder?" Rex asked.

"I think you were right, Rex. I think between Jesse and I talking to everyone, that word has gone down the grapevine this rash of drown victims isn't accidental," Joe pointed out.

"At least we've done some good," Jesse said. "Investigators will be more alert to the murder possibility of a drown victim. They've taken the body down to the morgue if you gentlemen want to go have a look see?"

Rex thought Jesse seemed awful perky over this continued excitement, but his stomach got queasy at the mention of the morgue.

"As much as I'd love to spend an evening with you, Jesse, I think it's time for me to say goodnight," Moe said.

"Yeah, you gotta go make peace with Ma. She's not to happy with the day she's had and her sons running out on her dinner."

"What can a guy do?" Moe asked as he turned to leave.

"Oh, and Moe?" Joe called. "Thanks for the call."

"No problem, brother. Looks like you've got your work cut out for you. See ya!" Moe disappeared into the shadows heading back to Front Street.

# CHAPTER TEN

Rex was having second thoughts about visiting the morgue, and he thought Jesse had become all business. The smell of formaldehyde made him queasy. Rex didn't think the sight of dead people or the gore of sliced body parts were the causes of his anxiety. He had witnessed death's arrival for as long as he could remember. Death came in many ways and forms. But after death, when the human was gone from the being which once had been full of life; when the body was laid upon the stainless steel tables (with their sucking tubes and drains); when the examiner started the dissection using powered knives, drills, and saws; that was the part of death that gave Rex the willies.

Rex contemplated his anxiety while Jesse told the resident to take an extended lunch, or dinner. This left the three of them alone to examine the body. Rex preferred having more live beings in the vicinity, but he didn't want to appear squeamish, so he held his breath as much as possible and tried to act normal. He couldn't start acting like a ninny in front of the two people who were counting on him to defy this string of deaths.

"Grab a lab coat off the tree, and then find a splat hat, goggles, and gauze mask from the drawers there. I'll have to find some gloves that'll fit those huge paws of yours," said Jesse with a smile. Rex thought Jesse might feel right at home here, but he couldn't be casual.

"You sure we need all that stuff?" Rex asked in a rush.

"Yeah, I'd hate to have something splatter on your clothes that won't wash out."

Rex made an audible swallowing noise to indicate this was not what he had in mind when he agreed to visit the morgue and view the body. He'd envisioned himself standing in a separate room from the dissection area while gagging on stale donuts and slurping cold coffee. He envisioned Jesse doing the slicing, stabbing, drilling, and poking of this cadaver while he watched through a TV monitor, bulletproof glass, or some sort of separating material. He had not envisioned himself standing table side with nothing but stinky air between him and the cadaver.

Jiminy Christmas how he hated morgues and autopsies.

Rex found a couple XX-large lab coats on the tree, and passed one to Joe. Rex was amused as he watched Joe do his imitation of Lou Ferrigno becoming the Incredible Hulk. Joe tried on his coat but the flimsy material ripped out of the back and shoulders. Joe finished off the coat by flexing his biceps and bursting the seams of the sleeves.

During Joe's struggle, Jesse stood in the background wearing a quirky grin. Rex saw she was finding this less than entertaining. When Joe finished hulking out of the lab coat, Jesse bounded past them without a word and disappeared behind a door marked, "Storage."

Rex stripped the shreds of the lab coat off Joe, and while trying to see things on the bright side, Rex said, "Hey, these would make neat morgue rags."

Joe frowned.

"No really, you never know what kind of spills you'll find in the dissection room of a morgue, do ya? An absorbent strip of cloth could always be handy around a leaky body."

Joe cracked a smile.

Jesse popped out the storage room with what Rex first mistook for a drop cloth draped over her arm. But after Jesse threw the drop cloth at Joe, Rex could see it was a white coverall of the size a Sumo wrestler might wear during a food fight in a sushi restaurant.

"Put those on," Jesse barked in a manner that made Rex jump. "If you don't, I guarantee you'll be throwing away the clothes you're wearing by the time we finish," Jesse stated as if she was a drill sergeant instructing first day recruits.

Rex was just as edgy as a first day recruit and he leapt into his suit and buttoned it up to his neck. Rex watched as Joe still struggled to get into his suit, and Joe was not wearing a smile.

Next, Joe and Rex tried to stretch sanitary skullcaps onto their heads. Joe had no problems, but this was a nightmare for Rex with his stitched scalp, Mohawk-do, and ponytail.

Rex's skullcap rested an inch off his head and he had to hold it with both hands just to keep it there. He turned to look at Jesse with his head down and a save me expression on his face.

"Oh, don't bother," Jesse told Rex with a grin. "It won't be that often that I squirt or spurt something in your direction anyway, and I hope you'll have the good sense not to scratch your head or get too close to the cadaver."

"Don't touch yours!" Jesse commanded Joe when she saw Joe moving to take off his splat hat. Joe rested his hands in a hurry.

"Goggles?" Jesse ordered.

Rex and Joe scrambled to the drawer where they'd seen Jesse get hers, and they each snatched a pair. The goggles looked like a clear plastic diving mask without the nose piece.

"Neat-o," Rex proclaimed. Rex felt some separation from the body after putting on his goggles but when he glanced up at Joe, Rex thought his partner looked like a mix between a deranged surgical nurse and a big balloon about to pop. He figured his own appearance was not any more appealing.

Next was the brief, but cloudy, battle at the talcum powder box while donning their gloves. Rex managed to disguise all three of them as ghosts when a slippery glove full of talcum snapped out of his control and pouffed the three of them in a cloud of powder.

"Oops!" Rex muttered.

Rex glanced up in time to see how Jesse would appear standing in a Michigan blizzard.

"You knothead," Jesse spit and sputtered. Rex nodded in agreement that was an appropriate description of him.

Joe burst out in laughter.

As hard as Jesse tried to wipe away the powder off her face she only managed to smear it around. Her clown appearance caused Rex to laugh with Joe.

"This isn't funny," Jesse griped.

"Have you looked in the mirror recently?" Rex asked in between giggles.

"This is your fault, Bana!" Jesse exclaimed before she burst into laughter as well.

Finally, the air cleared and the laughter subsided.

"Oh, that was a good one," Jesse hitched. "I haven't had this much fun down here since the Christmas party when we played hide and seek with the cadaver parts." Jesse giggled a bit while Rex and Joe stopped laughing altogether.

"Oh ... Never mind," Jesse waved her hand in the air. She walked over to the cabinet, grabbed a few of the rags Rex had made and passed them around so everyone could clean up.

"Shall we get back to business, gentlemen," Jesse stated. Rex noticed that Jesse stressed the "gentlemen" part in a manner that suggested they were anything but.

Rex forced himself to look over at the stainless steel-plated table on which the body of interest had been laid. The first thing that struck Rex was how small the victim looked on the big examination table. Rex would have mistaken this man for a child had he not known differently.

This brought another fact to his mind that he'd noticed in the files he'd examined earlier. Of the fourteen files Rex held out as possible criminal cases, thirteen of them had been women. The majority of them were of less than average height. But the single male had not been diminutive. Rex would have to check the files again, but he thought the majority of the victims would have stood less than five foot two inches. This could not be a coincidence, but an important clue to these killings. Rex knew he was onto something here, but darned if he knew what it was.

Was some wacko going around killing short people?

Then why kill the victim who wasn't short?

Rex admitted he knew some short people who were obnoxious, but certainly not to the extent of planning an elaborate method to murder them. At this rate it was going to take a hell of long time to eliminate all people of this world under five foot two inches. Rex had also noticed that all the victims were scrawny or weak-looking in their autopsy pictures. Even the taller ones looked frail to Rex.

Jesse's voice attracted Rex's attention. She had been examining the body while Joe and Rex had kept their distance. "There appears to be strap marks from the diving harness on the victim's shoulders and across his stomach, but these may have been caused after death since there appears to be no bruising. It's not immediately apparent whether there was any type of struggle before death or not," Jesse was saying.

"And it's difficult to use the facial features to tell if there was a struggle since this body has been floating for at least two days, and much of the soft tissue of the face appears to have been eaten off by marine life. This would indicate the victim wasn't wearing a mask or that he tore it off while drowning."

"He wasn't naked when they found him, was he?" Rex asked.

"No, the clothes, or in this case ... let's see here ..." Jesse read from the file. " ... Nope ... this guy was scuba diving, or at least was wearing scuba gear when they found him ... strange though ..."

"What's strange?" Rex asked not wanting to get any closer than he needed, but still curious.

"Well, I go diving nearly every day and consider myself an avid diver ..." she trailed off as she searched more thoroughly through the file.

"And?" Joe prodded.

"Ah, if this guy was scuba diving, he was either new at the sport or pretty dumb." Jesse stopped there and closed her eyes as if she was in deep thought.

Jesse's eyes popped open and she continued, "Ya know, a lot of those other victims were diving as well. This hadn't occurred to me before."

"What?!" Rex shouted. He was ready to start pulling out his hair.

"Oh, sorry, I was just thinking to myself out loud. I do that often since there's usually not anyone down here to talk to except the bodies. Yeah, I know it's a scary thought ..." Jesse went back to looking at the file.

Grinding his teeth, Rex hissed, "What did you find strange?"

"Oh ..." Jesse looked up catching his glare. "Ah, well, that this guy wasn't wearing a bottom timer, no compass, nothing. It's like this guy went diving with the absolute minimum of equipment. There aren't even any fins or a mask listed, but those could have come off after he died. Or he pulled off the mask while he was drowning like I said."

"Where's the equipment they took off the cadaver?" Joe asked.

"Oh ... It should be right around here." Jesse looked around for a moment. "There it is ..." she pointed, "... over by the wash basin."

Joe headed toward the wash basin at the far end of the room. Rex was close behind, but as they passed the examination table where the corpse was laid out, Rex made sure Joe was in between him and the table.

Rex thought for Joe this evening must seem as if he was a cop out a dinner and he was just doing his job. Rex felt like a caged animal rather than someone passing time for money. Rex knew there was no logical reason for him to fear morgues or dead bodies, so he fought down any urges to bolt for the nearest door.

Once they reached the far end of the room, Joe heaved a large plastic tub from the wash basin over to an examination table nearby, and then switched on the overhead lights.

Rex peered over the edge of the tub to see what was inside. "Not a whole lot," he said. It certainly wasn't like the accumulated pile of neoprene, silicone, regulators, rubber hoses, steel tanks, lead weights, knives, scissors, rope, air bags, batteries, lights, cameras, fins, masks, dive computers, pressure gauges with attached gadgets, and gizmos he took when he went diving. *Hell*, Rex thought, *when I go diving, the Hummer is packed so full of my stuff I couldn't fit in a diving partner.* Rex reminded himself that he tended to be a tech person that always had to have the latest equipment in redundant quantities. Even when he bought new equipment he always took his old stuff along for good luck or just in case he needed it.

"Nope, not much to work with," Joe commented.

Rex saw inside the container was a scuba tank with attached first and second stage regulators. There was a hard back harness holding a 50 cubic inch tank with a Velcro strap rather than the standard 78 cubic inch rental tank found in most of Maui's dive shops. Rex reached in and poked around a wad of black material that was in one corner of the tub. Rex grabbed the thing with both hands and then held the dripping wad at arm's length in front of him.

"Yuck," was Rex's description for the poorly made swimming trunks he held out. They reminded him of something Migisi might wear. The "yuck" wasn't over the poorness of the suit maybe as much as it was over Rex's mental picture of Migisi in it.

Rex thought the swim trunks felt heavier than the wet material would allow, so he gave them a shake and was rewarded when a dark object fell out of the shorts into the container. It landed into a puddle at the bottom of the container and splashed liquid which hit Rex in the forehead and chin.

"Yikes!" Rex yelped jumping back from the scene while spitting and sputtering. He thanked his lucky stars his mouth hadn't been open just then.

"Damn, Rex." Joe chuckled. "It doesn't take you long to get into trouble, does it?"

Rex dried off his face with one of the rags Joe had created, while Joe reached into the container and pulled out the black object. Joe unfolded a leather wallet which was about to fall apart. Shifting the wallet around, Joe pinched out a laminated card which Rex figured to be a driver's license.

"Wow, and I thought I took a scary-looking picture for my driver's license." Joe laughed, holding the card at arms length as if it might bite his nose. Squinting, Joe brought the license in closer for inspection before looking over at the cadaver again. He looked back and forth a few times before nodding his head and saying, "Yeah, that could be the ugly critter on the table, I guess. But it's hard to tell since he doesn't have much of a face anymore. Still, the hair looks right. Says here the guy lives in Hartford City, Indiana. Ever heard of the place, Rex?" Joe asked before passing the license over to him.

Rex took the license gingerly, looked at it, puffed out his cheeks as if he might vomit, then he passed it back to Joe. "Nope. It's probably one of those hick towns you find all over the Midwest. You drive through town without blinking in fear you might miss something or hit a pig crossing the road."

Joe chuckled again while rifling through the wallet. Rex saw a couple a credit cards, a substantial amount of cash and coins, and a few business cards which had turned into pulp. The business cards were unreadable.

"Do you see a scuba certification card in there?" Rex asked.

"Good point," Joe acknowledged as he looked at the credit cards and checked for hidden compartments.

"Nothing, huh?" Rex asked.

"Nope, nada." Joe carefully refolded the wallet and placed it on top of the swim trunks in the container.

"You don't think they'll check any of that stuff for prints?" Rex asked.

"Naw. Not the way they've handled this stuff."

Rex gazed into the container, and he thought there was something odd about the equipment. Something didn't seem to fit to him. Rex knew if he wasn't having these creepy feelings about being in a morgue that his head would be clear, and he'd see what was bothering him in an instant. What was it about this stuff?

"Hey. This equipment is all brand new!" Rex exclaimed.

"Yeah, now that you say that, it does look new," Joe commented.

Rex continued. "That's odd. I know anytime I've rented a scuba tank here, or anywhere else, the stuff is beat to piss and looks like it's been used a million times," Rex recalled.

"This stuff doesn't have a mark on it. The chrome is shiny, the paint on that tank looks as if it's still wet, and look at the Velcro on those straps. It doesn't have any garbage stuck in the fibers. It's not even crushed like it would be if it had been used a bunch of times."

"Maybe he just bought the stuff. Based on that driver's license, I'd say the man was a tourist." Joe speculated.

"Hey, isn't there a way to use the DOT (Department of Transportation) number stamped on the tank to trace it back to the manufacturer, and then to the retailer? We might be able to find out who bought this tank," Rex said.

"Yeah, we'll have to get someone started on that," Joe commented without much enthusiasm.

"It's a lead," Rex said, wondering how Joe was going to get someone to track down the tank when he was supposed to be on vacation. Plus, this case supposedly didn't exist in the sheriff's mind. Then it occurred to Rex that these were the same thoughts Joe was having and that was why he was being so quiet.

"Okay, gentlemen!" Jesse said loud enough to make Rex jump.

"What's up?" Rex asked.

"More like what's out," Jesse said. She took a glass slide from the cadaver's head over to one of the microscopes. Joe followed and Rex even hustled around the cadaver.

"After forcing some liquid out of the lungs, I took a sample."

"Anything in particular you're looking for?" Rex asked.

"Yes. Different types of water are easily identifiable once you get them under a microscope. I wanted to do a preliminary look-see to make sure it was saltwater that filled our victim's lungs."

"Good point," Joe said. "We'd definitely have a case for murder if it was pool or toilet water in this guy's lungs."

Jesse bent over the microscope for a couple minutes with her butt waving back and forth. Rex stood at attention a few feet behind her, and he started to rock toe-to-heel in his impatience.

Rex wanted out of this place. It was obvious to him this woman was going to drive him nuts with either her tantalizing appearance or while showing him around this scary morgue. He didn't dare look at Jesse's rear as it wiggled back and forth in front of him. He was afraid of what the sight might arouse in him at this most inappropriate time and place.

"Hmm," Jesse exclaimed. She studied the slide still wiggling her butt.

Finally, Jesse broke away from her microscope and raced off while holding her finger up to shut off any questions.

Rex's body motions increased dramatically with her departure. He tipped forward, tipped back————tip forward, tip back, blowout, inhale, blowout…

Jesse returned with a huge red reference book. She dropped the book on the counter next to the microscope with a slam that startled Rex before she began flipping through the pages.

"Yup!" Jesse cried out with the excitement of a cheerleader.

She fingered a picture of something in the book, and then she peeked back into the microscope.

"Voila!" she exclaimed. Jesse stepped back from the microscope and did a twirl in celebration as if she'd just discovered something important to the case. Rex's patience had reached its limit and he could hardly contain himself.

"What's a matter, Rex? You look like you're getting ready to pull out your hair," Jesse asked in the sweetest voice.

"Oh nothing." Rex sighed as he relaxed his face and hands. "It's just some Indian thing I do every once in a while ... dancing about while pulling on one's scalp. It helps—ah—relieve tension," Rex said in the calmest voice that he could.

"Oh really, I'll have to try it," remarked Jesse.

Joe was snickering.

"What's with him?" Jesse thumbed at Joe.

"Nothing. I think it's past the detective's bedtime and he's getting a little punchy. What'd you discover?" Rex asked.

"Well, our victim did drown," Jesse stated. "He drowned in the ocean, and he drowned at night." Jesse stared into Rex's eyes ending his impatience.

"Drowned at night? How do you know that?" Joe asked.

"Go look in the microscope," Jesse invited as she stepped aside while still maintaining her look into Rex's eyes trapping him where he stood.

Joe jumped at the chance and bent over the microscope.

"What am I looking for?" Joe asked.

"See those little mushroom shapes?"

"Ah ... yeah."

"Those are coral polyps. They're coral babies one could say, and they're only secreted by these particular Hawaiian corals at night."

Finally, Jesse tilted her head and broke her glance with Rex. "Take a look at the picture," Jesse pointed at the reference book next to the microscope. "You'll see that the polyps I took out of the victims lungs are identical. You can read about their rarity in Hawaiian waters and their times of excretion from the coral."

"So if those were in this victim's lungs, you can prove he drowned in seawater and at night," Rex reiterated. "I think this could help prove this man was murdered."

Joe asked, "How's that?"

"Well, I think if we checked with all the certification agencies, we'd find that our victim was not a certified scuba diver," Rex responded.

"How can you be sure of that?" Jesse asked.

"There's a multitude of reasons. For one thing;" Rex said looking back into Jesse's eyes. "... we went through the man's wallet, which in itself is weird. But there was no scuba certification card in his wallet, and a C-card would have been mandatory for anyone buying, renting, or using scuba tanks.

"The weird thing is, who takes their leather wallet diving?"

Jesse and Joe shook their heads.

"One point is that no certified diver ever dives at night without safety lights tethered to them. There's no evidence this guy was using any sort of dive light or even flares."

"And another thing is that a certified diver knows you don't dive alone, especially at night. You always have a dive partner. You haven't heard any reports of someone losing their diving partner, have you?"

Joe shook his head.

"Jesse, any idea how long this guy's been floating?" Rex asked.

"Not before doing some blood tests and internal temperature readings. It's very difficult to tell once a cadaver has been in seawater for a time. The water extracts body heat at four times the rate of air. But if I had to guess, just on the amount of rigor and knowing what overexposure to ocean water can do, I'd say somewhere between 24 to 72 hours."

"But there's been plenty of time for someone to make a report to the police about losing their dive partner, wouldn't you say?" asked Rex.

"Yes. I think it's safe to say there was plenty of time to call 911, or radio the coast guard, to say one had lost their dive partner. But what if this guy didn't dive with a partner? That's the trend these days. I know I prefer to dive alone when I don't have someone around that I know and trust to be my dive partner."

"You've got a point there," admitted Rex with a nod. "If this guy came to the island alone, that might be a very good point. Still, without a C-card I don't see how this guy would have gotten a scuba tank without someone's help. We'll need some background work on this guy that I have a feeling we're not going to get with Joe on vacation."

"I'm not on vacation," Jesse said. "Plus, I'm my own boss, and I can snoop into police files anytime I want without someone getting too suspicious," stated Jesse.

"Again, we need to do a background check to see if this guy was certified, but I think there are at least two killers working here," Rex told Joe. "That, Deputy Sheriff Tweedy, is why I said you do not have a serial killer loose on Maui. Serial killers almost never work with partners."

"What makes you so sure there's more than one killer?"

"There's a few indications so far that more than one person is involved. But have you ever seen someone drown?" Rex asked.

Both Jesse and Joe shook their heads.

"Neither have I. But when I was a kid I took the course to become a lifeguard, and one of the things they stressed was the method you approach a person that's drowning."

"They fight like hell, don't they?" Jesse asked.

"Yup, even the smallest victim shows phenomenal strength and they go crazy not caring if they drown someone who's trying to save them."

"So you think it would take two people to purposely drown someone?" asked Joe.

"Definitely. But there are other factors that lead me to that theory as well. If these are murders, then they are very organized because it takes some planning to get an uncertified person into scuba gear and out on a boat to go diving at night."

"Either that, or the victim was drunk or drugged when they got into the water," Joe pointed out.

"Right, and that takes planning as well. Either the victim has to voluntarily ingest the drug, or it has to be injected into his system.

"Jesse? In your preliminary search of the body, did you find any puncture wounds to suggest he'd been injected with something prior to death?"

"No, and that's one of the first things I look for. Although I have to say I haven't turned the cadaver over to view the backside. Come on over and help, maybe we should do that now."

"Oh joy," Rex said, "I had to open my big mouth."

They joined around the table with Rex following last. Joe got to the table first and flipped the cadaver over so Rex didn't have to touch it. Jesse did a search of the body's backside while Rex faded off as if he was interested in the rest of the lab.

"Okay," Jesse said. "There doesn't appear to be any marking consistent with a needle puncture, but after floating about the ocean and having his flesh pecked at by the fish, it's very difficult to find any small wound."

Rex stepped out of the shadows, and said, "So more than likely this victim ingested whatever drugged him."

"Let's just say that if he was drugged or drunk, it's a possibility," Jesse cautioned.

"If we assume this man did come to Maui by himself, and he was taken out on a boat to be drowned at night, then we have to assume that he went out voluntarily," stated Rex.

"We know no boat operator is going to take a non-certified diver out drunk and on a night dive. They'd lose their license in a second," Joe pointed out.

"Right," admitted Rex.

"So this guy was taken out on the boat by someone that picked him up at his hotel and drugged him, or maybe at a bar where he was drugged or drunk and then led out to the killer's boat," said Jesse.

"That certainly fits the facts," agreed Rex.

"What makes you so sure this guy didn't go diving voluntarily with someone that had a boat? It could be someone that simply picked him up and took him out at night. Then when he disappeared, whoever took him out got scared and didn't report it, knowing this guy came to Maui on his own," pointed out Joe.

"That may have been, but what about the other bodies you have that died under similar conditions?" asked Rex. Joe didn't answer.

"You have to factor in this guy's courage, as well," pointed out Jesse. "This guy's build is somewhat fragile and weak. It would suggest that this man is no hero. Come to think of it, the other bodies were mostly sickly and weak in appearance. They were certainly not people who would stand up and fight an aggressor."

Rex was elated someone else noticed the weak appearance of the victims. That helped to confirm some of his theory.

"My point is that it would take a lot of courage for someone who isn't certified to get into scuba gear and go diving at night, and I would guess none of these victims had that type of mentality. That's only a guess on my part, but as Rex likes to say, 'It fits the facts.'" Jesse giggled at Rex's frown.

Rex strolled around for a moment in thought. His fear of the morgue was forgotten as his mind had something else to work on.

"Okay, let's work on the point on how these victims were picked up and taken out on the boat. This brings us back to the Lahaina pier. As you pointed out earlier tonight, the Lahaina pier is the only pier from which boats leave this part of the island. And you already agreed that these victims were probably taken out on a boat, right? That's the only way they got so far out to sea."

"And to have inhaled those kind of coral polyps," Jessie added.

"Okay. To get someone onto that boat at Lahaina's pier requires they walk down Front Street through town. You both know Front Street is packed with people walking around window shopping, bar hopping, or just people watching during the day and night, right?"

Both Joe and Jesse nodded.

"So, no matter what time of the day or night they walked down Front

Street, they're gonna run into other people. I doubt a killer would risk fighting with a drunken or drugged person while walking down Front Street ... somebody's gonna notice. This means the victim was voluntarily led to the boat."

"Or under hidden gun point," suggested Jesse.

Rex gave Jesse a look as if she had marshmallows growing out of her ears.

"You've been watching too much TV," Rex said bluntly. "A kidnapping is a highly tense situation. To walk through the town with people watching, the victim would have to act at least somewhat natural to go unnoticed by anyone.

"The point is that whenever someone goes through town, they get noticed by someone somewhere along the line. And the intelligent killer that has done this on numerous occasions must know this. If the killer is smart enough to have done this sophisticated planning, then they're smart enough to make the whole episode look as natural as possible. Therefore, the victim had to have played along and gotten on the boat naturally. It'd be too easy for the victim to simply start screaming or grabbing hold of a bystander or something."

"Hey ... I got it!" Joe exclaimed.

"Go ahead, master mystic and soothsayer," Rex said with a grin.

"Well, maybe I don't have it, but let me summarize this as I understand it so far. The victims are possibly drugged at a bar, where he or she was picked up by a killer or killers. Then the drugged or drunk victim is escorted through town, and down to the pier." Joe shrugged.

"BINGO!" Rex hollered making the Joe and Jessie jump. "But, is that all?"

"You mean there's more?" asked Jesse.

"Sure. Who drove the car, or drove the boat? Who killed our victim?" Rex asked.

"Well, I was thinking a two-woman team," Joe said. "You said that it would take two people to drown a person, and that the victim was lured onto the boat voluntarily. That would suggest he was following his hormones," Joe noted.

"Yeah, that's one way of putting it. But you're missing some important points about the other victims. Most of them were female, which would make two female killers working together weird or incorrect."

"So we add a male team as well as the girls," Joe pointed out.

"Please enlighten us since you seem to have this case all figured out." Jesse smiled at Rex.

"No. I don't have it figured out. I'm just stating what the facts suggest. Did either of you notice the fact that most of the victims were under five foot one or two inches tall? Jesse, how tall is our latest victim?"

Jesse didn't even have to look at the chart. "Five foot four inches."

"Okay, so there are some that were taller. But most of the victims were short, and the large majority of them were women, right? And Jesse, you said they were all fragile and weak in body structure, so I don't think this has much to do with stature."

"It has to do with overall body strength, right?" asked Jesse.

"Right again. All the victims were people who could be easily handled by two female killers. This is especially true if the victims were already drugged and complacent from the start."

"So you think two women picked up these victims at a bar where they were probably drugged and led like sheep to the boat?"

"No, see, I don't like the theory that we're working with just two women killers," Rex said. "There are too many female victims."

"You think there are more than two killers?" asked Joe while doing a good imitation of Rex relieving tension through hair pulling.

"Sure. Who got all the women victims to board your death boat?"

"One or two men," answered Jesse.

"One man, I would think. Two men would be a little intimidating in a bar scene," Rex pointed out. "But then, it might be two short men since we're dealing with short victims. That would seem to fit, one man and a two-woman team."

"So now you're saying that there is at least one man and two women killers loose on Maui?" asked Joe.

"It almost sounds like a conspiracy," mumbled Jesse.

"What?" Rex asked just to make sure he heard right.

"I said it almost sounds like a conspiracy."

"Wow. That wasn't so tough, was it?" Rex asked.

"What was?" Joe asked.

"A conspiracy?" Jesse asked. "Hell if I know what he's talking about. You're the one that suggested bringing on this lamebrain half Indian with piggy-tails. You deal with it," Jesse said with joking excitement.

Rex gave Jesse a frown over the Indian comment but continued anyway. He didn't think he knew her well enough for her to be making racial comments, joking or otherwise.

"What you have here is not a serial killer that kills for the joy of killing—personal satisfaction," Rex said seriously. "It appears we have a group of killers that are killing for a specific purpose—kind of like a hit squad if you catch my drift."

"Okay, so you think either one man or a two-woman team picks up the victim at the bar, right?" Joe asked.

"That's a very good possibility. The man or the women must find a way to drug their victim at the bar to make them more complacent and willing to do whatever they want. I don't see them picking the victims up while they're shopping, or walking down the street. It would have to be in a bar-type setting, especially if it's occurring at night when a drunk person being escorted down Front Street would seem more acceptable," Rex continued.

"Kind of sounds like the typical bar scene and pick-up routine," Jesse put in.

"Exactly," Rex exclaimed. "And that's what makes this whole scenario so scary. The killers' plan is so typical no one notices it's happening."

"And once the victims are subdued, they're led to one of the boats we saw out at the Lahaina pier. Then, once on the boat, the victims are dressed in swim wear or scuba gear and thrown overboard," continued Joe.

"Yup," Rex agreed. "Once they're on the boat and drunk, the killers might even be able to talk the victims into scuba gear, or at least swimming. Once overboard the victims could easily be held underwater and drowned. Did you notice the newness of this last guy's scuba gear, and his lack of proper gear for night diving?"

"Yeah." Joe nodded.

"In other words, those were just props bought and put on the victim to make the drowning look real?" asked Jesse.

"Yup ... this all fits into the fact that this was a sophisticated and planned murder. There is nothing about these deaths that suggests a serial killer.

"I also noticed there was no mention of sexual abuse in any of the files I looked at," Rex commented.

"Meat," Jesse started and then laughed, "Dr. Cook did all the other autopsies and if he checked, he made no comment."

"So in other words, we don't really know," Rex suggested. That squirmy feeling returned to his stomach with the mention of Dr. Cook's name. Something about the guy bugged Rex and he couldn't put a finger on it. There was just too much good in Dr. Cook to be true. Rex's apprehension must have showed through.

"You really don't trust Dr. Cook, do you?" Jesse asked.

"About as far as I could throw him, and that isn't very far."

"Well, if two women killed this victim, I don't think they were having much of a sexual relationship based on his penis size," Jesse noted while examining the victim.

Rex sucked in some wind. "Ewwww ... You're a cold woman, very cold," Rex laughed.

"How do you know it wasn't a battery-operated relationship?" Joe put in.

"Ah, kinky." Rex grinned.

# CHAPTER ELEVEN

Rex couldn't deny it had been one very long day. After he said goodnight to all, he welcomed the soft, cool comfort of the night's bed.

Rex stretched out naked beneath the cool sheet of the bed, and his body reminded him that he was no longer a child and that the mileage had been much rougher on him than the years.

Rex listened to the ceiling fan wobbling overhead. The fan provided soothing fresh air that blew lightly on his face and bare skin. The breeze through the window by Rex's head provided additional freshness and carried the sound of waves pounding upon the beach. Rex's mind was lulled into slumber listening to the continuous fan wobble and the drumming waves.

He fell into a deep sleep as all his physical and mental energy had been drained from his body and his subconscious was given freedom to play without inhibitions. Through much of the night his subconscious played its games of review and renewal, but near dawn his dreams took a twist.

Rex dreamt he was twelve years old, and he was in Deputy Madison's barn coop. This nightmare had been played so often through his conscious and subconscious level, both waking and asleep, that he no longer feared its bloody visions. It was like an old movie he'd seen so many times he was bored with the scenes despite the outcome that continued to torment him.

Yet, in this dream there was something different. And since it was different, it remained with Rex's consciousness to ponder.

The nightmare ran its usual course as Rex broke his restraints after seeing his mother's spirit and the buck's pounding life force. Rex watched himself grab Deputy Madison's gun and leap to Sara's side. Deputy Madison threw back the trapdoor and popped into the confinement. What horrified Rex was now the Deputy Madison monster had two heads and a bare-chested bodybuilder's body as it leaped into the confinement. The monster got done with its jabbering at Rex and charged. The Rex in the dream only shot one of the heads as he usually did to survive. This left one head on the Madison body to fly through the darkness and slam Rex into the wall. Deputy Madison was still alive as it pinned Rex and began pinching and clawing at him. As Rex hoarsely tried to scream for help, he awoke.

Rex lay there panting and blowing with his sheet and pillow wet with sweat, but the nightmare remained clear in his memory. If not for the peaceful crashing of the waves and the cooling breeze from the ceiling fan, Rex would have thought he was still ten years old and squished beneath Deputy Madison in the coop.

After relaxing with the sound of the wobbly fan and the waves, Rex got out of bed and used the facilities. Then, still naked and sweating, Rex stepped out on the balcony of his room and stared at the night around him. The cool breeze blew about his body while blowing his long black hair in a manner that was refreshing and relaxing. Eventually, his gaze turned to the mansion on the hill next door to Tweedy's manor.

Rex knew Dr. Cook, a.k.a. Meat, had recently moved into this magnificent twenty-seven-room mansion. Rex could see parts of the mansion were brilliantly lit like a fortress awaiting an attack. Rex looked down and saw the black electrical fence Dr. Cook had installed around the property. He huffed as he thought of all the dangers, prowlers, and monsters Meat must fear to put up such security measures on the tranquil island on Maui. Then it occurred to Rex that maybe Meat wasn't attempting to keep things out of his property. What if he was trying to keep something within that electrical fence? Either way, Rex thought the man was weird.

Rex wondered how much money it took to run such an estate. Not that it was any of his business anyway. What was he doing being so nosy in the middle of the night?

Rex realized he was standing there naked flaunting himself on the balcony. His dick was hanging out in plain sight for all the neighbors to see. It occurred to Rex that Meat had good reason to put up that electrical fence. Meat had neighbors that stood on their balconies waving their privates in the early morning wind. With that thought, Rex headed back to bed and let his mind drift to different concerns.

Rex laid in his cold, wet, sheets, and he wondered about the significance of the two headed Deputy Madison with the bodybuilder's body. His subconscious was trying to tell him something with the second head and built-up body in an old nightmare. Something was different. Something was wrong. Rex wasn't the kind to pass up a warning.

Rex knew one had to read all the road signs when one traveled the road with Death. With the question of the second head and the body still unanswered, he returned to an uneasy sleep. But now Rex had been warned and was wary of what the future held.

# CHAPTER TWELVE

"What a great idea you had," said Rex, standing next to Moe as Moe maneuvered the *"Mickey Fin,"* Moe's thirty-nine foot luxury dive boat, out of Lahaina's harbor.

"This way Joe, Jesse, and I can finish talking about our business without any interruptions," said Rex.

"Hey, I like to get out once in a while without having to cater to ten passenger's whims and do some diving on my own," commented Moe. He pushed up the throttles to three-quarter speed. The Detroit diesels roared and Rex noted the compass on the dashboard showed they were traveling on a south-southwest heading—toward the Molokini Crater.

"It must be great living on a tropical island like this and having both business and pleasure right at your fingertips. What the hell am I still doing in Michigan anyway?" asked Rex in a louder voice so Moe could hear him above the wind, the slapping sea, and the growling of the engines.

Rex wondered about his sanity sometimes. He knew if it wasn't for Migisi and Sheriff Bana that he'd leave in a minute—maybe.

"Is this dive business of yours paying off?" Rex continued to pry.

"Yeah, it's a goldmine for the right operator," Moe said, looking around to make sure no one was listening. "The Feds are making a pretty penny out of this operation. They'd probably rather have me attend to this business more than working undercover to catch the Yakuza."

Rex got the impression the Yakuza was a subject Moe would like to speak about since he seemed to have such a keen interest last night while they talked about Joe's case.

"Speaking of which, do you really think the murders Joe's investigating has anything to do with the Japanese mob?" asked Moe.

"Well, we've come to the conclusion that these murders are a conspiracy of some sort, and I think it's too much of a coincidence that the Yakuza have an ongoing operation on this island at the same time these murders are occurring," said Rex.

"So you're saying that these killings are contract killings?" asked Moe. Joe and Jesse came through the cabin door as Moe was asking his question.

"Coffee?" Joe asked as he passed a deep steaming mug to Rex. Jesse gave another to Moe.

"Gee, thanks. Ya know, this is one thing I miss back in Detroit. We don't have Kona coffee unless ya pay a premium price."

"I know I couldn't live without it." Jesse laughed. "Moe, this is a really great idea you had. I really appreciate you calling and inviting me."

"Hey, the pleasure's entirely mine. I was just telling Rex that I love to get a chance to go out occasionally, without passengers, and do some diving on my own. But the real reason I called you was so I'd get to see that beautiful body of yours in a wetsuit," stated Moe with a grin.

"Always thinking of yourself, aren't ya, Moe?" Joe said as a joke. Jesse pushed Joe in the arm.

"What makes you think I don't like to show it off? A lady always appreciates the eye of a worthy man," Jesse said as she wrapped her arm though one of Moe's.

"Oooafff. Now I've seen it all." Joe waved to dismiss the subject. "What was this you guys were saying about contract killings?"

"Oh yeah. What I was saying last night was these killings don't fit in the serial killer categorization, but appear to be more like contract killings. Ya know, killings made not for the killing, but with a goal in mind."

"What's more interesting is what I was telling Moe about the rumor there's a Yakuza operation on this island," Rex said.

Moe shuffled his feet about. He suddenly became interested in the beautiful Maui mountains off to their left, but he didn't say anything. Rex figured he was digging too close for Moe's comfort.

"Yakuza?" mumbled Jesse as if she'd gotten something awful tasting in her mouth. "Isn't that a motorcycle or something?"

Rex laughed, but when no one answered immediately Jesse continued.

"What or who are they?"

Rex answered since the Tweedy brothers had lost their tongues. "Well, the easiest description is to say that they're the Japanese version of the mob. They're organized crime that operates all over the world, but their origins are deep in Japan's past. And it's believed they have some sort of operation going on here on Maui."

"Yeah, but no one knows all they're into," Joe started. "There are a lot of rumors they're involved with Maui politics, including what goes on in the Sheriff's office." Joe revealed his deepest worry.

"Really?" Jesse seemed astonished.

"Yeah. Some say the Yakuza helped elect our Sheriff to office, and for once, I tend to agree." Joe moaned.

Rex could see them getting off the subject and quickly interrupted. "My point was these killings seem like a conspiracy of some sort, an organized crime, and the only organized crime I know of on this island is the Yakuza. If they really exist at all."

"Oh, they exist all right," Joe stated in a loud voice. "So you think the Yakuza might be doing these killings?" Joe raised his eyebrows.

"I think it fits all the facts. But we have to figure out why the Yakuza are killing people at random for it to make sense. By killing the victims we've seen so far, the killers are definitely not acting as if they were a crime organization seeking chaos and authoritative power. The motive for these killings is very obscure to me. It's not like they're killing pillars of society. It appears that they're doing just the opposite. The Yakuza are killing prostitutes, runaways, and loners, people no one will notice when they disappear."

"If their motive isn't to disrupt society and aid their position for money and power, and they're killing in a way they hope will never be traced to them, then they have to be killing for the bodies themselves," suggested Joe.

"Maybe. Why do you say that?" Rex asked.

"Because the Yakuza's main operation on the island appears to be the Maui Funeral Home."

"Joe." Rex laughed. "You're sick. You think the Yakuza's motive for knocking off prostitutes and loners is just to drum up business?"

"No, but after this Sheriff was elected into office, he ordered any body disposal business on the northwestern side of the island, that wasn't being handled by relatives or friends of the deceased, to be directed to the Maui Funeral Home.

"This wasn't a big deal since there are only two funeral homes on this side of the island. But the county was doing most of its business with the other funeral home since we suspected the Maui Funeral Home was run by the Yakuza.

"You could say this showed the Sheriff's hand. A lot of the deputies were suspect about the way this guy was elected to office over a fifteen year incumbent. The whole department and the popular vote seemed behind the old sheriff. This suggested Erp had ties to the Yakuza, and this was one of his ways of paying them back for getting him into office."

"Wow. Those are strong allegations, Deputy Tweedy," Jesse said.

"Let's leave the Maui politics alone for a minute and get back to my point. If we assume the Yakuza are committing these murders, and if they are killing short or sickly people, which they're doing off a boat from the Lahaina pier, what is there motive for killing these easy targets?" Rex asked.

"To know that, you'd probably have to ask the Yakuza," pointed out Joe. Moe remained taut and tight-lipped throughout this conversation.

"That's going to be our problem. I don't suppose this sheriff of yours would sign a search warrant so we could go have a look see at what they're doing in the Maui Funeral Home?" Rex asked half heartedly.

"Erp!" hiccupped Joe. "No way, no how. If he even heard I wanted to stick my nose in the Maui Funeral Home business he'd have my job."

"Erp?" Rex asked. "Don't tell me the sheriff's first name is Wyatt?"

"You got it. Sheriff Wyatt Erp lives again. Except this guy spells 'Earp' by dropping the *a*. He spells it *E, r, p*." Joe laughed.

"Oh, come on. You guys are pulling my linguini," Rex complained.

"Nope, that's his name," Jesse confirmed.

"I did some background work on Erp," Joe started. "It took me a week, but Erp didn't seem to notice, or care."

"After getting his social security number, which he's never changed, the whole process was simple. The social belongs to a man by the name of Arnold Webster, and it wasn't difficult to get a driver's license on Webster with a picture that matched our Erp."

Rex was nodding since he knew the process of doing background searches all too well. Moe remained concentrated on their course, and Jesse was doing her normal string of facial expressions from surprised to shocked as she listened to the latest county gossip.

"Webster's a con man, a card shark, out of Las Vegas. There are some people back in Nevada with questions for Webster about a large sum of money left in his care as security manager for one of the hotels. Webster and the money went missing shortly before Erp reportedly turned up on Maui."

"How did he end up here?" Rex asked.

"Same as a lot of the criminals we get on Maui. For some reason criminals think a South Pacific Island is far enough away to hide from authorities on the Mainland. The case would have to be handled by the Feds, and so far, he's not done anything illegal for them to pursue. Erp isn't about to sign extradition papers on himself back to Nevada.

"Anyway, Webster changed his name, and found his way into the hands of the Yakuza. Or it's the other way around. Webster came to Maui, got tangled with the Yakuza, and then changed his name to Wyatt Erp. Whatever the truth, I have yet to find enough proof to make a case, and these murders have taken priority over getting Erp out of office."

No one seemed ready to interrupt him, so Joe continued. "I think using the name 'Wyatt Erp' is just another way for the Yakuza to thumb their noses at authorities on Maui. They're showing off their power by fixing the Sheriff elections and putting their own man in place. And to make it obvious they're the ones in charge, they gave their man a fictitious name out of America's past."

"Gee, and I just came here looking for a serial killer." Rex laughed.

"If you're saying the Yakuza are involved with these murders, then you're dabbling in a very big mess," confirmed Joe.

"And here I am just taking over as Medical Examiner of Maui County. How delightful." Jesse laughed.

"If we assume that it's the Yakuza that are committing these murders, then I think we need to get into the Maui Funeral Home and find out what they're doing with these bodies," Rex pointed out.

"And tomorrow would be a perfect time since the coroner's office will probably send the remains of the last victim over to the Maui Funeral Home to be put in cold storage or disposed of, depending on what I write up in the post autopsy report," Jesse stated.

Moe finally broke his silence. "You guys wanna lighten up? It's Sunday, and it's gonna be a beautiful one at that.

"Okay, boys and girls, this is where we tie up for some fun in the Sun," Moe said. He throttled down as they neared the Molokini Crater Marine National Park.

The luxury yacht coasted into the tranquil waters protected by the top of the cone of the Puu Olai volcano which partially broke the water to form a C-shaped islet. The cliffs of this islet rose so sharply out of the ocean's depths that the land mass was uninhabitable by humans. Rex noticed the seabirds had found a paradise of their own. The birds were everywhere, and the sheer cliffs surrounding the cove were covered in bird crap.

"Looks like a good place to be wearing a wetsuit in or out of the water," Rex suggested as he exited the cabin and had to duck as a seagull swooped over the boat too close to his head for comfort.

Once he stripped down to a huge pair of colorfully-flowered shorts, Joe cannon-balled off the diving platform to tie the boat line of the *Mickey Fin* to a buoy. Rex didn't want to be far behind. He was excited to get into the water since a good percentage of the fish he would see were indigenous to the Hawaiian Islands. He certainly wasn't going to see beautiful antler and finger corals while diving the murky and cold Great Lake waters of Michigan. Plus, Rex was dying to go diving and experience the relaxing feeling of weightlessness beneath the placid surface of the ocean. There was nothing like losing two hundred and twenty pounds in an instantaneous and comfortable manner.

The bow of the *Mickey Fin* seemed to lift as Joe hauled himself aboard the stern diving platform. Once Joe was aboard, Moe gathered everyone around the equipment lockers amidships.

"I have to admit there's a second reason I invited you all out this morning," Moe said.

"Ah, now his true intentions become evident." Joe laughed.

"See, sometimes dive companies send me some of their equipment to test underwater in hopes that I'll invest in the stuff and rent it to my passengers," Moe started.

"Oh no, this sounds dangerous." Rex laughed.

"Not at all. Merely a bit ... uncomfortable." Moe laughed in defense.

"Okay, brother, spit it out. What are we being used as guinea pigs for?" Joe asked seriously.

"You'd be considered a full-fledged hog," Rex pointed out and then had to duck as Joe took a half hearted swipe at him.

Moe stepped back into the cabin and then carried out a shipping box. "I think they only sent one set of these, so only two of you will have the honor of telling me how you like them," Moe said. He plopped the box by the dive equipment locker. "These are underwater communication devices so you can talk to each other."

"Hey ... Neat-o." Rex giggled, always the kid when it came to electronics and gadgets.

"I figured you would get a kick out of these. Who else wants to talk to him?" Moe asked.

"Hey, I'm game for anything," Jesse said. "Besides, this'll be my way of paying you back for inviting me on this expedition."

Moe went about setting up the experimental equipment. Rex noticed Moe had all the manual dexterity of an old man with arthritis. It was painful just to watch him work on the small contraptions with his huge fingers that were more accustomed to holding large spoons of food or a beer bottle rather than delicate electronics.

Fortunately, Rex didn't feel he had the same lack of mechanical dexterity and grabbed one of the earphones. He quickly had the batteries installed. Next came the attachment of a waterproof microphone that was set into a mouth mask and the attachment of an air regulator. Rex had his set completed in no time and was satisfied it would work.

Moe was stressing out the plastic milk crate he was using as a seat, and he had the instructions trapped under his flipper-sized foot so they wouldn't blow away.

Moe's tongue was sticking out the side of his mouth and he was staring at the diagram with such intensity Rex was waiting for laser beams to come shooting out of his eyes. Rex was surprised to see Moe not only put the contraption together, but probably put it together better than he did, since Rex didn't take the time to read the instructions and had a few extra parts.

Eventually, all was assembled and they had a chance to test their contraptions. Rex felt as if he was a kid again at a birthday party.

"Testing," Rex said into the mouth mask he'd put together.

"Ouch!" Moe hollered as he pulled the earphone away from his ear.

"I guess we need to adjust the volume, huh?" Rex laughed watching Moe dig his pinkie around in his ear.

"I'd have to say you're right on that one." Moe moaned.

"Would you guys quit clowning around? It's getting awful hot on this deck. Let's get into the pool," Joe whined.

"Is there anything special we might see down there?" Rex asked.

"There's a five foot white tipped reef shark that hangs around here occasionally, but I haven't seen it in the last couple of weeks."

"Oh, great," Jesse whined in dismay.

"Oh, don't worry about Sam. If he does show up, more than likely he'll ignore you," Moe instructed. "Just don't molest or pester him."

"You don't have to worry about that." Jesse sighed.

"There's also a Hawaiian monk seal that hangs out around here. They're pretty rare these days, but this one seems to like the divers and you used to be allowed to feed him, but now it's illegal."

"Cool," Rex exclaimed.

"One word of caution about Herby ..." Moe started.

"Herby?" Jesse and Rex asked in unison.

"Herby's the name the dive masters gave the seal." Moe continued to laugh. "Herby seems to be perpetually ... ah ..." Moe hesitated as he appeared to be thinking of the proper word to describe Herby's behavior. "Well, Herby gets horny. I guess that is the easiest way to say it," Moe commented while looking down at his hands as he spoke. Everyone laughed with Moe's embarrassment.

"It's not funny," Moe continued. "There's been more than one occasion where we've had to pull Herby off divers and snorkelers."

"Really," Jesse exclaimed with a wide eyed expression on her face.

"I had to pull him off this one lady's back last month. He was hugging her with his flippers and humping away on her like a dog in ..." Moe hesitated. "Well, you know.

"Anyway, as these monk seals mate, they bite each other ... ya know ... just sort of nibbling like a pinch ..." Moe reached over and pinched Jesse's bare skin on her shoulder blade to demonstrate what he was talking about. Moe's pinching made Jesse squawk and giggle.

"Anyway, they bite hard enough to leave a hickey on human skin." Moe laughed. "They don't try and hurt you or anything. I guess it's their way of showing affection.

"Well, I pulled Herby off this lady's back, and she had all kinds of hickeys on her neck and shoulders." Moe laughed. "She looked like a teenager coming home from a movie marathon at the drive-in.

"But she came back to the shop the next day to tell me her husband saw the hickeys and they got into a big argument cause the husband thought she was off screwing around behind his back."

"Ooooo ... Kinky." Rex laughed but kept the rest of his thoughts to himself.

Finally, Moe finished the assembly of Jesse's mouth mask and gave it to her to adjust the volume to her liking. She also needed to get used to using the contraption since it was different from normal scuba diving. Rex struggled into his gear, figuring they could do the rest of their testing in the water.

Rex savored the relief from the burning sun by jumping into the water. The sun was merciless on his dark skin since they were so close to the equator and out on the reflective waters.

Rex had a real urge to scratch the stitching out of his head, but that subsided. He figured a long bath in the saltwater would do the wound some good anyway.

Rex had to admit it was awkward diving with this mouth mask contraption. Rex waited until Jesse had jumped into the water before he started yaking away at her.

Moe had been right. Looking at Jesse in a wetsuit had been worth the ride. Rex was conscious of Joe's comment this morning during breakfast that Jesse showed aggressive body language towards Rex. Rex had hardly been listening since eating breakfast with the Tweedy brothers was an experience in itself.

As Rex contemplated Jesse's mannerism toward him he assumed they were common since he didn't have much experience around women and women often approached him in a similar manner.

Joe suggested that Jesse's way of touching Rex when she talked to him, or the way she constantly stood in Rex's "personal" space even though there was plenty of room to move about, was an indication Jesse was coming on to him.

Even though Rex was in his thirties, he had skipped the part of his life where a male learns to come onto a female, or vise-versa, recognizing when a woman was coming on to a man. He'd never spent the time for those things, and now it was coming back to haunt him.

Floating down to forty feet Rex looked about him in awe. The visibility was close to two hundred feet in warm crystal clear waters. This was unheard of visibilty while diving in Michigan.

Rex was used to diving Michigan's many ship wrecks in the frigid Great Lakes. The visibility there was considered excellent if it reached twenty feet. It never failed to amaze Rex when he dove in Maui's waters where one could actually see where one was going, and one didn't have to navigate by a compass to get from one place to the next.

"How's tricks?" Rex asked Jesse who was floating ten feet away. Jesse quickly moved the earphone away from her ear at his question.

Pushing the microphone button on her mouth mask to speak, Jesse returned, "NOT SO LOUD!"

This time it was Rex's turn to pull the earphone away from his ear. Rex decided they hadn't gotten the settings right on these earphones yet.

Joe and Moe made their cannon-ball plunges off the boat and were descending at an undesirable rate for anyone inexperienced in diving. To Rex they appeared as meteorites splashing into the ocean before sinking to the bottom. Rex still couldn't figure out how they equalized the water pressure on their ears and sinus descending so quickly. But then, Rex figured most of what the Tweedy brothers did was beyond him, so why worry?

Letting air out of his buoyancy compensator, or BC, Rex slowly descended feet first. "Going down?" whispered Rex.

"AFTER YOU!" said Jesse, sounding like she was shouting into his ear.

Rex held his hands up to his ear and shook his head. Jesse got the message and whispered, "Sorry," along with a bubbling laugh. He gave her the okay sign rather than risk further damage to his eardrum.

Reaching a depth of seventy feet, Rex remained five feet above the coral reef. He was surrounded by a variety of trigger fish. Some of the fish appeared black with flimsy white fins, which Rex knew were called Whiteline trigger fish. Other trigger fish had distinct geometrical designs along their backsides and fins in different tones of brown to black.

Rex was aware that light was fragmented when it hit the water, and the human eye detected few colors beyond ten feet beneath the surface. Unless artificial light was shown on these fish at seventy feet, Rex couldn't distinguish the many colors of the underwater habitat. However, he could make out the different shades of darkness.

For Rex, this was heaven. It felt so marvelous on his tired bones and muscles to be weightless. It was a total body massage on his weary body, and he hadn't realized how much the last couple weeks had taken out of him until he started to relax. At the same time, he was able to float along and watch the varied life so different from the life that went on above the surface. From his perspective it was incredibly peaceful here, even though he knew life on the reef was quite the opposite.

Rex didn't want to think about his position in the food chain. He wanted to relax and watch the interesting and sometimes comical antics of the reef inhabitants as they went about their daily business. For the most part the critters ignored or flirted away from him since he was a noisy bubble blowing shadow intruding upon their complicated struggles with life.

Rex also kept a close eye on Jesse. Other than the pleasant reasons of watching her, it was important he kept track of his dive partner. Surprisingly, now that they were down here, neither Jesse nor Rex took advantage of their ability to speak to each other underwater. It was so peaceful, neither one wanted to disturb each other's thoughts.

For awhile Jesse and Rex swam about the reef enjoying the beauty and the peace. When Jesse did break the nearly silent solitude of their diving, it came out as a shout in Rex's ear. "WHEN ... BREAK INTO ... FUNERAL HOME?"

*Whoa ... where did that come from,* Rex wondered as he grabbed the earphone away from his ear, and looked around to see who else heard Jesse. Then it occurred to him they were the only ones that could hear each other's conversation.

"Again?" Rex asked softly.

"When ... you ... into Maui Funeral Home ... see what's going on?" Jesse whispered. Rex was having problems hearing everything when Jesse wasn't shouting in his ear. He stopped his floating about, let air out of his BC, and descended five feet to the bottom. Jesse followed, and they came together kneeling on the sandy floor facemask to facemask. Rex tried to see Jesse's face, but her normal expressions were hidden by scuba gear so that only her eyes were visible. He felt weird hearing her voice but not seeing her lips move or the movement of her facial expressions as she talked.

"You have striking eyes," Rex bubbled as they came together.

"... making ... pass ... me?" Jesse bubbled back.

"What makes you think I want to break into the Maui Funeral Home?" Rex asked.

"That ... direction ... headed."

"Do medical examiners often break the law to find evidence?"

"No ... seemed ... easiest ... to get evidence."

"One could get into trouble breaking into Yakuza houses."

"Since when ... you ... consider trouble ... acting?"

"Touché." Rex laughed. Laughing underwater was a new experience. He thought, *Hey, I might get to like these contraptions.*

Jesse closed the gap between them and grabbed his arm. "Where ... me ... touch ...?" she asked.

"No ... I said 'Touché', not touch me," Rex bubbled. Whether Jesse understood or not, she continued to caress his arm with her free hand. Again, Rex felt the excitement of a teenager's first physical contact with a girl on his own.

"When will you send this last body over to the home?" Rex asked while speaking too fast and breathing too heavily. Jesse must have noticed the effects she was having on him and she stopped her stroking—she left her hand on his arm.

"Tomorrow ... okay?"

"I don't think we need to break in," whispered Rex. "We need to form a plan with Joe."

"... think Joe ... go for it?"

"Not sure, but he's the law. We can't go against the law to solve this case."

" ... understand," Jesse said.

Rex gave her the okay sign rather than talk. He thought about where he'd like to put his hands, and he didn't think Jesse would mind, but this wasn't the time or place. They might get away with secretive talk while floating above the reef, but Rex doubted they'd get away with passionate sex at seventy feet beneath the surface of the ocean and in scuba gear.

Still, the mental image of them trying such a thing was kind of funny, and it got Rex bubbling. That's when it occurred to Rex the image they must be presenting while floating facemask to facemask and groping for each other amid a cloud of bubbles as they talked.

Since Rex had Jesse right there, he checked her gauges to see how much air she had left. They'd been underwater for thirty-five minutes and it was about time to return.

"About time to go up," Rex told Jesse as he gave her a thumb like a hitchhiker.

She signaled okay.

Heading back while eyeing Jesse in her descriptive wetsuit, Rex contemplated how each of the Tweedys would react to a search of the Maui Funeral Home. At first, Rex figured Moe would be all for it. Then he thought about how much Moe had already put into the project and how he might think this was an intrusion on his case since it could cost him not only his job, but possibly his life.

Joe had stated his position. If it was found out Joe was messing in the funeral home's activities the sheriff would have his job. The more Rex contemplated this, the more he thought this might be a shoe in with Joe to incriminate the sheriff, if Joe was willing to chance it.

Joe said he thought the sheriff had illegal relations with the Yakuza. Maybe Joe could use the sheriff's connections with the Maui Funeral Home as a method of ousting the sheriff from office. But this would mean it would have to be proven the sheriff was involved in some illegal business in connection to the Maui Funeral Home. It was a long shot, and Rex realized that everything had to be done by the books. Unfortunately, this added another fish to fry besides the Yakuza, making a difficult job impossible. The job relied too much on the ill-fated hand of Luck, something Rex didn't trust to use when he was betting his life and the lives of others. "Whatever happened to the simple proposition of finding a serial killer?" Rex bubbled.

# CHAPTER THIRTEEN

Rex faced west as he gazed through the game room window of Tweedy Manor and watched the vast red-yellow sun burn its way through the dark bubbling clouds surrounding the mountains of Lanai. The blue sky had turned a pumpkin orange, and Rex laughed to himself, thinking he was probably the only one on Maui who was reminded of Michigan's fall and pumpkins while gazing at one of the most stunning visions of the sunset on Earth. He turned back to the game.

Rex and Joe were alone and sipping on their Strohs' while playing a game of eight ball. Rex was feeling the remnants of jet lag and the long activities of the previous few days. His body muscles were relaxed like over-boiled linguini noodles after the weightlessness of going diving. His mind was in a suggestive and dreamy mood.

Mentally, it seemed a lifetime since Death gave him a haircut on the front lawn of Norman Lipshitz, but his body remembered it clearly. And yet he realized he was being kept buoyant by a feeling to which he was unaccustomed—his emotions regarding Jessica Achew. His thoughts wandered toward images of Jesse. His mind echoed with her seductive voice saying his name. He kept wondering how it would feel to run his fingers through her thick hair. He imagined sticking the wet tip of his pinky in her ear and then covering her mouth with his lips and inserting his tongue when she became startled and complained. Just the thought of holding her hand seemed thrilling. His dick was constantly semi-hard making it hard to pee, and there was a warm sensation in his stomach he figured others would call a cozy feeling. But at the moment, all these new emotions and rising hormones where throwing his pool game right into the crapper.

"Rex, buddy, I think that bullet wound across your scalp did more damage to your head than you think." Joe laughed after Rex missed another easy shot on the twelve-ball and merely sighed rather than rant and rave his usual string of four letter superlatives.

"Oh, I guess my mind must be lost on this case," Rex said, backing off the table and grabbing his Strohs which had remained full for ten minutes, a personal record.

"Uh huh," Joe responded, and expertly slammed the two ball in the corner pocket.

"Yeah," Rex said more alertly. "Have you considered what our next move must be?"

"Been thinking of little else." Joe banked in the five-ball in a manner that suggested he'd been thinking more of his pool game.

"Jesse and I were talking on the way back from Molokini…"

"Yeah, what were you two love birds talking about all cuddled in the corner there?" Joe asked. He shot the four-ball in the corner from across the table. Rex winced. He was getting slaughtered his second game in a row.

"I'm getting there," Rex answered irritably. Joe sipped his beer and came around the table looking at the five-ball which, Rex thought, was sitting pretty. "We're going to have to get into the Maui Funeral Home somehow to have a look around while they have this Roger's body, and I can't think of a nice way to do it."

"God bless America!" Joe exclaimed, having miscued and scratching the felt when Rex mentioned the funeral home. Joe reluctantly pulled the four-ball out of the corner pocket and spotted it on the table. But he didn't say anything else as Rex took the cue ball down to the end of the table.

"You know it's what we have to do," Rex stated. He slammed the nine-ball into a far corner pocket.

"Showoff," Joe muttered.

Then Joe hollered, "YEAH," scaring Rex and making him top the cue ball so it followed the eleven-ball into the corner pocket. "Maybe we can figure some way in there to take a peek. But they already know me." Joe grinned. He removed the two balls from the corner pocket, spotting the eleven behind his four-ball. Then he marched to the shooter's end of the table with the cue ball. Rex thought he looked as happy as an elephant on a peanut farm.

"We're going to have to get in there while they're working on a body that we've classified as a murder victim to see what they're doing," Rex said while Joe considered his next shot. "Jesse says the Roger's corpse will be ready to go over tomorrow afternoon. Obviously, she doesn't have to go over with the delivery, but she could make an appointment to do so just to introduce herself as the new medical examiner."

"Naw, that won't do much good," Joe said, still not moving to make a shot. "If she went there on an announced visit, they'd be sure to have everything cleaned up and by the book. She wouldn't see anything but what they wanted her to see."

"I wasn't too keen on that idea myself, and obviously I have no reason to go there to snoop around and ask questions either."

"Nope," Joe agreed as he put down the cue ball and lined up to shoot the one-ball. He missed. Rex grinned.

Rex took a sip of his beer and cleared his throat before continuing. "I did have one idea, but I'm not sure how you'll take it."

"Yeah?" Joe responded. His big belly jiggled under his Hawaiian shirt as if he'd hiccupped. "Pass it by me, I'm ready for anything."

"Okay..." Rex's muscles tensed in preparation for flight, and he continued with all the caution of a youngster making his first public address. "But remember, you asked for it." Rex paused to lick his lips. "Alright, here goes. How would you like to take Lilly over to the Maui Funeral Home to shop for her funeral arrangements?"

"Rex!"

"I'd be going with you," Rex quickly added. "And all Lilly has to do is act like she wants to see the facilities and how things are done. She could say she wants to compare embalmment to cremation or something."

"But Rex—"

"And while you two act as a distraction, I could get lost going to the restroom and do some snooping around."

"But Rex, my mother?" Joe asked. Joe came around the table with a serious look on his face.

"Come on," Rex said, staring Joe in the eyes. "The only other alternative is breaking and entering to look around, and I always thought two wrongs don't make a right. Besides, whatever evidence we found during a break-in couldn't be used in a courtroom."

"No..." Joe shook his head vigorously enough to make his jowls shake. "I can't break the law to try and prove something that might not be provable."

Rex let Joe contemplate while he shot in the ten-ball, skipped around the table and banked the eleven-ball into the corner pocket. Not seeing another easy shot, Rex said, "Joe, we have to act quickly while the Yakuza have a body to work on. I'd hate to wait around until someone else was killed to get the evidence we need to support our case."

Joe made no response.

"Besides, if we waited until the Yakuza murdered again, we'd still be in the same position," Rex pleaded.

Joe stared back at Rex with intense eyes. Joe was squinting as if he was aiming a gun at a target. Rex could feel his muscles tighten, while his stomach made bubbly noises. He couldn't read Joe's intentions, but they didn't appear hospitable.

"Hey!" shouted Joe. "I got it! I can't believe I didn't see this before." Joe relaxed and started marching back and forth along the pool table using his pool stick as a walker. His head was down and he was pulling on his lips while he appeared to be thinking something out. Rex had jumped when Joe shouted, but when he saw Joe wasn't going to attack him he settled back to leaning on his cue stick. Rex was stalling before his next shot.

Finally, Joe stopped and looked back at Rex. "Why not wait to see how the Yakuza dispose of the body? If we find out what they do with the body, then we'll know the why."

"Nope, I already thought of that," Rex said with a frown and shook his head. "I looked into the files to see how all the bodies were disposed, and they all say they were donated to educational institutions for study. That means they're packed up and closed tight according to Department of Transportation requirements and shipped by an approved carrier service to whatever destination ... normally an educational facility."

"So?"

"Well, we have no legal means of interrupting that carrier service and opening a casket in the middle of who knows where to see what's in there.

"Even if Jesse used her Medical Examiner's credentials to stop the shipment, and we didn't find evidence of illegal doings, you know word would get back to Sheriff Erp and he'd figure out you were digging around in something you weren't supposed to during your vacation."

Joe frowned, but Rex felt he was coming around to his line of reasoning.

"I thought about catching the casket at the receiving point of the shipments to see what the recipients opened. But that wouldn't be any good because we'd need a legal reason and documentation for being there. That would require authoritative approval, and word would get out that we were snooping around.

All of this would be illegal anyway without someone's approval," Rex finished.

Joe sighed in defeat. "So we're back to square one."

"No, now we've covered all the bases, and it's a matter of deciding how to proceed," Rex said with a smile.

Rex shot the thirteen-ball where there wasn't a pocket, but he maintained his smile since he didn't think he left Joe a shot. Joe didn't seem to notice anyway. Rex figured it was Joe's turn to be distracted.

Rex saw he was correct as Joe bent over the cue ball with a glazed look in his eyes, like he wasn't paying attention to what he was doing. After duffing his shot and spreading the remaining balls around, it was Joe's turn to look out the darkening window.

Rex hated doing this to his friend and using his friend's mother in a manner that could prove to be dangerous. He knew how he'd feel if the tables were reversed. Although he didn't remember his mother that well, he remembered Namid to be a lively person. He thought Namid would jump at a chance like this: to help her son, and to save the lives of those who might be murdered if this chain of killings wasn't stopped. Rex decided Joe was being selfish in not allowing Lilly the opportunity to assist, but he'd never force the issue.

Finally, Joe turned from his reflection in the window and marched directly to the bathroom without saying a word. Rex sighed and thought about rearranging the balls on the table to his advantage. He heard the toilet flush before he got around to fixing the game. His mind had slipped away to how it felt to touch Jesse's arm in her wetsuit, and how her face appeared on the way back to the dock with the wind blowing her hair straight back. The tightness in his boxers told him it would be awhile before he was able to use the facilities—for their intended purpose at least.

Rex's hand had slipped into his baggy shorts, and he was playing a little pocket pool, when Joe burst out of the john to say, "Yeah, I can see how it could work."

Rex jumped and asked, "What'll work?" quickly removing his hand from his pocket to use it to cover his mouth as he coughed.

"Using Lilly to snoop around," Joe responded while giving him a strange look as if he guessed what Rex was doing in his shorts.

"Great," Rex said with more exuberance than appropriate. He quickly made for the table and bent over the cue ball to hide his embarrassment. He made an easy shot on the fifteen, and then another on the fourteen as the table started to clear.

Taking a break to sip his beer, Rex asked, "Do you think it's time to involve

Moe? We would be making this sort of a family matter, even though I don't see how Lilly would be endangered in any way."

Joe huffed, turned his back, and began to walk around the pool table. "Just walking into that place is endangering one's life."

"I think a shopping trip would be innocent enough. I could go along as a friend and a non-beneficiary trustee of Lilly's estate. You know, like the way we did the paperwork on Sara's Garden."

"In that case, we would definitely have to involve Moe, since Moe would be an obvious trustee to Lilly's estate. But I don't think me showing up with Moe would be such a good idea. The less the Yakuza see Moe and I together the better. We don't need them associating Moe with law enforcement, even though they must know about our relationship."

"Then I could go along as a friend of the family on vacation who had nothing better to do, and whose only interest is to see that things are done right for Lilly."

Again, Joe blew out his cheeks and huffed. "I can see how this would be a way to go, but I'm not sure we would see anything that would be of use to the case. I mean, they're not going to do anything illegal while we're there, especially if they realize I'm a deputy of Maui County."

"Yeah, but at least we could learn how their embalming process is done, and see where they do it. We could learn something that might give us an idea what they're doing with these bodies and why they need a body every three weeks to a month," Rex implored.

Joe looked at the floor still huffing and puffing, so Rex continued. "It's not like they'd ever consider Lilly a candidate for murder. All the victims so far have been fragile, weak, and probably drugged during a bar pickup scenario. Lilly doesn't fit into any of their criteria."

"Yeah, but Rex, we're talking about my mother here. If our places were reversed, would you send your mother into a situation knowing you were endangering her life?"

Rex understood how hard of a question this was, so he didn't respond immediately. "Well, I was just thinking about that. It's a rhetorical question to begin with, and I hardly knew my mother, but from what I remember, I'd say she'd do it. Namid was a believer in life and creating life, and I think Lilly is as well. She might jump at a chance to assist in the ending of this murder spree.

"You have to respect a person's age, their wisdom, and their sight, Migisi once told me, and Lilly might see something all of us are missing."

Joe shrugged his shoulders. "I guess there's only one way to find out. But we better have a good plan of action before we even bother her."

Rex bent over the table. "Eight ball in that corner there." After banking the eight ball off the bumper with the confidence of a pro, they both watched as the black Cyclops smoothly rolled into the appointed pocket as intended. "Game," said Rex with a smile.

"Damn, I've been hustled," complained Joe.

Rex continued to grin.

# CHAPTER FOURTEEN

Monday morning came to the world as usual, but for Rex, the Maui sunrise always seemed more special. It was time for Ester Gomez to visit Sara's Garden, and the morning was always extra special for Rex when he came to the garden. The foyer of the converted church had become a lobby where pictures of many smiling faces were hanging on the walls. The pictures were of children and women that had stayed at Sara's Garden. Many of the women and children in these pictures had continued happily with their lives.

Although the lobby appeared cheerful, Rex was always reminded of Sara. When Rex saw the pictures of the smiling faces he felt gratification knowing he'd assisted in putting those smiles on those faces. Rex hurt because Sara's picture wasn't among those smiling faces that moved on to happier times and places.

Rex entered with Joe, Jesse, and Ester, and they were greeted by the Reverend Mother Makuahine, the holy woman who ran the daily activities of the Garden. Rex was happy to see the Rev. Mother. He wasn't sure why. She seemed older than God Himself, and more Holy as well (at least to Rex). Maybe it was the fighter he saw in her. Rex knew the Rev. Mother had been born on Maui and had never left the island as she had dedicated her life to helping the homeless and abused. Rex trusted her judgment and her ability to run the Garden the way she saw fit. Rex knew Mother Makuahine's managerial skills exceeded his own, and Sara's Garden may have gone bankrupt if not for Mother Makuahine's wizardry at stretching a dollar.

The Rev. Mother was in her eighties. She might have been even older but no one knew for sure, nor did anyone have the nerve to ask her when she was born. Her age was another concern to Rex, since he knew there was a need to replace her directorship of the Garden.

As Rex looked upon the Rev. Mother Makuahine, he saw her face was creased with smile lines, and she returned his gaze with beady black eyes that revealed none of her thoughts. She had a large flat nose that overshadowed teeth that were brown with coffee stains. Rex had no idea what color her hair might have been beneath the white cloth covering her head, and she was always dressed in white with long sleeves and a baggy gown that fell to just above the floor. Rex glanced down from her intense look and saw she still wore block heel black shoes that he thought she must shine every night since there was never a mark on their leather. The Rev. Mother's shoulders seemed more bent to Rex than the last time he saw her and her back was more bowed; but she still moved with the lightness of a creeping house cat, and seemed ready to outrun the quickest child in her care.

"Rex, how good it is to see you." Mother Makuahine smiled.

"It's good to be here," Rex said as he took Rev. Mother Makuahine's hand into both of his. Mother Makuahine moved on to greet Joe and Jesse. Rex looked around the lobby.

"This is Ester Gomez. She's the one Rex spoke to you about on the phone." Joe introduced Ester to the Mother Makuahine.

"Pleased to meet you, Rev. Mother," said Ester in a quiet and formal tone.

Mother Makuahine grasped Ester's hand warmly. Rex had noticed that Mother Makuahine always looked into the eyes of the newcomers, as if she was searching their minds. She did this with Ester. Rex always wondered what ran through Mother Makuahine's mind during her searching looks. Rex had never been able to read Mother Makuahine's expressions, and this was an enigma to him. He could never discover her thoughts.

"I'm so happy to meet you, Ester," Mother Makuahine started. "Joe and Rex have told me what they know about you, and I see now how you must have shocked Rex on the airplane."

The Rev. Mother reached out with her gnarled hand, and gently pushed back Ester's hair so she could get a better look of Ester's face.

"You bare a striking resemblance to the girl for which this place was named. Although, I've only seen Sara in photographs."

"Here, look at this painting." Mother Makuahine directed everyone to the large portrait of Sara which hung in the center of the lobby.

"She's beautiful," gasped Ester.

"As are you," Rex whispered as he came up behind Ester and gently massaged her shoulder.

"Can you see the resemblance now?" Rex asked.

"Sí ... I can see that we look similar, but I'm nowhere as beautiful as her."

"Well, you're underestimating your beauty, and I think the artist kind of spruced up Sara. You're just as beautiful as she was." Rex smiled.

"What a shame such beauty was taken away so early in life," said the Rev. Mother as if she was reading Rex's mind.

"Well.... let's not dampen this bright day and the welcoming with sorrow," continued Mother Makuahine. "Let's give you the grand tour and you can decide for yourself if wish to stay. We also have employment counselors if you're able to work, and of course there are counselors if you just want to talk to someone."

Mother Makuahine ushered everyone down the hallway to show them the leisure area. This was a large room with comfortable couches and chairs and an old TV hanging in one corner. There were two nuns with two women and four children playing in the room.

"Will you be volunteering your services, Dr. Achew?" asked Mother Makuahine.

Some of the children and the two women were watching the group with obvious interest. Rex thought this was perfect timing on Mother Makuahine's part since one woman had a swollen face and a black eye, and one of the children's arms was in a cast. Rex felt his stomach muscles tighten and adrenaline run through his veins since he knew the stories on both families. These were repeat cases many times over and Rex wondered if maybe he wasn't in the wrong business.

"Yes, of course," Jesse said.

*Who could resist such painful looking pleas? Mother Makuahine certainly knows what strings to pull*, thought Rex.

"In fact, that's part of the reason I came out today. To see the facility again and talk about what services I could provide."

"The sisters are well-trained in first-aid, and they won't bother you with any whim. But occasionally we get a case where the battering has been bad or one of the children is sick and they would call you on those things," Mother Makuahine spoke quietly.

"If the State knows there's a qualified physician on call, then their funding is much more generous. That's an important point since we couldn't operate much of a shelter without the county and state funding. It also gives the shelter some legitimacy which helps in raising funds. Fund-raising is one of our primary efforts."

"And you'll find Mother Makuahine is a real campaigner when it comes to fund-raising," said Rex. "I'm kind of surprised she didn't have more children down here begging at your feet."

"Oh Rex ..." huffed Mother Makuahine. "I'm not that bad. But I'm glad to hear we have a physician to replace Meat ... Oops ... Dr. Cook." Mother Makuahine put her hand over her mouth and her whole body shook with suppressed laughter. Having regained control of herself, Rev. Mother continued. "Rex ... you're going to get me into trouble yet." She laughed. "But he did give me the ... what was it you called it, Rex?"

"The willies?" Rex returned.

"That's it ... the willies. Meat gave me the willies, too. Lord save me, but for all the good that man did here, I can't deny I'm happy to have you replace him, Dr. Achew," said Mother Makuahine.

Joe and Ester looked at Rex to say Gesundheit, but he just stood there and grinned.

"Please call me Jesse," invited Jesse.

They toured the entire facility, spending most of their time in the garden that was surrounded by the dorm. It was a quiet and peaceful place with a trickling brook that contained twenty-pound gold fish and a few cod swimming under the flowering lily pads in a shallow pond.

Rex thought Lilly Tweedy had it right when she'd said that one could stay here forever. Rex simply enjoyed taking off his shoes and walking in the cool grass with the sea breeze blowing over the wall.

By chance, Ester was introduced to some Hawaiian girls about her age, and miraculously they hit it off at once. Ester was full of questions for the girls. They ogled at Rex and whispered secrets back and forth before they all broke out in a giggling fit. Rex had to pull Ester along when it was time to continue the tour.

The nun involved with employment placement was also there. She guaranteed Ester that if Ester didn't mind working for minimum wage, there were two or three places that would take her today.

Lahaina was a town that lived by its serving class with its many restaurants and clothing stores. Ester could work whenever she wanted; in the meantime she could stay at the Garden for a while. But the nuns stressed that those who were able to work, should work. Rex knew not only did work keep one's mind occupied, but it also helped build self-esteem and confidence. These were two things he knew battered women and children needed the most.

During the tour Ester was often close to Rex's side. She would even hold onto his arm. Rex didn't resist this closeness, but he knew they were coming to a hard parting.

Before coming to the Garden, Rex had taken Ester into town and bought her some clothes and a suitcase. Those purchases were still in the car, but it was Rex's hope Ester would stay here. The Tweedys were nice people, but Rex knew they couldn't start taking in the homeless whenever they saw them. Everyone had their own lives to lead.

Returning to the lobby, Rex said, "Well, Ester... what did you think? You have to start someplace."

"I have money. I could stay at a hotel," Ester said lamely.

"That would be sort of a waste. Why not stay here until you have work and an apartment somewhere? Besides, if you stayed at a hotel, I wouldn't have time to see you every day. I spend a good deal of time here when I'm in town." Rex tried to compromise.

Fortunately, Rex saw that Ester appeared to have made her decision, so he didn't have to do too much selling. "You promise to visit every day?" pouted Ester. Rex thought the pout was a put-on.

"Or call if I'm out of town." Rex smiled.

"Come on, Ester, we'll get your stuff out of the car while Dr. Achew and Rex get things squared away with Mother Makuahine," said Joe, pulling Ester towards the door. Rex was never so thankful for having Joe around as just then.

After they'd left, Jesse and Mother Makuahine made their arrangements and exchanged phone numbers. Rex was elated since he'd gotten two worries off his mind. Now he wouldn't have to babysit Ester, and they'd found a doctor to replace Meat.

*Wow, what a gratifying morning*, thought Rex.

Then Mother Makuahine pulled Rex to the side for a moment.

"I see you're still carrying a heavy burden, Rex," said the Rev. Mother.

When Rex didn't respond, she drew his eyes to hers, and said, "Let it go, Rex. There's nothing more you can do for Sara in this life."

Still Rex didn't respond. He wasn't sure how to respond.

"That's evil work you're doing, Rex, and one of these days, evil will take you if you let it."

"What am I supposed to do, just stop?" Rex glared down at her as anger rose within him.

"Yes!" croaked Mother Makuahine. "Stop now while you still have a life. A life that can give in so many other ways. You've been hunting the Devil's children for too long, Rex. Doesn't this Sara lookalike say anything to you? You couldn't save Sara then, but you've saved this Sara now, just like you've saved so many others. How much more does it take to show you that?"

Again Rex said nothing but looked at his feet.

"I hate to ask this, but are you starting to enjoy the killing?"

"NO!" Rex shouted. His shout echoed in the lobby and disturbed the others. Rex softened his voice. "No, I'm not."

The hardness in the Rev. Mother's face softened as did her tone. "Why don't you close up your business in Michigan and move to Maui? You know we could always use your help here. There's always work for a man's hands in this old place."

"But I still have my father and grandfather back home who need my care, although they claim they don't," Rex said while nodding his head, knowing Mother Makuahine was right. "I've been thinking about that a lot recently. You've hit upon a sore spot right now that needs consideration."

For a moment they stood in silence. The Rev. Mother had her head bowed as if she was looking for whatever Rex was kicking about on the floor. Her arms crossed her thin chest in a defensive manner.

Finally, the Rev. Mother looked up at Rex's face again before saying, "You're a good man, Rex Bana. The Lord put you here for a purpose, so you think about it. I won't pester you anymore."

They returned to the group, and Ester said her goodbyes for now. "You promise to visit every day?" Ester asked tearfully.

Rex gave her a hug, and said, "I'll visit you, but I imagine before too long you're gonna be too caught up in your own life to have time to see me. And don't go running off without telling me where you're going."

"Never," Ester said as she reached up and gave Rex a little kiss on the cheek. "I thank the good Lord for bringing you to me, and I hope He continues to watch over you."

"So do I. I'll see ya tomorrow, my little chickadee." Rex turned and left before anyone else said anything. Geez ... It was getting hard to get out of places without some emotional tie-up.

# CHAPTER FIFTEEN

After leaving Sara's Garden, Rex, Jesse, and Joe returned to Tweedy Manor. Lilly was waiting with lunch, and Rex wanted to show Lilly her fine cuisine would not be wasted a second time. Rex was a man who enjoyed few home cooked meals.

They sat down to a meal that began with mushrooms stuffed with crabmeat and topped off with cheese melted to a light brown crown. Next, Rex enjoyed a thick swordfish steak grilled to perfection and covered with a macadamia nut sauce. As a salad, Rex ate an entire pineapple chilled and chopped into large chunks. This was all washed down with a fruity Chardonnay with which Rex was unfamiliar. Not that he was a wine connoisseur, but when he asked Joe about the label, Joe spit and spewed a response Rex didn't understand and he didn't care to ask again. Rex ate his swordfish with relish, but the wine's aftertaste made him think of smelly feet squishing sour grapes in an old wooden bucket. He was too embarrassed to ask about the vintage.

Later Rex searched the trash and found an empty wine bottle on which the label was handwritten in a difficult to decipher scribble. Rex managed to make out it was a wine made on Maui in 1999. After burping, Rex imagined two huge Polynesian women giggling while holding their skirts up to their hairy armpits as they stomped grapes with their bare feet in a wooden wash tub.

Just as Rex surmised, Joe wouldn't leave the table without dessert. Lilly brought out his favorite, a huge bowl of homemade chocolate pudding that had been chilled overnight to give it the proper consistency. Again, Rex packed it in before he walked away from the table feeling as if he was ready to pop. He decided it was a good thing he'd eaten the pineapple—things would pass along easier this evening.

Conversation shifted away from politics as they began to clear the table, and Lilly asked, "Jesse, nani wahine, pretty woman, when you going to settle down and hoʻâo, marry, one of my boys so I worry no longer about them?"

"Mâmâ!" Joe yelped.

Lilly maintained her gaze on Jesse. Jesse looked down at her feet in shyness before taking a sideways glance at Rex.

"Ha! Silly me. I must be makaʻalâ in my old age." Lilly let out a gale of laughter before heading to the kitchen.

Eventually, Rex, Joe, and Jesse made it down the hall, through the living room, and into the game room. Jesse continued to look at the floor as if there was something special there to find.

Once in the game room, Rex started to rack up the balls while Joe asked, "Anyone for a beer?"

Rex yelled to the affirmative, but Jesse remained silent.

Joe stopped in mid-stride and spun back to Jesse with a questioning expression on his face. Jesse looked up and smiled in a non-laughing manner, then asked, "Got anything stronger?"

"Sure," Joe responded. "I can whip up a pitcher of martinis if you'd prefer. I make some good ones."

"Sounds perfect." Jesse nodded. Joe made off to prepare his concoction.

"Joe's the perfect host and bartender," Rex commented. He gazed at Jesse for a moment to discern her preoccupation. "Has Joe filled you in as to why we asked you to lunch?" Rex asked before going back to separating the balls for a game of nine-ball.

"Huh?" Jesse asked after a moment as if she'd been lost in thought. "Ah, no." She moved around the table and parked her butt on the table right next to Rex and went about studying her nails as if they were a new science project.

Rex stopped playing with the balls and caught Jesse's green eyes that appeared a little browner as she looked up. He saw something there that confused him. There was an expectant look, like a puppy looking at him for its next meal. It was a wanting look which confused Rex in a way that he had no experience on how to respond.

Rex thought he'd like having Jesse up to his room where they could bounce their heads off the headboard for awhile, but he knew he could never do that in the Tweedy's house, especially while Jesse was wearing this hungry puppy expression.

Bending over and leaning on the pool table to hide his thoughts, Rex asked, "You know our next move has got to be looking around the Maui Funeral Home?"

"Ah, right," Jesse said in a distracted manner. Rex wondered if she was thinking of the same thing he was about doing some noggin knocking.

"Have you thought of how we can do that legally?" Rex continued.

"I haven't come up with anything, no," Jesse said with a slow sigh.

"Joe and I talked about it last night, and we think the only way to do it would be for us to take Lilly in to shop for her funeral," Rex said candidly.

"What?!" Jesse exclaimed coming back to life.

"What's going on?" Joe asked coming back into the game room with a glass pitcher of martinis on ice that had an island of olives floating on top. He set it up on the bar before returning to the fridge to get a Strohs for Rex.

"I was just telling Jesse about taking Lilly on a shopping trip," Rex stated. Joe handed Rex the Strohs before returning to pour two martinis.

There was a silence while they waited for Joe. As an afterthought he put out a box of toothpicks so no one had to gulp for their olives.

"You can't be serious," Jesse said to Joe. "Thank you very much." Jesse nodded as Joe handed her a martini glass complete with spiked olives. She looked long into her glass before bringing the drink up to her lips for a tentative sip. Nodding, she plucked out the olives and gulped the martini in one tilt. Jesse's eyes flew open and she pounded her breastbone before popping the olives into her mouth with a look of satisfaction on her face. "Ah ... perfect," she said in a husky voice.

"Told ya I make a good martini." Joe smiled before taking a mild sip of his own. "Ah, that hits the spot. An excellent idea, Jesse."

"A couple of lushes," Rex mumbled before tipping back his long neck and downing half the bottle.

"Rex convinced me that taking Lilly was the only way to get a look see around the funeral home short of breaking and entering," Joe started.

Jesse headed back to the bar to grab the martini pitcher. "That was my idea. Breaking in, that is. But Mr. Bana pooh-poohed that notion right off."

"'Pooh-poohed'?" Rex asked. He was surprised by Jesse's formal use of his name. It felt to him like he'd either missed or done something wrong, and now he was the one that was pooh-poohed.

"And I agree with him there," Joe said. "We can't be doing anything illegal to discover evidence we'd never be able to use in court."

"We figured you making an appointment to introduce yourself as the new

M.E. wouldn't get us anything since they'd hide anything illegal knowing that you were coming," Rex said to Jesse.

"Yes, I'd thought of that too," Jesse agreed as she returned with her martini.

"So that leaves us with going on a shopping trip. If we go unannounced, while they are working on the Rogers' corpse, we might see something that tells us what they're doing." Rex finished his beer.

"How are we going to know when they'll have the Rogers' corpse out to be working on it?" Jesse asked before sipping her drink, shaking her head, and putting it back on the bar.

"That's where you come in," said Rex. "How long does it take a mortician to prepare a body? We need to pick your brains to get the inside scoop on dead person preparation."

Jesse grabbed her glass for another sip.

"Yeah, and it looks like we better do our picking quickly before your brains are pickled," Joe remarked. "What's with you, Achew? You have been acting squirrely since Lilly asked her nonsense question about marrying one of her boys. She was just kidding."

"No, your mother has a keen sense of what is going on around her, and I don't think she would joke around about something like that to me. But that's beside the point. How long does it take a mortician to prepare a corpse, you asked. That all depends on what they're planning for the corpse—"

Rex interrupted. "All the files say the corpses were donated to science or education. So we need to know what the mortician would do to a body to prepare it for scientific examination."

"If that's what they're really doing with them. When we close a file as dead—"

"Joe!" cried Jesse.

"Oops." Joe slapped his hand across his mouth and then dropped it. "When the final disposition of a John or Jane Doe is decided, the Sheriff's Office doesn't check up on the disposal just to make sure the body really went to some university or whatever. So they may be doing something else with the cadavers we've never checked on."

"That's a good point. Doesn't Sheriff Erp have to sign off for his department with these John and Jane Does?"

"Yup." Joe smiled. "That would mean Erp has to know something about what's happening with these stiffs."

"And he acted so surprised when we brought all these files to his attention," Jesse stated sarcastically.

"Okay," Rex said. "Go on with what you were saying, Jesse."

"Well..." Jesse thought for a moment. "If a mortician is preparing a body for study, that would involve replacing the body's decaying fluids with fluids meant to preserve body tissue. But since Rogers was autopsied, as were all the others, most of the preliminary work will have been done for the mortician. Things like removing the brain, and what blood we could get was withdrawn to test for toxicity, and we would have removed, weighted, and examined all the major organs, and so on. Naturally, we put it all back in basically the right order."

Jesse's comments had Rex turning green, even though he knew she was just joshing with her direct words and facial expressions.

"Since most of the work is already done, and there's no need for cosmetic work, it'd probably take less than an hour for an experienced mortician to prep the cadaver," said Jesse.

Rex sucked down the rest of his beer, but he decided that was it for now if he was going to remain clearheaded. Jesse had stopped for a moment and appeared to be thinking, so Rex and Joe remained quiet.

Finally, Rex lost patience and asked, "When do you think the mortician would start on the body after it's delivered?"

"That's what I was thinking about right now," Jesse started. "The work load on Maui is minimal, and Joe, you said they had two morticians. Still, it's possible they'll wait for a time after delivery. Rogers had no relatives. The medical examiner and Sheriff's Offices have signed it off as a drown victim not pending further investigation, and then they're free to wait as long as they want. The county will have paid for the services, and the timing is indefinite as long as the body doesn't become a health hazard."

"But since we believe they're doing something illegal with the body, more than likely, they'll do their work immediately," Joe pointed out.

"Yes, that stands to reason," Jesse said. She returned to the bar for another sip on her martini.

"You say the Rogers' body is ready to go over to the funeral home whenever we're ready?" Joe asked.

"Yupper." Jesse responded with a grin. She'd done her job.

"Then I think it's time to call in Lilly," Rex said. "Joe, you might find Lilly's in a bigger hurry to go back to Honolulu than you think." Rex laughed and Jesse smirked, but Joe didn't appear amused as he left to get Lilly.

# CHAPTER SIXTEEN

Lilly entered the game room still drying her hands with a dishtowel, and wearing the smile Rex had come to expect on a Tweedy. Rex noticed for the first time that when Lilly unpinned the hair which had been rolled up to her neckline, a braided pony tail as thick as a woman's forearm was released and cascaded to her expansive rump. Her hair was lava black intertwined with grayish stripes.

"Whoa. Now there's some pretty hair," Rex commented. After the boob incident at the airport, Lilly still eyed Rex with suspicion whenever he expressed any comments about her appearance. Rex was finding that this incident was becoming legendary already, and he felt humbled whenever Lilly was present.

"What is so important that Rex needs to talk to me now? Did my boy do something wrong?"

Lilly walked around the pool table to meet Rex. Rex had been sitting on a barstool, but he stood up since he'd never forgotten the feeling she was going to attack him. Lilly had pressed her lips together, making her smile disappear. She glared defiantly at Rex.

"No. In fact, Joe should be commended for his courage while acting on a case no one else would take," Rex stated as he returned Lilly's glare.

This put the smile back on Lilly's face.

"I need to ask you for a favor," Rex started.

"As I said before, 'Koʻu hale ko kauhale', my house your house. You do not need to be nervous about asking me a favor," Lilly said.

Rex's nervousness had nothing to do with asking Lilly a favor. He noticed that Jesse and Joe were hovering in the background and not providing any support.

Rex started pacing. "Lilly, we, I, need you to assist in this case that we're working."

"What?!" Lilly exclaimed.

"We'll explain the whole case to you, but basically we need an elderly person to go into the Maui Funeral Home to shop for their funeral—ah, that'd be you."

"Rex!" Joe bellowed. Rex had gone straight for the throat. He didn't sugarcoat his words well.

"While you keep the home personnel occupied, I can look around to see what illegal activities they might be doing," Rex stated bluntly.

Rex stopped and was looking at Lilly when he made his statement. Lilly didn't say anything, but she dropped her eyes from Rex's; the corners of her mouth were straight, but her lips didn't disappear. Lilly seemed to be thinking about what Rex was saying for a moment.

"Is that all?" Lilly asked.

"No, that's not all," Joe said coming over to face his mother. "We believe the funeral home is really a headquarters for a Japanese crime operation that has committed fourteen murders over the last year or so. Basically, Rex wants to snoop around while you and I price caskets."

"So there's potential danger to your life if you do this," Jesse was quick to point out.

Lilly tilted her head with a quirky smile and looked Rex up and down as if she might be judging him for the fit of a straightjacket. Rex was tempted to tilt his head to the same angle as Lilly's and stick out his tongue—the moment passed.

"Sure," Lilly said while straightening her head. "Is that what all this tight air is about—you asking me to shop for my own funeral?" Lilly shrugged her shoulders and held out her palms as if it was no big deal to her.

"Tell me when you want to go so I can make myself presentable." Lilly laughed and left the room.

The game room went silent and Rex sat down like a deflating balloon. He was amazed not only at how calmly Lilly had taken his request for her to sit on the hot seat, but also how perfect and unaccented her English became when she was serious. There was far more to Lilly Tweedy than a wide girth and platoon-sized flat feet.

"Geez," Joe huffed while puffing out his cheeks.

"No kidding," Jesse said, returning to the bar, retrieving her martini, and gulping it down as she had done with the first one.

Rex grinned at Joe in a satisfied manner as if to say, "I told you so."

Rex knocked around the pool balls while Joe and Jesse recovered from Lilly's easy capitulation. Rex was mostly eyeing Jesse and not paying attention to what he was knocking around.

"Well, now we have to do a little planning so we don't waste this opportunity," Rex said to break up the moment of contemplation.

Neither Joe nor Jesse offered any immediate responses so Rex continued. "Do either of you have an idea of the layout to the funeral home?"

Jesse shook her head. "I haven't had a chance to go into the place much less meet the principals that operate it."

Rex nodded as if seeing how that could be.

"Well I can't say the same," Joe replied. "Before Jesse came to me with these files, one of my pet peeves was discovering what the Yakuza were doing. So I've got a whole file on the place. Since I work in the county building, I even went down to the Building Department and got the final blueprints on the home itself. I also have the names of the officers of their corporation with their local tax forms from their last two years showing their employment numbers, their names, etcetera. Those parts aren't current, and I'll have to stop down to the office to get them. That part might be a little sticky since Erp is bound to find out that I'm in the office and likely will want to know what I'm doing there on my vacation."

"Can't you simply go down there later in the evening when he's not in the office?" Jesse asked.

"Yeah, I suppose I could do that. I'd still prefer no one knew I came to the office, and I'm going to have to sign in to get to my floor."

"Isn't there any back way? I mean, we're talking about the county building and that place is huge," Rex said.

"Why don't you tell me where to look in your office?" Jesse asked. "The building is free access to county personnel, especially someone with my credentials. They should let me in with no questions asked. I could go in during shift changes like I was looking for you. I've done that enough times in the past where no one should ask any questions," Jesse pointed out.

"Yeah, I guess that's a good enough plan. I'll have to give you the combination to my desk safe however, and that could be the sticky part. If someone caught you going through my personal files there might be some eyebrows raised," Joe said.

"She could tell them she was retrieving information for you so you didn't have to come down to your office on vacation," Rex pointed out.

"That might work, but Erp might still find out and suspect something," Joe answered.

"Oh, let him find out. It's not like the close relationship Joe and I have is secret," Jesse said as she waved off the whole thing as if it was nothing. She eyed her empty martini glass.

It was going on four-thirty in the afternoon by the time Rex, Jesse, and Joe finished their plans. They decided the best time for Jesse to enter the county building was at five-o'clock when the secretarial staff was going home and the patrol persons were changing shifts. Rex hoped that any intruders to Joe's office would be lost in the shuffle.

"I have the county Bronco, so why don't I drive?" asked Jesse.

"I get shotgun," Rex said. He jumped at the chance for the priority seat in the Bronco.

"I think I'd prefer the rear seat anyway, Rex. It has a wider bench seat," Joe grumbled.

"You've obviously never tried to get into the backseat of a Bronco." Rex laughed.

"This Bronco is particular since it's been modified to carry a gurney. Joe, given your dimensions, it would be easier if I opened the back and let you crawl in and play the cadaver." Jesse smirked.

Rex would remember the drive to the county building as one of his more memorable experiences in his life. First, there was the concern Jesse had been drinking too much, but Rex figured two gulped martinis after the huge lunch wasn't enough to impair Jesse's driving ability. He had different ideas by the time they got to the county building.

Rex knew the county building was in Wailuku, and the only road to Wailuku was Highway 30. Driving down Highway 30 involved many thirty and forty-five degree turns as it snaked around a volcano the Hawaiians had named Puu Kukui. Rex was anxious traveling Hwy 30 at any time, since on the land side one had to be wary of falling rocks from the volcano. On the other side one tried not to drive off the steep cliffs into the Pacific Ocean. It wasn't a trip for the lighthearted or those who got carsick. He was about to find out it wasn't a trip to be riding in a vehicle driven by Jessica Achew.

Rex decided Jesse's driving problems stemmed from her inability to talk and drive at the same time. Her driving coordination was probably horrible to begin with, but after drinking it got worse since now she felt the need to talk to everyone.

Joe crawled in the back of the Bronco where he sat on a half-seat that normally folded up to make room for a gurney. Rex strapped into a rickety captain's chair in front that might have been comfortable in the 1980s. Rex discovered the swivel lock to the chair didn't work, and that if he tucked in his knees to avoid the console, there was enough room for him to twirl around and around as if on a merry-go-round.

Rex might have enjoyed this seat if it hadn't been for the smell of formaldehyde coming from the seat cushions. The smell reminded him of the autopsy room and death which were things Rex didn't care to think about with Jesse talking and driving at the same time.

Rex saw Joe was confined with his head behind the Captain's chair, so Joe's view through the windshield was blocked. The large side windows of the Bronco had been replaced with paneling so a cadaver on a gurney didn't become the main attraction at a stop light. When Rex glanced out the rear window, he found it was either tinted or too dirty to see much of anything.

Rex knew they were in trouble when Jesse rounded the turn out of the Tweedy's neighborhood. She was going twenty miles over the speed limit and made a sharp left turn on an orange stoplight to get onto Highway 30.

"Weren't we supposed to stop back there?" Deputy Tweedy wanted to know. Then he yelled, "Ouch," as his head was thrown against the side of the truck during the sharp left turn.

"Oh boy," Rex muttered, and he buried his face in his hands.

"Hey, what's going on up there?" Joe wanted to know, but Jesse punched the accelerator to roll Joe to the back of the Bronco—there wasn't a seatbelt back there since the half seat wasn't meant to be used while the vehicle was moving.

Jesse pushed in a CD to drown out any further talk. Loud instrumental music shook the closed windows of the truck from a seven-speaker sound system.

"What's this?" Rex asked. He reached over and turned down the stereo system so he could hear a response.

"It's the overture to the movie *Armageddon*, from back around the year-

2000. Remember when everyone was terrified the world would end and everyone would die?" Jesse yelled with a smile. She leaned over and turned up the volume again while swerving down the wrong lane of the highway.

"How appropriate," Rex mumbled. He covered his eyes again.

"Isn't this a great sound system?" Jesse hollered after she turned down the system enough to be heard.

"Just dandy," Rex replied. Behind him, Rex could hear Joe yelling about something, but he couldn't understand what it was and he lost interest as Jesse took a curve a little wide. Rex peered out his window to see the waves of the Pacific smashing on huge rocks a hundred feet directly beneath him.

"Yahoooo!" Rex yelled. No one seemed to notice as they got back onto the highway with the Bronco's big mag tires spinning and shooting up the gravel from the shoulder.

"I put it in myself," Jesse yelled.

Rex turned down the volume again and asked, "What?!" His voice cracked.

"I put in the stereo, silly," Jesse shouted after turning toward Rex. When Jesse turned her head to talk, the Bronco slid into the next lane and began to play chicken with a loaded pineapple truck.

"Haaaaa!" Rex yelled. He tried to lunge from his seat but was stopped by the safety-belt as he jerked the steering wheel toward him.

"Hey, who's driving here?" Jesse asked while she slapped Rex's hand off the steering wheel. Rex wanted to ask that same question.

Joe's head and shoulders popped up in between the two captain chairs. Rex saw his partner's eyes were wide and his face was sweating. "What's going on up here?" Joe asked.

Jesse was startled by Joe's appearance and looked down at Joe while allowing the Bronco to veer over into the other lane again. Rex saw Joe's mouth drop open in a silent scream while his eyes widened until they appeared they might roll out of his head. Rex turned to follow Joe's view. Looking through the windshield Rex saw they were going head to head with an eighteen-wheeler, and they were so close he could see the dragonflies and other bugs squished into the front grill of the MACK. His eyes moved higher to focus on the huge **O** on the truck driver's face. This time Jesse recovered in enough time to swerve back to her lane, but it was so close the wind blast from the truck slammed the Bronco onto the shoulder again. Rex recovered to look at Jesse, and he was amazed to see she was bee-bopping to Aerosmith rocking to "I Don't Want To Miss A Thing," as if her driving was nothing unusual.

Rex thought Jesse was doing a decent job of trying not to miss a thing herself. As they sped down a straightaway with nothing coming from the other way, Rex and Joe exchanged glances which asked if they were still alive.

They came upon the part of Hwy 30 which Rex feared the most even when he was driving. Now Jesse would have to steer the Bronco through the steep curves that began near Papalaua Wayside Park and Lookout Point. Lookout Point was a tourist stop and viewing area on the south side of Hwy 30. Rex knew tourists could park there and view the Maalaea Harbor far below. The site was high enough to see beyond the harbor into the city of Kihei which had been the main tourist hangout on this southwest side of the island before Hwy 30 opened up a faster passage to Lahaina.

There was considerable amount of traffic on Hwy 30, and Rex noticed Jesse enjoyed tailgating cars before slamming on her breaks when she saw the car's taillights flashing red. Rex found this practice a bit unnerving. He was getting a whiplash, and Joe was being slammed into the back of Rex's chair. Rex grasped the handgrip by his head as if he was a mountain climber clutching his lifeline after losing his footing. Rex slammed both feet on imaginary brakes so hard he was surprised he didn't stomp through the floorboard, and having Joe's huge mass hammer the back of his chair gave Rex's legs a workout.

Jesse closed on a train of five vehicles turning and dipping through the tight curves. The car before them was a four door Ford Escort rent-a-car that had seen too many trips down Hwy 30. Its rear-end was crumpled from previous experiences, and its small engine whined like a sewing machine running amok as it struggled up the small hills and then zoomed down the valleys loaded down with four passengers and their luggage.

Rex could clearly see through the Escort's large rear window. He saw there were two youngsters, a boy and a girl in the back seat, and their faces of fear and excitement were obvious as they watched Jesse pull within inches of the rear bumper of the Escort. Rex could see the boy turn his head back and forth as he looked from the snarling grill of the Bronco to the back of his father's head. Then the boy hammered and pushed the back of the driver's seat to get his father to drive faster. There was nowhere for the Escort to go in the traffic and winding curves. Rex watched as the mother leaned back and smacked the boy upside the head to quiet him down.

The girl turned and made faces at Jesse and Rex. She stuck out her tongue; she shoved her fingers up her nose to make her look more like a pig than she already did; she picked her nose and then tried to finger paint on the rear window with boogers; she pulled her eyelids inside out—typical kid stuff. Rex understood why he never wanted kids of his own, and he was beginning to wish Jesse would give the Escort a little knock and pitch it over the cliff into Maalaea Harbor. Then, the little girl yanked her shirt up to her armpits to show off her tiny tits. Rex was shocked beyond words.

If Jesse saw any of this she didn't make any adjustments to her driving habits. Fortunately, they made it through the steep curves and cliffs, and came down onto the lush green plains of Maui that divided its two-volcano crests. These plains were full of sugarcane and pineapple fields. Most of the car train turned right toward the airport while Jesse remained going straight along a wide and even highway. Rex could finally relax his hands which had become stiff and white-knuckled holding onto the seat supports.

Rex was amazed when Jesse finally parked in front of the county building without mishap. He sighed and wiped his brow while thinking, *There are things in this world which one might experience that are more frightening than serial killers.*

Jesse knew where Joe's office was in the investigative staff's general section of the building, and Joe told her the combination to his desk safe. Rex went along just to see Joe's office, and to be Jesse's lookout while Jesse dug through Joe's safe. Jesse took in her empty briefcase to carry Joe's files. This way she could grab the files without anyone seeing what she was taking out of the office.

Jesse was dressed in a casual pair of brown slacks and a loose white sleeveless blouse which showed off her natural beauty and flowing hair. She was a double-take in anyone's eye. Rex was a double-take for opposing reasons. He looked as if he belonged inside one of the county's prison cells. His middle-of-the-back-length black hair, topped with the spiked stitching from his head wound, was a scattered mess after the drive with the open Bronco window. His Native American features, smoldering black eyes, and bull neck gave him a sinister appearance. Rex's paint-splattered cut-offs, flipper sized flip-flops, and muscles abounding out of a black T-shirt that read: "Property of Alcatraz Football Team," made Rex appear as if he was a bouncer at a punk rocker concert looking for some heads to crunch.

Rex figured Jesse and he appeared as an attorney with her convict as they entered the investigative branch of the Sheriff's Office. Rex heard necks cracking as every head in the office swivelled to focus upon them. He counted five green metal desks, but he thought there were twenty people either seated at a desk or walking between the desks wearing serious or bored expressions. On the right side of the office were large windows looking out onto the ocean and the beautiful afternoon. Rex couldn't imagine sitting inside with this kind of view. On the left side were four doors with detective's name plates in the middle. Rex noticed the name plates were set in retractable holders so the names were easily changed. Three of the doors were closed, and Rex didn't see any light coming out of the doorjambs, so he assumed the other three detectives were out of the office.

Rex was most interested in the fourth door. This was the door to Joe's office, and it was open.

In front of them, across from the entrance, were two doors. One door held Sheriff Erp's name plate; the other door simply read "Office." Unfortunately, they would have to walk straight until they reached Erp's office, and then turn left to get into Joe's.

Right off the bat, Rex knew this wasn't going to work as they planned. He almost turned tail and left the job up to Jesse, but the male in him wouldn't allow him to abandon Jesse in case Erp was hovering around somewhere. So trying to look as menacing as possible, he stared down the onlookers and followed Jesse down the aisle between the desks.

The officers and other personnel in the office seemed to know Jesse and they all greeted her warmly. All Rex got was cruel glances before the lookers turned away from his glower.

Rex was surprised to see that Joe's door was open since Joe told them he'd locked it up before going on vacation. He'd left no files in his office so there was no reason anyone should be in there. Rex figured the janitor had left it open or something.

They were making great progress. No one had stopped them to ask what they were doing. They rounded the corner of the aisle and Rex had a chance to pop his head into Erp's office to have a quick glance. He was relieved to see the office was vacant. Rex was impressed with his glance, however. The sheriff's office was nothing like his father's back in Salem Township. This office was enormous in comparison. Two of the walls were glass with a beautiful view of the ocean. There was a twelve foot Marlin sailing across a side wall, and Rex had to admire the huge walnut desk that he figured to be an antique, along with its equally large black leather executive style chair.

Rex would have gone in for a better look, but Jesse didn't hesitate to ogle. She continued across the office to Joe's open door, so Rex had to catch-up.

Rex stepped right behind Jesse, and he was eagerly looking over the top of her head, into Joe's office, when he saw why the door was open. There was a bald and pot-bellied man rifling through Joe's desk. This was no janitor. This guy was wearing pointed and hand-carved leather cowboy boots. He had on worn blue jeans that hung low on his hips, but his pants sagged in the rear because the man didn't have a butt. He wore a blue Levi's work shirt with bucking horses stitched across each shoulder. Rex's first impression was the man belonged in Texas, and they should call him, "dude."

Jesse came to an abrupt halt upon seeing the dude in Joe's office. Rex rammed into Jesse since he was looking at the dude rather than paying attention to where he was going. The dude kneeled with his back to them, showing his crack, as he used a screwdriver in an attempt to force open a desk drawer. So far the dude hadn't noticed them.

Jesse obviously recognized the dude, since she stiffened at the sight of him and Rex heard her whispered oath. Jesse did an about face, and would have rushed out had Rex not been standing in the way. Rex had figured out who this dude was, and he had no intention of letting the dude break into Joe's personal files. Instead, he went on the offensive.

"Sheriff Erp, how nice to finally meet you," boomed Rex as he turned Jesse back around and shoved her into the office.

Sheriff Erp shot up from his squatting position as if his hemorrhoids had been electrocuted. He was so startled he dropped his screw driver and did a little jig on the spot.

Rex pushed his way into the confined office with his right hand out and a cheek to cheek smile that showed all the sincerity of a piranha's grin.

"What kind of asshole scares a person like that," Erp said as he whirled about to face them. Rex saw Erp's balding head was sweating, and he had the face of a chicken. His large pointed nose and sharp chin made a good imitation of a beak. It didn't help that Erp wore glasses that magnified his eyes and he had a tiny mouth with little teeth and wet lips. *This is not a face that could command authority over others, or even threaten them*, Rex thought.

Taking in the rapidly approaching Rex, Erp's eyes grew even larger, and Rex almost broke out in laughter at Erp's expression of confusion and fear.

"I'bid, who'ka," Erp babbled.

Rex grabbed Erp's sweaty hand, gave it a crushing pump, and then threw it away as if it was something out of last month's kitty litter.

"Charley Sims, at your service, sir," Rex bellowed in a loud voice to ensure Jesse caught the change in his name. "Joe Tweedy has told me so much about his esteemed leader."

"Eck. Ur. Esteemed? Leader?" Erp asked, and looked more baffled. This time Rex couldn't hold back his chuckle.

"Yes, sir. He said you were his mentor." Rex grinned as he came around Erp and slapped him on the back hard enough to make Erp stagger forward a step. By this time Jesse appeared to have gotten over her shock at finding Erp in Joe's office and she had to cover her mouth with her hand to hide the giggle.

"Ma—Ma—Mentor?" Erp seemed dumbfounded. He puckered his wet lips to make him even more amusing to gaze at.

"Yes, sir, his leader in all his life's endeavors." Rex wrapped his left arm around Erp and gave him a bone-popping hug. "Shall we step over to your office so I can elaborate? Maybe you can give me some pointers on law enforcement."

Rex push-pulled Erp out of Joe's office while completely ignoring Jesse was there. He stopped just past the entryway and slammed Joe's door closed with Jesse still inside wearing one of her expressions of dismay. Then Rex ushered Erp into Erp's office and slammed his door closed behind them.

Once Rex had Erp alone in his office, he continued to badger the big chicken look-a-like. "You see, Sheriff Erp, I'm an old friend of Joe's and a fellow officer of the law from the fine city of Detroit. I'm here sharing my vacation with my old buddy, and he's done little but talk about you ever since I got here." Rex pushed Erp over to his executive chair and slam-dunked him into his seat.

Erp made no attempt to put off his giant compadre, and Rex thought he appeared to be frightened into capitulation of his sanity. Rex stepped back around Erp's large desk and spotted a cigar box. Not waiting for an invitation, Rex opened the box and grabbed a cigar.

Behind Rex, he heard Erp mumble, "Mentor?"

Rex bit off the tip of the cigar and spit it out with a whack against the far window where it left a splatting spit mark.

"Are you sure we're talking about the same Joe Tweedy?" Erp asked while spinning his chair around to speak to the pacing "Charlie Sims."

"A heavyset Polynesian fellow, about six foot six or so. Three hundred fifty pounds round about," Rex said through clinched teeth that were biting down on his cigar.

"That'd be the Joseph Tweedy I know," Erp agreed, trying to do a southern accent that was obviously false.

"Yes, sir, Joe and me met up at Michigan State University when we was college students," Rex said, sucking on his cigar.

"Joe went to college?" Erp asked as if this was news.

"Why yes, sir. I did think it was a prerequisite to becoming an officer in this here county."

"Ah yes, I suppose it is. Sorry, I haven't kept up with the hiring requirements lately," Erp said thoughtfully.

"And what fine school did you attend, sir?" Rex asked knowing he had Erp here.

"Ah, ah—University of Arizona."

"No kidding? Well, I'll be darned," Rex boomed, scaring Erp again with his loudness. "That's were I did my gratuitous work," Rex continued, wondering if Erp would even catch his missed speech. "I'll never forget my evenings at Harry's bar right there on University Street in front of the Union."

"Ah, yeah. I liked that place as well." Erp gulped.

"Was Harry bartending when you were there?" Rex asked while chewing on his cigar.

"Harry? Sure, all the kids loved Harry."

"Tell me, did Harry ever get that glass eye of his replaced, or was he still popping it out and leaving it in people's beer glasses?" Rex asked with a laugh.

"No, I never saw him do that, so he must have had it replaced." Erp gulped. "But I'll never forget that waitress, Sue," lied Erp.

"Sue? You don't mean Mad Susan Jacobs?" Rex asked putting on a scared face as he continued to pace and gnaw on his cigar.

"Yeah, her last name might have been Jacobs," Erp commented.

"You didn't ever visit her apartment, did ya?"

"Naw, I was never so lucky."

"Wow!" Rex yelled loud enough for it to echo off the walls and make Erp jump in his seat. "Good thing for you," Rex said shaking his head. He spit a chuck of tobacco onto the shiny floor then rubbed it in with his flip-flop.

"Why's that?" Erp asked. He was nervous enough to grab one of his cigars.

"Didn't you hear?" Rex asked with big eyes of astonishment.

"Ah, no, what?" Erp bit off the tip of his cigar and spit it onto the floor.

"Mad Susan was arrested and convicted on fourteen counts of first degree murder!" Rex exclaimed with a look of horror on his face.

"She what?" Erp gagged in astonishment.

"Yeah—I'll never forget the late night I turned down her invitation to join her up at her apartment. She acted like she wanted me so bad it was scary. Drunk as I was I said no thanks.

"The next semester they arrested her after a neighbor complained about the stench coming from her apartment. They found fourteen shriveled cocks and their testes nailed to her closet wall.

"Man, my balls crawled up into my stomach for a month after that," Rex gulped in faked fright.

"I'll bet," Erp said, staring out into space while unconsciously putting his hand on his crotch as if he was checking to see if his dick was still there. The room fell into a scared silence as Rex and Erp were both lost in their separate fears. Rex was worried about what was taking Jesse so long and how much more bullshit he had to conjure, while Erp appeared to be lost in fear of losing his testes in an imaginary lie.

KNOCK! KNOCK! KNOCK!

The banging on the door startled both Rex and Erp out of their lost places.

"It's just me," Jesse said as she popped her head through the door.

"Oh, yeah," Rex commented bounding across the room to grab Erp's hand, and giving it a hearty pump. "Like I said, it's great to finally meet ya."

Rex leaped around the desk and was out the door before Erp could respond. He slammed the door and was ushering Jesse down the aisle in hopes of getting out of the office before anyone else had anything to say to them.

As they neared the end of the aisle, Rex heard Erp's door open and Erp holler, "Sims?! Mr. Charlie Sims?"

Rex came to a skidding halt, and whispered to Jesse, "Get outta here." He pushed her toward the door.

Rex chewed on his cigar and turned around to see Erp stalking down the aisle toward him. Rex couldn't read Erp's expression. He felt every eye in the office was on them with some expectancy as if they were about to witness an execution.

As Erp came within steps of him, Rex heard the office door open and close behind him. That meant Jesse was out with her briefcase and the goods. Erp confused Rex when he cracked a smile and extended his right hand. Rex accepted the sweaty chicken claw as Erp slapped his left hand on top of Rex's. *Yuck, I hate sweaty hand shakes*, Rex thought.

"I want to thank you for conveying Deputy Tweedy's praise," Erp was saying. "Ya know, in the stress of the office setting, sometimes people's true feelings about their fellow workers aren't readily apparent. I'm afraid I've misread Deputy Tweedy's feelings.

"I was under the impression Joe was upset about my filling the Sheriff's

Office over the incumbent sheriff," Erp said with a big smile. Rex noticed Erp had lost his cigar, but a piece of it had stuck to his front teeth making it appear as if he had a gap where one of his front teeth should have been. Rex tried to ignore the problem rather then bursting out in laughter.

Still locking Rex's hand in his, Erp swung his left arm across the office before he continued. "Maybe I've misconstrued the feelings of my other fine employees as well."

Rex pushed his cigar over to the other side of his mouth and bit down. Erp finally dropped his hand. "Well, I just wanted to thank you for airing out Joe's feelings," Erp said as he slapped Rex on the back and appeared to be about to hug him before Rex spun out of the way.

"Yeah, well, I'll convey your appreciation to Joe. See ya!" Rex said. Then he darted out the door before Erp got all huggy and kissy.

Once Rex was out on the steps of the county building he threw the cheap cigar into the trash and he said to himself, "Jimminy Christmas, that man is one of the dumbest people I've ever met."

The ride home was more terrifying than the ride to the county building. Jesse told Joe all the things Rex told Erp about Erp being Joe's mentor and idol in life. Joe moaned all the way back as if he had the greatest of toothaches. Rex smiled and patted Jesse on the arm. "We did it! We actually got in and out of there with no one being any the wiser. We did it!"

Jesse punched Rex in the arm while driving into the other lane and forcing another small rent-a-car off the road.

To Rex, getting Joe's records was more than a minor victory. This modest feat proved they could work as a team and get things done. No one panicked to the degree that they couldn't function. The fact they could work together held the biggest promise for Rex since he knew they'd be doing a lot more of it, and he was accustomed to working alone.

"I just can't believe you told Erp he was my mentor. Rex, what were you thinking?" Joe griped as he unfolded his reduced copy of the Maui Funeral Home's building blueprints out on the pool table.

Rex had gone through one beer. He didn't care if it was a Strohs or not. He was just happy to be alive after Jesse's daring drive back from the county building.

"I was thinking of making your life easier. If Erp thinks you're on his side, so much the better," stated Rex as he went for another beer.

"I'll take one of those," Jesse called after Rex, knowing where he was heading in such a hurry.

"And I still can't believe Erp had the balls to try and break into my desk," Joe said while shaking his head.

"Oh, you should have seen how Rex handled Erp. It was amazing. The man never knew what hit him." Jesse laughed.

"Ha. You didn't hear the stories I told Erp to keep him occupied." Rex giggled as he handed Jesse her beer. "Oh, Joe. Just so you know. You now have a good friend in the Detroit Police Department by the name of Charlie Sims. And Charlie is here vacationing with you right now."

"What the beep-blooper are you gabbing about now?" Joe wanted to know.

"Charlie Sims is the name I used to introduce myself to Erp."

"Why not use Rex Bana?" Jesse asked. "You almost threw me for a loop there."

"Cause I couldn't risk Erp having heard my name before—either from Joe, or some stupid militant magazine article he'd read."

"I'm not sure Erp can read, but that was good thinking anyway. The less he knows about you the better. I don't want him to know what I'm really doing on vacation.

"And you say he didn't even notice you, Jesse? I find that hard to believe," Joe stated.

"I'm sure he knew I was there, but Rex did such a fine job of bullying and baffling Erp he didn't have time to acknowledge my presence."

"Let's put it this way," Rex started. "Erp was left thinking about anything but what he was thinking when we caught him trying to break into your desk. And I imagine he was looking for those files you and Jesse had showed him earlier."

"I don't know what else he could have been thinking, but I wouldn't put it by Erp to be trying to rob my desk for lunch money." Joe sighed.

Rex and Jesse joined Joe at the pool table where he'd unfolded a much used copy of the blueprints of the funeral home. Rex looked down at the blueprints that were shiny under the pool table lights. The copy appeared to have been made of a heavyweight paper that had been laminated. He saw a few food crumbs in the folds. It occurred to Rex the blueprints reminded him of a treasure map—one that had been unfolded, examined, and refolded countless times—someone's obsession.

Rex thought, *Joe's obsessed with the Maui Funeral Home. This is his crusade—his goal in life to getting some wrong righted. Wow, no wonder he's giddy about taking Lilly in there to shop for her funeral.*

"If I take Lilly in there, they'll probably show us around these rooms here," Joe said pointing to the first level of the plan that showed five rooms and a bathroom.

"These three rooms are used for viewing, and that fourth room, the bigger room, is for the mourners to congregate.

"The fifth room in the back, that's the kitchen. The one small room there is the bathroom, and right next to it you'll notice the stairway that leads to the basement. If you can call it a basement.

"I've never been down there, but that's where they do all their mortician work."

"Look at the dimensions of that basement," Rex said. "Let's see—forty-eight feet by forty-eight and a half feet. That's—ah—shit—that's almost twenty-five hundred square feet of floor space. There's enough room down there to fit a good sized house."

"Yeah, and I talked to the contractor who built the place ten years ago. He says they built the basement like a bomb shelter. The walls were made eight inches thick from solid cement. It even has a kitchen and living quarters.

"They put in all sorts of heavy duty wiring and two electrical generators. It's got its own underground air duct system that can be closed off from the inside. Both the generators are diesel powered with their own air intakes. Each one of the generators can produce more electricity than would be needed to power the house itself—including the refrigerators."

"Aw, Joe, always thinking about your stomach." Rex laughed.

"I think he was talking about cadaver storage, Rex," Jesse commented. Rex winked at Jesse to show her he knew that and was just joshing.

"You think they're building a Frankenstein monster down there with these cadavers?" Rex asked halfheartedly. No one laughed.

"Whatever they're doing down there, you can't dig, shoot, or bomb your way into that basement from the outside," Joe noted. "And who knows what kind of building alterations and installations they had done without filing for the building permits."

"I'm a little baffled by why they need the bomb shelter and all this electrical power," Jesse stated with a thoughtful expression.

"I asked the building contractor the same thing, and he said he was curious about that as well. He was told by the architect that it was the Japanese mistrust of Americans, and the Japanese efficient way of being prepared for any accident. As far as the generators go, they said they didn't want the embarrassment of rotting cadavers if there was an extended power outage after a typhoon or something—ya know, like that one that hit Kauai about fifteen years ago. They said it would cause an 'irreparable loss of face'."

"Boloney," Rex grumbled. Joe shrugged.

"And that's the area I want to get down to, huh?" Rex asked after taking a sip of his warming beer.

"My guess is that's where you'd find the Rogers' corpse after delivery," Jesse said.

"See where they have this rear loading dock and elevator that leads to the basement area?" Joe pointed.

"More than likely they'd immediately take the gurney and corpse down to the refrigerators and put it in the deep freeze for a time since the stiff will have started to warm-up during the trip from the morgue," Jesse said.

Rex gave Jesse a disgusted look for her comment about warm stiffs.

"What about this third floor?" Rex asked.

"I've been up there once," Joe said. "You can see how it's four rooms and two bathrooms. The time I was up there I was only able to go into this first room by the stairwell. It's a sophisticated computer and communication room."

"Why the hell does a funeral home need a sophisticated computer room?" Rex asked.

"My thoughts exactly. By sophisticated I mean it contains a good sized mainframe computer that's installed into a side closet area. I would imagine the computer has an equally powerful modem capable of handling a worldwide data communication system.

"There were three separate terminals that were occupied at the time I was there, and these appeared to be personal working cubicles. Ya know, each one had personal pictures and hang-ups, just like anyone's private work space. That's what really surprised me."

"No kidding," Rex said thoughtfully.

"What are the other rooms used for, I wonder?" Jesse asked.

"I'm not sure," Joe answered. "Personally, I feel they're living quarters."

"Why's that?" Rex asked.

"Well, it's really more than a guess. I've staked out that place on a couple of different occasions, and no one arrives or leaves at what would be normal business hours. I've rarely seen anyone leaving for as many people as I saw working there. If you check their parking lot, there are usually no more than three cars at any time, and the tax records show eight employees working there."

"What about the hearses?" Rex asked.

"The Maui Funeral Home has two hearses registered, and they're both kept in this four car garage here." Joe pointed it out on his diagram. "As far as I can tell they have two drivers who also serve as mechanics, as well as other things. I believe the drivers live in these quarters here above the garage."

"Jeepers-creepers, Joe." Jesse laughed. "Is there anything you don't know about this place?"

"Oh, we've only touched the tip of the iceberg of my knowledge about this place and its inhabitants. You might say cleaning out the Maui Funeral Home has become my life's ambition. Just as Rex has his crusade against serial killers, I want to eliminate this cancer that's eating away at my home and haven." Joe spoke these words with determination and vengeance.

"Hail, brother! Rock-on!" Rex hooted as he strutted over to Joe and gave him a high-five. Jesse looked at Rex and Joe like they were crazy. Rex laughed again, and hollered, "Ya gotta love it! Yes, sir, ya gotta love it!"

"Is he normally this nutty?" Jesse asked Joe.

"Hell, woman, I'm only getting warmed up," Rex answered for Joe. "Okay, Joe, let's have the goodies—let's hear about the bad guys. I know you've done checking on the principals operating this place."

"I thought you'd never ask," Joe said as he delicately folded his blueprints and pulled over a thick folder that opened like a harmonica.

Rex saw the harmonica was full and knew Joe truly was obsessed with the Maui Funeral Home. There were eight by ten pictures of Japanese people, of cars and hearses, of the funeral home from every side plus down-the-street views. Rex wasn't surprised to see an aerial view photo of the home. There were copies of tax records, building permits, and fuel bills. But mostly there were pages hand written both loose and stapled. Rex saw Joe's handwriting on most, but there were sheets in another bold script that Rex didn't recognize.

Finally, Joe pulled out eight leather bound, five by seven inch notebooks that appeared to Rex as if they'd been through a few food fights. Rex thought the padded cover notebooks must have cost a relative fortune on a detective's salary. Each notebook had a thick red rubber band around it that appeared to be used as a page marker. Across the middle of each book was a two inch wide strip of athletic tape. Large letters were written on the tape with a thick black magic-marker, but Rex couldn't read the words from his angle. Rex was reminded of diaries when he looked at the books and he wasn't surprised when Joe said that's what they were—in a sense.

As Joe organized his paperwork in preparation for what looked to be a major presentation, Rex noted, "You said you've only done a couple stakeouts on this place—which I assume were on your own time… What's with all this stuff?"

"Yeah, Joe. You been holding out on me?" Jesse asked.

"Jesse, we hadn't connected the Yakuza with your murder case until Rex pointed it out, and like I said, the Yakuza have been a thorn in my side that I've wanted extracted for a long time. You could say I've been doing some studying in extraction in preparation for the big operation. I knew we'd catch them doing something sometime, so let's just say I've been preparing for this moment."

"With your huge thighs that must be a hell of a thorn." Rex chuckled.

"Did you do all this information gathering yourself, on your own time?" Jesse asked. Rex leaned across the pool table so Joe could see he was interested in the answer as well.

Rex saw that Joe was going to evade Jesse's question by shuffling around with his notebooks for awhile and preparing his presentation. He was wearing the expression he always used when he tried to bluff his way to the poker-pot; his head was held back, his eyes were heavily lidded, while his forehead and cheeks remained slack. Rex knew there was no way Joe accumulated all this information himself; this had to be a family operation—Moe had to be involved somewhere, some way.

Still shuffling through his stack of notebooks, Joe pulled out the notebook that appeared to have been used the most. It had more food stains and smudged finger prints on its cover than any of the other notebooks Rex had seen. Rex had to believe the brown smudges were chocolate, but he didn't say anything. They could have been blood, but chocolate was the first thing that came to mind. He did notice the red rubber band in this notebook was nearly on its last page, and the writing on the pages was in a heavy hand with small sloppy scribbles that seemed to be about to cut through the paper.

Rex saw that on the front cover of this notebook was written what he assumed was a Japanese name. Below the Japanese name was written "Black Devil," and Rex wondered if this was a joke. The Japanese name read, "Kuro Akuma."

Joe started. "I believe the leader of this group is the president of the Maui Funeral Home organization. His name is, Kuro Akuma."

Joe pulled off the rubber band and thumbed through the pages as if he needed to remind himself of something from his notes. Rex noticed that some of the notes were in a script from a different hand.

"What's with the 'Black Devil'?" Rex asked.

"That's the basic English translation of Kuro Akuma." Joe laughed. "It's a rough translation someone down at the office gave me."

"You're kidding, right?" Jesse asked.

"Nope. You'll recognize him when you see him. He has a black fu-man-chew mustache, small pointy ears, and slicked black hair that he pulls into a shoulder length ponytail. Kuro stands close to six feet, which one might think is tall for a Japanese descendant, and he always wears black a black suit. Physically, he appears to be in excellent condition." Joe said this while looking down at his notebook on the Kuro, but Rex thought Joe didn't need to look at the notebook.

Then Joe looked down his shirt and said, "I always thought he appeared graceful and smooth in his movements and actions."

"You almost sound like you're in love, Joe," Rex ribbed.

Joe looked up and replied, "No, not in love. I respect the man, however. Just looking at him demands respect for his authority, and if you watch those around him, you'll see they cater to him as if he was a king or something. But I also have to believe that he's capable of being a killer or the mastermind behind the killings—But I don't know what he's capable of doing. My impressions are he's a master of his mind and body. So put him at about your caliber, Rex."

Rex looked down at his feet, unsure how to take this comment.

"I said that as a compliment, Rex. I don't know anyone with your intelligence and mastery when dealing with death."

Rex still didn't appear to take this well and downed the rest of his beer. "Anyone for another beer?" Rex headed for the refrigerator. Since no one responded he brought back three more beers.

Joe continued. "Anyway, Kuro is our first concern. The others are followers trained in their own methods, and lacking Kuro's higher intelligence—I think the organization would collapse without him."

"Here's a good picture of Kuro," said Joe. He pulled out an eight by ten black and white photo of a tall Asian who appeared as Joe described. Rex looked at the blown-up figure and had an instant dislike for the character. Rex didn't like the way he couldn't see the man's eyes. He was obviously Oriental, but his eyelids came down so low that Rex couldn't tell where the man was looking. Rex didn't like not being able to see an enemy's eyes.

"So what's with the 'Black Devil" name?" Jesse asked. "That can't be his real name."

"I would think not, but bear with me as I read off these other names," Joe replied.

"Kuro has a mate in this crime ring. At least, I always positioned her as Kuro's mate, since she gives orders to the others with the same authority as he does.

"Her name is Hi Onna. Simply translated, her name means, Fire Woman.

"Here's a photograph of her I caught last year when she was coming out of the Maui Funeral Home." Joe pulled out another of his eight by ten photos.

"You might not be able to see it in this photo, but she's a tall woman, about five foot eight or so."

"What's wrong with her face? Her cheeks look scarred ... the kind of scars caused by second and third degree burns," Jesse pointed out.

"You might be correct. I don't know her personally, so I don't know what maimed her face. But her face and her hands are the only flesh she shows in public, and she rarely comes out of the funeral home—I mean rarely. I, myself, have only seen her twice, but other people have seen her giving instructions to the others or walking about the funeral home.

"You can't see it in the photograph, but her hands are scarred as well, so I would imagine that most of her body is scarred and that's the reason she doesn't show herself much."

"I wouldn't walk around in public with a face like that either," Rex said with a chuckle.

"Rex! That's mean," Jesse said. She slapped him on the arm.

"Oh, I guess it was a little mean. I'm sorry. But these are killers, Jesse, remember that."

"I wonder why she never had plastic surgery to improve her appearance?" Jesse asked as she rubbed her hands up and down her cheeks.

"Kuro has two female assistants. I believe these two women, sisters, to be highly proficient killers as well. In fact, all the names I read off are killers if we go along with Rex's theory.

"The two assistants' names are Migi Te and Hidari Te. Anyone want to take a guess at how these names translate into English?"

Joe pulled out another black and white eight by ten photograph that was blown up to such a degree that Rex couldn't tell where it was taken. In the photo, Rex saw, stood two Japanese females shown from the chest up.

One stood half a head taller than the other with more defined and thinner features. Both the women had long black hair which grew beyond their shoulders, but the shorter one reminded Rex more of a Native American than Japanese. She had wider cheekbones and a flatter nose.

Since no one hazarded a guess at the translation of the two names, Joe carried on. "The taller one, named Migi Te, stands for Right Hand."

"And Hidari Te stands for Left Hand, right?" Rex asked.

"Right on," Joe answered.

"Geez, nothing like making it obvious," Jesse said.

"Exactly. That's why I think giving the sheriff the name Wyatt Erp was done on purpose as well. They're thumbing their noses at us. They use these names to laugh at us and see what we'll do about it," Joe said.

"I assume their work papers pan out," Rex stated.

Joe huffed and looked down in frustration. "That's out of my jurisdiction, and I've never been able to study their original paperwork. I have to assume that they do. I can't get to them without higher authority, and we already know I will never get that," Joe said with a sigh and a frown.

Perking up again, Joe said, "Okay, on to our two driver/mechanics. The first one, Yama Korosu, or Mountain Killer, is another joke of a name. You'll recognize him immediately when you see him." Joe pulled out his next photograph.

"Yikes!" Rex exclaimed.

"Dido." Jesse laughed.

"Dido?" Rex asked.

"Well, he's ugly, isn't he?"

"Yeah, but I was thinking more in line with Frankenstein, not Dido."

"Go on, Joe. This man obviously has an impaired Frankenstein brain sloshing around between his ears." Jesse laughed.

"Yama is one of the two that have international criminal records. His real name is Yamamoto Sumisu. He stands six foot nine and has cropped bleached hair. Yama also has a knife scar that's very noticeable down the right side of his face. It starts on the right side of his forehead and runs down his right cheek to his lips. The right eye is milky." Joe ran his index finger down the right side of his face to show them where Yama had his scar.

"Why do you have *Lurch* written beneath his name?" Rex asked.

"Just my personal name for the ape," Joe said with a shrug and a smirk.

"What's his criminal record for?" Jesse wondered.

"It's never been proven, but he's believed to be an international hit man.

He's been arrested a few times in different countries for his believed association in the assassinations of powerful political and business figures. But he always has alibis for being in a different place when the murder takes place, and there's always been big money behind him to get him out of jail. He's an enigma for international law enforcement.

"However, he's been here for almost three years as if he was in retirement or something," Joe said.

"Retirement, or doing something really big," Rex commented. "Besides, you can't beat the weather."

"Yama's assistant, and the other driver, is Chiisai Desu, or Little Hurt. Both Yama's name and Desu's are rough translations and may even be wrong, but that's the way we think they're supposed to be translated," Joe pointed out. "Desu also has a record and has been seen working with Yama before they came to Maui. But I don't think there's any love lost between Yama and Desu. Watching them together doesn't give the impression of love for one's fellow man.

"Desu might get his name because he's only five foot three inches tall, and just the opposite of Yama. Although he has a boxy build, his Interpol records suggest he's a swift and agile killer. He's been arrested on numerous occasions both abroad and on Maui for assault and battery.

"I've followed Desu one night to a sleazy bar. Since I know the owner and occasional bartender, 'Lefty' Sullivan, I went in—"

"You mean to tell me that Maui has a sleazy bar, as in hookers, druggies, and drunks?" Rex asked with a grin.

"Note that he doesn't drink. He likes to find the roughest bar in the area to pick fights. Also note he never kills in these fights. He uses his bare hands to incapacitate and cripple. It's as if he enjoys watching people suffer. Desu is definitely someone to stay away from, although he's never been arrested carrying any sort of a weapon."

"Likes to work with his hands, does he?" Rex grinned in a menacing manner. "I've got the perfect cure for that. He's like many serial killers. They like to torture and kill with their hands, or use some sort of instrument like a knife, a wrench, something up close and personal. Yeah, I've dealt with his type before."

"And with success, you should add," Jesse said in all seriousness.

"Well, I've only lost one fight, and it's the one I've always sought to avenge," Rex said grimly.

"Before you get Rex all riled, let's go over the last two employees, shall we?" Joe interjected. Rex was heating up, and it wasn't the appropriate time to go over old war stories.

Rex slumped back to his barstool without so much as a huff.

"Okay. The last two are the morticians, and they're twins," Joe said as he showed them another photograph. The photo was another blow up and the background of the picture was a blur.

When Rex heard "twins," he leaped out of his chair to study the photograph. He was thinking about his dream with the monster that had two heads and the bodybuilder's body. Rex never thought of the possibility of fighting twin murderers.

The photograph showed the twins smiling with short black hair, small noses, perfect white teeth, and the same high cheekbones which made their eyes disappear when they smiled. The photo was in black and white as were all the others. The twins were wearing shorts and T-shirts. To Rex they appeared as if they were Japanese tourists just enjoying their vacation.

"Their names are Naifu and Kiru Otoko, and don't ask me to tell you which one is which, cause they both look the same to me," Joe said.

"Do they have a record?" asked Rex.

"Ya know. That's the biggest surprise of this bunch. These two are as clean as a whistle. They were written up by the University of California Police for doing something with a human leg during a college fraternity prank a long time ago, but that's all I can find on them. And those are their real names as far as I can tell. They went to college at the University of California, and they're registered morticians in the State of Hawaii. You couldn't ask for cleaner cut boys." Joe laughed.

"You're being morbid now, Joe," Jesse commented.

"But that's the lot of them. Sometimes someone will come to the funeral home and stay a few weeks, but these are the main characters that have been there since we started picking up on them as a possible crime unit."

"Just out of curiosity ... how did you peg these guys as part of the Yakuza organization?" Jesse asked.

"Oh ah...Word came down from the Feds that Yama and Desu were bad news, and that we should keep an eye on them. That sorta started a whole ball of wax that we best not get into," Joe said while shaking his head.

"I'll bet a good deal of your information comes from the Feds," Jesse continued, as if she was onto something.

"Oh we occasionally work together..." Joe said while looking away from Jesse.

"Could you use your federal connections to assist us on this case … this case that supposedly doesn't exist?" Jesse asked as she followed Joe around the pool table to not let him get away.

Rex remained on his stool and out of the way. Secretively, Rex knew Jesse was on the right trail, so he sat there and waited to see if Joe would crack and fess up as to who was his federal connection.

"That'd be kinda tough, Jesse," Joe said in a slow manner while acting like he was going through his files again. "Ya see, my connection is an undercover agent who's also working to bring down this Yakuza operation… whatever that operation might be."

"Ah, so you're afraid of exposing this agent?" Jesse asked.

"Exactly."

"But how many lives is it going to take before your contact comes out and makes a bust?" Jesse asked in an angry tone.

"Well, first of all," Joe started in a defensive manner, "no one had made the connection between the Yakuza and those bodies until one Mr. Bana showed up on the scene to show us all how to do things, right? And I'm not saying that in a sarcastic manner. I mean, we were going about this all wrong until Rex had a chance to work these files a bit."

Rex got up off his stool finally and said, "I appreciate the acknowledgment and all, but I think my part has been over stated and over used. We still haven't proven a damn thing, nor have we caught any criminals. And on that note, I think I'll use the facilities and ease some of this internal pressure."

"Okay, what did you all come up with in my brief absence?" asked Rex in a thundering voice as if to wake up bored students.

"We've concluded our personnel review—" Joe started.

"And a mighty fine job you and … ah … the Feds did," Rex said. "Now that we know the individuals, we need to know how they function as a unit. I mean, who's going to greet us when we take Lilly in there, or better said, who should we be asking for when we walk through that front door?" Rex smiled then picked his teeth with his thumbnail.

"If we walk in with Lilly unannounced, and I'm sure they get a lot of casual customers that just walk-in, then we'll probably be greeted by one of the Te girls, or maybe Kuro himself," Joe answered.

"And you'd be going in on this second level on your diagram," Jesse pointed out.

"Yup," Joe confirmed. "We'd have to pass right by the dragons, the two front doors, which appear as if they belong on a twelfth century castle, and into the entryway or lobby."

"Dragons?" Rex perked up. "You said dragons, didn't you?"

"Relax, here, look at this picture."

"Oh, you mean statues." Rex wiped his brow. "It's bad enough we have to fight an international band of terrorists without bringing dragons into the picture."

"Ya know, that's true. I never thought of them as an international band of terrorists before," Joe said. "I always considered them just a foreign pain in my ass. And no comments from you, Mr. Bana." Joe shook his finger in Rex's direction.

"Yeah, too bad we can't bring in some big boys from a federal anti-terrorist group," Jesse said sarcastically.

"Don't worry about the Feds, Jesse. They're aware of the situation," Joe said.

"They are?" asked Rex.

"Well, sort of." Joe squirmed.

Rex saw this was no time to be goofing with the federal issue. It was a closed case as far as he was concerned—the feds weren't coming.

Rex knew he had to help out Joe here and steer Jesse's hound nose off into another direction.

"Okay!" Rex started in a loud voice. "You, me, and Lilly are met by Kuro, and the suave and graceful headsman has shown us around the second floor while enlightening us with their different methods of internment."

"Sounds about right so far," Joe agreed.

"Well ... what's next?" Rex asked.

At this Joe huffed in frustration. "You were the one that was supposed to provide us with that part of the show," Joe said to Rex.

"I guess this was my idea, wasn't it?" Rex grinned. "Well, here's my best plan so far. I'll take along my whoopee cushion and hide it under my shirt. After we've been there a while I'll fake some farts that everyone will hear, then I'll complain about having intestinal flu ... and could they direct me to the rest room in a hurry please. I can even put some water in the whoopee cushion to give it that runny wet fart sound. No man on Earth, no matter what nationality, is going to deny the directions to the rest room to someone with wet runny farts."

Both Jesse and Joe had burst out laughing when Rex introduced the whoopee cushion idea. By the time he was finished, they were knee-slapping, snot-running, tear-jerking laughing.

"I'm serious," Rex exclaimed.

Their laughter came to an abrupt halt.

"Rex, that's preposterous. We're talking about taking my mother into a possibly death threatening situation, and you want to play childhood pranks? You have to have something better than that."

"Like what?" Rex asked. Rex thought it was a perfect plan.

"You guys are taking this too seriously," Rex said getting off his stool and starting to circle the pool table like a shark looking for a meal—he kept Joe and Jesse inside his circle.

"Remember the Maui Funeral Home is an operating business that has people walk into their building every day. It's not like you, me, and Lilly are going to be any different to them than any other walk-in customer.
It's like going to the grocery store, for Pete's sake. Lilly was right. This is no big deal."

"Rex, you heard Joe's personnel evaluations. Those people are experienced killers," Jesse said.

"That's just it, Jesse. We're trained killers as well," Rex pointed out.

"Speak for yourself. I've never killed anyone in my life," Jesse grumbled. She gave up trying to watch Rex and stared at her empty beer bottle instead.

"Neither have I," Joe said solemnly.

"Joe, at least you're trained to kill people."

"No," Joe countered. "I'm trained to protect people. There's a big difference."

"Okay, fine." Rex threw up his hands. "I'm the bad guy now. I'm the one who's done all the killing." Rex appeared to be huff-puffing mad.

"I think I need a walk. See ya!"

Rex did an about-face and stalked out of the room.

# CHAPTER SEVENTEEN

"I think I'll let them stew for a time... thinking I'm mad. Maybe that'll get them off their keisters and quit all this postulating and planning," Rex said while he walked down the lawn waving his arms back and forth as if he was trying to shoo away a swarm of gnats out of the dark, starlit sky. He stopped abruptly and kicked off his flip-flops which he threw on the drive where he wouldn't forget them.

"I'm tired of sitting, waiting, and planning. This working with a team is driving me bonkers; everyone wants to study everything, every way, from here till next Tuesday with all the ifs, ands, and buts answered to their own perfection."

"This sure as hell isn't Michigan grass... ouch!" Rex hopped on one foot after stepping on a rock. "I guess this Maui thatch isn't grass, it's more like crabgrass. Maybe I shouldn't have been so hasty taking off those flip-flops." Rex pondered his feet for a moment—a man deep in thought.

"Hell, maybe I shouldn't have stomped off to begin with. Maybe they're right to be so cautious and planning. I'll bet neither of them walks off into the night like a madman and talks to themselves either." Rex put his hand up to his chin as he continued to make for the beach. "Okay, so the whoopee cushion plan is a little childish..." he muttered and thought some more. He was nearing the Koa trees that separated the lawns from the beach. "The fact the whoopee cushion idea is so childish in such a dangerous situation ought to make it work. Who the hell would walk into a house full of killers with a set of whoopee cushions under their armpits? It's perfect, no one would expect that!" Rex stopped short of the tree line because he was waving his arms about like a maniac again and realized how he must appear.

He quickly made it through the string of Koa trees and onto the Tweedy's private beach. The tide was in and Rex walked down into the surf to where the waves splashed up his calves. Overhead, there was a spectacular display of stars in the moonless sky. "Wow, the water feels great, but look at all those stars. This is amazing."

Rex lost any thoughts of his troubles and stood in awe while gazing above him at the black velvet blanket studded with millions of sparkling diamonds. His view of the stars extended all the way to the horizon, a view Rex had rarely seen, and the lights from the heavens were reflected upon the black carpet of the ocean creating a display which was overwhelming. There were so many stars he couldn't begin to innumerate or class them.

Rex ambled west till he ran out of sand. He came to a small rising made of glistening black lava rocks and boulders that were eternally pounded by the waves. The rocks built up to a small cliff that was easily climbable if one was wearing shoes, but without them Rex knew the sharp lava rocks would cut his feet to shreds.

Rex peered over the cliff and up the green hill which led up to Dr. Cook's mansion next door to Tweedy Manor. He leered at the black wire fence which stood out even in the darkness. The fence was an amazing contrast after pondering the magnificence of the open sky. To Rex the fence looked ugly and out of place as it ran across the hill, cutting off any exit down to the sea, or any entry up to the mansion. Rex noticed the lights were on all over the Cook's estate, and again he wondered what Meat was hiding and why he should need this security. Rex turned about disgusted with the sight and the waste, and he headed back down the beach, kicking the sand and loving the cool wash of the waves. Rex had reached close to the entryway through the Koa trees and his mind was lost in the stars again.

"It's an awesome sight, isn't it?" Jesse asked.

"Yahoooo ... Look out!" Rex shouted and jumped backward three feet. Jesse scared the bajeebees out of him as she lay on the beach—without much clothing.

"Don't just stand there with your mouth open, drop on down here and have a seat," Jesse invited as she patted the sand next to her nearly-bare bottom.

Rex came forward. He was staring as he eased down and crossed his legs before Jesse's bare form.

"I'm sorry," Rex mumbled and shook his head. His voice was washed away with the waves and the hiss of their approach up the beach.

"Sorry? Sorry about what?"

Rex blew out his cheeks and spoke louder. "Oh, I'm sorry for being rude and staring at you."

"You can stare all you like. Like I told Moe; a lady always appreciates the eye of worthy man."

"Well, I've never seen a woman as beautiful as you in a... ah bikini; if you could call it that."

"Thank you for the compliment."

Rex glanced around to see if anyone else was watching this scene. He spied Jesse's clothes hanging from a tree branch nearby. Rex figured Jesse had a good notion and he stood up again. He ambled over to the tree and slowly removed his t-shirt before hanging it next to Jesse's clothes. Rex felt invigorated by the sea breeze upon his chest and blowing through his long hair as he strode back to Jesse's prone figure camouflaged in the night sand. He was aware of her examining his naked torso and thighs.

"Care for a swim?" he asked.

Rex put out his palm to help her up.

"I could use some cooling off, I suppose." Jesse smiled. She grasped his hand although she bounced to her feet as light as a feather.

"I almost feel we should dance," Rex said while standing in front of Jesse, and holding her by her fingertips. Jesse twirled into Rex's embrace. She threw her head and arm back while lying in Rex's arms as if stricken. Rex effortlessly tossed Jesse across his chest and caught her with his right arm so she could lie in the same stricken position with her head and arm dangling toward the ground. Jesse giggled and Rex laughed as he gazed down the hollow of her stomach, her protruding ribcage, and towering breasts that were capsized by pointy nipples barely concealed beneath a bathing top smaller than two band-aids. Rex couldn't help but be aroused by her beautifully sculptured body.

"It's time for a cold shower," Rex announced.

Rex lifted Jesse and tossed her over his right shoulder as she screamed and screeched. Rex carried Jesse in a fireman's carry while he charged the crashing waves and plunged himself headfirst into the swelling ocean.

Jesse had been screaming like a howling hyena, but all the noise was lost when Rex's head dove into the shockingly cold waters. He submerged into darkness and most of his senses were dampened. Rex's aroused nature was purged from his body as his testicles shrunk in search of some body warmth and his dick shriveled out of pure fear of the coldness in the water.

Rex released Jesse after submerging her beneath the oncoming waves not desiring to drown her if she hadn't been prepared for the plunge. He imagined Jesse was more accustomed to night diving and swimming than he was since she lived here, and he soon discovered Jesse was as comfortable in the night's ocean as a playful dolphin.

Rex reemerged and he was shocked to find Jesse with both her hands on his shoulders, dunking him beneath the surface again. Rex had only gotten a gulp of air and was surprised to find that he was already too deep to touch the sandy bottom while keeping his head above the water. He figured war had been declared and she was going to pay for sneaking up on him and slamming him beneath the surface.

Rex didn't resurface, but instead swam in a circle he thought would go around Jesse's previous position and allow him to pop out of the water behind her. The night water was too dark for him to see Jesse even if he was brave enough to open his eyes in the salty swill. Rex reemerged and was amazed when he didn't find Jesse's head bobbing right in front of him. He whirled around in search of Jesse, but he was unable to find her anywhere on the surface. The laughter he'd been holding faded as he continued to twirl about but he was not able to locate Jesse anywhere along the surface.

Rex would have jumped out of the water with fear, if it was possible, when something pinched his butt with sharp nails. He swept his hand across his backside but he couldn't locate anything. He kicked this way and that way, but he still wasn't able to find any obstruction or person who might have pinched him. Jesse still hadn't surfaced.

"Jesse!" Rex yelled while still treading water and starting to get tired. The only sound that came back to him was the sound of the crashing waves on the shore. Rex thought of returning to the beach in hopes of being able to see more from that vantage point.

"Jesse! Come on, you're starting to scare me."

Someone wrapped their hands around his right ankle and jerked his head beneath the surface. Again, Rex was surprised to feel Jesse's powerful hands clamp onto his shoulder muscles and push him further beneath the water. Rex thrashed about beneath the water, but he still couldn't make contact with Jesse or anything else.

"SHIT!" Rex bellowed beneath the surface. He surfaced again to try and locate Jesse. Again he was at a loss.

"What are you, some sort of a mermaid?" Rex hollered and sputtered into the dark swells. This was starting to scare Rex who was a mainlander that didn't swim on a daily basis and to whom the ocean was still fearful in the darkness of the night.

"Okay ... I've had enough. I'm going in," Rex shouted into the waves as if Jesse might hear him. He started a slow breaststroke toward the beach with his head above the water so he could see if Jesse reappeared. Jesse's head popped up from beneath the surface not three feet in front of Rex scaring a double-bubble out of him.

"Wow, where'd you come from?" Rex sputtered as he stopped to tread water again.

Jesse just smiled, showing her glowing teeth in the starlight of the night. Rex could barely make out her complexion other than the whites of her eyes and teeth. Even as he spoke she disappeared beneath the surface with barely a ripple in the coffee-like surface.

"Shit," Rex sputtered and swallowed some seawater this time.

Rex coughed out the water and began his breaststroke again, but this time he swam in earnest with powerful stokes that swiftly carried him toward the beach. Rex had started his fourth stroke when he was pounded in the middle of the back from above, and he was driven beneath the surface. Rex found his legs tangled with what seemed to him like a powerful octopus. When he tried to kick he found his calves were twisted around those of another. Rex was appalled at Jesse's strength. He'd never encountered a female with legs as powerful as Jesse's, and he quickly found out her arms and chest were also equal to the task.

Jesse hugged Rex from behind by wrapping her arms beneath his armpits and around his chest. As they sank into the depths, Rex tried to break the hand-locked grip Jesse had around his chest, but the combined effort of her hold on his chest and legs defeated him. Rex gave up and used his powerful arms to swim back to the surface.

Rex took a deep breath upon breaking the surface before re-submerging. He did a somersault in the water and reached around to find Jesse's bare bottom. He thought, *Two can play at this game*. Rex pinched Jesse's right cheek and was rewarded by an underwater yelp.

Jesse did not relinquish her hold in the least, so Rex was forced to grab her right ankle in both his hands and pull it off from around his own leg. His grip was tremendous and was meant to be painful.

Jesse released Rex's chest in an attempt to regain her ankle. Rex released one of his hands so he could swim to the surface again. Rex held up his right hand as he broke the surface so he could see the foot he'd caught. Jesse had released all holds she had on Rex and she surfaced to thrash about while trying to get out of Rex's grasp.

"Rex! Le ..." Jesse spit before going under a swell.

Rex floated with the swell and continued to hold Jesse when she came up sputtering and laughing. Jesse thrashed about before splashing Rex in the face. The next swell passed, dunking Jesse again. This time Rex submerged as well in search of Jesse's other leg. It wasn't difficult to find and he locked her calf beneath his armpit before kicking to the surface.

This time both their heads popped out of the water. Rex looked toward the beach and saw they were getting close. He kick-dragged Jesse along by her legs until he got close enough to the shore to plant his feet on the sandy bottom. It was difficult to keep Jesse afloat with the increasing strength of the waves and the riptide, but Rex managed and he was having a grand time holding Jesse's thighs around his stomach and chest. Occasionally, the swells would push Jesse's butt into Rex's thighs, and this pelvic pounding aroused him. Jesse oohed and aahed during these encounters, so Rex figured she was being aroused as well. She only fought to stay afloat and didn't make an effort to escape his provocative grasp.

After a large wave, Jesse sat up and wrapped her arms tightly around Rex's thick neck and smacked him with a long and hard kiss. To Rex the kiss was a long time coming. It seemed like he had thought of nothing else since before he'd even met Jesse, and he felt she had wanted it as well. They stayed this way with their pelvises thrusting and their tongues twisting.

After breaking from their kiss, Jesse said, "I have to warn you. I was raised with four older brothers, and all of them were college athletes, so I know how to beat on bigger men." She laughed.

"Oh yeah?" Rex dunked her again.

Jesse came up sputtering again, and locked her arms around Rex. Another large wave knocked Rex off his feet and they were submerged until neither could hold their breaths any longer. Breaking the surface out of breath and increasingly horny, Rex reached around beneath Jesse's rump and stretched her cheeks so his erection could rub her in between her thighs. They went into another long kiss.

Jesse broke off their kiss and moaned. "I think it's time to move to the beach."

Rex did an about-face and was pushed/pulled in toward shore by the ocean. They didn't make it in far beyond the top of the waves before Rex kneeled and gently laid Jesse upon the beach before him with her legs still wrapped around his waist.

While still embraced in Rex's deep kiss, Jesse reached down and undid the ties to her bikini bottoms. After she did this, Rex stopped the kiss and sat up on his knees. He undid his cuts-offs and dropped them to his knees. Rex sucked in his breath as Jesse reached up and palmed his erection to feel its hardness.

Rex got off Jesse and rolled onto the sand close to her side. He reached down and felt a slippery wetness between her legs that had nothing to do with the ocean. Rex bent over, covered her mouth, and sucked out her breath while rubbing in between her thighs.

Rex and Jesse used their hands to massage each others sexes, and then Rex stopped to untie Jesse's top and suck her nipples into their highest projections. But Rex had to pull himself away from Jesse's grasp to allow him to settle down—this was coming too fast for him. It seemed to him that Jesse had much more tolerance than him and was more experienced as well.

When Rex was calmed, he spread Jesse's legs and lay on top of her. He gently pushed inside Jesse's eagerly awaiting self. Jesse accepted Rex with a small cry, and she tightly wrapped her legs around him. Rex's groaning and moaning rapidly increased as it wasn't long before he was aroused again. Jesse seemed more aroused and it seemed to Rex that she quickly reached an orgasm. Unable to control himself after Jesse's body went stiff as a board and she let out a near scream, Rex allowed himself to relax and come. His body contracted to such a degree he felt Jesse's back pop in his tight embrace. Even though Rex came, he didn't stop his rapid pumping as his cock remained stiff. Jesse screamed louder as she reached a multiple orgasm.

Finally, Rex was completely soft and he slipped out of Jesse. Jesse shuddered with his withdrawal as if she was ticklish. Then, for what seemed like the longest time, they lay there, with Rex on top just kissing and sucking in wind. Slowly they relaxed, and Rex rolled off Jesse to lie on the cool sand. Again Rex stared at the stars and was more amazed at their beauty now as his body felt so tremendously relaxed.

"That was a magnificent feeling, Rex."

"I know. I have no complaints," Rex laughed.

Jesse reached over and punched him in the ribs. "You pig!" Jesse laughed.

"Okay, it was alright." Rex laughed some more.

It seemed to Rex that he'd fallen asleep after awhile. Jesse woke him up by playing with his penis. Rex looked up and saw she was already dressed again.

"How about getting dressed and going for another quick swim," she asked. "We've been away for over an hour and a half," she said pointing to her underwater watch.

Rex yawned and said, "Well, that will never do. They'll know what we've been up too."

"I don't think that'll be too hard to guess anyway. I think I'll go straight to my car after this so they might think you've been out here by yourself."

"I doubt that'll work. Joe's too aware of things. He'll hear your car for sure," Rex pointed out.

"Not if you push it all the way up the drive first." Jesse laughed as Rex got up and started to put on his shorts. Before he got them up, Jesse reached up and tenderly stroked his penis again.

"Oh, better not start something again. Push your car up the drive? Are you nuts?"

"Nuts about you," Jesse said tenderly as she got up as well.

"Ditto," Rex laughed.

"Ditto?"

"Yeah, ditto. I owed you a 'ditto' at a bad time, remember?" Rex pointed out.

Jesse reached up and gently kissed his lips.

Rex wrapped his arms around Jesse and held her tightly before she could get away. Then he gave her a wet and sloppy kiss. Having finished, he bent down and lifted her by her back and legs and carried her back into the cold ocean.

After dunking each other a few times to clean away the sand, they ran out of the water and back toward the house. Rex was freezing by the time they were indoors. He was amazed to find the house dark, as it appeared Joe had figured out what was going on and had gone to bed.

Rex went and got two clean towels and they dried each other off. He wasn't surprised to even find sand in his crack. He knew he'd have to take another shower before bed. He hated to think what Jesse was going to find in her shorts. He hoped that dip in the ocean turned out to be a good contraceptive. Then Rex took Jesse out to her car and they kissed each other good night.

"Ya know, you're something special Bana. I've waited a long time to meet someone like you."

Rex was taken aback by this statement. His inexperience with women was evident. "Jesse, there's something you should understand about me. I have little experience with women and relationships. I've spent my life on the hunt and killing men. I've never really had much more than one night stands with a woman, and I don't think I've ever truly been in love."

Jesse didn't release her grip nor turn away her eyes. Instead, her gaze seemed to bore into Rex with meaning and understanding that Rex couldn't comprehend from someone whom he'd just met. "Then maybe it's time you learned to love. I see a huge heart in you, Rex Bana. I see a heart that's yearning to be loved in return and to give rather than take." Jesse sighed. "I also see someone that's afraid to give because he's seen so much death and unhappiness in his life. I see someone that's only seen the take from life of the madmen he's hunted—someone who's seen the evil of the world. I can only ask that you trust me as one that's seen as much of death as you have. I've seen every type of tragic death that's humanly possible, and I've seen its effects on those who adored those that were lost."

Rex looked long into Jesse's green brown eyes for some lie, for some dishonesty where she was making fun of him. Instead, he saw the sadness of one who truly knows the haunting hurt of death. He saw the truth he himself often felt so deeply. Rex looked away from those eyes rather than have to face them tonight. He'd had enough emotion for one day. Jesse reached up and turned Rex's face back to hers for a moment. "Rex, I understand what kind of life you've lead, and until you can understand the good things in life, I'm asking you to trust me and let me show you there is a good side to living and loving. If anything, you should already know there's a good side since you have such a good friend in Joe Tweedy. They don't come much better than him."

"Yeah, he's a good egg, I guess." Rex hiccupped to hold back his emotions.

"Well, you think about what I said. If you need any proof that there's goodness in you, just think of all the happiness you've brought to those at Sara's Garden, and the deep friendships that you have already. In the few days I've known you, I'd say I could be with you for eternity, and I do know the gives and takes of loving someone."

Again, she reached up and kissed Rex on the lips.

Rex took hold of Jesse. He ducked his head to her shoulder and squeezed her tightly. Finally, he whispered in her ear, "Thanks for your kind words and confidence. I'll hold them dearly and ponder their meaning."

"You'll ponder?"

"Yeah, you know—I'll think about what you've said to me."

"Okaaay. See ya tomorrow, Rex Bana." Jesse said as she turned about and headed for her car.

Rex watched her drive away. He knew he'd goofed in some way, and probably hurt some feelings. He stood in the driveway gazing at the stars again for a long time. His thoughts wandered near and far, but mostly he wondered how such a vastness could exist in the heavens when just here on Earth, in his very own head, body, and soul could exist such turmoil of knowledge, lack of knowledge, and emotion. He knew he'd never understand a human being, much less the infinite existence around him.

# CHAPTER EIGHTEEN

The time had come.
Rex, Joe, and Lilly put on their finest and headed to the Maui Funeral Home. Jesse called to confirm the Rogers' corpse had been delivered first thing in the morning. Rex rented a Ford Town car for the trip. If they'd gone in Joe's unmarked police cruiser, someone was going to have to sit in the backseat where there was a steel screen between the front and back seats. Although there were times Rex would have liked to put Lilly in that cage, without any door handles to get out, he couldn't see doing that and forcing her into the Maui Funeral Home afterwards. Once she got out of there she was liable to tear off somebody's head. So Rex rented a plush riding Town car made for long legs and wide bodies.
The morning was another of Maui's finest. The sky was a perfect blue and it appeared as if the temperature might reach the mid-80s. The ocean was cobalt and calm.
Rex felt uncomfortable in his suit jacket and tie, but it served a purpose as well. First and most importantly, it covered his shoulder holster and his Glock 20. Joe had provided him with hollow point ammunition even though it was illegal.
"When we're protecting my mother's life, nothing is illegal," Joe had told Rex with a stern face. "Not that I want you blowing away the place. But having some insurance never hurt."
The other thing the suit coat hid was a mini-digital Minolta spy camera so Rex could take pictures if he felt it was necessary to provide some evidence

about something. Rex carried his whoopee cushion apparatus around his side and stomach area.

Rex parked the Ford on the expansive asphalt parking lot under a large Banyan tree that provided a comforting shade. They had to wait a few minutes for Lilly to get her big bottom out of the car. Rex thought he heard some cussing and swearing from Lilly by the time she wrestled and lifted herself out of the backseat. He thought it was a shame he hadn't rented one of those four door pick-ups where they could have pushed her out the side door, but he kept his mouth shut.

While he waited for Lilly, Rex found himself thinking of Jesse and the night before. He was still a bit tired and sore from doing exercises his body was not accustomed to doing. He was also finding that warm feeling in the pit of his stomach was growing warmer as he thought about that woman.

"Hey, Rex, ya want to join the party?" Joe yelled. Rex was surprised that Joe and Lilly were already halfway across the parking lot, and he'd been daydreaming.

"Shit," Rex muttered. He jogged to catch-up to them.

"Got your mind on that woman, eh, Rex?" Lilly laughed.

Rex looked into her chocolate-brown eyes and smiling face. He couldn't lie.

"I suppose," he admitted.

Lilly amazed Rex by putting her huge arm around his waist and drawing him near to her side as they walked. "You do okay, Rex Bana. You good man. I think she good woman too. You make each other happy."

"Oh, geez," Rex heard Joe say. Rex didn't say anything.

Lilly dropped her arm and marched forward. "Let's get this thing out of way. We meet you back at the car afterward, if needed, Rex." Lilly instructed, she didn't follow.

Rex wondered with all this goodness going on in his life, if this wasn't the day things went terribly wrong. Rex looked up beyond the dragon statues and stone steps. The large wooden entrance reminded him of the doors of a church or a castle. Yet, Lilly provided the strength to march forward. Steadily, but surely, Lilly climbed the steps up to the front doors. Joe was already at the doors and he pulled one open for Lilly and Rex to enter.

After Joe opened the door, Rex looked inside. He enjoyed the coolness of the air conditioning, but he could see nothing in the darkness. Rex followed Lilly and entered the home. Rex was surprised how well-lit the interior was after his eyes adjusted from the sunlight. The huge door banged shut as Joe entered and Rex heard chimes going off to tell everyone there were guests at the front entrance.

For a few moments, Rex, Joe, and Lilly stood alone in a tall, long, and dark hallway. There was a dark Persian rug laid out before them on top of dark gray marble floor.

Rex had the impression he was entering the Vincent Price horror film, *The Pit and the Pendulum*. But then he decided he was being a chicken. He looked about the dark wooden paneled walls and saw dark tapestries hanging of peasants at work. It struck Rex there was nothing Polynesian or Oriental about the interior. He decided that went along with Japanese running an American funeral home. He wondered if they did Buddhist and Hindu funerals as well.

In between the tapestries were two doors on the right wall, and two doors on the left wall. Presently, the farthest door on the left opened and Kuro stepped out in a tailor-made, three piece black suit. He appeared impeccably dressed to Rex. Rex wasn't much for clothes or the latest fashions, but he did notice Kuro was wearing diamond studded cufflinks and a diamond tie pin.

As Kuro walked toward them with a curious smile on his face and an upturned nose, Rex noticed what Joe meant when he said the man was graceful. *Kuro walks with the flowing smoothness of a tiger on the prowl*, thought Rex. *I know I'll have to do something to knock down that nose a degree or two.*

Rex noticed that Kuro appeared to be searching each of their faces as he approached, but it was difficult to tell what Kuro was looking at since Rex couldn't see the pupils of Kuro's eyes. Kuro's eyelids hung so low he couldn't see where Kuro was looking. Rex was forced to follow Kuro's upturned nose to determine who Kuro was addressing. Rex thought it was obvious that Kuro recognized Joe, but Kuro's nose quickly pointed at Lilly. Kuro nosed Lilly briefly, before he flicked it at Rex.

Rex didn't enjoy Kuro's nose pointing since it was so hard to read Kuro's facial expressions. By the same token, Rex didn't think Kuro enjoyed what he nosed in Rex's eyes, although they looked eye to nose the longest, and Rex felt he was nosed with close scrutiny.

Rex's eyes were wide open and easily read, while Kuro's eyes were slanted and heavily hooded. Rex took this glance as someone that was hiding something, yet Kuro's even smile never faltered.

"Deputy Joseph Tweedy. To what do I owe the honor of your presence?" Kuro asked as he came up to meet them. Rex noticed that Kuro spoke in perfect English although Joe had told them he was a Japanese national.

"Mr. Kuro, may I present my mother, Lilly Tweedy, and a close family friend, Mr. Rex Bana," Joe announced as he shook Kuro's hand formally.

"Madam Tweedy. It's a pleasure to meet you. I have worked with your son on and off through the years, and he has always proven to be an honorable man and a fine peacekeeper." Kuro took Lilly's hand and lifted it to his lips and kissed it. Rex found this action peculiar for a Japanese person.

If Lilly was impressed, she didn't show it. "Those be kind words," Lilly said before she retracted her hand and wiped it off on the side of her flowered, dark blue Mumu.

Next, Kuro stepped to Rex and pointed his nose at one of Rex's eyes Rex was not sure which eye Kuro was looking at. Rex glared back at Kuro's nose and found it offensive. The man needed to trim his nose hairs. Still, it was a glare that a mongoose might give to a cobra.

Rex was the first to speak. "Have we met before, Mr. Kuro?" Rex asked, knowing they hadn't met.

"Maybe in a different dimension," Kuro answered. Rex thought this was a strange response. "But in this place your face is new to me."

"Your face is familiar to me. Maybe we'll meet again under different circumstances," Rex said, trying to be equally mysterious.

"There are infinite possibilities in this world, Mr. Bana," Kuro said, raising his eyebrows but not producing any eyeballs for Rex to see.

"Ah, Mr. Kuro?" Joe broke the spell.

Kuro flared a nostril at Rex and replied, "Yes, Joe-san?"

"I brought my mother in today to look into arrangements—for——ah—well…"

"You seek advice regarding Mrs. Tweedy-san's eventual internment?" Kuro asked in a soft voice.

*The man's a snake*, Rex thought.

"Exactly," Joe answered with a smile.

"You are a wise family to plan ahead of time," Kuro pointed out.

"We learned with Joe's father," Lilly said. "I would learn your burial process before I decide on my type of burial."

"Absolutely," Kuro said, now attentive to business. "I'm sure you would like to examine the different expenses involved as well."

"Yes, cost is a factor," Lilly admitted.

Abruptly, Kuro did an about-face before he nosed up to Rex again. "And what is your function in all this, Mr. Bana?"

Rex was caught off guard by the question, but he quickly recovered. "I'm one of the executors of the Tweedy's estate. I'm here to make sure Lilly gets what she wants should something happen to Joe during his hazardous employment as a police officer."

"Excellent idea. I see that you've planned this out already. Excellent, really excellent. I find too many families unprepared for the eventuality of death," Kuro said with the same smile as he rubbed his palms back and forth as if to warm them.

Rex noticed Kuro's immaculate manicure.

"Please, come this way. We'll start with the caskets where you can see the fine and durable materials they're making these days. We prefer to call them 'eternal beds,'" Kuro said as he led them down the hallway. Lilly went first with Joe following while Rex brought up the rear.

The casket-showing rooms were in the back of the second floor just where Rex wanted to be. He knew from Joe's diagram the room at the end of the hallway was the kitchen area. Once he got into the kitchen, there should be two doors on his right. One was a bathroom and the other was the door leading to the basement. He had to make it to the kitchen to make it to the basement. It was fortunate the bathroom on this level was in the kitchen right next to the basement doorway.

Rex had opted to use two whoopee cushions in this operation since if he farted all the air out of one cushion, and no one noticed, then he'd be out of farting material, besides doing the real thing. And Rex didn't want to trust Lilly's life on his ability to fart on command. They didn't want to have to make this trip twice, so it paid to be prepared in redundant quantities.

After viewing a few caskets and listening to Kuro's salesmanship, Rex moved in close to Kuro and lightly pushed the whoopee cushion on his right hip. The resulting fart was small but audible. This caused Kuro to pause in his speech as everyone gave each other an accusing glance.

Rex maintained a straight face, but Joe was unable to hold back his grin. Lilly saw this grin and back handed Joe in the arm as if he was the one that let the fart. Joe grinned and shrugged his shoulders. Kuro acted as if he didn't notice.

*Shit*, thought Rex. *Now everyone thinks it's Joe who's got gas.*

Then it occurred to Rex they'd never told Lilly about the whoopee cushion scheme. She knew Rex was going to suffer intestinal flu and ask for the rest room, but they'd forgotten to clue her in on the bathroom "signal," as it was. Now what was he going to do?

Kuro slid along with his silky sales pitch, and Rex thought Joe and Lilly were either doing a great acting job, or they were really interested in what Kuro had to say. He figured Joe wouldn't get out of here without buying something. *Kuro's pearly voice and presentation sounds as if he could sell an anchor to a drowning victim,* Rex thought.

Having examined the economy casket models in the first showroom, Rex and company adjourned to the second room that contained the mid to luxury caskets. Rex figured the sales job would be over by the time they finished this room. He needed to work fast if he was to escape while Kuro still had a good deal of negotiating to do with the Tweedy's. The longer those three pushed around the poop, the longer he would have to nose around the house. What worried him the most was the fact that he hadn't seen anyone else since they had arrived. *Where are all these terrible killers?* Rex wondered.

Rex also noticed something else that they hadn't discussed in their preparations—the home's security and monitoring system. Strange, now that Rex saw the monitoring cameras in two corners of the room, that's the first thing he should have been thinking about. If the place had a mainline computer, it would be simple to control all the cameras and security system around the home. Rex figured he wasn't very experienced in investigating buildings with high security, but this mistake was obvious. *Tsk, tsk, you're losing it,* Rex thought. *Naw, it's from too many knocks on the noggin.* Rex reached up and rapped his knuckles on his head just to prove it was still there. Kuro turned and caught Rex in the act of abusing his noggin. Rex grinned back at Kuro and waved his fingers to show him he was still there—*Yeah—I'm a moron—just standing beatin' my brains for no reason.* Kuro turned back to the customers without so much as a change in expression.

They had reached the far end of the room, and Rex figured it was now or never. Rex was standing at the top and open end of a luxurious and plush eternal bed. By the looks of the coffin, it was the most expensive eternal bed offered. Kuro had everyone bending over to see the lead shield along the bottom that would last, "forever," he claimed. Rex wondered how many caskets Kuro dug up that had been in the ground for an eternity to prove that point, but he decided it wasn't in Lilly's best interest to wonder about such things aloud.

Kuro neared Rex's position. Rex had been swallowing air for the last five minutes. This was a prank he hadn't pulled since he was a kid, and he wasn't sure he could still pull it off. Kuro inched closer and closer until his head was just before and below Rex's, but Kuro was still turned away from Rex while he spoke to the Tweedys. Rex swallowed some more air, but he couldn't hold it any longer. With little effort; Rex vocalized his stomach air in an all-American belch. The burp came with an added treat of Rex's spit and some spittle splatted on the shoulder of Kuro's impeccable black suit coat. The milky spit was an added effect Rex had not thought of, much less planned on achieving—sometimes he surprised even himself.

"Oh, excuse me!" Rex exclaimed in mock horror, as he placed his hands on his stomach and made a face as if he was in pain. Kuro gave Rex the most contemptible expression Rex could imagine on the man's smooth face. Kuro pulled out his handkerchief and wiped away Rex's dribble. Rex saw he was losing his desired effect on Kuro. He quickly bent over while pushing the whoopee cushion under his right armpit. At the same time, he accidentally farted for real and it came out as a real cheek flapper. Kuro was standing directly in front of Rex, and he had to have noticed that these flagellations were coming from both Rex's North and South Poles. Rex could only groan and act as if he was suffering deep intestinal illness.

While Rex was doubled over groaning, he kept his mouth closed and pinched his nose. Then he filled his cheeks with as much air as he could until his eyes were bulging so much he feared they might pop-out of their sockets. Kuro placed a hand on Rex's shoulder to see if he was alright. Rex belched again, and then stood straight with a red face, watery eyes, and drop of spit hanging off his lip. He looked ill, possibly rabid.

"Are you okay, Bana-san?" Kuro asked in a concerned tone.

"Rex has had the flu the last couple days," Joe quickly cut in. "Do you have a rest room he could use?" Rex had covered his face with his hands and wasn't saying anything. He was just glad Joe got his head out of the clouds and remembered why they were here.

"Certainly, come this way," Kuro said as he gestured with his hands. Joe was right behind him, but Lilly and Rex remained. Rex watched Kuro through his fingers, and as soon as Kuro turned to see what the delay was, Rex made a burping sound like he was about to lose his lunch, then he made a mad dash for the plush open casket.

Kuro realized his danger for potential loss. He whirled about with the speed of a mouse with its tail on fire, and made a move on Joe that would have put him in the John Madden Hall of Fame, as he rushed to intercept Rex before he could reach the casket.

Kuro didn't make it.

Rex hit the side of the casket hard enough to wobble it on its stand, an impressive charge. Kuro arrived in time to see Rex clinging to the edge of his finest casket. Rex had his face buried in an embroidered silk pillow while making muffled noises like someone who was really delivering the goods.

Rex tried to look sick when he finally came up for air.

"A most unfortunate accident." Kuro grimaced.

Rex sighed and put on his widest grin. At last he'd gotten Kuro to drop that nose a few steps. *Got ya*, Rex thought.

"Oh, lighten up, Mr. Kuro. I didn't do anything. I just had to get out some intestinal gas is all. See?" Rex held up the silk pillow to show it wasn't covered with lunch.

"But I really should hit the head before something else arises." Rex gave Kuro a weary grin and loosened his tie.

"If you mean the rest room, please come this way—and hurry, Mr. Bana. Our top of the line eternal sleeper is not the proper place for your—refuge," Kuro pointed out.

Rex and Kuro set out for the bathroom before Kuro stopped and turned to Lilly, "Ma'am, if you'll give me a moment while I attend to our ill visitor here. I shall return immediately."

"Better move along then. I seen what that man can do on a full belly," Lilly said with a wide smile.

Kuro looked so shocked at this statement that Rex thought he might see some eyeballs, but they were a no-show. Kuro ushered Rex out of the room at a trot.

Rex was shoved and pushed down the hallway to the door at the end of the hall—the first door toward his goal. Rex had the strangest urge to ask, "What's behind door number one, Monty?"

Rex burst through the kitchen door at a fast walk. He was leery of Kuro pushing him and touching his coat since it was easy to feel his shoulder holster strapped across his back and under his arm pit. If Kuro pushed the right places he might even get a fart from one of the whoopee cushions.

After Rex busted through the door, he took two steps and came to a halt with Kuro right behind him. Rex prepared for Kuro to run into him, and he was surprised when Kuro came to a halt even faster than he did.

The reason Rex came to a stop was because he'd discovered where the rest of the home's personnel were hiding. Rex quickly counted six people in the kitchen enjoying a hot drink that he believed was tea and some delicious smelling pastry. He tried to put names to the faces from the photographs Joe had shown him, but he didn't have time.

"Don't mind them, Mr. Bana," Kuro said. This time Kuro patted Rex in the center of the back where he must have felt the strap of Rex's gun holster.

Rex jumped at Kuro's touch, but he knew he was too late. Kuro had to know about the gun Rex was hiding by now. Strangely, Kuro stepped around Rex and continued to lead him toward the bathroom without a change of cadence. Rex was hesitant to act as if he already knew where the bathroom was and followed slowly. The other reason for his slower gate was because he wanted a good view of the other six people in the kitchen who were eyeing him with their own curiosity.

The most outstanding individual was Yama Korosu who seemed to dominate the room with his mere size. His bleached crew-cut hair stood well above the others, and his huge shoulders seemed to throw a shadow of their own over those around him. Just looking at him made Rex's balls curl-up in search for a hiding place.

Rex had met many evil men in his life, but Yama appeared to top them all at first glance. Yama oozed evil. As if he felt Rex's gaze, Yama turned to stare directly at Rex. For a moment, Rex hesitated in his step to return the monster's gaze. To Rex, the scar down Yama's face looked like a red stab of lightning, and Rex could see how the scar was cut in half by a white orb which had been Yama's right eye.

While many might be terrified of Yama's face, Rex took it as a good omen. The fact that Yama bore such a horrid scar proved that he was vulnerable in some way and could be hurt. "The bigger they are the harder they fall," Rex mumbled.

"A true saying, Mr. Bana. However, do you possess the power to cause such a fall?" Kuro asked.

This question startled Rex out of his daydreaming as he was not aware that he'd spoken aloud, nor that Kuro had silently snuck up on him. He was losing it.

"This way, Mr. Bana, if you've gotten what you came to see," Kuro commented with a smile. Rex looked down at Kuro and thought it was too bad he couldn't see Kuro's eyes and figure out what the man was thinking. Rex thought maybe Kuro was on to him and what his true mission was on this morning visit.

Silently, Rex turned his back on the motley crew and followed Kuro. It might have been his imagination, but Rex felt eleven eyes studying his back as he walked away, and it made his skin crawl.

"Here are the facilities you so desperately need, Mr. Bana," Kuro said as he opened the door to the bathroom. This door was exactly where Joe's diagram had shown it. More importantly, there was another door next to the bathroom door that led to the basement. Rex saw this door was shut.

"Thank you for your kindness, Mr. Kuro. I'm not sure how long this'll take, so please don't wait on my account," Rex said with a grin so wide it made his cheeks hurt. He decided he needed to practice grinning. He didn't do it often, and he was finding a good grin to be a required tool for politics and playacting.

"Then I will return to Mrs. Tweedy and Deputy Joseph. As soon as you are ... ah, finished, please come directly to the room we left and do not wander. The home is large and I would not want you to lose your way in your ... ah, condition," Kuro said with a grin nearly as wide as Rex's.

Kuro had the practiced grin; it looked perfect, polite, while not revealing a thing. Rex needed that grin!

"I'll do that," Rex said with a squeeze of one of his whoopee cushions for added effect. As Rex closed the bathroom door he caught the grimace on Kuro's face.

As Rex locked the door he heard Kuro saying something sharply in Japanese to someone in the kitchen. Rex knew little Japanese and he couldn't understand what was being said, but based on the tone, Rex would have to say that Kuro was mad about something or at someone.

Rex heard another deep male voice murmuring something to which Kuro gave a snappy reply. Then Rex could hear the floor creaking as everyone seemed to be on the move in the kitchen. Sitting on the toilet seat, Rex heard someone open the door next to him. Rex started counting when he heard the door open and he got to a slow eight count before the door was closed again. Based on the long period that the door was open, Rex figured most, if not all, the group from the kitchen had gone down to the basement.

Rex looked around the small bathroom. He was surprised on how clean it was, but Japanese were fanatics for cleanliness, he thought. Rex studied the white walls looking for any sort of listening device. He knew someone would be monitoring him and he needed to cut off that monitor, or at least block its range of vision before he could do what he wanted.

Since Rex couldn't find anything that might be a camera or a listening device, he assumed they were in the ceiling light which was well out of his reach. He decided hopping on top of the toilet seat would only make him look foolish and would only give away that he was on to their monitoring equipment. Not wanting to give himself away, Rex pushed the last gas out of his whoopee cushions. Anyone listening got a good dose of his flagellation.

Rex decided if he couldn't reach the light to disable the monitoring equipment, then he'd simply turn off the light. This way, unless they had an infrared camera, they'd be in the dark as much as he was. Naturally, they'd still be able to hear him so he had to play out his part to some degree.

Rex turned out the light, turned to the toilet, and lifted the seat cover. Bending down as he would to throw up, Rex grabbed the edges of the toilet and made bellowing noises into the bowl so it sounded as if he really was hurling his lunch. Then, spitting into the toilet a few times, Rex ripped out his whoopee cushions and quietly inflated them with his head still hanging over the toilet. Rex blasted away with his two balloons. He particularly enjoyed the way the farting noises echoed in the toilet bowl, and gave them a more authentic and sickening sound. To add to this, Rex groaned and moaned as if it was Sunday morning, and he was sitting down to read the comics.

Rex was satisfied that he'd played his sickness part to the full extent; now it was time for the job he came to do. He stuffed his whoopee cushions back down his shirt while still bending over the toilet. He hoped that if there were an infrared monitoring device in the ceiling light, that he had blocked all his whoopee cushion shenanigans with his head and body.

Rex stood and dropped the toilet seat before flushing. After adjusting his coat, Rex turned on the lights and straightened his tie. To finish off his act, Rex went to the sink, looked in the mirror, and stuck out his tongue. He turned on the cold water faucet hoping, but not getting, some cold water.

"It's the little things ya miss from home," Rex mumbled to whoever was listening. Rex splashed water on his face, in his hair, and even scrubbed behind his neck with a wet paper-towel. Using more paper towels Rex dried off his face and patted his hair.

Now came the main event. First, Rex had to make an appropriate exit since he didn't know if anyone was still in the kitchen. He hadn't taken more than five minutes in the bathroom, so it was possible someone was still drinking tea and eating pastries. Thinking of this, his stomach growled in hunger.

Opening the door, Rex wasn't surprised to see Yama standing across the kitchen with his eye staring right at him. When Rex emerged Yama stiffened to his full height, and again, Rex was awed by the man's size.

"Hi'ya," Rex waved at Yama and smiled.

If Yama noticed Rex's greeting, he ignored it. Stepping with the slowness of a Frankenstein monster, Yama closed the distance on Rex.

"Mr. Kuro awaits you in the showroom," Yama said in what Rex thought was fairly decent English.

"Fine." Rex smiled. "I'll be on my way, then. No need for an escort, it's only down the hall."

Rex was walking away as he said this, and he was glad Yama didn't follow. When Rex made it to the swinging door, going in the opposite direction that he wanted to go, he turned around to have one last glance at Yama. To his dismay, Yama still had his eye on him. As Rex hesitated, Yama lifted his arm and pointed in the direction Rex was supposed to be going. Rex saw he had no choice in this matter, so he went through the door and back into the hallway.

Rex could hear Kuro still slinging his sale's pitch as the door closed silently behind him. Rex had played all his cards and not reached his goal. He decided it was time to improvise. He had succeeded in getting himself into a limbo position where no one was watching him—unless the hall was actively monitored.

Rex wondered how long Yama would wait in the kitchen. He figured Yama had other activities to attend to rather than watching over sick customers to ensure they didn't go astray.

Rex counted slowly to ten. He figured that was long enough for anyone to leave the kitchen. Then Rex counted another ten since he'd seen how slowly Yama walked.

Rex couldn't wait any longer. He popped his head back into the kitchen. "Yes!" he whispered with vengeance as he saw the kitchen was clear of people. What was more, he saw the door to the basement had been left ajar, an open invitation.

Rex tiptoed across the kitchen to the basement door. When he reached it, he decided it was better to act more casual since he figured this whole place was monitored. More than likely it wasn't monitored, but Rex preferred to act safe rather than be sorry. Besides, everything was more fun if he thought people might be watching. Any kind of nincompoop could sneak across a funeral home kitchen on a bright cheerful morning without the possibility of being seen. Rex preferred to think there was more thrill to life— somebody had to be watching.

Rex reached into his inside pocket and palmed his little camera. It occurred to him he better shut the bathroom door in case Kuro came looking for him. *You're stalling, Rex*, he told himself.

Unsure whether to sneak, or to not sneak, Rex decided to hell with it, he needed to get into that basement. He shut the bathroom door, turned about, and opened the basement door as if he was in his own house.

Rex stopped momentarily because he heard voices coming up the curving staircase. Rex also stopped to marvel at the staircase itself. The stairs appeared to have been carved out of a huge slab of volcanic rock taken from the Puu Kukui volcano itself. Rex was awed by the beauty of the black stairs, and yet he saw they remained slightly rough so no one would slip.

As Rex moved down the winding stairs—from which he could see diddly-squat before him—he found that, acoustically, the stairway was perfect for eavesdropping without anyone being able to see him. Unfortunately, most of what Rex heard was in Japanese, but there was an American voice down there as well—a male voice.

Rex could pick out this Yankee voice easily from the fluid dialogues of the others. Besides, the man had a tendency to resort to some English four letter superlatives that Rex wasn't even sure were possible.

Rex had heard the American voice somewhere recently, but in his nervousness, the memory section of his brain refused to fork over the connection. Rex decided not to worry about it. He needed to see what was going on down there.

Rex sat down on his step so he could look around the center beam of the stairway without his body being visible. Slowly, Rex looked around the stair beam until only one eye was peeking. One quick peek gave him an eyeful.

Rex saw a brightly lit surgical auditorium with a center stage of three dissection tables surrounded by supporting cabinetry with sinks, Bunsen burner connections, and computer stations which appeared to be built into the cabinets so one only had to flip the cabinet open and pull out the monitor and keyboard. Rex saw that beyond the dissection tables were the refrigerated cadaver trays. This was a wall of stainless steel cubical units in which the dead were held. Rex saw a group of people hovering over an opened cadaver tray that held an unzipped body bag.

The alleged criminals were less than fifteen feet from Rex's eyeball. Rex's eyeball widened when he realized who he was seeing. He saw the twin morticians were there, Naifu and Kiru Otoko, and Hi Onna, who Joe thought was the second-in-command. But most of all, Rex's eyeball widened when he saw good old Sheriff Wyatt Erp.

Rex saw Erp was examining something that was kept in a black plastic pouch about the size of his hand. Erp was holding the pouch in his left hand while he stuck his right thumb and index finger into the pouch to pluck out something.

Rex saw Erp was holding a diamond, or some sort of crystal. Erp held the rock up to the light as if he could determine its worth with his naked eye. When Erp held it up, the diamond refracted brilliant white streaks of light.

Erp replaced the diamond in the black bag and sealed up the zip-tie bag. Rex watched with increasing interest as Erp gave the bag to Kiru. Rex saw that one of the Otoko brothers had reopened the chest cavity of the corpse. Kiru took the bag and placed it inside the chest of Rogers' body.

*Oh this is just too good*, Rex thought. Yet Rex knew he only had a moment or two. Rex set the camera in his left hand in a manner which he could push the shutter button with his thumb. Then he stuck his hand around the corner in a position he thought he could get a good shot of the whole bunch before he pushed the button.

With a flash of light, Rex knew he had the picture.

*SHIT!* He almost screamed. He forgot about the flash on the camera. That had to have been seen. As if to acknowledge his thoughts, Rex heard some exclamations in Japanese, and Erp hollering, "Hey, someone just took a picture of us from over by the stairs!"

Rex was running back up the winding stairs as Erp spoke. He whipped around the last corner to find Yama standing in the doorframe and blocking his exit. Rex continued his charge forward figuring he had the advantage of being beneath Yama. Rex recalled his days of old, when running with the football meant it didn't matter how big the defender was before him, he was going to move forward with the ball no matter how hard he was hit.

Rex continued to run forward with his head and shoulder lowered, and he rammed Yama in the stomach with all he had. Fortunately, Yama either wasn't expecting such a charge or wasn't used to having smaller people attack him. As Rex charged Yama stepped back, but he wasn't fast enough. When Rex hit Yama, he grabbed Rex's arm as he fell, causing Rex to fall with Yama. Rex winced under the strength of the man's grip.

They hit the floor like a bomb blast. Rex thought the entire house shook as he and Yama hit ground-zero. Rex landed on top of Yama, and was rewarded with an "Oaf!" from a man as big as a king-size mattress. Yama released his hold and Rex bounced up in a hurry. He was on the run and back through the swinging door as he heard people yelling up the stairs behind him.

Rex ran down the hallway and he could still hear Kuro yammering away in the second showroom. Slowing down, and trying to act casual, Rex rounded the corner to see Joe, Lilly, and Kuro were at a desk in the far corner of the showroom. Rex thanked his lucky stars when he saw Kuro had his back to him and couldn't see Rex.

Rex saw he had been correct when he thought Joe wouldn't get out of this place without buying something. It appeared that the Tweedys and Kuro were going over some paperwork.

Joe was seated facing Rex as he rounded the corner, and Joe looked up at Rex. Rex quickly drew his index finger across his neck while opening his eyes as wide as they would go and drawing his lips straight so Joe could see his teeth. With Joe still watching, Rex looked back toward the kitchen, then back at Joe. Rex started running in place to indicate they really needed to go, as in now.

It would have been simpler for Rex to run out to the car and take off—leaving the Tweedys to take a taxi. But Rex wasn't about to leave the Tweedys behind if there was going to be trouble, and he was sure there was going to be trouble. Rex had a photograph of Sheriff Erp doing something illegal with the Rogers' corpse, and the Maui Funeral Home was definitely involved. Besides, once Yama got his big ass off the kitchen floor, Rex was sure he'd have something to say, or do, to Rex.

"Ah, excuse me, Mr. Akuma. We're going to have to cut this visit a little short," Joe stated in an authoritative manner as he stood and motioned Lilly that she should stand as well.

"Is there a problem, Joe-san?" Kuro asked surprised.

"No problem with your service or salesmanship, Mr. Akuma. But it appears that Mr. Bana has returned and has signaled me he needs to leave immediately. I imagine he needs his medication," Joe said as he grabbed Lilly's arm and began to leave.

Kuro turned around and saw Rex holding his crotch while grimacing his teeth. "Yes, I see Mr. Bana is in dire need. You are best to rush him to be medicated."

Lilly and Joe were by Kuro and were nearing Rex when the swinging door burst open and Yama squeezed through.

"Uh oh," Rex said as Joe and Lilly joined him. "You guys better get to the car as fast as you can. Your life may depend on it."

Joe didn't ask any questions as it was clear by the fury on Yama's face that he wasn't coming down the hall to bid them a fond farewell.

"Oh shit!" Lilly exclaimed when she saw Yama. Rex and Joe looked at Lilly with surprised expressions on their faces.

"Mom?" Joe asked in amazement.

"Rex say it all the time." Lilly laughed. "Last one to the car is a rotten egg." Lilly took off at what could be considered a fast walk for her.

Joe was pounding the Persian rugs behind her all the way down the hall. Rex followed shortly afterward, but he stalked backwards with his right hand buried in his coat as he unclasped his holster and pushed off the safety on his revolver.

Kuro appeared out of the showroom to meet with Yama. Yama bent over and said something into Kuro's ear before starting down the hall after Lilly, Joe, and Rex. After Kuro heard whatever it was that Yama had to say, he turned and nosed at Rex. Rex thought Kuro's nosing could be considered a glare if Rex could have seen his eyeballs.

Kuro grabbed Yama's arm and said something in Japanese that stopped the big man's chase. Rex was still walking sideways or backwards while trying to keep an eye on both the Tweedy's progress and of anyone from the funeral home that might be following them. Kuro surprised Rex when he stopped Yama from pursuing. Yet what really got Rex's attention was when Kuro turned to Rex with a hint of a smile on his face and bowed at Rex as if in respect.

Rex could see there would be no chase, and he withdrew his hand from his coat. Turning about, he could see Lilly and Joe were at the front entryway and pushing open the huge doors. Not understanding why Kuro was allowing them to leave this easily, but not wanting to look a gift horse in the mouth, Rex turned about and hurried after Lilly and Joe.

"Hurray! We did it!" exclaimed Rex as he got to the Towncar and opened the door for Lilly. As Lilly came around the door, Rex stopped her, bent over, and gave her a granny hug.

"Thank you very much for your assistance, Lilly. I think we've solved this case, and it couldn't have been done without you," Rex said.

"Oaf, you give too much praise," she mumbled. If Rex could believe his eyes, he saw Lilly blushing.

"Come-on Rex, let's get outta here," Joe whispered in a harsh tone. Joe was already squeezing himself into the front seat. Rex knew they weren't going anywhere fast as the two Tweedy's struggled into their car seats and fastened their safety belts. Wearing a safety belt is a law in Hawaii, and Joe insisted on enforcing it.

After much huffing and puffing, pulling and pushing, squeezing and sucking, Lilly was able to fasten her seatbelt. Now Rex could close her door and they could go home.

*What would we have done if someone was coming after us?* Rex wondered.

# CHAPTER NINETEEN

They were halfway home before Rex was sure there was no one following them and he finally got a chance to relax. Joe had contained himself up till this moment, but after Rex announced the coast was clear, Joe almost popped. "So what'd ya see, what's going on? Come on, talk, man. Why was Yama so pissed off?"

"Cause I knocked him on his ass in the kitchen," Rex said smugly.

"You did what?!"

"Like I told Kuro, 'The bigger they are, the harder they fall.' He was standing in my way as I came running back up the basement stairs."

"And you just bulldozed right over him, huh?"

"No, I don't think he was expecting me to hit him. It was sort of a cheap shot." Rex shrugged his shoulders. He'd take them anyway he could get them—especially against a man as big as Yama.

"So what did you see in the basement? And what did you mean when you told Lilly we'd solved the case?"

"Yeah…This I want to hear too," Lilly said from the back seat.

"Well, I saw a couple of things. We're going to have to wait until we can get on your computer so we can see the picture I took. I think the Yakuza are using the dead bodies as smuggling vehicles."

"What're they smuggling in dead bodies?"

"I'm not sure. But I'd say large quantities of diamonds. Professional grade and already cut."

"Oh, it makes perfect sense. Why didn't I think of that earlier?" Joe said.

"But that's not the best part. Guess who was examining the diamonds before shipment?"

"I dunno, you got me."

"Sheriff Wyatt Erp."

"Erp! You're kidding. Oh my god, this is terrific. ALL RIGHT!" Joe yelled.

"And I have it all on a picture." Rex smiled.

Joe reached over and tried to give Rex a hug, but fortunately the seatbelt restrained him.

When all had settled down a bit, Lilly set the party to the right tune when she said, "Now the bad men will be after you."

Hearing this, Rex and Joe stopped smiling, and Rex returned to thinking about why Kuro let them get away so easily. Did he not realize what Rex had seen and taken a picture, or did he know but didn't care what Rex had seen and knew. If he didn't care, why didn't he care?

It occurred to Rex that Kuro might have known from the start what was going on with Lilly's visit, but he allowed it to happen, thinking there was no way Rex and company could stop Kuro and company's illegal actions. He could be right about that.

The more Rex thought of this, the more he thought he was correct. The Yakuza had shown nothing but supremacy and arrogance toward the authorities during their whole operation. And with Erp, the alleged authority on the island in their pocket, they had no reason to worry. Yup, Rex thought, why make a scene at the funeral home, the Yakuza's place of business, when the Yakuza knew that they would control everything since there was no one that could stop them? Kuro had reacted with intelligence rather than brawn and allowed them to escape as if to prove their indestructibility.

Rex knew history had proven that even the most invincible could fall from power, beaten by even the smallest of forces. No one and no group was indestructible, and Rex was dying to get back to a computer to see how this digital photograph turned out.

# CHAPTER TWENTY

"Here it is, boys," Joe said as he pushed the print button for three copies as well. Rex, Moe, and Joe stared at the digital picture on Joe's nineteen inch monitor. This presented a larger and more visible picture for them to scrutinize.

"Wow," Moe whispered.

"Holy Shit!" Rex exclaimed. "It came out!"

"Hallelujah, brothers! Hot damn! There it is!" Joe yelled with enough excitement for all of them.

The photograph showed Naifu, Kiru, Hi, and Erp surrounding the Rogers' corpse in perfect clarity, and Erp still had a black bag in his hand. The chest cavity of the body was open, but it wasn't readily apparent what they were doing.

"Shit!" Rex exclaimed.

The Tweedy bothers both looked at Rex in surprise.

"What does this photo really show or prove?"

Both the Tweedys looked confused for a moment. Rex thought it didn't take much to confuse these two when they decided to turn off their thinking caps.

"It doesn't prove a thing," Rex stated. "All it shows is Erp, two morticians, and a member of the funeral home staff standing over a corpse that the Sheriff of Maui County has every right to inspect since it was an unsolved drowning."

"It all looks perfectly legal, doesn't it?" Moe asked.

"It sure does," Joe said.

"Shit," Rex repeated.

"Well, don't go throwing our trip away as useless," Joe commented. "At the very least we now know what the Yakuza are up to, and what they're doing with the bodies."

Moe backed away from the computer, and said, "Yeah, and I can testify that those black bags contain some sort of rocks. Probably diamonds, as Rex saw."

Joe whirled around on his desk chair and asked, "What do you mean, brother? You knew about these black bags all the time?"

Moe didn't answer, but he paced back and forth with his head down as if he was thinking.

"You've been picking up these pouches for the Yakuza, haven't you, Moe?" Rex asked. Joe turned to Rex as if Rex knew something Joe did not. Moe continued to pace, but now he was nodding his head while still looking at the floor.

"WHAT!" Joe was out of his chair and charging Moe with such quickness Rex barely had time to react.

As Joe's three hundred and fifty pounds of Hawaiian beef went stampeding by Rex, he jumped on Joe's back, sliding his arms beneath Joe's sweating armpits and trying to lock his hands together behind Joe's neck. Unfortunately, Joe's back was so wide Rex couldn't reach around to get his hands together. Instead, Rex was forced to use brute strength to stop the charging bull. In a move that would have easily flipped a lesser man, Rex threw his hips into Joe's expansive butt while hauling back with his upper body.

While Rex could not manage a flip with his maneuver, he did manage to get Joe's attention. Joe halted his reckless charge upon Moe and came to a standstill with Rex's puny two hundred twenty pounds hanging from his back like unnecessary luggage.

"Would you kindly get off my back, Rex?" Joe asked in a more normal tone.

Rex dropped to the floor. "Anytime, big fella." He laughed and patted Joe on the back a few times. Then Rex bent over and used his cut-offs as a towel to clean Joe's sweat off his arms.

Moe had been making a hasty retreat when he saw his brother coming. Rex figured Moe had seen the look of murder in Joe's eyes before Joe had come to his senses. *Joe has a right to be upset*, thought Rex. Moe has been assisting the Yakuza all along without knowing it apparently.

How much Moe knew was up in the air for Rex, but he thought it was time that Moe come clean before there was another murder. Now it was obvious these were murders, and the Yakuza were committing them in order to smuggle whatever they wanted in those pouches. Whether they were diamonds or rock cocaine in those pouches was a mute point to Rex. The Yakuza were murderers all the same, and Rex was itching to get at them to put them out of business.

"Yeah, I've been picking up bags about the size of mailbags out at the Molokini Crater for a good ten to eleven months now," Moe admitted with his head down.

"Didn't you ever wonder what was in those mailbags?" Joe asked, gritting his teeth to control himself. Rex could see he was still hopping mad at Moe.

"Sure it occurred to me!" Moe exclaimed. "I think of little else." Moe stared at Joe with eyes rimmed with red fury.

Moe continued his pacing. "But for me to get at the higher-ups in the Yakuza organization, I have to gain their trust by doing the smaller odd jobs first, and that means picking up these pouches exactly as they asked me to do, without opening them or acting suspicious.

"I reported all this to my section chief and he agreed that I should continue. I can tell you that more than likely it was diamonds in those pouches," Moe said.

"How's that?" Rex asked.

"I told my boss how I was picking up these pouches, but there was no way I could look into the bags without the Yakuza knowing they'd been opened. So we arranged for a fake Coast Guard search of the *Mickey Fin* during one of the pick-ups out at the Molokini Crater. Captain Ahab and his crew—"

"Captain Ahab?" Rex asked.

"Yeah, you'll have to meet the guy, he's a riot. But anyway, Captain Ahab and crew stopped the *Mickey Fin* and secretly took the pouches back aboard their ship where they had an ultrasound machine. Ya know, like the ones they use for airport security?

"But anyway, we put the pouches through the ultrasound and found them to contain precious stones. So I figure you really did see Erp holding a pouch of diamonds."

Rex watched as Joe's eyes and body position relaxed. Joe went back to sitting in the chair.

"Yeah, I understand," Joe said softly. "I apologize; I shouldn't have gotten so riled. I know the work you do is much more dangerous than straight law enforcement. It's just that I see those dead faces in my dreams. It infuriates me these assholes are out there acting so smugly, and they've been out there doing this shit for so long but we haven't shut them down yet." Joe made a fist and pounded on the desk hard enough to make the computer monitor wiggle.

"Those are big words, big brother." Moe came over and massaged Joe's tense shoulders. For a moment, both the Tweedys stared at a point on the wall as if they saw something intriguing there. Rex was smart enough to let the brothers have their time together. His memories went back to his sister, Sara, and how it felt to be next to her, having her hold him when he was troubled. Rex remembered how thick blood could run; how thick it ran in him. Wasn't he still fighting a battle to save Sara?

The moment was broken when Joe finally spoke again. "Okay." He huffed and shrugged off Moe's kneading hands. "We now know for sure what the Yakuza are doing in that funeral home—"

Moe interrupted, "We know one of the things they're doing. They could be doing all sorts of illegal activity that we're not aware of."

"Right, brother. We know they're smuggling things off the island by using the corpses of people they kill."

"But you can't prove any of this based on a picture," Rex pointed out.

"At least it tells me what resources we can't use," Joe said. "I was thinking of getting some of the other deputies involved that I trust, but now I don't think it'd be wise to approach anyone in the department."

"So what does that leave?" Rex asked.

Both Joe and Rex turned to look at the pacing Moe. It was a moment before Moe noticed the silence, but eventually he looked up.

"What, you think I'm full of resources?" Moe asked.

"A lot more than just me and Rex."

"You're leaving out Jesse," Rex pointed out. "I don't think she's gonna want to be left out after coming this far."

"Yeah, but Jesse doesn't have any resources behind her to combat this," Joe said.

"I just meant we shouldn't forget the person who brought all this together in the first place."

Joe and Rex both looked at Moe again. Moe didn't say a word.

"Well, how are we gonna prove what the Yakuza are doing?" Rex asked. He had an idea, but he would rather someone else suggest it.

Neither of the Tweedys said anything. They were just shaking their heads, and to Rex, that made them appear as if they were losers. And Rex knew neither of these two were losers.

"Are we gonna wait until the Yakuza strike again ... murder someone else?" Rex asked.

Still just head shakes from the Tweedys.

"Then we need some sort of a plan," Rex said.

"Well, you're the one that busted this whole thing open," stated Moe. "What do you suggest?"

"Have the Yakuza approached you for another pick-up yet?" Rex asked.

"No, but I just did one a couple days ago. It might be another couple weeks before someone drops by the shop. Why?" Moe asked.

"Isn't it obvious?" Rex asked, but the Tweedys continued their head shaking.

"We're going to have to put on a sting operation to catch the Yakuza red-handed and connect them to the murders," Rex stated.

"Sting operation?" Joe asked. "Rex, you been watching too much late-night TV. How are you and I going to con the Yakuza to catch them red-handed?"

"You keep leaving out Jesse," Rex reminded.

"Boy, you really got your heart set on that girl, don't ya?" Joe asked.

This comment broke Rex's concentration. Now he was thinking about Jesse, and there seemed to be no room in his mind for the hunt while thinking about Jesse.

"Oh...I see a dazed and lost look in your eyes, Rex old buddy. Yup, you're off daydreaming about Jesse again," Joe said.

"What'da ya mean, 'again?'"

"Oh, come off it. Every time you think of Jesse you get this dopey look on your ugly mug. Your eyes glaze over, and you get this bulge in your shorts." Joe laughed.

Rex looked down and Joe was right. Rex had been thinking about Jesse and a bulge, a good feeling bulge, had arisen in his cut-offs.

Moe grabbed Rex's arm and turned him sideways so he could check out this bulge as well. "Yes, sir. This man has a class A boner if ever I've seen one, and I think I've seen my share."

Rex backhanded Moe on the arm, and said, "You guys attend to your own privates, and I'll look after mine. We still haven't come-up with a plan on how to catch the Yakuza."

"Don't forget Erp," Joe pointed out with a smile.

"You're really gonna enjoy seeing Erp take a ride, aren't ya?" Rex asked.

"Probably about as much as you'd like to take Jesse for a ride." Moe laughed. Rex backhanded Moe again, only this time there was some punch in the smack.

"Ouch!" Moe cried.

"Serves you right, little brother." Joe laughed. "Rex, did you have a plan in mind, or are we just going to sit around and act like you don't."

"Of course I have a plan in mind, but it isn't all figured out yet because it's going to involve some resources we don't have—yet."

"Like what?" Moe asked.

"Well, we're gonna need some heavy duty sea support to stop the Yakuza in the process of drowning someone. Do either of you have any connections with the Navy or the Coast Guard? How about this Captain Ahab guy? Moe, you seemed impressed with him."

"Oh, no. I don't want to deal with that nutty Captain Ahab again," Joe said, shaking his head.

"Come on, Joe, you're only judging Ahab and his crew from that one incident."

"Yeah, but that one incident was enough. He almost killed those people. Let me think on this one, Rex. You just continue planning as if you have your sea forces. We'll come up with something. Right now I think it's time for some food."

"You guys go eat your hearts out. I have a personal call to make on Ester," Rex said.

# CHAPTER TWENTY-ONE

Again Rex woke with a start. The two-headed Deputy Madison had been bearing down on him with the bloody cleaver. It was the same nightmare from the previous nights.

Rex got out of bed, and took a leak before deciding it was too late in the morning to go back to sleep. The two-headed Mr. Madison had even scared the morning boner out of him. Rex knew his subconscious was trying to tell him something with this rerun of an old nightmare and the inclusion of two heads on Deputy Madison with a bodybuilder's body. What did the two heads of the killer tell him? And what did the bodybuilder's body mean?

This was a continual nagging problem in his mind. Maybe if he brought it out in the open someone might understand the meaning ... or maybe someone would think he was a loony-tune, and that's all he needed.

After standing under the shower, Rex headed down to the kitchen. It was already eight in the morning. Yet, to his body it was 1:00 p.m. with the time difference between Detroit and Maui. It'd been a late night and Rex needed the rest.

Rex entered the kitchen to see the Tweedy brothers beginning their day with their morning feast. Moe was leaning against the counter next to the sink eating fresh pineapple chucks straight from a huge bowl. Rex judged there to be at least three or four pineapples cut up in that bowl. All Rex could see of Joe was his humongous butt swaying in air while the rest of him was bent over and buried in the refrigerator. Rex had to reach over Joe's wide back just to get the juice and milk cartons off the top self of the fridge.

Rex put the juice and milk on the kitchen table, and returned to the counter area for a glass, a spoon, and a cereal bowl. Rex was aware both the Tweedy's chugged directly from the milk and juice cartons like he did at home, but he was a guest in this house, so Rex tried to show some table manners—not that anyone noticed.

He went back to pluck some cereal boxes off the top of the fridge. Rex sat down at the kitchen table for a long bout of cereal crunching while facing the two Tweedy brothers in the kitchen area.

"What's on your agenda today, Mr. Bana?" Moe asked. Moe spit pineapple pieces at Rex while he talked. *The battle begins*, Rex thought.

Rex moved his two 20-ounce cereal boxes so they were strategically placed between himself and the Tweedy feeding machines. He did this for his own protection before he replied, "Well, we obviously need to set up that sting operation to catch the Yakuza red-handed. Otherwise, we don't have the evidence to take them to court."

Rex shoveled some cereal into his mouth and pretended interest in the back of one of the boxes, but he really was watching Joe. Rex became more and more interested in what Joe was doing in the refrigerator. *Did the man ever come up for air?*

"Are you suggesting a joint operation between the local police and the FBI in this matter?" Moe spit, but was defeated by the cereal box on Rex's left.

Rex thanked his lucky stars and ducked lower.

"That's entirely up to you two. I came here to lend a hand in catching a serial killer. As far as I can see, you don't have one. You have a powerful crime organization running an illegal and effective smuggling operation that involves high members of the Maui County Sheriff Department. And that's only at first glance. We've stumbled onto one minor Yakuza operation. It's hard to tell how far the corruption and crime goes on this island."

At this Joe popped out of the refrigerator for the first time. Joe's jowls were puffed as he chewed. Rex had the mental image of a two-legged dinosaur that popped to attention and looked around while it gorged itself on a kill. Rex only needed to imagine a tail to perfect the picture.

"Are you saying you're cutting out on us?" Joe asked in an excited and muffled tone that spit and spewed chunks of something Rex didn't hazard to guess. Fortunately, the cereal boxes held off Joe's advance, but Rex was clearly aware of the rapid—thump—thump—thump—thump—of something striking his cereal box defense.

"Not at all," Rex called from his position halfway beneath the kitchen table.

He'd slouched so low in his chair it was getting difficult to shovel the cereal into his mouth. But every time a Tweedy spoke, they spurted. Rex had no intention of being in the middle of a sputtering spit match if the Tweedy brothers got argumentative and started jabbering back and forth while shoving food into their mouths for ammunition.

"So you're saying that this sting operation has to be set up and run by the three of us basically?" Moe spewed and sputtered.

"Won't the FBI get involved?" Rex swallowed and asked.

"Shit, Rex, with all these budget cuts, the only reason it's still an on-going investigation is because the dive store makes money," Moe pointed out with flying pineapple punctuation. The cereal box on the left wobbled back and forth as if it would concede defeat, but Rex quickly grabbed its side to lend a supportive hand in a time of need. The box held steady.

"Well, there is evidence the Yakuza have crossed state lines smuggling illegal goods," Rex threw out, knowing it wouldn't get too far.

"Sure." Moe swallowed. "We can go on that. Just as soon as you produce enough evidence to convince the assistant director it's time to blow my cover and provide the manpower to bring about your plan."

"That obviously serves no purpose. So the FBI wouldn't get involved?" Rex asked again.

"I can alert some people to standby in case we need a back-up to save us. But it'll cost me my career if we're wrong. I'll be blowing my cover as a dive shop owner/operator the second we ask for assistance from outside."

Joe had backed out of the refrigerator and was wiping off his mouth. Joe closed the refrigerator door, making the ultimate sacrifice. Rex saw this as an indication Joe was finished with his breakfast. Good, Rex thought, now he could eat his own breakfast in peace.

"Obviously they can't count on the Maui County Sheriff's Department to help us," Rex stated in between cereal shovels.

"Oh ... I trust most of the detectives," Joe said. "It was Erp I never got along with. He's the new boy in town. Still, you're right. I've lost confidence in who's on the take down there."

"What about medical examiners?" asked Rex.

"Dr. Cook or Jesse?"

"Either one. Is Meat still in town?" Rex asked.

"You can go next door and knock. I'm not sure," Joe said. "But I wouldn't involve Dr. Cook."

"Why's that?" Rex asked.

Joe sighed, and said, "He's the one that overlooked these murders to begin with. It was Jesse who made the discovery after the fact. It's almost as if Cook was protecting the Yakuza. He might be another one to watch out for."

"So no Meat," Rex stated. He continued to shovel cereal into his maw while trying to find his way through the maze on the back of a cereal box.

Rex completed the maze and added, "Ya know, we're gonna have to include Jesse in whatever we do. I mean, she's not going to want to be held out of the process now that push has come to shove. And this has nothing to do with my personal reasons," Rex added when smirks appeared on both the Tweedys' faces.

"I'd be glad to have her," Moe said. "Ya know she'll always get my vote."

Rex chuckled over Moe's enthusiasm as he finished his cereal. "It might not be a bad idea to keep an eye on Meat, just to be safe."

"You sure you're not reacting to some impulse that you simply don't like the guy?" Joe asked. "Cause at the moment, I don't see how we have the manpower to do a sting operation on the Yakuza, let alone keep an eye on Dr. Cook."

"Let's concentrate on the Yakuza and see what happens." Rex sighed.

"Oh, goodie." Moe smiled. "I was hoping you'd say that."

"Why's that?" Joe asked.

"Cause I think something big is going down with the Yakuza. I went back down to the shop last night to close up, and the big shot, Kuro Akuma, dropped by just as I was locking the door. It was like he'd been waiting in the alley until closing and to make sure everyone was gone before appearing.

"He asked me to do another pick-up. This guy was suave and complementary on the fine job I'd done so far without any hassles. He was talking about what a great relationship we'd established, and how the rewards for my service would be much greater in the future. Kuro did a real sales job…the brilliant smile, nodding his head all the time, and that deep voice he has. It would have been more effective if I could have seen the bastard's eyes. Man that drives me crazy."

"Yeah, the guy's a salesman, a con artist," Rex commented with disgust on his face.

"Was anything different about the pick-up?" Joe asked.

"No. It sounds like it'll be pretty much the same, except there's to be two bags this time. He says it can easily be handled by one diver, but it was imperative that I bring the pouches directly to the dive shop where they'd be waiting for me. So whatever it is, they must think it's important."

"You sure you're not being set up?" Joe asked.

"Set up for what, and by whom?" Moe asked with a shoulder shrug. "The Feds aren't going to bust me, at least I hope not, and Kuro has too good of a thing going on to mess with me. He'd have to charter a boat and get his own divers if he wanted someone else to pick up his pouches."

"Exactly," Rex interrupted, "and that won't tie the Yakuza into the murder and kidnapping charges either."

"What'da ya mean?" asked Moe.

"Well, if we're gonna catch the Yakuza and Kuro red-handed, we not only have to catch them with diamonds in those pouches, but we need to catch them during their kidnap and murder routine as well. Smuggling or illegal transportation of goods isn't going to put these guys away. It'll be the murder and kidnapping rap that sinks them."

"So you're suggesting we have someone playact the roll of a prostitute, or a runaway, so the Yakuza can kidnap them with the intentions of murdering them? And all the while we're backstage watching this whole thing?" asked Joe.

"That sums it up, yup," Rex started.

"But we'd have to have that person in the right place at the right time, and hope the Yakuza picks our person up," Rex schemed. "It doesn't sound like a reasonable plan, does it?" Rex added.

"Well, they have to be looking for someone to murder for this pick-up they want me to do tomorrow," Moe pointed out.

"So it's a perfect time to wave a piece of meat in front of them, and hope they'll take the bait," Rex said.

"Who do you suggest we use as bait?" Joe asked.

"And where do we place the bait?" Moe added.

"Hey, remember, this bait is a human being," Rex stated. "Based on the files, the Yakuza seem to prefer women who are on the short side, or men that are on the weak side. That immediately negates any of us as the so-called bait," Rex pointed out. "I knew I didn't feel like a worm to pierce with a hook this morning," Rex mumbled.

"So if we're looking for a prospect within our little crime fighting group here, that only leaves Jesse," Moe suggested.

"Yup, she's the obvious choice, unless you or Joe is willing to get all dolled up in nylons, heels, and miniskirts," Rex put out there for the Tweedys to ponder. Rex got a mental picture of Joe trying to squeeze his size fifteen foot into nylons and heels, and it sent him into a storm of laughter.

When Rex finally dried up, he got a peek at the pouts on the Tweedy's faces and it sent him into another gut-busting, knee-slapping, button-popping giggle. It occurred to Rex he must appear insane to the Tweedys, but this only renewed his merriment.

Rex's emotional outburst came to a screeching halt when he heard a gong sound that rang his ears and reminded him of a fat Chinese man bashing his thumper against a huge suspended oval of copper. The gong echoed throughout the house; and in his current mood, Rex was tempted to jump up and say, "It's the Gong Show with your host, Jooooe Tweedy." But the Tweedys were giving him strange looks already, so he kept his mouth shut for a moment.

Joe explained, "We have a visitor."

"Holy shit. That was your doorbell?" Rex asked.

"Yupper…I'll check it out," Moe said. "You keep an eye on your friend there." Moe patted his brother on the back before rushing off with an eager look on his face.

"You expecting company?" Rex asked.

"Nope, and you're not skirting the question any longer. What's the hub-bub, bub? What's wrong wit' you?"

Rex managed to keep a straight face and get his mind centered on the task at hand. "I dunno Joe—I—"

"Hey, Rex Bana!" Moe yelled from down the hall.

"Yo," Rex responded while heading out of the room with a sigh of relief. Joe followed.

Rex saw the Special Delivery man there holding a letter pouch, a clipboard, and tapping his feet as if every second counted at the front door.

"Are you Rex Bana?" asked the young delivery man.

"That'd be me."

"This is a requested signed receipt package, sir," the delivery man gave Rex the package. "Please sign on—ah—yeah right there. And once again right here." The man gave Rex his clipboard and pointed to an "x"ed line.

Rex signed his life away without reading a thing. The Special Delivery man said, "Thank you, sir." He ripped the top receipt off Rex's package, yanked back his clipboard and pen, twirled about on one foot and hollered, "Too-da-loo." He made several other noises Rex associated with bird songs as he headed off.

Before Rex looked at his packaged letter, he watched the delivery man skip to his truck. He was amazed that the guy hop-skipped-jumped into his cabin and was off.

"Wow," was all Rex could say.

Moe shut the door with a sigh and a shake of his head, while Joe said, "It's the West Coast, man. Fries people's brains." He laughed.

Moe appeared to care less. "What's in the package, Rex? Come on, let's see." Moe tried to grab the package from Rex's hand before Rex slapped him away and told him to bugger off.

After flipping the twelve by fourteen inch package over and looking at it from all sides as if it might contain a letter bomb, Rex said, "I can't imagine who'd even know I was here to send me a package." The package had no return address on it.

"Come on, let's open it in the office." Joe motioned everyone back down the hall to a room Rex had only visited on occasion since it seemed not to be used.

After Joe turned on some overhead lights, Rex saw a small room lined with dark wooded bookshelves crammed with hardback and soft back books, and piles of periodicals. Rex had noticed most of the literature was regarding crime and its prevention, although he wasn't surprised to find a large stack of "Mad" magazines that had been carefully preserved throughout the years. To the left of the door, against the far wall, was a large roll top desk with a personal computer on it. The monitor was set up so the roll top wouldn't close, and before the desk was a comfy looking leather executive chair that reminded Rex of a king's throne on wheels. Rex also noticed two leather covered chairs against each side wall. Neither looked as if they'd fit a Tweedy.

The wall behind the door and across from the desk was a wall of hardback novels—an entire bookcase. Rex was surprised to see so many novels, reference books, and periodicals stuffed in this room because he never saw a Tweedy holding a novel, much less reading one.

Joe grabbed the package as Rex took a gander about the room again. He went to the desk and rummaged through the top drawer. After producing a letter opener which appeared as if it was large and sharp enough to be an executioner's sword, Joe swiftly sliced through the top of the package and handed it back to Rex to open.

Rex opened the package as the other two crowded in with their hot breath and big bellies. He slid out a black folder which had a full page illustration of the Maui Funeral Home on one side. Paper clipped on top of the folder was a business card for the funeral home with the name of Kuro Akuma on it.

"What the hell?" Rex muttered.

"It's from the Maui Funeral Home? From Kuro himself?" Moe asked.

"So it appears..." Rex trailed off as he began turning the pages through the notebook.

After a letter of introduction, the other pages showed detailed pictures and blueprints of the Maui Funeral Home. There were eight by ten studio photographs of each of the Yakuza Joe had on his list, plus a few others Joe hadn't talked about. After each photograph, some of which had been touched up, Rex thought, there were short dossiers on that person. These backgrounds and profiles appeared to contain more information than Moe and Joe had accumulated during their own research.

Rex didn't see anything about criminal activities in the dossiers, but he thought the pictures were a hell of a lot better then Joe's. Finally, the notebook contained various pictures of the morticians at work. These were very vivid photos Rex could do without. But Rex could see in the photographs the morticians were placing black plastic bags in the cadavers, just as he'd seen them do while hiding on the staircase, just as his photograph showed them doing.

Flipping through the notebook was only the preliminary review. Rex took his notebook to the executive chair where there was more light, and plopped the notebook open to the introductory letter. The Tweedys each took one shoulder behind Rex and read along. The room had become uncomfortably warm, and it seemed awfully small to Rex. Having seven hundred pounds of Polynesian curiosity hanging over him was a new experience for Rex. What bothered him most was that Moe was reading semi aloud, and he was a very slow reader.

Rex concentrated on the short letter. He saw that it was addressed to him at the Tweedys address, but below that address was his home address in Michigan. They went as far as adding not only his home phone, but also the phone number Rex only used for business. This was his private line that was unlisted and only rang in his study. Few people knew this number existed.

"What's that second phone number?" Joe wanted to know.

"Ah, oh nothing important," Rex mumbled.

"Bullshit. They didn't go through a lot of trouble to pull these numbers just to write them on here," Moe pointed out.

Rex still tried to shrug off Joe. "Oh...you can get these phone numbers by simply calling Michigan information and asking for me," he muttered.

"Beep! Wrong again. You've got an unlisted number you don't give out, don't you?" Joe inquired.

"So, what of it?" Rex uncharacteristically exploded.

"Hey, lighten up, little boy. We're just curious," Moe said. Rex felt two hands clamp down on the thick and stiff muscles at the back of his neck and shoulders and start a squishing massage. Rex pictured Magella Gorilla was massaging his shoulders and he relaxed with a giggle. "That's better, my boy," Moe said. Rex returned to the letter, although his head was repeatedly being pushed forward then pulled back by Moe's massaging. This made it difficult to read. He saw after the greeting to him, "Dear Mr. Bana," Joe's name was included in parenthesis as: ("Deputy Sheriff Joseph Tweedy.") There was an "et al" after the parenthesis which Rex assumed meant "and others" in this case. *Smart ass*, Rex thought.

"Smart ass," Joe said.

"My sentiments exactly," Moe added.

The letter read as follows:

Greetings from the Maui Funeral Home, Mr. Bana.

I hope your health has improved. I had the impression your illness was a temporary mishap.

I have learned of your desire to photograph our facility.

We are not a tourist event.

Please find enclosed diagrams and photographs of our operations at the Maui Funeral Home. I enclosed photographs of personnel employed at the Maui Funeral Home, including information of their backgrounds. I hope this satisfies your needs and curiosity.

Had you made it known before you arrived that you were hunting for something in particular, it could have been arranged. I was sorry for your hasty retreat, yet I understand the callings of nature.

Mr. Bana, our encounter was brief and unworthy. I feel we have much in common, and a discussion in a professional manner might be advantageous to both of us. I would be honored if you would meet with me at: 127 Hinau Street, in Lahaina, 7:30 this evening. We may sit in an atmosphere more to your comfort, and we can discuss something of mutual benefit. Since our discussion will only involve you, please come alone.

Govern yourself accordingly,

Kuro Akuma.

"Notice how he doesn't sign the letter?" Moe asked.

"I'll bet there aren't a whole lot of finger prints on that notebook either," Joe pointed out.

"Well, there are now," Rex said as he slowly started turning the pages to see what else the notebook contained. Moe had stopped kneading Rex's neck and shoulders, and now his neck felt so weak he wondered if his head might not roll off. He briefly thought of taking Moe home with him as a masseuse, but then he thought the grocery bill would stiffen him up again.

The Tweedys remained behind Rex puffing and blowing down his neck, and Moe would occasionally read out loud as Rex slowly thumbed through the pages.

Rex thought he couldn't have asked for a better description of an operation as he looked through the notebook. He didn't think it was put together with haste as it provided a more in-depth profile of the operation than Joe and Moe could have put together after all their hours and days of work staking out the place and risking their lives while trying to remain undercover. Everything they wanted to know had just been handed to them in this notebook. Rex thought Moe's boss at the FBI was going to freak after seeing this and finding out how Moe got it. Moe was going to have to keep this file to himself until Rex was out of the situation and the case was solved, but there was nothing like going over to a crime syndicate and asking for them to cough up the goods about their organization and potential for crime. And yet this file proved nothing.

"Geez-O-pete," Rex said, shaking his head as he turned the last page. Blindly, he passed the notebook behind his head before someone could ask for it. It was quickly snatched, pulled, yanked back again, and pulled before Rex heard the smacking noise of flesh upon flesh and all the shenanigans halted.

There was a moment of silence.

"So, are you going to go?" Moe asked in a low voice. Rex figured Moe lost out on the notebook or he wouldn't be asking questions.

"Of course I'm going to go," Rex said to the roll top desk.

"Do you know where this place is?" Moe asked.

"Nope," Rex said making a church and steeple with his hands, and then resting his forehead against the church's front doors.

"That's Lefty's Saloon on Highway 30," Joe threw in.

"What?" Rex finally reacted and twirled the big chair around.

"127 Hinau is the address for Lefty's Saloon right off Highway 30, just outside of town," Moe said as if this was common knowledge.

"Now I understand the part in Kuro's letter about meeting in an atmosphere more to my liking," Rex laughed, and he also understood why Joe and Moe knew the address right off the batt. Kuro must have had the same idea. *Smartass*, Rex thought.

"Going to Lefty's would be more to my liking," Moe nodded as if to confirm Rex's thoughts.

"But you ain't going—not even near the place," Rex said. "I think I'll call Jesse for a dinner date."

"Damn, Bana, I was just thinking how one of their large double cheese, double pepperoni, and stuffed crust pizzas would taste right now," Moe pleaded.

"With a pile of those Parmesan breadsticks on the side," Joe added as he smacked his lips and drooled.

"And a tall pitcher of beer with a frosty mug to wash it down," finished Moe.

Rex heard a grumbling squishy noise that came from Joe's stomach. It was a stomach that had a life of its own, and it seemed to have been awakened by their conversation of delectable foods. Rex's mouth dropped open in surprise when Joe's tummy grumbles were answered by the squeaky-squish noises coming from Moe's stomach. Back and forth, the two stomachs communicated to each other—grumble—squeaky-squish—grumble—squeaky-squish...

Rex's neck muscles tangled and bulged as his head rotated back and forth while he listened from stomach to stomach. *You guys just had breakfast for-crying-out-loud*, Rex thought. He wondered how they could possibly be hungry after that store's worth of food he'd seen them eat. Then his stomach growled.

"Hey, that was a good one." Joe laughed.

"Excuse me, I have a phone call to make," Rex said as he lifted himself out of the executive chair and made his moves for the doorway.

"There's a phone right there," Joe pointed out.

Rex halted. He turned to look at the phone on the desk, but Joe's stomach growled something fierce and Moe's stomach roared in response. Rex shook his head and he continued towards his room.

Rex went up to his room and closed the door. He sat on the bedside for a bit listening to the ocean waves outside and relaxing in the cool breeze coming through the windows. In the quiet and comforting coolness of the room, Rex thought he could easily take a nap and forget all his troubles. Looking briefly out the window and up the hill toward Dr. Cook's mansion, Rex felt a cold chill that made him shiver despite his attempt of self control.

Something was holding him back from making his call to Jesse and he wasn't sure what it was—he just wasn't sure he could acknowledge it. It could only be himself, he finally decided. No one was holding a gun to his head. He wondered why he might be hesitant to call the doctor, and then his stomach did that funny flip-flop thing it had been doing earlier when he thought of Jesse.

"Huh? I wonder what that's all about?" he said to no one.

The waves continued to crash outside and the breeze blew in through the windows despite whatever his thoughts might be. *Time passes on*, Rex thought. *Time passes with or without me. My thoughts and feelings are unimportant to the passage of the world around me.*

*My, aren't I the philosophical one this morning.*

Rex was startled out of his musing when the phone next to him screeched as if it were a Condor chick being raped. Rex dove for the phone so he didn't have to listen to the shriek a second time and because he had the premonition the call was for him.

"Tweedy residence," responded Rex in a deep, clogged, voice.

"Rex?" asked a soft female voice.

"I'm so glad you called," Rex answered in a warm tone.

"You are?" Moe asked.

"Get off the phone, ya numb-nut! This one's for me," Rex yelled into the phone.

Rex heard a click.

"Okay, Joe. You can get off the line as well," Rex growled.

"Aw, shit. I like to hear that love'y dovey stuff," Joe muttered before there was another click.

"Lilly?"

"Yes, Rex?"

"Ms. Achew and I would like to have a private conversation if you don't mind."

Rex heard another click through Jesse's shaky laughing on the other side of the phone line. "How'd you know they all picked up the phone?" Jesse asked.

"I didn't. I was just being careful. So how are you?"

There was a pause before Jesse said, "Oh, I don't know. I guess I've had better days. You know how it goes."

"No, I don't," Rex answered. "At least, I don't know how things go with you. You've been a new experience for me from the moment I heard your name."

Another pause.

"Am I?" Jesse asked.

Rex thought she sounded on the verge of tears. Her trembling voice gave him cause to stop and think before answering. He felt his answer would be important to Jesse right now, and he didn't want to hurt her or confuse her in any way regarding his emotions.

"You are the most important person in the world to me, Jesse," he said finally, surprised to hear his voice have as much emotion as Jesse's.

Jesse's response was immediate this time, but it didn't come in the form of words. Rex heard a heavy sigh from the other end, as if Jesse let out something she was holding in for a time. Then he heard her give a shaky chuckle.

"Are you ok?" Rex asked.

"Yes," Jesse responded after a moment. "But it was you just now that made me ok, maybe better than ok."

Rex thought they shared the same emotions about each other, and they were too shy or too new with the experience to express themselves in words. These emotions and feelings were new and different for Rex, and he liked them.

"Rex? Are you still there?"

"Ah, yeah. Yes! Sure I'm here." Now and forever, Rex wanted to add before deciding that was a bit premature.

"Well, I was just calling to say…" Jesse choked up before finishing her thoughts.

"You wanted to say our relationship has gone beyond our involvement with this case… I hope. And I think you were worried I'd pack up and go home when the case was over." Rex tried to put his emotions into a form they could both talk about—at least over the phone.

"What are you doing? Reading my mind?" Jesse laughed.

"Nope, just listening to my own mind for once," Rex said with a smile. Yes, this was a good feeling he'd like to capture and hold for awhile. It was something worth fighting to save.

"Can we meet? Ya know, get together without the Tweedy brothers on our back?" Jesse asked sounding apprehensive.

"You bet your booty we can," Rex said. "I was about to call you to ask the same thing."

"So you *are* reading my mind."

"Great minds think alike, they say," Rex said.

"What does that have to do with this conversation?" Jesse asked with a laugh. Rex was glad to hear her laugh. It was Jesse's normal laugh.

"Speak for yourself, Achew." Rex laughed along with Jesse.

"Gesundheit."

"Alright, you've rubbed that one in enough," Rex said. "When are you off work?"

"Oh, I could probably leave any time, it's not like people are dying to see me," Jesse said.

"Well, why don't I pick you up from work so we can be together for a while? We have to be at Lefty's on Highway 30 by about seven, and I have to appear as if I'm alone."

"Why, what's up?" Jesse asked in a more enthusiastic voice.

"I'll tell ya when I pick ya up. When can you be ready?"

"Well, I wasn't quite honest when I said I could leave anytime. There's a mound of things that need to be signed off today. Let's say one o'clock."

"Sounds terrific." Rex was hyped.

There was another pause.

"Okey dokey, pokey. You're in my palm pilot."

"Pokey? Is that all I am to you?" Rex laughed.

"Wait until one, and you'll find out." Jesse giggled in an evil manner.

"I'll be there," Rex said.

"Is that ok with you guys?" Jesse's voice came hollering out of the phone.

"Ouch. Ya didn't have to yell, Jesse," Moe cried.

Rex heard a click on the line.

"How' bout you, Joe," Jesse asked.

(*click*)

"Lilly?"

(*click*)

"See ya at one," Rex finished.

(*click*)

# CHAPTER TWENTY-TWO

Rex started up the steps of the county building at quarter to one. He would have been earlier, but Joe kept fussing over points of the case and different possibilities, causing a delay. Rex almost missed seeing Jesse as he ran up the stone steps with his head down. She was hidden in the shadows of one of the columns before the front entrance to the building. When Jesse popped out from the shadow and Rex caught sight of her, he was surprised and unprepared. He wasn't sure why he felt unprepared. Maybe it was her physical beauty that surprised him after not seeing her for a while. Rex was surprised because even in her baggy work clothes, that took away any sense of her figure, she was more beautiful than he remembered. He stopped on a step and peered up at Jesse with her looking down on him.

"Wowzers!" Rex laughed and smiled. "You look prettier today than yesterday."

Jesse came down the steps until she was one step higher than Rex. Jesse's smile turned from a grin to a wide open row of teeth as she walked down the stairs, and finally into outright laughter. Rex grasped her in his arms and gave her a tight hug. He eventually found her lips and they kissed.

"Don't you think it's time to get off the steps of the county building?" Rex asked as he broke his grasp on Jesse.

"Only if you're going with me," Jesse answered.

Rex didn't answer, but swept her down the steps toward the parking lot. Rex thought, *What the hell did I wake up to this morning?* A tiny voice in the back of his head said, *Too much, Too soon.*

Jesse asked, "Where're we going?" once they were back on Highway 30 and heading south.

"I assume you're talking about today, as in now?" Rex asked back. Jesse nodded and gave him a funny look.

"Oh, I thought we'd take a picnic over to the 14-mile marker. You know where it is?"

"Sure, good choice, except I hate all the black sand that sticks to everything."

"It's not a problem with the tarps I brought to lay down. Ya didn't happen to bring your swimsuit, did ya?"

"To work? Ah, no. But they always say, 'Where there's a will, there's a way.' Ya know what I mean, jellybean?" Jesse laughed.

"No, but I figured you didn't take a swimsuit to work, so I went down to see Moe on the way to pick you up, and he gave me a diveskin he thought would fit you. Plus I bought a bikini suit, if you'll wear it."

"Oh really, Moe knew my size?"

"I think he's been doing a little staring, and has your body imprinted upon his mind."

"And what else did you bring along?" Jesse asked as she craned her neck about to see what was in the backseat.

"Well, if we're going to go diving, I wanted to have all my stuff. It's all back there in the trunk."

"Sounds like you've got the whole day planned out."

"Up until 7:30 this evening."

"Oh yeah, you said we had to be at Lefty's by 7:00. What's that all about? And what'd you mean you had our case solved?"

"Well, we got a delivery from Kuro this morning. It was a package that had diagrams of the Maui Funeral Home and dossiers of all the home personnel," Rex said. "Everything Joe has been looking for over the years he's been working the case," Rex laughed.

"You're kidding."

"Nope, Kuro's on to our plan of wanting to find out what's going on at the funeral home."

"Shit." Jesse slapped her leg.

"Don't worry, he doesn't know about your involvement." Rex tried to comfort her.

"He only knows about me and Joe. At least I think that's all he knows. Have you and Kuro ever met?" Rex asked.

"Nope, I've never been in the funeral home. That was one of the things I was going to get around to in the next month or so when I finally got situated. Why do you ask?"

"Oh, that's for later."

They were driving through the curvy part on Highway 30 that bordered the cliffs over the Pacific on one side and the falling boulders on the other side. It was Jesse's turn to hold on tight and turn green as she waited to either be crushed by a huge rock or pitched into the ocean.

Both Rex and Jesse got quiet as they concentrated on the road. Rex was better at handling the big car through the curves and staying well behind the car in front of him, but he was still happy to see Jesse be anxious through this part of the drive as a payback for what she'd put him through earlier.

It wasn't far after the curves at Papawai Point that they reached flat land again and the 14-mile marker on Highway 30. Across from the marker was a two mile stretch of beach that was famous for its snorkeling and diving. What made this stretch of beach famous was the coral that grew within feet of the beach and the tranquil waters of the cove that surrounded the shoreline. The most novices of snorkelers could float about here and see the beautiful coral and reef fish. The area was so shallow one could swim well out into the ocean and still be in shallow water. The only problem that Rex had ever discovered here was finding his way through the maze of coral that grew to the surface. One could ride an ocean swell over a strip of coral only to find themselves trapped in a coral room where the walls reached the surface and there was no way out, and it wasn't the type of coral that one could walk on.

Rex pulled an illegal U-turn and parked at the far end of the beach. There were cars parked along the side of the highway, as many tourist and locals had the same idea of how to spend their afternoon.

When Rex opened the trunk, Jesse could see that he hadn't been kidding about coming prepared. The trunk was filled with a couple of small coolers, two scuba tanks, fins, towels, and whatever else Rex thought of for a beach picnic.

"Good thing you brought a big car," Jesse noted.

"Everything a camper could need. Grab those beach towels, if you would."

Jesse did as she was told while Rex grabbed two tarps and the coolers. They made their way onto the beach and plopped the tarps beneath the coolers. Jesse laid the towels on the coolers as Rex roamed the thin beach for some rocks or heavy driftwood to hold down the tarps.

It wasn't long before they had the tarps laid out and weighted down with dead coral and small volcanic rocks against the strong Pacific breezes. Jesse laid out the towels as Rex took off his shirt.

"I wish I could do that," Jesse said.

"Oh, I forgot. Come on back to the car." Rex smiled.

Popping open the trunk again, Rex pulled out a travel bag and handed it to Jesse.

"You'll have to change in the back. I'll look out for you, and I promise I won't peek."

"Like it would matter." Jesse huffed. "What's in here?" she asked as she held up the travel bag.

"You'll see. Go on, the coast is clear."

Jesse got into the back seat, and Rex leaned his back against the back driver's side window, with his arms across his chest while looking around him to see if anyone was coming.

Rex heard Jesse laughing inside the car. He could imagine what she was laughing at, but he was glad she wasn't unhappy with his choice of swimwear.

Rex had purchased a bikini bathing suit off the racks at Moe's Dive Shop for Jesse while Moe had been gathering the equipment for this afternoon's festivities. He hoped it would fit her. He couldn't decide about the fit seeing how there was little to put on. After seeing some girls with good figures walking the beaches in similar suits, Rex figured this suit was the "in" thing to be wearing. Moe had looked at it and smiled, but he didn't disagree.

Jesse opened the car door and popped out again all smiles and giggly as if she was embarrassed. Rex could see the top half of the suit fit her well, if one could call it "fitting."

"Wow! You look spectacular!" Rex said.

"Who picked out this suit?"

"I did. Don't you think it fits you perfectly?" Rex asked.

"Yeah, like a band-aid over a mosquito bite. There isn't much here to cover me." Yet Jesse smiled as she ran her hands up and down her body.

"Nope, but it looks good on you." Rex ogled.

"I don't think I would ever have the nerve to buy one of these for myself," Jesse said. She scooted up next to the car so it was hard for anyone to see her flesh.

"Well, come on. You can always wear the diveskin and no one will see a thing." Rex was disappointed Jesse didn't want to show her figure. Putting himself in her position, Rex figured he might get embarrassed as well.

Rex's body was sweaty by the time he lugged everything from the car. Jesse was on her beach towel sipping on a cold beer. Rex looked out and studied the diving boats parked outside the reef area. He knew this was a popular spot for dive-masters to take people who had never been diving, and the middle of the afternoon was the time most dive shops sent the novices to paddle about in calm waters.

Rex noted two of the smaller thirty-foot dive boats. Rex knew dive shops used these boats for short trips along the coast with novice divers. He was surprised to see a forty- to fifty-foot luxury boat parked just to the right of where he knew the center of the reef to be. This vessel appeared as an aircraft carrier in comparison to the smaller boats. Rex thought it was a good thing he brought his waterproof binoculars along so he could take a better look at the monstrous craft. Rex dug through his duffle, brought out a pair of black rubber coated binoculars, and spied on the large ship.

"What's ya looking at?" Jesse was curious.

"I'm not sure yet. But I think I've seen that larger vessel in the Lahaina harbor a few times, and I always wondered who owned it since it's so nice looking."

Rex thought the boat looked a lot like the *Mickey Fin*, Moe's dive boat, and he searched the bow for the boat's name. There, in large black letters, outlined in red, was the name "*Tora*."

Rex recognized the name from the World War II movie about the bombing of Pearl Harbor by the Japanese back in 1941, and he thought that in the movie the word "Tora" had been the Japanese code word to say: "The target has been sighted, and they are unaware of us," or something to that nature.

If Rex was right about this, it gave him some indication of the boat's ownership—Japanese for one thing. He absently wondered if Tora meant something like: "We're attacking the enemy and they are unaware of our presence." Something Kuro might be saying right now. Then he decided he might have Kuro on the brain and was just relating everything to him right now.

These thoughts gave Rex more reason to study the ship. Unfortunately, the boat was far enough away that Rex was unable to distinguish the faces of the people he could see on the deck of the boat. There was one individual that seemed to tower above the rest of those on the deck and this gave Rex an uneasy feeling as he thought of Yama, the "Mountain Killer."

Jesse repeated, "What's ya looking at?"

Rex sat down next to her and handed her the binoculars. "See that bigger boat out there?" Rex pointed to the *Tora*.

"Yeah," Jesse looked through the binoculars. "It's a nice one. What about it?"

"I think that's the Maui Funeral Home's boat."

"Gee, talk about your coincidences."

"Yeah, it makes me wonder if they're out searching for another body or something."

"You mean as in producing another body?"

"Yup," Rex said absentmindedly, lost in his thinking.

Rex grabbed a beer and lay down to rest on his towel next to Jesse.

Together, they spent some moments not talking. They relaxed and sipped on their beers while marveling at another perfect day on Maui. Their silence was long enough to allow their minds to drift.

"Ya know, I don't understand why I waited so long to make my move to Maui, and live here permanently," Rex said while still gazing out at the ocean.

Jesse didn't say anything, and Rex waited for her to react to his words. Jesse took another sip of her beer, while Rex watched her out of the corner of his eye. He was beginning to think she hadn't heard him, or that maybe she didn't care.

Suddenly Jesse jumped as if a sand crab had pinched her butt.

"What's a matter? Something get ya?"

"Yeah! You want to repeat what you just said? I'm not sure I heard you right."

Rex turned to Jesse and she looked back at him. "I said, I've decided to make Maui my home. You know, move from Michigan to Maui, making Maui my permanent residence. I want to buy a house here. Live to stay, as in park my butt here for good. Get it?"

"Oh, you wonderful man, you," Jesse exhaled. She set her beer behind her, and rolled over to climb on top of Rex's reclined body. Jesse gave him big, slurpy, sucking kisses while she locked his head in a mighty hug. Rex spilled his beer, but he didn't care as he defended himself from this merciless advance.

"You are serious?" Jesse asked when they broke off for air.

"Never more serious."

"Yipee!" Jesse cried. She latched herself to Rex's face again like a starfish intent on opening a clam and sucking out the muscle.

The kiss and hugging went on long enough to get Rex's bodily fluids flowing.

Jesse twisted her legs into his and started some posterior pressure.

Finally Rex broke away, and said, "We are in public, you know."

"Who cares?" Jesse said breathlessly and uncaring.

"You're not wearing much of a bathing suit." Rex broke away.

"I know. That's what makes it more exciting," Jesse said before she renewed her advance.

Rex heard children laugh nearby in the ocean, and it gave him an idea of something more acceptable to play at the moment.

"Why don't we go diving? That'll cool us off a bit," Rex pleaded.

"I guess having sex on this beach would be kinda public, wouldn't it?" Jesse finally noticed.

"I'd have to agree with that." Rex sighed.

Jesse rolled back off Rex, and he felt sweet relief the moment their sticking bodies parted. A sea breeze cooled the sweat on his torso and forehead. *This woman is going to drive me crazy with desire*, he thought.

It took only moments to assemble and get into their diving gear. Jesse's equipment was rental gear from Moe's Dive Shop, and it looked like experienced equipment. The paint on their tanks was chipped away and there were nicks in the aluminum. Jesse's US Divers regulators, one black, one yellow to denote a safety second, and her buoyancy compensator, were models that were a couple years old and had seen better days; but Rex knew them to be of a reliable make and he trusted Moe to have kept them in good working order. Rex had checked everything out before leaving the shop, and he knew it all worked well.

Rex noticed that Jesse overcame her shyness of being seen in her skimpy suit since she opted to not wear the diveskin. Rex was sure there were many eyeballs bulging from the men along the beach as well as many envious female glares as they spied Jesse strutting about in preparation for their dive.

Once they had all their gear on, except for their fins, they walked into the ankle high surf and out to sea.

"I remember a way through the coral here to the left," Rex pointed out. "We can get in the water to about chest high before stumbling on the coral."

"Sounds good to me," Jesse said. She pushed the purge button on her regulator, emitting a loud hiss, and ensuring her air was on.

They were far down the beach, and not bothered with other snorkelers or divers. They walked out to chest level. Rex's muscles shivered until he was accustomed to the water's temperature. He felt someone pinch his butt. Rex turned about and looked down into the clear waters to see Jesse already beneath the surface putting on her fins.

"My, aren't you the anxious one," Rex said to no one.

Rex put on his mask and bit down on his regulator before sitting down in the cool aqua waters. Rex could see that Jesse already had on her fins and was floating patiently for him. Jesse gave Rex a wave with her fingers while Rex struggled into his fins and clouded the water by kicking up sand.

Rex got his equipment situated, and stretched out in the tranquil bathtub-like ocean water. The world above had been silenced as the water pressured against his eardrums, and his muscles relaxed as they were freed from his body weight by his underwater buoyancy. He was disturbed only partially by the sound of his own inhalations and the bubbles of his exhales which sounded explosive at his shallow depth. He was finning in a horizontal position with Jesse behind him when he saw the beginnings of a huge lump of Lobe coral. He knew this was the most common coral found around the islands and it existed mostly around the shoreline. Sprouting out of the Lobe coral were patches of bleach white Cauliflower coral. Rex had yet to figure out why it was called Cauliflower coral when it didn't look like any cauliflower he'd ever seen. To him it appeared to be tree branches of coral shooting out of a central hub. The Cauliflower coral appeared much more like deer antlers, but someone had already named another type of coral Antler coral so Rex couldn't describe Cauliflower coral like that either. The only difference he could see was that Antler coral had branches branching off its branches where Cauliflower coral didn't branch out. Rex shook his head in confusion and understood why he'd not taken marine biology as his major in college.

Rex saw Jesse finning around the coral in the direction of deeper waters. He followed after her while watching pairs of Arc-Eye Hawkfish with their orange skin and a white strip horizontally down their bodies; and some Redbar Hawkfish that were more reddish than Arc-Eyes but had multiple white stripes that were vertical along their sides. There were plenty of Achilles, Sailfin, and Yellow Tang Surgeonfish. There were Whitespotted, and Whitebar Surgeonfish; Goldring and Convict Tang Surgeonfish. Rex noted many of the Wrasse family of fish with their longer, more tubular bodies opposed to the pancake like bodies of the surgeonfish. Only ten feet beneath the surface, Rex saw fish with all the reds, deep blues, oranges, greens, and yellows designed in such a color display it appeared as if Walt Disney had thrown up.

Once Rex and Jesse passed the ten foot depth, many of the colors disappeared to their eyes as sunlight was refracted by water. What the fish looked like beyond ten feet was anyone's guess.

Rex tried to follow Jesse in a game of hide and seek between the small mountains of coral, but he didn't feel like playing games. He decided to float about and take advantage of the bliss of weightlessness, and let Jesse expend all her energy and air trying to find her way around the coral canyons and ravines. Rex hovered and watched the pecking antics of some Clown Butterflyfish as they appeared to be nipping at the coral. He floated on and saw the Hawaii State fish, the: humu humu nuku nuku apua'a; but trying to pronounce its name in his mind gave him a headache. It was the only fish for which Rex knew the Hawaiian name. In English, it was called the Rectangular Triggerfish for its angular brown blocks of coloring.

Rex checked his gauges and was surprised how time passed beneath the surface. They'd been down over twenty minutes. Even if it was no more than forty feet deep, most of it being in the twenty five to thirty foot range, it was still plenty deep to drown someone, so he had to pay attention to what he was doing.

Rex looked around him and he didn't see Jesse. In fact, he couldn't recall seeing much of her after the first few minutes when he'd been eyeballing her cheeks from behind in her new bathing suit.

*What's with this girl?* Rex wondered. He figured she might be used to diving alone, but he was not. Rex kicked himself for not keeping better track of his diving partner since it was his responsibility as well.

Rex was only a couple kicks from the surface so he decided to follow the diving rule when one loses their partner, and that was to surface. He did this if only to cover all the bases and see his position in relation to the beach.

Rex surfaced, but he didn't take off his mask. He spotted the beach right off, and found he was farther out than he thought. Still, the water was shallow. Rex thought the people on the beach looked like munchkins, and he could barely make out where their towels and coolers were sitting in front of the Towncar. Rex rotated about to see how close he was to the dive boats.

"Oooops," exclaimed Rex into his regulator. He was less than a hundred feet from the *Tora*. He could definitely read the boat's name, and see the fine lines of the boat's structure, but he was unable to see the boat's deck.

Rex let some air out of his BC and he sank fifteen feet beneath the surface. Rex figured this was deep enough to not be seen from someone on deck, and he kicked off toward the side of the *Tora*. He wanted a better peek, plus he wanted away from the boat's path in case the boat tried to run him over. He knew he was being paranoid, but when one was out this far from land, with no visible help at hand, Rex figured it was better to be safe than sorry.

Swimming until he was about mid-ship, based on what he could see of the keel of the *Tora*, Rex swam back toward shore, away from the *Tora*, before surfacing. He surfaced only a couple hundred feet from the *Tora*, still only letting his head pop-up with the minimum of ripples. His regulator hissed and blew bubbles enough to attract anyone's attention.

Rex had the sun in his face, thus the *Tora* formed a shadow on the water that would make his head difficult to see from the *Tora*'s deck unless anyone was specifically looking for intruders up close to the boat's side. This proved to be a disadvantage for Rex since the sun's reflection was in his eyes and he could only make out the silhouettes of the people walking the deck. Still, there was no mistaking Yama's high and hulking shadow, and Yama appeared to be looking directly at Rex.

Rex didn't think Yama could see his small head out here in the ocean, especially with only one eye. But his thinking proved to be off as he watched Yama point directly at him. Yama must have said something since another figure joined him to look out to where he was pointing.

Rex suddenly felt as if he was under the spotlight, although he knew it was impossible for them to recognize him from their position. Had he surfaced ten feet away they wouldn't recognize him with his mask on and regulator distorting his face. Still, Rex felt incredibly vulnerable. He was about to duck his head beneath the surface, and be rid of these boogers, when a third person joined Yama and his friend on the deck. What caught Rex's attention was this third person was wearing a headset and appeared to be talking into a handheld microphone. The microphone was connected to a small box by a wire. Rex thought the box appeared like a lunchbox strapped to the newcomer's waist.

All three of the Yakuza were looking directly at Rex, and the headset guy was talking animatedly into his microphone. The guy would talk into the microphone then look at his lunchbox, and then he'd talk into the microphone again. Rex got the impression they were trying to talk to him and were not succeeding.

To test his theory, Rex raised his left arm out of the water and dramatically pointed toward his left ear. After pointing at his ear a few times, Rex drew his hand back and forth across his neck. His intention was to say that his hearing device didn't work and he couldn't hear what they were trying to tell him. Hopefully, he could trick the guys on the deck into thinking he was the person they were supposed to be talking to.

After making these motions several times, the guy with the headset acknowledged Rex when he formed a big "O" by raising his left arm and tapping the middle of his head in the universal signal of "O.K." Then he stopped talking into the microphone and just stared at Rex staring back at him.

Rex had no idea what was going on here. He ducked underwater and allowed himself to sink to the ocean floor at thirty feet. He needed to think this one through.

It was obvious to Rex the Yakuza had someone in the water they could communicate with, but why didn't the Yakuza diver respond to the guys on the deck? Apparently, their communication system didn't work. Rex wasn't surprised that a communication system didn't work since wireless transmission between boat and diver, or even diver to diver, was not a perfected technology.

The Yakuza having a person in the water spelled trouble with a capital T to Rex. What else would that Yakuza diver's mission be on this fine Maui afternoon when one considered Moe was supposed to make an important pickup soon? Would that someone from the funeral home be out here diving for pleasure? *Ummmm, maybe. Anything's possible.* But Rex didn't think this was the case here.

Rex stopped his floating around and started finning toward the beach. He knew it would be near impossible to find Jesse amid the coral maze, but he'd never know unless he tried. Rex wasn't worried about Jesse finding the beach on her own, but if the Yakuza had someone out here diving to drown another victim, and they chose Jesse to be that victim, Rex would like to be around to put a stop to that action.

Finning through one coral opening after another, Rex recognized some of the coral clusters as clusters he passed on the way out. Hopefully, Jesse had followed the same path back. He realized he was using up his air in gulps, and he tried to relax his panic since he knew he couldn't fight if he was too excited and not thinking.

Rex looked at his air gauge and saw he had 800 psi left. In this shallow calm water, Rex figured he had plenty of air to get back to the beach while searching for Jesse as he went. He assumed Jesse would have used less air than he did, since women tended to use less air than men, so air would be no problem for her. The problem was finding the Yakuza diver, or divers, before they put the hurt on an innocent swimmer to produce another body.

As Rex made for the beach, he ran into two other divers, a dad and a son taking pictures of the fish. Rex wondered which of the Yakuza would be a good enough diver to be able to drown someone. He ruled out Kuro, based on the fact Rex didn't think Kuro would subject himself to this type of "wet" work. Rex also took Yama off his list since he'd just seen the bruiser on the *Tora*'s deck—not that he could imagine that hulk underwater. Nor could Rex imagine Hi Onna in the water, or doing much in the way of physical activity with all her scars and deformations. That left Chiisai Desu, Yama's partner. *Naw, the man was too short and ugly*, Rex decided.

There had been two men on the deck with Yama; the first guy Yama talked to, then the second guy with the headset. Rex figured these two guys were the Otoko brothers, Naifu and Kiru. These two were the only other men left on Joe's funeral home list and neither of them had the physical appearance of Kuro or Chiisai Desu. Rex would have recognized Kuro right off the bat, and neither of the men was short enough to be Desu. Having accounted for three of the eight Yakuza, and figuring three of the Yakuza wouldn't be underwater, Kuro, Hi Onna, and Chiisai Desu, that left only Kuro's assistants, Migi and Hidari Te. One or both of the women were swimming around down here, and Rex would bet on this being a tag-team job. That meant Rex was looking for two female Japanese divers who were swimming about looking for someone to drown, and what a perfect place to drown a lone victim. Rex had seen all sorts of novice divers and snorkels paddling about the shallows alone, and he didn't think anyone would notice if someone dropped beneath the surface and didn't come up again. Once that person was underwater, all kinds of mayhem were possible.

Rex thought it'd be simple for two healthy women on a mission to hold one of these lone swimmers beneath the water long enough for the swimmer to lose consciousness and eventually drown. Half these swimmers swam about as if they were drowning victims waiting to happen. *Yup, the Yakuza divers would have an easy time of their job.*

Still, Rex maintained a path back to the beach in hopes of finding Jesse. There was no way he could cover the entire stretch of coral reef and protect every swimmer, and he wasn't sure he wanted to run across the Yakuza divers by himself anyway. He wasn't sure he was a match for two strong women underwater if they were trying to hold him under.

Rex popped up to the surface and checked their tarp area on the beach. There was still no sign of Jesse on the shore. *Shit!* Rex submerged, but he was only in twenty feet of water. Looking about, he saw nothing but coral and a school of light green and white goatfish. Nothing too exciting there, and the water was getting cloudy with sand as he neared the beach.

Rex kicked around a coral mini-mountain, and spied two female divers. Rex stopped, and pressed near the coral to watch them for a moment. He noted their long black hair which was pulled back in ponytails and flowing with the motion of the sea. The diver closer to Rex was smaller than the diver next to her. Rex thought these two divers resembled the two Te sisters in body type that he'd seen in Joe's photos and later in Kuro's notebook.

As Rex thought of tagging these two divers as the two Yakuza women, he also asked himself what they were doing. They were both on their bellies upon the sea floor with their hands dug into the sand to maintain their positions when the surge from the waves passed overhead. To Rex they appeared as if they were watching their favorite TV show—if Yakuza killers did that sort of thing.

Rex couldn't figure out what the two women were doing, so he pushed himself backward until they were out of his sight again, and he finned around the coral so he was directly behind the two women yet still out of their vision. Rex floated off the sea floor enough so he could view what they were watching with so much attention.

It didn't surprise Rex to see Jesse's figure ten feet in front of the two Yakuza divers. Rex was ensured it was Jesse when he recognized the tank on her back as the one he'd picked up at Moe's Dive Shop. But just seeing her body in the skimpy suit he'd given her was enough for Rex to identify Jesse no matter what scuba gear she had on. *Oh, what a bod.*

Jesse had her back to all of them and she was also on her belly as she lay upon the sandy ocean floor. Directly in front of her was another coral mini-mountain. This coral grew to the surface, and had all sorts of antler outcroppings with small caves for marine life to stake out as homes.

Rex could see Jesse had a small branch of drift wood in her right hand and she was playing in the sandy ocean floor just before the coral mountain. To Rex, it appeared Jesse was trying to coax something out of its cave at the base of the coral with her piece of wood. All around Jesse were surgeon and tang fish waiting to see what morsels appeared out of the coral soup of sand she was stirring. Rex chuckled and bubbled watching the impatient fish darting in and about Jesse like a storm of birds diving and swooping for a meal.

Suddenly, a green moray eel as thick as Jesse's arm popped its head out of the cave with its mouth hanging open and showing dagger teeth. Rex figured the eel was what Jesse had been teasing. Jesse wasn't poking the eel or touching it. She was digging in the sand just in front of the eel's head and pushing aside small crushed shells and other debris the eel had pushed out of its cave after eating the shell's inhabitants.

Rex could also see Jesse was so intent on the eel and the cloud of fish that were surrounding her, she was unaware of her other audience. Rex wasn't sure what to do. The Japanese divers weren't doing anything to disturb the show, and yet Rex was sure their purpose here was not to be entertained. He could either wait until they made their move, or he could go pick up Jesse and head for the beach.

Jesse continued to poke in the sand and bubble away oblivious to anything outside her vision. Rex studied the two Japanese divers and saw they were wearing mouth-masks. They also were wearing hearing devices attached to their mask straps which hung over their left ears. Rex thought the mouth-masks and hearing devices explained why the man with the headset on the deck of the *Tora* had tried to talk to him. The man must have mistaken Rex for one of these two divers that had the capability to talk back to him through their mouth-masks while they were underwater. Rex again wondered why neither of the Yakuza divers had responded to the guy on the *Tora* when he had tried to talk to Rex. Rex figured the range of their underwater walkie talkies was limited, or they forgot to change the batteries. The technology used was so finicky there could be any number of reasons why the things didn't work.

As Rex pondered and watched, the Yakuza diver on the right, the taller sister, turned her head in a way which suggested she was talking to her sister. Rex could see bubbles blowing from the taller sister and the other sister turned her head in the talker's direction. Rex decided that although the Yakuza divers couldn't talk to the *Tora*, they could talk to each other, and they were in the midst of hatching some evil scheme.

Not trusting the outcome of a four way wrestling match, Rex decided it would be better if he picked up Jesse and called it a day. Rex didn't trust his luck to save Jesse if these two Yakuza divers decided to attack her. There were too many variables and he hadn't planned on meeting the Yakuza this afternoon and in this manner.

Rex kicked off the bottom and swam directly at the two Yakuza divers. They still had their backs to him and seemed to be yammering away to each other. Rex swam up behind the taller diver without her seeing him. He stopped long enough to give her flowing pigtail a hearty tug, and then swam around her right side toward Jesse. Rex heard the taller diver yelp and bubble in surprise of his yank, and he was sorry he didn't have time to turn around and see her reaction.

As Rex swam up to Jesse, the eel felt him coming and slithered back into his cave. All the fish around Jesse scattered with the quickness of rabbits disappearing into a magician's hat. First they were there and then—poof—they were gone. Jesse must have felt him coming as well since she turned toward him before he reached her.

For a moment their eyes met and Jesse raised her arm to wave at Rex, but then Jesse's eyes shifted as she saw something beyond Rex and her eyes widened as if she was scared. Rex saw Jesse's eyes shift and her scared look, and it gave him the impression someone was about to attack him from behind. Rex whirled around just in time to see one of the Yakuza divers descending upon him. Rex realized the crazy woman had a knife in her right hand and was planning on plugging him in the back.

This wouldn't do at all. Rex thanked his lucky stars that human motion was slower underwater as the woman was already on him. He might have been feeling a knife rack his ribs, but instead he was quick enough to throw up his left forearm and block the woman's hand as her knife sliced through the water with deadly efficiency. Rex grabbed his assailant's wrist with his right hand, as he knew this woman was no match for his upper body; especially in open water where she had nothing to use for leverage. Plus, Rex held no qualms about beating on a woman when she was trying to kill him.

Rex cranked the wrist he had a hold of with a mighty wrench in a manner he was sure it was not meant to go. He heard the dulled snap of a twig and a scream of pain from the woman as she dropped the knife. Rex knew he had broken one of her forearm bones, but he wasn't finished with the woman who would have killed either him or Jesse if the tables were turned.

While the woman grabbed at his hand to release her arm, Rex drove his left fist into her diaphragm, knocking the air out of her lungs. Then Rex quickly reached up and tore off the woman's mask before sweeping his hand down to knock off her mouth-mask. Then he released her to her pain and suffering.

The Yakuza killer wasn't dead, but she was one hurting lady that still stood a good chance of drowning. Rex brought around his leg and pushed her back into the ocean floor. As the sand and silt produced a cloud around the Yakuza diver, Rex turned to find Jesse still there behind him. Rex reached out and Jesse grabbed his hand. Rex could see her wide eyes through her mask, and he knew she was still petrified.

Rex pulled Jesse close to his body and wrapped his arm around her. He wasn't going to lose his dive partner again, not with the Yakuza around. Jesse hugged him back as they swam toward the surface just a few kicks away.

They broke the surface, but Rex didn't allow Jesse to slow down. Rex held onto the yolk of Jesse's tank and kicked just as hard as his powerful legs could kick. With his free hand, Rex pushed the air button on his BC, and he was gratified as air rapidly filled the diving vest around his chest and back. Now he was moving along faster and with less effort as the BC held him above the water.

They weren't far from the beach, and Jesse filled her own BC to make the swim easier. With both of them kicking toward a common goal, and Rex knowing his way around the coral mountains, they made it to the beach in excellent time. Rex was glad that he'd picked this far side of the beach where entry and exit from the water was as simple as standing up and walking out.

But they didn't walk out of the water. They staggered about like drunken sailors, both of them too out of breath to talk. Rex had to help Jesse to her feet after she'd taken off her fins, and he held her up as they made it to their tarp and towels.

Once on the tarp, Jesse dropped her fins and her mask before pulling the quick release belt around her waist and letting her tank fall to the ground.

"Oh...God..." heaved Jesse as she let herself fall on her towel. "Why was that diver trying to knife you?" she asked as she turned over on her back and threw her arms above her head to expand her lungs.

Rex had already slid out of his gear and was hunting through his gear bag for his binoculars. "Those were Yakuza divers hunting for another body," he said absently.

Rex found his binoculars and turned them on the *Tora* to see what was happening on their deck. Jesse caught her breath before she was back up on her knees and looking out at the *Tora* as well.

"What, you think that lady was going to kill you so they could eventually use you as another body to do their smuggling?"

"Naw. I think she was just pissed off and wanted to get back at me—crazy bitch. Oops, excuse my French." Rex laughed as he dropped the binoculars and looked down at Jesse.

"That's all right. Growing up with four older brothers that were all jocks kind of breaks a girl's ears in," Jesse said as she reached for the binoculars. Rex handed them to her without saying a word.

Finally, Rex broke their silence. "Oh, so you know what it's like to play with the big boys, do ya?" He laughed as he said this.

"I bet I could beat the snot out of you," Jesse came back, but only as a joke.

"Oh you do, huh?" Rex looked back out at the *Tora*, and he could see that their divers had reached the back of the boat and were getting out of the water.

"I saw the way you fought that woman. You were either very nice, or you don't know anything about fighting." Jesse handed the binoculars back to Rex.

Rex took the binoculars back and peered at the rear of the *Tora*. He saw one diver was up on the diver platform on the back of the *Tora*, but the other diver was struggling with only one arm. Rex smiled since he knew this diver wasn't going diving for awhile. He watched as Yama descended to the diver platform. He reached down and grasped the diver in the water by her tank before he lifted her clear out of the water. Yama tried to stand the diver on the platform but when he released her, she fell flat on her butt.

"Oow," Rex said, "that must have hurt."

Yama waved his hands at the whole thing and climbed back up the ladder onto the deck. Rex swept the deck of the *Tora* with his binoculars, but he only saw one man, who he figured was one of the Otoko brothers. No one else was visible. He figured Kuro wasn't into boat trips, or he was inside the boat thinking up some evil scheme to get his next body. Rex was sure Kuro would be pissed off to find one of his killing divers maimed and out of action for a while. This made Rex smile some more.

Thinking back to what Jesse had just said, yes, he'd gone lenient on that woman diver. But she had been a woman, and Rex had never so much as spanked a woman before. He wasn't sure how to fight a female, but that last one sure had come at him like gangbusters. He better be ready for the next one, or it'd be him that was hurting and not the woman.

"Well, I'll let you decide how I really fight," Rex said to Jesse. "You must think all the serial killers I've caught in the past were a bunch of sissies."

"I'm not calling you a sissy, ya big dope." Jesse reached over and swatted Rex's leg.

"Ouch, that hurt." Rex smiled.

"Well, now maybe I'm calling you a sissy. I hardly touched you."

Rex didn't see anything of importance on the deck of the *Tora*. He dropped the binoculars and paid more attention to what, in his opinion, was a far more pleasant view—Jesse.

"How about lunching with me, if I'm not too much of a girl for you?" Rex asked.

"I thought you'd never ask." But instead of going for the picnic basket, Jesse sat up and pushed back her wet hair. "I think I owe you an apology, and a thank you for saving my life."

"How's that?" Rex asked as Jesse moved closer and wrapped her arms around his shoulders.

"That diver you fought off was after me, wasn't she?" Jesse asked as she looked into his eyes.

"Oh, I don't know. I yanked her hair pretty hard when I was swimming past her. That must have pissed her off a little."

"You mean you knew she was there?" Jesse asked with a surprised expression on her face.

"Yep. You had quite an audience while you were teasing that eel."

"What do ya mean? There was more than one of those crazy ladies?"

"Right again. There were two Yakuza killers out there. They were both eyeing you, and they looked like they were getting ready to pounce when I showed up." Rex smiled.

For a moment Jesse looked long into Rex's eyes. Rex wondered if Jesse was thinking of a way to say thank you for saving her life. Rex figured this was a first for her and he didn't want to belabor the point or the moment.

"I guess I owe you in a big way," Jesse said quietly, looking away. "No one's ever saved my life before. I didn't even realize I was in danger."

Rex smiled. "That'll teach you to stay with your dive partner next time."

"I guess you can be my dive partner anytime."

Jesse turned about to draw Rex near and gave him a long kiss.

When Jesse pulled away from the kiss, Rex could see a single tear rolling down her cheek. He reached up with his thumb and wiped the tear away before she could turn her head down.

"What's with the crying? I thought we came out of that one on the good side of things. They're the ones that're hurting, not us."

"They don't have anything to do with it," Jesse said with a crying laugh. Not understanding, Rex looked back into Jesse's eyes as if to find an answer. What he saw was how much he cared for this woman, and he wasn't sure how to explain these feelings. How could someone come to care so much for another person in such a short time? Rex understood how a life-threatening situation could bring people together, but he'd faced life-threatening situations almost all his life and they'd never made him feel like this about someone.

"What is it you're feeling, Jesse?"

"Damn it, Bana, I don't know for sure," Jesse cried as she pounded on his chest. "There just hasn't been enough time for me to be feeling like this about someone. Feeling like I've never felt before."

"So what's the problem? I've never felt like this before either, but you don't see me fighting it, do you?"

"It's because I'm scared to death of falling in love with you, Rex. You represent so much of the world I hate, and I'm afraid that if I fall in love with you that it's going to be your face I see on my cold table sometime—your dead face."

Rex did not have an answer for this problem. He'd always lived day to day and always for himself. Living and answering to another person was something new to him. Rex looked away from Jesse and remained silent. Finally, Jesse withdrew her arms and sat on her towel.

"Still want to picnic with me?" Rex asked.

Gazing out at the beautiful horizon, Jesse smiled and wiped away her tears before she said, "Of course, you knothead."

That got them laughing and returned them to their earlier mood of jocularity and the joy of being together. Rex sat and opened the large cooler that was under the shade of a palm tree. Inside were a couple of submarine sandwiches, a plastic container of chopped fruit, a bag of Maui Chips, a bag of Oreos Double-Stuff, and some plastic plates and eating utensils. Rex pulled out the plates and divvied out some food. Jesse went to the other cooler to pull out a couple of Stroh's longnecks. Rex even remembered to buy a box of wet-wipes to wash their hands and use as napkins.

It was a fine and simple feast that would remain unforgettable for Rex. In the future Rex could not think of a time when the food had tasted better; the ambiance more beautiful and comforting, the beer more thirst quenching, and the company finer.

As they ate, Rex caught Jesse up on the investigation, but mostly it was small talk and learning more about each other. It sounded to Rex that he'd like Jesse's family, which lived back in California. And Jesse said she would enjoy meeting big Sheriff Bana and Migisi someday.

Rex's mind kept returning to the *Tora*, which had left after picking up the two divers. Rex was going to have to ask Jesse if she would play the bait in his plan for catching the Yakuza red-handed, and he was having a difficult time raising the issue. To use Jesse as bait was a tremendous risk to her life, and he wasn't sure he could do that. Even to ask Jesse to do something like he planned would hurt Jesse badly. Finally, Rex determined not to ask Jesse. The fact that he even considered asking her was disgusting. No, they would have to find another way.

After packing up, Rex noticed the time. It was going on 4 p.m., and Rex knew they'd have to be starting back so he had plenty of time to prepare for Lefty's Saloon.

"Jesse, have you been in Lefty's Saloon very often?"

"Lefty's? Are you nuts? That place is a dive. But yes, I've been in there before. Why do you ask?" Jesse laughed.

"Well, that's where I have to be by seven tonight, like I told you, and I wanted to know about the place. I've only been in there once for a quick beer, and I don't know that much about it."

"What's your business there?"

"I'm meeting with Kuro at seven thirty."

"You are kidding, right?" Jesse asked seriously.

"Nope. That's where he wants to meet."

"Of course you're going alone, right?" Jesse asked sarcastically.

"That's kinda up to you."

"What'da ya mean? You want me to go along?"

"That's the idea. Except I want you to enter separately and sit somewhere where you can see everything. Kuro doesn't know you or your involvement in this case. There should be no problems for you," Rex said.

"Oh, no problems at all," Jesse said with a sarcastic tone.

"Well, do you have any girlfriends that will go in there with you? That would be the best way to do it," Rex asked.

"Not on this late of notice. Plus, it's a work night."

"Alright, just forget it," Rex said.

"No, what is it you want me to do?"

"Really? You're not just saying it cause I just saved you from a certain death?" laughed Rex.

"Smartass."

"I need someone on the inside that can keep an eye on me. If something happens, I want that person to be able to call in Joe, who'll be outside somewhere as backup."

Jesse returned to looking out on the horizon. They were in the shade now and the Pacific breeze felt fabulous to Rex as it cooled the sweat on his skin. Rex looked down at his bare chest and saw that he had become much darker over the last few days. *Yeah, I could live here for good*, he thought. To him, this had become a paradise. For Rex, the fun of Michigan winters had deteriorated with age. Still, Rex thought, he'd grown up in Michigan and there was Migisi and his father to handle. But Migisi didn't recognize him more times than he did, and his father would probably welcome the move.

"Okay, I'll do it." Jesse squealed and made Rex jump.

"Huh? What?" Rex asked still lost in thought. He turned and met Jesse's face and eyes again. *God, she's the most beautiful creature on this Earth*, Rex thought.

"I said I'll do it. I don't know what you've done to me, Bana, but I've never been this happy in all my life. And my happiness is not infatuation, it comes from true love. I can't explain it, I only know what my heart feels."

Jesse scooted over so their bodies met. "Hold me, Bana. Hold me tight and tell me you love me."

Rex moved over and wrapped his arms around Jesse so that they were still sitting down, but they were chest to chest, face to face. Drawing Jesse in close, Rex whispered in her ear, "I love you, Jesse, but you can quit calling me Bana."

# CHAPTER TWENTY-THREE

Rex parked the Towncar in a parking lot between Papalaua Street and Lahainaluna Road next to a Japanese grocery store called "Nasko's," in Lahaina. It was a good three blocks from Lefty's, but it was in the middle of the dinner hour and Lahaina was crowded with tourists and their vehicles, making it impossible to find a parking spot.

Lefty's Saloon opened to the back alley behind Front Street. Lefty's was not on the tourist's maps or the places rich people stopped to enjoy the local environment. Lefty himself, a World War II veteran that'd lost his right arm at Pearl Harbor, was a small and mean old man, and he ran his bar like his personality...dark and dirty.

It was nearing 7:00 p.m. and night had fallen. Rex stuck to the alleyways, away from the crowds and the traffic. In this part of town there were no street lights and one had to be wary of where they walked and what they stepped in. On the left side of the alley was the back of the stores, the restaurants, and their dumpsters that fronted to Front Street. The right side of the alley was lined with rundown houses with tin roofs, junk cars sitting in makeshift driveways, and lawns full of trash.

Rex walked slowly in the darkness with a wary eye constantly roving the shadows for trouble, as it had occurred to him that this might be a trap. Rex had a slim waist holster with his Glock 20 stuffed in his khaki shorts and hidden beneath his baggy Hawaiian shirt. It wasn't a comfortable fit for his gun, but he figured it was a hell of a lot better than going unarmed, and this alleyway was the perfect place to set up a trap.

Rex was also contemplating why Kuro might want this meeting. Obviously, Kuro had done his homework on Rex, and Rex wondered if Kuro didn't misread his past and motivations and think him a rogue killer with his own laws. Maybe Kuro might want to hire his services. Moe and Joe had come to a similar conclusion—who knew more about murder and murdering people than Rex. If a crime organization was looking for a body producer in the area, who was better at it than Rex?

Rex hoped Moe and Joe were in their positions around Lefty's and provided good back-up if necessary. Supposedly, Joe and Moe had arrived by 6:30 to take a good look around while some light remained. Joe was to park his unmarked cruiser in one of the makeshift driveways close to Lefty's. He was going to wait out the meeting from the cruiser in case there was a need to chase someone down by car. Plus Joe's car had a police radio and he could call for backup if something serious happened.

Moe was going to walk the alleyways and hang out in the shadows to keep an eye out for any of the funeral home goons. No one expected Kuro to come alone, so they were better off coming prepared for anything. Jesse still didn't know about Moe's involvement in this case, so Rex hadn't told her about Moe walking the alleyways. She would wonder why Moe would want to stick his neck out.

Jesse was hyped for the mission. Rex had dropped her off on Front Street fifteen minutes ago with instructions to sit in one of the corner booths. Lefty's Saloon consisted of only two walls and a corner support. It was a back corner opening of one of the Front Street buildings that had a tourist information booth and burger restaurant on the Front Street side.

"The man calls a meeting then he doesn't show," muttered Rex.

Rex fished the hair out of his beer, drank it, and was about to call it a night. It was 7:45 when Kuro strode up to Rex's booth.

Rex figured Kuro's lateness was deliberate, just as his show of patience was going to be deliberate. Rex figured Kuro was late so he could verify Rex was alone, and to make Rex edgy so his thinking and reactions might be off—thereby giving Kuro the initial advantage.

Rex was anything but edgy. He might have been a bit miffed at not being able to get a new beer after the hair incident, but Migisi and his teachings were close in his mind this evening. Rex thought this might be because he thought his past and persona were about to be questioned by Kuro. If there was one rule Rex had learned from Migisi, it was to remain cool and calm when facing an adversary. Once one was calm and relaxed one could think and react accordingly—*then one can beat the piss outta them*. Rex added this last part to Migisi's rule due to personal experience.

Rex was looking for trouble, and he caught Kuro's entrance from the Prison Street alley like a flash of light in the darkness. To Rex, Kuro stood out like a neon tube in a light bulb convention. He was dressed as if he could buy Lefty's Saloon rather than settling for patronage between its two roach infested walls. Kuro was wearing a black three piece suit that was tailor fit and impeccably clean. Rex thought Kuro's attire was appallingly inappropriate for this hot humid place considering the rest of the patrons were in shorts and some sort of light top—most were dirty, unshaven pier workers. Rex wondered if Kuro got jock itch under those piled layers of clothing in this heat and humidity. But once Rex got the mental image of itching bacteria thriving on his confined testes and in between his sweating thighs, he had to reach beneath the table and claw at his balls.

Once Rex relieved his subconsciously irritated testes, he noticed Kuro was wearing a bright pink shirt and a rosy tie beneath his tailored suit jacket. He didn't even appear to sweat. Rex wondered if Kuro was trying to make a fashion statement here in Lefty's Saloon. *Good luck, pal*, Rex thought.

Rex saw Kuro was carrying a shiny black leather briefcase. Rex was intrigued with this briefcase as it suggested this was going to be a business meeting. Rex's curiosity was peaked, as he thought there could be anything in that case.

Kuro came straight to Rex's booth. There was no smile on his face, and Rex couldn't find the Oriental's pupils to make eye contact. This personal aspect about Kuro continued to boil Rex's oil. He wanted to reach across the booth and yank open Kuro's eyelids to see for himself if the man had eyeballs in his head. *People without eyes...How is one supposed to know what the person is thinking if one can't see their eyes?* Rex wondered

Before Rex could vent his frustration over Kuro's tardiness and lack of eyeballs, Kuro was before his table and was bowing, rapidly asking for Rex's pardon.

"Please forgive my late arrival, Bana-san," Kuro said bowing up and down—up and down. "One of my loyal employees broke her arm in a swimming accident." Up and down. "It was necessary to take her to the hospital. I left her in the physician's care so I could return for our meeting."

"Spare me your sob story," Rex said curtly. He had his elbows on the sticky table while he glanced around the bar to see who was taking notice of this bowing exhibition. Rex thought, *Kuro has chosen his meeting place well.* No one batted an eye in their direction. Most of the patrons appeared to be having enough trouble coping with their own lives without sticking their noses into other's affairs. This seemed good to Rex. Jesse would be watching from across the room in her corner booth, but Rex avoided looking at her in case Kuro noticed his interest in her direction. Rex turned back to Kuro who was still bowing like a toy bird bobbing for water—up and down.

"Will you stop that bowing crap—it's embarrassing," Rex hissed.

Kuro bobbed into an erect position and smiled at Rex like the Cheshire cat in "Alice in Wonderland." Rex tried to glare back at Kuro but those damn pupils simply weren't there to focus on. Rex figured he'd center his vision of the tip of Kuro's nose since he couldn't see those freakin' eyeballs. *Maybe staring at his nose will drive the booger batty*, thought Rex.

Kuro's smile was giving Rex a problem as well. Rex could see a lot of nice and brilliantly white teeth; but he couldn't see Kuro's eyes, and that made it hard for him to judge the genuineness of Kuro's grin. Rex could imagine Kuro wearing this same smile as he threw his manicured hands into the intestines of a cadaver just so he could get a gut feeling for death. *He'd just keep smiling away*, Rex thought.

After they'd finished studying each other (Rex *felt* Kuro giving him the once over even if he couldn't see the mobster's eyes), Kuro slid smoothly into the bench opposite Rex. The fine cloth of Kuro's suit cleaned the scum off the bench's vinyl as he slid. Kuro's slide also created the sound of a fake and longwinded fart. Rex hoped this was just the vinyl of the bench creating that sound or it was going to be a short meeting.

*Good*, Rex thought, *the sucker's gonna have to clean his suit after this meeting. He won't get away from here as clean as he came.*

Rex was kicking himself for wearing shorts which allowed the skin on the back of his legs to stick to the dirty vinyl bench. Besides the fact Rex made fake farting noises every time he moved, it was hard telling what kind of crap was coming off the bench and sticking to his skin. This said nothing of the way the vinyl was making his legs sweat, thus causing his fake farts to sound wet—a disgusting sideshow.

Kuro set his briefcase on the bench between himself and the wall. Rex figured this was an appropriate precaution considering the nature of the business that milled in and out of Lefty's Saloon. Kuro squeaked and farted with every move; however, he made no indication that he was embarrassed in any way.

"It is not a 'sob story,' nor is it an excuse. There is no excuse for tardiness," stated Kuro as if he was a protocol teacher. "Tardiness is a poor choice of priorities." He gave his speech on manners even though he was making farting noises with every adjustment of his buttocks.

"Exactly," commented Rex, as he leaned back into the darkness of his booth where it would be difficult for Kuro to see his eyes. "In other words, you wanted to check out the place before you entered, huh?"

"A precautionary measure, you must understand," Kuro said as he waved for the waitress. *Good luck on that one*, Rex thought.

"No, I don't understand. And I don't understand why you called for this meeting," Rex commented. He was enjoying the ability to look down at Kuro when they were both seated. He especially enjoyed that his head was in the shadows where Kuro couldn't see his eyes. *Two can play at this lack of eyeball shit*, Rex thought.

"Then why did you attend? A man of your talents and ambitions must have other things to do on such a beautiful evening."

"Curiosity, one might say," Rex replied. "Curiosity of why you know so much about me while I know nothing about you. I'm curious as to why you spend time learning about me at all, and to what extent you do know about me."

Rex knew Kuro was listening, but Kuro was trying to wave down a waitress again. This made Rex chuckle. Maybe Kuro had not been here before, but Rex didn't believe that. Kuro must have chosen this place for a reason, and knowledge of the clientele and service must have been one of those reasons. Rex wondered if Kuro was trying to make this meeting seem of little importance.

"Excuse me while I go get some refreshment," Kuro stated. Kuro was up and out of the booth before Rex even had a chance to ask him to get him another beer. Rex did notice Kuro took his briefcase with him, and he held it close to his body as if it was a prized possession. *He must have something of value in that briefcase*, Rex thought. *I'll bet it's some sort of payoff.*

"I would have taken another beer," Rex mumbled to no one. "One without the hair this time."

Rex twiddled his thumbs for a few moments. He stole a peek over at Jesse, and saw she was playing with an empty beer glass. He'd seen her order a pitcher of Lefty's finest brew when the evening started, and now he could see the pitcher was as empty as her mug.

"Shit," Rex said to himself. He wondered if he was going to have to carry her out of here tonight. That certainly was not the plan, and he didn't want to be worrying about her as well as Kuro. He idly daydreamed about having sex with her again. Something else that wasn't in his plans for this evening, but Rex found he couldn't help himself.

"Here you go," Kuro said startling Rex out of his thoughts.

Kuro set another mug and a large foaming pitcher of beer before Rex. In his left hand, Kuro carried his briefcase and a mug for himself.

"Well," said Rex, "this kind of sets the balances even for you being late."

Rex looked into the bottom of his mug. After he blew it out to ensure there were no hairs or flakes of dead skin in it, Rex poured himself a heady brew. Rex grabbed Kuro's mug and filled it as well.

"You didn't strike me as a beer drinker, Kuro," Rex commented.

"I am not—in your league—as you Americans would say." Kuro smiled his toothy smile again. *His smile seems to come to him automatically*, Rex thought.

"A wine drinker?" Rex asked just to make conversation.

"A good wine is enjoyable on occasion, yes," Kuro nodded. "I am not a drinker of alcoholic beverages, Bana-san."

"Not even sake?" Rex asked raising his eyebrows—which Kuro couldn't see.

"Yes." Kuro smiled. "I enjoy warm sake on occasion."

Rex nodded his head in agreement, looked into his beer and decided it was all beer before he took a long chug. Rex sighed with satisfaction after his swallow, and he glanced about the bar again. He was surprised to see a waitress delivering another pitcher of beer to Jesse.

Rex turned his head back to see Kuro nosing him closely. "What?" Rex looked down his nose back at Kuro. "Do I have a booger hanging outta my nose or something?"

"'A booger?'" asked Kuro. "I am not current with American slang. What is it you are asking? I see nothing hanging out of your nose. I can barely see your nose in this light."

"Nothing," Rex said as he wiped his nose and leaned into the light. "So, what's this meeting all about?"

"You."

"Me?" Rex asked, retreating to his hiding place in the shadows of the booth. Rex imagined from Kuro's viewpoint that he was only a voice speaking out of the darkness.

"Yes. I am interested in why a man such as you is on the island at this particular time." He took another sip of his beer. "I thought your skills would be useful to the Maui Funeral Home."

"I've never been one to play with dead bodies. Exactly what skills do I possess that you feel would be useful to the Maui Funeral Home?"

Kuro laughed at this question, and he drank some of his beer. Although Rex couldn't see the man's eyes, he could tell from Kuro's overall expression that he didn't enjoy the bitter taste of his Hawaiian brew.

"Ahhhh—There is much in life to be desired before drinking this—beer." Kuro sighed after his drink.

Rex came out of the shadows laughing. He agreed with the man there. But considering its source, Lefty's Saloon, one took what they asked for.

"No, it is not a salesman or mortician that we seek at the home," Kuro said.

Rex asked, "Well, what sort of job were you looking to fill?"

"I must beg your pardon again, Bana-san. I have never done this before. That is, hire a person such as yourself."

"What sort of person were you looking to hire? Based on that personnel package you sent me, I'd say you know how to hire the kind of person you want."

"The personnel you speak of were hired by our home office in Tokyo, and they selected me to manage this group. It was the management in Tokyo that suggested I attempt to hire your services as a first option." Kuro appeared to be looking at his beer glass in distaste before continuing. "If you will: There is not a job—ah—classification—for the type of work you do. Is this not true?"

Rex tried to ponder everything that had been said and how it related to him, so he didn't answer or say anything immediately. After drinking the rest of his beer, Rex poured himself another one.

So now Rex knew the Yakuza big wigs were interested in what he was doing poking around their Maui operation. Rex was impressed as well as shocked and afraid. He was impressed he could draw the attention of the higher ups in Tokyo, but at the same time he didn't want the worldwide and powerful criminal resources of the Yakuza releasing a death contract for his head. Refusing an offer after the Yakuza had taken interest in him was like yanking the dragon's tail while not wearing armor—one could be toasted.

Rex noticed Kuro had drunk at least half his brew. *So,* Rex thought, *Kuro isn't too comfortable with this meeting either.* The fact that Kuro himself was nervous about this meeting and its outcome stressed the importance of this discussion even more to Rex. Rex hid in his darkness and continued to think about this one. When he did speak again, it was slowly and deliberately.

Rex said, "No. I cannot say that what I do has been placed into a job category. But what is it you think I do?"

Rex couldn't read Kuro's facial expression, but the way Kuro cocked his head gave Rex the impression Kuro was nosing at him to ask if Rex was kidding. Come to think about it, Rex had never sat down and asked himself what he hoped to accomplish in life—What were his life ambitions?—What did he want to achieve during his lifetime?—Did he really kiss Julie McKay full on the lips in third grade?

Kuro must have been put off by Rex's verbal question since he didn't say anything immediately. "You…" started Kuro. Then he grabbed his beer and finished it. Rex was polite enough to fill his glass again.

"Yes?" Rex asked.

"You kill people," Kuro said directly.

Rex wasn't shocked by this statement. He was trying to provoke just such a statement out of Kuro so it was open and on the table what they were talking about. Yes, he had killed murderers. This was nothing new and different. The way Rex saw it, killing was a byproduct of his job, not the original goal, but it happened. Rex's original goal with each job was to capture the killer, if he could, but if the murderer was going to force the issue and attempt to kill Rex instead of surrendering, he'd kill the man without batting an eye.

"I've had to kill men on occasion, yes," Rex agreed. "Are you suggesting I'm a rogue killer?"

Now it was Kuro's turn to drink his beer and ponder the question asked. Rex stayed in his darkness and watched for any change in Kuro's facial expression while he thought about this question. Kuro's expression remained lax as if he had a stroke and lost any muscle control or feeling in his face. Kuro's pallid facial skin seemed to sag with gravity. This gave Rex the impression Kuro had little understanding of the value for human life. One simply didn't ponder such a question without some internal turmoil which would appear in their expressions.

Finally, Kuro spoke without any change in facial expression that Rex could see. "It is a difficult question. You kill men who are murderers and antisocial themselves. But at what point do you become an executioner, Bana-san?" Kuro asked this question with an even face. It was a simple question to Kuro as if he had asked what was one plus one.

This was a difficult question for Rex to answer. It was the question Rex had asked himself for years. Rex was glad to hear someone else ask it for once because he would like to hear someone else's opinion. Rex had killed multiple murderers in the name of the law. And innocent people had died during his captures or killings of serial murderers. Rex constantly asked himself at what point did he become the murderer? Or was he one already?

"Have you ever killed a person?" Rex asked Kuro trying to switch sides of the table and get an opinion of another human, even if that human was a murderer himself. Rex realized this was the first time he'd ever sat across from a murderer and discussed murder in a civil setting—as if it was an emotionless business transaction.

"We are not talking about me," Kuro stated curtly. Kuro's rush of emotion was evident to Rex. Rex watched Kuro's face gain some muscularity and control beneath his skin. Kuro's face cringed as he contemplated his status as a murderer. The meaning of the question was starting to sink into Kuro's thoughts—*maybe for the first time*, Rex thought.

"Ah—so you have, and you have a conscience." Rex grimly laughed.

Rex caught another cringe in Kuro's face for a second. It was a squint Rex was sure Kuro didn't even know he'd made. *So, Mr. Perfect can't always hide what he's thinking. You can break through that shield*, Rex thought.

"I cannot answer that question," Kuro stated while he turned his face around the bar for the first time as if he was trying to avoid Rex's glare.

"Don't worry. There's no one here recording what you say." Rex laughed. "I have no more desire to be judged by society and fry in the electric chair for my crimes against humanity than you do."

Still, Kuro pressed his lips together and remained silent.

"Time to spit it out, Kuro," Rex said with force as he leaned forward forcing his presence on Kuro. "What is it you want me to do? And what's in the briefcase?"

Kuro sank back into the booth as if threatened by Rex's advance. Again, Kuro made a grimace, but this time he hissed through his perfect teeth. He said something rapidly in Japanese that Rex didn't catch, before he put his arm on the briefcase as if to protect it.

"You are a murderer even though you do not consider yourself as one," Kuro said as he leaned forward on the table.

"So are you," Rex growled.

Kuro continued as if he hadn't heard Rex. "You kill men in the name of the society; men whom society has labeled murderers. But you kill human beings nonetheless. Yet you attempt to pass yourself for a moral man, a man doing his duty I would think." Kuro hissed at Rex like a snake.

"So if I'm killing in the name of society, under what pretense do you kill?" Rex asked.

Kuro took another gulp of his beer, but did not respond to this question. Rex went back to the shadows. "Worst of all," Kuro continued ignoring Rex's question, "is that you pass your own judgment on men and condemn them to death as you see fit. It is as if you act like your God."

After a moment of silence, Rex answered quietly from his darkness. "No, there you're wrong, Kuro. I don't have a god, so I can't act like one."

"Very good, Bana-san, very good." Kuro smiled as he leaned back in the booth. Rex realized Kuro was still trying to bait him into anger or self pity, and Rex knew even if he could see Kuro's eyes, they wouldn't match the smile on his lips. His eyes would be as unemotional as a dead man's. Rex feared that Kuro was nuttier than he was.

"Here is my proposal, Bana-san. In my briefcase is one hundred thousand dollars in fifty and one hundred dollar denominations. This money is clean. I will give you this briefcase if you give me your word that you'll be on a plane to Detroit tomorrow afternoon. A seat has been reserved for you on tomorrow's Northwest flight and there is a plane ticket in the briefcase as well."

"First-class?" Rex asked out of curiosity.

Kuro grinned, apparently thinking he'd made a deal.

"First-class," Kuro said.

"Huh. That's an interesting proposition. A hundred grand for doing nothing but fly home in style—if one could call Northwest's first-class going in style."

"That is not my only proposition. We could always use your skills at the Maui Funeral Home. You can take the money in this briefcase as a signing bonus," Kuro said. "As I have said, or you might have guessed, the people from home office have taken an interest in your skills and abilities."

Rex spoke from his shadows. "Can I see what's in that briefcase? You know, just to be sure you're on the level."

Kuro was hesitant, and he turned his face around the bar again. Rex rested his elbows on the table and took a peek around as well. Then he quickly looked away as Jesse raised her glass in his direction when she saw him looking in her direction. He could have sworn she even winked.

"You appear to have attracted someone's attention," Kuro said. Kuro had also seen Jesse's tilt of the glass and wink of the eye in Rex's direction.

"Huh?" asked Rex, playing stupid, although he thought there was no need for acting since that act of bringing Jesse along was stupid enough. What was he thinking asking a woman, whose habits he didn't know, to watch his back in a life-threatening situation. *This love business has its drawbacks*, Rex thought.

"That woman over there." Kuro pointed at Jesse. "She has been watching us all night, and now I think she has drunk enough to be courageous. She just winked at you." Kuro grinned.

*Good, Kuro isn't taking Jesse seriously*, Rex thought.

"Well—ah—I'll take care of the lady business after we conclude our business," Rex said, just shaking his head in disbelief. "Now come on. Show me what you've got there, and then we'll talk about our possibilities."

Kuro gave one more look at Jesse, who was laughing away to nobody, and blinking her eyes very slowly as if she was trying to wink, but couldn't manage it with only a single eyelid.

"Only in America," Kuro whispered.

"What's that?" Rex asked.

"Nothing," Kuro said as he slid around and lifted the briefcase onto the table. Rex moved his mug and the near empty pitcher of beer out of the way. Kuro produced a small key from his inner suit coat pocket. He twirled the briefcase and opened its two locked latches. Then, Kuro slowly put the key back in his pocket before cracking open the lid of the briefcase. Kuro opened the briefcase so the side of the case came open and blocked anyone's view from outside the booth.

Rex expected to see a mountain of money, but when Kuro opened the case, it was only three quarters full of tightly wrapped bills. Rex didn't get much more than a glance before Kuro snapped shut the case and closed the latches. Rex had also noticed the airline ticket sticking out of a pocket inside the briefcase.

"That's what a hundred grand looks like in cash?" Rex asked. He drank the rest of his beer, and then he emptied the pitcher into his glass.

"What? Have you never seen one hundred thousand dollars?" Kuro asked in surprise.

"Well—ah—yeah, but never in cash. Usually I'm paid by check or money transfer."

"I thought you had seen large sums of money before based on your account balances at Michigan National Bank. You have Swiss accounts too, I presume."

"Let's just say I have accounts outside the U.S. which neither you, or the U.S. Government, will ever see." Rex smiled, although he was surprised Kuro had access to information on his accounts in Michigan. *You learn something new every day*, Rex thought. *I might have to start putting my money in jars and burying them in the back yard. Of course, this guy might be putting me on, and just saying things he knows nothing about.*

"And you're just going to give me all that money so I'll go home, huh?"

"I think you have grasped the idea, as you Americans say," Kuro stated.

"What? Don't you Japanese have your own clichés?" Rex asked with a grin.

"None for this situation that make sense when translated."

Rex drank some of his beer. He was beginning to feel a bit tipsy, and he knew that wasn't good for the situation. Suddenly there was a crash and a scuttlebutt that caught Rex's attention. Rex nearly leaped from the booth when he saw what all the commotion was about.

Three rough-looking characters had surrounded Jesse's booth, and now they were pushing and shoving over some argument between themselves. Rex recognized and had dealt with their type before, and the conclusion was normally nasty. Rex liked to call this type of person a motorhead. To Rex, they were the type that got drunk every night and pissed away their paychecks. In Rex's opinion they were wastes for lives since they had no ambition to do better for themselves or others. Rex had no problems with those with limitations. To him, it was what they did with those limitations that made the difference. Getting drunk each night so they had the courage to abuse women was not Rex's idea of doing something constructive with their lives.

Rex was in the midst of sliding out of his booth to bail out Jesse, when he saw Kuro pop out before him, straighten his tie and suit jacket, then head for Jesse's booth. What surprised Rex more was that Kuro left behind his briefcase. The briefcase was unlocked, and if anyone wanted to steal it, here was the opportunity.

Rex wasn't going to be left behind in saving his own maiden. He jumped out of the booth and was right behind Kuro as Kuro arrived at the push-shove match in front of Jesse's booth.

*Alright! A good old bar fight. I haven't had one of these in years,* Rex thought as he stood beside Kuro. The three molesters had their backs to Kuro and Rex. Rex saw the three were wearing oil-stained ball caps with a company logo on them. They were wearing stained white gas station shirts with the sleeves pulled off to show their meaty arms, and they wore dirty and baggy blue pants. Each of the motorheads stood in heavy black boots with black grease oozing out from beneath their soles. Rex figured each of these gentlemen would have an IQ lower than toilet mold, and the social manners to match.

These three were drunk. The booze had boosted their self esteem high enough to make them feel worthy of taking any woman they thought was defenseless and available—to take any woman who would prove their manliness this fine evening. That was the one thing they lacked proof of the most in their minds, their manliness. And once they'd taken that woman, with or without her participation, then by God, they were real men in their minds.

Rex felt Kuro looking up at him. He looked down at Kuro and wondered if Kuro might be another Jackie Chan. Then Rex thought, *Naw, Jackie Chan wouldn't be working for the Maui Funeral Home.* But if Kuro could fight as well as Jackie Chan, then they might make short work of these three slops. It was a positive impression. Kuro nodded at Rex. Rex winked at Kuro which made Kuro do a double take. Rex turned his attention on the back of the irritating person in the middle.

"Hey, pal," Rex said as he forcibly laid his right hand on the guy's left shoulder. Rex felt the shoulder was hot and sweaty, but hard with muscle.

With the quickness that he was expecting such an action, just dying for someone to grab him, the guy beneath Rex's palm whipped around to face Rex. Rex looked into the brown, bloodshot eyes of a life-long loser. Rex thought he was looking at the face of a man who had nothing to lose from the trouble he created. For the meanness, the pettiness this man created in the world, Rex saw this face deserved what it received in return from the world around him.

It had been days since Rex had confronted death in the eyes of Norman Lipshitz, but when he looked into the eyes of this troublemaker, something in Rex awoke like a crazed beast dying to burst out of his skin.

"The lady doesn't need your type of company," Rex said quietly and slowly.

The loser stepped back under the pressure of Rex's hand on his shoulder, and yet Rex knew he'd just pushed the right buttons to egg this guy into a fight.

"Who-ah-are ya-you ta sa-say what the lady needs," the loser said the last part in a rushing breath. His eyes blinked at about half the speed they were supposed to move.

*Yup, you're drunk, ya loser*, Rex thought. *Easy meat.*

"I'm a friend who has come to pick her up, and take her home," Rex said with an easy smile. By now the loser's two buddies had turned to surround Rex and cut him off from Kuro. It was as if they hadn't noticed Kuro at all, which Rex found strange since Kuro was dressed in a three piece suit and didn't belong in this place.

"Wa-well ma-maybe she dah-doesn't want to ga-go home wit ya-you," said the imbecile on Rex's left. Rex thought this guy acted as if he was on some drug, not drunk. This was scary since Rex knew one could beat someone on drugs all night and they just kept coming back at you.

"Since I brought the lady here, I think she will want to go home with me,"

Rex said, still smiling but feeling the tension increasing by the second.

"You brought the lady here, man? And you left her all alone?" asked the lunkhead on Rex's right. *Hey, this guy almost sounds coherent*, Rex thought. *He might have his wits about him, but he wasn't the leader of the group, and he'd follow the wave*, Rex figured.

"I had other business to attend to, not that it's any of your business. Now please move aside so I can escort the lady home," Rex said without moving. None of the three moved either.

"I-I don't believe ya," sighed the loser.

"I don't care what you believe. Now I'm asking you for the last time to step aside, because believe me, you're asking for more trouble than you think if you don't move along," Rex said in a quiet and icy voice.

"W-What? Trouble from an Injun?" The loser laughed before his mates joined in his laughter.

"Oh, now you're getting personal, and I don't like that," Rex said, dropping the smile and standing to full height. He was taller than any of the three, which forced them look up to him.

"Since when does it matter what a white man says to an Injun?" asked the loser. Rex noticed the loser had sobered up some now that he was looking at real trouble. But the drunkenness was still giving him dumb courage and was going to get him hurt.

"You have something against Native Americans, punk?!" Rex spat through gritted teeth. Rex took a step toward the loser, stepping into the loser's personal space, and glared down at him. The loser had no room to turn since there was an empty table behind him, but the booze kept him brave, and he stood his ground even if he was looking up into the meanest-looking eyes he'd ever seen.

"Yeah—they stink. They smell like an old woman's asshole," said the loser with a quirky laugh. His two buddies laughed along, and in the laughter Rex heard a clicking sound that was so quiet it would only be noticed by someone familiar with the noise and its meaning.

Rex leapt backward even as the clicking sound reverberated off his eardrums. Rex was suddenly aware that this loser was crazy enough to be one step from becoming a murderer like the ones Rex hunted for a living.

Rex looked down and saw the loser's right arm swinging out from behind his back. At the end of this swinging arm was a hand holding a long blade that caught whatever light there was in Lefty's Saloon. It flashed and flickered before Rex's eyes as the loser twirled the switch blade in his hand. The loser looked dead sober now, his eyelids at half mast, and Rex was sure he meant business. Rex judged the blade to be a seven inch slicer that was sharp enough to give him a shave.

The loser's buddies were sober enough to back off, as it appeared they wanted no part of this type of evening.

"Come get your girl, ya red-skinned scum," the loser growled.

But even as the "scum" came out of the loser's lips, Rex caught some movement out of the corner of his eye. The knife was kicked out of the loser's hand and went flying beneath the empty table behind him.

In the blink of an eye, Rex was now looking at a stunned loser who was grasping his hand in pain without knowing what hit him. As the loser stood there wondering where the kick had come from, another kick of a polished shoe caught him under the chin and laid him out on the empty table.

"Wow, that was quick and neat," popped out of Rex's mouth without thinking.

"Hey! Hey! That's enough rough stuff in here. Take it out in the alley or I'll call the cops," shouted a bull-looking bartender from behind the bar. Rex turned to see the bartender had a baseball bat in hand and looked mean enough to use it.

"No problem here," Rex said holding up his hands as if to say, "I didn't do anything."

Turning back around, Rex saw the loser's two buddies were rushing out of the bar on the Prison Street side. The loser was out cold, and Rex was amused to see Kuro had disappeared as fast as the two kicks he'd used to end this scene.

Looking over at Jesse's table, Rex saw that she was gone. Oh shit! Rex twirled about to see Kuro was returning to their table. Rex decided to join him since he was going to have to wait and see if Jesse had run to use the ladies room while he and Kuro were entertaining her would-be escorts.

Back at the booth, Rex found Kuro grabbing his briefcase as if he was going to leave.

"Is our meeting over?" Rex asked from behind Kuro's back.

Kuro whipped around with the same quickness as when he fought. Rex thought he must have surprised the little man and he held up his hands again to show he wasn't trying to do anything.

Kuro smiled his smile almost immediately upon seeing Rex. "You Americans talk too much. One should settle their disputes and be done with it," Kuro said.

"Does that mean the meeting's over?" Rex asked again.

"Yes. It is, I believe," Kuro said, before bowing once and turning back to the booth to grab his briefcase. When Kuro turned back to Rex he said, "That was a close call. I do not wish any interference with the authorities."

"But you went over to help that lady knowing it was going to end in a fight; a fight which would have attracted the police."

"A fight such as this one has no honor as you seem to think. You seem to think that you're saving of a damsel in distress. In reality those three men were about to fall on their faces out of drunkenness and drugs. This has no honor, am I not correct?"

Rex sighed. "Yeah, I guess you're right." Rex blew out his cheeks. "But it was going to be fun." Rex laughed.

"For you, maybe that would be enjoyable," Kuro said. "For me, it was nothing more than taking out the garbage at the end of the day. It is a nasty and meaningless chore, but one that needs to be done. I do these chores as I see necessary. I do not find enjoyment in their doing."

Rex remained silent and looked down at Kuro. He respected the little guy who seemed to have all his thoughts in order. Rex preferred to have a man like this on his side rather than facing him as an enemy.

"So, you gonna let me have the briefcase?" Rex asked.

Kuro smiled as if he was a salesman making his most rewarding sale. "You plan on leaving the island tomorrow," he stated.

Rex reached over and grabbed the briefcase out of Kuro's hand. Kuro offered some resistance, then he let go of the briefcase. Rex stepped back with his new bundle gripped in his hand and a smile on his face.

"You are going to leave on tomorrow's flight?" Kuro asked, now seemingly uncertain.

"Tomorrow? Oh, tomorrow's another day, and I've just become a hundred thousand dollars richer. I guess you'll have to go to the airport to see if I go, won't you?" Rex grinned and then walked away.

"You will find Yama waiting at the Tweedy residence to take you to the airport tomorrow afternoon," Kuro said to Rex's back.

Rex stopped and turned back around. "I don't think that would be a wise idea. Joe's on vacation and I don't think he'd be amused to find one of your henchmen at his doorstep. You're better off sending Yama to the airport if you want to see me board that plane."

"Why is it I feel we have made no progress tonight and Yama will be wasting his time tomorrow?" Kuro said, standing there with his hands held together before him.

"It must be the nature of your work that makes you paranoid." Rex smiled and headed back over to Jesse's booth.

Rex took a seat at Jesse's booth and waited. Before him was an empty mug and pitcher. Looking over at the booth where he'd left Kuro, Rex saw Kuro nose him suspiciously and then take a seat in the booth to watch. *Well, whatever*, Rex thought.

Next, Rex glanced over at the table next to him where the drunken loser remained out cold. Jesse popped out of the rest room and came back to her booth slowly as she looked all about her. She had a silly grin on her face.

"Oh, boy." Rex sighed.

Rex got out of the booth with the briefcase and grabbed Jesse before she piled into a table of drunks and got into real trouble.

"Hi ya, Rexy-pooh." Jesse giggled as Rex grabbed her right shoulder and turned her toward Prison Street. Jesse wrapped her arm around Rex's waist and laid her head on his shoulder as if it was the natural thing to do.

Rex knew Kuro was watching their exit, but he didn't bother to look to see Kuro's expression when it became obvious Jesse knew Rex. *Maybe this'll teach Kuro he isn't right about everything, and that he doesn't know everything that's going on*, thought Rex as they exited onto Prison Street.

As soon as they were in the shadows of Prison Street and no one could see them, Jesse popped up and resumed her normal walk. "So how'd I do?" she asked as perky as if she'd drunk a gallon of coffee.

"Wow," Rex stepped sideways so he could get a full view of Jesse. "Ya mean you're not drunk?" he asked in surprise.

"Me? Naw," Jesse said with a grin. "I didn't drink a thing while I was watching. Geez, how was I supposed to keep an eye on you if I was drunk?"

"But the empty pitchers and mugs ...?"

"Aw, those. I made a deal with the waitress, Mary, nice girl, to have her deliver full pitchers and mugs of beer and then replace them with empties later on so it appeared as if I was drinking that nasty stuff."

Rex walked on with his mouth open in surprise. He'd been fooled by someone who'd never done anything like this.

"I'm losing it, man," Rex grumbled.

"What's that?" Jesse asked as she came to his side and walked with him.

"Ya sure fooled me." Rex gaped at Jesse. "Great job, I mean, really, an excellent job. I think you had the entire bar fooled. Wow."

"Not the entire bar; Mary and the bartender knew what was going on and they were keeping an eye out for me."

"Yeah, that's the first time I've seen a bartender in Lefty's breaking up a fight. You must have paid him well."

"Oh, he was well paid, but not in cash, if that's what you're thinking."

Rex stopped again to look at Jesse in surprise. "What did ya give the man to keep an eye on you?"

Jesse stopped and looked up at Rex. "Oh nothing that won't wash off." Jesse smiled. When Rex frowned and appeared as if he wasn't going to take another step until he found out what Jesse had given another man, she came to Rex, leaned up and gave him a peck on the cheek. "There, the bartender got nothing better."

Rex grinned.

"I'll take you as an undercover back-up anytime," Rex said as he laughed and continued toward the Towncar.

"That sounds serious." Jesse laughed.

"More than you know," Rex said.

# CHAPTER TWENTY-FOUR

"So, how was your first undercover outing, pretty lady?" Joe asked as Rex and Jesse entered the pool room of Tweedy Manor.

"How'd you guys get back here so fast?" Rex asked before Jesse could answer. He had given Moe and Joe the okay sign as he and Jesse exited Lefty's and come directly to the Tweedy Manor, yet here were the two brothers playing pool and drinking beer as if they'd been home all night.

"We kept the necking and smooching to a minimum on our way home," Moe joked.

Rex didn't bother to justify that comment with an answer. Instead, he walked to one side of the pool table and laid out his new briefcase. Moe was lining up on the one ball in the best game he'd played in ages. He looked annoyed when Rex scattered his pool balls about the table, but his eyeballs nearly burst from his skull when Rex opened the case and he saw what was inside.

"Oh my gosh!" Jesse said. She drew next to Rex and laid her hand on his shoulder.

"This is how good she was!" Rex laughed pointing at the money. "We came outta Lefty's with a hundred thousand dollars more than when we entered," he puffed out his chest and boasted.

"Oh mother of pearls, will ya look at that," Moe said abandoning his pool stick.

"Jumpin Jehovah," Joe muttered with big round eyes and raised eyebrows.

"Rex! Kuro just gave you all that money?" Jesse asked, bouncing up and down on her toes with a greedy smile that said, "Gimmy gimmy gimmy."

"All that money, a nice leather briefcase, and a plane ticket back to Detroit scheduled for tomorrow afternoon." Rex grinned.

"Geez, all I got out of him was a kick-boxing lesson." Jesse laughed.

"He did put on a fine show, didn't he?" Rex smiled.

Joe looked confused, and asked, "What're you two gabbing about?"

Rex turned back to face him. "Oh, not much. Kuro saved Jesse from being mauled by three grease monkeys while we were in Lefty's. You know, the usual pond scum that hangs out in that place."

Moe was still eyeing Rex's loot when he asked, "What were you doing while Kuro was saving Jesse?"

Rex had to turn back around to answer Moe. "Beating my meat, I guess." Jesse slapped him on the arm. "Kuro said we Americans talk too much."

Jesse stopped her bouncing enthusiasm and turned from the prize money. "Well, *you* were just standing there doing nothing. Those guys were arguing about who was going first once they got me outside, Rex. You never said anything about getting raped on this undercover job."

"Oh, for Pete's sake, no one was gonna take you outside and rape you," Rex griped.

"No, cause I would've busted the balls of the first one that touched me," Jesse said, starting to get her whistle blowing. "You—you men think you're so macho and shit. Ha!" she stamped her foot and glared defiantly at Rex. Rex clutched his balls in defense.

"Jesse, I was simply trying to get the motley crew to move along without further trouble. We didn't need police coming on the scene at the time. There would have been too many questions," Rex said, turning and putting his hands on his hips so he could bend over and glare back at Jesse up close and personal.

"You, Rex Bana…" Jesse spat back at Rex. "… talk someone out of trouble to avoid a fight? I think not," Jesse retaliated.

Rex stood erect, twisting his head toward Moe or Joe for support. Both were examining the paint job on the ceiling. Rex sighed in resignation. "Yeah, well, that's sorta what Kuro said too," Rex grumbled.

He was not enjoying how this conversation had turned against him for reasons beyond his knowledge. Why was everyone pointing a finger at him and yelling, "killer" or "troublemaker?" He was the one they called to help them out of a difficult situation. If not for their request, he'd still be home chasing down some murderer, and possibly killing that murderer. *Wait a minute*, thought Rex, *this isn't coming out right.* He was back to square one: Asking himself if he wasn't the killer.

Moe was ogling the cash. "So, big guy, what's ya gonna do with all this spending money?"

"Not that it's any of my business," Joe cut in, "but as an officer of the law, I'm diligently bound by my duty to warn you that you can't fly back to Michigan with that much cash in hand."

"I don't know?" Rex stated.

"I suppose it's yours unless you want to turn it over to the Maui County Sheriff's Department," Joe said.

"Yeah, right, and see it all disappear into the hands of one major thief, Sheriff Wyatt Erp," Rex said snidely.

"Hey, you asked. I know I'll never admit I saw it. As far as I'm concerned you've earned a nice fee for this job that you'll never see out of my salary," Joe said.

"Or mine," Jesse added.

"But I feel guilty taking this money. I'm doing this job because it needs to be done, and out of friendship," Rex said. Then his eyes lit up as if he had an idea. "Never mind. I know exactly what I'll do with this money."

"I thought it would eventually occur to you," Joe said with a wide smile.

Rex closed up the case. "I'll be right back," he said and disappeared up the stairs.

As Rex went he heard Jesse asking, "What's he going to do with it?" But he never heard an answer since he was up in his room and sliding the case beneath his bed for safe keeping. Then Rex returned downstairs to hear Jesse giving her frightened version of the three creeps that tried to pick her up.

Rex laughed at Jesse's excited tale since it was somewhat exaggerated.

"So what is it Kuro asked you to do?" Moe asked.

"He said I should take the money and board the plane to Detroit tomorrow and forget I was ever here. That was one option."

"You took the money," Jesse said. "Does that mean you're leaving us to do this job by ourselves?" There was a worried look on Jesse's face as if she was sure that was what he was going to do.

"What did I tell you earlier this afternoon, Jesse?"

Jesse frowned and looked at the floor for a moment, lost in thought. Then she looked up, and Rex saw her face light up as if by magic. She laughed and said, "How could I ever forget? All this excitement today has blown away my mind."

"What?" asked Joe as he was caught in Jesse's excitement. "What'd he tell you this afternoon?"

Jesse stepped forward, wrapped her arms around Rex's waist, and looked up into Rex's face for a moment. Then she said, "I think that news is for Rex to tell you. All I can say is that it's news that will change my life."

"It'll change my life as well." Rex laughed as he wrapped his arms around Jesse and gave her a hug for making that change in his life.

"I'm moving my business to Maui," Rex stated.

"You're moving to Maui?" Joe asked with a slap of his leg.

Rex nodded as he continued to look down at Jesse with a happy smile.

"Hot diggity dog!" Joe laughed. "Alright!"

"There goes the neighborhood!" Moe bellowed.

Joe strutted over to the Rex and Jesse's hugging match and held out his right hand. "Let me be the first to welcome you to your true home. At least this is where you belong and can do the most good."

Rex took Joe's hand and gave him a long look in the eye as if to understand what Joe was talking about. Rex didn't know what he was going to do when he moved to Maui.

Moe came around and shook Rex's hand as well, but he didn't say anything, and he backed away quickly. Rex got the impression Moe was thinking the same thing he was thinking: What exactly would Rex do on Maui? And if he continued his current employment of hunting men, how was that going to go over with Joe and the Maui County Sheriff's Department?

Joe asked, "How did Kuro take you grabbing the money and leaving?"

Jesse unleashed herself and stepped away from Rex.

"Well, Kuro suggested I was a man without integrity or honor. That was the real reason I took the money. I was counting on him not to have the balls to start something against me without an immediate back-up. And for a second there I thought I was wrong. In the end he released the briefcase, still not knowing what I have planned. I figure Kuro is kicking himself in the butt for allowing me to walk out of Lefty's with the case. He doesn't know if he was set up or not. He didn't realize you were with me, Jesse."

"I thought I saw a surprised look on his face as you escorted me out of Lefty's. I don't think he knows I was with you. I think he believes you were helping out a woman who was in the wrong place at the wrong time. You were playing the knight in shining armor."

"You may be right, but Kuro will never think of me as a knight in shining armor. I know one thing, however. Kuro is going to be one P.O.'d kitten when he discovers I'm not taking that plane back to Detroit tomorrow afternoon," said Rex, shaking his head.

Moe laughed and said, "You're damn right about that. In fact, we might expect a visitor tomorrow afternoon. It might be a good afternoon to take Lilly out on the boat ride that she's been wanting."

"Well, shit. I couldn't just leave that money there. Kuro would have suspected more than ever what I was doing on the island at the moment. I had to give him something else to worry about."

A silence fell on the room with which Rex was uncomfortable. Finally, it was Joe that broke the quiet. He said, "No one will blame you for anything that happens, Rex, if that's what you're thinking."

"No, not at all," Moe put in while wearing a serious face for once.

"If anything, you're the one that has carried us through this case. We wouldn't have learned as much as we have, or made as much progress if not for you," said Jesse. "What're you going to do with that money? It's driving me batty."

Rex broke the tension by exploding with laughter. "Make a huge anonymous donation to Sara's Garden, of course. Or maybe I'll make it in the name of the Maui Funeral Home. Wouldn't Kuro just love getting the thank you note from Rev. Mother Makuahine for that one? Ha!"

They all laughed and agreed the Maui Funeral Home donation would be the best and the most ironic.

"Okay, that's what it'll be. A donation from the Yakuza themselves. Oh, I love it. I only wish I could see Kuro's face when he finds out how that hundred thousand will be used," Rex said.

Moe racked up the pool balls and they made small talk over a few games of eight ball. They drank a few beers, and the evening wore on. Moe continued to be miffed by Rex and Jesse's pool play. Jesse was not only a looker, but an outstanding pool player. "You learn a lot from four older brothers," Jesse offered.

Rex found nothing but joy when watching Jesse play pool; both in looking at her beautiful body and at the way she could sink a pool ball. *Yeah, everything feels right at the moment*, thought Rex. But he knew there was something missing, some task undone that needed doing before Jesse went home for the night.

Finally, it was getting late, and Rex needed to ask the question that he'd set out to ask at the beginning of the day. Jesse had just dropped the eight ball leaving Moe and Joe with an abundance of striped balls still on the table, when

Moe said, "I quit. But I'll say, I couldn't bow out to a prettier opponent."

"Why, thank you, Moe. I didn't know you cared," Rex said while hiking his shorts up to show off a hairy leg and buttock.

"Yes, sir. I believe I'll call it a night as well. Tomorrow's going to be here awful early for this little girl."

"Ah, Jesse, before you leave, there's something we need to talk about," said Rex as he put up his pool stick.

"Wedding plans already?" Moe laughed as he began to collect the other sticks.

Rex gave Moe a nasty look.

"Jesse. Why don't we take a walk on the beach? All the stars should be out by now."

Jesse nodded her head.

"I'll see you gentlemen later. Thanks for the beer and the pool games," said Jesse, heading toward the back door.

"I'll play pool with you anytime. Besides, you owe me a chance to redeem myself," Moe said.

"You better practice up first," Joe said. "See you guys later. There're some beach towels in the closet next to the backdoor. You better take a couple with you so you don't get a bunch of sand in your shorts again. See ya."

"You're disgusting." Jesse laughed, but she took a couple towels out of the closet anyway.

Rex and Jesse walked across the Tweedy's lawn without saying anything. Rex was too caught up in the sky to say much.

"So what's up, dream boy?" Jesse asked.

"Dream boy?"

"Yeah. You were lost in some sort of dream while you stared at the stars."

"I wasn't necessarily dreaming. I was wishing I didn't have to ask you this question I'm going to ask."

They went down the steps onto the beach. Rex put his arm over Jesse's shoulder. She hugged the towels, and they both gazed upon the spectacular scene before them. Again, it was another awesome sight for Rex.

"Okay, dream boy. What's this important question that you won't speak of in front of the Tweedys?" Jesse spread out one of the towels as she asked her question. She plopped the other towel on top of the one she spread out and then gracefully sat cross-legged as Rex continued to walk along the beach close-by for a moment.

When Rex turned around he looked at Jesse and smiled. "You're such a beautiful woman. You know that, don't you?"

"Oh, this must be a really bad question. You're starting out with compliments. This has been bothering you all day, so spit it out and get it over with."

Rex laughed at the way she could read his mood and his mind so easily after only a few days.

"Well, you know that if we are going to catch the Yakuza red-handed, in the act, as it were," Rex started out slowly, "...we're going to have to pull our own sting operation. We have to let them pick-up a person at the bar, watch them kidnap that person, then follow the Yakuza as they take that person out in their boat and try and drown that person. It's the only way we're going to catch them with enough evidence to put them away for good."

Jesse said nothing, so Rex continued to roam a close area of the beach. He continued to speak slowly and directly, as a teacher might instruct a student...trying to give that student all the material she needed to figure it out, but allowing her to make her own conclusions.

"For us to get the Yakuza interested in our particular person, we have to put someone out there that has all the qualifications as their other victims, right?"

"Qualifications of victims? Rex, that doesn't sound right."

"Okay," Rex said patiently. "I goofed on the proper word. Let me start again." Rex saw she was looking at her hands with great interest.

"Well, that person is going to have to appear alone, first off. That person will have to appear weak and easily intimidated, as well. So more than likely it'll have to be a woman..."

"Oh, cut the shit, Rex!" Jesse burst out. "I know where you're going with all this. You're just afraid to ask me: Will I play the bait for your little scheme?"

Rex stopped in his tracks and stared at Jesse. Maybe his eyes tricked him for a second, but Rex could have sworn he saw flames in Jesse's eyes when she yelled at him.

"Did I ever tell you one of my hobbies is finding the English definition of a person's name and then comparing that translation with that person's lifestyle?" Jesse asked.

Rex stopped his pacing as if he was surprised by the change in subjects.

"No," he said, and sat down cross-legged so he could be eye level with Jesse. Jesse smiled, and looked down at the towel as she sniffled and wiped the tears from her eyes. It was a cautious look.

"Well, I do. I translate a person's name into its English meaning so I can compare how their name, their label for life, compares with their lifestyle or what they have done with their lives," she said with a sniffle.

"I looked through my books on name origins and meanings. Do you know what I came up with for your name, Rex Bana?"

Rex shook his head. He hugged his knees and wondered if his destiny was about to fall upon him whether he liked it or not. Part of him wanted Jesse to stop now—*Don't tell me what my name means*—*It's gotta be bad*—but another part of him was saying—*Yeah, gimme the goods. I need to know.*

"We'll start with your first name. This part I'm sure you'll like," Jesse said, hugging her knees as well, and moving her face to sit upon them. "'Rex' is Latin for 'king.' You know, Tyrannosaurus Rex—the king of all dinosaurs—top of the food chain—king carnivore," Jesse said.

Rex said, "Okay. I knew that one. I figured it out when I was a kid. And you're right; I read about it while studying dinosaurs in the library. After learning the definition, the Tyrannosaurus Rex was always my favorite dinosaur." Rex smiled, although he was confused about what this discussion had to do with anything. Still, he added, "King—I can live with that."

"Yeah," Jesse acknowledged, and she paused for a moment in thoughtfulness. "It's interesting that T-Rex is your favorite dinosaur." Jesse let the statement hang for a moment. "I figured you'd enjoy the translation of Rex."

"But 'Bana' was tougher to translate," Jesse said. "I finally found its roots in my Anglo-Saxon listings. You know, King Arthur and the round table kind of thing. You know what the name 'Bana' means?"

"I'm sure you'll tell me."

"'Bana' means 'Slayer', as in 'Killer.'"

Jesse stopped there as if she wanted to watch Rex figure this one out for himself. But Rex showed no immediate reaction, so Jesse carried on. "So, in English, your name is: 'King Slayer,' or the slayer of kings, or maybe the king of slayers." Jesse stopped again. Rex had not moved a muscle since she had said "Slayer."

Rex was still staring back at Jesse, but it was as if she wasn't there anymore. It was as if he was seeing right through her. Jesse shivered and hugged her knees tight. Then she continued. "The only reason I bring this up is so you understand the meaning of your name. If you're going to continue to be important to me as you are now, I must know in my mind that you understand what it is you do."

Rex was stunned, and yet, he wasn't surprised. It was as if he knew this but hadn't expected it to be voiced by someone else. He had a feeling as if the missing piece of his life had been gently put in place for him by the first thing he'd loved. His very name pronounced his destiny—his fate in life. He was the king of killers, the king of slayers. He was King Slayer.

As the pieces meshed, Rex felt his mind, his self, pulling away from the body and burying itself within. Jesse and the world outside grew faint. All of his life's questions barreled in on him at once.

Was that all he was? A king of slayers?

Was that all he was meant to do with his life—kill others until he himself was killed?

These were questions which had been running through his mind for years, and now they had to be answered. His fate had been determined since his beginning. At birth Rex had been labeled as a slayer. In fact, his whole lineage on his father's side had been labeled slayers. Did they know that?

As far as Rex could see, he'd lived up to his label. Rex didn't create new life; he didn't create things at all. He was a destroyer, someone that killed life—a human Grim Reaper.

Worst of all, when Rex was given the chance to love and create something new, he twisted it into another method of death and destruction. Rex had taken the first woman he found worth loving in his adult life and asked her to be bait so he could continue to kill and destroy.

Suddenly, Rex knew his destiny had become clearer to him than most men would see during their lifetimes. Now the question became: was Rex happy with the fate that had been dealt to him, or was he strong enough to write his own fate and achieve his own desires?

Jesse came closer to Rex.

After a while, Jesse said, "I'll do it."

As if he was awaking from a deep sleep, Rex asked, "What? What did you say?"

"I'll play the bait as long as you promise to protect me."

"No, no..." Rex shook his head. "I made a stupid mistake even asking you to do such a thing. We'll think of something less dangerous."

"That's just it, don't you see?" Jesse asked. "If I don't play the guinea pig that means some other unsuspecting girl will be picked up tonight or tomorrow.

She might be killed before we can save her. I don't think I could live with that on my conscience. No, I think my love and my faith in the King Slayer will pull me through," Jesse said, giving Rex a tight hug.

For a long time they sat in silence. It was the silent world Rex was accustomed too. If Rex was going to change this sort of world he lived in, he knew that he'd have to let Jesse in at some point. Otherwise, he'd remain the solitary slayer that everyone saw. Yet Rex felt what everyone saw was not right.

Rex always sought to not be the killer that had been forced on him in Deputy Madison's barn. That was a matter of kill or be killed, and Rex never killed serial murderers unless they gave him no choice. Still, he had to ask himself if he didn't force the situation. Didn't he stand there and poke the snake until it tried to bite him and then he had to kill it?

Maybe it was time to drop the gun and find some other employment. But Rex knew he still had to complete this job. It might all be a moot point if he was killed trying to shut down this Yakuza operation.

Rex's thinking came back to the task at hand. "Ya know it's not just going to be me and Joe covering you on this job?"

"What?" Jesse asked in a dreamy voice. She moved away from Rex so she could see his face.

"I said that it will not only be Joe and me covering you through this whole thing."

"What? Is Curly going to show up so I have the Three Stooges covering my back?"

Rex laughed. He was glad to see Jesse maintained her sense of humor since he thought she was going to need it.

"No. We might end up looking like the Three Stooges, but Moe and some of his party might show up."

"You mean Moe Tweedy?"

"Yup."

"Who's he going to bring along, the salesgirl of the month?" Jesse snickered.

Rex didn't laugh, nor did he say anything for a moment. He wanted Jesse to figure it out for herself. That way, he could say he never told anyone that Moe was a Special Agent for the FBI.

"Not talking, huh?" Jesse asked. "Okay, I'll figure this one out by myself. Let's see, who do you know on this island that could offer assistance to a lady in need?" Jesse rested her chin in her palm and gazed at the stars as if she was thinking, or maybe she was expecting the answers to be written in the heavens some where.

"Dr. James Cook, a.k.a. Meat," Jesse guessed.

Rex peered up at the mansion with all its lights and the electrical fence, before saying, "Nope. You were on the right track with Moe Tweedy. Stay with him."

"You're not saying that Moe really is an agent for the FBI, are you? Is that why you guys looked so relieved when I said there was no way Moe could be an FBI agent?"

"You're right, but I didn't tell you, okay?" Rex said.

"Moe works undercover for the FBI?" Jesse asked. "But if I know, I would imagine all of Maui County knows."

"What you should know is that there will be a lot of professionals out there to keep an eye on you at all times and to protect you. I believe Moe will have someone from the Coast Guard following you if they take you out on a boat, as well. In fact, Moe, Joe, and I will be following in the *Mickey Fin* if it gets to that point."

"All this for me!" Jesse said with a giggle.

"All this for you. God, Jesse. I wouldn't want a hair on your head hurt. Boy, didn't that come out sounding stupid."

"Stupid or not, I'm in. I put my life in your hands," Jesse said seriously.

Rex frowned at this, but he didn't say anything. Eventually, he nodded his head as if he agreed to Jesse's terms.

"Come on lets tell the Tweedys the good news," Rex said as he started to get up.

"Good news? Me, being bait at the end of a sharp hook is considered good news?"

"Well, you know..." Rex said.

"No, I don't know, but come here a second." Jesse waved Rex toward her.

"What?"

"Gimme a little smooch under the beautiful stars," Jesse said as she puckered up like a fish.

Rex laughed at Jesse's face and then he leapfrogged on top of Jesse to give her smooches and then some.

It was a half-hour before either Jesse or Rex bothered to look at the stars, and it was only when they were putting their clothes back on that Rex realized they had to stop meeting this way.

While Rex attempted to shake out his shorts, and Jesse cleaned off the beach towel, a bright spotlight froze them in their positions.

Rex's first impulse was to run, but then he remembered Jesse was next to him and he couldn't run off without her. Rex stood his ground and held up his hand to ward off the glare of the light so he might see who was pointing it at them.

For a moment, Rex felt as if he was an animal caught in the headlights of a speeding car. Then he realized the light was coming from the direction of the ocean, and it had to be a large dive light to be coming out of the waves. Abruptly, the light went out.

"Sorry," said a deep voice that made Rex shiver. Rex's eyes had yet to adjust to the darkness, but he could tell an inhumanly large person was stalking towards them from the ocean.

Rex felt his chest tighten, and Jesse whispered, "Who is it?"

"My name's James Cook. You know me as Dr. Cook, ex-pathologist of Maui County. How nice to see you again, Jesse," said a mountain of a man that came to a halt a few feet away from Rex.

A few moments passed as each party assessed the other.

"I see the cat has your tongue as usual, Rex Bana. You should see a doctor about that; but then, you're surrounded by doctors already, aren't you?" Dr. Cook smiled. Rex could see the sparkle on ivory in the middle of a dark moon which was blocking his vision of the stars.

"No, I was momentarily tongue-tied when I saw an upstanding citizen of Maui, a protector of Maui's sovereignty, out spear-fishing in the middle of the night," Rex said. When he finished his speech, Rex flashed his own cheesy smile at the doctor.

"Ya caught me, Rex. I was out fishing," Dr. Cook bellowed.

"You do know it's illegal to spearfish in Maui waters," Rex came-back.

"As usual, you have jumped to the wrong conclusion concerning my activities, Rex. I wasn't spear-fishing. Hell, I never even cocked the damn thing. I only take it along in case there's an adventurous reef shark. I saw a fourteen foot Mako out here one night, and that's when I started carrying a spear-gun on my night dives. It's believed that Makos are nocturnal feeders, and they like to come up from behind and beneath you where you can't see them coming."

"Sneaky devils, huh," Rex pointed out.

Jesse continued picking up and folding the towels through this odd conversation without saying a word. When Rex saw she was done, he knew it was his cue to say, "Buenos noches compadre y adíos."

"Before you run off, Rex, may I extend an invitation for you to stop in for a chat? Well, it's really a long overdue talk," Cook said. He still hadn't moved a muscle since starting this conversation, and again Rex felt a shiver build up along the back of his neck. He was forced to shrug his shoulders and roll his head to keep from shuddering all over his body. It was as if someone scratched a chalkboard every time he thought of Cook.

"What's this conversation to be about?" Rex asked once he got control of himself.

"About you, but I don't want to spoil the surprise by saying too much. Besides, I believe that you two and the Tweedy brothers have some business to take care of first."

Rex was taken aback by Cook's implications and he wondered how Cook could have come across his knowledge. Rex asked, "What business is that?"

"Oh, don't worry. The Yakuza won't hear a thing from me. In fact, this is a great relief to me. I hated leaving that burden behind for Dr. Achew to find out for herself."

"Gesundheit," Jesse said.

Cook burst out in laughter. "Ah, that's a good one. Sorry, Jesse, but you caught me off guard. I don't mean to laugh at you."

"I'm glad there're some gentlemen left in the world," Jesse said while kicking Rex in the shin.

"Really? Let me know when you find one." Cook laughed. He laughed a deep hearty laugh of a man without a care in the world as he turned and headed back to his side of the beach and back to his mansion.

"Don't forget about our talk, Rex," Cook yelled back at them as he climbed up the stairs to his expansive yard.

"I hope he fries himself on his electrical fence," Rex grumbled.

"I HEARD THAT," Cook bellowed from an ungodly distance. "GOOD NIGHT."

Laughing, Jesse grabbed Rex's arm and started dragging him toward the Tweedy's stairway. Rex looked as if he was ready to charge after Cook to have his "talk" right then and there.


Rex and Jesse found Moe and Joe at the pool table just as they were earlier in the evening.

"Geez, don't you two have other lives to live?" Rex grumped as he headed for the fridge to get a long-awaited beer.

Jesse danced around the pool table and poked Moe in the side again. "Ouch! I wish you wouldn't do that, woman. I bruise easily."

Jesse continued to stand there staring at Moe with a grin on her face. "What's with you, lady? Did Rex go and fill your panties with sand again?"

Jesse punched Moe's arm. "There, I hope that does leave a bruise for all the mean things you've been pulling on me."

Rex came around the bar with a couple bottles of beer and handed one to Jesse.

"What's she talking about, Rex? What'd you two talk about down on that beach?" Moe asked with a worried face. Rex shrugged.

"I didn't tell you a thing about Moe being an FBI agent, did I Jesse? Honest to God, Moe. I didn't say a word," Rex said.

"I figured it out myself a long time ago, anyway. It's not really much of a secret. Even your neighbor seems to know."

"Who, Cook?" Moe asked.

Rex nodded.

"That doesn't surprise me," Joe said. "I talk to him on occasion. He's an odd character, there's no doubt about that, but nothing happens on this island that he doesn't seem to know about—I mean nothing. He knows about the Yakuza operation and everything."

"Yeah, I've noticed some strange characters pulling into that estate. Some people come in limos and others come in beat-to-shit pick-ups. He seems to know everyone on the island, and I'm sure that's the tip of the iceberg," said Moe.

"I would imagine he has the money to pay for any information he wants to know," Rex commented. "I just can't imagine why he wants to know."

"I understand that he's a war hero and was a Recon expert from the Vietnam War. I know he was highly decorated for something. Maybe he still likes to dabble," suggested Joe.

"Well, he seems awful paranoid to me," Rex stated, sipping on his beer.

"Are you guys trying to change the subject or something?" Jesse asked anxiously.

"Change it from what?" Moe asked still trying to play the innocent.

Jesse smacked Moe in the arm again.

"Ouch!" Moe complained. "I tell ya, woman, you do that again and I'm gonna smack you back."

"Oh yeah! You just try it, buster. You just see if you're fast enough to catch me," Jesse said while taking a step backward, just out of Moe's arm reach.

"We were discussing our next plan of action, weren't we? Now that I know you work for the FBI, maybe you can fill me in about what you know about the Yakuza that I do not," Jesse asked.

As Moe started, Joe passed around fresh beers and returned the empties to the bar. "Well, Jesse, I hate to disappoint you, but I don't know much more than you already know. I've spent the last year just getting them to trust me, and trying to get in closer with the higher-ups, one might say."

"This whole operation of yours, ours, is frustrating since Rex has discovered, and gotten more into the Yakuza's confidence than I could have done in a few years. His actions and reputation have plopped him right in the middle of this section of the Yakuza Empire—that was my goal within another couple years," Moe said with a sad frown on his face as he shook his head.

Rex hadn't really seen it this way, but now, as he looked on at Moe, he saw how Moe was right. For someone like him, a newcomer to the Yakuza, it would take years of service under the Yakuza's ever-watchful eyes for him to become trusted within their infrastructure. Rex realized this was an extensive operation the FBI had planned. It was an expensive plan to allow their mole to dig deep into the Yakuza operation over the years, and discover as much as he could before making the bust.

Moe saying his name brought Rex back from his pondering. "In less than a week, Rex has managed what the FBI, and a shitload of government money and assets, couldn't manage to do in three years. He's gained the Yakuza's trust and even has them thinking he's on their payroll. You're not going to become a double agent and take up with the Yakuza, are you?" Moe asked Rex. Rex saw no laugh in that Tweedy face.

Rex moved out from under that gaze and came around the pool table to place his hand softly on Moe's shoulder. Rex looked directly into Moe's eyes before he spoke. "I would never betray the trust of a friend, Moe."

They looked into each other's eyes for a long count.

"Then it's true what Joe said," said Moe in a throaty voice.

"What?" Rex asked.

"Rex Bana is a blood brother," answered Moe.

Rex turned his head to look at Joe. "You said that?" Joe shrugged, but he didn't look away nor was he smiling.

"Then I guess that makes us thick as blood," said Rex.

"What're you guys going to do, slit your palms and do the brotherly handshake or something?" Jesse asked with a laugh.

Rex turned toward Jesse. "Hey, that sounds like a good idea. We'll all slice our palms and shake to make this a crime-busting force like no other—blood sworn to keep the peace. Yeah!"

Quick as a flash, Rex whipped around and grabbed Jesse's forearm with one hand, then he wrapped his other arm around her waist and pulled her in close to his body.

"Where's the knife, Joe?" Rex asked as he fought to contain the giggling wildcat.

"Oh no…I don't what any part of this." Joe laughed. "But you two ought to look into renting a room sometime, you're making a spectacle of yourselves."

That was enough for Rex. He released his laughing playmate. Rex felt a bit excited after that brief wrestling match with Jesse, and it was going to be hard to keep his manlihood in his shorts.

"Okay," Rex sighed. "Phew! I guess it's time to get down to business." But instead of talking business, Rex caught a glimpse of everyone's low beer level and made a run to the fridge. Moe and Joe went back to playing pool, while Jesse sat on a bar stool to finish off what beer she had.

Rex moved amongst them and completed his doling duties before he got serious. "Okay, boys and girls, it's time for the first piece of good news," Rex started. The Tweedys put aside their cues, and Jesse perked up on her bar stool.

"Jesse has agreed to be the enticement that will allow us to catch the Yakuza red-handed."

"Really?" Joe said. He stepped over and gave Jesse a pat on the back and a little hug.

"You're kidding?" Moe said. He started to move toward Jesse, but Joe beat him to her. "Alight! Now we're cookin'."

"I thought that would make everyone's day." Jesse gave everyone a grim smile and sipped on her beer.

"Have you guys figured out where they're picking up these victims?" Rex asked.

"Joe and I have talked about that," Moe said. "Kuro has met me twice at Lefty's Saloon, and nowhere else. Plus, he picked Lefty's as a place to meet Rex."

"Yes, and he must be comfortable with Lefty's since he walked in there carrying a large sum of money," Jesse pointed out.

"I've also followed some of the Maui Funeral Home people into Lefty's on various occasions," Joe pointed out. "Although they've frequented a number of other bars and restaurants besides Lefty's as well when I've followed them."

"I would imagine that Kuro is smart enough not to use the same bar all the time," Jesse noted.

"Yup, you're probably right there. I know if I were in his position, I wouldn't hunt the same place every time," Rex said.

"We have to start someplace. I vote we try Lefty's first. It gets so dark in there you can't really see anyone's features anyway," suggested Moe.

"Anyone disagree?" Rex asked. There didn't appear to be any dispute. "Lefty's it is. For now, let's call it a night. I'm pooped."

"I would think so," Joe squawked like a mother-hen.

"Remember, I'm supposed to be catching a plane back to Detroit tomorrow afternoon. And I expect you," Rex pointed at Joe, "… to be taking me to the airport."

"That's right!" Jesse exclaimed. "You're supposed to leave with your money." Jesse clapped her hands to her face.

"And I *will* leave, just as Kuro expects. Cause ya know someone from the Maui Funeral Home is going to be at the airport to ensure I get on the plane."

Jesse, Moe, and Joe stared at Rex for a moment. None of them wanted to ask, "Are you really going to leave?"

"I'll be right back, of course," Rex claimed. "I shouldn't be gone more than a few hours. It all depends what I can get to fly back, and I won't know that till I make some calls tomorrow morning." Rex watched as Jesse's, Moe's, and Joe's faces went from sighs of relief to bewilderment.

"Shall we plan on starting our operation tomorrow night?" Rex asked.

"Well, are you gonna be here or not?" Moe whined.

"Of course I'll be here, ya ninny. Ya don't think I'd let you guys have all the fun, do ya?"

"How are you going to get on a plane bound for Detroit and get back here in a couple hours?" Joe huffed.

"Ah, but you must not be familiar with the route this Northwest flight takes to Detroit," Rex said.

"No, I'm not as well traveled as you. Would you care to enlighten us as to what you plan?" puffed Joe.

"It's simple, really. Don't work up a lather, Joe. I'll get on the flight to Detroit to satisfy the curious Yakuza. But that flight stops in Honolulu to add more passengers and fuel. It's about an hour layover, and the passengers can leave the plane to roam at will."

"Oh, I get it!" Jesse clapped her hands together before her face. "You're going get off the plane in Honolulu, and then fly back here. Oh, I love it." Jesse clapped her hands together again and giggled.

"You're the winner of the sixty-four thousand dollar question." Rex pointed at Jesse.

"You really think that will work, Rex?" Moe asked in a serious tone. "What if they have someone on the plane to watch you? What if they plan to escort you all the way back to Detroit, then see you safely to your home?

"We're not dealing with a local problem, Rex. The Yakuza organization is world wide. If the big guys in Tokyo were aware enough to pay you off, then you can bet your bottom dollar they're going to be sure they get what they paid for." The smile had dropped from Moe's face.

Rex looked about him for a moment as if an answer would pop out somewhere, then he said, "All I can tell you is that I'll deal with it as it comes."

"Jesse, it's late and I'd hate to see you driving all the way back to Wailuku," Joe said. Rex grimaced as he caught a mental image of Jesse driving home with her surround sound speakers blaring; swerving all over the road to her music; coming up on those curves; Ewwww, what a nasty thought.

"We've got too many bedrooms upstairs that never get used, so why don't you stay here tonight?" Joe asked.

"That would be nice," Jesse started. "You sure your mother won't mind?" Jesse asked with a look on her face as if she'd just stepped on a sharp rock.

"Naw, Ma won't care as long as there's no fooling around… if ya get my drift."

# CHAPTER TWENTY-FIVE

"I can't be sure, but I think we've been followed," Joe commented with sarcasm in his voice. He made the turn into the Kahului airport.

"Oh yeah." Rex laughed. "What gives you that idea?"

"I'd have to say it was the black hearse with the Maui Funeral Home painted on the driver's door. I spotted it outside our house after eating lunch, and it's been behind us ever since we left," Joe said.

"Naw, I think you're being a little paranoid." Rex laughed as he turned around to take a peek at the black Continental limousine hearse that was taking the turnoff behind them yet was a discreet distance away.

"Have you seen who's driving?" Rex asked.

"It looks like it's just Yama and Desu, but I couldn't see through those tinted windows. It's possible the whole home staff could be behind us just to bid you a fond farewell," Joe said.

"Yeah, I wonder just how fond that farewell might be. I also wonder if I'll have an escort beyond this airport." Rex frowned.

Joe handled the crazy drivers zig-zagging in and out of the airport entrance by squawking his siren, flashing his police lights, and shouting a string of profanity out his window with such proficiency Rex was embarrassed. It occurred to Rex that Joe must be awful nervous about their tailing party to be bellowing such vulgarity.

"Hey, I really appreciate you driving me down here this afternoon and seeing me off," Rex commented in earnest.

"You're welcome." Joe sighed. "But I'm also interested in seeing who is coming down here to see you off and just how far your escort is going to go."

Joe pulled his unmarked cruiser into a handicapped parking spot close to Northwest's sign. He popped open the trunk and flicked on his police flashers. Red, white, and blue lights lit up the area like a rock concert light show, and Rex got out of the cruiser ducking his head, as it seemed everyone in the airport was looking at them to see what was happening.

After Rex hauled Kuro's briefcase and his carry-on out of the trunk and closed it, their freak show became a three-ring-circus. The Maui Funeral Home limousine pulled up behind Joe's cruiser. Rex stood agape as Yama opened the driver's side door, stiffly unfolded himself from behind the wheel, and stuck a yellow flashing light on the limousine's roof. Rex waved to the tall and scarred Yama, without getting a response, while the short and stocky Chiisai Desu got out on the passenger's side. Rex was relieved to see no one else got out of the limousine. *Good*, Rex thought, *Kuro only sent his henchmen and didn't come himself.*

Joe wasn't going to stand for this blatant display of Yakuza supremacy over the authority of the Sheriff's Office with this illegal parking at the airport. He reached into the cruiser and radioed dispatch.

Rex figured they had some time to spare, so he and Joe leaned on the trunk of the cruiser and waited until a Sheriff's patrol car pulled up a few minutes later to park beside the limousine. Two deputies squeezed out of their cruiser. Rex's first impression of the deputies was that a couple of grizzly bears had escaped the zoo, shaved off their fur, and dressed in sheriff's uniforms. Their overbearing appearance brought Yama down to size and made Desu look dinky.

"They must be hell at the donut counter," Rex muttered to himself.

"What's that?" Joe asked. He was standing shoulder to shoulder with Rex.

"I asked: Are those your boys?"

"That's not what I heard, but, yeah, they're a couple youngsters that joined the force a couple years back. Good honest workers." Joe sighed.

The deputies waved at Joe. Both Joe and Rex waved back. Then one of the deputies pulled out his warped ticket writing book from his back pocket. He pointed at the limousine as if to ask, "Is this the one?" But Rex couldn't read the deputy's expression behind his mirrored sunglasses. Rex did see a small smile appear on Joe's lips as Joe nodded in agreement with the deputy. The deputy's face lit up with an ear-to-ear smile that had Rex looking for pointy teeth.

The deputy proceeded to question Yama. As Yama dug through his wallet for his driver's license, and Desu hunted through the glove compartment for the limo's registration, Rex and Joe proceeded through the agriculture screening and on to the Northwest's first-class ticket counter to check-in.

"Those deputies know the Maui Funeral Home story, and they must be overjoyed to get a chance to do a full car search of that limo. It'll be awhile before they'll let Yama go." Joe laughed. "And Yama better have all his 'i's dotted and his 't's crossed or those deputies will haul the whole kit-and-caboodle down to the station for questioning about possible smuggling operations."

Rex looked across the airport lobby and saw the limousine was still parked between the two police cruisers and their flashing lights. He also saw that while one deputy checked out Yama's and Desu's driver's licenses, the other deputy proceeded to open all the limousine's doors and give the car a thorough search. Yama picked up Rex's glance and he gave Rex the evil eyeball. Rex continued with his childish manner by sticking out his tongue.

"Nifty thinking there, Joe," Rex commented as they made their way from the Northwest counter to Rex's gate.

Joe laughed. "What, you mean with the parking ticket and car search?" Rex nodded. "Yeah, I felt it was only my duty. I mean, what gives them the right for special parking privileges?"

Rex smiled to himself as he thought about Joe parking in the handicapped spot and turning on his police flashers, but he didn't say anything.

"Looks like your Little Hurt is still with us," mumbled Rex to Joe as he stood up after using the drinking fountain next to his departure gate.

"What do you mean?" Joe asked.

"Desu is skipping down the lane toward us."

Joe didn't turn around to gape at the little man's tailing tenacity, but Rex saw him sigh in resignation of escaping the Yakuza's dogged determination to see their project to the end.

"Man, they just keep coming, don't they?" Joe said with some weariness in his tone. Rex sensed something was troubling Joe beyond the heat of the day and the persistence of Desu.

"What's up, big boy?" Rex asked. He switched his carry-ons to his right hand so he could reach his left arm around the shoulders of his best friend.

"What'da ya mean?" asked Joe, doing a ballerina twirl to escape from beneath Rex's arm while barely missing a fragile granny who happened to be walking past.

"You haven't been yourself today. You been cussin' and swearin' at people, nearly pancaking old ladies..." Rex said, pointing at the elderly woman, "... and I'd say you're weirding out."

"Does it show that bad?" Joe asked.

"Yup," Rex replied as he joined the crowd at his departure gate. Rex was relieved to see the big DC-10 parked at the gate, and that they would be boarding the plane through a tunnel entrance rather than having to go back outside and climb up a mobile staircase like when he arrived on Maui. He rubbed his jaw in memory of when Lilly clobbered him after he accidentally grabbed her boob.

Joe sighed heavily as they got to the gate and he turned to see Desu standing by one of the concession stands reading a newspaper. "Oh, I guess I'm not used to these continual stressful situations like you are," Joe started.

"Stressful, huh? You ain't seen nothing yet, my man. No one's shooting at us." Rex laughed as he people-watched.

"It's just that this is a case in a lifetime for me, Rex. This is the biggest thing that's ever happened to me, and probably will ever happen."

"You're worried about me leaving, aren't ya?" Rex asked.

"Yeah, I guess that's a big one. There are just too many loose wires flying around—too many variables, if ya know what I mean. There's too much going on and I hate to see our best chance of survival, you, leaving the den for even a few hours."

Rex looked Joe in the eyes to be sure he had his attention before saying, "You worry too much, Joe. You have to learn ya can't plan for everything in these situations and you have to let fate do its thing. If you sweat all the little details you'll go crazy."

"Yeah well, at the moment I'm going crazy."

"Have some faith, big boy," Rex assured with a pat on Joe's back. He stared back at Desu for a moment and winked at the short fart. Desu went back to reading his paper with a scowl on his face.

"How do you think Moe and Jesse are holding up?" Rex asked.

"That's another thing that's bothering me. I mean, Moe seems to be taking things too lightly and doing things too easily," Joe said. Then he shrugged and said, "But then he always has.

"I'm worried about this back-up operation we have going with the Coast Guard," Joe continued as he huffed and puffed while pacing about in a small circle. "Moe made a couple of calls, met with some strange people, and voilá: we've got this lunatic Captain Ahab and his nutty crew aboard a recommissioned WWII mine sweeper that's gonna back us up if the Yakuza take Jesse out to sea and try to drown her," Joe jabbered. "Ya know how big those freaking mine sweepers are? I mean, we might as well bring out the whole Navy."

"Captain Ahab, huh?" Rex shook his head in bewilderment. *Why couldn't we just get a Smith or a Jones for once? Everyone's gotta have their weird titles around here,* Rex thought.

Joe nodded. He stood there with his huge arms crossed and resting on his huge belly.

"Rex, I never envisioned this case taking on the proportions it has. I mean, we're talking serious usage of federal property and manpower, and someone could be killed."

Rex ignored Joe's panic attack.

"Captain Ahab is a bit of a flake," Rex started. This made Joe huff and glare back at him in disbelief. "But ya gotta admit the guy's a humanitarian and willing to do anything to save a life. I mean, anyone who would shoot holes in a Japanese whaling vessel to save a whale has gotta have some guts and daring in him if nothing else.

"No, I think if we have to go out to sea with our sting operation, Ahab is the perfect back-up. I know he'd do his damndest to save Jesse's life if there's trouble. And I don't think he favors the Japanese either—just for their whaling practices alone."

Joe sighed as if he was resigning to fate.

"Yeah, I guess we could do worse than Ahab," Joe started as he looked down at his shuffling feet. "Jesse," Joe continued to speak his thoughts. "I don't know her that well. Sometimes she seems like the ultimate professional and knows exactly what she's doing, and then there's other times when she seems like the girl next door just goofing off."

Rex mused for a moment. "I get the feeling we've only seen the tip of the iceberg with Ms. Achew. I think after growing up with four older brothers that we're going to find she's a lot tougher than she might act at times. Shit, just being a county pathologist at her age should prove something to us.

"But you're right. She does have her off the wall side. I think this scheme of ours will be the real test of courage for her, and I imagine this case is the biggest thing that's happened in her life. But I doubt this is the biggest thing that will happen in either of your lives. Those things should be happy events, not something ugly like crime and murder."

"So, you've finally let a woman into your life," Joe blurted out with a grin.

Rex was taken aback by the statement, and looked long into his friend's eyes as if he was searching for a joke. He didn't find anything there except maybe honesty and the truth. Rex didn't say anything.

There was a loud announcement that they were boarding the first-class passengers for Rex's flight. It was time for them to do their acting job of Rex departing for good.

Rex wrapped his arms around the Polynesian and gave him a tight hug as if he wouldn't be seeing him for another age. "See you in a few hours," Rex whispered into Joe's ear.

"You better," Joe said squeezing Rex back.

They ended their embrace and both turned to look at Desu. Rex wasn't surprised to see Yama had finally caught up with Desu and they were both staring back at him and Joe. Joe went to the window to see the plane off.

Rex was the last of the first-class passengers to board since he wanted to see what Yama and Desu had planned. He laughed and entered the tunnel to the plane when he saw that Yama and Desu walked over to the gate's window to watch the plane depart along with the rest of the crowd. Neither one appeared to make an attempt to board the plane as if they were going to follow Rex back to Detroit.

Rex walked down the tunnel and neared the door of the aircraft. He was struck with a sudden impulse, and he didn't stop to think. A maintenance man had just entered the tunnel from a door off to the right of Rex. Rex was momentarily alone when the man entered the plane and headed for the cockpit. Rex looked and saw the plane attendants had their backs to him. Rex seized this chance, and dashed out the door from which the maintenance man had entered.

Suddenly, Rex was blinded by the bright light of the afternoon and punched by its heat and humidity. Yet it was the noise that nearly overwhelmed him. The sounds of jet engines running dominated Rex's hearing, and gusts of wind straightened his ponytail.

A thought passed through Rex's mind that this was a dumb idea and he should just go back in and take his seat in first-class. A vision of a good looking stewardess serving him an icy beer flashed into Rex's mind, but it blipped out of focus as soon as he noticed that the beer wasn't a Strohs— *Oaf, one could never live with that.*

Rex looked to ensure he wasn't visible from the departure gate's window. He was relieved to see the tunnel blocked the vision of anyone standing at the window to see the plane off. Next, Rex contemplated his method of getting off the landing. There wasn't a mobile staircase like the ones passengers used; there was only a rusty ladder that appeared to end a measurable distance from the tarmac.

Rex realized time was ticking. The maintenance man would be back any second, plus there were maintenance people on the tarmac which might be coming by and spot him. He knew he appeared as if he was a dorky tourist lost and stuck out on a limb. To add to his urgency, he was sweating under the Maui sun and the baking heat floating off the asphalt tarmac.

The landing was gated all around except for the ladder exit, and Rex rushed to that exit. He swooned at the sight of the drop-off to the tarmac, but he grabbed the gate to steady himself in time.

Rex sat on the metal landing, and then leaped to his feet again as his butt burned and he screamed, "YIPES! Jesus that's hot!" Rex recalled the maintenance man had been wearing gloves, and now he understood why.

Rex regrouped for another attempt at the ladder. This time he used the briefcase to sit on, then he reached his Nike cross-trainers down to the ladder's third rung, heels first. After hooking his carry-on over his shoulder, Rex reached across and grabbed the right side of the ladder with his right hand. Gripping the ladder burned him for a moment, but his calloused hands took the heat. Next, Rex did a little twirl while pivoting on his right hand, swinging his butt out into the air, and grabbing the top rung with his left hand so now he stood facing the ladder. Rex grabbed his briefcase and was down the ladder before his hands got toasted. He thanked his lucky stars for wearing his Nikes rather than the old flip-flops he had in the briefcase.

Rex was on the tarmac under the plane. The noise was deafening and rattled his senses. The crosswinds were powerful enough to blow the briefcase away from his leg, and then slap it back with painful punishment. Rex looked about to try and familiarize himself on the tarmac. He knew that when he'd arrived they had walked across the tarmac to an outside baggage claim area that had an easy exit to the street. Then Rex recalled that had been on Hawaiian Airlines and an island hopper flight. He was standing beneath a Northwest plane bound for an international flight. The two airlines were probably on the opposite sides of the airport from each other, and Rex figured that exit onto the street wasn't nearby, let alone easy.

In front of Rex was the gate itself, even as he watched a mechanic or someone from the airline rush out a door and come right at him.

"Oh shit," Rex said, although he was sure no one could hear him.

Rex had barely made his condescending statement when the man approaching him looked up and noticed Rex just standing there looking back. Rex took the initiative and began walking toward the airline employee.

"I'm sorry," Rex yelled when he got nose to nose with the man. "I was looking for a Joseph Tweedy in maintenance."

"You should not be out here, come on," yelled back the man while grabbing Rex's arm and escorting him to the door from which he'd just come.

Rex followed eagerly so the man let go of his arm. Rex even opened the door for the guy, but he waved Rex off and ushered Rex through the door. As the door slammed shut and relative quiet ensued, Rex found himself alone on a stairway landing. His escort had stayed outside. Directly ahead of him was a door leading off to somewhere on the same level. There was a sign on the door that read, "Authorized Personnel Only." To his left was a stairway that Rex figured would lead to the next level where people were watching the plane depart. Rex knew for certain he didn't want to go back up to the gate and be caught by Yama and Desu. He decided to see where the door on his level would take him.

Rex found that the door was locked, but after a little work, he managed to break into the door with hardly any trouble at all. "Huh," Rex muttered out loud. "So much for airline security around here."

Rex found himself in a huge garage that housed a few airline pick-ups, baggage haulers with trailers, and large tractors used to tow a grounded airplane around the runway. He also saw maintenance people working on the machines.

Rex strutted toward the other side of the garage like he belonged there but had an urgent errand. He kept his head down and walked briskly down the center aisle of the garage carrying his briefcase in one hand and holding his carry-on over his left shoulder—just another guy finished with a job and ready to go home.

As Rex neared the other side of the garage, he spotted a door which seemed to be the entrance/exit to the garage. He figured that was his route to freedom. The only problem was there was an office with large windows looking out onto the garage that was next to the door. There were a few important-looking men in the office wearing white Oxford shirts, black ties, and had a dozen pens in their shirt pockets. These guys were wearing hardhats and safety glasses while looking out those windows and one of them had taken notice of Rex's approach.

Rex kept his head down and continued to walk briskly toward the door. When Rex did look up he was horrified to see the guy that had taken notice of him was still staring at him. To Rex's dismay he saw the guy had a badge of a security guard or policeman clipped on to his breast pocket beneath his pen and pencil set.

Rex looked at his badge, and he kept right on walking toward the door. As Rex passed the office he saw the security guard/police officer break from his group and start toward the exit of the office to intercept him. Rex stepped up his pace in order to reach the door before the cop stepped out.

Rex hit the doorway and was running up a stairway when he heard the office door open. "Hey, you," someone shouted from behind Rex.

Rex didn't respond, but he hurried up the next staircase as he heard two doors closing behind him. Rex stopped to listen for pursuit, and it was only a moment before he was rewarded with the sounds of someone huffing and puffing up the staircase behind him. Rex looked over the banister and saw a yellow hardhat making its way up the stairs.

"Shit!" Rex hissed under his breath. He was on a landing with a door. There was no where else to go but out the door, and Rex knew it had to lead out to the gate from which he'd just departed. He didn't want to be spotted by Yama and Desu, but being stopped and questioned by this security guard was bound to get everyone's attention, including Yama and Desu who might be interested in what the commotion was all about.

"Let's hope everyone is still watching the birdie," Rex muttered as he opened the door and peeked out.

Rex found himself near the water fountain where he'd gotten a drink earlier. He slid all the way out the door and closed it as he heard the security guard reaching the staircase to his landing.

"Hey, you. Hold on a second," yelled the security guard as Rex closed the door.

Rex looked to his right, down toward his departure gate, and he spotted the huge back of Yama and the broad back of Desu. Their hands were in their pockets, and they were still staring out the window at the DC-10. Rex also saw Joe sitting off to the side eating a candy-bar, but Joe wasn't looking toward Rex. At a fast walk, almost a jog, Rex mixed and mingled with the crowd to lose anyone that might be following. He made his way back to the entrance of the airport where Joe had left his cruiser with the lights flashing.

Rex exited the airport. He hurried over to the cruiser and threw his luggage in through the open driver's window. Then, Rex reached in and pushed the power locks to unlock the backdoors. He took a glimpse around to see who was watching, and to ensure Yama and Desu weren't on their way back to their car. It appeared that the security guard had been lost as well.

Rex opened the backdoor of Joe's police cruiser and jumped into the rear seat. Rex slammed the door shut and lay down on the backseat of Joe's car after taking another quick glance around. He was thankful Joe's car didn't have steel mesh between the front and the rear seats, and the rear doors had handles on the inside so one could open the door. Rex figured no one would see him lying on the backseat, so he pushed the power locks back on and took a nap until Joe came back. It seemed to Rex that he'd barely closed his eyes when Joe returned.

"What the hell's all this shit," Joe exclaimed as he opened his car door and saw Rex's carry-on and the briefcase.

"I'm back," Rex sang from the backseat without getting up.

"Holy Cow!" Joe exclaimed as he jumped back from his car as if it was going to bite him. Joe looked around to see if anyone had seen his fearful hop, or if they even cared.

Joe must have realized Rex was in the backseat hiding since he quickly gathered his wits and jumped behind the driver's wheel. Joe started the cruiser without saying a word, turned on the siren, and bullied his way through the airport traffic.

"Are we clear?" Rex yelled from the backseat.

"Hold on till we get to the highway and I can be sure no one's following us," Joe hollered back. "Man, you scared the living shit out of me hiding back there."

"Do we need to stop at a restroom?" Rex asked, still lying down in the backseat with his head behind Joe. It was kind of comfortable and Rex was thinking about that nap again.

"Naw, but how the hell did you get back there?"

"You left your doors unlocked, so I just jumped in. It seemed more convenient than calling for a cab, and I didn't want to be seen."

"No, I mean how'd you enter that tunnel to the plane and then get back here without anyone seeing ya?"

"Oh, people saw me. Let's just say a maintenance man showed me the way out of the tunnel. I got down to the tarmac and walked back to your car."

"Well, Yama and Desu fell for it, hook, line, and sinker, cause they were still watching the plane depart when I left."

Joe pulled the cruiser onto Highway 31, and sped toward Lahaina.

"You can sit up now," Joe said as he rolled up his window and kicked on the air conditioner with the blower turned on full blast.

Rex popped up and let out a huge sigh of gratification as he felt cool air blowing on his hot face and down between the silk of his Hawaiian shirt and his wet skin.

"It looks like we're back in business," Rex said while looking out the back window.

"Yup, that was a nifty move you pulled. Now what about tonight?"

Rex thought for a moment, and then said, "If Kuro believes I'm no longer on the island, I would imagine he's hot to pick up another loner to kill."

"So you think it's time to pull our sting operation?"

"Is Captain Ahab ready to sail tonight?"

"According to Moe, Ahab said he and his crew are ready twenty-four hours a day, anytime we want…unless he's already on a rescue mission, of course. Ahab knows our situation and he's just as anxious as we are to capture these guys. His crew is experienced in boarding hostile vessels, and they have the authority to use force in a kidnapping or smuggling operation.

"All Moe has to do is tell Ahab when we're going to start our sting. Ahab claims he's already familiar with the *Tora*, the Yakuza cruiser. Apparently, he's followed the *Tora* out of Lahaina harbor when it leaves late at night with all its lights turned on. Ahab suspected something illegal was going on, but he never had the proof that would allow him to stop the vessel and board her. Yup, Ahab said he wouldn't mind taking a few shots at the *Tora* during a kidnapping siege."

"He's our man." Rex laughed.

# CHAPTER TWENTY-SIX

Rex felt a scream of horror building in his lungs when he walked into the game room and saw this woman talking to Moe. He knew he was looking at Jesse, but the woman he saw before him did not appear to be the Jessica Achew he'd met only days ago.

"Holy Shit! What happened to your hair?" Rex hollered. He was looking at Jesse who had been made-up to play the part of the loner. Jesse had cut her hair to shoulder length and put some gel in it to make it look greasy. As Rex drew close to Jesse he smelled the aroma of frying bacon. His stomach agreed with his nose by making growling and gurgling noises.

"How do ya like my makeover, Rex? Does she look like a whore?" asked Moe.

Jesse turned about and slapped Moe's big arm.

"I'm not a whore," Jesse said with all seriousness.

"I wouldn't suggest you were," Moe said. "I just asked Rex if your appearance could pass for one."

"But your beautiful hair? You cut it all off. And how'd ya make it look so greasy?"

"That's another of Moe's ideas," Jesse started. "He said if I really wanted to attract men, I should start with their stomachs." Jesse laughed. "But in this case I tend to agree, so I wiped some lard in my hair."

Rex's face puckered in disgust. "But you cut off all your hair."

"No, it's only a trim job. The grease makes it look shorter. Besides, I can always grow it back."

Then Rex looked at Jesse's face and saw Moe's artistic work. "Well I'll be damned. Just look at you," he exclaimed. "That nose looks real as can be, and I know something else is different with your face."

"Yup. Moe expanded my chin just a tad. You like it?"

"Yeah! Oh Yeah! There's a definite improvement in your appearance. Gee, I don't see how we'll keep the men off ya, Jesse."

"Oh, you boob," Jesse said as she stepped over and smacked Rex in the arm.

"I'm just kidding. Moe, you did an excellent job. I don't think I'd recognize Jesse in the darkness of Lefty's bar," Rex claimed.

"I'm glad you like it, but will it fool Kuro and company?" Moe asked.

"I don't see why not," Jesse said. "I've never met any of them personally, so they won't recognize me."

"Ya never know what they might have up their sleeves," Rex commented. "I just hope none of your co-workers come to Lefty's and blow the whole thing."

"Don't worry about that. It's the middle of the week and everyone thinks Lefty's is a disgusting establishment anyway."

"We better get rolling," Rex said. He put his arm around Jesse to guide her to the door.

# CHAPTER TWENTY-SEVEN

Rex was beginning to think he might enjoy this stakeout. This was new for him. He figured it beat the hell out of sitting in the tree across from Stormin' Norman Lipshitz's house. Rex was sitting cool and pretty in a massaging leather executive chair inside Lefty's "office." This comfort beat the hell out of sitting cross-legged in a deer blind and leaning against a knobby tree trunk for three days in the Michigan freeze. *Hell yes, hallelujah, brothers and sisters.* Rex took another swig of ice water.

Rex confined himself to drinking ice water from pitchers that one of Lefty's waitresses brought up the ancient stairs to Lefty's office and left for him on the landing in front of the door. Rex thought he'd better leave a large tip for the waitresses for trusting their lives on those dark rickety stairs just to bring him water.

A soothing breeze was blowing across Rex's head from an air conditioner which cooled Lefty's computer and the array of TV monitors. Rex was using the TVs to keep an eye on Jesse through closed circuit TV as she sat on a barstool beneath Rex and played the kidnapping bait for the Yakuza.

Rex knew to do his surveillance of Jesse he only needed to watch the 35-inch monitor which was seated before him. Yet Rex found it increasingly difficult to concentrate on Jesse slurping tonic water when Lefty had so many toys to play with in his personal electronics room. This problem was growing in size since none of the Yakuza had entered to take the Jesse bait.

After deciding to use Lefty's Saloon as their initial setting to capture the Yakuza, Joe arranged an appointment with Lefty at his bar. Introductions were made, and they took seats in one of Lefty's less repugnant booths that were away from the bar. Then Rex, Joe, and Jesse acquainted Lefty with the Yakuza's murder and smuggling scheme without partaking of Lefty's hospitality to enjoy a few beers with hairs in their glasses.

They weren't surprised to learn Dwight "Lefty" Sullivan lost his right arm in the Japanese attack on Pearl Harbor in December of 1941. Although no one shed a tear at Lefty's loss, he remained anxious to get some payback from any present day law breaking Japanese while using his bar as a stage for kidnapping and murder.

Lefty told them, in his stuttering speech, many ladies of the evening (cough, gag) met their escorts in his bar. Lefty claimed that since these ladies brought more business he looked the other way. Rex thought if Lefty had been Pinocchio his nose would be about two feet long by now.

Lefty went on to say that recently these ladies hadn't been coming into the bar. Joe advised Lefty that some of his ladies had become victims of the Yakuza scheme, and they wouldn't be picking up any johns in this dimension. The other girls had probably been frightened away.

Joe showed Lefty morgue photos of the victims that were believed to be prostitutes and Lefty agreed the photos were of girls that frequented his bar. Lefty wouldn't say anything to confirm the victims were prostitutes, and he didn't seem too broke up over their demise.

Joe had gone on to show Lefty pictures of the Maui Funeral Home staff, and Lefty agreed that each face was a regular customer, except for Hi Onna. It didn't surprise Joe that Hi Onna was never present since he'd never seen her leave the funeral home due to her marred features.

Lefty agreed the funeral home members came in groups of three or four, although he could never recall them leaving, nor the company they took. Lefty admitted he never stayed till closing since he tired easily these days and needed his rest.

Lefty was as excited as a stooped old man could get when Rex told him his plan to capture the Yakuza in the act. Lefty had warmed to Rex's plan, especially after Rex showed him a roll of Kuro's money as proof there was a monetary reward for assisting in the operation. Lefty demanded half payment up front.

There was so much good spirit going around that Lefty had shown Rex up to his "office."

"Na-na-now ya-ya st-stay po-poo-put," Lefty wagged his index finger at Joe. Joe and Lefty knew each other well, and they didn't see eye to eye. This had nothing to do with Joe's six five height over the old man's stoop. When standing, Lefty did his talking to either Joe's ass or his zipper.

Lefty had also taken an interest in Jesse (besides the fact she was the County Medical Examiner and could close down Lefty's establishment with a wink of her eye). Lefty swore on his mother's grave no harm would come to Jesse in his bar. Rex wondered if Lefty knew who his mother was, let alone where her grave might be.

To ensure Jesse was taken care of during the operation of his scheme, Rex gave generously from his stash of Kuro's money to bribe the bartenders, waitresses, and bouncers—especially the bouncers. Rex estimated both Polynesian bouncers to be in Joe and Moe's weight range, but these two boys were fresh out of college and had recently seen the use of a weight room. If it came to hand to hand combat, Rex figured either bouncer would be a good match for Godzilla. Lefty received the largest of Rex's donations since they were using his bar for their purposes.

At first, Rex was the one to be anxious as Lefty pulled him from their booth and yanked him up some rickety wooden stairs. Lefty fumbled for his keys to the door to his office in the dark, on a landing at the top of the stairs. Then he showed Rex into what could be better labeled an "attic." Rex entered a room stuffed with old boxes and crates which appeared to date Lefty. The cobwebs hanging from the ceiling and walls were thick enough to require a machete to cut one's path, although there was a tunnel cleared at Lefty's height.

Rex bent over and followed the old man so close to his ass that if Lefty farted Rex would have lost some facial features. Rex followed Lefty through an aisle that zigzagged through the old boxes and crates to come out to the back wall of the room. Before Rex could get the cobwebs off his face and out of his hair, Lefty seemed to fall at Rex's feet. Rex saw Lefty hadn't fallen, but kneeled to play with something on the floor. As Rex bent down to assist Lefty, there was a sucking sound which came from the back wall as if a refrigerator door had been opened. Surprised, Rex looked up to see the unbelievable.

Before Rex, a portion of the back wall slid away, and florescent lights began to blink on in an area behind the sliding wall. Rex caught his first glimpse of Lefty's electronic game room.

"Hot-diggity-dog," Rex exclaimed.

As Lefty erected himself to his stoop, he said, "Ya-ya-ya can do bet-bet-better than that."

"Neato!" That was the best Rex could blurt out at the moment. His mind was too filled with his vision of this room of electronics and arcade games. The gadget part of Rex awakened and he was dumbfounded as he stepped through the threshold of the room and saw a complete kitchen, a pool table, and what he figured was a porta-potty over in the far corner.

"Ya-ya didn't tha-think I'd stuffed all me money bee-bee-beneath me mattress, did ya?" Lefty had asked.

"Na-nanaa," Rex started to respond. "Shi-ah-it, now ya got me stuttering," Rex stammered.

"I-I-I ga-ga-gots just tah tha-thing for tha-tha-that," Lefty came back.

"What's that?"

"Cah-Close ya-yeas eyes."

Rex turned to face Lefty and closed his eyes.

"Ya-Ya rah-ready?" Lefty asked. Rex felt some spit land on his arm, but didn't do anything to wipe it away.

"Yup."

Lefty reached up and gave Rex a feeble left-hook on the side of his head. Rex was so shocked at the knock to his head he nearly fell backward.

"What the freakin' hell do ya think you're doing, old man," Rex yelled as he advanced on Lefty to give him a powder in return. But he stopped when he saw that Lefty didn't cower away. In fact, Lefty was giving Rex something that could be considered a smile, a revolting display Rex could add to his nightmares, but it was a smile none the less.

Lefty raised his hand to halt Rex's advance, and asked, "It worked, didn't it?"

"Well—ah—I guess so." Rex smiled.

"Works for me too." Lefty spat.

Rex was amazed to hear that Lefty had stopped stuttering, at least for a while. Over the next half-hour Lefty showed Rex how to use all his gadgets and gizmos. Rex figured the room was Lefty's pride and joy, and Lefty was dying to show it off to somebody. Rex figured the old fart probably didn't have a whole lot of friends at his age and with his demeanor and appearance.

Lefty showed Rex how to use the cameras that were strategically placed about the bar and outside areas so Rex could scope out anything of interest that happened in or around Lefty's Saloon. Using the remote control, Rex could zoom in on any table or barstool and use three different light settings. He could watch using the normal lighting; or he could try the infra-red to pickup everyone's heat signatures; or he could use a magnified night vision which showed everything magnified 3x in green light (similar to Rex's night vision goggles). Rex could record what the cameras were seeing on CD as well. Rex knew these recordings could be critical as evidence in a trial.

At the moment, Rex enjoyed the massaging of the executive chair and Lefty's gadgetry. He was supposed to be watching out for Jesse. Lefty had disappeared an hour or so earlier, leaving Rex to be massaged and to manipulate the cameras on his own.

Rex zoomed in on the breasts of a disguised Jesse as she sat alone at the bar fingering her tonic water with her tiny drink umbrella. Her breasts sat up perky and exposed in the tight shirt she wore with its large looping collar. Since Jesse was supposed to be playing the part of a whore her breasts were exposed to nearly a naked extent.

Rex had experimented with the zoom button on other women's breasts. Rex was perturbed while testing the infra-red mode on one woman's breasts which appeared particularly voluptuous. When he zoomed in the screen had gone grayish and darker as if he was viewing objects that omitted a low amount of heat.

Rex questioned Lefty about this, and Lefty replied, "Imps."

"Imps?" asked Rex.

"Implants," Lefty repeated. After that, Rex was amazed at the number of "imps" he saw. Rex decided to keep his breast-zooming to a minimum and only watched Jesse's breasts when the urge struck him.

Rex zoomed back, and moved the camera to examine Jesse's face in the normal lighting. Although the light was poor, Rex thought Moe and Jesse had done an outstanding job of changing Jesse's facial appearance. No one would recognize her as Jessica Achew with her change in clothes.

Only fifteen minutes had passed since they'd set up at Lefty's when a Latin-looking man started buying Jesse drinks. The Latin grabbed Jesse's rear after the first drinks were served and this caused Jesse to jump. Rex had gotten a bit hot under the collar at these swipes, but the bouncers were quick to hustle Jesse's solicitor to other entertainment. Rex later learned the Latino was escorted to the dumpster in the alley. The bouncers added a couple punches to ensure the Latino wouldn't be mistreating women in Lefty's Saloon again.

The Latino was the first in a long list of Jesse's solicitors through the evening, and Rex noticed the wide grins that passed between the bouncers whenever they'd done a particularly fine job of roughing up one of Jesse's unwanted drink buyers. Rex thought he'd have to curtail the bouncer's enthusiasm on future nights before they killed someone just for asking to refresh Jesse's tonic water.

It was an hour later when Rex saw Kuro enter the alley entrance with Migi and Hidari Te. Not far behind came Naifu and Kiru Otoko.

"Wow, just about brought the whole crew. Something must be up," Rex muttered to himself.

The Yakuza squished into a booth right behind Jesse, but they waved away the waitress. *Kuro must know Lefty puts a hair in every drink or leaves something unappetizing floating in the foam of the beer*, Rex thought. Rex watched the group intently. It wasn't long before Jesse craned her neck and saw the Yakuza gang as well. She quickly did an about-face to the bar and Rex saw her back straighten with tension.

Rex saw from Kuro's position that Kuro could see nearly the entire bar room and everyone who entered or left. Rex figured they had been correct in thinking Kuro had scouted his kidnapping areas well, and he knew exactly where to sit to get a good view of potential victims.

Rex watched Kuro and company settle into their booth. He looked into their faces, and he saw the professional determination each one of them took in completing their task.

Rex felt a nervousness which he hadn't known before. Rex felt a real fear for Jesse's life. As time passed he watched his opposition. Rex welcomed the adrenaline of the hunt, yet his preoccupation with Jesse bothered him.

Rex thought the Yakuza appeared to be all business. None of them drank or ate. If they talked to each other, Rex didn't see their lips move. It was obvious to Rex the Yakuza had come to the bar in search of victims. They weren't going to be socializing. It was also obvious to Rex that Kuro was in charge of the group. Each face was turned toward his as Kuro surveyed his surroundings. Rex got the feeling Kuro was searching for a loner, a victim.

Rex concentrated on the job at hand. There were so many variables that could go wrong when working with other people that Rex knew he had to be at his absolute best. Otherwise, Jesse could end up dead.

It was strange, Rex thought, Jesse didn't appear nervous or scared for her life. She appeared uptight when she first noticed the Yakuza in the booth behind her, but now she was back to appearing bored and playing with her ice cubes and drink umbrella.

On the other hand, Joe and Moe had seemed very nervous when the time had come to leave this evening. Jesse must have a different attitude regarding death, Rex figured. Either that or she must have complete faith in Rex that nothing was going to happen to her. If this was the case, Rex wished he could feel the same confidence. Rex knew every job had its surprises, and he never went into a job feeling invincible.

Rex noticed how late it was getting. The bar had cleared and Jesse appeared lonely sitting by herself. Rex was thinking nothing was going to happen when he saw Kuro say something. Naifu and Kiru left their booth and took up barstools on each side of Jesse.

Rex's nervousness returned as he thought of Jesse in peril. This nervousness surprised Rex and he fought it down by studying the monitor and watching every move the Otoko brothers made on Jesse. It seemed obvious to him that Kuro had made a choice, and Jesse was to be the next victim. The Yakuza were taking the bait. Rex watched as Kiru waved for the bartender and ordered drinks for everyone.

Rex was relieved to see the bartender returned with tonic water for Jesse, but Rex watched as the bartender poured an exorbitant amount of rum with just a splash of coke into two rum and cokes for the two Yakuza gentlemen. Rex laughed as Kiru and Naifu made sour faces after sipping their drinks. The bartender flipped a thumbs-up at one of the cameras to show Rex he was on the job.

"Dumb-ass," Rex growled.

Rex watched as the two Japanese made idle conversations with Jesse. Jesse appeared to be playing the part of a drunk as well as she did when she fooled both Rex and Kuro. She was swinging on her bar stool, or leaning heavily on the bar, and she wiped at her eyes as if she was having trouble keeping them open.

Naifu and Kiru drank their drinks and continued to buy Jesse drinks of her own. The Japanese were swinging about on their stools and leaning heavily on the bar after three rounds. Rex laughed until his sides hurt when he saw Kuro's face squished in frustration at the Otoko brother's drunkenness.

Next, it was the Te sister's turn to join Jesse's party. Rex was pleased to see that Migi Te had a greenish cast on her right forearm and hand. The cast didn't seem to slow Migi down a bit. Rex had a vision of Migi using the cast as a weapon to club her victims. This hadn't been in his plan at all.

The sisters pushed Naifu and Kiru over to the next chairs and closed in tight with Jesse. Neither Migi nor Hidari ordered drinks for themselves, but they ordered another drink for Jesse and coffee for the Otoko brothers. Rex was happy to see the bartender laced the Otoko brother's coffee with clear liquor which came from a bottle without a label. Rex assumed this was a homemade brew which would probably knock their socks off. Rex was glad to see this since the fewer of the Yakuza that he had to deal with the better.

Now there were four Japanese crowding around Jesse, all patting her on the back, messaging her neck, and maintaining constant contact with their victim to be. It occurred to Rex this was their way of making Jesse appear part of their party—make it appear she was one of them. Worst of all, Jesse appeared.to be having a jolly good time.

This explained to Rex why the Yakuza had picked Lefty's Saloon to carry out their kidnappings. No one in this place seemed to care what the hell the next guy was doing, and they'd probably only get trouble for butting into other's affairs if they tried to help out.

It was outwardly apparent that Jesse was absorbed into the Yakuza group at the bar as if she was just another member of their party. This wouldn't do if Rex was going to witness a kidnapping. Jesse couldn't just go along as one of the gang, and Rex prayed Jesse wouldn't join the group.

Finally, the test came. Kiru bent close to Jesse and appeared to be whispering into Jesse's ear. Rex figured Kiru had asked Jesse to leave with him and Naifu because Jesse shook her head in a violent manner. Jesse's movements were so exaggerated Rex would have thought she was plastered.

Rex watched as Naifu leaned over and whispered into Jesse's other ear. Rex wanted to know why the Otoko brothers thought they had to whisper. It wasn't as if these clowns were exchanging national secrets, and it didn't appear as if either Kiru or Naifu were going to get Jesse to move. Jesse continued to shake her head at their whispers, and Rex noticed she was even holding on to the bar.

Rex caught a glimpse of Kuro's face on another monitor, and Rex thought Kuro appeared tight-lipped and anxious.

The Te sisters got serious and Rex almost blew his cool. While the Kiru and Naifu looked around to see if anyone was watching the Te sisters each got one of Jesse's arms and yanked Jesse off the bar stool.

As Jesse opened her mouth to complain, Migi elbowed Jesse in the diaphragm and knocked out her wind. This made it impossible for Jesse to utter a peep. Rex waited for Migi to drop her arm and cast across the back of Jesse's head to complete the beating. Before Jesse could double over in pain the two Te sisters had her by the armpits and were escorting Jesse out of Lefty's. Kiru jumped out in front of Jesse, while Naifu brought up the rear. The Yakuza surrounded Jesse so Rex couldn't see her in their midst.

Rex watched, too shocked to believe his eyes, as the Yakuza congregation huddled Jesse out of Lefty's before anyone noticed they were leaving. Rex could see how fifteen people had been kidnapped out of this place without an alarm being raised as he looked around for his other "watchers." Rex looked for the bartender, but he couldn't find him. The bouncers were talking to a couple of girls and hadn't noticed a thing. Lefty had already gone to bed.

Rex watched Kuro for a moment. Kuro appeared to check for anyone taking notice of his group or their exit. Kuro slid out of his booth, straightened his suit jacket and tie, and then briskly walked out of Lefty's.

Rex sat there for a moment. He was astounded by the precision and practiced efficiency in which the whole kidnapping was carried off. And it was a kidnapping. There was no doubt in Rex's mind about that. Jesse had been carried out of Lefty's Saloon against her will. What irked Rex the most was that no one had done a thing to intervene. People just didn't care anymore. At least Rex had recorded the kidnapping on a CD.

Rex shook his head and remembered that he still had a major part in this whole thing. He hustled down the stairs and went after Jesse and the Yakuza.

He hoped Joe was in position with his car.


Rex exited Lefty's by the north alley and was able to see the Yakuza as they shuffled down the alley toward Front Street. Rex was careful not to run up too quickly on the group and be spotted by Kuro. Kuro appeared to be keeping a sharp eye out for anyone that might have noticed the kidnapping.

"You have no idea how much trouble you're heading into, Kuro," Rex said softly to himself.

The Yakuza bunch disappeared into the darkness of the alley. Rex knew where they were going, so he followed by running from one dumpster to the next, always staying in the shadows. Rex figured that Kuro would not be able to see him in his black clothing and shoes, his black hair knotted in a ponytail, and his dark tanned skin. Rex was wearing soft soled shoes, and he moved silent as a snake while keeping an eye on the Yakuza.

Kuro issued a sharp hiss which stopped the group. Rex stopped sneaking, but he was caught in the middle of the alley with no cover. Rex squinted so even the whites of his eyes weren't visible. He moved only his eyes as he watched Kuro turn around and take two steps toward him. Rex held his breath for what seemed an eon, and his heart pounded like a bass drum as Kuro looked back down the alley.

Kuro issued another hissing order. The kidnapping group hurried ahead double-time, but Kuro remained facing Rex. Rex couldn't figure out if Kuro saw him or not. Certainly he could see Kuro, but Kuro was wearing a white shirt beneath his black suit jacket. Kuro stood out like a light bulb in the alley's darkness.

Kuro said something aloud in Japanese that Rex thought might be meant for him, but he didn't understand the words. Kuro turned around and quickly followed his group. Rex's heart was really pumping. Rex blew out and took a couple of deep breaths before moving again. He hoped he hadn't blown his cover and revealed to Kuro that he had never left the island.

Rex followed more carefully and with more distance. Rex saw the Yakuza had reached the end of the alley. He stopped and hid behind the last dumpster. Only Kuro ventured out onto Front Street, and he only took a few steps onto the sidewalk. Rex saw there wasn't the crowd on Front Street as there would be during the day or evening. Everything was so quiet Rex could hear the ocean's waves splashing against the seawall on the other side of Front Street.

Rex watched as Kuro waved at someone or something down the street. Rex wasn't in position to see who Kuro was waving to. The black limousine hearse which followed Rex to the airport pulled into the alley. Rex had just enough time to duck behind the dumpster before the limousine's lights lit up his position. Rex heard the limo's doors closing, and he decided he'd be spotted if the limousine drove straight down the alley rather than backing out on to Front Street.

Rex squeezed down behind the dumpster with his back scraping the wall, and his hands slipping on something squishy which had been growing on the back of the huge trashcan. While Rex thought of losing his lunch over this oozing texture, he heard the roar of a motor coming from the Front Street entrance of the alley. Rex prayed the limousine didn't hit the dumpster. The limo accelerated down the alley.

•

Rex squeezed back out of the dumpster and ran down to the Front Street end of the alley. As he got there, he was nearly run over when Joe's unmarked cruiser turned into the alley. Rex jumped around the hood of the cruiser and into the front seat.

"Good Lord, what did you step in?" Joe asked as Rex seated himself.

"I dunno," Rex said. He reached into the back seat and was happy to find a roll of paper towels to wipe off his hands.

"We're not following anyone with that stench in the front seat. Pheweee!" Joe complained. He slowed the car so Rex could toss the defiled paper towels into one of the dumpsters. They were back in business.

"Do they have Jesse?" Joe asked as he accelerated the cruiser down the alley.

"They took the bait, hook, line, and sinker. They turned left at the end of the alley," Rex directed.

"I got'um," said Joe reaching for his microphone.

"I've got a code 10-55," Joe said into his microphone. After a few heartbeats there was a double-click as Moe acknowledged Joe's call. Moe was on the *Mickey Fin* listening to his police scanner for Joe's call that the bait had been taken and the operation was on.

"Code 10-55? Isn't that the code for a 'coroner's case?'" asked Rex.

"Yup. And I hope no one responds but Moe."

Rex knew this would be a short trip if they were heading to the pier. Again, Rex thought about Moe's decision to leave his FBI superiors in the dark about this operation. Rex thought it was a heavy decision, but he had to respect Moe's wishes if Moe was going to help and provide the use federal property that was needed for this phase of the sting. Rex had the impression Moe didn't think the Yakuza would pick up Jesse, and thus the whole operation would be a bust. If the operation was a bust, Moe didn't want his superiors knowing he was screwing around with the FBI's plans and equipment. On the other hand, if the sting operation worked, it could appear as if Moe had taken the initiative to organize the local police, the Coast Guard, and plan his own sting operation. Moe would appear the hero of the hour as far as the FBI was concerned. Rex was only concerned that Moe did his part as planned, and that the Coast Guard showed up as Moe had directed. If Moe came out looking like a hero, so what? First, they had to get through this thing alive.

Joe followed the hearse out of the alley with his headlights off. They turned left into a larger alley behind the Front Street stores. Rex and Joe grew anxious since now they were heading North and away from the pier. They held their breath as the limo turned right onto Papalaua Drive, heading toward the highway. There wasn't another moving car on the street. This was making Joe's cruiser obvious to the people in the hearse.

Joe stopped at this point because Papalaua Drive hit the intersection to Highway 30 only two blocks up. This intersection had a stoplight and the area was well lit. Joe couldn't sneak up with his lights out and not expect someone in the hearse to notice them.

The light turned green and the limousine turned right, disappearing from view. Joe flicked on his headlights, raced out the alley, up two blocks, and slowed down as he took the right turn onto Highway 30. They came out a few hundred yards behind the limousine.

"I thought you were going to lose them there." Rex sighed.

"You and me both. I knew we should have gotten a backup somehow," Joe grumbled.

"Oh, we were through all that. We don't know who is on the take, so the fewer people that know about this screwy operation the better," Rex said. Rex had barely finished talking when they watched the limousine's right blinker go on.

"Oh good. They're turning onto Prison Street." Joe grinned.

"Just where they belong, huh?" Rex asked.

"You betcha." Joe's grin broke into that wide smile Rex had always liked to see.

"Prison Street leads back to Front Street right in front of the pier, doesn't it?" Rex asked.

"Yup, it looks like they're heading to the pier. They're just taking a long way around."

"I'll bet he's looking for a spot to park that hearse for a few hours," Rex suggested.

"You might be right. The only place he'll find a legal parking spot for that monster is either on Front Street or maybe Dickerson. Both streets are near the pier."

Rex watched as the limousine turned right onto Front Street and came to a smooth stop next to the curb across from the pier. Joe stayed at the corner of Prison and Front streets since he was partially hidden behind the outside tables of an ice-cream shop and the cars parked along Front Street.

"You always could pick 'em," Rex grumbled, meaning Joe parking next to a sign of a huge ice-cream cone.

"What?" Joe asked.

"Always thinking with your stomach."

"They're getting out."

With Rex watching, and Joe looking at the huge ice-cream cone, Yama unfolded himself out of the driver's seat of the hearse. Desu stepped out from the front passenger seat. *They look like they're ready for a funeral*, Rex thought.

Rex glanced over to see what was between Front Street and Lahaina Pier. He saw a block-sized park or square with patches of mangy grass and a floor of reddish brown volcanic clay. In the left hand corner of the park were the coral corner stones of a wall that was once part of an ancient Hawaiian fortification. Sidewalks crisscrossed the square, and at their intersection grew the largest and oldest banyan tree on the island of Maui. Hundreds of mini-trunks surrounded the huge central trunk and held up the tree's many limbs. Rex knew that during the day, the park would be crowded with people eating ice-cream cones beneath the tree's shade and carrying packages that held the treasures they'd bought in the tourist shops along Front Street. At the moment, the park was empty and dark shadows hid anything under the tree's limbs. Front Street remained as devoid of humans as a main street in ghost town at midnight.

Both Yama and Desu took good looks around their surroundings before moving to the backdoors of the limousine. Desu opened the backdoor on his side for Hidari Te to bound from the limo as if she'd been goosed. Hidari was followed by an elegant woman in a black leather body suit. She wore her long black hair as if it was a cape, which she used to cover her face. Rex hadn't seen this woman before.

"Holy shit! That's Hi Onna. I've never seen her out in public," Joe said in awe.

"That's the fire lady, right? The one that had her face maimed in a fire or something?" Rex asked, although he knew he was right.

"Yup. That's her alright. Something special must be going on."

"For Jesse's sake, I sure hope not," Rex muttered. He was getting a bad feeling about this. He felt he was missing something.

Yama came around to the back of the hearse with his slow gait, and he opened the rear door of the hearse. The Otoko brothers popped out of the hearse instead of a casket. Rex bit back a scream when he saw Jesse remained prone in the back of the hearse. Migi Te was at her side. Rex thanked his lucky stars when Jesse sat up and took her time to scooch out the rear of the hearse. Rex saw Migi prod Jesse along with her cast, and he smiled that he'd dealt at least a small blow to the murderess.

"Nice job on breaking Migi's arm," Joe said as he patted Rex on the back. "Picking on women now, are we?"

Rex twisted his head around and squinted at Joe with a sour expression before turning back to the kidnapping. Joe leaned toward the scene, and blew his hot breath on Rex's neck.

"I don't know how we're going to handle Yama if he decides to resist arrest," Joe whispered.

"If it comes to a fight, we'll let Moe handle 'em," Rex said to the window. "He had to pick up some mano a mano combat training at the FBI academy, right?"

Rex twisted around to look at Joe, forcing him back in his seat.

"Come on, Rex. Moe? Even I can give him a wedgy in no time flat." Joe shrugged and stuck out his lower lip as if to say: "You gotta be kidding."

Rex frowned and nodded before turning his head back to see Yama and Desu closing the hearse doors. He watched Jesse gaze about her as if she was looking to see if Joe and Rex were on the job and following this, but the Otoko brothers each grabbed one of her arms and escorted Jesse across the street in the direction of the pier. Rex was surprised when Yama scrunched himself back into the driver's seat of the hearse and drove away as if he'd done his job and was going home.

"Aw shit! Where's Yama off to?"

"'Aw shit' is right. I been looking forward to arresting that bastard for a long time," Joe hissed.

"Well we can't follow Yama and save Jesse at the same time," Rex said.

Rex watched the rest of the Yakuza crowd around Jesse and the Otoko brothers, making her disappear into their midst again. To Rex they appeared as a close group of mourners shuffling quietly across a graveyard on their way to a funeral. Rex realized it would do Jesse no good to scream since there wasn't anyone around to hear her.

Once the Yakuza and Jesse disappeared behind the banyan tree on their way to the pier, Joe pulled his cruiser around the corner and parked on Front Street. Joe and Rex quickly got out of the car and hustled across the park. It didn't take them long to find the Yakuza entering the pier's gate. Rex and Joe slowed down to maintain their distance. It was obvious that the Yakuza were heading toward the *Tora's* slip at the end of the pier. Rex and Joe wanted to get to the *Mickey Fin* which was more toward the front of the pier. Rex still had the nagging feeling he was missing something.

Rex and Joe tip-toed like a herd of elephants as they tried to be stealthy on their way to the pier entrance. But at this time of night, when there was no one on the pier, any arrival was made a scene in itself. It wasn't surprising when the old night watchman crept up on the dynamic duo and scared the living bajeebees out of them.

"Hey! What are you two up to!" the watchman hollered. Joe and Rex jumped as if they were kids caught raiding the refrigerator. The night watchman showed his light on Joe. "Deputy Tweedy! What are you doing sneaking around my pier in the middle of the night? You're not working on a case are ya?"

"Could you hold it down, Hank?" Joe hissed. "We're trying to follow that Japanese group which just came through."

"Oh, you mean those funeral home creeps," Hank said in a moderate tone. "Yeah, they passed by here. "You know, they do a lot of sneaking around at night just like you're doing," Hank carried on.

"Hank!" Joe exclaimed. "Look! Someone's trying to steal the Simmons's yacht!" Joe pointed with excitement toward the opposite end of the pier.

Hank fell for it and jogged off into the night.

"You ought to feel ashamed of yourself," Rex said as they hurried off toward the *Mickey Fin*.

"Oh, come on. That probably made the old man's night."

Then it occurred to Rex what he'd missed back on Front Street, and he came to a screeching halt. "Hey, where's Kuro?"

Joe stopped, turned around, and looked thoughtful for a moment. "Aw, puppy poop! I don't know."

"Puppy poop?"

"Damn, Joe. This whole operation is going to hell. I know Kuro got into that hearse outside of Lefty's, so he must have still been in it when Yama drove off."

"That means our two most important suspects just slipped out of our fingers cause we've gotta go after Jesse," Joe whispered.

"Damn! This calls for some real foul language, not 'puppy poop,'" Rex wheezed.

Joe started moving toward the *Mickey Fin* with Rex slowly following. As much as he tried, Rex couldn't think of an alternative to their plan that would both save Jesse and catch Kuro. Rex knew it would take all three of them to save Jesse from a watery grave. That was an alternative he wouldn't consider. But letting Kuro get away might be more costly to them all in the long run rather than following after Jesse.

# CHAPTER TWENTY-EIGHT

Joe and Rex tiptoed to the *Mickey Fin* without further complications. Rex was glad to see Moe had the *Mickey Fin's* engines warming up and the engine noise was a mere grumble which could barely be heard on deck. There was no use in tipping off the Yakuza they were there with loud engine noises.

While Joe threw off the lines, Rex went on board and up to the pilothouse to assure Moe the Yakuza had taken the bait and the plan was going as scheduled. Joe boarded, yet he stayed on the main deck in preparation of leaving the dock so they could follow the Yakuza on the *Tora*. Moe had bad news for Rex when he climbed up to the pilothouse.

"Bana," started Moe, "you're not going to like this." Moe frowned. "Lilly called to say Mother Makuahine has been trying to track us down all night."

"Who died?" Rex asked since he couldn't think of any other reason Mother Makuahine would rush to track him down.

"No one died," Moe huffed. "Ester Gomez hasn't come back to Sara's Garden since the night before last, and Mother Makuahine was worried since Ester is a newcomer. Mother Makuahine waited all day for Ester since she's been working late nights at Lefty's."

Rex was surprised to learn Ester was working at Lefty's. He thought it was too nasty a place for an eighteen-year-old to be waitressing, especially an attractive girl like Ester. This was not good, and it deepened the anxiety Rex was already feeling.

Moe continued. "Since Ester was new on the job, Mother Makuahine figured she might have stayed late or something, but when Ester didn't come back to the shelter for another day, Mother Makuahine got worried and called Lefty. Apparently Lefty asked around and discovered Ester left at closing last night, but he wasn't at the bar that late so he couldn't say for certain. He did say he hadn't seen Ester since yesterday."

"We didn't see Ester or Lefty tonight. Didn't Lefty say anything else to Mother Makuahine?"

"Yeah. One of the waitresses told Lefty that Ester left with Dr. Cook on the nights she worked late. Dr. Cook was her escort back to the shelter."

"Shit!"

"You want to stay here while Joe and I look after Jesse?" asked Moe. "You could run by Cook's house and find out what happened to Ester."

"No. We already know the Yakuza will kill Jesse if we don't intervene. I don't know what Dr. Cook is doing, but he's taken care of women from the shelter before. There might be something innocent going on there that Ester hasn't told us about…"

Suddenly, the early morning tranquility was rocked as the *Tora* started her twin Detroit Diesels by coughing the crap from her tubes with enough bang to wake half of Lahaina.

"It sounds like the *Tora* is getting ready to roll," Moe said.

"We better get out of sight," Rex suggested.

Moe and Rex ducked into the darkness of the pilothouse. They watched the *Tora* rumble her diesels and back from her slip. The *Tora* advanced slowly, passing the other dark boats. Then she rounded the pier breakers and made for the open seas.

Rex wondered if they were trying to be sneaky by leaving the harbor without any lights, but then the *Tora* turned on enough lights to rival a Steven Spielberg UFO production. Rex had to squint his eyes to look at the *Tora's* lighting effects as they sliced through the darkness of the night.

"It's not like they hide their presence," Moe commented.

"You got that right."

Joe scampered on the deck and untied the *Mickey Fin*. "All clear," Joe said in a harsh whisper up to the pilot house. Moe took the wheel and adjusted the throttles to pull the *Mickey Fin* from her slip. Moe kept off his lights as the *Mickey Fin* followed the scar the *Tora* cut through the sea.

Moe picked up his microphone to contact Captain Ahab of the Coast Guard and ensure they were in their appointed positions. Rex knew most of Ahab's crew would be sleeping and would have to scramble to their positions to get their vessel ready and in position once Moe had given the signal to Captain

Ahab that the operation was on.

Rex listened over the intercom to take in the developing situation: "Coast Guard: This is the *Mickey Fin*, come in, over," Moe said into the microphone.

There were a few tense moments before Ahab himself responded.

"Ahoy *Mickey Fin*! This is Captain Ahab of the United States Coast Guard! Over," the intercom shouted back.

"Jiminy Cricket," Rex hissed. "Could we make it a little louder so my deaf aunt in Wisconsin can hear it too?"

Moe rolled his huge shoulders and shook his head.

"Captain Ahab, the *Mickey Fin* is in position and in pursuit of the target vessel, over," Moe called back.

"Aye, *Mickey Fin*. I have you in my glasses…" Rex covered his ears with his hands and twirled around the pilothouse as if stricken in the head. "…Our forces are in position. This includes two inflatables at your stern. Maintain vigil on your course and wake. Suggest no contact till target vessel drops anchor. Then will secure position to assist. Will lower *White Whale* for observation and backup. Over."

"*Mickey Fin* acknowledges. Good whaling. Over and out," Moe said before he put the microphone back.

Rex was at a loss as to what that conversation was all about and he was still shaking his head over Ahab's yelling.

Moe must have seen Rex's confused expression and pointed to the *Mickey Fin's* stern, "Can you even see the Coast Guard vessel?"

Rex looked astern to pick out the Coast Guard vessel on the horizon. Ahab was running without lights on a moonless night, and Rex thought the coast guard vessel was ghost-like since it was white and appeared to float above the horizon. Rex had difficulty maintaining the outline of the coast guard vessel as it merged with the misleading horizon, so he didn't think anyone on the *Tora* could see it. Rex prayed to his lucky stars the *Mickey Fin* was equally as difficult to see at this distance.

"What was that deal about lowering the *White Whale*?" Rex asked Moe.

"Oh that's just another of Captain Ahab's gizmos. It's a white two-man submarine the Coast Guard uses in search and rescue missions.

"After the *Tora* anchors, Ahab will lower the *White Whale* into the water to reconnoiter the area and to aid in the rescue attempt if it's needed."

"Wow. Here I thought I went overboard with my high tech arsenal of weapons and gadgets. Geez." Rex grinned and decided he might like this Ahab character.

"If you think the two-man sub is something..." Moe went on, "... I understand Ahab called in his nephew, who is a Navy S.E.A.L.. This guy and three of his buddies have been freshening up on some training over at Pearl Harbor. Apparently Ahab's nephew and his bunch do pretty much what they want, and these four guys jumped at the chance to do some real life enforcement. Anyway, they're following us in two motorized inflatables. That's what Ahab meant when he said the inflatables were in position. We have to keep an eye on our course, and make sure we don't run them over."

"You're kidding," Rex spit out. He jumped over to the side to see if he could spot any commandos in their inflatables. Looking around, Rex had difficulty seeing anything with detail in the surrounding black waters. Rex thought of his night vision goggles that were in his deployment bag, but decided he didn't feel like playing around at the moment.

"The Yakuza won't go out too far if they want the drowned victim to float back into Lahaina Harbor," Rex commented as he headed below to the equipment locker.

"Right," Moe agreed. "We'll keep a close eye on the *Tora*. It's hard to miss with all the lights they've got turned on."

Rex looked astern again to see the bow of the Coast Guard vessel making white waters as it drew in tight with the *Mickey Fin*. To Rex, the Coast Guard vessel appeared huge compared to the *Mickey Fin* and the *Tora*. It was a comforting feeling to know the Coast Guard was on his side. He hoped they weren't spotted.

The wheels were in motion, and there was nothing Rex could do but prepare for the hunt. Rex, Moe, and Joe had to be ready to jump into the water as soon as the *Tora* anchored so they were there when the Yakuza got Jesse in the water and tried to drown her.

Rex returned to the equipment locker to get ready for diving into the ocean's black water with only a flashlight. His feelings of anxiety were increasing as he worried about Jesse. What kind of fool sends the woman he loves off to be killed by the killers he's trying to capture? *Look on the bright side, buddy*, Rex thought. *If we make it through tonight the rest of our relationship should be smooth sailing.* Rex was so caught up in his thoughts that he didn't hear Joe coming up behind him over the monotonous growl of the boat's turbines.

"Are you sure that you're comfortable with these full face masks and ear attachments?" Joe asked from directly behind Rex. Rex nearly jumped out of his skin at the sound of Joe's voice, and mentally went on the defensive.

*What kind of idiot does Joe take me for,* Rex wondered as he looked at the complex tangle of high pressure hoses, silicone mask straps, rubber coated electronics, 80 cubic foot air tanks, and full face masks which had a microphone and a listening device attached. It was an arrangement that could confuse the most experienced dive master in this darkness and these threatening circumstances.

"Sure I'm comfortable, aren't you?" Rex asked.

"I know all about these full face masks, but this Buddy Phone system is new to me. You and Jesse had a chance to try it with the mouth mask system, but I've never talked underwater."

"Oh, you'll love it," Rex said, trying to console the big guy. "But it does take some adjusting to get the correct volume level; otherwise you'll blow out the ears of anyone that's listening to you."

"Okay, guys. I think the *Tora's* laying anchor," Moe called down from the pilothouse. Rex felt the engines being throttled back to maintain a safe distance from the *Tora*. Rex watched from the deck as Moe positioned the *Mickey Fin* as close to the *Tora* as he thought was safe yet out of sight. Rex thought the closer the better since he knew they would need to swim the distance between the *Mickey Fin* and the *Tora* to save Jesse.

"Can you see what's going on?" Rex asked with apprehension.

"Not really. If I pull up too close they'll see us. All I can tell is that they've stopped and I don't want to pull closer and be spotted," Moe said in a hushed tone.

"Oh! I've got something we can use to see what's going on over there," Rex said. He darted back to the equipment locker to dig through his deployment bag. He pulled out his GEN III Navstar 3000 Pocket Scope, and said, "This scope has a built-in infrared illuminator with a focus range of one foot to infinity. Right now it's set up with a three times magnification lens that will help us see what was going on over there." He raced up the ladder to the pilothouse before putting the scope to his eye and pointing it at the *Tora*.

"Yup, this thing will do the trick for ya. You could look up a mouse's asshole from fifty paces with this scope."

"We don't need to look up any mouse assholes," cracked Moe. "Can you tell what they're doing on the decks of the *Tora*?"

Rex's stomach muscles tightened as he gazed upon the decks of the *Tora* and saw Jesse. "It looks like they're holding a scuba tank up for Jesse to put on. Yup ... now it looks like they're forcing the tank on her," Rex said tightly.

"*Mickey Fin*! Come in, *Mickey Fin*, Over!" squawked the intercom.

Moe picked up the microphone before it bit him and responded, "*Mickey Fin* here. Are you in position, Captain Ahab?"

"Ahab here. Aye, *Mickey Fin*. We are in position and lowering the *White Whale* to reconnoiter. Have seen rescue victim on deck of target vessel. Victim is struggling. Our mates are surrounding target vessel to ensure protection. Over!" the intercom screeched.

"*Mickey Fin* acknowledges. Proceeding per plan. Over and out," Moe finished.

"Damn Moe, can't you turn that thing down? They got to be hearing Ahab halfway ta Tahiti." Rex swore as he continued to watch the action on the *Tora*.

"It's not me, Rex," Moe complained. "It's Ahab. I've got the intercom set to low. Ahab must be screaming into the microphone or something."

"Well, drop anchor here. We better get suited up and head on over in their direction cause it looks like things are about to take place."

Moe didn't need instructions from Rex. He dropped anchor and waited as it caught—the *Mickey Fin* was parked.

Rex came back down to the deck with Joe. Joe had his equipment on, and he helped Moe and Rex with their equipment.

The only piece of equipment Rex was unfamiliar with was the Maxx Stealth Scooter. They needed these yellow torpedo shaped scooters to haul them through the water between the *Mickey Fin* and the *Tora* since swimming the distance would take half the night and consume their resources. Rex prayed all this new equipment worked because if it didn't Jesse was fish food. Rex hated to think of Jesse as fish food. It only strengthened his determination and increased his anxiety.

The three of them made ready to dive off the stern of the *Mickey Fin* with only the starlight to see what they were doing. Rex took a final glance at the *Tora* with his night scope, but he was unable to tell whether Jesse was still on board or whether they'd made her walk the plank.

When it came time to jump in the pool, Rex, the ultimate techno-geek, got flustered. The idea of using the Divator MKII Full Facemask, the Buddy Phone Kit, and the scooter, was bad enough. But diving with all these new contraptions, into water as black as a cup of coffee, made things kind of scary. Rex knew he was stalling, so he slid into the water.

Rex didn't start his scooter right off the bat. He shivered and bobbed as his wetsuit filled with cold ocean water. His BC held his head just above the surface, so he became a head with a yellow mask strapped on his face. His breathing seemed noisy to him in the darkness. It either hissed or bubbled as the ocean swells passed.

Rex did high knee bends to get his circulation going as he watched the Tweedy brothers slide quietly into the calm waters. The Tweedy boys bobbed on the surface like shiny black apples and made Rex bubble in the wake of their entry. Before anyone could submerge, two inflatables crept out of the darkness heading toward the *Tora* using silent electric motors. Each inflatable bore two commandos dressed in black and hooded wetsuits. There was just enough light for Rex to see that each commando wore a rebreather. These were scuba units that reused a diver's breath and were therefore bubbleless. Rex knew the commando's equipment was perfect for sneaking up on an enemy underwater during the night.

Rex also noted that each commando had some sort of machine gun tightly wrapped in plastic and strapped across his chest. Rex couldn't tell what other weapons the commandos were carrying in the darkness, but he imagined they were armed to the teeth.

Looking into the eyes of the commandos, Rex saw that these were veterans. He couldn't see their expressions due to the black grease paint smeared across their faces, but their eyes appeared hard and determined.

Rex reminded himself that he was a professional as well, and he'd fought more battles, killed more men, and seen more people die in tragedy than these young men might experience in a lifetime. There was something to be said about that thought, but Rex wasn't sure he wanted to sort it all right now. Instead, he felt the heat of the hunt boiling in his blood. If anything he was more intensely excited than he could recall ever being. He put this down to Jesse's involvement, and then he lost all other thoughts and worries to concentrate on the job he faced.

As the inflatables passed, the commando at the front of the first inflatable gave Rex the "ok" sign, which Rex returned. Then he watched as the commando turned and gave the other inflatable some sort of a sign, and the inflatables split up. One inflatable headed around back of the *Tora*, while the other inflatable stayed on the *Mickey Fin* side of the *Tora* and headed for its stern.

Rex turned about to see where the Tweedy boys were. He didn't have any problems hearing the Tweedys since Moe had fixed the microphones so that they were always "hot."

"Are we ready for some action?" Rex asked.

Huffing and puffing came back into his earpiece. He was going to have to listen to the Tweedy brothers breathing during this whole dive. Rex wasn't sure if he was up to it. At least neither of them had a cold. Rex thanked his lucky stars.

"Moe here. I'm ready and steady."

"Joe here. Ready when you are."

"Okay. Let's submerge and meet at the anchor. No further communication until meeting unless there's a problem," Rex said.

Rex pulled on the deflation cord of his BC, and he began his descent feet first. His head disappeared into the cold darkness.

God, it's dark, Rex thought before he reached up and turned on his headlight. This was a small light with rechargeable batteries and a neoprene headband that strapped around Rex's forehead like a third eye.

Rex had always felt nervous diving at night, and the experience could be scary if he let his imagination wander. Normally, he dived at night only in shallow waters that he knew, and with the moon and stars providing some eerie illumination. With this light night diving wasn't all that different than a day dive—except all the nocturnal feeders came out at night for a bite to eat.

This night was moonless and the water held no illumination. Rex looked into the darkness beneath the surface, and it was easy for him to imagine all sorts of creatures and monsters that would appear out of nowhere to taste his human flesh.

Rex tried to concentrate on the hunt. Night diving on the hunt was a whole new world for him. Now, not only did he have to worry about the dangers of night diving itself, but he also had to worry about the two-legged finned murderers which might be floating around in the darkness. If these murderers were finning through the darkness, his headlight would act as a beacon telling any enemy where he was and making him an easy target for a shot with a spear gun.

Besides adjusting himself to the cool water, which sucked out his body heat at four times the rate than he lost it in the open air, there was the adjustment to neutral buoyancy—total weightlessness—the loss of gravity.

Although Rex had experience with this feeling from diving during the daylight hours, he didn't have any reference points to see at night. Without reference points, diving at night made the feeling of floating weightlessly in a void almost overpowering. Rex knew this was enough to make some people sick—make him sick. So he used his light to give him a point of reference and counteract the feeling of floating in a total void. But no sooner had Rex imagined his fears, when they were dissipated. Abruptly, the *Tora* lit its underwater lights. Rex was shocked as the ocean surrounding the *Tora* lit up as if a star had fallen from the heavens. Rex thought the *Tora's* underwater light show rivaled the light spectacle she put on above the surface.

*Nothing like making it easy for us to see where we're going*, Rex thought. He was hesitant to use his Buddyphone and speak to the Tweedys in fear of experiencing another earache. Rex had been hearing the Tweedy boys blowing and sucking since they had donned their equipment and entered the water.

Rex had scheduled an equipment check with the Tweedys near the anchor of the *Mickey Fin* after everyone had entered the pool. Rex knew he'd have to find the anchor line first.

After tugging on this strap, pulling on this other strap, making sure his open heeled fins were on as tight as they could be, Rex fiddled with his gauges to ensure his dive computer was functioning and to see how much air was in his tank. His compass was unnecessary since the *Tora* turned on its underwater lights making his target visible. Still, Rex marked the compass at his current position since he would need to know which direction to head to return to the *Mickey Fin* through the darkness after picking up Jesse.

Rex didn't know if the Tweedys had gone through all these checks since he could no longer see them. He would have wondered if they were even out there if not for all the puffing and sucking noises they made in his left ear.

Rex had an underwater speaker attached to his mask strap forcing him to listen to everything that was said or even breathed into the "hot" microphones inside the Tweedy's full face masks. On the other hand, Rex was wearing the same kind of mask and the Tweedys had to listen to his breathing—when he talked to himself—or even if he decided to sing a tune. He decided to hold off on the singing until after the operation was successfully completed.

Initially, Rex felt he was getting the raw end of the deal since the Tweedys were snorting and blowing in his ear like a herd of elephants with sinus infections. Then he decided it was better this way since he would always know they were out there and he wasn't alone in this void.

Rex popped his ears to adjust to the pressure change as he descended, and he looked around to see two light beams beneath him and to his left. Rex thought that would be the Tweedy boys. He flipped over in their direction, triggered his scooter, and away he went.

The *Mickey Fin's* sonar had shown the ocean's depth to be no more than seventy-feet in this area, and Rex considered this to be a big plus. He used the ocean floor as one boundary to the nothingness that surrounded him which was better than attempting this operation in the open sea. The close sea floor was another point of reference in the darkness.

The sonar had also shown a picture of the bottom, so Rex knew it was sediment and sand down there with a few small rock or coral out-cropping. He didn't have to worry about the seafloor pitching off into an abyss.

Rex figured the Yakuza had selected their sight well, not wanting their prize body to plummet 1000 feet into a sea abyss where it would never be discovered. Rex was also conscious of a current which headed back toward shore. This current would catch a floating body and carry it back toward land rather than out to sea. *Yup, the Yakuza did their homework*, figured Rex.

He arrived at the sea floor next to the anchor and found the bubbling and bobbing Tweedys waiting for him. Rex checked his own equipment first. His analog depth gauge pointed out that he was between sixty and seventy feet. His air gauge showed almost 2900psi—almost a full tank of air.

Moe was closest to Rex off to his left. After greeting Moe with an ok sign, Rex grabbed Moe's gauges to verify they read about the same as his and they functioned normally. After he'd verified Moe's gauges were okey-dokey, Rex repeated the same procedure with Joe's gauges. Both the Tweedy's equipment appeared to be performing normally.

As Rex did his checks on the Tweedys gauges, the Tweedys were doing the same with his gauges and each others. While this was common sense and a normal scuba diving procedure, the three of them passing each others gauges back and forth led to a chaos of tangled hoses. The effort to sort out the hose entanglement evolved into a pushing and shoving match which ended in a snarled mass of arms and legs bubbling madly in a cloud of sediment and sand.

"STOP IT ... JUST STOP IT!" Rex shouted.

"Hey, I didn't start it!" Moe whined.

"Well, ya sure were tugging on my depth gauge awful hard," Joe retorted.

"I was ..."

"SHUT-UP!" Rex yelled.

Rex pleaded, "Are we ready now?"

"Always have been..." Moe mumbled after a moment. To Rex it sounded like Moe was chewing on something as he spoke.

"A-Okay, here," Joe blew in.

"Then lets get to the show," stated Rex as he turned to face the light beneath the *Tora*.

Rex inhaled sharply when a white-tipped reef shark ripped through his light beam just out of his reach. Rex whipped around in circles, but he couldn't locate the shark again. This bothered him immensely. He liked to keep all his bad eggs in the same basket, and he found that wasn't possible in this freakin' darkness.

Rex knew there was a high possibility of human blood entering the water if the rescuing of Jesse got messy. Rex pointed his scooter in the direction of the *Tora*. Yet every time a large fish passed through his beam of light, Rex jumped, and thought it was a shark until his mind registered the shape of the fish.

Rex scooted closer to the *Tora* and its light show. The light show made him feel as if he was sitting in the balcony of a theater about to see a play on a brightly lit stage. After seeing this underwater sensation, Rex turned off his headlight. Rex bubbled with energy as he knew the black waters of this night would hide them from human attackers rather than hinder their approach on the *Tora*. He only worried about the sea life that might rip out of the darkness to feed or defend their territory. The white-tipped reef shark's presence was an ever present churn in his stomach.

Still, Rex was thrilled with the rush of being a torpedo as he stretched out behind the scooter and sped through the dark waters toward his target.

During this rush forward, Rex could feel his body gearing up for action. Like a runner before the race, Rex felt the adrenaline pumping through his veins and his muscles shaking off any cold or stiffness. Not only did it feel great to be on the hunt again, but just the action and going into the unknown made it so stimulating that it was fun for Rex. For a moment, he forgot about the shark.

"AHOY THERE, MATES!"

"WHAT THE FUCK!" Rex yelled without thinking.

Rex took a hand off his scooter and tried pulling the ear phone away from his ear, but he couldn't get the ear phone far enough away without pulling off his entire mask.

"THIS IS CAPTAIN AHAB, OVER!"

"THIS IS MOE TWEEDY, PLEASE LOWER YOUR VOLUME, WE'RE READING YOU LOUD AND CLEAR, OVER!"

Rex bubbled and shook his head trying to clear it.

"SORRY ABOUT THE VOLUME, MOE. WE PICKED YOU UP AT 33kHz AND WANTED TO COORDINATE OUR ATTACK. WE'VE GOT THE TARGET IN THE WATER; REPEAT, TARGET IS IN THE WATER! OVER!

"CONFIRMED TARGET IN WATER," Moe seemed to bellow. "WE HAVE VISUAL AND WILL CALL IF NEED ASSISTANCE, OVER!"

"AH—ROGER THAT, MOE—WILL STAND BY TO ASSIST—

HAVE LOWERED *WHITE WHALE* TO RECONNOITER, OVER!"

"WILL YOU GUYS SHUT THE FUCK UP?! YOU'RE BLOWING MY BRAINS OUT!" Rex hollered into his mask. "OVER!"

Everything went silent. Rex couldn't even hear the Tweedys breathing.

"Thank you. Over," whispered Rex.

Loud sucking noises were followed by explosive exhalations in Rex's ear, but he was glad to know the Tweedys were breathing again even if the noise drove him batty.

Rex grabbed hold of his scooter with both hands and was off toward the *Tora* again. Rex felt as if they were covering the underwater distance between the *Mickey Fin* and the *Tora* in good time as the water rushed by him. As Rex drew closer to the greenish glow of the *Tora's* underwater lights, he could make out three female divers descending along the *Tora's* anchor line. He was still too distant to see which one was Jesse. Yet, in their skin tight diveskins, he could tell they were all female. *Ohoooo,* Rex thought, *maybe I can get Jesse to strut around in that diveskin some more when this is all over.*

Then Rex's breath was caught in his throat when he saw a seven foot white-tipped reef shark swim leisurely through the lighted area beneath the *Tora*. Rex watched to see the shark's back and dorsal fin did not appear arched, nor did its pectoral fins appear stretched out suggesting aggression on the shark's part. He mentally kicked himself for his limited knowledge of sharks. The shark factor; the possibility of a shark feeding frenzy, had not been in his game plan.

Rex racked his brain for any knowledge of shark behavior beyond what he'd seen in the movies. He found pitiful amounts of knowledge that would aid him in facing a situation that might become bloody and dangerous. An additional chill ran down his spine as the only thing he could recall about sharks that might be of value were memories of watching a shark behavior documentary on the Discovery Channel. Rex had only learned the behavior sharks would exhibit before attacking their meal. A shark swam with its back arched and stiff, and it would have protruding pectoral fins as it stalked its prey.

But Rex had also seen sharks while diving in Maui's waters in the past. These had always been exciting, yet fleeting, moments when a small shark would pop into his vision and then disappear into the deep. As Rex watched this shark, he was reminded how effortlessly they moved through the water. It was nothing like watching a shark on TV.

Rex saw this shark appeared not to notice the divers. *Just passing through*, he thought. Rex had also learned many sharks were nocturnal feeders, and the blood, combined with excited motion of a kill, would change a shark's cool reflection into heightened aggression in an instant.

As the shark disappeared out the *Tora's* light, Rex returned his attention to the three divers. He took his hand off the scooter's trigger and turned about to ensure the Tweedy brothers were following.

"THIS IS AHAB!" Rex groaned. "TWO MALE DIVERS JUST DOVE OFF THE *TORA*. BELIEVE THEY WERE CARRYING SPEAR GUNS. YOU BETTER MAKE YOUR GRAB AND QUIT CLOWNING AROUND. OVER!"

"Joe and Moe. Those two guys are all yours. I'll take care of Jesse. Over!" Rex said in a tone that spoke he was taking command and the Tweedys should do as they were told.

"Gotcha, Master Bana-san. Over," Joe came back.

"Alright," Moe followed. "Over."

As the two Tweedys headed toward the stern of the *Tora* to come around behind the two Yakuza divers with spear guns, Rex restarted his scooter and headed down to where the three female divers were nearing a sandy bottom towards the bow of the *Tora*.

The three female divers were at the edge of the ring of light provided by the *Tora's* generators. They began to follow a weighted string of lights that was next to the *Tora's* anchor line.

Rex was close enough to tell Jesse was the diver in the middle of the pack, and he saw she wore no fins. Rex noted that one of the divers had her forearm in a black plastic bag. He figured this was to protect her cast from getting wet. *That diver must be Migi Te, making the other Yakuza diver Migi's sister, Hidari.*

Migi and Hidari each had one of Jesse's arms and Jesse was yanking and pulling the sisters all about to get her arms back. Rex could see Jesse was fighting tooth and nail as the three neared the bottom.

Rex's initial impression was that the three women couldn't get into too much of a ruckus seventy-feet beneath the water. Jesse apparently had some ideas of her own. She managed some leeway from Hidari and turned to her left to knee Migi in the crotch.

*Oow, that had to hurt*, Rex thought. He watched as Migi released Jesse and doubled over in a cloud of bubbles as if she was going to pray. At the sight of so much pain, Rex reached down to check his athletic supporter and cup. His cup was the only armor he could wear underwater, and it didn't feel like it was nearly enough. Rex made a mental note to try his Special Opts Vest in the bathtub when he got home.

Rex saw Jesse had one advantage over the Yakuza divers in underwater hand-to-hand combat. She wasn't wearing any fins. Jesse's bare feet were slicing through the water with speed, and they were delivering forceful blows. It crossed Rex's mind that the Yakuza were being kinda chintzy for not giving their victims fins to go with the rest of their props. Talk about penny pinching.

As Rex moved in on the bubbling threesome, Jesse threw back her freed elbow to punch Hidari in the diaphragm. To Rex, the punch appeared as if it was delivered in slow-motion, and he was surprised to see the Hidari's regulator pop out of her mouth with an explosion of bubbles. Rex even heard the "Oooafff" escaping Hidari's mouth as Jesse freed her other arm.

Jesse had her arms back—she was free. All she had to do was swim to Rex. Yet she didn't take this chance to swim for her freedom. Much to Rex's dismay, Jesse turned to finish off her assailants. She was a bubbling storm of kicks and punches assaulting the Te sisters with the scary vengeance of one female upon another.

"Yeah—payback time," Rex said as he grinned behind his mask.

Something splashed on the surface that caught Rex's attention. He saw the bottom of the commando's inflatables as they entered the ring of light surrounding the *Tora*. The two commando's inflatables came circling in from both sides. They were boarding the *Tora*, Rex figured. *Good*, he thought, *let the commandos deal with Yama, the seven foot freak.*

Rex decided it was time to break up this underwater cat fight. Yet as he turned back to Jesse, another splash on the surface next to the *Tora's* hull captured his eye. Rex didn't know what he was seeing at first other than what appeared to be a spreading pool of blood. He thought it might be shark chum; someone was throwing shark chum over the side of the *Tora*.

*Oh, Shit!*

To Rex this didn't make sense. Neither the attackers nor the attacked were in a position where they would want to attract and antagonize sharks.

Then Rex noticed what appeared to be a suit jacket in for a cleaning. He realized it wasn't pieces of fish and scraps that'd been tossed overboard; it was a body which had come in pieces. It had to be one of the Yakuza the way it was dressed. Rex thought he recognized the clothing, and guessed from the small body that Chiisai Desu had not surrendered peacefully. Desu was about to become fish food.

Rex figured Desu had either been gutted, or he had been riddled with bullets based on the dark cloud that was spreading around his body. *This guy is a bleeder*, Rex thought.

"Oh shit!" escaped Rex's lips in a whisper that must have been heard by everyone else at the higher volume. Rex watched the bleeding body sink into the middle of the drown Jesse scene, and he recalled something else about the inclusion of blood into the water.

"Sharks—Sharks! We gotta grab Jesse fast. That blood will start a feeding frenzy with all this commotion in the water!" Rex yelled, not caring whose ears got blasted.

Rex thought they couldn't be in a worse situation than diving at night during a shark feeding frenzy.

Suddenly, a giant shadow appeared in the ring of light skimming along the sandy bottom at the stern of the *Tora*. Rex kicked himself for thinking things couldn't get worse.

"Holy Moly! That's a Mako shark!" one of the Tweedys screamed in Rex's ear. Rex figured they must be down by the stern.

"A fourteen-footer," whispered the other Tweedy.

This was the first time Rex had seen a Mako for real. *Looks like a Great White*, he thought as he saw the angled tip of the shark's nose and the mouth filled with teeth that never seemed to close. With its slack jaw, it appeared as if the Mako was perpetually preparing to eat.

Rex had also learned from the Discovery Channel that although Makos were smaller, they were as aggressive as their larger cousins—the Great White sharks.

Rex could see that this Mako had a smorgasbord from which to choose. There were Japanese, Polynesian, and even plain old American entrées swimming about this evening.

Rex floated and watched in terrified fascination as the Mako slowly passed through the *Tora's* ring of light toward his position. Rex froze in fear, and he hoped the shark would not be interested in a stiff piece of meat that smelled like it just peed its pants.

Apparently, the Mako was checking to see if the dinner table had been set in accordance with its desires, since it turned to the side and swam out of the light ring without showing interest. *Just window shopping for a bite to eat*, Rex figured—hoped.

Abruptly, two reef sharks appeared from opposite directions into the light ring that was becoming increasingly cloudy due to the blood and fluids gushing out of Desu's riddled body. The view was also clouded by sediment and sand kicked up by Jesse and her wrestling partners.

Rex hoped these were the same two reef sharks he'd seen in the last couple minutes and not two additional sharks. His anxiety upgraded to heavy breathing and heart pounding when he saw both sharks had their backs arched and were sticking out their pectoral fins as the aggressive sign that they were about to dine.

"Strike!"

"Shit! That was a STRIKE!" Rex screamed into his mask.

The larger reef shark had swooped up from beneath the cloud of blood to chomp down on Desu's upper arm. The shark shook the body back and forth in an untamed attempt to grab a bite to eat. The shark's viciousness spread the remains of Desu into a larger cloud of blood and guts as the shark ripped away an entire arm and hand entrée. Rex could see more blood gushing out of the body into the water from Desu's bone white arm socket.

The shark took its arm and hand selection and turned tail before darting back out to the darkness. As Rex watched, the disembodied hand appeared to wave bye-bye to him. He was so horrified by the scene that he waved back.

Once the shark had disappeared, Rex turned his sight back to the three female divers who were still scratching, kicking, and punching it out in an all-out match for the Woman's Underwater World Wrestling Title. Engrossed in their own clash of the titans, the women wrestlers hadn't noticed the saucy consumption of Desu's body that was still taking place ringside.

Rex moved in to grab Jesse away from her playmates since he figured the girls had enough play time in the sandbox—*time for Daddy to take you home, Jesse dearest.*

Rex scootered forward, and he saw the ugly nose of the Mako shark as it poked into the ring of light. The Mako apparently had decided on a meal after its window shopping, and it zeroed in on the women wrestlers.

Rex continued his advance, not knowing what else to do. The wrestling women had also seen the Mako's intentions, and they would have made Rex laugh with the quickness of their dispersion had he not been involved in their plight himself. To Rex, it appeared the two Sushi divers disappeared in a blink of an eye, and left Jesse as the only dish available to the Mako.

Rex was too distant to assist Jesse, yet he was close enough so that he could see the Mako in detail. Rex felt as if he was an audience in the front row peering onto a brightly lit stage. Jesse and the Mako were the actors, and Jesse was so close to the Mako's gaping mouth any move to escape was fruitless.

Rex had triggered his scooter in a race to snatch his love, his new life, before the Mako could bite, rip, and tear Jesse apart. Rex's senses were so heightened that time seemed to slow so he might catch every detail, and scrutinize every possibility. At the same time his body and the physical world took months, years, to react to his thoughts.

Rex looked into the Mako's black eye as he had always looked into the eyes of murderers. This stare down was far different than any eyeballing Rex had done with a human killer. This eye of death was famed for its lack of emotion during a kill. Rex thought he saw a great deal in that black eye. He saw his life passing before him, the life he had hoped to share with Jesse, his whole future...

The black eye rolled white.

"NOOOOO!" Rex shouted.

The Mako's yawning maw stretched open into a cavern of hunger and desire. It was ringed with dagger sharp teeth that had saws along their edges to rip apart Jesse's soft flesh. Rex was horrified to see there were strips of white flesh stuck between the shark's teeth.

Rex was amazed to see the Mako's mouth open wider as it expected to chomp down on large prey. Jesse's legs were inches from the sharp snout and open mouth, and Rex knew their doom had fallen from a direction he hadn't even considered.

Jesse had other thoughts.

Terrified as she must have been, Rex saw Jesse's legs spring into action even as the Mako's mouth began its bone crushing chomp. Jesse kicked faster than the Mako's bite. She booted the Mako's nose with enough force to turn up its angled snout and shock the shit out of the shark. Jesse planted her feet on the shark's stunned schnoz to spring away from the snapping mouth. The shit only clouded the water further, and the shark's reaction was swift as it turned a cheek and made for Rex.

Seeing the Mako's jaws snap closed onto nothing, and then reopen to a gaping eating assault brought down on him, Rex's reaction was immediate.

"AHHHhhhhh," he screamed.

He realized he was just floating there with a ton of muscle, cartilage, and teeth, arched in preparation for another strike. Rex knew he was dead. He'd never faced an opponent like this one—nature's perfect killing machine. *I didn't see a shark do this on the Discovery channel*, Rex thought.

Rex stiff-armed Mako's nose, and allowed the shark to push him along at arm's length. While the Mako's nose pushed him back, Rex felt his legs being sucked into the meat grinder. The huge beast threw Rex down and the destruction machine chewed and bit. The Mako was only able to crush down on the scooter Rex shoved into its hole.

The Mako's teeth broke and snapped off as the immense power of its bite crumpled the plastic and metal of the scooter with all the ease that Rex might squish a beer can. Now that Rex's hands were free he was able to push himself away from the chewing mandibles.

As he cleared the way for the giant shark to pass, Rex was amazed that Jesse decided she still had payback to deliver. She kicked the Mako upside the head a second time risking life and limb. *That's my girl*, Rex thought. Rex figured he'd better stay away from that lady's feet when she's angry.

This was too much for the carnivorous giant. Jesse's kick had caught it in between its eye and gill, an area as sensitive as being kicked in the nose. Rex figured the Mako didn't usually get this sort of retaliation from a prospective meal.

Jesse took one more swipe at the shark's tail, but she missed and settled into a crumpled mess of arms and legs upon the seafloor. The Mako swam out of the light ring still chewing on the crushed scooter, and Rex hoped it was swimming out of their lives.

Rex wasn't sure how long the Mako would be satisfied with that tasteless, hard-to-eat scooter, and now that he had Jesse, he figured it was a good time to get out of the pool. No more fun and games tonight.

Rex hadn't forgotten their other adversaries, and he swam over to scoop up Jesse. Rex tried to wrap his arms around Jesse's warm body, but she hauled back and elbowed him in the ribs with enough force to make him cough.

"Jesse, its me," Rex tried to yell even though he knew she couldn't make out what he was saying.

Rex released Jesse, and as she whipped around he saw her eyes widen in recognition and then soften with apology. Although—he thought she might have been laughing as she bit down on her regulator and bubbled.

Jesse approached Rex and gave him a hearty hug that hurt his now bruised ribs. *Boy, that woman packs a whoolap*, Rex thought. *I better not ever get her mad at me. I've seen how she beats up on women and sharks; I'd hate to see what she does to men. I wonder how her four brothers fared against her.*

"I have Jesse. Time to scoot," Rex announced into his microphone as soon as he had verified Jesse was okay. *Too bad about the scooter, we could use it now*, he thought.

Before adventuring into the darkness and unknown again, Rex glanced about him to find the Tweedy boys. Although he could still hear their sucking and huffing, the sounds had become background noise while he had been concentrating on Jesse and the Mako. Now that Rex was shooing Jesse along, his mind was free to hear the Tweedys again. Since Jesse didn't have any fins she was slower than a sea slug. At this rate, it would be next week before Jesse made it back to the *Mickey Fin*.

Rex gazed around for the Tweedys, but he only spotted two Yakuza divers, the two with spear guns that Ahab had warned them about. Rex figured these two divers were the Otoko brothers, Naifu and Kiru. They were coming in Rex and Jesse's direction through the blood and gore cloud that had formed around the body of Desu. They didn't appear to mind finning through the innards of their fellow employee; but then, Rex remembered they were morticians by trade, and bathing in blood wouldn't be anything new for them.

Desu's body had stopped its descent after the first shark strike and remained floating halfway to the surface. Rex glanced up farther as he saw little streaks of bubbles entering the sea in quick succession. Someone on the surface was shooting into the water, the morons. Rex knew the bullets wouldn't hurt anyone seventy feet beneath the surface, but it concerned him that someone was trying to shoot the sharks just beneath the waves.

Rex could see a reef shark was on the surface next to the *Tora's* hull. Some idiot, by plan or stupidity, was taking pot shots at the animal. Rex also noted new sharks circling into the light around the Desu's cadaver. They swam into the lit area with a swiftness that was scary to see. Rex knew they were coming in at a speed no human was going to out swim—especially without fins.

Some sharks made for Desu, while some made for the surface where the trail of blood started. The sharks swimming along the surface were pelted by gunfire from the *Tora*.

"Ahab—stop those gun happy idiots from shooting the sharks. They'll start a feeding frenzy!" Rex yelled into his mask loud enough that he hoped he'd gotten Ahab's attention.

Rex stayed and watched as more sharks entered the light ring, and still he got no response out of Ahab. The sharks were all over the place. Rex knew what was going to happen, and he knew they had to get out of the water now. The Yakuza divers and their spear guns were the last thing Rex needed to worry about.

Rex grabbed Jesse's hand and began to kick with strong straight legged kicks he knew would use his fins most effectively. His plan was to hug on the ocean floor where they were smaller targets for the variety of assailants they faced. *Where are the good guys?* Rex wondered.

As if they were reading Rex's mind, Rex looked up to see two immense shadows appear in the light ring just above the Yakuza divers with spear guns. Rex laughed as he watched these shadows descend through the water like boulders hurled from the sky.

"Tweedys to the rescue!"

Rex stopped to watch the festivities while placing Jesse behind him. He knew they weren't going anywhere fast anyway. Moe and Joe descended on the Otoko brothers as if they were hawks swooping down on field mice. It was Tweedys versus the Otokos. The Tweedys came from above and behind the Otokos where they wouldn't be seen. The Tweedys pounced on the smaller Otoko brothers hard enough to throw off the Otoko's aim. Whether on purpose or due to the Tweedy's attack, both Naifu and Kiru shot their spear guns at the moment the Tweedys pounced. Rex thought the spears had been aimed at him, but one spear zipped off harmlessly into the darkness, while the other spear struck a nearby reef shark in the gills.

That did it.

Suddenly, the scene of semi-tranquil sharks exploded into a wild frenzy of feeding. The speared shark squirmed, snapped, right and left at an unseen assailant, while fresh blood from its wound squirted into the waters. The erratic convulsions of the dying shark acted like a magnet, attracting other sharks as if they were slivers of steel.

Sharks flew into the light from every direction. They hit the speared shark with incredible ferocity. Their gray white bodies of muscle twirled, squirmed, ripped, and bit to get a piece of meat. Rex saw that it didn't matter where the meat came from either, the sharks bit each other just as often as they bit the speared shark.

To Rex it appeared as if the sharks formed a huge squirming ball of Death with the speared shark as the main entree. To make things worse, the *Tora's* lights allowed Rex to see the burgundy redness of the gore that surrounded the squirming ball. The sharks became so intertwined, Rex couldn't tell where one shark began and another one ended as they twisted, turned, and bent in their attempt to eat, defend themselves, and survive.

Rex had witnessed dog fights and cock fights, but this was by far the most vicious animal fight he'd experienced. Rex didn't know whether to be terrified or horrified, but awesome seemed to intertwine with scared shitless to produce a stunned still position for the moment.

The Tweedys and the Otokos had been whirling around in a struggle of their own. Yet none of them were dumb enough to remain next to Desu's body as this frenzy began.

Rex saw the Tweedy-Otoko wrestling match break up even as the sharks began to strike Desu's body again. The Tweedy's breathing had become a typhoon in Rex's ear, and he had no doubt they were as terrified and excited as he was at the moment.

Rex had dropped Jesse's hand in his awe of this incredible battle of nature. Yet Jesse reminded Rex that she was still there by wrapping her arms and legs around him from behind. *I can keep track of all her limbs this way at least*, Rex thought.

Suddenly, the lights went out.

"Whoa," escaped Rex's lips.

"Son-of-a-bit..." Rex heard in his ear. Then the slurping and puffing was renewed in chorus. Rex figured by the higher breathing rate that both the Tweedy's anxiety had gone up another notch to match his own. Jesse reminded Rex she was there by scrambling off his back and coming around to his front side.

He reached to turn on his headlight when someone—Jesse?—started clawing at his mask. He saw part of a hand—a palm and some fingers—as they were plastered against the tempered glass before his eyes. If Rex's hand hadn't been right there to turn on his light that someone would have pulled his mask clear off his head.

Rex grasped the wrist that went with the hand, and he managed to keep his mask on his face. Yet the pull had been enough to allow the cold Pacific to fill up his full face mask, making it impossible for Rex to see or breathe.

Rex didn't panic, although the flooding of the full face mask was a new experience for him. The cold water that was now confined around his face went up his nose and into his eyes, yet instinctively his mouth had remained closed and he didn't inhale. His conditioning took control and kept things from getting worse. Rex told himself to relax and think. What are you supposed to do when your mask floods? *Come on Rex, this is an easy one*, said the voice in his head.

While still holding onto the wrist of the person that was trying to kill him, Rex used his other hand to find the purge button on the second-stage of his regulator. The button wasn't hard to find since it was large and close to his face. Feeling the soft rubber that covered the purge button, Rex pushed down with his thumb. A blast of cold air filled Rex's mask, forcing out the water. The blast was so powerful it even straightened his eyebrows and blew back a few nose hairs.

"Wow—what a head rush," Rex growled. He pushed the purge button again just for kicks. Another blast of frigid air blasted across his face and out of his mask. "Hey, this is fun," Rex commented, and then he recalled where he was and what he was doing.

Rex reached up and turned on his headlight using his free hand.

"Now who the hell am I holding onto?" Rex asked.

Rex yanked his capture into his light beam and was surprised by the meanness he saw in the slanted eyes of Hidari Te behind a high volume mask. Hidari's eyes were as black as the Mako's, and having seen both, Rex preferred the Mako's unemotional eyes to this cold stare. There was more intelligence and intention in Hidari's eyes. As Rex stared, and wondered what had become of Jesse, a fist flew into his face, smashing into the tempered glass of his mask. The glass didn't break, but Rex was rocked, and before he could recover a knee hammered him between the legs.

"Oooaff! That must have hurt," Rex grunted. He wasn't the one experiencing pain after the knee job. Rex had come expecting and prepared for those kind of tricks.

The knee to the crotch was the undoing of the Hidari murderess. Now her body was next to Rex's, and he used his hold on her wrist to whip her around so he had her scuba tank in his chest and his arms were wrapped around her abdomen. Rex performed the Heimlich maneuver on his captive with one quick and powerful jerk. Hidari coughed up her regulator along with a barrage of bubbles. Rex didn't think he'd broken any of her ribs, but he'd just knocked the breath out of the woman seventy feet beneath the surface of the ocean, and that was going to occupy her time and attention. Rex pulled off her mask before he kicked her in the ass and shoved her out into the darkness where she was shark bait like everyone else.

"I took care of Hidari Te. Over." Rex said into his mask if anyone was listening or cared. No one responded. Rex remained where he was since this was the last place he held Jesse. At least he thought it had been Jesse he held. It might have been Hidari who was wrapped around his back.

*Oh shit, where the hell is Jesse?* Rex wondered.

Rex knew Jesse didn't have fins so she couldn't have gone far. The Tweedys were still sucking and blowing in his ear, and Rex thought it was strange that they weren't talking. He expected them to be jabbering away.

Rex's light stabbed through the darkness, but the beam was so thin it didn't show him anything he wanted to see. Sharks continually passed through the light, yet they appeared more interested in the feeding frenzy rather than with Rex, who was hugging the ocean floor.

Rex tried to calm himself and think. He checked his pressure gauge and was surprised so much air remained in his tank. Then it occurred to him that with all this action it seemed like he'd been down here all night, yet when he checked his bottom timer he saw that he'd been down only sixteen minutes.

Rex figured this was good news since it meant Jesse wooldn't be running out of air too soon unless she began with less than a full tank of air. He knew, in general, women consumed less air than men, so she ought to be okay.

Just where the hell was she?

"ANYONE SEE ANYTHING! OVER!" Rex yelled into his microphone.

"Nope. Over."

"Nada. Over!" *Smartass.*

Rex's anxiety over Jesse's whereabouts increased his anxiety for his own safety. He knew he stood out as if he was a beacon for everyone, or thing, that could see his solitary light slicing through the black void of their environment. Rex imagined himself as a floating phosphorescent wiener; defenseless against anything that charged out of the inky waters to grab, beat, or devour him.

"You're gonna have to turn on your lights so we can find Jesse—or so she can find us. Over."

"If we turn on our lights, won't that make us floating targets in a hog shoot? Over," Moe asked.

"Speak for yourself. Over!" Joe said as he turned on his light. Moe followed suit, and there were three beams of light slicing through the dark water. It was the Three Stooges doing an underwater light show. Light beams slashed this way then that way as Moe, Joe, and Rex looked every which way to find Jesse. Rex swore to himself, thinking Jesse had been right. The three of them couldn't protect themselves, let alone her.

Rex knew they had no protection against the shark feeding frenzy, and this worried him the most. He tried to look everywhere at once as he twisted about in the water, but he was only catching fleeting glimpses of a shark or an occasional fish and then they were gone. *This is no good*, thought Rex.

More and more he felt like the proverbial sitting duck. There were more Yakuza divers out there and they might have knives or something worse. Rex was sure at any moment a Yakuza diver would attack him out of the darkness if a shark didn't bite off his head before then.

Rex's ear exploded as Moe yelled, "I GOT ONE! OH, SON-OF-A-BITCH... HOLD STILL, WILL YA!"

Rex couldn't figure out what was going on.

Had Moe been speared?

Moving his head and light about, Rex caught sight of the strangest battle he'd ever seen.

Highlighted by his light, Rex watched Moe wrestle with a Hawaiian Monk Seal that must have been attracted by either the blood in the water or Moe's underwater light.

Not finding Jesse, Rex decided he'd better help Moe before the mating process got serious. As Rex swam to assist Moe, a hand clinched around his ankle with a frightening grip. Whirling around, Rex kicked to free his leg, but he couldn't shake his gripper off.

Rex tried to swing his head around to put some light on whoever was clutching his ankle, but his attacker released him. Rex made his biggest mistake as he figured it was Jesse fooling around and he relaxed. Suddenly, he found himself in a frantic struggle with what felt like a vicious octopus.

Rex felt two legs wrap around his own from behind, locking them up in a tight hold. Before Rex could call for help, an arm roped around his neck cutting off his air. Rex knew one of the Yakuza divers had wrapped themselves around his back and had him in a death grip.

Rex couldn't get a grip on his attacker with all his equipment on. He'd never felt so helpless in his life, and he figured it was at the hands of a Migi Te since she was the only Yakuza diver in his vicinity when the lights went out. Apparently the broken arm had done nothing to slow Migi down.

Rex twisted and somersaulted, trying to grab a hold of the leach on his back who was about to kill him here in this cold and total blackness. He frantically whipped his arms around and tried to kick his legs free. Rex still couldn't get that witch off his back, and with each frantic movement he used up his air. Slowly the inky water about him was becoming even darker, and Rex realized he was losing his eyesight due to lack of air. In a last ditch effort, Rex dove and twisted around with the hope of scrapping his parasite off on the sea floor.

Rex kabonged his head into the sand hard enough to make his neck crack, but he knew Migi had been smashed into a coral rock outgrowth. Rex was rewarded when the arm around his neck slid away and allowed him to breathe again.

"WILL SOMEONE HELP ME GET RID OF THIS DAMN SEAL...OVER!"

Rex gagged and coughed before he whirled around to aim his light on his opponent, but Migi had vanished into the darkness. Rex rubbed his hand across his Adam's apple, and he coughed-bubbled again with a dry throat. His heart was still going bumpity-bump in his chest; faster than it had when the Mako had almost chomped his legs for an appetizer. This was one night dive to remember, and it wasn't over yet by a long shot, he figured.

Rex took a moment to collect himself before he began swimming over to help Moe—the mating pair. Rex hadn't kicked his fins more than twice before something huge whooshed by him in the darkness. Rex felt he'd been pushed aside by some giant creature swimming past him. Then he heard the wishy washy sounds of a clothes washer and realized this was the swishing turbulence of propellers passing close by him. The waters before Rex were suddenly ablaze with the brilliant lights coming from Ahab's *White Whale*.

"What the hell is that?" Rex yelled in his astonishment. "Over!"

The *White Whale* came to the rescue from out of nowhere. Rex watched in fascination as the submarine spotlighted one of the Otoko brothers. The submarine moved much faster than Otoko could swim in retreat. The sub swooped down on him, and extended its two mechanical claws. The submarine reached out with one claw and clamped onto the arm of the Otoko brother who was still holding a discharged spear gun. The other claw reached up with deadly precision to pluck the regulator out from the diver's mouth. The first claw released the diver's arm, and then cut off the diver's air hose to create a hissing, flailing, snake-hose that spewed pressurized air bubbles and whipped Otoko's head and shoulders for all the trouble he'd caused.

The two claws released Otoko, came together, and made a shooing motion to bat away the Yakuza diver as if he was a pesky fly. Rex's blood boiled as he thought they were being too nice to these murderers.

Still there was no sign of Jesse. Rex prayed that she wasn't hurt.

"I GOT ANOTHER ONE. OVER!" hollered Joe in everyone's ear.

Thinking of Moe's continuing struggle with a seal, Rex had to ask, "ANOTHER WHAT? OVER!"

"ANOTHER YAKUZA DIVER IN A BLACK WETSUIT. WHAT'D YOU THINK? OVER!" Joe asked in a surprised tone. Rex figured Joe hadn't seen his brother wrestling with the monk seal.

"HAS ANYONE SEEN JESSE? OVER!" Rex asked. He was starting to panic.

"NEGATIVE!" Joe answered. "I JUST SENT ONE OF THE OTOKO BROTHERS TO THE SURFACE WITHOUT A MASK OR ANY AIR."

"WILL SOMEONE HELP ME GET RID OF THIS SEAL?" Moe whined. "I THINK IT'S GETTING ROMANTIC WITH ME. OVER!"

"AT LEAST SOMEONES GONNA GET LAID TONIGHT. OVER!" someone said. Rex thought it sounded like Captain Ahab.

Suddenly, Rex was rocked as another attacker struck him from behind and wrapped an arm around his neck. Rex could not react before the arm around his neck relaxed. A hand slid down his thigh groping for his cock but only finding his sport's protector.

Rex grabbed the hand groping between his thighs, assuming it was Jesse. This time Rex wanted to make sure it was Jesse so he dragged her into his light where he could see her face. Rex saw two beautiful green-brown eyes squinting back to him through a voluminous mask that showed Jesse's features clearly. Rex could even tell Jesse was wearing her victory smile despite the regulator in her mouth. A heat that was almost sexual passed though Rex's innards now that he had Jesse safe in his arms.

"JESSE—OH JESSE!" Rex hollered. "HEY, GUYS? I FOUND JESSE. OVER!"

"IS SHE OKAY? OVER!" Joe asked in a concerned voice.

A warmth filled Rex's belly and his penis filled his athletic supporter and cup beneath his wetsuit. Rex sighed, "Ah—yeah—she seems in good spirits."

Jesse and Rex became the highlight of the underwater show as Joe and the *White Whale* threw their spotlights on Rex and Jesse's underwater dance. One spotlight turned off immediately, and Joe said, "Yes, I see you have things well in hand, there."

"Ah, Roger that. Over!" Rex spoke with contentment. The powerful spotlights from the two-man submarine didn't go away even after Rex tried to wave them off. The two perverts in Ahab's submarine wanted a free peep show.

"HEY YOU GUYS," Moe continued to plead. "HEY YOU GUYS CAN'T LEAVE ME DOWN HERE WITH THIS SEAL. HEY YOU GUYS…"

"Captain Ahab, are you still monitoring these communications? Over!" Rex asked while squinting into the bright lights of the *White Whale*.

"Aye, this is Ahab. I'm not only monitoring these escapades, the *White Whale* is recording a visual for some late night fun. Over!"

"Could you have the *White Whale* take Jesse and I back to the *Mickey Fin*? Over!"

"Aye, that looks to be the safest route. Over and out!"

"HEY, YOU GUYS CAN'T LEAVE ME DOWN HERE WITH THIS SEAL. HEY, YOU GUYS..."

Rex saw the *White Whale* turned in the direction of the feeding frenzy for a few moments, lighting the gory spectacular and probably taking video. Rex didn't think Ahab would get any late night jollies out of that video, but it did make a whale of a tale.

The *White Whale* finished its documentary of sharks and their table manners, then maneuvered beneath Rex and Jesse. Rex looked into the nose bubble of the submarine and was surprised to see a pimply young face that could pass for a teenager serving fries at McDonald's. The kid was in a white Coast Guard uniform with some impressive-looking strips on his sleeve, so Rex figured he knew what he was doing. The kid pointed upward, so Rex decided the kid wanted him and Jesse to get on top of the submarine.

Then Ahab came back to torture Rex's ear and give directions, "Sit your fannies around the conning tower and straddle the whale if ya can. Use the footholds in the sides of the tower to hold on if the ride gets too rough. This is Ahab signing off to attend to other duties. Over."

"Thank God," Rex whispered more to himself.

"I HEARD THAT!" came back Ahab. "OVER!"

Rex pressed his hands to the sides of his head, squinched his eyes shut, and mentally started counting to ten. He didn't make it to five. Jesse started tugging on his elbow to move him toward the submarine. Then Joe was shouting in his ear, "Rex baby! I've seen it all tonight! We might have to reserve a honeymooner's suite!"

Rex's body jolted in a muscle spasm at the talk of wedding bells. *Sure Jesse and I have been fooling around a little*, he thought, *but certainly nothing that might constitute matrimony*. "Come again," he whispered while succumbing to Jesse's tugs of his hand and moving toward the submarine.

"I think Moe has found his one true love!" Joe hollered in everyone's ear.

"I have not. Quit fooling around before she comes back!" Moe screamed.

"Uh oh, you're talking about Moe. You mean the seal, right?" Rex asked sounding relieved.

"What'd you think I was talking about?" Joe asked with interest.

"Nothing. Quit screaming in my ear," Rex whispered.

"You quit screaming in my ear!" Joe yelled.

"Are we set to ascend? That seal could be back any second and I still have my headlight on," Moe cried.

"I wouldn't worry about the seal," Rex said. "There's sharks in the dark dying for a meal, and I hear they like Hawaiian takeout." Although the feeding frenzy had been lost from Rex's sight in the darkness, the carnivorous ball of death was still clear in his mind's eye.

Rex and Jesse positioned themselves on top of the *White Whale*. Rex sat straddling the top of the submarine as if he was riding the back of an actual whale. He hugged the conning tower, and held tightly to the footholds as suggested. Jesse straddled tight behind Rex and gave him a breathtaking hug. Rex groaned. His ribs remained sore from Jesse's earlier elbowing.

When Rex got in position he saw he had a perfect view into the submarine through one of the conning tower windows. Rex could see the back of the pimply kid up front busy manning a console of controls, and he was surprised to see another youngster lounging behind him while reading the latest addition of "MAD" magazine. Rex bubbled since he hadn't received his addition before leaving home.

Rex banged on the hull with his knuckles, and instantly regretted it. He shook his hand in pain. The pimple kid twirled and spotted Rex in the window before giving him the okay sign. Rex returned the okay sign. Then he saw as the second mate slapped his knee and rolled with laughter. Rex imagined the sound of the mate's laughter and wished it was his. Suddenly the *White Whale* whooshed forward in smooth but rapid motion compared to Rex's journey on his Maxx Scooter. Jesse hugged Rex tighter as he white knuckled the foothold in the conning tower, and yelled, "And away we go!"

"Jackie Gleson just rolled over in his grave," Joe yelled. "Quit screaming."

While the *White Whale* remained on a level course following the ocean bottom, Rex worried whether the submarine's pilot would have enough sense to remember Boyle's Law and maintain a slow ascent in consideration of his passengers. Boyle's Law defined the inverse relationship between pressures on a gas's volume. Rex's particular worry was that as the submarine went up and the water pressure on his body went down, the air in his lungs would expand. As the sub got closer to the surface, his lungs would act like a balloon being blown up with air. If Rex and Jesse didn't exhale this expanding air fast enough their lungs would explode. Rex wasn't interested in testing this law, and he prayed Jesse remembered the danger as well. Since the submarine had a pressurized cabin, the sub's inhabitants didn't need to worry about the interior pressure of the sub's cabin changing and their lungs exploding during a rapid ascent. This meant it would be easy for the submarine's driver to forget his passenger's dangers outside the sub's cabin.

Rex was relieved as he noticed the bow of the submarine begin to point toward the surface in a gradual ascent that didn't exceed the quickness in which the air bubbles of his own exhalation moved toward the surface.

"WHOA! DID YOU SEE THAT?" Moe shouted in Rex's ear.

"AHHHHH!" Joe screamed.

"JOE! JOE! ARE YOU ALRIGHT?" Moe shouted.

"WHAT'S GOING ON?" Rex yelled.

Rex didn't know why the *White Whale* wasn't tuned in to their transmissions, but it continued with its course regardless of the catastrophe that was occurring.

"JOE, ARE YOU OKAY?" Moe repeated.

There were a few moments of anxious silence. Then Joe came back with a breathless response. "YEAH... YEAH...I'M MORE SCARED THAN HURT."

"WHAT THE HELL HAPPENED?" Rex asked. He was literally still in the dark since he couldn't see either of the Tweedys.

"THE SHARKS HAVE EXPANDED THEIR HUNT," Moe cried.

"A SHARK JUST BIT MY AIR TANK, BUT THEN LET GO!" Joe said, still sounding shaky. "THAT SUCKER PACKED A WALLUP!"

"Where are ya? I can't see ya," Rex asked.

"ON THE OCEAN FLOOR TO YOUR RIGHT," Moe said. "WE CAN'T CATCH UP WITH THE SUB!" Moe said in a voice that sounded terrified in its amplification. Rex whipped his head all about trying to see into the black depths behind him and to his sides. The once bright and all showing lights of the *White Whale* didn't seem to light enough area for Rex. His fears were passed to Jesse and she hugged even closer and tighter to his body. Suddenly a large reef shark zipped through the lights of the submarine. It was quickly followed by two more as if they were playing a game of tag.

"WATCH IT!" Joe screamed, but Rex didn't know who he meant to be on the look out. Rex's body whirled this way, then that way, as if he was a fighter pilot searching for an enemy fighter on his tail he couldn't shake off. Suddenly, the ascent rate of the *White Whale* seemed agonizingly slow and steady. Rex's sense of being the sitting duck in the darkness returned with vengeance. Rex had the sensation as if he was creeping up a dark basement stairway knowing a monster was racing up from the depths to rip him apart; yet he could see nothing in the blackness and his legs wouldn't move any faster. The skin on the back of his neck was crawling and he shuddered involuntarily.

Rex caught some sudden movement through the submarine's lit window before him. He focused on the motion inside the submarine and panicked to see the lounging mate rolling with laugher at a magazine cartoon without a notion or interest of what transpired outside his own watertight world. Rex had the urge to bolt toward the surface to escape the deadly and unbeatable predators on the scent of his blood. It was only Jesse's tight grip that reminded him of his other responsibilities that were more important than his fears. Rex's terror turned to frustrated anger to fight his terrifying opponents that he couldn't see or defend himself from even if the beasts were visible. The tensions of this day were beating down his strength and endurance to focus and react to the threats which surrounded him. Rex began to kick the sides of the *White Whale* with his heels as if he was riding an immense mule that stubbornly refused to move faster than a lazy amble. The lazy mate inside the submarine gazed up through the window with annoyance, then returned to his magazine.

Again a shark raced through the lights of the submarine, and Joe yelled, "LOOK OUT, MOE!"

"WHERE? I CAN'T SEE THEM!" Moe screamed.

"THIS IS AHAB. WHAT'S ALL THE SCREAMING ABOUT? OVER!"

"THE SHARK FRENZY HAS EXPANDED. YOU NEED TO GET THE SUB TO RETURN TO THE OCEAN FLOOR FOR THE TWEEDYS. THEY'RE UNDER ATTACK. OVER!" shouted Rex.

"UNDERSTOOD. WILL RELAY THE MESSAGE AND SEE IF I CAN GET THE SUB TUNED INTO YOUR FREQUENCY. OVER!" Ahab replied.

"WE'RE DIRECTLY BENEATH THE SUBMARINE … OVER!" Moe added.

Ahab didn't respond, but after a moment the sub driver was yelling in everyone's ears. "THIS IS CHIEF PETTY OFFICER TODD. UNDERSTAND WE HAVE A SHARK PROBLEM. OVER."

"YOU COULD SAY THAT. OVER!" Joe said in an amazingly calm voice.

"THIS IS TODD. WILL DESCEND UNDER SAME COURSE. CAN YOU REACH THE *WHITE WHALE* ON YOUR OWN? OVER!"

"THAT'S AN AFFIRMATIVE. HOLD YOUR SPEED TO A MINIMUM. WE'LL APPROACH FROM YOUR STARBOARD TO YOUR BOW. OVER!" Moe answered.

"ROGER THAT. OVER!" responded Todd.

"STRADDLE THE BOW AS YOUR MATES HAVE DONE ON THE STERN. LEAVE ROOM FOR ME TO SEE OUT THE BOW BUBBLE. OVER!"

Rex noticed as the *White Whale* began a slow descent before it took a more direct dive toward the ocean floor. All this was handled with amazing professionalism and maturity, Rex thought, considering Todd's young personal appearance and his mate's lack of interest. Rex did notice the mate had dropped his magazine and was ogling out the bow bubble over Todd's shoulder once he'd heard about a possible human dinner platter about to be served to the sharks.

Just as Rex thought they might escape without further trouble, the ocean floor appeared in the light and they seemed to in the middle of the shark frenzy. Gray streaks flashed through the sub's lights seemingly by the hundreds, while sharks swam past Rex so close he could feel the wake of their passing.

Jesse held Rex in a terrified grasp, and for the first time he heard her screaming into her regulator in fright. Rex sucked hard as Jesse had nearly forced the air from his lungs with her renewed hold.

Rex understood the Tweedy's concern for their safety as he was now concerned for his and Jesse's safety as well. Thinking of the Yakuza divers they'd sent struggling to the surface, Rex doubted that they had made it to the safety of the *Tora*. If they'd made any attempt to escape on the surface Rex was sure they were dinner appetizers. Rex was surprised how little concern he felt for the Yakuza's plight.

The *White Whale* leveled and hovered just above the ocean floor. Rex thought they were fish food since there were sharks everywhere. He felt as if he had a sign stuck on his back that read: "EAT ME! FRESH FLESH! GET 'EM WHILE THEY'RE HOT AND THE BLOOD'S STILL PUMPING!"

He realized his initial plan of making it back to the *Mickey Fin* while hugging the sea floor would have been ludicrous. They would have been shark ka-bobs before they reached the surface.

Then two figures appeared next to the submarine that didn't have the sleek shapes of sharks. Rex recognized Joe and Moe as they made their way to the sub's bow as if there were sharks chewing their hiennies.

"GO, JOE, GO. THERE'S ONE ABOUT TO BITE YOUR ASS!" Rex screamed, although he was joking. Rex giggled as Joe went frantically trying to shoo the shark away from his bottom while scampering onto the sub's bow at the same time.

"JUST KIDDING, JOE!" Rex laughed.

"ASSHOLE!" Joe replied.

Rex saw the Tweedys were straddling the bow before he pounded the submarine's window and signaled Todd all was okay. Immediately the submarine began its ascent at the same slow and maddening rate as before. The sharks continued to swarm, and Rex was terrified to see some were striking the submarine's hull in their insanity.

Abruptly, Rex was slammed against the conning tower by a powerful push from Jesse on his backside. Before Rex realized what was happening, Jesse's grip around him went limp and he felt her begin to slide away.

Rex released his grip on the conning tower while hugging the submarine with his legs for all he was worth. Quickly, Rex twisted his body around to catch Jesse's now struggling body before she fell off the *White Whale*. Rex realized a shark had struck her from behind and knocked the breath out of her. He saw Jesse's regulator had been blown from her mouth and was free flowing above her head like a drunken snake. In her breathless panic, Jesse was unable to reach her air supply. Rex twisted around and pulled Jesse toward him. Then he grabbed her bubbling regulator, and shoved the regulator back into her screaming mouth with bruising force. Jesse double fisted her regulator and did some deep inhalations for a moment. As she began to relax, Rex gave her the okay sign and she looked into his eyes with contempt before returning the sign that she was okay. After Jesse returned her tight grasp around Rex's middle she pinched him for good measure. Rex twisted back to grip the footholds of the conning tower. The sharks continued to swarm around them. Rex saw they all had the protruding dorsal fins and arched backs of sharks ready to attack a meal.

Officer Todd must have become concerned since he elevated the planes and had the submarine ascending at a brisker pace. The sharks followed as if they sensed dessert was to be served. Rex had to pop his ears to equalize their pressure so he knew they were ascending at a good rate and he could only hold tight and wait till they reached the surface and safety.

Rex stretched and peeked around the conning tower to see how Joe and Moe were faring just a few feet before him. Their breathing had been huffing and puffing at an alarming rate but Rex had been too occupied with Jesse and the sharks to notice. Rex peered toward the bow and was amazed by what he saw.

Joe and Moe were straddling the *White Whale* just as he and Jesse were, but they were separated by a few feet and duking it out with swarming sharks as if they were legless prizefighters. Every time a shark came within their reach, Joe or Moe would jab and swing their gloved fists to deliver a scaring blow to the shark. Rex saw them bop a few sharks in the head area before wondering why the sharks weren't approaching him and Jesse. They were striking all about the *White Whale*, and Rex thanked his lucky stars he and Jesse had only that one strike.

Suddenly something slammed Rex's head into the conning tower with such ferocity his faceplate was cracked open to the sea. Rex remained conscious long enough to feel the warmth of blood on his face before his mask was ripped off and a regulator was shoved in his mouth. He felt someone pinching his nose and nestling his head into something soft and comfortable. Rex passed out thinking how comfy and cozy it was sucking on mommy's milk and having such nice pillows to dream upon.

# CHAPTER TWENTY-NINE

"Come on, Ester, wake up!" shouted young Rex.

Young Rex started out kneeling beside the prone figure of Ester who was lying in the same position Sara had lain in the attic of Deputy Madison's barn. Ester was dressed as Rex had seen her on the plane from Honolulu, but as much as young Rex shook Ester's side and called her name, Ester didn't respond. The two-headed Deputy Madison with the muscular body came charging at them.

Young Rex had shot away one of Deputy Madison's heads, but that only set the monster back a few steps. Then, young Rex's patrol pistol transformed into a strange looking .50 caliber machine gun.

"Time to do business," young Rex notified Deputy Madison as he gazed at the odd-looking gun. He didn't know how he could use his huge and heavy machine gun with his right hand while pushing Ester back and forth as she lay on the floor with his left hand. Rex pulled the gun's trigger, and the big .50 caliber exploded with unbelievable firepower. The gun's explosiveness threw Rex against the wall and kept pounding on his right shoulder as it shot.

Young Rex became infuriated when he saw his .50 caliber bullets become Hostess Twinkies as they were shot and bounced off, or were squished, upon contact with Deputy Madison. Deputy Madison's deflated head regained shape, but it blew up like a Moe head while the other head popped like a balloon to become a Joe head. As the heads became Moe and Joe bobble heads, Madison's body sported a Hawaiian shirt with a wide girth.

The machine gun continued to slam against Rex's shoulder with each

Twinkie it ejected, and the two-headed Moe Joe thing continued its assault heedless of the Twinkie gun. Young Rex realized the monster was after the Twinkie gun now instead of Ester as Joe and Moe's appetites took control of their behavior.

Young Rex was very confused. He became aware of his name being called from out of nowhere.

"Rex!"

"Rex!"

"Rex!"

Rex opened his eyes as Jesse's face was diving upon his own. "Rex," she said softly.

Before his scattered thoughts could be realized, Jesse's lips were glued onto his open mouth and her tongue was dancing among his dental work. Rex returned the kiss, and he rolled his eyes to see four large feet on a wooden deck. Rolling his eyes the other direction; Rex saw Jesse's breasts through an unzipped wetsuit, and he realized he was lying on the deck of the *Mickey Fin* with Jesse kneeling at his side.

"That's not the way I learned CPR," Joe said. Jesse was kneeling over him and sucking on his face as if she was the one needing air. Rex felt a warmness building in his loins, and he was wondering just how long this face sucking had been going on—and if it would continue.

"Yup, he's alive," Rex heard Joe say as Joe apparently saw the movement just below Rex's waist since Rex was wearing a dive skin. Jesse and Rex continued to dine on each other's faces, and Rex felt Jesse's hand pressing on his shoulder just like the Twinkie gun had been doing in his dream.

Abruptly, Rex broke off his kiss and sat up. "Ester ... what happened to Ester?" asked Rex. For a moment, the world darkened around him, and he felt a queasy feeling in his stomach. Looking down into his lap he was surprised to see a few drops of his blood drip from his left cheek. Rex brought up his fingers to find the origin of the blood, but Jesse grabbed his wrist and pulled his hand away.

"Ya went and got it bleeding again," Moe said as he passed a wet and bloodied towel to Jesse who applied it to Rex's cheek. Rex tried to look around him. He remembered how his cheek had been cut and the last moments before passing out. Yet he couldn't recall how he'd gotten onto the *Mickey Fin*, but that didn't seem to matter at this point. Rex saw everyone was on board safe and with all their legs, arms, hands, and fingers. What was more, they were all smiling.

"You did it, Bana," Joe shouted with glee while stamping his feet upon the deck and rocking the boat. Rex saw his big buddy had his happiest smile. With a few cobwebs still mucking up his thoughts, Rex asked, "I did what?"

"Hot-damn! He doesn't even know what state he's in," Joe laughed.

"We're in Mich... Maui. But if you want to get technical, we're really in the South Pacific Ocean just off the coast of Maui," Rex managed to say through the towel pressed to his face. He found talking made his face hurt, and he tried wincing, which only made his face hurt more.

Rex wanted to look up at the people around him, but every time he tried to move his head there was sharp stabbing pain along the back of his neck. Rex felt a good neck cracking would settle his muscles back into their proper places.

"Can ya help me stand?" Rex asked while holding up a hand. Joe squished Rex's hand in his huge paw and hauled Rex to his feet as if he was picking up a small tree limb. Joe released Rex and the world suddenly grayed around him again. Rex knew better than to shake his head. He waited a moment and things cleared with no problems.

"Are you okay?" Jesse asked as she came around in front of him and looked up in his face. There was a beautiful smile on her face which brought warmness throughout Rex's body. *Jesse is safe, yeah, Jesse is safe. Things are going to be alright*, Rex thought.

"Are *you* okay?" Rex asked as he reached out and gave her a hug. He recalled someone ripping off his mask and shoving a regulator in his mouth before tilting back his head into something soft. He knew that someone had been Jesse, and looking down, he realized the soft something had been her breasts. *Yeah, Jesse is okay.*

"I could never be better." Jesse jumped up and down while clapping her hands together. "And we *did* pull it off," Jesse said with a smile and a glint in her eye.

"Yeah, I guess we kind of pulled it off." Rex tried to smile, but that split open his face and started the blood flowing.

"We're going to have to get you back to the hospital, Rex," Moe said with concern.

"THIS IS AHAB, CALLING THE *MICKEY FIN*. OVER!"

Moe left the group and rushed up the ladder to the pilothouse.

"*MICKEY FIN*, COME IN, PLEASE. OVER!"

"Damn, I wish he would quit shouting," Rex said as he took the towel away from Jesse, pressed it against his face and started for the pilothouse. "This is the *Mickey Fin*, Over!" Moe said.

"AHOY *MICKEY FIN*. THIS IS AHAB. CONGRATULATIONS ON SUCCESSFUL COMPLETION OF OPERATION 'WATERLOGGED!' ALL SUSPECTS SAFE AND ACCOUNTED FOR EXCEPT ONE CASUALTY. HE HAS BEEN IDENTIFIED AS CHIISAI DESU. OVER!"

"We couldn't have done it without you and your crew, Captain Ahab. Special thanks to Chief Petty Officer Todd and the *White Whale* for their recovery efforts," Moe responded.

"HAVE FIVE PRISONERS. CREW IS JUST BEGINNING SEARCH OF *TORA*, BUT REPORTS A MAJOR BUST. HUNDREDS OF THOUSANDS OF DOLLARS AND OTHER MONIES ALREADY CONFISCATED FROM *TORA'S* SAFE. THERE ALSO APPEARS TO BE A LARGE AMOUNT OF COCAINE AND OTHER DRUGS STOWED IN FRONT CABINS. HAVE LOCATED A COUPLE OF POUCHES THAT CONTAIN LARGE CUT RARE STONES AND GEMS! THIS WILL BE THE LARGEST BUST TO BE MADE IN THIS REGION. SO IT'S OUR THANKS THAT GO OUT TO YOU, MOE! OVER!" said Ahab with laughter in his voice.

"I'll make a special commendation in my report to my superior and to Washington about your efforts, Captain Ahab. Over."

"FORGET WASHINGTON. JUST TELL THE WET HEADS AT PEARL WE WERE ON THE BALL AND OF PROPER ASSISTANCE. HOW'S YOUR CASUALTY? OVER!"

"Rex Bana has minor facial cuts and probably a concussion. But he is up walking the decks thanks to the *White Whale*. He'll survive. Thanks for asking. Over!"

"AND THE LADY IN DISTRESS? HOW DID SHE FARE? OVER!" Ahab asked.

"She's in perfect condition, and in a hurry to get into some warm clothes. Thanks again, we're heading back to Lahaina pier. Over!"

"EXCELLENT SAILING WITH YOU, CAPTAIN TWEEDY. WE'LL HAVE TO GET TOGETHER AT LEFTY'S TO SWAP STORIES. THIS IS AHAB. OVER AND OUT!"

Moe returned the microphone and then jumped after turning around to find Rex behind him crowding the pilothouse. Rex had climbed the ladder to hear what Ahab had to say although he was sure anyone within a mile radius caught

Ahab's yelling.

"So they've recovered the crew and are heading back to port as well?" Rex asked when Moe settled back on his feet.

"Yup. It looks like this part of the case has been concluded with satisfaction," Moe responded while still holding a hand on his chest. Moe was wearing a huge grin as if he was happy with the way things had gone. Rex was not smiling.

"We have to get back to port as quickly as possible," Rex stated in an urgent tone.

"Sure, Rex," Moe said with a frown, before he turned to the controls of the *Mickey Fin*. "We'll get you to the emergency room, but your face is already looking better."

"Oh, that," Rex said drabbing at his face with the blooded towel. "That's not what I was concerned about. I'm worried about the safety of Ester Gomez."

Moe stood for a moment as if considering Rex's words and their tone. Moe leaned over the side of the pilothouse. "Joe! Pull up the anchor so we can get underway. And step on it, Joe. Rex is worried about Ester Gomez."

"Gotcha!" Rex heard Joe holler from below. Rex felt the heavy footsteps of the Hawaiian as he plodded across the deck toward the bow at a rapid pace.

"I'll get us back to port as fast as we can, Rex," Moe said with concern. "You head back down to the deck and see if Jesse can doctor up your face. It looks like the night's not over yet."

Without a word, Rex made his way back down the ladder. He swayed a bit, but put it down to the passing swells. He was happy to hear the throaty growl of the *Mickey Fin's* twin turbines as they fired up in anticipation for their race back to shore. Rex was even happier to feel the warm and safe hug of Jesse as he reached the end of the ladder and she steadied his step onto the deck.

After their brief hug, Jesse's smile disappeared as she saw the concern on Rex's face. "You really feel Ester's in danger?" Jesse asked.

"Yeah. But if I told you my reasons for worrying, you'd think that hit on my head left me with brain damage."

"Oh, Rex." Jesse closed in and wrapped her arms tightly around his body. "I could never doubt you. I trusted you with my life and the King Slayer came through," Jesse said into Rex's chest.

"Please don't call me that," Rex murmured.

Jesse pulled back, nodded, and said, "You're right. It's not a name I care to call you."

Again they embraced each other, but Rex felt the anxiousness of the hunt returning to his chest. There were too many loose ends left over from this operation. Rex felt the real killers remained at large, and he wouldn't be able to find peace until Kuro and Yama had been caught and accounted for. A more immediate concern was what had happened to Ester Gomez. Rex felt in his heart that his path lay with her destiny. The Sara look-a-like couldn't be a coincidence; there had been a purpose for Ester popping into his life at this moment in time.

Rex walked hand in hand with Jesse over to the starboard railing and felt his spirits lighten as the wet wind from the *Mickey Fin's* accelerated pace hit his face, and made it sting. Rex felt they were headed into the part of the night which held something important for him, and he was anxious to meet it. There seemed to be a job left undone, and he wasn't sure what it was. Then again, he figured, the hit on his head might have confused his thoughts.

Jesse continued to hug Rex's waist as they looked at the approaching lights of Lahaina, and Rex felt something was clicking into place for him mentally. Something was right, yet he could only see the wrong. What happened to Ester Gomez and Meat? How could they rest with Kuro and Yama still on the island?

# CHAPTER THIRTY

The *Mickey Fin* closed on Lahaina Harbor and Rex was worried about what to do next as his head throbbed and he felt dizzy. How was he going to act to a deadly situation if he couldn't even stand on his own two feet?

If he had to face James Cook as a killer, he had his doubts of surviving. He felt the shark attack had taken its toll and he was amazed his head was still attached, let alone barely maimed. The back of his head should have cuts as well, but the thick rubber from his full face mask strap incurred most of the damage. Rex figured the shark had to have been a small one since it didn't simply yank off his head. He thanked his lucky stars again and his daily weight lifting program which maintained his bull neck.

Closing his eyes, he dared to shake his head back and forth. An audible popping noise came from his neck as he felt the kinks in his muscles loosen and his head seem to fall back into place.

"Ahhh…" Rex said in relief. "Oh, that felt great." Rex started to smile before he felt the scab on his cheek start to crack, and held his smile to a grin.

"Are you crazy? You could have just snapped your spinal cord if that had been a serious injury," Jesse cried.

"Oh well." Rex sighed. He'd had similar injuries during his football years, and he knew the strain on his neck would disappear after a few days of soreness. Nothing to worry about.

"Don't 'oh well,' me, buster. I didn't stick my neck out for you so you could pull some stupid stunt like that and become a paraplegic," Jesse scolded.

Rex abruptly twisted about while dropping to a squatting position in an experiment of physical dexterity. He managed the move correctly but wobbled in his squat as the world around him swirled before becoming level again.

"Whoa," Rex said as he whirled his arms and jumped back a step before regaining his stance. "Better try that a little more carefully next time."

"Why are you trying it at all? You should be in bed lying down," Jesse said with anxiousness in her voice.

"Time to get dressed for my second mission of the night," Rex said as he headed below to a cabin where he'd stored his deployment bag.

Jesse wouldn't be left behind. "You *did* bring my extra set of clothes, didn't you?" she asked.

"Bring 'em? Hell, they hogged my whole bag," Rex complained behind his back.

Rex was bent over digging through his bag as Jesse turned on the cabin light and came over to smack his rump. "So, now I'm a hog, am I?" she asked.

Pulling out her wear and passing it to Jesse, Rex responded, "I said nothing of the sort. You've got the most beautiful body I've ever seen in real life." Rex ducked for cover back into his deployment bag and searched for his own clothes.

Rex rummaged around for a moment or two through all the additional equipment he brought but hadn't used. "You really think so?" Jesse asked in a quiet seductive voice.

With his head still in his duffle, Rex heard Jesse's question, her tone, and he knew he was in trouble. He figured the excitement of the night had not been lost on Jesse either. Slowly he stood erect to see Jesse had slipped out of her wetsuit and set aside the clothes Rex had given her. She was only wearing the clothes she was born with, and Rex had to agree with his earlier statement.

"Yup, that's a big 10-4, pretty lady. That's a body no man could turn away from. Could ya close the cabin door at least?"

Rex dropped the clothes he'd grabbed and moved toward Jesse. The light of the cabin gave Jesse a yellow-white aura in Rex's vision. He felt he was approaching an angel.

Rex felt Jesse's nakedness as he embraced her in a fierce hug. Although Rex's heart felt otherwise, his head told him there wasn't time for playing kissy-face. Rex backed off Jesse and reached for her clothes. "Here, you better put these on before the Tweedys start wondering what we're doing down here."

"Ah Rex, you're no fun anymore. You use me then just throw me aside like used meat." Jesse laughed.

"Meat is exactly why we can't do this right now," Rex said as he started to dress in his street clothes. "If it wasn't for Meat, I'd be banging your head against the hull there, and you'd be hollering 'More! More! More!'" Rex did his impression of a woman having an orgasm.

"Promises, promises..." Jesse giggled before disappearing into a billowing football jersey. Rex saw the jersey was green with the white number "89" on the front and back along with his name across the back of the shoulders.

"Hey, that's one of my old State jerseys," Rex cried. "How'd you get that?"

"I'm just putting on the clothes you gave me, like you said." Jesse smiled.

"It looks a bit large, but I suppose it belongs there," commented Rex while dressing himself.

"Oh, it belongs here, huh?" Jesse asked getting into her shorts, then heading to Rex's bag for her sneakers.

Rex was about to make a comment but the *Mickey Fin* bounced lightly against something, and Rex figured they were docking.

# CHAPTER THIRTY-ONE

The night was waning as Rex and Jesse returned to the deck, and he was correct in assuming they had regained the port. Joe was already on the pier tying the *Mickey Fin* to the dock, and Rex heard Moe shutting down the turbines.

To Rex, the night felt like an early morning in Michigan during late spring. There was a bite in the air that would make goose bumps on the naked flesh and the air was heavy with dew. To him it felt refreshing and clean.

"Geez, it's colder than a witch's tit," Moe grumbled as he came down from the pilothouse.

"You've felt a witch's tit?" Jesse asked from behind Moe.

"Oh, sorry, Jesse. I didn't see you there." Moe reached behind her and gave Jesse a one-armed hug while rubbing his hand up and down her arm to warm each other.

In no time at all, Rex ushered everyone back up the pier, across the quiet park, and headed toward Joe's cruiser on Front Street. Rex was concentrating on what Dr. Cook could possibly be doing with Ester Gomez. Rex continued out onto Front Street with his head down and hurting. He wasn't paying attention to the world around him, nor did he immediately acknowledge the screams from his friends.

Thinking of something else and looking up to see where he was, Rex saw the grill on the speeding limousine close enough to read the "Ford" emblem. Without thought, Rex's body reacted. He leaped backwards with his butt landing on the trunk of a car parked on the curb. Rex did a sliding somersault in a continuing motion from his leap and flopped hard on the sidewalk beside the car. Rex didn't hear them, but later Joe told him shots were fired from the limousine's driver's window even as he was tumbling backward over the car.

The roar of the car's engine continued down Front Street before Rex realized what happened. Rex peeked behind him to see Moe, Joe, and Jesse dusting themselves off and looking around after getting up from the dirt floor beneath the huge banyan tree where they'd dove for cover. Rex got to his knees with a grunt and checked the street for more ill wishers. He saw Front Street was devoid of life again and decided it was safe to stand like a real person again. The others soon joined him.

"Are you okay?" Jesse asked anxiously.

Rex brushed himself off and nodded before looking Jesse over to see that she was okay. "Was that who I think it was?" Rex asked.

"If you were thinking of the Maui Funeral Home limo, then you got that right," Joe said.

"Did you see who was driving?" asked Rex.

"Nope, but I would guess it was Yama," Joe said.

They all looked up and down a street they'd once only considered dangerous to the slow moving shopper. Now they realized one could be run over by a car or shot at as well as being trampled beneath the feet of tourists with fat bellies and third-degree sunburns.

"I wonder if Kuro was in the backseat. I don't think he was," Jesse said.

"Why do you say that?" asked Moe.

Rex answered instead. "Kuro would never have allowed such open violence. He's more of the planning, sneaky type."

"Exactly, but now it's a sure thing that Kuro will find out that you never went back to Michigan and you stole his hundred thousand dollars. Oh I just love it when crooks get screwed," Moe smiled.

"You think we should try and go after him?" asked Joe as he pushed the party down Front Street toward his cruiser.

"You can do whatever you want, Joe. I'm going after Ester Gomez," Rex said.

"I'm with Rex. I say we go find out whether Dr. Cook is a crook or a saint," said Jesse.

"Whatever he is, he ain't a saint," Rex grumbled.

"I'm with Rex. I owe him a few after tonight. I might make Section Chief after this job," Moe said, all puffed up and strutting.

"Well, I'm the one with the car keys," Joe said with an evil grin. For a moment their excitement bubble deflated. "But I guess I owe Mr. Bana the rest of the evening at the very least. Come on, boys and girls, let's go catch ourselves some Meat!" Joe hollered.

While motoring down Highway 30, Joe kept an eye on his rearview mirror and tracked the other cars. He didn't want to approach the winding curves of the highway and have that limousine on his tail. The ride went smoothly, if not calmly. Only Rex appeared anxious as he wondered about his own stability and his ability to react to an intelligent killer; if that's what Cook was. Rex also worried about Ester. He had promised her safety on this island and it appeared he'd failed miserably at his task. He still felt woozy.

"Tell me how you plan to approach Dr. Cook, Rex. He *is* one of the Island's leading citizens and benefactors," Joe said.

"Huh? Oh, Meat?" Rex responded rather sluggishly.

"You sure you're okay, Rex?" Jesse asked.

"Yeah, just tired I guess. Tired and a bit overwhelmed with all that's gone on tonight."

"I guess I'm too elated we pulled it off. I feel sort of chipper," Moe said.

"Chipper, huh?" Joe asked. "So what about it, Rex? How do we approach the big Meat?"

Joe was already pulling into their driveway, and as Rex looked over at the neighbor's mansion, he was surprised to see all the estate lights were turned off. Meat's mansion appeared as if it was an ancient European castle set on top of the hill under a moonless night. All that was missing from his view were the moors and the packs of wolves. When goose bumps reappeared on Rex's flesh, he didn't think they had anything to do with the coolness of the night air.

Rex thought, *All we need is to stick Yama into this picture; dress him in a dark shabby suit that's too small, give him some black platform shoes, and away we go! A real Frankenstein monster*!

"It's not Halloween, is it?" Rex asked as Joe put the cruiser into park. The others followed Rex's gaze and peered up at Cook's Castle.

"If it is, I'm not trick or treating at his house," Moe whispered.

There was an eerie silence that lasted much too long for Rex.

Rex could hear the pinging and hissing noises from the cruiser as it settled for the night. It occurred to Rex it was his imagination spooking him at the moment, and he wondered if the others were scaring themselves as well.

"You still haven't told me your plan of action, Rex," Joe said in a husky whisper that shattered the silence as if shooting off a gun. It took another moment of silence for everyone to settle down and Rex to answer.

"Joe, I haven't told you my plan of action because I don't have one," Rex said to the back car window as he glared at the haunting scene.

"Do you know why you dislike Dr. Cook so much, Rex?" Moe asked in a curious tone.

"I have no idea, and that's what really bothers me. I mean, I should hug the guy and give him a bunch of kisses for all the things he's done at Sara's Garden."

Jesse's expression turned to one of someone that had just drunk bad tasting medicine.

"There's something between me and Meat. I feel there's a connection I've never understood and it gives me the willies." Rex shuddered.

Joe blew up his cheeks until Rex thought his head would explode, and then Joe let out a lip-flapping sigh that sounded like a toy motor and splattered the windshield. Finally, he spoke. "Lighten up, Rex old buddy. You came here and did your damndest for Moe and me. You broke the case of a lifetime for us—whether you believe it or not. So if you're lost on this one, I think Moe and I can help you out.

"We have witnesses that claim Ester was last seen in Meat's company. And since I *am* the law in this town, I say we go pay Meat a visit." Joe huffed and snorted.

"Just give him a little knock on the door and ask what's cookin', Dr. Cook?" Rex joked.

"Yes, sir. Now there's the old Rex I's looking for. Come on, let's boogy," Joe rallied.

Joe unlocked the shotgun from the cruiser's dash, and jumped out of the car ready to take on an army—of ants maybe. Moe followed suit by grabbing his brother's police utility belt and taking the Smith and Wesson .9mm out of its holster before bouncing out of the car himself. Rex saw Moe shove his brother's revolver into the huge pocket of his shorts.

Rex and Jesse stared at each other in the backseat of the cruiser.

"You should stay here in case there's trouble," Rex said.

Jesse slapped her knee and said, "Ha! That's a good one, Rex!" She threw open her door and bounded out.

"Jesse…" Rex started to say something, but Jesse was already gone and the door was closed.

"Shit," Rex growled. Now he was stuck alone in the car. It was dark, but

Rex did not fear the darkness of the backseat—there was something else he feared. Grabbing his Glock 10 and a spare ammo clip, Rex was ready to fight; he just prayed it didn't come to that.

# CHAPTER THIRTY-TWO

"Should we try the front door, or sneak in through the beach entrance?" Joe asked. He was standing behind the cruiser with his shotgun thrown over his shoulder.

"I would think the front door would be more appropriate at five a.m.," Rex said. "We're just asking questions, aren't we, Deputy on vacation Tweedy?"

"Sounds appropriate. Do most killers answer their doorbell?" Joe asked.

"Sometimes," Rex said with a serious face.

"Not gonna lighten up, are ya?" Joe asked.

Rex responded with a dead stare. Then he started down the drive toward the street. The others followed in a close group, although no one seemed in a hurry.

"Ya know. I've never really noticed how high this fence is," Moe remarked as they hit the street and started the block long walk to Dr. Cook's front gate.

"Can you imagine the monthly electrical bill?" Jesse asked to no one's attention.

"I still haven't figured why Dr. Cook thinks he needs all this security. I mean, he does have two law officers as neighbors," Joe said.

"No. He was supposed to think he only had one law officer as a neighbor," Moe reminded.

"Oh, come on, Moe. Half the people on the island know you work for the FBI," Jesse joked.

Rex was the first to reach the gate. As he studied the entrance the others crowded around him. Rex saw the twelve-foot high iron rod gate was held up by fourteen-foot brick and mortar posts, and it ran on a thin rail track so it could slide open. He noted the gate sunk into the drive. It appeared impervious to him.

"Anyone got an M-1 tank we can borrow?" Rex asked quietly.

No one cared to respond.

Looking around, Rex found an intercom box with a remote control sensor and a ten-button numerical keypunch. Rex pushed one of the white unmarked buttons and heard a quiet buzzer noise. Moments passed. Rex heard the whine of small electric motors and looked up to see cameras mounted to each post aimed at the entrance. He figured these must be remotes to see who was at the gate while one watched the monitors inside the house.

Although it was obvious the cameras were focused on them, no one responded to the door buzzer. Rex shuffled around for a moment. He was sure the other three were having second thoughts of disturbing the good doctor at this time of the morning.

Rex knew they didn't represent the fairest looking congregation to ring the doctor's buzzer, but surely the doctor recognized his two neighbors. The Tweedy boys were hard to miss in any crowd. And Rex figured Meat would recall him from their interactions both at Sara's Garden and on the beach with Jesse. Certainly, Dr. Cook would recognize his successor, even if she did look like she'd just gotten out of the shower. Jesse was dressed this time, and that might throw Cook for a loop, figured Rex.

Impatiently, Rex pressed the buzzer for an obnoxiously long time. His experience with serial killers was that they never answered their door when the authorities were standing on the front porch. Meat's delay in answering the door only made Rex more certain that something fishy was going on here. Rex was determined to figure out what that fishy thing was and just how bad it smelled.

"Come on, Rex," Joe started to whine. "Maybe we just ought to call the doctor. The guy's still in bed."

"And if he's not?" Moe stood up for Rex's thoughts, or he simply found another way to pester his big brother. Rex knew Joe was thinking with his stomach. The big guy could not have eaten for hours and his hunger must be ravenous.

Just as Rex reached up to ring the buzzer a third time to notify the doctor they had no intentions of leaving his gate, a deep angry voice boomed through the intercom, "Who the hell is buzzing my doorbell in the middle of the night?"

Before Rex could give his desired response to the doctor's indignation, Joe stepped over and pushed the intercom button. "Ah... Doctor Cook, this is

Deputy Sheriff Joseph Tweedy of the Maui County Sheriff's Department..."

"Yes, I have cameras at my entryway and I recognize you and your brother, Deputy Tweedy. And what's with the shotgun?"

There was a moment of silence.

"We are neighbors, after all," continued Cook. Joe looked up at the camera with a surprised expression on his face. "But what do you want with me in the middle of the night?"

No one made a response.

"If I'm not mistaken, that's Dr. Achew standing behind you, but I don't recognized that villainous character next to you. Who is he?" Joe chuckled while Rex glared back at the camera. Rex was sure Dr. Cook recognized him and knew his intentions. Rex figured that Meat was stalling for some reason.

"Oh," Joe said acting surprised that Dr. Cook didn't recognize Rex. "That's Rex Bana. He's ..."

"Yes, I know what he is," Dr. Cook interrupted in a tone that sounded like he was wiping something undesirable off his shoe. "Is Mr. Bana the one that led you to my doorstep at this ridiculous hour?"

"Ah, well, some of his logic was used to bring us here. Sir, I just have a few questions. If you'd kindly allow us to enter, I'm sure we can clear this whole matter up in a few moments."

"Mr. Bana? You may recall I invited you into my home the other evening so we could discuss subjects which would have cleared up this entire matter. You refused then, and now you come banging at my gate during unsociable hours. What if I don't allow all of you to invade my privacy?" Cook asked in a voice that sounded like a man beaten upon and weary to his last end.

"Then I'm afraid, sir, I'll be forced to get a court order," Joe responded. "Please believe this is not my intent, but if you force it, I have enough evidence to get a court order and police reinforcements by just using the cellular phone in my pocket. I won't even have to leave this gate. And I will not allow you to leave this estate until such time as that order and reinforcements arrive. So it would be in everyone's best interest if you would simply answer these questions and we'll be on our way." Joe made his speech in a stern official voice Rex had never heard him use. Rex glanced at his friend as if he was seeing something new in Joe, and he was happy to have the big guy on his side.

Again, static noise responded from the intercom, then in a stronger voice Cook responded. "All right, Deputy Joseph Tweedy. I invite you, Special Agent Moe Tweedy, Dr. Jessica Achew, and Rex Bana into my home. But I warn you. You enter here at your own risk, and you'll be ruining a major surprise that involves each and every one of you in a close way. You may enter now." There was a loud buzz and the gate rolled aside with a crushing slowness.

"Just who on this island doesn't know I'm an undercover agent for the FBI?" Moe asked as the group proceeded up the drive.

"Obviously very few." Rex snickered at Moe's indignation.

Still, Rex wondered how Meat got his information, and how he was related to these murders. None of the murders were discovered until Cook was replaced by Jesse. If Meat was still the medical examiner of Maui County these random murders might have continued to occur. Rex noticed some of these thoughts might be going through Moe's mind as well. Moe's face was squished with thought. Rex watched as Moe dug into his short's pocket to reassure himself his handgun was easily accessible.

Rex tried to keep an eye on Joe as they walked. He knew whatever happened these next few minutes would depend a great deal on Joe's reactions to the situation as it unfolded. Joe was in charge here.

Over their long friendship together, Rex learned Joe had a multitude of facial expressions which consistently gave away what he was thinking at the time. Rex found these expressions to be highly advantageous during poker parties, so he'd never said anything to Joe about his study and knowledge.

Rex could tell Joe was struggling with an inner dilemma right now based on his facial expression. Joe was wearing the face he always did when he was trying to bluff his way to the poker pot. His head was held back, his forehead and cheeks were slack and possibly sweaty. Joe's eyelids were nearly shut, and he would even close his mouth in reverence of the situation. Rex was sure Joe couldn't have liked the way that conversation had gone at the gate. At least he didn't think Joe had received the answers he would have liked to have heard from his next door neighbor.

Then, Joe's expression changed and Rex knew Joe had reached a decision in his dilemma. Joe opened his eyes and he creased his forehead. Joe pressed his lips together until his mouth disappeared into a thin strip. Sure enough, a moment after Joe's expression changed he reached down and flicked off the safety of the shotgun.

For his part, Rex was cautious about this approach to a possible serial killer. He was more worried about the other lives that he'd dragged into this situation. Rex had needed Joe to get through that fence, and Moe was always good backup, but Rex figured Cook knew who he was and understood why Rex Bana was banging on his front door. This man had to be the most intelligent killer Rex had confronted. Rex was glad to have all this assistance, yet he still worried about their safety.

Surely, Jesse shouldn't be here. She didn't have a gun or any knowledge of how to defend herself. Rex would have to hang back with Jesse and let Joe do the talking here. Rex couldn't go blasting forward or Jesse might easily become another of Cook's innocent victims.

They arrived at the massive double oak front doors of Cook's mansion. Rex wished they'd driven the cruiser over after their long night. His face hurt, his head ached, and his limbs felt weak. Looking up at these enormous doors made Rex feel more like a medieval knight approaching a castle entryway to save his lady in waiting than a twentieth-century bounty-hunter who was about to bring a terrible killer to justice. The doors remained closed when Dr. Cook knew he had guests waiting on his doorstep.

Rex stepped forward to pound on the door, but Joe held him back, "Wait a second, Rex. I'm the law here, and everything has to be done by the book or it's no go. Let's do this thing right."

Rex backed down and held Jesse behind him. At least this way, Jesse was out of the way should Cook prove to be a madman and come out shooting. Cook said they were all in for a big surprise, and Rex didn't like surprises in a situation like this. Rex liked to confront the killer directly and ask his one simple question. How the killer answered that question was when the problems began to develop.

So when the door opened and Rex stepped forward to ask his question, "Dr. James Cook, are you holding Ester Gomez against her will?" not only was Rex surprised by the response he received, but also by the way this serial killer appeared.

While it was apparent this killer wasn't a bum, neither did James Cook have on his robe and jammies as if he'd just rolled out of the sack. Rex's vision of millionaires was they slept till late in the morning and had their maid bring them breakfast in bed. Yet this was an odd perception for Rex considering he was a millionaire himself.

Rex was running out of murderer profiles to pin on this guy. Dr. Cook was a huge man, a sculptured body-builder, standing toe to toe with him in a sleeveless gray sweatshirt with the word "Champion" inked across his bulging chest. Cook wore gray cotton sweatpants cut off above his knees that were stretched around his massive thighs. Sweat dropped off his chin and glistened off his brown stretched skin. He was dripping with sweat as if he'd been exercising. Rex asked himself, *This isn't your typical serial killer, is it?*

"No," James Cook said simply. "Is that what all this is about?"

"Ah, yeah," Rex said shifting from one foot to the other and feeling like a fool under this gigantic man's stare.

Cook talked down to Rex as he said, "I thought you might be the reason everyone came calling at my door at this hour. Have you been ill recently, you look much smaller than your magazine pictures show you."

"Ah, no," was all Rex could think to say at the moment. Rex felt even smaller as Cook seemed to tower over him. *Come on*, Rex thought, *where's that great surge of power, that surge of confidence like nothing can defeat you?*

Jesse stepped forward and said, "Dr. Cook. We're looking for a young Latin girl named Ester Gomez; and she was last seen with you leaving Lefty's Saloon where she works."

"Oh, so it's the nosey crew down at Lefty's Saloon that turned me in, is it? Tell me you didn't give anyone money for that information."

No one answered.

Cook redirected his attention to Rex. "I suppose, Mr. Bana, that Ester was to contact you sometime yesterday after work to assure you she was safe?" he asked.

"Ah, yeah."

"Don't they teach you Michigan State graduates a more diverse vocabulary? I know at Purdue University one can get a respectable education, but I've often wondered about the rest of the Big Ten, or Eleven, whatever it is these days."

Joe stepped up with his chest all puffed-up, "Sir, you seem well informed about us, and our backgrounds, but you still haven't told us where Ester Gomez went after she left you."

"What makes you think Ester ever left me?" Dr. Cook asked.

"Then she is here?" Rex asked anxiously.

"Of course she's here." James Cook smiled. "Unlike you, Mr. Bana, I didn't trust the quiet streets of Lahaina after midnight. Ester should never have been made to work, let alone walk home from Lefty's Saloon in the wee hours of the morning."

Rex was ready to crawl under a rock, but Dr. Cook continued. "No, no, no—Mr. Bana. Had I allowed that to continue, then indeed, Ester might have fallen into the hands of the Yakuza or some other evil people."

Cook was smiling. Rex couldn't believe it. The guy was smiling like he was really getting a kick out of this.

"By the way, Deputy Tweedy and Special Agent Tweedy, let me extend my congratulations," Cook said as he continued to hypnotize his audience.

"Congratulations for what?" Joe asked.

"Well, Joe, it's early to say, but I do believe you will be elected as the Sheriff of Maui County after you clean up the mess Erp made of the job," Cook replied and smiled with big white teeth which reminded Rex of the Mako shark's yawning maw he had seen not too long ago.

"What?" Joe started, but Cook cut him off by lifting the palm of his hand to silence him.

"All in good time, Deputy Tweedy. First, I have to relieve Mr. Bana's frustration before he pees his pants—or worse."

"Come on inside. I'm being a terrible host."

Cook waved them all in as he did an about-face and retreated into his domain without looking back. Seeing no immediate need for his weapon, Joe unloaded the shells from his shotgun and dispersed the ammo in the pockets of his baggy shorts. Joe parked the shotgun leaning on the side of the house. Moe continued to play with his pistol in his pocket. Rex had never met a serial killer that could talk down the weapons of his capturers like this. Rex's impressions of James Cook and his motives were going to the crapper, and his perceptions of how to continue on the hunt were confused.

Rex entered a foyer with cathedral ceilings while the others crowded in behind him. Rex stopped to gaze at tapestries hanging from the walls that stunned him with their size and beauty. The tapestries painted a picture of Polynesians progressing upon a pleasant beach with sharp edged mountains in the background.

The rays of the early morning sunlight shot through the colored glass windows high above, and the white marble entryway was lit by gold, yellow, and green shafts of illumination. Rex was shocked by the beauty of the entryway. He never imagined Cook having artistic ambitions and acquisitions.

Before them spread an interior that was wide, spacious, and airy. Although the light was dimmed in the early morning, what spread before them could only be described as a section of Eden's garden. There were the healthiest trees, ferns, and green grasses. There were colorful flowers in bloom of every sort, and Rex even saw some striking butterflies fluttering about. He found it incredible to hear the singing of birds as they chattered and chirped with their morning's excitement.

Rex never suspected that such a combination of man's artistic architecture and Nature and could exist so harmoniously right beneath his nose. And he knew that this place had been constructed while the Tweedys had lived next door oblivious to its creation.

Rex turned and saw the others mirror his expression of awe and disbelief. He turned and followed Cook along a brick walkway until the five of them entered into a garden. Rex was accustomed to hunting in Michigan's forests, but here they came to a small meadow with a mound that was covered with finely trimmed grass. Rex saw a statue crested this rising. Behind the statue was a waterfall with sparkling waters that misted in the morning sunshine. At the base of the waterfall Rex could see a bubbling brook that twisted and turned over mossy rocks then disappeared into the garden. Rex had to remind himself this was all under a roof of man's creation.

He could see at this time of the morning that the colored shafts of light fell most directly upon the knoll and the statue. Gazing now on the mound and its statue, Rex stopped dead in his tracks and felt his heart miss a beat.

Rex gazed in wonder at the white marble icon on the mound. The statue was a representation of an angel descended from Heaven. The angel held open its arms to assist those who would come into the garden. Rex was stuck, not only by the statue's beautiful appearance and meaning, but that the statue had a remarkable likeness to Sara. As Rex stood there in wonder and awe, a warm hand fell on his shoulder, but Rex was so involved with looking about him that he wasn't startled by this approach.

"You see, my friend..." Dr. James Cook said in a soft voice, "... your desire to help can be done by other methods. I am only carrying forward an image you struck in my heart many years ago when I first learned of your personal crusade to assist the needy and abused children of this world."

Rex just stood there with his mouth agape and his mind mystified by both Cook's words and the creation that surrounded him.

"I see you're still confused." Dr. Cook smiled.

"Ah... yeah." Rex laughed.

"Do you have a speech impediment?"

"Ah... no," Rex returned.

"Just a man of few words?"

"Ah... yeah."

"Well, we can work on that if you'll agree to come and work for me."

"Ah..." Rex sputtered. He felt like a self-centered, egotistical boob next to this guy. He remained speechless.

"Whatever. Come and let me show you the new Sara's Garden I have created. I was going to announce it to the public within the next few weeks. So your arrival has been very timely, and yet I don't know why I didn't anticipate it. I did invite you here for a chat. By the way, Ester has been a big help in the final details we are having installed in the shelter. Come, we'll find her first. She has been very moved and changed by her relationship with you."

Rex was even more confused. He turned to look at Jesse, Joe, and Moe. They had stood there with his expression of the bewilderment; now the three of them shrugged at his questioning gaze.

Rex put his hands on his hips and changed his expression as if to say, "Well, a lot of help you guys have been." Then he huffed and turned to follow Dr. Cook before Cook disappeared and they were all lost in this botanical jungle.

Coming out of the garden area, which Rex assumed was the entrance to this huge edifice, they entered another large open area with more ceilings that reached to the sky. Rex saw the garden atmosphere prevailed as this room resembled more of a botanical restaurant or cafeteria setting with large wooden tables and sturdy chairs. Rex thought there was enough room before him for a small army to sit and eat, and he was awed to see full-grown oaks and maples that he knew were indigenous to his homeland in the North. Yet here the trees seemed to thrive between the crisscrossing walkways and picnic furniture beneath a high roof.

The early morning sunshine illuminated this room with the earthy tones they'd seen in the entryway. Rex continued to ridicule himself for busting in here like a barbarian demanding justice. Obviously a man who created such beauty was not a daily mass murderer.

Having realized his error, Rex followed the doctor through the cafeteria and down a side hallway. The others followed Rex at a slower pace. Rex saw Dr. Cook waiting at a door as if he waited for everyone to catch up. Rex thought Cook showed patience and he enjoyed the various expressions of wonder and amazement on the faces of his four "guests."

"Come along." Dr. Cook ushered. "This door leads to the 'Aquatic Appreciation' area. Anyone who enjoys the Ocean and its inhabitants should have a field day in here." Dr. Cook laughed as he showed them into the new area.

Rex caught up to Cook and he saw that he *could* be more awed as they entered the Aquatic Appreciation area. Rex was speechless at what lay before his eyes. He saw an Olympic-sized pool centered in a dome-covered room, and in that pool Rex spotted a dark-skinned girl in a black racing swimsuit as she sheared through the water while doing an effortless freestyle stroke. Rex admired the girl's excellent swimming abilities.

"She's quite a swimmer, did you know that, Mr. Bana?" asked Dr. Cook. Rex watched the slender body of the swimmer slice through the water as if she was a mermaid slipping through the morning sea.

"My God!" Rex huffed and pointed toward the mermaid. "That's Sara! I mean Ester." Ester heard his exclamation and looked up to see the group watching her.

"Rex!" Ester cried. She dropped her towel to run up the lava rock steps and meet the group. Before Rex could say anything, Ester jumped into his arms.

After giving Rex a tight, wet, and sloppy hug, Ester looked up and said, "Oh Rex, isn't it beautiful?"

Rex looked down at the dripping, smiling face, and he saw only happiness. Although his heart was still banging against his chest, he was unable to say a word.

"Ah, Ester?" Dr. Cook asked. "Were you supposed to keep Mr. Bana informed of your whereabouts?"

Ester's face squinched up into a prune as she realized her mistake. "Mr. Bana and company are here to keel-haul me because they believed I might have taken you against your will and possibly harmed you," Dr. Cook continued in his most diplomatic of roles yet.

"Aí ya aí..." Ester hissed and she stepped away from Rex, shaking her left hand as if she was trying to fling something disgusting off her fingers. "Oh, Rex... Aí aí aí... Lo siento mucho ... I'm sorry, Rex Bana...I goofed."

Not wanting to see his chickadee so tormented, Rex finally found his tongue. "It's okay Ester. I just wanted to know you were safe."

Then, while looking at Dr. Cook, Rex added, "I almost made a terrible mistake to a man that deserves much better. Words can't describe how sorry I am for this intrusion."

"No apologies necessary, Rex. Your intentions were far nobler than what many would have done with a runaway they'd just met. Besides, I learned long ago you are a man of action rather than words; and like I said, I think you were meant to be here today." Dr. Cook smiled.

"Ah..." Rex started, but Dr. Cook silenced him by lifting a palm.

"Let's find someplace more comfortable where we can talk and can get some refreshments for our early morning callers," Cook said.

"I'm genuinely happy to see you're safe, Ester," Rex said. He could not help it as he continued to gaze about this new "room." Glancing all about him like a kid at the circus, Rex was fascinated with the "Aquatic Appreciation Area" as Dr. Cook had called it.

Before Rex were huge two walls made of see through material. Rex was sure the walls were not made of glass due to their tremendous size and the water pressure that was being exerted upon them. One of these walls measured more than the length of the pool and cornered to the other translucent wall that measured the pool's width and then some. There were only thin walkways between these walls and the pool. It was from behind these clear walls that Rex found the most stunning habitat he'd ever seen—he saw that they appeared to house a complete oceanic environment.

As the group continued down the walkway, Rex noted that if a person was swimming in the pool they could have the illusion of swimming through the ocean at depth. Inside these "aquariums," Rex could see healthy coral growing on a sandy foot-deep bottom. All about the coral swam the typical fish Rex saw while diving out at the Molokini Crater. The room represented the visual beauty one would find diving in the shallow Hawaiian waters.

Rex became so entranced he stopped walking. This caused the other three to crash into him while they continued their pace and looked on in astonishment.

"Hey, watch where you're going," Rex mumbled, not really caring who bumped into him.

"Come along, group," Dr. Cook said with impatience. "There will be plenty of time for looking about once Mr. Bana agrees to our discussion."

Dr. Cook's wording snapped Rex out his trance, and he continued to follow. The doctor led the group past the aquariums and off to a conference room. Rex entered a room that reminded him of the kind of place a board of directors would gather to discuss their business strategies.

Rex gazed about the room and felt deadness, stillness, a feeling of a soundproofed room where no one would be disturbed. In the room, Rex saw enough electronic gadgetry to control a NASA lunar mission. There were two huge screens on each of two walls, while smaller screens crowded together on a third wall. On the fourth wall was a huge two-dimensional map of the World with major cities being highlighted by TV monitors. In the center of the room was the largest one-piece table Rex had ever seen. It wasn't a square table since it tapered off on each end, but it occupied enough space to appear as if it was the deck of an aircraft carrier. Rex imagined people sitting around the table would need intercoms to talk to each other. Along each side of the shiny black table were black leather executive chairs with puffy arms. Rex noticed the chairs even had rollers so they could scoot across the polished hard wooden floors.

"This is the Control Center of the operation," Dr. Cook stated with his nose turned up a notch. "From this room one could communicate data, have audio-visual contact with anyone…anywhere in the world… or you could just pick up the phone and dial. From here, Rex Bana, you could control the establishment of shelters for the abused anywhere on the planet as you desired."

Rex heard someone behind him mumble it looked like a control room out of a Matt Helm film. Rex found his voice and asked, "What is all this? What's the purpose of this beautiful building?"

"Isn't it obvious, Rex?" Dr. Cook asked.

"It might be. But let's assume I'm brain-dead, and don't have the slightest idea what this is all about," Rex responded.

"You do set yourself up nicely for ridicule." Cook laughed. "But I won't partake of the opportunity to belittle you further, Rex. I'm sure you do that enough yourself." He still left Rex's question unanswered.

Cook took a seat at the head of the vast table. In front of each chair was a fold out monitor with a keyboard which Rex figured was linked to a mainframe somewhere. Rex wondered what kind of video games he could play on one of these terminals. He glanced around the terminal in front of him to see if he could find a joystick.

"Okay. Here we go…" Dr. Cook clapped his hands as each of them took a seat at the table except Ester who remained wet and standing.

"Excuse me," Cook continued. "Ester, would you fix some refreshments for our guests? The Tweedy boys look famished and they've had a busy night. You know were everything is now, right?"

"Well, if I'm not back in half an hour, you'll know I got lost again." Ester giggled, and then quickly made her way from the room.

"Okay. Mr. Bana and company…" Dr. Cook started. "I did say that I invited each of you into my home for a reason, although you've barged in prematurely…"

"Call me Rex, if you please," Rex interrupted.

"We'll see about that." Dr. Cook smiled and began again. "I'll start with a story and try to make it short since you may know a great deal of it anyway." Rex got the feeling that he was thirteen years old and sitting on the parquet floor of Smith Middle School again—with another adult about to give him a sermon on what he should and should not do.

Dr. Cook sat back in his chair and gazed at something above Rex's head. Rex was tempted to look behind him, but he continued to eye Dr. Cook. In the corner of his sight and across the table, Rex could see Jesse seated with her hands on the table as she watched him. To Jesse's right sat Joe, while Moe had taken a seat to the left and behind Rex.

"Back in the late 60's early 70's, I was a hunter, a killer much like you, Rex Bana. By the way, your name fits you perfectly." Dr. Cook smiled. Rex could have sworn there was a flicker of light reflecting from his dark eyes.

"I recently learned it's meaning," Rex said, looking down at his hands.

"Don't be ashamed of your name, Rex. It's not like you had a choice in picking what fate would call you or demand of you.

"To this day I don't know who my parents were or what my heritage might be, since I was raised an orphan on the island of Molokai in a colony of lepers..." At this Jesse shuddered while the Tweedy boys grimaced.

"No, I can assure you it wasn't a pretty place, Ms. Achew..."

"Gesundheit," escaped from Rex's lips before he could stop them.

"My sentiments exactly." Dr. Cook laughed. "But that joke is getting old on me.

"I left Molokai and volunteered for the US Marines at the age of fifteen. I have a slight glandular imbalance which brings out the male characteristics of the human body. In short, I looked much more mature than my age, and the Marine Corps weren't picky about who they enlisted in those days. You all may be too young to remember, but it was a time of trouble and strife for this great country.

"I doubt the Marines even looked at my fake birth certificate. So I went to Vietnam an innocent child to learn to be a killing machine, Rex. I had a knack for killing other humans while going uninjured myself. Much as you've experienced, I'm sure."

Rex said nothing, so Cook continued after a pause.

"I did three tours of duty, and I loved every minute of it. I was so much a part of the jungle, an animal, that our troops couldn't track me if I didn't leave a trail."

Rex could only nod as if he was becoming hypnotized by Meat's voice or just bored sleepy.

"Then, during a covert operation, I was captured. Tricked by my own people and I spent months in a living hell, as I was starved, beaten, and tortured. This time it was me who was the recipient of all the evils one man can inflict upon another. I learned what it was like to be the victim whose only desire was to survive somehow, some way for another minute, another day."

Rex listened as Cook said these words in a neutral tone, but he saw the doctor's neck muscles growing more taut beneath his deep brown skin. Rex glanced at Dr. Cook's hands and saw his skin was stretched white over his knuckles as each hand clutched the armrests of his chair.

"And fate came to my rescue," Cook continued with a sigh. "Eventually, our POW camp was repatriated and I was rescued."

Rex watched Cook's body sag and yet the doctor's gaze remained distant and lost somewhere else.

"But what had they rescued?" Cook asked with a painful expression. "Emotionally, I was a mess. I was no more than a starved beaten animal.

"I was nothing more than the Meat and bones you've seen fit to call me, Rex." Cook laughed. Laughing appeared to be the best way for Cook to release his heavy emotions.

It was obvious to Rex that Ester had told Dr. Cook about the "Meat" nickname Rex had given him. Rex glanced under the table for a good spot to crawl.

"Rex, you can't crawl under the table," Meat said, reading his mind. "Actually, I like the nickname because it's so appropriate for me. I *do* have a glandular imbalance, like I said, that brings out my physical muscularity without me having to work out much. So I don't mind you calling me 'Meat.'"

Rex was relieved when Ester returned with a tray laden with fresh fruit and a large pitcher of iced tea.

"Please, Joe and Moe, help yourselves." Meat gestured toward the fresh fruit. Rex felt Meat was dismissing the Tweedys from the conversation. That was something Rex couldn't do. Rex knew the Tweedy boys had not eaten since the night before. They were famished. Rex turned to face Meat completely and put his back to the Tweedys, but still the sound of the Tweedys grazing through the fruit basket carried forward to his ears.

Rex saw that Meat looked around the table with an expression of amusement, but not distaste, or superiority. He appeared to be simply enjoying the company of others. During this break in Dr. Cook's story, it occurred to Rex what kind of loneliness and solitude a man of James Cook's intelligence must have experienced throughout his entire life.

Yes, Rex could see the similarities in their paths in life. But James Cook had turned his life around. James Cook had gone from the killer to the builder of life's stories. Rex wondered what had occurred to change this man's life so completely. Certainly he didn't appear to have "talked to God," or found faith in any deity.

"You see, Rex..." Dr. Cook recalled his attention, "... I was fortunate enough to have survived man's hell and learn the marvelous healing qualities of the human spirit. I spent two months on a hospital ship that came back to Pearl Harbor from Vietnam with the wounded bodies and souls. I had a lot of time to contemplate my role in life. I'd seen life's struggle from both the predator's and the prey's vantage point, and I knew I never wanted to be the prey again... or see any other human be preyed upon. The end result was that I didn't want to live anymore because I saw no future for the human race or myself. Oh, I had the intelligence and the ability to do much in this world, but I had lost any fire, or will, to continue. So I lay on my hospital cot, rotting away, and I distantly hoped to die.

"I say distantly because I must have still held some hope. I maintained interest in the world around me. I read the newspapers and magazines from the States whenever I could get them.

"One day, just before we reached Pearl, I picked up a copy of *Stars & Stripes* that was on the floor and had been kicked all about.

"I picked up the magazine because a pair of eyes on its front cover caught me in their grasp. The kind of look that was in those eyes, glaring out at me from that magazine cover, will haunt me till the end of my days.

"In the jungle, in the villages of Vietnam, I'd seen the same look in the eyes of men and women that'd seen so much horror and death that they were scared out of their minds and they didn't care about life anymore. I saw those same eyes whenever I cared to look into a mirror.

"Yet the eyes on the magazine cover were the eyes of an American child. It was a black and white photo of the most unforgettable child I'd ever seen. In his eyes, I saw the terror and the dread of many of those soldiers I'd left behind in Vietnam. But this was only a child, and this American child was being proclaimed a hero. I wondered how this child in America could have seen the type of Hell I'd seen. How could this child in the land of the Free and the Brave have been as tortured as the children of Vietnam had been? These were the questions I asked myself."

Rex did the arithmetic and he knew whose picture Cook had seen. It was a photo of him. Rex remembered the photo being taken in front of Deputy Madison's barn.

Everyone tried to act as if Rex was a hero for killing Deputy Madison. Afterwards, the newspaper people wouldn't leave Rex alone until they had the full story. But Rex didn't feel like a hero.

Rex had talked to his father and said he was sorry. He was sorry that he had failed to save Sara. There probably could not have been a more painful time in his life. Some jackass had to take his picture. They wouldn't leave him alone until they had their freaking picture.

"Rex, when I saw your picture on the front of that magazine, I thought to myself that there was someone as pathetic looking as I felt."

"And yet you were only a child of twelve years; an American child who so many of us had fought and died for; fought and died so these children would remain safe, happy, and innocent. America's children weren't supposed to see Hell in reality."

"I felt like I'd been stabbed in the back. Not by the idiots that protested the war. Those people were so out of place they didn't see the problems they were having in their own homes. What about these abused American children we'd fought so hard to protect?"

"I read the story about Rex Bana and his attempt to save his sister..." Cook stopped because Rex had dropped his face into his hands and his shoulders were shaking with emotion. Jesse started to rise, but Rex raised his head and plopped his chin on his palms. He wore a down turned expression of someone mentally hurt, but he sat straight and spoke.

"When you talked about that picture I relived what I was feeling after Sara died."

There was a moment of silence in which no one knew how to respond. The Tweedys even stopped their chewing.

"You have to accept her passing, Rex," Dr. Cook said.

Silence followed and Rex nodded his head before leaning forward to place his elbows on his knees and his head in his palms. First Rex stared at the wall, and then he looked at Meat.

"But you've already done more than enough to keep her memory alive."

Dr. Cook got up from his seat, and Rex could see he was getting riled as he started to pace. Rex didn't hurt his neck trying to follow Meat pace about the room. He saw the others were occupying their attention to something on the table or themselves.

"Rex, I was a basket case until I saw how an innocent boy showed me that there was hope if one was willing to fight for the precious lives one loves. So you see how one small person can make a difference in the lives of so many by his single act of courage and hope." Again Meat expected some response from Rex that was not forthcoming.

Rex felt tired, drained from the events of the night. They'd found Ester in secure surroundings she seemed to enjoy. Ester was safe, and one less worry. As far as Rex was concerned with the immediate future, life was great and it was time for beddie-eddie.

Meat wasn't having any of it. Rex had stormed his gate in the middle of the night, so he was going to get an earful whether he was tired or not.

"There are many ways one could take your story, Rex, but I chose one to use my talents in a way that I could try to save abused children as you had. I have no delusions of changing the world, but I knew if I could save just one child from suffering, then there was value in living and continuing on. Besides that I was too chicken to commit suicide.

"So you see, Rex, in a way you saved my life. In a way you showed me the light to a new beginning. In your courage, I found the courage and purpose to start again. Except I had already learned that the future lay not in spreading the death, but in renewing life. I began my mission to save the abused children of the world that I could.

"And as fate would have it, I found I had the same knack for making a killing in business as I did in the jungle. I used my VA benefits, I studied medicine, and I started to build my fortune."

Dr. Cook paused in his dialogue to laugh at himself. Those at the table were mystified until Dr. Cook explained his reggae.

"And yes, Rex, you saw my skills as a medicine man. I'm afraid some of the butchery of my war days carried over and I made a terrible surgeon. That's why I stuck to pathology. That way I would have a steady income while my other income ventures profited or lost."

At this, even Rex had to laugh as he thought of some of Cook's autopsy reports and how he'd come up with the nickname of "Meat."

"You might be wondering why I never said anything about all the drown victims that were accumulating over the last year. It wasn't that I didn't notice what was happening. Indeed, I know more about this island's politics than most. I've developed a web of paid informers on the islands that keep me informed of everything that happens. I mean everything.

"Still, it has only been a month or so since I discovered what the Yakuza were doing. I had my head buried in my own concerns and really wasn't paying attention to what happened down at the morgue. When I did figure it out, I had no idea what to do.

"Although I had the means to do something, I knew I couldn't approach Sheriff Erp, and I didn't know who else was on the take… including the

Tweedy brothers. I knew Moe was an undercover agent working the case, so I didn't want to just bust in and spoil whatever he had going on.

"When you resurfaced, Rex, as a grown man, I was deeply hurt to learn that your methods of assisting the abused were by taking it directly to the source in such a deadly manner. And while no one can condemn your reasoning, or your methods, to me this was destroying life instead of adding to it. I knew we already have enough destroyers of life in this world.

"But fate would prove to me that I was on the right track and that someday we would meet. Eventually you and Joe developed Sara's Garden in Lahaina. There I saw my opportunity to start repaying you by continuing with my goal of assisting abused women and children. I knew it would only be time before you would come knocking at my door. The only question that remained was the method of our meeting."

"You were the anonymous donor who set up a trust fund to make the whole deal at Sara's Garden work, aren't you?" Joe asked.

"Ah... yup." Dr. Cook nodded. Rex just nodded as he could see how that whole puzzle fell into place. Without Dr. Cook's trust fund Sara's Garden would never have survived its initial years. Rex had no idea how many anonymous donations Dr. Cook had made to keep Sara's Garden running. Rex had always thought Mother Makuahine had a direct line to God's wallet. Well, maybe this was it.

"So now you know my whole story, Rex. Do you still wish to end my life as you have so many others, Rex?"

Again Rex could only bury his knoggin in his hands and shake it back and forth.

Looking up again, Rex looked directly at this benefactor of so many and said, "Lord, no. I've been such an idiot for so long. How could I ever want to hurt another soul?"

"Don't condemn yourself, Rex. All those you put to death deserved exactly what they got. Although I could hardly speak for the Lord above, I have to believe you were fated to do what you have done. I believe you acted as God's hand and saved many innocent lives from the agents of the Devil. So don't hate yourself or your actions.

"But now my fate is to move on to do other things and it seemed to me that you were brought to Maui at this very moment to take over the direct supervision of Sara's Garden and continue your own work in a non-violent capacity.

"So if you haven't already guessed, I ask you now, King Slayer. Will you set down your sword, move to Maui, and supervise the new Sara's Garden?"

Rex felt everyone's eyes upon him, yet he could not answer this question outright. Rex stiffly got up from his seat. It felt like he'd been sitting for days and his body ached. He stretched, and then walked around the head of the table to where Jesse was seated.

Jesse turned and looked up at Rex. Rex kneeled before her and took her hands in his. After looking Jesse in the eyes for a thoughtful moment, Rex asked, "If I do this ... if I move to Maui ... will you marry me, Jessica Achew?"

"Whoa," Joe exclaimed. "Now that deserves a gesundheit."

Jesse's eyes widened as she took in a sudden deep breath. Tears brimmed along her eyelids. Finally, Jesse's face broke into laughter. "Oh thank God, yes. Rex, nothing in this world could make me happier."

Standing again and pulling Jesse to her feet as well, Rex hugged Jesse and gave her a long loving kiss. Then, breaking out of Jesse's arms while still holding her hand, Rex turned to Dr. Cook.

"Then, Dr. Cook, I would like nothing better then to return to this place I call my paradise and take over what you've started."

Cook rose and took Rex's hand and shook it with a huge smile on his face. "At last, Rex, after all these years, I am indeed happy that we can join forces together to save some that deserve so much better. You, Rex Bana, have made one of my life's dreams come true as you have for so many others."

The Tweedys gathered around and gave Rex and Jesse huge hugs in congratulations. Joe admitted it had always been one of his hopes for Rex to move from Michigan to Maui. Now they would be together again.

Finally, Ester came to Rex and looked up at him with teary eyes. "Congratulations, Rex, I'm very happy for you, and I'm happy that now we'll see each other all the time."

"Then why the long face and tears, my chickadee?" Rex asked with a smile.

Ester didn't answer the question, and Rex was about to ask again, when Cook stepped over and answered for her. "Rex, you've lived alone too long. Don't you recognize a teenager's crush when you see it?"

Rex remained confused. "What? You mean you have a crush on me?"

Ester looked down at her feet and nodded. "I wouldn't call it a 'crush'." She looked up at Rex again with tears streaming down her cheeks. "I love you, Rex.

I've loved you since the day we met on the airplane. I know you are old enough to be my father, but that doesn't help at all." Again she looked down at her feet.

Drawing her in, Rex gave Ester a hug and ran his hand through her beautiful black hair. "Ester, I love you too," Rex said. "You will be one of the closest things to my heart till the day I die. But I love you as a sister."

Pulling away from Rex, Ester said, "I understand. I guess I've always known this to be the truth. But just like you finally mourning Sara, I had to admit it to myself and it hurts."

Hugging Ester again, Rex said, "You'll always be my chickadee, and I'll always care for you, and I'll try to do a better job of protecting you." Rex gave Cook a grin.

# CHAPTER THIRTY-THREE

"I hate to spoil the party," Dr. Cook announced. "But aren't you forgetting a couple of villains which escaped your operation last night? What did you call it? 'Operation Waterlogged'?"

"Ah... shhh..." Joe started before seeing the frown on Meat's face. "Kuro and Yama are still loose."

Rex's head ached at the thought of the two killers they were unable to capture. To him the whole operation was a failure without having captured the leader and head assassin of the Yakuza's team.

Rex felt the screws turn tighter when Dr. Cook pointed out, "They're more dangerous now than when you started your investigation. Now, they know they're known criminals, so they'll kill without prejudice or doubt."

Rex took a seat. These last 24 hours had played mayhem with his emotions and mental processes. "Sorry, folks, but I'm too wiped out to go chasing after anyone tonight... this morning... whatever. I'm sure we all need our rest anyway," Rex stated.

"No, you can't go after them now. You will need a plan of action; have your goals set in mind; and have your senses on maximum alert. Kuro is a highly intelligent killer and will be difficult to capture alive. Yama is an overgrown bully who kills for his own enjoyment. I'm surprised he's lasted as long as he has," Dr. Cook said.

Rex looked to Jesse, then at Joe, and finally at Moe. Moe and Joe appeared exhausted and drained, but Jesse seemed to have some internal generator that kept her percolating and a pleasure to look upon.

"Give it a break and get some rest," Dr. Cook advised. "While you do that, I'll scrounge around to get an idea of where Yama and Kuro are hiding out. Who knows? If I meet up with the right person I might find out if they've left the island, or plan to stay around in an attempt to regain face back in Japan by killing you."

"If we're going to take a break to sleep, will someone come with me?" Jesse yawned. "I don't want to go back to my place alone."

Before Rex could respond, Cook said, "Why don't you all stay here? This is about the last place they'd look for you. It's this type of situation I must have had in mind when I put up that silly electrical fence."

"Then I take it you don't care for the fence either?" Moe asked with a chuckle.

"No," Cook replied as he shook his head. "I'm not sure what I was thinking when I signed for that fence, but after they put it up I saw what an eyesore it was, and how much it made me appear as a wimpy old man hiding in his hole."

Everyone got a chuckle out of that comment.

"I have to go next door first," Moe said. "If Kuro or Yama come to our house looking for us, my mother is there and she has no defense. Kuro would kill her just to get back at us."

"I don't know, Lilly's one tough cookie," Rex grumbled, rubbing his jaw while recalling the incident on the airplane.

"Why don't you invite Mrs. Tweedy up here?" Cook asked. "As you can see..." he threw his arms wide, "... there's room for everyone, and it safer here than anywhere else on the island. Besides, Ester tells me your mother is a great cook, and I have a state of the art kitchen for her to play with."

Joe interjected, "I still have to go downtown to ensure the Yakuza we captured were arrested correctly and are properly celled. I still have to keep an eye out for Sheriff Erp. He has the authority and could walk into the jailhouse to set the whole bunch free."

"After we get Lilly squared away, I need to report in to my Section Chief what we did tonight," Moe said with a frown. "I'm not sure I'll have a job in the morning since Yama and Kuro got away."

"I know Section Chief Robert Doherty well, Special Agent Tweedy," Dr. Cook said. "If you have a problem with him, let me know. My influence with the federal government goes far and wide."

Moe and Joe exchanged glances before leaving the table. "You're welcome to use my telephones to call anyone anywhere," Dr. Cook said pointing at one of the terminals in the table. " ... Or you can use my PCs to communicate on the Web."

"Dr. Cook, is there anything you can't do?" Rex asked in a whimsical manner. Cook regarded Rex with a somber expression and shook his head as if to say, "This is not a joking matter."

After the uncomfortable silence that followed, Rex said, "Then I'll spend some time here with Jesse resting, but I still need to return to the Tweedy's as well."

The Tweedys headed back out of the vast conference room and back through the Aquatic Room. Cook followed after them, apparently to ensure they didn't get lost. Ester had disappeared after her emotional scene with Rex, so this left Rex and Jesse alone. Rex glanced at Jesse while giving her a grin.

"You want to come with me for a change of clothes?"

"I'll come with you. I like wearing your jersey, but there's one small problem," she said, returning his grin. Jesse stuck her nose into the right armpit of the jersey. After making the face of someone who'd just been skunked, she said, "You didn't use a whole lot of deodorant while wearing this, did ya?"

Rex got up and pulled her into his arms. "It's nearly twenty years old and was just a practice jersey. If you want to know the truth: Yes, my shit stinks on occasion."

Giggling like irresponsible kids, Rex and Jesse followed Dr. Cook through the Aquatic Room. Here, Rex had to stop for a moment to ogle at the magnificence of the aquatics before Jesse yanked him forward again. As Rex walked, his step felt lighter, his emotional burden was lessened.

Then they were going through what Rex thought of as the entryway to this massive production. Again, Rex marveled at the statue which appeared so much like his older sister he wanted to go out and touch the stone, but Jesse held fast to his arm and pulled Rex onward again. The Tweedys were already out of sight and Meat had a long head start on Rex and Jesse.

Walking through the golden light of the room, Rex felt the tiredness melting away from him. Strangely, he felt as if a heavy burden had been removed from his shoulders ... *the burden of carrying Sara*, he thought. He felt clearness in the spot where he thought of Sara.

Rex felt his feet were rejuvenated and the aches in his leg muscles loosened and disappeared with each step he took. Rex broke from Jesse's embrace long enough to look back at the statue of the angel. His entire body felt relieved of its pain. Rex was feeling revived, and he knew his future would be brighter than black. Rex felt he could lay down his guns and work on healing wounds rather than causing them.

They neared the front door where Dr. Cook stood waiting. Moe and Joe had already passed through. Rex figured they were in a rush for Lilly's breakfast spread.

Rex and Jesse stopped as they neared Meat at the front door. Rex said, "This place has amazing recuperative and healing powers. I feel better already."

Cook looked down on Rex and nodded with a smile. "Is it the healing powers of this..." Cook raised his huge arms and rolled his head around his massive shoulders, "... this building, or," he lowered his arms to look Rex in the eyes, "is it possible that you've left behind a heavy burden you've been carrying for most of your life?"

Rex smiled and said, "Sorry, I'm not up for psychology debates at the moment. All I know is that when I came here my brain felt like a melon mush, and my body felt as weak as boiled linguini. After spending only a short time in Sara's Garden, I feel rejuvenated." Rex and Jesse moved on down the drive.

"Didn't I tell you the human mind had amazing healing powers?" Cook said to Rex and Jesse's back.

Rex turned and walked backwards and said, "We'll see you shortly. Maybe after I've slept and recovered we can talk mind games. My grandfather, Migisi, could yak at ya about that stuff till your toes curled." Rex laughed again when he saw Dr. Cook showed renewed interest in his toes. Then he turned around to catch up with Jesse.

"We'll see you all in a bit," Meat said at the doorway.

Rex and Jesse waved back as they exited. The Tweedy boys were already hustling down the drive. Rex had glanced up at Meat's face as they passed. Now as he moved on, Rex thought Meat was giving Tweedy Manor an odd stare. Rex could have been wrong, but he thought he saw Meat lift his head and sniff the breeze that was blowing from Tweedy Manor toward his front door. This made Rex shiver as he walked down the drive.

"What's wrong?" Jesse asked when she felt Rex shiver.

Rex waited until he was well out of Meat's earshot before answering. "Dr. Cook still gives me the willies," he said. "If it isn't Dr. Cook, then something else is wrong with this situation."

Jesse said nothing else as they neared the end of the drive, but her perkiness was subdued and she glanced about her as if looking for someone that might be following her.

"Did you see that mansion? Wow, was that something or what?" Rex rambled, but it was obvious his mind was elsewhere.

"You think something is about to happen, don't you?" Jesse asked.

Rex didn't answer right away. He was watching the way Moe and Joe were goofing off up in front of them. *They shouldn't be playing around like this whole thing is over,* Rex thought. *Kuro is a very cunning killer and he's going to make us pay a price for ruining his operation if he gets a chance.*

"I don't like the way the Tweedys are passing this off. I think we need to keep on our toes while Yama and Kuro are loose. Especially when we know the sheriff's department is in shambles and won't help," Rex said.

Jesse moved closer to Rex and she put her arm around him. "At least I'll always have you to protect me," she said. "That makes a girl feel more secure."

Physically, things did look better to Rex. The sun was up, and it appeared it would be another sunny day in his version of paradise. Most of all, Rex was thinking of his future. He thought of his future with Jesse. It was a future with life and hope, no more death or killing. That warm feeling inside him that he felt whenever he was around Jesse was growing as he knew she'd always be there.

Rex looked up at his bedroom window as they walked up the drive. It was the window from which he'd gazed after the nightmares of a two-headed Deputy Madison. He was surprised to see the bedroom light was on this early morning. Rex knew he'd turned off his light before leaving since the light switch included the ceiling fan's "on" and "off." Rex had never gotten the controls correct, and it had irked him, being a gadget person and all, that he couldn't figure out the switches. So it was a memorable moment when he finally got both the fan and the lights turned off. He had even done a high kneed dance in the hallway in celebration of this feat.

The light being on not only meant someone had been in the room after he'd left, but that they were more astute than he was when it came to electronic switches—and that really ticked him off.

Normally, Rex wouldn't consider the light being turned back on to be that out of place. After all, it wasn't his house. But with only Lilly at home… Lilly, a person who didn't climb stairs… this meant that someone who could climb stairs, and turn on his light, was in the house that they didn't know about.

Rex unconsciously slowed his pace as he gazed at the window and thought of how the light could have been turned on. This left Moe and Joe enough time to enter the house before he could warn them. When Rex noticed the boys had entered the house without them, he quickly pulled his Glock out of its holster and flicked off the safety.

"Rex, what's wrong?" Jesse asked as she dropped into a crouched position like a trained professional. Rex put his index finger to his lips before crouching down himself. Rex glanced at the house then waved at Jesse to follow him. Rex shuffled in a shooter's stance and eyed the house, while Jesse ran after him in a doubled over position. Her knee knocked her in the forehead and nearly dropped her to the pavement, but they reached the rear of Joe's cruiser. After a brief halt, they slid around the side of the cruiser to keep it between them and the house. Jesse rubbed her forehead, and Rex turned to see she was sporting a red area on her forehead that was swelling into a bump.

"Something's fishy," Rex hissed. "I turned off my bedroom light before I left and now it's on again."

"Couldn't Lilly have gone in there to change the sheets or something?" Jesse asked trying to reason things out. Rex shook his head.

"First of all, Lilly wouldn't change my sheets if her life depended on it. Oops, I probably shouldn't have said that.

"Second, Lilly's too heavy to manage the stairs, so she wouldn't go up to my room."

Sitting down and leaning her back on the rear wheel of the cruiser, Jesse huffed and asked, "You think Kuro and Yama are in there?"

Rex was kneeling next to Jesse and peering through the windows of the cruiser to keep watching the house. "All I know is Lilly Tweedy didn't turn on my bedroom light," he stated. "The tooth fairy might have left it on when she left, but I think it stands to reason that Yama and Kuro got into Tweedy Manor before we did."

"So what do we do?" Jesse asked.

"I'm working on it. Just give me a minute." Rex peered into the morning sky as if his answer was written in the clouds. He had no idea what to do next. Handling a hostage situation was not one of his strong points.

Rex stood up and cupped his hands around his mouth before he yelled, "Yaoooo Joe!" Then he crouched behind the cruiser and watched the house for a response. Rex was mystified by the response he received from his yodeling, since it came from behind his back. Jesse snickered and then broke out in knee-slapping laughter.

"What's so funny?" Rex asked while still looking at the house and expecting a different response.

Jesse snorted, giggled some more, and then pinched her own cheek to stop her hysteria. "Sorry ..." sniff, "But when we were kids, my brothers were really into playing Gi-Joe, remember him?"

Rex turned his head to say, "Yeah, sure, I remember old Gi-Joe. I did all sorts of gruesome missions with him."

Jesse nodded as if she should have expected as much from Rex, and said, "My brothers were always yelling 'Yaoooo Joe!' until I was certain their yelling would be embedded on my eardrums and my brain."

"Okay, here's another one just in case Joe missed the first one." Rex stood up again and hollered, "Yaoooo Joe!" loud enough to be heard in Lahaina.

Jesse didn't giggle this time since it was obvious something was amiss in Tweedy Manor. Rex thought Tweedy Manor, his paradise away from home, looked uninviting. So Kuro had gotten some of his payback already.

"Yeah, but I have his hundred thousand dollars," Rex muttered to the cruiser window.

"What was that?" Jesse asked. Rex didn't respond.

He squatted next to Jesse, and his knees popped off like a couple of popguns. "Okay, girl, do you have your running legs on?"

"No, silly, you said we were just going to play in the water last night so I only brought my fins."

"Those will have to do." Rex smiled at her lack of fear. "I want you to hurry back to Meat's mansion and tell Dr. Cook the Tweedys have been captured by the Yakuza. Tell him they are either being held hostage or dead. I hope his infinite resources can come up with something in a hurry, cause all I have is this..." Rex pulled his Glock out of his shoulder holster to show her "... and I've only got nineteen loads."

Jesse got up on her haunches, and stared Rex in the eyes. Before she could say anything, Rex held up his palm. "The faster you notify Cook, the faster relief will come our way." Jesse made to say something, but Rex gave her a mean stare and she was off quicker than a hunted fox. She never looked back.

Rex watched Jesse sprint off to Cook's mansion and safety before he turned to look at Tweedy Manor under siege. His eyes widened when he picked up movement in his bedroom window. Rex popped up to place his arms straight on the roof of the cruiser while aligning the aim of the Glock at the shadow he'd seen. Rex didn't shoot randomly. He took his time to turn on the Glock's aiming laser sight. Instantly the red laser line pinned someone leaning out the window and throwing their arms in every direction to get his attention.

A brilliant red cross appeared on Ester's forehead before Rex recognized his chickadee and turned away his weapon. For a moment, Rex stared into Ester's crying eyes as he tried to assess the situation, then he ducked behind the cruiser realizing he might have signed Ester's death warrant if Kuro or Yama had seen his actions and noticed where he was aiming. Apparently the killers didn't know Easter was in that bedroom. The why, when, and how she got there was beyond him at the moment; but as he visualized Ester's waving arms, Rex thought she was trying to point at someone downstairs.

Rex flopped back onto the Tweedy's drive in a seated position. For the second time in his life Rex was hit with the emotional burden of having people close to his heart being persecuted and it appeared he was their only salvation. Rex knew he was more experienced this time, and he knew there was no time for emotional bellyaching.

"Looks like I get a second chance at saving Sara after all." He laughed grimly. Rex recalled the ways his father and Migisi had taught him to hunt. He knew one of the keys to survival was remaining calm and not wasting energy with fear, and anger during the hunt. Rex safetied and holstered the Glock. Then he relaxed his mind and body while drawing three deep breaths and exhaling. Rex tied his pony tail in a knot as he felt the heartbeat of the beast growing inside him—the desire to live coursed through his veins.

It was obvious to Rex he wasn't going to get a shooting match out of Kuro from the house. It was all going to be up close and personal, a true serial killer's methods. It occurred to Rex to search the cruiser for additional weapons, or anything else that might be useful in routing out Yama and Kuro. *Some tear gas grenades would do nicely*, he thought.

Opening up the front passenger door he didn't see much that was useful. He thought about using the cruiser's radio to reach dispatch at the Sheriff's Office to call in reinforcements, but decided by the time he contacted the correct people, the wrong people would have done their dastardly deed and been on their way to Tahiti.

Rex recalled Joe taking the riot gun out of the cruiser. He only saw the radio. Rex wondered if the cruiser was equipped with an amplifier so he could yell at Yama and Kuro to discuss a peaceful resolution.

"Naw, it'd never work even if I did figure out how to turn the thing on. I'm sure Yama and Kuro didn't come here to give up.

"Jiminy Christmas, I hope these two aren't suicidal." Rex continued to babble his thoughts as they came. He was losing his concentration. "Look at all the freakin' candy wrappers down here," he said after seeing what was beneath the seats.

Knowing there'd be nothing useful in the backseat, Rex checked the glove compartment and popped open the trunk. He got his first real fright of the morning when he opened the glove compartment and it exploded with candy bars and candy wrappers flying all over the floor and the seat of the cruiser. Rex would have laughed had this occurred at a different time. Joe certainly did not maintain a waistline. "If he could even find his waist." Rex huffed before he jogged back to the trunk.

Rex glanced at Meat's mansion as he threw open the trunk lid, but saw nothing new. He knew the clock was ticking. He thought again about the possibility of Kuro and Yama committing murder without thought of their life or security, and it wasn't a happy thought at the moment. But what he saw in the cruiser's trunk brought a sparkle to his eye and a mischievous grin to his face.

The cruiser's trunk was a shambles by any organizer's definition, but in the mess Rex saw a goldmine. Joe's Kevlar Special Ops vest was on top of the pile, and his riot helmet equipped with a face shield was stuffed in one corner. Rex prayed for some weapons, but he could find nothing more explosive in the trunk than some highway flares.

Rex hid behind the uplifted trunk lid as he donned Joe's Special Ops vest and tried to adjust its fit. Rex was a big person physically, but his size was nothing compared to Joe's. "Damn, Joe, they must have special ordered this thing for you," Rex grumbled as he tried to shorten the side straps between the chest/abdomen plates and the rear plate. He noticed his fingers were shaking with nervousness as he went about this tedious task.

Rex almost chucked the vest back in the trunk when he realized it might inhibit his motion. Wearing the vest would make it impossible for him to duck, tuck and roll. If he fell down with this thing on, he might not be able to get up with any speed. He'd struggle like a turtle on its back until someone shot him in the head.

Rex had a greater fear of being shot or knifed, so he strapped on the vest as tight as he could while he felt his heart pounding with anxiousness. The vest still made him feel as if he was wearing pieces of plasterboard on his front and rear.

Rex strapped on Joe's riot helmet and face shield, and then stuffed four highway flares under the lower back of his Special Ops vest. The pockets of his shorts proved useless. He had even taken off his at his cup and jock strap earlier, so John Henry was going to have to wing it with the hanging crouch protection of the Special Ops vest. Finally, Rex pulled a police baton out of the trunk and strapped its lanyard around his left wrist. He was as ready as he could be under the circumstances to face whoever was in Tweedy Manor, if there was someone in Tweedy Manor. He was going to feel awful foolish if he popped into the kitchen and the Tweedys were sitting there sipping tea.

Rex peeked over the trunk lid to take in the scene. Before him he saw the front and west side of Tweedy Manor. Joe had parked the cruiser about midway up the half circle drive which led passed the main entrance of the house. Rex glanced at the detached three car garage at the top of the drive on his right but figured it would have little inside to either assist or deter him.

Rex knew Joe and Moe had entered their house from the side entrance between the house and the garage. This entry opened to the large kitchen area. Rex didn't think the Tweedys were so engrossed in their breakfast that they wouldn't have responded to his yodeling from twenty yards away. But the kitchen area was too open to provide cover for two attackers, especially an attacker as large as Yama. Rex figured he'd try this side door rather than the front entryway since it was an entrance into the house and he knew he could see nearly the entire room as he entered.

Having thought of his initial options, Rex slid along the side of the car then rushed to the side entrance heedless of anyone watching through the three large living room windows. He bounced/crashed into the wall next to the side entrance and he was surprised to see the door remained open. Joe and Moe must have been expecting Rex and Jesse to enter right after them. Rex could see clearly through the entryway into half of the kitchen area. As his eyes adjusted to the inner darkness, they were drawn to the red luminous clock and the steam rising from the Mr. Coffee coffee maker sitting on the counter top next to the commercial size refrigerator to his right.

*Looks like someone's brewing a pot of coffee*, Rex thought. But he couldn't decide if that was good or bad news. The counter tops remained clean, and pineapples remained in the large fruit bowl. Rex knew Lilly enjoyed fresh pineapple every morning. *So Lilly had time to turn on Mr. Coffee but no time to slice pineapple or make breakfast*, Rex figured.

The swinging door on the left side beyond the refrigerator, which led to the dinning room, was closed. Rex knew the Tweedys normally left this door open for rapid access to the kitchen from the game room that was beyond the living room. Rex disliked the idea that he couldn't see farther into the house. This didn't tell Rex much about how everyone was faring this fine morning.

This half of the kitchen appeared safe to Rex, so he slowly edged his way into the door with his gun leading the way. Whipping his eyes side to side, Rex saw the whole kitchen. There wasn't a living soul within sight, an oddity for a Tweedy kitchen. Rex saw the hallway door to the kitchen was also closed, another first in his memory.

Rex relaxed a little and he entered the kitchen. He kept his gun level at shoulder height, but he remembered to relax and think of the situation. Yama or Kuro could bust through either of the doors blazing away with who knew what kind of weapons, but Moe and Joe had entered here without making any more noise than their heavy feet and growling stomachs. No one had fired a weapon on them, and yet they hadn't responded to his calls.

"MOE ... JOE!" Rex yelled, not worried about giving his presence away.

Mr. Coffee burped and Rex whipped the Glock around at the noise. He intermingled his red gun sight with Mr. Coffee's red clock light. "Oh, I almost punched your clock there, Mr. Coffee," Rex said without a smile. There remained no human response to his call.

Rex stopped for a moment to think of the house layout and where Kuro might hold hostages. He ruled out the second floor since Ester had been up there, and apparently of her own free will. As Rex visualized Ester in his bedroom window, he thought he remembered her pointing downward as if someone was downstairs.

He knew both of the kitchen doorways would eventually lead to the living room and the attached game room beyond that. Rex decided to follow the path Joe and Moe might have taken to find their mother. If the Tweedy boys hadn't found Lilly in the kitchen, they would have assumed she was in the master bedroom which was connected to the far side of the game room. Rex marched with determination to the door beside the refrigerator, and then he paused to take a deep breath and relax. He reached out and pushed the door, opening it partially to the right. This blinded Rex to the dining room, but allowed him to see most of the living room. Rex peeked through the door crack between the door and the door jam to see no one was hiding behind the door or in the dinning room. He exhaled slowly after he realized he was holding his breath.

Rex stood sideways to the door and squatted down in a shooting position while double fisting the Glock before his face shield in preparation of jumping through the door. He blew out a breath and said, "Shit." His hot exhalation had fogged up the face shield. Rex decided Joe wasn't up to speed on the latest defogger juice, or he didn't use it on his face shield. What a great time to make that discovery, he thought.

"This is the last time I storm hostile territory while using someone else's equipment." Rex spit, adding more gunk to the inside of his face shield. He decided to quit talking since the noise boomed around his head as if he was wearing a tin trash can over his noggin.

Rex reached up and tried to wipe off the condensation inside the shield. His dirty greasy hands smeared things enough so it was difficult to see. Rex only prayed he didn't sneeze. Standing back up, Rex pushed back the shield and turned into the kitchen to find a towel or something to clean off the shield. A roll of paper towels next to the sink did the trick.

Then Rex spit on the inside of the face shield and wiped the mucus around with a paper towel. He wiped away any wetness. Rex knew spit was a proven defogger when push came to shove, so now he could see without the worry of future fogginess. As he did this operation, Rex noticed his fingers weren't shaking anymore. His hands felt strong and ready to rip and tear.

Rex put on his party hat and strapped it down tight. He moved back to the door with his usual smoothness and tried to peek to his left around the door jam and into the living room. Again the helmet gave him problems with its size and gawkiness, but he refrained from cursing out loud or even taking deep breaths. Seeing nothing so far, Rex moved around the door jam to see the rest of the living room. It was silent as toe-jam squeezing in a tennis shoe, which Rex found disgusting, but he was more frightened by the lack of people he'd found so far. *Where does one hide a ton of Tweedys?* Rex mused.

"Lilly! Joe! Moe!" shouted Rex. He received no response, but he was glad to see his face shield didn't fog. Then, as the echoes of his yells began to recede, he heard a voice. Rex was sure it was a human voice, but he couldn't tell whose it was or where it came from since the helmet distorted his hearing. Rex decided he'd had enough of this blinking helmet, but he left it strapped to his head as he moved forward. Experience had taught him one could never have enough safety equipment when entering a shootout situation.

Rex trotted to the wall of the living room on his right. This exposed him to the end of the hallway and the game room for an instant, but he went fast enough so he didn't allow time for someone to line up a shot. The right wall was a solid wall all the way to the corner. If he moved down the middle of the room or on the partial left wall, he would have been visible to anyone in the game room. This was where he feared Yama and Kuro were waiting. Rex didn't mind Yama and Kuro knowing he was there, but he didn't want to set himself up as if he was an obnoxious turkey on Thanksgiving Day. He slid down the wall without event, and saw no one in the open foyer at the end of the hall on his left.

Rex drifted slowly from the right wall to the connecting entryway between the living room and game room. He was listening for signs of where Kuro and Yama were waiting to jump him since he felt they had to be in the game room if they were there at all.

Rex stopped at the right side of the connecting entryway; unfortunately this gave him little vision into the game room itself. Rex was close enough to hear the silence in the room. Rex knew Joe and Moe had not come back to pop a few beers and play some pool. Rex wouldn't have put it past them, and he honestly wished they were horsing around.

Figuring any surprise had been lost, Rex yelled, "Joe! Moe!"

Again his damn face shield fogged a bit as he discovered his spit hadn't been uniformly spread. Rex decided the yelling and hoping for a response was a dumb idea, but not one to give up on a dumb idea, Rex tried one final holler: "Kuro! Yama!"

"We are all here, Mr. Bana. Please stop all your noise and join us," a voice invited from the game room. Rex thought it had to be Kuro's voice since he knew Yama didn't speak English with such a pearly tone.

"Are you going to shoot me?" Rex asked as he stepped around the connecting entryway to come fully in the game room with the Glock point stretched out in front of him. Before Rex had a chance to drop his left foot onto the floor something huge flew into at his face with all the force of a swinging crane ball.

Rex saw four huge knuckles slam into his face plate hard enough to send him flying back through the entryway and onto his butt. As he crashed on his ass his rear armor plate bounced off the floor and hit him in the back of his helmet. The helmet was thrown forward over his eyes and bashed into the bridge of his nose with crushing force. Rex found himself on the floor. He was blind, and his nose was squirting blood. He knew this was only the beginning since he'd found his enemy and now had something to fight. He felt something akin to relief as his body reacted to the assault and he rolled off his behind to his left. He whipped his right leg over and planted it on the floor to stop his roll. Then he kicked off his right leg and stood in a retreating stance. Rex continued to twirl like a ballerina with the Glock pointed out with his right hand while using his left hand to throw back his face shield and helmet.

The helmet hampered Rex's visibility when he saw a huge shadow coming right at him. He threw his left hand back and gripped beneath the rear of the helmet. This violent motion bounced the helmet off his nose a second time, but Rex managed to get the damn thing off. He was hammered in the chest by a shocking blow. Rex was thrown back again but instinctively he pulled the trigger of the Glock and shot into the middle of an advancing shadow he assumed was Yama.

Rex's ears were shocked by the loudness of the Glock's firing in closed quarters as he bounced off his rear a second time. Rex dropped the helmet and twirled into a shooter's squat a little breathless. He wiped away the sweat and blood that distorted his vision to see Yama falling to the floor. Yama's right thigh was torn apart just above the knee. Rex saw Yama was clutching the thigh with two bloody hands, but glaring back at him with a wide eye of surprise.

Rex tasted blood and swallowed. As he tried to peer into the game room, he licked his lips to clear away the two streams of blood that were squirting out his nose. Rex knew this was a problem that had to be dealt with if he was to continue. It was not his desire to find the Tweedys at their time of need and then faint before he could rescue them.

"Shit, if it isn't one thing, it's another," he sputtered. Rex grappled around his short's pocket and pulled out a paper towel. Rex kept his eye on Yama, who appeared to be in no mood to attack at the moment, so he holstered the Glock. Rex tore his paper towel in halves before rolling each half into a cone shaped plug that he gingerly stuck in each nostril. As he did this, he felt some things moving around in his nose that had not been mobile in the past. His eyes watered and the pain was nauseating.

Rex's vision cleared in time to see Yama begin to get to his feet. Yama was a seven-footer and Rex figured it would take awhile for him to erect himself with his thigh injury. Rex didn't need to see Yama erected, so he bounded two steps and kicked Yama's head as if he was a punter kicking a football. His foot was accurately placed as the topside of Rex's right sneaker made contact under Yama's chin. Yama's head was whipped backward by the blow and his towering torso was thrown to the floor unconscious. Rex hoped he hadn't broken Yama's neck, and he regretted kicking Yama's bowling ball of a head since his right ankle and foot became useless after the kick.

"Aw shit that hurts!" Rex said and he doubled over to grasp his ankle and foot in pain. He forgot about the challenge that remained from the game room.

"Mr. Bana, what am I to do with you?" Kuro asked from a corner of the game room. Rex could hear Kuro's calm voice, yet he couldn't see him through the connecting entryway. Rex stood erect while drawing his Glock, now heedless of the pain in his face, ankle, and foot.

"Please come closer so we can see each other while we talk. Do not bother with your weapon since I can easily shoot you if I wished," Kuro to droned on.

"I..." gag, cough, and spit, "... I like to keep it handy in an affectionate way.

Ya know, kinda like a teddy-bear," Rex sputtered in a nasal tone. Rex limped through the connecting entryway and entered the game room figuring if Kuro wanted to kill him he'd have done it by now.

"I underestimated you in many ways, Mr. Bana."

"It's an easy mistake," Rex mumbled as he tried to fixate on Kuro.

The game room was darker than usual since the vertical blinds were closed, but Rex followed the sound of Kuro's voice in the left hand corner. Rex knew there was a large leather recliner in that bend, and he could make out a darker shape of a man seated within its shadow. It was taking a moment for his eyes to adjust to the light of the room, but two things were impossible to miss even in this darkness and Rex stumbled forward.

"Do not worry, your friends are not dead," said the voice in the corner.

Rex holstered his Glock and ignored Kuro's voice as he limped to the pool table. Joe and Moe where sprawled horizontally across the table with everything below their knees bent over the side. Their arms were neatly stretched at their sides as if they were cadavers. They each appeared prepared for burial. Then Rex detected the shallow rise and fall on their big bellies and he was relieved to see they remained alive. Rex hobbled over to his right side of the pool table and laid his hand gently on the top of Joe's head as he bent over to examine it. Joe looked almost comical with his head turned sideways. His eyes were closed as if in slumber, but his tongue was sticking from his mouth as if it had been yanked out.

"You will notice I pulled their tongues out of their mouths so they didn't swallow them and choke to death," Kuro said from his corner.

"Yeah, you're full of surprises," Rex puffed through his paper towel plugs. Rex couldn't see anything physically wrong with either Tweedy. They almost appeared as if they came in here, noticed how dark it was, and decided to lie down on the pool table for a power nap.

"Lord knows it's been a long night," Rex whispered.

"Pardon me?" Kuro asked.

"I said, it's been a long night," Rex repeated louder and in his new nasal tone. Finally, Rex looked up and caught a good look at Kuro.

Rex thought he should have guessed what he saw, but his vision still came as a surprise. Here was the second head of his Deputy Madison nightmare. Here was the highly intelligent serial killer he thought he'd hunted down at Cook's mansion next door. Here sat Kuro dressed in what Rex guessed was a black three piece suit, but Rex couldn't see the lines of the man's clothes in the shadows. Rex could see Kuro's pale hands were neatly clasped together in his lap, and he saw Kuro was wearing his usual smile which seemed to glow with all the ivory of his teeth.

Rex imagined how he must appear to Kuro and he could understand why the man was smiling. Kuro must see a disheveled head of sweaty black hair; a blood smeared face with two paper towel plugs hanging from his nose; and a sagging body that hid inside an oversized Kevlar vest. But Rex figured if Kuro was still smiling, then he didn't see the burning desire in his watery eyes.

Rex placed both his hands on the pool table and leaned his torso forward to relieve the ballooning pain in his right ankle. He tried to relax and ignore the pains of his face and ankle so he could think of how to act, but his heart continued to rattle his chest and his breaths were still coming in huffs and puffs. Rex knew he was in poor condition to handle this high class killer. Rex also knew Kuro was aware of Rex's poor condition and Kuro would milk Rex's agony all he could.

"What do you want?" Rex asked stalling for time.

Kuro got out of the recliner and stood out of the shadows. He moved and seemed to glide to the side of the pool table opposite Rex. Rex saw he was in his tailor-fit black suit. Rex noticed the bright red tie which collared Kuro's black silk shirt. Kuro placed his manicured left hand on one of Joe's knees, and Rex was surprised to see a large diamond pinky ring that he hadn't seen before. Rex saw Kuro maintained his right hand across his chest, hiding it in his dark suit jacket. Rex leaned on the table with his head tilted back as if he was a boxer entering the 15th round with plugs holding up his nose. Joe and Moe lay between Kuro and Rex as if they were poker chips whose life depended on the winner of this fight to come.

"I want many things, Mr. Bana, but first let us talk for a moment. I feel you must understand how futile your life has been," Kuro stated in a level tone. "Before I kill you, I wish you to understand that your efforts have only been an inconvenience to a much larger operation. What was it that you believe we were doing with those bodies, Mr. Bana?"

"Oh, so you confess to murdering those people to have their bodies." Rex coughed.

"I confess to nothing, Mr. Bana. We used the bodies of people who did not exist even to themselves. They were runaways, or physically ill people who had no futures. I ask again: What did you think we were doing with these cadavers?"

Rex had to think of a way to stall this murderous bastard until help arrived, so he played along to gain all the time he could get.

"No one was sure what you were doing with the cadavers. That was one of the questions of the investigation. In any case, those people were murdered. They weren't slabs of meat for you to do as you pleased."

"Oh, you make me sick, Mr. Bana. You, the killer of killers. You are calling me a murderer? Those people are nothing to me personally, and I did not do as I pleased with them; whereas you saw fit to do what you wanted with these men you judged and dispatched so easily," Kuro spit these word out like a venomous snake.

These words thrown at Rex hurt him as much as his physical wounds. He almost raged back out of anger, but he paused and took a few deep breaths to control his emotions.

"You mean to say these bodies had no value to you as modems of transportation for smuggling jewels?"

Kuro jumped, and seemed surprised at this statement as he cut off Rex. "Ha! You think all we were doing with these cadavers was using them to transport stolen goods to the Mainland?"

Surprised, Rex asked, "Isn't that what you were doing with the bodies?"

"Maybe I'm overestimating you, Bana. Maybe you're as stupid as I originally believed?"

"Why don't you fill in this stupid oaf before you kill him so I might go to Heaven a little more enlightened than when I was alive?"

Kuro grinned. "I doubt your soul will be going to your heaven, Mr. Bana. But I will lighten your ignorance to show you how little you have accomplished in your life. You, Rex Bana, are an ignorant killer of men. You are a destroyer of life. What we are doing is just the opposite. We are not all stupid animals such as Yama and yourself. Those cadavers truly were donated to science. Our part of the organization simply helps cadavers reach the proper laboratories. In these laboratories, under the hands of skillful scientists, these bodies will do more good for humanity when they are dead than when they were alive. You Americans still live to satisfy your personal lives. In Japan, where resources have always been limited, we learn that one must sacrifice for the better of all."

Rex huffed at this baloney just looking at Kuro's dress habits. "You can stuff the morality crap, Kuro. I don't see you sacrificing anything for the good of the many. You'd kill your mother if it was to your advantage."

Kuro stiffened as if Rex had hit a sore spot. Kuro continued his sales pitch with a deeper tone. "No doubt you have read in the newspaper what is being accomplished by cloning cells. Maybe you also know about the increasing demand for donor organs so that ill or injured people can go on living when the organ donor cannot. There is a tremendous market for organ transplants, Mr. Bana. People will pay anything to continue their lives. The American health system proves that."

Rex was stunned. "What the hell are you talking about? You want to clone people for the organs?"

Kuro smiled, and it pissed off Rex that he couldn't see the man's eyes. "Nothing so inefficient. No, Mr. Bana; we have some of the best scientists in the world working to clone the organs themselves. Smuggling the jewels is only part of the financing. Currently, we use the organs for experimentation. Our ultimate goal is to grow the organ from the person who will need it—self regeneration.

"So you see, Mr. Bana, our operation creates life and allows the living to continue. The operation is so large that your assault on the Maui Funeral Home is not only trivial, but it was wasteful to this process of rejuvenation."

"Is that all you want?" Rex puffed as he started down the right side of the table using his hands to limp along.

"I want my hundred thousand dollars back," Kuro stated.

"Huh! Your hundred thousand dollars?" Rex asked as he arrived at the bottom corner of the pool table. Rex watched, but Kuro didn't move other than the angle of his face to keep his nose on Rex's struggle around the table. Quick as a snake strike Rex reached for his Glock. Kuro jerked a gun from his coat and shot at Rex's head even as Rex fumbled for his Glock beneath his oversized armor. Kuro missed. Rex could not free his gun from beneath his armor. Joe Tweedy extended his left leg and booted Kuro's gun hand. Kuro's next shot went astray and his gun was kicked from his hand. Kuro drove his elbow into Joe's thigh making Joe scream, "Hallelujah!" Kuro dropped to the floor and rolled beneath the pool table. Rex yipped and he frog-leaped onto the pool table. He gave up on extracting his gun. Rex crawled over Moe's inert body and pushed Joe into a seated position so he could see if Kuro was escaping from the other side of the table. Rex shoved Joe too hard. Joe rolled off the table and hit the floor with a loud, "Oooaff!"

Kuro popped out of the side of the table where Rex was waiting to pounce. Rex hopped off the table to land knees first on Kuro's spine and pancake him to the floor. Rex's momentum was excessive and he rolled off Kuro's back. Kuro struggled into an erect position gasping for breath, and Rex got to his feet in time to receive a solid kick to the chest from Kuro. Rex surprised Kuro by absorbing the kick with his body armor and catching Kuro's foot with both hands.

Rex hauled back on Kuro's leg, forcing Kuro to hop along on his other leg as they retreated into the room where they'd have more space to play. Rex stopped. He held his position, still grasping Kuro's ankle. They stared eye to nose at each other while Kuro grinned as if he had Rex exactly as he wanted him. But Rex was reminded of an old playground game as he continued to pull Kuro's leg in a fashion that got Kuro hopping around him in a circle. Rex leaned back and pulled harder forcing Kuro to hop faster and faster. The merry-go-round turned with more speed, and Kuro began to fly through the air between hops as he twirled his outstretched arms to maintain his balance. Rex was happy to see Kuro's expression change to one of alarm. Rex was happy to see Kuro was unable to kick at Rex and maintain his balance.

"Don't … you look … stupid … in that … three piece suit … playing games," Rex hollered.

They twirled faster until Rex was getting dizzy and Kuro completely lost his balance. Kuro went smashing to the floor. His leg ferociously twisted in Rex's grip, but Rex was prepared for the roll. Rex maintained his grasp upon Kuro's leg and picked up the pace to pull Kuro bouncing off the floor by his head, chest, and arms. Their sluggish drag wasn't enough for Rex as the rage of his anger was fueled and he pulled harder and harder.

The speed of the merry-go-round reached a point where Kuro didn't descend after a good torso bounce. Rex began to laugh like a kid as Kuro took flight, and Kuro began screaming for his savior with his arms stretched over his head. Kuro's impeccable appearance had been tossed to the wind. His shirt was billowing over his head, and Rex caught sight of Kuro's belly that was so smooth and pale it reminded him of looking at dead fish bobbing in the water.

Rex began to wobble as he got dizzier, but during one of his twirls he noticed a dark figure emerge from the living room. It slowly approached from the opposite side of the pool table where Rex thought Joe had plopped to the floor. Rex's vision was poor and he was unable to define the approaching shape. He thought it was Yama, and he became certain after one twirl where he saw Joe pop up behind the figure. Rex twirled again to see a struggle had begun between Joe and Yama. Rex decided he had enough of the Kuro twirl.

Rex aimed and released Kuro. It was a perfect Kuro-toss. Kuro flew over the pool table screaming before he descended upon Yama and broke the choke hold Yama had on Joe. Rex tried to stand still but his head continued to whirl and his body followed until Rex spun to the floor. Rex rolled on his rump and immediately regained his feet. He stumbled sideways as if he was drunk and brought his hands to the sides of his head to hold it still. He wobbled sideways for another moment before the ground seemed to grow steady for him.

Suddenly, the bedroom door burst open and Lilly Tweedy charged out with a baseball swinging behind her head.

"Not hurt my babies!" she hollered as she rushed and brought her bat down on Yama's neck with crushing force before he knew what hit him. Yama was cast down by Lilly's cracking blow and he banged his head on the pool table as he fell.

"Yeah! One for the…" Joe said before he sank to the ground knees first. Joe fell forward across Yama's reclined position, and Lilly slowly descended to her knees to attend to her son.

Suddenly, Kuro popped out the other side of the pool table as if someone had tossed him from a hole. Kuro was completely ignorant of Yama, Lilly, Moe, and Joe and pointed his nose at Rex. But Kuro leaned sideways before he then stood erect again as if he was having problems with his balance. Kuro brought his hands to the sides of his head just as Rex had done before and he steadied himself.

Rex started to the right around the pool table; he had no weapon to shoot Kuro and would have to use his bare hands to catch or kill the evil munchkin. Kuro seemed to welcome the chance to beat on Rex since he smiled his sales smile before stepping toward Rex's advance.

Ester popped out of nowhere and Rex saw her sprinting through the living room from the hallway stairs behind Kuro's back. Kuro never saw her before Ester leaped through the air and smashed onto his back sending them to the floor.

"Oh great, now everyone's into the act," Rex said as he hobbled around the pool table to save Ester. He didn't find Ester since she rolled beneath the pool table, but Kuro bounced right back to his feet. Rex threw a sweeping right cross at Kuro, but Kuro ducked beneath his swing and Rex twirled about until his back was to Kuro. Rex had just enough time to think he'd made a big mistake before he felt a swift kick on his Kevlar-covered ass.

"That was a good one, as you Americans like to say," Kuro mocked as Rex turned to face him. "Come. Let us *duke* it out, as you say," Kuro sneered and he put up his fists before his face. Kuro threw a jab in the air with his right hand like a prize fighter. He smiled the whole time.

"If that's the way you want it," Rex said, laughing at Kuro's comical stance. He found it even more amusing that Kuro's once impeccable suit was now in total disarray. Rex advanced slowly on his smaller opponent while squatting down and drawing his hands into his protective armor.

"No guns," Kuro hissed.

"No guns," Rex agreed, and he left the Glock in its holster. Rex could hear Lilly asking Joe how he was in the background. Joe didn't respond.

As Rex advanced, Kuro began to hop and dance while jabbing at the air with his right, then his left, while still retreating into the living room as Rex followed him. After crossing into the living room he made a rapid step forward and whirled about to kick Rex in the head. Rex had anticipated Kuro's kick and he held up his loose Kevlar armor as soon as he saw Kuro's move. Rex was jolted when the kick landed but he was not injured. He was starting to believe the oversized armor vest was a plus until he found himself falling backwards when Kuro swept his legs. Rex was thrown flat on his back, and he had the wind knocked out of him before he even realized Kuro had thrown his sweeping kick. Then Kuro was standing on Rex's armored chest. Rex couldn't breathe. He saw Kuro raising his right foot that he would bring down into Rex's nose and end his life.

Suddenly Kuro vanished from Rex's sight and his weight was gone from Rex's chest. Something snatched Kuro into the air and made him disappear into the heavens without as much as a squeak. Rex didn't contemplate this miracle as he struggled to regain his breath. He shut his eyes and prayed to his lucky stars for air while his hands clawed at the sides of the body armor the clasped releases. His hands knew their way around, and they were able to pop the quick releases around his neck, shoulder, and sides.

Rex's chest muscles finally relaxed and lungs were able to draw air again. With no immediate attacker, Rex closed his eyes and sucked wind for all he was worth. His hands tossed aside the body armor on his chest, and Rex lost all interest in what was going on around him.

"Rex! Rex, are you okay?" Rex heard the sweet voice of Jesse calling his name. "Oh Rex, your poor nose."

He opened his eyes to see Jesse's face hanging over his, and for a moment he didn't understand how she could be there. She was supposed to be getting help. Then Rex remembered Kuro and he sat up so fast he conked his head against Jesse's.

Rex shook his noggin thinking there was another bruise to consider later, and he quickly gathered his wits. Rex ensured he wasn't about to be attacked, and that help had arrived in a big way—a very big way.

Rex saw he was ringside to what he thought was going to be one humdinger of a fight. Kuro stood with his legs armpit apart at the other end of the Tweedy's living room. From what Rex could see Kuro had no interest in him at the moment. He saw the beating he tried to give Kuro had only ruffled his suit a bit. The man wasn't even sweating, but now he had a deep frown on his face which Rex took as a worried look. Rex still couldn't see Kuro's eyes so it was still hard to read his expression.

In Rex's corner—on his side of the living room—stood Kuro's new opponent. Dr. Cook had tagged with Rex for the chance to beat on Kuro, and Rex was glad to have someone else get into the room.

Dr. Cook had thrown his shirt aside to demonstrate his hormonal imbalance to all. Meat was indeed meaty. His body was deeply tanned and his muscles were huge even by Rex's standards. Rex added in Meat's height and imagined he was seeing the Incredible Hulk in real life. *Meat might not be green*, Rex thought, *but he looks twice as mean*. Dr. Cook was not wearing shoes or socks and the only garment that could cover his mass was a pair of cut-off gray sweatpants that were tied around his waist and dropped to his massive knees. Meat seemed to fill the entire room from Rex's vantage point.

Rex felt an arm wrap around his neck and he almost panicked before he realized Jesse was snuggling up close behind him. Rex made to get up but then thought better of it since he couldn't think of a better seat to watch Kuro being thrown to the lions.

"I have no quarrel with you, Mr. Cook," Kuro weaseled with his usual smile.

"But I have a quarrel with you, Huri Yammamoto," Cook said with a smile.

Kuro took in a sharp breath before replacing his smile. "I see you have learned my true name."

"It wasn't difficult to discover once your bosses in Tokyo offered contracts for your head," Dr. Cook said as if he was ordering a pizza. Rex knew this was a bluff, but Kuro's smile finally disappeared. Rex admired the way Cook used his intelligence and brought mind games into the exchange.

"I suggest you surrender. They can take you to the safety of an American jail, and you'll be saving yourself a beating you might not survive."

"The bigger they are, the harder they fall. Isn't that an American saying, Dr. Cook?" Kuro asked with a sneer.

"I wouldn't..." Cook began. As Cook was speaking, Kuro tried the kick he first used on Rex. If Cook saw Kuro's foot coming he made no effort to turn away. Kuro's black shoe whirled at Cook's head, but Cook swatted it away as if it was pesky fly and threw Kuro sprawling across the floor. Now Cook had the advantage, but he made no effort to attack. He stood his ground and waited. Rex had time to wonder if Cook had turned pacifist after all these years. Somehow he couldn't imagine Cook turning the other cheek.

Kuro bounded back to his feet and rushed Cook with an expression of hatred on his face almost as mean as Rex had ever seen. *If I could only see his eyes*, Rex thought.

Kuro took a flying leap at Cook with his feet before him, yet Cook stepped aside as if he was a matador sidestepping a bull. Expecting resistance, Kuro flew through the air with a comical expression and landed in a crumpled mess before Rex. As Kuro made to stand up, Rex returned Kuro's kick in the fanny and sent him flying back towards Cook.

Cook reached down and wrapped his huge left hand around Kuro's neck before Kuro could recover. In a move Rex had only seen Darth Vader do in movies, Meat straight-arm lifted Kuro off the floor by his grip around Kuro's throat. Rex didn't hear any bones being crushed like in the movies, but Kuro spit as he wrapped his hands around Cook's forearm and his tongue popped out of his mouth as he gagged. Cook held Kuro at arms length with a mean smile on his lips. Rex watched with awe at Cook's inhuman strength. Kuro hissed and tried to kick Cook, but he couldn't reach. Rex could see that Kuro's face was as purple as a tick stuck on an artery, but Rex didn't move a muscle to stop it.

"Now, little man, you were saying something about bigger men falling harder?" Cook asked. Getting no verbal reply, Cook released his grip and let Kuro fall to the floor with a solid thump. Kuro looked like a crumpled mess in black cloth and shoes while lying on the floor, but he didn't move. Rex figured Kuro had passed out after having his throat crushed. The mere thought of strength in Cook's grip around his throat made Rex gulp to make sure his Adam's apple was still bobbing.

Cook looked down at the mess at his feet and nodded. Then he turned and walked towards Rex with a smile on his face. Rex was aware of Jesse's head resting on his right shoulder, but that uneasy feeling had not left Rex's stomach as he glared at the rumpled heap that had become Kuro.

Slowly, Rex reached over with his right hand and grasped the handle of the Glock. Rex saw the smile drop from Cook's face either from seeing Rex reach for his gun or some hunting instinct Cook retained. This time Rex freed his gun with lightning speed, even as his brain realized he had been staring at a gun barrel poking out from the crumpled black mess of Kuro on the floor.

Rex knew Kuro was aiming at one of them but he couldn't squeeze the trigger fast enough. Finally the Glock exploded, releasing Rex's shot. Rex thought Kuro shot simultaneously, but no one would ever know. Kuro's aim was off and his bullet went harmlessly into the wall. Rex knew his shot was true as he saw Kuro's gun jump from Kuro's hand into the living room, and out of reach.

Kuro made an effort to sit up as someone screamed in Rex's ear. Rex squeezed the Glock's trigger again as Kuro's face appeared above the pile of black cloth; but then he pulled back the barrel and thought for a moment. Rex twirled the gun and shoved it back in his holster.

"Good shot," whispered Jesse from his right shoulder, but Rex couldn't hear her praise since his ear was ringing from her scream and the gunshots.

Rex started to get to his feet as he saw Kuro struggling to do the same. Jesse's arm tightened around Rex's neck and shoulder forcing him to lift her weight as she tried to keep him down, then she dropped away after Rex regained his stance. Jesse apparently wasn't ready to give up since she hugged Rex around his chest as if he was a buoy and she was lost in a monstrous storm at sea.

"Just where do you think you're running off to, big boy?" Jesse said in a muffled tone behind Rex's back.

Cook, who'd jumped for cover when the shots were fired, now turned to see that Kuro was on his feet again.

"Haven't had enough, have we?" Cook asked as he turned full around to face Kuro. Hearing Cook's renewed interest in stopping Kuro, and given the desires of his lead-legged attachment, Rex stopped his advance.

He turned his head sideways and said, "I'm not going anywhere, or so it would seem."

Jesse briefly tightened her hug before nudging her head beneath Rex's right arm pit and popping out on the other side to see what was happening.

"Leave this one for me," Cook growled. "I can almost imagine Yammamoto as one of those North Vietnamese officers who enjoyed torturing me, and I've longed to repay my agony with interest."

"What do you mean?" Kuro shrieked.

Rex got to see Kuro's eyes for the first time as they bulged with fear. Rex decided Kuro's eyes didn't appear worth the wait. Kuro's eyes showed his true emotions just as Rex thought they would. Kuro was terrified.

"What are you talking about?" Kuro asked with a whine in his voice. He began to retreat as Cook stepped forward.

"As we Americans like to say: It's payback time!"

Rex coughed through his dangling nose plugs.

Cook leaped across the room and grabbed Kuro by the back of his shirt as Kuro attempted to escape. Rex couldn't see what happened next since Cook made an effective shield to what he was doing to Kuro. But Rex could see Cook's huge back and arm muscles bulge as Cook worked over Kuro. Rex could also see between Cook's legs which were set shoulder width apart. Cook hunched over Kuro, and Rex could see Kuro's legs kicking around as if he was showing off a highly energetic dance step. Rex noticed how quiet it became, and Jesse snuck her whole body under his right arm.

A high-pitched scream broke the silence like fingernails screeching down a chalkboard. Rex shivered with the sound and gazed at Cook who was slowly straightening his back. Kuro's legs rose into the air, and he kicked violently before his scream stopped as suddenly as if someone had turned it off. Kuro's legs went limp. The silence was renewed, and it lasted long enough for Rex to find it creepy. Then Rex heard sounds he couldn't describe in words since he'd never heard them before ... but Jesse, the pathologist, was there to provide commentary.

"It sounds like he's snapping bones. Oh, that was muscle and cartilage tearing, I'm sure ... and that was another bone snap. Euww, that was a good one. Oh! No, I've never heard that noise before," Jesse said in the same tone she used to record her actions during an autopsy. She looked up at Rex with her perky grin as if she was just happy to be alive. Rex looked down at her as if to check her sanity, but then looked back up when he heard a wet-sounding thump.

"Oh, lord," Rex whispered, and he suddenly believed everything Dr. James Cook, a.k.a. Meat, had told them about his killing abilities in Asia, and why the Vietcong had feared him so. Rex watched as Dr. Cook retreated, back-stepping from the twisted body he'd dropped on the floor like a crumpled piece of paper. Rex knew the disorganized heap, from which blood and stenchy fluids were now leaking, had to be Huri Yammamoto, a.k.a. Kuro Akuma, but he'd never seen a human body configured in such a way except on a cartoon drawing.

"Rex, you look pale. Are you okay?" Rex heard Jesse ask at his side. Abruptly he remembered she was there. *How can anyone remain perky after hearing the dismemberment noises of a human?* Rex wondered.

"Yeah, I'll be fine as soon as we leave the room, or someone cleans up this mess," Rex said.

"Aw, that's nothing. You ought to see a bad car wreck." Jesse laughed. "Rex, aren't you happy? We did it! We finally solved the case!"

"Ugh," was all Rex could say as he struggled to get up.

"Here, let me help," Dr. Cook said.

Before Rex could complain or escape, Meat grabbed Rex by the armpits and hauled him to his left foot as if he was lifting a child.

"Wooow! That's one set a biceps you got there." Rex laughed nervously.

"I ate my Wheaties this morning," Dr. Cook joked.

Sirens could be heard outside. As Rex listened, it sounded as if the whole Maui County Sheriff's Department had arrived as well as all the island's ambulances.

"What's going on outside?" Moe asked from behind Rex.

Rex put his arm around Jesse for support and they both did an about face to see Moe and Joe standing next to Lilly. As they watched, Ester popped out from behind Moe.

"Hey, you guys woke up just in time," Jesse said.

"What is that mess on my clean floor!" Lilly boomed as she stomped toward the Kuro remains.

"Lilly, I wouldn't get any closer to the mess than you are if I were you," Rex said. But Lilly was never one to listen, and she walked a few more steps until she recognized the mess was a tangled body of a dead man.

Lilly made a funny noise in her throat and puffed out her cheeks in a way that was comical to Rex so he laughed. Rex's smile died when he caught a glimpse of the nasty look Lilly gave him for laughing. He looked at the ground to escape Lilly's reprise.

"Just what in tarnation is going on here?" barked a new voice with a Southern accent from the living room.

Rex recognized the voice instantly even though he'd only heard it twice before. "Oh boy, when it rains, it pours. Hot diggity dog." He smiled.

Rex looked over to see Sheriff Erp leading the police brigade coming from the entryway.

Erp barely passed the living room entrance when he caught sight of Kuro's mess on the floor. Erp was not a man with a strong constitution, and his brief glance was too much for him to constitute. Erp stopped in mid-step, and quickly dropped his ten gallon hat over his pale face and bulging eyeballs. Then he turned tail and headed back in the direction he came. Unfortunately, the two grizzly bear deputies that Rex had seen at the airport were right behind Erp and they were now blocking his exit. Erp turned back, saw the Kuro mess again, made a retching noise, then he turned back to the deputies again. Erp was forced to use his ten gallon hat before the deputies could even get out of his way.

Rex watched all this in painful fascination and he even got a laugh when Erp ruined his hat. He had to give the guy some credit. At least Erp hadn't made his mess in the Tweedy's house like Kuro had done.

"I think it's time to get back to work and do my job by arresting Sheriff Erp or whatever his name is today," Moe said as he passed by Jesse and Rex. "Thank you kindly, Dr. Cook," Moe added as he passed by Meat. "We'll have to have that neighborly chat as soon as we get some things cleaned up here."

"I would enjoy that," Dr. Cook returned.

Moe appeared almost perky as he walked quickly after Sheriff Erp.

"I guess the Feds will have fun with old Sheriff Wyatt Erp," Rex said.

"Deputies!" bellowed Joe from the entrance of the game room. "Would you please assist me in arresting this... this thing that's soiling my floor," Joe pointed at Yama.

The two deputies briskly went about their business while giving a wide berth to Kuro's mess. Rex thought the young deputies looked like grizzly cubs compared to Meat. Rex laughed through his pain when Meat barked as the deputies passed, making them jump all the way over to Joe.

Dr. Cook laughed a hearty laugh at his joke. Rex figured he was just letting off some of the emotions created in killing Kuro. Rex thought he could use a little of that letting off himself.

# CHAPTER THIRTY-FOUR

Rex sat in a booth in Lefty's Saloon with a big grin on his face. His best friends and his new family sat all around him in celebration. *So this is life*, he thought, *I kinda like it*. His grin grew wider.

"What are you grinning about now?" Jesse asked.

"Oh...Nothing in particular..." Rex kept on grinning.

"Is he always this way?" Moe asked.

"He's been this way ever since we got married and went on our Honeymoon," Jesse said.

Dr. Cook refilled everyone's glass with the cheap champagne Lefty had provided for this afternoon get-together-celebration.

"I thought you guys vowed to never come in here again," Moe said.

"Naw...We figured we'd come by and see how Ester is making out on this job, and to see if Lefty was keeping things respectable," Rex came back.

"I didn't know you'd sent her back to work, Dr. Cook," Joe commented.

"Yes, we both agreed that she needed to do work on her own if she was going to earn money so she could go to the University of Hawaii in the Fall," Meat replied.

"But she's still living at the new Sara's Garden?" Moe asked.

"Yup...she's become somewhat indispensable there," Rex replied. "I'm thinking of hiring her on as an office manager to get her away from Lefty's. I think she's learned enough about life to not have to be constantly exposed to some of its worst. Besides, I think Reverend Mother Makuahine is due for retirement, if that's possible in her capacity. Ester might be able to fill the Rev.

Mother's duties, but I'm not sure how that'll go over with the other personnel working at Sara's Garden. It's something I've been thinking about."

"I'm not sure you'd get Ester away from here," Joe commented. "She appears to be having too much fun."

They all looked at Ester as she laughed away with one of the customers she was serving a couple of tables away. To Rex, she certainly appeared to be able to hold her own.

Jesse leaned over to Rex and whispered that it was time. Rex grinned again and nodded. Using his knife, Rex tinked on his glass a few times to get everyone's attention.

"Uh-oh," Joe grumbled, "I think someone already has an announcement to make after barely returning from their honeymoon."

"Yup!" Rex beamed. "Mrs. Rex Bana and I have an announcement to make, if you please." Rex's grin was so wide it looked like it hurt, but it did appear as if he was getting that politician's grin perfected.

"I'm not sure how much more good news I can handle today," Dr. Cook claimed as he stared at another full glass of champagne. Rex noticed that Meat was somewhat of a novice when it came to drinking. Dr. Cook already had a red nose and shiny eyes.

"Well, you'll probably only have to do this one time. Go ahead, honey... tell everyone the news you've been dying to tell," Rex said to Jesse.

"I'm pregnant!" Jesse exclaimed.

"Congratulations!... Great!...Wonderful news!..." came in from around the table from everyone. Rex had to tink his glass again to quiet down the crowd. Jesse wasn't finished with her announcement.

When all had grown quiet again, Dr. Cook said, "Don't tell me, Rex, you're pregnant too."

"Nope... It's not quite that earth shattering," Rex said, but he continued to beam.

Jesse continued, "The ultrasound they did to confirm the pregnancy showed we're going to have triplets. With any luck there's going to be three little Bana's running around in about eight months."

"There goes the neighborhood." Moe laughed.

"A toast to the Bana's," Dr. Cook suggested and everyone drank.

"And a special toast," Dr. Cook continued on a serious note, "To the spirit and courage of Rex Bana. He was once known as King Slayer, a destroyer of evil lives. Now he's proven he can be part of the creation of life, as well as a savior." Rex grinned his grin.

"Here, Here... Amen..." arose from around the table as they all downed another one.

"Another toast if you please," Rex announced while all the glasses were refilled. "Here's to the appointment of Joseph Tweedy as the Maui County Sheriff in interim, and to his success in becoming the permanent Sheriff in the up-coming elections."

Everyone drank again.

"What happened at the Indictment Hearing of Arnold Webster, a.k.a. Wyatt Erp?" asked Dr. Cook.

Joe began. "Erp pleaded guilty to the lesser charges of fifteen counts of conspiracy to commit murder and one count of embezzlement of County monies. This was in exchange for his testimony against a total of six Yakuza members," Joe started. "I don't know what all the charges will be and how many Yakuza members will remain in custody. We're still sorting that one out since they have so many different and confusing testimonies from the different Yakuza members. It seems some of them want to turn State's evidence for unsolved crimes we hadn't even linked to them."

"Yeah..." Moe interrupted. "That's just the State's cases against them. There still are all the federal indictments that have to come down. This case may be going on for years."

"Which brings us to another toast," Rex cheered.

"Oh no," Dr. Cook sighed. "I do believe I'm getting drunk."

"That's okay." Rex laughed. "You can stay at the Garden tonight. Jesse can even drive home since she isn't drinking, and believe me; you'll want to be drunk for that ride... OUCH!" Everyone laughed as Rex rubbed his shin after being kicked under the table.

"Rex, what about Kuro's ravings in the end there... about a Yakuza operation cloning organ transfers?" Dr. Cook asked.

"Kuro was right. That's out of my ballpark, ask Joe." Rex shrugged.

Joe said, "As long as they don't do anything illegal in my jurisdiction I suppose I'll never know how that operation pans out either—or even if Kuro was telling the truth. Ask Moe." Meat rolled his eyes while Moe pretended not to hear, and the subject was dropped. Rex figured Moe's head was lost in the clouds of dreams come true.

"Next," Rex said to revive the celebration. "We have to toast to Moe's retirement from the FBI."

"Yeah... I'll drink to that." Moe smiled.

"Here's to his health and prosperity! No more undercover cases for him," Joe encored.

"To the creation and prosperity of T.C.B.Inc.," Dr. Cook said in slow manner.

"I'll definitely drink to that!" Moe jeered.

They held their glasses high before throwing back their toast. They didn't bring their glasses together in celebration in fear of breaking Lefty's "fine" goblets.

"Hey, where's the hair in my glass?" Rex asked, feeling cheated.

"Are you sure you don't need any help working Moe's Dive Shop?" Rex asked. "There isn't that much for me to do at Sara's Garden with the Rev. Mother still on the job. Ester gets most of my work done, and since Joe won't allow me to do more than talk to the wife and child beaters, I have to restrain myself from pummeling some of these saps."

"Remember your promises," Joe said sternly.

"Well, anyway..." Rex continued, "... here's to the creation of Tweedy, Cook, & Bana Inc." Again another round of cheers rose from the table.

"I think buying Moe's Dive Shop away from the Feds and the creation of T C B, Inc. is one of the best investments I made," Meat claimed in a joyous tone.

"I hope so," Jesse commented. "It's certainly the first major investment I've ever made. I'd hate to see it go down the dumper."

"I couldn't ask for better partners," Moe stated. "Are you all sure you trust me running the shop?"

"Here's to the best dive shop manager one could ask for," bellowed Dr. Cook a little too loudly. The cheer that followed was equally loud.

"Moe, you ran the shop with such success over the years, why should we worry about you operating it now?" Rex asked.

"That was when it was the Feds money, and it really didn't matter whether I failed or not. Now it's partly my money and part of yours. This time it counts," Moe said in a worried tone.

"Don't fret it, Moe. You know what I used to do to people who pissed me off in the past." Rex laughed. At this there was another roar of laughter.

"Hey, if you guys don't calm down over here, Lefty's threatening to call the police," Ester hollered over their continued cheering. This announcement brought even more jeers and cheers.

Dr. Cook sat up straight and said in a serious tone, "We all know that is the past, Rex. Let's leave it there until the time the need returns. Something tells me the Yakuza are not finished with this group."

Cook's statement brought a sober taste to all sitting in the booth. The chatter settled down, and Rex hugged Jesse for the millionth time in the last six weeks.

In the background the beat-up jukebox sang:

"Here I go...

"Playin' star again...

"There I go...

"Turn the page," *click*.

"Turn the page," *click*.

"Turn the page," *click*.

"Turn the page..." Rex heard someone swear before kicking the jukebox to make Seger stop stuttering. For a few moments Rex was twelve years old again and he was walking home along Napier Road from Salem Middle School. He shivered and squinted his eyes to protect them from the icy needles of the sleet. Rex remembered the warmth and comfort of Sara being alive, and he thought of how much his life changed that day. Rex was lost in these thoughts when he heard Jesse laughing in the background and felt her living warmth so close beside him. He thought of how much his life had changed these last weeks.

"Turn the page..." Rex muttered.

The End.